THE CHRISTINE BROOKE-I

CHRISTINE BROOKE-ROSE was born in
Somerville College, Oxford and Univers
worked in Intelligence at Bletchley Park
War, and as a freelance reviewer and writer during the 1950s and 60s. She is the author of a number of works of academic criticism and translations, as well as novels, one of which, *Such*, received the James Tait Black Memorial Prize in 1966. Christine Brooke-Rose taught at the University of Paris, Vincennes, from 1968 to 1988 and now lives in the south of France.

Also by Christine Brooke-Rose from Carcanet

Amalgamemnon
Xorandor
Verbivore
Textermination
Remake
Next
Subscript
Life, End of

THE CHRISTINE BROOKE-ROSE OMNIBUS

Four Novels

Out

Such

Between

Thru

CARCANET

First published in Great Britain in 1986 by
Carcanet Press Limited
Alliance House
Cross Street
Manchester M2 7AQ

This impression 2006

Out (1964), *Such* (1966) and *Between* (1968) were originally published by Michael Joseph Ltd., London; *Thru* (1975) by Hamish Hamilton Ltd., London.

A CIP catalogue record for this book is available from the British Library
ISBN 1 85754 884 1
978 1 85754 884 6

The publisher acknowledges financial assistance from Arts Council England

Printed and bound in England by SRP Ltd, Exeter

CONTENTS

OUT

Resettlement Camp No: 49 **File No:** AS/239457/Z

Ex-nationality: Ukayan

Ex-occupation: humanist

Re-training: fitter

Observations:

DISCHARGED

Labour Exchange No: 174 **Card No:** 3BL/4963/81

Ex-nationality: Ukayan

Ex-occupation: Ph.D.

Re-trained as: odd job man

Employment history: unsatisfactory, see D.P.I.

CONFIDENTIAL

State Hospital No: 897 Southern Region

File No: PSY/L8I5325 NOT TO BE HANDLED BY PATIENT

Ex-occupation: ~~psychopath~~ gardener

Present occupation: unemployed

Present address: Settlement No 4512(c)

Local doctor: none, see letter from Mrs. D. Mgulu

Seen by: Dr. Fu Teng

Recommendation: Psychoscopy

Observations: Biogram attached

1

A FLY straddles another fly on the faded denim stretched over the knee. Sooner or later, the knee will have to make a move, but now it is immobilised by the two flies, the lower of which is so still that it seems dead. The fly on top is on the contrary quite agitated, jerking tremulously, then convulsively, putting out its left foreleg to whip, or maybe to stroke some sort of reaction out of the fly beneath, which, however, remains so still that it seems dead. A microscope might perhaps reveal animal ecstasy in its innumerable eyes, but only to the human mind behind the microscope, and besides, the fetching and rigging up of a microscope, if one were available, would interrupt the flies. Sooner or later some such interruption will be inevitable; there will be an itch to scratch or a nervous movement to make or even a bladder to go and empty. But now there is only immobility. The fly on top is now perfectly still also. Sooner or later some interruption will be necessary, a bowl of gruel to be eaten, for instance, or a conversation to undergo. Sooner or later a bowl of gruel will be brought, unless perhaps it has already been brought, and the time has come to go and get rid of it, in which case –

– Would you rather have your gruel now or when I come back from Mrs. Mgulu?

The question is inevitable, but will not necessarily occur in that precise form.

– Two flies are making love on my knee.

– Flies don't make love. They have sexual intercourse.

– On the contrary.

– You mean they make love but don't have sexual intercourse?

– I mean it's human beings who have sexual intercourse but don't make love.

– Very witty. But you are talking to yourself. This dialogue will not necessarily occur.

The straddled fly stretches out its forelegs and rubs them together, but the fly on top is perfectly still. Soon the itch will have to be scratched.

– Hello, is there anyone there? It's Mrs. Tom.

– Who is it? Oh, hello, Mrs. Tom, did you get my message?

– Yes, that's why I came, and how are you?

– I was delayed this morning by Mrs. Ned's tub, it was broken you see, so I was too late to catch Mrs. Jim. But Mr. Marburg the butler kindly offered to get in touch with you.

The itch is scratched very gently, so as not to disturb the flies. The fly on top trembles, quivers and sags, then stretches out its left foreleg to flicker some reaction out of the straddled fly, which, however, is now quite still. Sooner or later the knee's immobility will undergo a mutation, a muscle will twitch and the flies will be disturbed. But for the moment they are dead to the world, even to the commotion made at the door by the coming interruption, the question which sooner or later must occur, in some form or other.

– That was Mrs. Tom.

– I know, I heard her.

– She got my message in spite of everything. You see I was late at Mrs. Mgulu's this morning, on account of Mrs. Ned's tub.

– Look, two flies are making love on my knee.

The squint seems bluer today, and wider. The pale eye that doesn't move is fixed on the two flies, but the mobile eye wriggles away from them, its blue mobility calling out the blueness of the temple veins and a hint of blue in the white skin around. Then this eye too remains fixed, reproachful perhaps.

– Mrs. Mgulu looks quite ill you know, at least, as far as one can tell, with that wonderfully black skin. Yesterday apparently the doctor changed all her medicines, so she said I could have her old ones. This is for the thyroid. And this one's for the duodenum, look.

– Don't come too near, you'll frighten them.

The pale fixed eye stands guard over the flies. The other moves along the print.

– *Duodenica* is an oral antacid buffer specially prepared for easy absorption by the sick the aged and the very young its gentle action provides continuous antacid action without alkalisation or fluctuations reducing gastric acidity to an equable level of p H 4 which is sufficient to relieve pain and discomfort with practically no interference with the secretory balance of the stomach or other normal digestive mechanisms. *Duodenica* is particularly recommended in cases of over-alcoholisation supersatiation ulceration hyperacidity dyspepsia *Duodenica* is NOT a drug one capsule twice a day during or after meals NOT to be taken without a doctor's prescription.

In the sudden silence the fly on top is very still, so still that it seems dead under that pale policing eye.

– Would you rather have your gruel now or in a little while? It makes no difference to me, I have things to do.

– Sooner or later I shall have to disturb them.

The mobile eye shifts towards the knee and back, but the two flies lie quite still, as if dead to that extra light of awareness briefly upon them.

– Where's your fly-swatter? Ah, here.

– Don't! . . . frighten them.

– There's hundreds of eggs in that fly. Think of the summer. It's the winter flies you have to kill. Well I'll leave the thyroid thing with you, and the *Duodenica*. There are some suppositories too, let's see, anti-infectious therapeutic and tonifying by means of bacteriostatic properties of four sulphonamides selected among the most active and least toxic, together with – ah no, that's for dogs, how silly of me.

The winter flies lie quite still, dead to the removal of that pale light of awareness briefly upon them. Sooner or later there will be a movement to make, a bladder to go and empty and a bowl of gruel to go and eat. The fly-swatter is made of bright red plastic. Through it, the high small window looks trellised in red, a darker red against the light, almost a wine-red. Through the trellis the winter sky is blue and pale, paler than the summer sky. But it is difficult to re-visualise the exact degree of blueness in the summer sky without interposing picture postcards as sold in the city streets. No sky is as blue as that, not even here in the South. It is difficult to re-imagine the exact degree of heat, and picture postcards are cold. The winter flies lie quite still, dead to their present framing in a circle of dark red plastic, dead to the removal of the red plastic frame around the light of awareness on them. Sooner or later they must be interrupted, but now there is only immobility.

The knee lowers itself gently, an earth transferred, a mountain moved by faith. The leg stretches slowly to a horizontal position. The elbows on which the recumbent body rests have to straighten out so that the body can rise from the mattress on the floor, using the hands to lean on. In the process the knees bend up again slightly. The winter flies take off, locked in a lurching flight, at eye-level, then, together still, they sway up towards the high small window a long way from the floor, and land their conjugal bodies on the transverse bar, where they lie very quiet, so quiet they might be dead.

Even at eye-level the flies lie quiet on the transverse bar, so quiet they might be dead.

The kitchen door is framed by the bedroom door. At the end of the short dark passage, almost cubic in its brevity, the kitchen through the open door seems luminous, apparently framed in red. The doors however are of rough dark wood. The walls of the passage are at right angles when curving is desired.

The circle of steaming gruel in the bowl is greyish white and pimply.

A conversation occurs.

A microscope might perhaps reveal animal ecstasy among the innumerable white globules in the circle of gruel, but only to the human mind behind the microscope. And besides, the fetching and the rigging up of a microscope, if one were available, would interrupt the globules. If, indeed, the gruel hadn't been eaten by then, in which case a gastroscope would be more to the point. And a gastroscope at that juncture of the gruel's journey would provoke nausea.

– Mrs. Mgulu looks quite ill, you know, but then she will complicate life for herself. She was expecting toys for the children this morning, and it was important they shouldn't see them arrive, so they were sent out with the nanny and Mrs. Mgulu stayed home, so that delayed her, and by the time she got to town she was late for the hairdresser and he kept her waiting, though really, she doesn't need it, her hair looks lovely and smooth, in the middle of all those preparations, and pheasants too, and seven servants away ill. Well, she was grateful to me, I can tell you, she even gave me a bonus. So I bought a tin of pineapple fingers. You never know when it may come in useful.

A rectangle of light ripples on the wooden table. The wrinkled wood inside the rectangle seems to be flowing into the wrinkled wood outside it, which looks darker. If the source of rippling light were not known to be an oblique ray of winter sun filtering through the top segment of the slightly swaying beads over the doorway, the wrinkled wood might be thought alive, as alive, at any rate, as the network of minute lines on the back of the wrist. But the minute lines on the back of the wrist do not flow as the wrinkled wood seems to flow. A microscope might perhaps reveal which is the more alive of the two.

The rectangle of light is only a refracted continuation of the oblong thrown on the red stone floor between the doorway and the table. The beads ripple the light of this oblong also, turning the red stone floor into a red river. Sometimes it is sufficient to envisage a change for the change to occur. The hanging beads are still, however, and the red river is only a stone floor.

– Take one or more tins of Frankfurt sausages allowing two per person gently split each sausage down the middle and insert one pineapple finger into each split simmer in pineapple juice for two to three minutes meanwhile open a tin of either spinach or garden peas and warm up but do not boil in thick bottomed saucepan serve the pineapple sausages piping hot on a bed of spinach or garden peas. That sounds very good. Would you like some more gruel?

The circle of gruel in the bowl is greyish white and pimply. It steams less, and appears quite flaccid. In the rectangle of rippling light a fly moves jerkily.

The squint is not so blue, or so wide, in the luminosity thrown by the oblong of moving light on the red stone floor and the rectangle of rippling light on the wooden table. It is good that the gruel was not brought but come to, arrived at. Sooner or later movement, which is necessary but not inevitable, will lead to attainment. Yet, frequently, the gruel is brought.

– Mrs. Ned's tub was broken, you see, and I helped her mend it. So naturally I arrived too late this morning to catch

Mrs. Jim. Mr. Marburg the butler said she waited as long as possible, but then she had to go or she'd get the worst of the market. Because of course she knew from yesterday that I would have a message for her to give to Mrs. Tom, but she didn't know that Mrs. Ned would delay me with her tub. So then when she got back I hadn't been able to give her the message. Well in the end it didn't matter because Mr. Marburg the butler was most obliging and said he would contact Mrs. Tom and himself give her the message, but he charged me for the call, pocketing the money no doubt because I can't see that Mrs. Mgulu would know one way or the other, but he said she keeps a careful check on such things.

Some of the gruel's globules remain attached to the rounded white sides of the bowl, which looks like the inside of the moon. Nobody has ever photographed the inside of the moon. To see inside a bladder the instrument is called a cystoscope. The inside of a bladder is framed in pink.

Yet frequently, the gruel is brought. It has then been sufficient merely to imagine movement for the movement to occur. Or not, as the case might be.

The skin around the eyes, both the mobile eye and the fixed eye, is waxy. But the eyelids are the right colour. More so, at any rate, than usual, at least in the luminosity thrown by the oblong of moving light on the red stone floor.

– Yes, I am pale, but look at my eyelids, they are the right colour, for the time of year, I mean.

– So they are. It is a pity, of course, that the colour has gone out of fashion.

– Very witty. But you are talking to yourself. This dialogue does not necessarily occur.

The waxiness is due to a deficiency in the liver.

In the rectangle of rippling light on the wrinkled wood of the kitchen table there is no fly.

– Did you bring the *Duodenica*? It said during or after meals, or was it before? What does it say?

The formula printed on the bottle marked *Duodenica* is

Aluminium glycinate (dihydroxy aluminium aminoacetate) 850 mg. light magnesium carbonate B.P. 150 mg.

– I think you ought to take this, not me.

– Oh thank you, I was hoping you'd say that. Then you can have this heart extract, o point two grammes of heart extract, corresponding to o point eight o six grammes of fresh organs. Or this one. It's for the bladder. Hexamethylene tetramine crystallised and chemically pure both preventive and curative diuretic it constitutes an active dissolvant of uric acid especially for all infections of bilious and urinary ducts colitis angiocholitis pyelitis pyelonephritis etcetera its antiseptic powers are reinforced by a minimal addition of potassium citrate to the hexamethylene tetramine. By the way did you go to the Labour Exchange this morning?

The waxiness could even be due to cancer.

The bedroom door is framed by the kitchen door. In the short passage, almost cubic in its brevity, the lavatory door to the left is certainly another possibility. To the right of the kitchen door, facing the lavatory door, the door to the front verandah room, where the lodgers live, is not a possibility. If the waxiness were due to cancer then the eyelids would not be the right colour, but of course the colour of the eyelids might have reflected the luminosity from the rectangle of rippling light. On the other hand, the luminosity thrown by the rectangle of light would also have affected the waxiness of the skin elsewhere around the eyes. A microscope might perhaps reveal, a teinoscope might perhaps reveal, from this position between the small high window and the mattress on the floor, through the cubic passage and the angular framework of the kitchen door, that the squint is less wide and less blue, less noticeable in the luminosity thrown by the oblong of moving light on the red stone floor. A telescope might perhaps reveal a planet off course, a satellite out of orbit.

The transverse bar of the window is dark and flaking with age. At eye-level it is empty of flies. The old wood has cracked considerably, as if the flies had caused much commotion in their wintry love-making. Flies do not make love, they have sexual intercourse. Only human beings make love. The transverse bar at eye-level is quite empty. The vertical bar is empty too, and the window-sill, and the window-panes, and the vertical wall around the window, and the other three walls, and the low cracked ceiling, all are empty of flies in their wintry occupation.

– Occupation?

– I am a builder.

Behind the trellis the bland black face looks patched like wet asphalt with curved oblongs and blobs of white light.

– A builder? But your hands. They look such sensitive hands.

– Ah, but have you seen my eyelids, they are the right colour.

– You know very well this dialogue cannot occur. Start again. Occupation?

– I am a builder.

– The truth is after all unimportant in a case like this.

– I haven't actually built for a long time, you see. I am as you might say a master builder, a man of ideas, which others carry out. No, well, they haven't for a long time, it's true. In my country they did, before the displacement of course. I had many people under me. I built many houses, in many different styles, as for example the miniature stately home style. That used to be very fashionable you know. I lived in a miniature stately home style house I built myself. I also built office blocks. The old glass house style, you seem to like it here. I was very successful –

– Look, since you're inventing this dialogue you ought to give something to the other chap to say.

– But I must get all those facts in.

– He won't let you, he exists too, you know.

– I suppose so, with his beautiful bland black face patched like wet asphalt in curved oblongs and blobs of light. And the facts, anyway, are not true.

– I know. You must be more realistic. Say for instance that you were trained at a Resettlement Camp.

– I built the tower of Pisa and it leant.

– Inside it spirals. A bronchoscope might perhaps reveal –

– Oh shut up.

At eye-level through the window, about three metres away, and to the left of the fig-tree which overlooks the road, there is Mrs. Ned's bungalow. Some people would call it a shack. The windowless clapboard wall immediately opposite is dark with age and the cunonia at the corner of it is dead, its dark red spike dried up. To the right, at the front of the bungalow, the verandah looks dilapidated and at the back the straw shed over the wash-tub is crumbling down. The wash-tub has a bar of new pale wood nailed along its top edge. The shack is exactly similar to this bungalow and exactly in line with it, but too close, for it blocks the view. Some people would call the verandah a porch.

– Well, you started it, your dialogue gets out of hand.

A telemetre might perhaps reveal the distance to be three and a half metres, or even four. The view to the right, if it were visible from this position at the right of the window, would be the fig-tree. The view obliquely to the left is of the corner of the porch belonging to the shack next to Mrs. Ned's. The view ahead, if a view were available, would consist of innumerable bungalows in small bare gardens where nothing grows very tall. Some people would call them shacks. The shacks would be low and spare with slightly sloping corrugated iron roofs that straddle the smaller roofs of the entrance verandahs. The insulating paint on most of the roofs would have flaked away leaving brown patches of rusting ripple. The gardens would be small and flat.

– You're incapable of preparing any episode in advance. You can't even think.

At least that is the view from the kitchen window over the sink, which faces the South East side of the Settlement, unblocked by Mrs. Ned's shack. If Mrs. Ned's shack were not in the way, all the innumerable other shacks to the South West would be visible from this window also, unless all the shacks save this one had been removed, or destroyed, in the walking interval between the kitchen window and this window. It is sometimes sufficient merely to imagine an episode for the episode to occur. A periscope might perhaps reveal a scene of pastoral non-habitation. It would be sufficient merely to move two steps to the left for the window to be filled, in an oblique way, only with the fig-tree.

– I am a builder. I received Vocational Training at a Resettlement Camp after the displacement. Since then, however, I have only been spasmodically in labour. Since then, however, I have only been employed intermittently.

Frequently, after all, the gruel is brought. It is sometimes sufficient merely to imagine movement, in the walking interval between the kitchen window and this window, for the movement to occur, though not necessarily in that precise form. The gardens, when visible, are too small and the shacks too close for health. Every shack, climbing over its own verandah, might be a fly straddling another fly. It is sometimes sufficient to imagine a change, but in this case the shacks, if visible, would merely be shacks. Some people like to call them bungalows.

Beyond the closed wrought-iron gates the mimosas up at the big house are in bloom, gracefully draping the top of the white pillars on either side of the gate. Single branches also droop over the white wall that separates the property from the road. Beyond the tall wrought-iron gates and beyond the mimosa on either side the plane-trees line the drive, casting a welcome shade. One half of the tall wrought-iron gates may be ajar, might perhaps be pushed open with an effort of the will. It is sometimes sufficient.

Here however the fig-tree's thick grey twigs poke upwards into the sky. The branches bearing them are contorted, like the convolutions of the brain. The darker grey trunk leans along the edge of the bank at an angle of forty degrees, inside which, from a standing position, the road may be seen. One of the branches sweeps downwards out of the trunk, away from the road, forming with the trunk an arch that frames the piece of road within it. The thick and long grey twigs on this down sweeping branch grow first downward also, then curve up like large U-letters.

In summer, from ground-level, nearer to the fig-tree, the arch formed by the leaning trunk and the down-sweeping branch frames a whole landscape of descending olive-groves beyond the road, which itself disappears behind the bank. In summer the grey framework of trunk and branch is further framed by a mass of deep green foliage.

At the moment, from a standing position, it is only a piece of road which is framed. At the moment the fig-tree looks blasted.

If the fig-tree here looks blasted then the mimosas up at the big house cannot be in bloom. The two events do not occur simultaneously. It is sometimes sufficient to imagine but only within nature's possibilities.

Beyond the closed wrought-iron gates the plane-trees line the drive, forming with their bare and upward branches a series of networks that become finer and finer as the drive recedes towards the big house, made now discernible by the leaflessness. First there are the vertical bars of the tall wrought-iron gates, flanked, behind the two white pillars and white walls, by the feathery green mimosa trees which are not in bloom. Beyond the vertical bars of the closed wrought-iron gates there is the thick network of the first plane-trees on either side of the drive. Beyond the thick network of bare branches there is a finer network, closing in a little over the drive, and beyond that a finer network still. The network of bare branches functions in depth, a corridor of cobwebs full of traps for flies, woven by a giant spider behind huge prison bars.

It is not true that the mimosas cannot blossom while the fig-tree looks blasted. The small nodules just visible on the straight long twigs of the fig-tree may already represent the first, January round of buds, the edible ones which do not produce leaves and fruit. Therefore the mimosas could just be in bloom. Unless of course the fig-tree does not look as blasted as all that. The nodules could already be the buds that produce leaves and fruit, in which case the problem does not arise.

– Oh anyworrourr slishy ming nang pactergoo worror worrerer-er-er-er whinnyman shoo. Oh no. Fang hang norryman, go many wolloshor-or-or nang – Oh, how silly of me, tharrawarrapack hang norryman.

– Is it you or me you're talking to? Because I haven't heard a word.

– I was talking to myself. I was just saying that I forgot to ask Mrs. Jim to buy me a packet of gruel when she went to the market this morning. I couldn't go myself because Mrs. Mgulu wanted the sheets changed in three of the guest-rooms, her friends from Kenya are leaving you see and others are arriving. She didn't say where from. And then I remembered that I had an extra packet stored away behind the tins for just such an emergency.

It is not, however, January. Early December must be the latest possible time for flies to make love. For flies to have sexual intercourse. Unless perhaps a certain period has already elapsed since that episode, if indeed it occurred. The flies may have been a product of the fine network that functions in depth, in which case they will certainly have got caught in the cobwebs.

The squint, very wide and very blue, hovers in the doorway, a planet off course, a satellite out of orbit. The skin around the eyes, both the mobile eye and the static eye, is waxy. There is no reproach in the mobile eye. The emotion expressed is nearer to concern. The static eye expresses only off-ness, since it is static, and it is this off-ness which emphasises whatever emotion the mobile eye is expressing.

– Would you rather have your gruel now or later? It makes no difference to me.

– I'll be along in a few minutes.

– I can bring it to you here if you like.

Sooner or later the other question will occur also.

– No, it's all right.

Most eyes are an octave, one note repeating the other. These are a ninth, sometimes an augmented ninth. The two waves of light, like the two waves of sound, are not quite parallel, and may cause the minute voltages of the neural cells to rise from five microvolts to ten for example. An oscillograph might reveal curious fluctuations. These would not, however, represent the waves of light or sound emanating from the eyes or from the augmented ninth.

– The only snag about hiding things for emergencies is that one forgets, either that one has hidden them, or where one has put them. It was just by chance that I took down a tin of curried chicken to read the recipe – it's a rather succulent one and I wanted to cheer myself up a bit – and there behind it I saw the extra packet of gruel.

– I used to be an electrician, actually.

– I thought so, from your delicate hands. Now let me see, there is a temporary vacancy for an oscillographer up at Government House. In the Gallup Poll Department. I take it you play all the instruments?

– Was there anything at the Labour Exchange this morning?

– I didn't go.

– Oh, you said you would. You haven't been for three weeks.

– And before that I went for eighteen months.

– Well at least you got the unemployment pills. Just look at you. Well, I promised Mrs. Mgulu you would go up and see her head gardener this afternoon. It's very kind of her to have arranged it, you know. She takes an interest.

Beyond the tall wrought-iron gate the mimosas are in bloom, gracefully draping the top of the white pillars on either side. Single branches also droop over the white wall that separates the property from the road. Beyond the mimosas the plane-trees line the drive, casting a welcome shade. No. Beyond the mimosas the plane-trees line the drive, forming with their bare and upward branches a series of networks that become finer and finer as the drive recedes towards the big house, discernible through the leaflessness. One half of the tall wrought-iron gate is open, by remote control perhaps, unless it has been pushed open by an effort of the will.

– You have to go round the back, past the kitchen garden, you know. There's a black painted door in the wall, and you ring the bell, it's a cottage really, the head gardener lives there. He's expecting you at three.

Sometimes the gruel is brought.

Mrs. Mgulu sits graciously at her dressing-table, brushing her thick black hair into sleekness and she takes an interest. Mrs. Mgulu sits graciously at her dressing-table, having her thick long black hair brushed into sleekness and she takes an interest. She takes an interest in the crackling electricity of her hair which is being brushed into sleekness by a pert Bahuko maid, whose profile is reversed in the mirror. Mrs. Mgulu does not choose to be touched by sickly Colourless hands. In the tall gilt-frame mirror the smooth Asswati face smiles, mostly at the front of the head framed by the long black hair, with self-love in the round black eyes and in the thick half-open lips, but occasionally with graciousness at the reflection of the white woman changing the sheets on the bed behind the head framed by the long black hair. The white woman can be seen in the mirror beyond the pert profile and beyond the smooth Asswati face, whose smiling black eyes shift a little to the right, with graciousness, and then a little to the left, with self-love. A psychoscope might perhaps reveal the expression to be one of pleasure in beauty, rather than self-love. The scene might occur, for that matter, in quite a different form. The personal maid, for example, could be Colourless after all.

– Oh, no. I mean, she'd have to assist me in my bath. Oh, no.

– Why not? says somebody or other representing something dead, but there is no person in the mirror.

– Even my husband Dr. Mgulu, who stands on an Internationalist Platform, would not let his white boy assist him in his bath.

– And yet, says somebody or other, his eyelids are the right colour.

The waxiness is due to a deficiency in the liver. The waxiness, hovering in the doorway, hides behind a curling wisp of steam. There is no reproach in the mobile eye, the emotion expressed is nearer to concern, veiled a little by the curling wisp of steam.

– The post has come. There's one for you, it's the Labour Exchange. I've got a letter too, I can't think who from. It gets on my nerves the way Mrs. Ivan opens tins and leaves them out on the table in there. It smells even in the corridor. I wonder how they haven't poisoned themselves. I can't read the postmark.

The circle of steaming gruel in the bowl is greyish white and pimply.

– I know this writing, I know it very well, but I just can't – let's see – oh I do believe – yes it's from Joan Dkimba née Willoughby, she was at school with me. You don't know her, she married very well, dear Lilly I've been meaning to write for ages but I've been so busy I wonder how you are, well I hope, here all is well too except that the children all had measles one after the other instead of all together according to our records you have not reported to this Exchange for three weeks a terrible bout of gastric trouble but I'm better now, poor thing I must send her some *Duodenica*, Denton is doing very well he is Chief Spokesman now you must have seen his name he travels a lot too and unemployment benefit cannot be administered retrospectively. We cannot keep any person on our books who does not report daily. Your group's reporting time is: 8 a.m. Daily from 8 a.m. a gnarled left hand lies immobile on the next human thigh at the Labour Exchange. Sooner or later a name will be called out and the thigh will slope up in a vertical position, slowly or suddenly according to this terrible wave of unemployment which I hope hasn't reached you in any shape or form you being *such a very active person* well at least she remembers that about me, isn't that nice, and er-er-er-er – ever down your way I'll look you up though at the moment it seems unlikely. *However* one never knows and in the meantime do let me know how you've been faring yours ever Joan.

Some of the gruel's white globules remain attached to the rounded white sides of the bowl. Sooner or later there will be a movement to make, a raising of the haunches, a shuffling of the feet, an emptying of the bladder. Sooner or later a name will be called out, and the next human thigh will slope up into a vertical position though not necessarily in that precise form.

– I am a gardener. I received Vocational Training at the Resettlement Camp after the displacement. Since then, however, I have only been intermittently employed.

– I am a gardener. I specialise in tending fig-trees. I eat the first crop of buds, in January, they make me strong and virile. I tend the second crop with secret knowledge handed down by generations.

– What does your letter say?

– I must report daily from 8 a.m.

– Nothing else?

– It's a printed slip. The time is handwritten.

– Oh I see. Well, that's lucky isn't it? You could do with

the benefit pills. It's nice to hear from Joan. She always played the part of the fairy princess in the school play. And she's done very well. You never know, she might be able to help you, indirectly I mean. Not that I'd ever ask her, but she takes an interest. Would you like some more gruel?

The white globules – sometimes it is sufficient simply to speak, to say no thank you, or yes please, as the case might be, for the sequence not to occur.

The black nodules on the bare branches of the fig-tree which, close up, does not look blasted, seem to represent the first crop of buds. A simple test would be to taste one, or even several. From here inside the curve of the downsweeping branch the sky is entirely filled with long grey twigs that poke into the eyebrow line topping the field of vision. In the lower part, on either side of the nose, the branches that bear the twigs are thick and grey and contorted. To the right of the nose, with the left eye closed, the thickest branch sweeps horizontally below the starting-line of the yellow grass patch, where Mrs. Ned's shack begins. To the left of the nose, with the right eye closed, it underlines Mrs. Ned's shack, as if Mrs. Ned's shack were built on it. The fig-tree does not look blasted, for the rough grey bark is wrinkled in the bend of the trunk like a thigh of creased denim shot with darker thread. The rough grey bark is shot with black lines running parallel down the length of the thicker branches, in high relief but discontinuous and made up of black dots. These lines are interrupted by the thick transverse cracks where the trunk curves, or by crinkly craters where branches have been cut away. The smaller branches are like curved spines, knotty but smoother in between the bumps, and with the transverse lines more regularly marked. The dots are paler and more scattered. To the carelessly naked eye the dots of these smaller lines are not immediately visible. But a microscope would certainly reveal a system of parallel highways all along the branches in discontinuous black blobs like vehicles immobilised. Or neural cells perhaps.

The bud tastes sweetly insipid on the tongue, but sharper on the palate. One step forward and Mrs. Ned's shack is framed in a trapeze of black twig and branch. The branch runs below, thickly, like a censored caption, and sweeps down to the right towards the grass, where the long grey twigs it bears grow first downwards and then curve up, in large U-letters. The buds taste distinctly sharper after they have passed beyond the taste-buds. The mimosas could just be in bloom.

Mrs. Ned's shack grows big. A red and white blob floats in the darkness behind the verandah window, grows big and becomes presumably Mrs. Ned, though without a head. The rectangular frame of the verandah is itself still held in the rounded frame formed by the line of the eyebrow and the line of the nose, to the left of the nose with the right eye closed, to the right of the nose with the left eye closed; below, there is the invisible but assumed line of the cheek, which becomes visible only with a downward look that blurs the picture. The frame of the verandah expands beyond the rounded field of vision as Mrs. Ned grows unmistakably into Mrs Ned, who is ironing in the small front room. She bends her white face downwards, more than is perhaps necessary for ironing, and shows therefore mostly the top of her brown head, with the thin untidy hair emerging now from the dark background. She is cut across the chest by an oblong bar of light reflected in the glass. The frame of the verandah engulfs as Mrs. Ned looks up and smiles, with eyebrows raised perhaps more than is necessary for the occasion. A camera with a telescopic lens used on approach might perhaps have revealed that Mrs. Ned had in fact looked up and out of the verandah door, but only to the human mind behind the lens, and besides, the rigging up or even the mere carrying, at eye-level, of such a camera, if one had been available, would have caused Mrs. Ned to look up, thus proving nothing. The bar of oblong light reflected in the glass vanishes. Mrs. Ned is no longer cut in half but framed by the open door, whole and unmistakably

Mrs. Ned, in a white apron and red cardigan. The cardigan's collar half hides the goitre to the left of the neck.

A conversation occurs.

The ironing-board rests on the backs of two kitchen chairs. The smell is of steamed soap. A basket of unironed things lies on the floor to the right of the ironing-board. To the right of the verandah door, facing Mrs. Ned, a crisp white overall hangs on a hanger from the left hand knob on the top drawer of the tall dark chest of drawers. A shining but faded green blouse hangs from the other knob. And over the big brass double-bed in the left corner behind Mrs. Ned clothes and towels are neatly folded and regimented. Mrs. Ned's four grown daughters, who are out in service, use the bed in turns of two and Mrs Ned sleeps in the small back room. Alternatively three of the four grown daughters who are out in service sleep in the big brass double-bed, the fourth sharing the small back room with Mrs. Ned. Or two, and two, Mrs. Ned using the big brass double-bed perhaps. The walls look like the surface of the moon. The smell is of steamed soap. The hard eyes stare but strike an octave. At most a tonic chord. The phrase what a surprise has come and gone, unless perhaps it formed part of the merely tonic chord, the expected notes, which have not in fact been played.

– if you don't mind, I mean.

– No, I don't mind.

The tall dark chest of drawers is pocked with worms. The passage, with walls at right angles where curving is desired, is almost cubic in its brevity. The smell of soap remains behind as the nose follows Mrs. Ned, who smells of freshly chopped onions and washing-up water. Her legs are thin and very white, which, in a black man's world, has more than adulterous appeal, the tender, incestuous appeal of love within minorities. To the left, the kitchen is not luminous, nor is it framed in red. The kitchen is spick and span but colourless and Mrs. Ned herself smells of freshly chopped onions, sweat and washing-up water. Her arms throw her voice about, it rebounds against the walls and she catches it. The kitchen is colourless and mottled. The hanging beads over the doorway are mottled and make a crackling sound.

– So you see this top bit keeps coming off and that's just where I beat the washing, it can't take the strain I suppose.

The wash-tub is a rounded hollow of zinc encased in dark sodden wood which has cracked. Along the top in front. A new but bent board of thin wood lies on the ground in front of the tub, with nails sticking out of it. Next to it lies a hammer.

Sooner or later the bent board of thin soft wood will embrace the tub. The eyes of Mrs. Ned strike a tonic chord of expected notes. The arms no longer throw the voice about, the voice is quiet and the white arms naked to the elbow rest along the edge of the tub. The vertical upper arms, after the elbow, are wrapped in red and the fresh air absorbs the smell of washing-up water and sweat. The red cardigan partly conceals the goitre on the neck. Sooner or later a movement will have to be made. The kitchen, through the hanging beads, is dark.

Sometimes it is sufficient merely to speak, to say perhaps or I don't think so, as the case might be, or even, in this instance, to hammer a nail into the bent board over the dark sodden wood, for the sequence not to occur. Such as, for example,

– Ooh! You gave me a shock, that went right through me.

– I don't think so.

The white forearms move away from the edge of the tub, but one hand remains on it with the arm arching over.

Up at the big house, the mimosas are in bloom. Beyond the tall wrought-iron gates they rise and gracefully drape over the white wall separating the property from the road. The mimosas –

The conversation, during the hammering, takes the form of excited squeals and giggles.

– Ooh ! You gave me a shock.

– Did I , my dear? And what would you say to this?

Or rather, the conversation, during the hammering, takes the form of admiring murmurs and modestly expressed advice. One hand remains on the edge of the tub with the arm arching over. The right leg stands so near that it would be possible to stroke it all the way up, thin though it is. The right leg is very white and granulated with black dots.

– The nails don't get a grip. The wood is too sodden.

– I know. I need a whole new casement really.

The bent board of soft wood embraces the top of the tub. The hammer lies on the edge, then falls with a clatter into the rounded zinc tub, pushed by a careless movement. Both arms dart in to retrieve it, and the hands touch.

Beyond the open iron gates up at the big house the plane-trees line the drive, forming with their bare and upward branches a series of networks that become finer and finer as the drive recedes towards the house, made now discernible by the leaflessness. The network of bare branches functions in depth, a corridor of cobwebs full of flies.

– My tub seems to have broken, do you think you could come through to the back and have a look at it? If you don't mind I mean.

The passage is almost cubic in its brevity, with walls at right angles. To the left, the kitchen is not luminous, but muddled and mottled, nor is it framed in red. A tape-recorder might perhaps reveal this to be the phrase that came and went, through the short dark passage with walls at right angles. There is otherwise no explanation for the lack of lodgers in the front verandah-room or for the lack of the red framework, or for the colourless mottled kitchen. Beyond the colourlessness the kitchen has once been painted in cream and green. The hanging beads over the doorway are mottled and make a crackling sound.

During the hammering, the arms no longer throw the voice about, the voice is quiet and the white forearms hang limp down the white apron, continued a little lower by the marble veined legs, thin and about one metre away.

It is sometimes sufficient to say nothing or, in this instance, to hammer a nail into the bent board over the dark sodden wood, for the sequence not to occur, if indeed, the circumstances have been brought about at all in that precise form.

– The nails don't get a grip. The wood is too sodden.

– Did you say something?

– The wood is too sodden.

– I know. Your wife helped me with it earlier but it came off. I need a whole new casement really.

The bent board of soft wood embraces the top of the tub. The hammer lies on the edge.

– Were you winking at me as you came up to the bungalow? You were making such peculiar faces.

– I don't think so.

The hammer falls with a clatter into the rounded zinc tub, pushed by a careless movement.

Beyond the closed wrought-iron gates of the big house the mimosas are just beginning to blossom. Feathery green branches droop like ferns over the white wall that separates the property from the road, scattered here and there with yellow dots. The white wall is gently rounded as the road curves and continues to curve, but almost imperceptibly. It is impossible at any one moment to see whether things are any different round the corner.

Mrs. Mgulu, on the other hand, takes an interest.

In the white wall, the glossy black door opens suddenly and a jet of icy cold water shoots out at face level.

- Ice!

Or alternatively,

– Aaah, sprtch, grrr brrr expressing iciness and force of water on face.

– Ha-ha! You dirty! You need washing.

Or alternatively,

– Oh, you poor man you. This was not intended. You look sick. Have some *Duodenica*.

– No.

– Ha-ha! You dirty! You need washing.

The Bahuko face grins behind the pursuing jet of water which seems to spray out from between the two rows of white teeth, though in fact two black hands must be holding the hose, which is made of red thermoplastic, and a dark but pink-nailed index finger must be on the empty nozzle-holder to make the jet spray instead of pour.

– Hee-hee-hee-hee.

The laugh is that of a delighted child.

The red thermoplastic hose lies inside the flower-bed like a snake. The brass nozzle-holder has no spray-nozzle and out of it the water pours gently around the stem of a laurel bush. The red thermoplastic hose curves out of the flower-bed and all the way up the path, then turns behind the white corner of a small house.

– Oh, you poor man, you look wet. Is it the bladder troubling you? Have some colimycin.

No, that's the wrong one.

The other one laughs like a delighted child and says you dirty, you need washing.

In the white wall the glossy black door opens at last. Good afternoon, I'm the new gardener. But the reality is a negative of the previous images. Instead of the black man clothed in the pursuing jet of water, a woman stands framed in the whiteness, dressed in a black cotton overall, pale face, pale eyes that strike no note, pale hair. The waxiness is due to a deficiency in the liver. Behind the woman in the white frame the background is brown and cypress green.

– I've come about the gardening job.

– Oh, yes. My husband's somewhere about. Come in.

The path leads straight up to a small white cottage. On either side of the path runs a narrow brown flower-bed and a cypress hedge. The converging greenery engulfs the woman in the black overall, which may after all be a dress, or a black rectangle on two white pillars, moving up the path. The path is made of pink hexagonal tiles, slightly elongated like benzene rings.

– Wait here. I'll go and call him.

The left foot in its dirty canvas shoe is wholly contained in a benzene ring, the other, a little less dirty, has its big toe on the top dividing line like a carbon atom. If there were a single carbon atom at every angle the result would be graphite, soft and black. A little further up, two steps away perhaps, the left foot steps on the dividing line like the two shared carbon atoms of naphthalene, or for that matter the two shared carbon atoms of adenine, but no, the right-hand tile would in that case be pentagonal, more or less, with complex extensions to the right. Nevertheless the left foot angles off on the line that holds the atoms of the molecules together, linking the nitrogen atom to the carbon. The right foot makes a V with it, linking the nitrogen atom to the carbon and hydrogen. The cement between the sides of the long pink hexagons is thin and grey. In this manner, with the appropriate enzyme, represented perhaps by the left heel in a ribose molecule to the South East and a whole series linked by two energy-rich phosphate bonds, the energy can be quantitatively transferred from one molecule to another so that the backward and forward reactions are thermodynamically equivalent. Under biological conditions, however, the reaction is virtually irreversible. The forward reaction is attended by a large loss of energy in the form of heat. Unless perhaps –

– Good afternoon.

The head gardener is shocking pink, almost red, under a wide-brimmed hat. He looks ill, too, not like a gardener at all.

Perhaps he only ordains the gardening. Quite clearly it is not radiation, or even kidney trouble, it must be his heart. As a dark pink man he is employable.

– I believe Mrs. Mgulu –

– What? Speak up, I can't hear you.

– I believe Mrs. Mgulu –

– Ah yes. She told me about it. You know Mrs. Mgulu well?

– No. Oh no. It's my wife, she –

– Oh, I see. Well isn't that nice. I'm all for everyone helping each other especially us. Yes. I always say to Polly, that's my wife, forty-four years we've been married and we've seen plenty I can assure you. I always say to Polly in these difficult times we must all pull together and sink our ex-differences as Westerners, don't you agree?

The dialogue slowly but smoothly runs along the kindness of his blue eyes and many flowers are mentioned. The red network of veins over his face is very fine, especially on the cheeks where it forms a darker patch like a flower. The dialogue falters and comes to an end. The face turns the red network of veins away, leaving only the broad-brimmed hat and a deeply lined red neck. The voice starts up again, slow, deliberate. A monologue moves away on the other side of the moving hat and the red neck.

– That is poinsettia on that wall over there to the right. It will be coming out shortly. Now, did you know that the red flowers, or what appear to be red flowers, are not flowers at all, but leaves? The flower, now, is a modest little yellow thing, inside the red leaves, looking like a mere pistil. These are zinnias, or rather they will be zinnias, in due course. Here the winter irises are out.

– And the mimosas. I much admired your mimosas on the way here.

– Oh mimosas need no real care. Just sandy soil. The soil is very sandy here. Too sandy for almost everything we want. But modern chemistry is wonderful.

The left foot is inside another adenine molecule, the right foot having blotted out one of the energy-rich phosphate bonds East of ribose. The energy-rich bonds cannot be directly used for biological work of any kind, unless transferred to adenesine diphosphate so as to generate new triphosphate molecules. The phosphate radicals –

– I'm afraid that once a triphosphate molecule has shed its terminal phosphate radical its life as energy-donor is at an end. In my country –

– In your country men were lazy. That is why they lost the battle for survival. It is an article of faith.

– This dialogue is out of place, he's nice, he likes you.

– They're conceited, lazy, unreliable.

– We don't bother with them here, they're a typically temperate flower, you know. Mrs. Mgulu says that chrysanthemums remind her of damp December funerals in the North. But she's fond of begonias, as you can see, and laurels. These are the young orange-trees. They have been wrongly planted though, in round hollows, instead of on mounds of earth. The water should drain away. They should never be allowed to soak. The gardener who did that seems to have been out of his mind, or drunk perhaps. Well, he was ill, actually, of the malady, he died last week I believe. He was supposed to know. The heel of the left foot is in the ribose molecule, the toe, which is wearing out the canvas, is in the adenine, no, that's no use, they are pentagonal, it could, however, be oestrone, obtained from stallion's urine. The right foot is wholly in the elongated hexagon, as in a coffin, during the rainy season. Quite likely they will have been seriously harmed. You would not be replacing him, however, he has in fact already been replaced. I want you, rather, for the watering, not now, but when the dry season begins. Here is one of the hoses, it is kept stretched along the inside of this flower-bed right back to where you came in. In the other direction, however, it will also reach as far as that wall, beyond the olive grove. There are six other hoses and six taps.

The thermoplastic hose is green after all that, and slithers along the left flower-bed. The feet move obliquely towards the phosphate energy-rich bonds East of ribose, it takes four or five hours, because of course every plant must be watered individually. Some plants like the spray, you see, and some prefer a plain jet, on the root, or even, some, around the root. These little castor-oil plants, for instance, they grow up large and massive, like those over there, but while they are so small and delicate the jet must not touch them at all, the stem would break. So it's better not to use the spray-nozzle, but just to put your finger over the nozzle-holder whenever you need to spray. There is a spray-nozzle, however, for certain beds. You need not know much about gardening, but you will have to learn the whole drill. It must be done in the correct order, otherwise some beds get forgotten. The cactuses don't need direct watering.

Both toes are in one large oblong paving stone. Each heel is in a smaller stone, and the line of cement runs between them. The heart beats reach the throat suddenly.

– I am a gardener. I received Vocational Training at the Resettlement Camp after the displacement. I –

– Did you say something?

– I am a gardener. I received Vocational Training at the Resettlement Camp after the displacement.

– Oh. But Mrs. Mgulu gave me to understand that you had no training, and no experience. An odd job man, she said. This is an odd job you understand.

– In my country –

– Excuse my asking but was your country Ukay?

– I was head gardener at the White House, I had twenty men under me.

– The white house. Which white house? The Ukayans have long had a bad reputation as workers, you know. However, I am not one for generalisations, as I always say to Polly, one must not be hide-bound by dogma, come what may, it's the particular that counts. I understood from Mrs.

Mgulu that your wife had told her you had been a politician in – er – London, would it be?

– That's not true. Never. No, no, no. I was a gardener –

– I see. Well, it all comes to the same thing in the end, doesn't it. I mean I'm not one for prejudice in these matters. One of my best friends was a Uessayan of Ukay extraction. On the other hand there is no hurry about this particular job. The hot season is not yet due, and much planting remains to be done. You may wish to think about it. I'll let you know.

The feeling is one of heterotrophism. The left foot treads the length of a cemented line. Between the tiles, the right foot carefully selects another line of cement parallel with the edge of the path. The amount of free energy that becomes available for the performance of useful work does not correspond to the total heat change but is equivalent to about ten thousand calories per gram. molecule, the remaining two thousand being involved in the intra-molecular changes of the reaction. It is possible to walk on such parallel lines only, almost without touching the diagonals. It is possible, but difficult, and a little slow, for the molecules are closely linked and have to be either skipped or touched, democratically, each and every one, which leaves little choice. A periscope, held backwards, might perhaps reveal whether the turning away of the red network of veins and the moving off, beyond the red poinsettias, of the broad-brimmed hat over the deeply lined red neck has been totally accomplished, or whether there has been another turn, and a pause, and a watching there still. The green thermoplastic snake lies along the inside of the right-hand flower-bed, about twenty centimetres away from the cypress hedge, quite straight, and very long, leading towards the glossy black door in the white wall. The green thermoplastic snake comes to an end by a laurel-bush, pointing its brass nozzle-holder at the stem, without the spray-nozzle attachment. There is no water coming out of the hose. The glossy black door in the white wall, on this side, is painted yellow.

The end of the green thermoplastic hose, held downwards with the right hand six centimetres away from the brass nozzle-holder, and with the left hand further away still, pours an imagined jet of water straight at the spot where the strong stem of the laurel-bush comes out of the earth. The pressure of the water in the hose is not strong. It can be made stronger by holding the hose higher, about a metre or more above the plant, so that the jet of water goes straight down into the root, making a slight hole in the dry earth around the strong stem. The earth drinks quickly. It has been baked all day by the hot sun and it is thirsty. A small puddle forms around the laurel-bush. The baby castor-oil plants are next. The hose must be held much closer, the brass nozzle-holder almost touching the earth around each plant but not touching the plant itself. Held at this height, it gives a jet which does not remove or disturb the earth but flows gently into it.

The right hand has jerked. The right arm is a model of still control, and yet the hand that holds the hose six centimetres away from the brass nozzle has jerked sideways, so that the jet, following the movement, has fallen on the delicate reddish stem of the smallest castor-oil plant. The stem has not broken but the plant is uprooted. It is possible, however, to replant it quickly in the now softened earth.

– Conceited, lazy, unreliable. It is an article of faith.

– Ha! You dirty, you need washing. Ha!

– Aaah, sprtch, grrr, brrr, stop, shshtop, prshsh.

– Hee-hee-hee! The laugh is that of a delighted child. You have a heart condition. Symptoms? Verbal diarrhoea, sanguine complexion. Did you know that the dark patches on your cheeks are not flowers at all, but blood, belonging like words to the element of fire, quench it, quick, water, water, help fire. I am a doctor you see. Drench, drench.

The white wall is gently rounded as the road curves, and continues to curve, but almost imperceptibly. It is impossible ever to see whether things are different round the corner. The bougainvillaea clusters over the top of the wall, backed by young palm trees that sway a little in the luminosity of the white winter sky, and the white wall continues to curve along the curving road. It is impossible to tell when the mimosas will come into view. Sooner or later they will flare brightly into view. The red flowers of the poinsettia, or what appear to be red flowers, which will be coming out shortly, are not flowers at all but leaves. Did you know that? Well of course, I am a gardener. Feathery green branches droop down like ferns over the white wall that separates the property from the road, clustered here and there with yellow dots. Beyond the closed wrought-iron gates the mimosas are just beginning to bloom. Sooner or later they will be a mass of yellow. Sooner or later they will be a mass of gold against the post-card blue sky. It is difficult to revisualise the exact degree of blueness in a summer sky, or to re-imagine the exact degree of heat. You may wish to think about it, I'll let you know. The hot season is not yet with us and much planting remains to be done.

– Yes, well, as a matter of fact I would like to think about it. I hadn't quite visualised the exact degree of, I hadn't quite visualised the degree of heat that would be applied. The fire of cosanguinity is excessive. The pressure of the water is low. Pulse diagnosis shows that the plant is uprooted, although the delicate stem has not been actually broken. It would be possible to replant it quickly in the now softened earth.

– Yes, well as a matter of fact I would like to think about it. I hadn't quite visualised the degree of – servility implied. I am a doctor by training, and although circumstances have, through no fault of theirs, forced many of my countrymen to open the great wrought-iron gates, slowly, by remote control, the plane-trees lining the drive form with their bare and upward branches a series of networks, like a map of the nervous system, that become finer and finer as the drive recedes towards the big house, just discernible through the leaflessness. Beyond the thick network of bare branches there is a finer network, closing in a little over the drive, and beyond that a finer network still. The network of bare branches functions in depth, a corridor of cobwebs full of traps for flies. At the distant centre of the corridor of cobwebs the spider is advancing.

The spider is advancing with sparkling teeth bared in a wide flattened grin that blares white as it catches the luminosity of the white winter sky. Nearer and nearer it smoothly advances, apparently stretching across the whole width of the drive, broadening as the drive broadens, approaching with an engulfing threat to the wrought-iron gates until suddenly the gates dwarf it with their own tall fangs that close slowly behind it as it passes through. A pale blue face floats in a blue glass globe above the wide metallic grin. Beyond it, outlined against more light, more glass and moving fronds, a cavern-blue chin-line curved like a madonna's and pale blue teeth flashing in wide mauve lips under a wide mauve hat of falling plumes, all of it cut, swiftly, by a shaft of light reflected in the glass, and then away, only a purple blob in a moving bubble of quickly shifting blue and green. The number of the vehicle is 24.81.632. There is no numerical significance in such a number. Beyond the vertical bars of the closed wrought-iron gates there is the thick network of the first plane-trees on either side of – oh hell. The number of the vehicle is, the number of the vehicle, the number of the vehicle is gone. The number of the vehicle is insignificant.

Daily from 8 a.m., at the Labour Exchange, a gnarled left hand lies stretched like a claw on the neighbouring human thigh. A fly straddles the high blue vein that comes down from the middle finger towards the thumb. The vein must seem like a rampart to the fly, unless perhaps the fly has no conception of a rampart, any more than it has of love, and does not even know that the vein is blue. Sooner or later the thumb, or even the whole hand with a flick of the wrist, will twitch the fly away. Sooner or later a group of five names will be called out and the thigh will slope up into a vertical position, slowly or suddenly according to the age and the humour and the health, according to the degree of sanguinity or melancholia, according to the balance or imbalance of hope and despair.

Dear Madam, your head gardener. Dear Madam, in an age of international and interracial enlightenment such as we have been privileged to witness and partake of on this continent since the displacement, it is a shock and a disappointment for me to have to report to you that your head gardener. Dear Madam, you will only know the name at the bottom of this letter through my wife who serves you, and for whom you were kind enough to arrange an interview with your head gardener. And on behalf of whom you were kind enough. And for whom you were kind enough to arrange an interview between me and your. Between your head gardener and. For whom you were kind enough to ask your head gardener to see me with regard to a job. Dear Madam – you will only know the name at the bottom of this letter through my wife, who works for you, and for whom you were kind enough to ask your head gardener to see me with regard to a job, as I understood it, a job presumably as assistant gardener. In an age of international and interracial enlightenment such as ours, the gnarled left hand lies on its side, with the fingers curling in under the stretched out thumb, as if the hand were holding a bunch of flowers or a stemmed glass. The high blue vein from the middle finger curves upwards towards the thumb.

In an age of international and interracial enlightenment such as we have been privileged to witness on our continent since the displacement, the fly moves jerkily on the canvas shoe of the left foot, between the bump made by the big toe and the first hole of the grey shoe-lace. The shoe-lace though grey, is brand new. The blue of the canvas is faded, the shoe is well worn but not in holes. The other shoe, half hidden by the left foot which is crossed over it, may be in holes.

The fly takes off. Perhaps the left canvas shoe has twitched slightly with the long waiting. The fly climbs up the air as if the air had steps, and at each stage it rests a little in a state of comatose suspension. From about eye-level it swoops to land on the left knee of the neighbouring human thigh whose leg has a foot that wears a blue canvas-shoe, well-worn but not, to the naked eye, in holes. The fly lands about fifteen centimetres away from the hand that holds an invisible bunch of flowers. Sooner or later a group of five names will be called out. It is a shock and a disappointment. It is with dismay that I have to report to you that your head gardener is still governed by reactionary prejudice. Ha! you dirty! Aaah, grrr.

– Please?

The neighbour's face is as gnarled as his left hand. His eyes – the tiled floor is mottled. Up by the counter some twenty men stand in four short queues of five at each of the four grilled partitions. Further towards the door men mill about in murmuring groups of mostly Colourless faces, some detaching themselves to go out, some detaching themselves to come in. Above the door the notice says Do Not Spit. A Colourless boy pushes through the groups, looks around at the benches along the walls, hesitates then walks towards one of them along the opposite wall. The fly has left the mottled floor, frightened, perhaps, by the banging of metal cupboard doors and filing cabinets. The sound in the air, however, is mottled with human voices. It is all the more astonishing in view of the fact that your head gardener seems to be, to all appearances, himself an ex-Ukayan. The only possible explanation I can think of is all the more astonishing in view of the fact that the wall is dirty green and peeling. The portrait of the Governor on the far wall beyond the strong black heads of the employment clerks at their grilled partitions, the portrait of the Governor with his vain Asswati face, the fly sits like a wart on the corner of the Governor's stalwart lips. The fly is reflected in the glass, like two warts. Unless perhaps it is a different fly, there being one fly inside the glass and one outside, the female fly seeking its mate on the mottled floor, the male fly on the Governor's portrait, contemplating its image. The only possible explanation is that your head gardener is of a sanguinary complexion still uncontrollably radiating a reactionary prejudice.

Dear Mrs. Mgulu.

The neighbour's gnarled hand that held an invisible bunch of flowers stretches out and lies flat on the left thigh. The far hand, which is also gnarled, and which may or may not have held an invisible bunch of flowers or even the stem of a glass, does the same. There is a tension in both the hands, as if the human mind in control of their movements expected at any moment to use them, perhaps for raising the body by means of pressure on the two knees. The thighs are thin and tightly trousered in faded denim. Creases starring out from the loin vanish under each wrist.

Dear Mrs. Mgulu. I hope you will not mind my writing to you, but through my wife I feel I am already acquainted with your great kindness and generosity and understanding. No doubt you know a little about me also. It is therefore in appeal to your well-known humanity-y-y-y

– You feel all right?

– Why?

– You groan much. It is long waiting.

– I'm in a state of comatose suspension.

– Please?

– I am happy with my thoughts.

– Excuse me.

The fingers drum a little on the thighs. The blue denim

calls out the veins on the back of the hands. The chin crumples into a crumpled neck.

– Very witty. But unkind.

– He didn't understand. He's a foreigner.

– So are you.

– The dialogue will not take place, anyway.

– Sometimes it is sufficient just to be bloody rude.

– Sometimes it is sufficient merely to speak, to say perhaps or I don't think so or how very interesting, as the case might be, for the effect to be bloody rude and the sequence, therefore, not to occur. Or to hammer a nail into the bent board over the dark sodden wood.

Dear Mrs. Mgulu.

The fly lies comatose on the Governor's stalwart lips, unless it is contemplating its image. The Governor stares fiercely out regardless. The Governor gazes benignly down regardless. His dark eyes meet all eyes that meet his, but the meeting is not compulsory.

– Well I couldn't help it, sir, I didn't know. I wasn't told.

– You people are all the same. You should have known and you could have found out. Listen you lot, this is the sort of thing I'm up against with you. This fellow says he's a builder. He was sent to mend a roof-flashing which had got torn up by the gale and what did he do? He nailed it down into the wooden beam with ungalvanised iron nails. This in the rainy season. Needless to say they rusted immediately. The damp got into the beam and is rotting it.

The employment clerk hammers on the counter to make his voice louder and louder. The man on this side of the counter is puny, with a ginger head. Like a crooked ungalvanised nail he seems to sink into the tiled floor with every hammering of the employment clerk's hand which is the colour of an old oak beam, startlingly braceleted with a white cuff-edge. The hall is silent. The silence of the hall is broken by coughs and shifting feet. The ginger head is raised again.

– I didn't have no galvanised nails with me.

The bland Bahuko face shines, patched with curved oblongs and blobs of white light. The cuff-edge moves again, upholding the fly-flicking gesture of dismissal that must cause the ungalvanised nail to disappear from the floor.

There is a murmuring in the hall. The puny man with ginger hair shuffles past the row of sitting thighs and their belonging feet. His face is oxidised copper. Oxidative metabolism is a more efficient source of adenosine triphosphate than is fermentation. The greenish colour, however, is due to over-production in the gall-bladder, and gall-stones are the tomb-stones of bacteria. This is a good topic with which to go into reverse and bring about the sequence that has not yet occurred, should the non-occurrence of the sequence prove unbearable. Or not, as the case might be.

It is easy enough in the negative. It is more difficult to bring about than to prevent. Is this proposition true? Sometimes, anyway, the gruel is brought.

– Poor man.

– I beg your pardon? Smile to make up for tone.

– That man. He look sick.

– Oh, yes. He's bilious. Over-production of the gall-bladder I should say.

– Please?

– I said, trouble in the gall-bladder.

– Were you doctor then in your country?

– Well, in a way.

– But why you queue here? They need doctors, many many sick, of the malady.

The fly, where is the fly? The Governor gazes benignly down regardless. Dear Mrs. Mgulu.

– Well. It's a bit complicated. And you?

– Schoolmaster. Iranian. Useless here. Speak no good Asswati. Work on roads. Better for you, speak Ukayan, second language, and medicine better.

– Well. Not really.

– You ex-Ukayan?

– Yes.

– I see.

The sequence has occurred.

At home, a recipe would be read. At home there would be a remedy. It would occupy the air. Or a letter from someone possibly. According to our records you have not reported to this exchange for three weeks. Retrospectively a name will be called out daily from 8 a.m.

– You get slip?

– Er, yes.

– Doctors also?

– Well. Not quite. It's a bit complicated.

– I understand.

– I wasn't complaining.

– No. But sad. Excuse me. You take your dole pills?

– I haven't reported for three weeks, just as it says.

– I have extra some. I collect but keep for big pep booze. You wish one?

– No, no. Thank you. Very kind.

– Please.

At home there would be a remedy. A remedy would be read out and it would occupy the air. It is more difficult in the negative, more difficult, that is, to stop than to bring about. Sometimes, however, a group of names is called.

– It is not really as you think, anti-Ukay. Look at me, Iranian. And that man up there now, ex-Uessayan, every day he come. And there is ex-French. And him Portuguese.

– Of course, all Colourless. But the head gardener up at one of the big houses is bright pink. Mauve even.

– Pink is a colour. Yellow is a colour. Beige is a colour.

– That is an article of faith.

– I understand their attitude. White is the colour of the mal –

– Waxiness is due to a deficiency in the liver. A greenish colour is –

A group of names is called out.

– Excuse me.

The gnarled, blue-veined hands press the tightly denimed knees as the thighs change to a vertical position. There is a nod high up.

At home there would have been a recipe. Dear Mrs. Mgulu. I hope you won't mind, I hope you will not mind my writing to you, but in an age of international and interracial equality such as we have been privileged to witness and partake of since the great displacement, it is a shock and a disappointment for me to have to report to you that the two hands clasped together between the next human thighs are brown, dark brown like strong and tudor beams. The two index fingers point up cathedrally, touching at the tips. The two thumbs touch, pointing dihedrally towards the loin. A lodge is formed, with porch and gate, pink within, brown without. Pink is a colour. Brown is a colour. Black is a colour. It is an article of faith. There is a movement in the neighbour's neck of one who is about to talk, to show that despite everything he is in the same boat, temporarily at least. They should know that people with kidney trouble find it difficult to use their voice, the voice gets lost and little. People with kidney trouble do not like people. It is easy enough in the negative.

– What job are you hoping for?

– Oh, anything, odd job. And you?

– What were you before?

– I was a schoolmaster.

– Uessayan?

– No, no, Iranian. And you?

– How very interesting. Ah, that's me. Goodbye. Good luck.

The fly moves close to the white leather shoe on the mottled floor. Brown is a colour. Sooner or later, however, the correct identity, the Colourless identity that belongs, will be, is called out. The fly takes off swiftly. The left foot whose big toe is wearing out the canvas steps squarely into a mottled tile. The mottled tiles merge, move fast. Through the metal trellis the bland Bahuko face is splintered. It is not bland and not Bahuko but lean and brown and Berber, granulated like basalt rock, with hooded eyes over white slits that vanish. The Governor stares fiercely out regardless.

– Ex-occupation?

– Schoolmaster.

– Speak up, I can't hear you.

– Schoolmaster.

– Ex-nationality?

– Iranian.

The brown hoods lift.

– That is two of you in five minutes. It is statistically improbable. What was your occupation?

– I used to be a joiner.

– We have you down as a philosopher.

– No, no, no. That's not true.

– Well, it all comes to the same thing in the end.

– Why ask then?

The white cuff-edge encircles the brown wrist like a bracelet. The finger-nails along the golden pen are pink and well rounded. Whereas no amount of positive evidence can ever conclusively confirm a hypothesis, one piece of negative evidence conclusively falsifies it. Discuss fully, making detailed reference to your set texts. Dear Mrs. Mgulu.

– We have you down as an odd job man.

– Well it all comes to the same thing in the end.

– Don't be impertinent. We're doing all we can for you people but it isn't easy.

Framed by the square in the middle of the metallic trellis the lean basalt face bears a wart above its well-chiselled lips. To the left of the nose, with the right eye closed, the left side of the trellis square divides the face almost exactly in half with a vertical bar. To the right of the nose, with the left eye closed, the bar moves to the left of the face.

– Oh, now wait, someone rang through about you. I didn't connect the name. Where are we? Yes. That's it. From Mrs.

Mgulu of Western Approaches. Apparently there was a misunderstanding.

– A misunderstanding?

– That's what's written on the pad. Misunderstanding.

– Did she say that?

– Well, no, it was the butler, or someone. She wants you to start work tomorrow. In the garden.

Hee-hee-hee of a delighted child, the jet shoots out, the feet are apart, the index finger covers the brass nozzle-holder and the jet sprays out over the sliding blue globe in which against the moving palms a cavern-blue chin-line curves like a madonna's, underlining a blob of mauve beneath a wide mauve crest of falling plumes, drowned in the water and away bearing a lucky number. Beyond the tall wrought-iron gates the mimosas are difficult, you see. We have no prejudice that's an article of faith. But there is an irrational fear of the Colourless that lingers on, it's understandable, in some cases, even justifiable, with the malady still about, well, it makes them unreliable. However, good luck to you. Oh, wait, here's your unemployment pill, you're entitled to it as you're not working till tomorrow.

Whereas no amount of positive evidence. Dear Mrs. Mgulu, I know you won't mind my writing to you in this way. The peeling walls are painted green. You must understand, we do all we can. Men move aside. Above their heads the notice says Do Not Spit. This lady takes an interest, as you should know, since your wife, the floor is mottled. A young palm tree mops the luminous white sky, framed darkly by the door.

Inside the avenue of the mind that functions in depth, Mrs. Mgulu sits back on the cushions of the vehicle as it glides towards the tall wrought-iron gates. The tumbling purple plumes of the wide hat shade off the cave-blue face, call out the wide and purple mouth.

To the right of the driver's cap, far ahead, a man is standing beyond the wrought-iron gates. The sun flickers through the quick plane-trees. The iron gates grow and the man moves to the left behind the driver's head. The iron gates open towards the vehicle, forming a guard of lances. The man stands in the road, shabbily dressed. He is Colourless.

– Who was that, Ingram, did you see?

– I'm afraid I didn't, ma'am.

– I do believe it was the husband of one of my maids, she has often described him to me.

Mrs. Mgulu turns her black madonna chin-line towards the rear window just as the vehicle slides along the rounded corner.

– I wonder what he was doing there.

Ingram is silent, his eyes fixed on the coming curve of the road.

– I do hope the head gardener didn't upset him, he is so very insensitive. A sanguine temperament. I really ought to get rid of him. But he is old and I am sorry for him. No, this would only be a thought. Mrs. Mgulu thinks, I do hope etc. Ingram, she says aloud, you didn't hear anything in the servants' quarters about the head gardener interviewing someone for a job as assistant gardener did you? I mean could anything have gone wrong?

– No ma'am, at least, nothing specific.

– What do you mean, nothing specific?

Ingram looks cryptically into the driving-mirror, sees her mauve mouth and stares at the curve in the road ahead.

– I only know that he came into the servants' hall just before I left for the garage. He seemed rather angry.

– Oh dear, what a nuisance.

The olive-trees move slowly along, tinged by the sunset. It is difficult to tell the exact colour. The knowledge of their normal silvery green interferes with the absolute result of being tinged. And yet the road is pink. Not underfoot, where the immediate familiarity with its normal greyness makes it grey, but further ahead, receding even, the pinkness of the road recedes beyond the greyness covered. The white house on the hill is pink. The pink house higher up is flame-coloured. At eye-level, the shacks come into view. Three of them are on fire. Three of them are having a party. The glass verandah doors of three of them reflect the setting sun in dazzling orange. Some people would call them bungalows.

It was the glass that was blue of course, making the hat look purple and the face cave-blue and the wide mouth mauve in the avenue of the mind. The hat inside the vehicle must be pink. The wide pink hat of falling plumes calls the wide and dark pink mouth out of the chin-line that is charcoal smooth. In the driving mirror Ingram glimpses the crimson mouth and stares at the wrought-iron gates that grow as the man beyond them moves to the left. The iron gates open, forming a guard of lances. The man stands in the road, blue through the glass.

– Who was that, Ingram, did you see?

– No ma'am.

– I do believe it was Lilly's husband, I have seen him before on this road. I wonder what he was doing there?

– Oh dear, what a nuisance. I did promise Lilly. Lilly is such a very excellent woman.

We can make our errors in a thought and reject them in another thought, leaving no trace of error in us. Comment and percolate. Sooner or later the bladder must be emptied, leaving no trace of urine in us. Explicate and connect. The grey base of the olive-tree darkens and steams a little.

Sooner or later a bowl of gruel will be set down on the wrinkled wood inside the rectangle of light. Unless perhaps it is set down in a round pool of light.

Mrs. Ned's bungalow is on fire. The glass verandah doors

of Mrs. Ned's bungalow reflect the last rays of the setting sun, but the other bungalows are extinguished. The fig-tree looks blasted. Its thick black twigs poke upwards into the dusk, out of contorted branches. The dark trunk leans along the edge of the bank at an angle of forty degrees inside which, from the road, the lower section of the brown clapboard wall next to the verandah may just be seen, that is, with the help of the knowledge that it can normally be seen from this position. One of the branches sweeps downwards out of the trunk, away from the road, forming with the trunk an arch that frames the lower section of the wall within it, the frame merging into the darkness of the clapboard wall. The thick long twigs on this down-sweeping branch grow downwards first, then up, like large U-letters, almost invisible against the dark patch of grass and the dark wood of the bungalow beyond. It is the knowledge of their shape which makes them visible. Discuss and titillate.

The glass door of the verandah reflects a green light, in which a filmy monster shifts into view, cut into three sections. The top section frames a jellyfish, the middle section a tiered hierarchy of diagonal wobbles, the lower section two thin trunks, wavering like algae. The lower section two thin trunks as still as trees; the middle section a tiered hierarchy of frozen diagonal zigzags with two arms that can lift away out of the tiered zigzag to form two angles of forty-five degrees, two angles of ninety degrees, two angles of a hundred and eighty degrees, continuing the two thin trunks up into the top section on either side of the jellyfish. Sooner or later the identity will be called out. And here is Mr. Blob in our studio tonight. Mr. Blob, you've been cutting yourself into three sections of different wriggling shapes for twenty years now, beating your own record year after year. Can you tell us why you do it?

– Yes. I can no more help doing it than breathe, you see. It's something inside me that drives me. Like climbing a mountain, one must get to the top, you see. Of course one could give up and go down again, but it's so much more satisfying to go on, however difficult, it gives one a sense of purpose, you see.

– But isn't there a very real danger of complete disintegration?

– I might of course disintegrate, but that is a risk worth taking.

– Worth taking for whom, Mr. Blob? What can really be the point of an activity which costs one and a half million every time and keeps two hundred and ninety-seven people fully occupied all along the operation assembly line just seeing to it that you don't disintegrate?

– In these days of severe unemployment Mr. Hatchet, I don't think that keeping two hundred and ninety-seven people occupied can possibly be called wasteful. They are all extremely loyal and believe in it tremendously, without them I would be as nothing and I must say that. It may look pointless to you but the ionization industry is backing it heavily. Each time, technical discoveries are made which help them considerably in their research. Ultimately however the greatest importance of my achievement – modest though it may be in scope – is that it adds to Ukayan prestige abroad and in the whole world.

– But Mr. Blob, this record for, what is it, I quote, standing still in near disintegration, it's your own record you keep beating. No one else has the slightest desire to compete with you.

– It doesn't matter whose record it is. I think you will find that in the long run any world record broken adds to Ukayan prestige abroad and in the whole –

– Mr. Blob: thank you very much.

– Eh!

The picture has been quite replaced.

– Oh, good evening Mrs. Ivan. Nice evening. Er, yes, I was just looking at the verandah door to see if, well, to see –

– Yes?

– To see myself, Mrs. Ivan. Not you I assure you. I apologise. I disintegrate.

– My verandah. Okay?

– Okay.

– Goodnight Mrs. Ivan. Thank you, thank you Mrs. Ivan. Goodnight.

The bead curtain crackles. The kitchen is rounded by the twilight. It is the knowledge of the shape and size of the kitchen table and chairs which make them visible. In absolute blackness, however, the knowledge of their shape and size would not make them visible, it would merely guide the sense of touch. Is this true or am I mad? Discuss and denigrate.

The remedy lies in the sudden pool of light, set down in the wrinkled wood. Behind the hanging beads the door is shut. The stone floor between the doorway and the table is dark brown and still.

The remedy is called Metabol. The light over the table makes a moon in the darkness beyond the window. Below the moon is the jellyfish. Closing in on the jellyfish it is possible to see deep within it, a rectangle of faint orange light, itself enclosed in the black trapeze-shape that is Monsieur Jules's shack and melts into the darkness beyond the kitchen window. Moving the jellyfish a little it is possible to capture other black trapeze-shapes deep within it. The view from the kitchen window, when it can be seen, is of innumerable low-built bungalows. The remedy is for emotional manifestations. But then, she will complicate life for herself, sitting back in the cushions of the vehicle as it glides towards the tall wrought-iron gates. Her face is cavern-blue.

– Who was that, Ingram, did you see?

– I don't know ma'am, a Colourless man.

– Oh but his eyelids were all right. I do believe he is a doctor, I have seen him before. Stop the vehicle, Ingram, I feel so ill.

Inside the jellyfish beyond the kitchen window, the night

engulfs. The conversation, during the hammering, takes the form of admiring murmurs and modestly expressed advice. The hanging beads over the doorway are mottled and still.

– Whatever were you doing at sunset on your verandah?

– At sunset?

– Well, it was just getting dark. You had your arms lifted up above your head and you were dancing about like a puppet on strings.

The trapeze shape is enormous and quite black.

– Mrs. Ned?

– Anyone at home?

– Hello, there?

– Mrs. Ned. It's me. I came to see if your tub is all right.

– Hello? Mrs. Ned. I've been given a job.

During the hammering the conversation is one-sided.

A tape-recorder might perhaps reveal certain phrases that came and went, leaving no trace of error in us. Everything that moves increases risk.

The first failure is the beginning of the first lesson. Learning begins with failure. The green thermoplastic hose, held downwards into the night, with the right-hand six centimetres away from the brass nozzle-holder, and with the brass nozzle-holder almost touching the night-black earth around the small castor-oil plant, would perhaps be black in the circumstances, and give a black or maybe silvery jet which does not remove or disturb the earth but flows gently into it. The dark jet must not touch the delicate stem and the right arm is a model of still control. The blackness, however, nudges.

– Oh, hello, Mrs. Ned. I've been given a job.

– Oh, hello. I didn't recognise you without the chip on your shoulder. Oh, hello, I didn't recognise you in the dark.

The letter is on the table, folded in four, next to the remedy. The handwriting on the top quarter is upside down which draws the eye to decipherment. The remedy is called Metabol. Nervousness and agitation irritability motor unrest insomnia hostility aggressiveness phobias and hallucinations.

Even though many personality problems characteristic of senility may be linked with organic changes in the brain
· · · any in · · · you reached · · · hasn't · · · hope · · · I which
· · · very a such · · · being · · · you · · · form · · · or shape
person. · · · active This terrible malady which I hope hasn't reached you in any shape or form you being of course their fear is irrational as it's not catching from people it's the radiation in the air and they merely resist better, but it's all very soul-destroying though I must cry it out aloud that they're being extraordinarily humane and generous about it. I must say I'm lucky to have married as I did, at least my children stand a sporting chance.

The light over the table makes a moon in the darkness beyond the window. Below the moon is the window-ledge. The pool of light engulfs the entire table and part of the red stone floor. The wrinkled wood is quite static in the light, as static, at any rate, as the network of minute lines on the back of the wrist. A microscope might perhaps reveal which is the more static of the two. The protozoan scene under the microscope is one of continual traffic jams and innumerable collisions.

– What was it you said?

– I was saying that Mr. Marburg the butler was most obliging today –

– No, before that.

– Don't forget to lick your spoon.

– Ah, yes, I knew it was something important.

The circle of steaming gruel in the bowl is greyish white and pimply. The squint seems blue tonight, and wider. The pale eye that doesn't move is fixed on the remedy, but the mobile eye wriggles away, its blue mobility calling out the blueness of the temple veins and a hint of blue in the white skin. A microscope might perhaps reveal a striking increase in the leucocyte count, due to a myeloid hyperplasia leading to an absolute increase in the granular leucocytes. Sooner or later immature and primitive white cells appear in the peripheral blood and corresponding changes in the bone marrow. Then the mobile eye too remains fixed, reproachful perhaps.

– Mr. Marburg just happened to mention it to me, I had no idea of course, and I would never have known if he hadn't come up to the guest wing just at the time that I happened to be there. I've never seen him up there I must say, it was the purest chance, unless perhaps he came specially to tell me, which is always a possibility. But why did you do it?

Sooner or later movement, which is necessary but not inevitable, will lead to attainment. That seems to be the general theory at any rate. Yet everything that moves increases risk. Sometimes it is sufficient merely to desire intensely.

The knock ushers Mrs. Ivan into the kitchen to fill her two large jugs of water. Phrases come and go, with and without smies, not at all, good evening, thank you, goodnight.

– Oh, Mrs. Ivan.

– Yes?

– I hope you don't mind my mentioning it, but could you use up and throw away your opened tins more quickly? They do smell so and anyway it's dangerous for your health. You may get food poisoning.

– Thank you Mrs.

– I mean if you don't eat the whole contents why open so many?

– Thank you. Thank you. Goodnight.

– Goodnight. She'll break my heart with those tins. Well anyway it was very awkward for me, I mean, I didn't know whose fault it was and I assumed naturally that it was ours in some way. But Mrs. Mgulu couldn't have been kinder. She really takes an interest you see and it's become a matter of principle with her. She said – I say are you listening? That thing is for doctors, not patients. I mean you want to be careful, listen to this, for instance. Care should be taken in prescribing other depressants of the central nervous system such as anaesthetics, analgesics and hypnotics since their effects may be potentiated by Metabol. Tachycardia and postural hypotension have occasionally been observed but these have rarely been sufficiently serious to warrant the discontinuation of the drug. Other side-effects reported in isolated cases are convulsions, constipation, anorexia, dyspnoea, epistaxis, insomnia and slight oedema. Well I mean it doesn't do to read that sort of thing, it's better to stick to posologies for patients.

The light over the table makes a moon in the darkness beyond the window. Below the moon is the jellyfish. Mr. Blob: thank you very much. Closing in on the jellyfish it is possible to see deep within it a black trapeze-shape that melts into the blackness. It is possible to see it, that is, helped by the knowledge that it can normally be seen from this position. Moving the jellyfish a little, only blackness can be seen. Knowledge certain or indubitable is unobtainable.

The gesture is one of benediction. The hands are pink. The earth is pale and dry. The plants are blackened by the frost.

Or something like that, the hands being brown perhaps and the flowers a mass of pink.

– Mrs. Mgulu says they remind her of damp December funerals in the North.

The flowers a mass of red.

The black hands out of the white cotton sleeves spread over the flaccid white belly, the third finger of one occasionally tapping the third finger of the other, flatly brown on the white flesh. No, it is the head gardener who is in question and his hands are definitely pink. The earth is brown and healthy.

– The dry season hasn't really begun yet, I don't know what to do with you. That's all I said you know. Well you could dig up those old bulbs, here, they should have come out two months ago, but the fellow who was to have done it died last week. As a matter of fact the best thing would be for you to get to know all the plants intimately before the watering begins. Every plant must be watered individually, you see. I'll have to take you round and introduce you, one or two beds a day for the first couple of weeks, or you'll never learn the drill. It must be done in the correct order otherwise some beds get forgotten.

– Those little orange-trees look wrongly planted, don't they?

– Oh, they're all right. Some plants like the spray and some prefer a plain jet on the root. Or even around the root. The important thing is to do them one at a time, remembering each plant's individuality. The little orange-trees now, they don't need watering every day, but every two or three days, and then you give them plenty, deep down into the root.

Above the gesture are the two mauve flowers. The red network is very fine.

Through the red plastic trellis made by the fly-swatter the winter sky in the rectangle of the shack window is white and luminous. It is difficult to remember the degree of luminosity in the summer sky. The summer sky being blue, which is in one sense almost the other end of the prism. The metal grid splinters the bland Bahuko face, which also shines with curved oblongs of white light, although the day is cool. No, this time it was a pale brown face, lean and Berber, granulated like basalt rock.

– Oh, now wait, someone rang through about you. Where are we? Yes, that's it. From this Mrs. Mgulu, of Western Approaches. She wants you to start work tomorrow. In the garden.

– In the garden?

– It is not however permissible. No. The job isn't odd enough.

The gesture is one of helplessness, palms flat and briefly facing upwards, paler, almost pink, and heavily lined. The gesture would be the same if the helplessness were faked.

– We have you down as an odd job man. This is a gardening job. The gardeners' union would object. What did you say you used to be?

– A fortune-teller.

– Yes well, there's no future in that, not nowadays.

The gesture is one of denial, palms up and vertical, paler, almost pink, and heavily lined. To live the gesture in immobility is to evoke it and therefore to have observed it. Or something like it, the palms being white perhaps, the head gardener's, and the earth dark and damp, swallowing up all gestures as realised and rejected, leaving no trace of error in us.

– You won't need the hose yet, at least not with water running through it, but you could practice with the dry hose. It's best to identify with each of the plants one at a time. Then you will know exactly what its needs are on any one day during the dry season.

– Excuse me but how can I identify without the water?

– That's a very good question. I congratulate you on having avoided the trap. What did you say your occupation was?

– Well at the moment –

– No, I mean, before the displacement.

– I used to be a welder.

– Oh, I see. Somebody told me you were a historian of sorts.

– That's not true. Oh, no. Never.

– Oh well, it all comes to the same thing in the end. The important thing is in the holding and the applying of the instrument. At least you'll be used to aiming correctly, whether it's fire or water.

– It all comes to the same thing I suppose.

– Don't be impertinent. We haven't built you up yet. There will be a period of initiation. At the moment all the plants are shrivelled and blackened with the frost. But the leaf is in the seed. That is an article of faith. It is with the seed that you must identify. This will give time for the black and white image to percolate. We can add the colours later, when they crop up. The process is known as osmosis.

– What is the catch, though?

– Well, there might be an explosion. Too many to the square centimetre.

– The flowers a mass of red.

– I don't know about red. In any case one type of explosion tends to cancel the other. The answer to the one is to fill the body's reservoirs with minerals like potassium or carbohydrate complexes found in seaweed, so that radioactive minerals are absorbed and passed out. This of course tends to encourage the other type, the population explosion. However, it is a risk worth taking, and square centimetres can be enlarged.

– I thought you said that it's best to identify with the plants one by one?

– That's a very good question. But these are mere statistics in time. You must learn to identify with the flux.

– It's an article of faith, I suppose . . . it is difficult to tell who's talking in this type of dialogue.

– If you must have your schematisations the job can go to someone else. There are other candidates for initiation. But Mrs. Mgulu made a particular point of taking a special interest.

The number of the vehicle has no numerical significance. The gesture is of holding a conventional weapon. A flame-thrower for example, or an atomic machine-gun. Sooner or later some such interruption will be inevitable. Under the fig-tree, however, as in a brain, there is only immobility. The sky is entirely filled with long grey twigs that poke into the eyebrow line topping the field of vision. In the lower part, on either side of the nose, the branches that bear the twigs are thick and contorted. To the right of the nose, with the left eye closed, the thickest branch sweeps horizontally along the edge of the grass patch, underlining Mrs. Ned's shack, as if the shack were built on it. To the left of the nose, with the right eye closed, it darkly cuts across Mrs. Ned's dark shack, cancelling it almost. Close up, the fig-tree looks blasted, filling the sky with its metallic trellis.

– The gardeners' union, however, would not object to your working overtime only. At overtime rates I'm afraid, which is quarter-pay at the moment.

– That's all right. What are the overtime hours?

– In the dry season twelve to three. In winter seven to ten.

– But it's dark at seven in winter.

– Yes well, as a matter of fact it's rather a nominal concession anyway, because as you know in this time of severe unemployment overtime is almost universally disallowed. We'd have to get a special permit for you. Oh, but wait now, someone rang through about you. Mrs. Mgulu, that's it. Oh well in that case the special permit might not be necessary.

The pinkness of the flower is its gesture. It is essential to hold on to that. The earth is dark with mould. As humus decays it yields carbon dioxide, which, dissolved in the soil water, attacks the mineral particles and makes available the phosphate and potash they contain.

In the white wall the glossy black door opens suddenly. The woman stands framed by the whiteness dressed in a black cotton overall. Pale eyes, pale hair, and the face is waxy. Have some Metabol. You dirty, you need washing. Behind the woman in the white frame the background is brown and cypress green.

– Good morning.

– Yes?

– I've come about the gardening job.

– Oh, yes. My husband's somewhere about. Come in.

The path leads straight up to a small white cottage. On either side of the path the converging cypress hedges engulf the woman in the black overall, which may after all be a dress, or a black rectangle on two white pillars moving up the path. The cypress hedges are trimmed flat and square at eye-level. On the other side of the left-hand hedge is the field of tomato plants protected from the heat by straw wigwams that stretch out like a vast encampment. On the other side of the right-hand hedge the tall cob-corn grows higher than the hedge.

– Wait here, will you, I'll go and call him.

The left foot, in its dirty canvas shoe, is in an elongated hexagonal tile like a benzene ring, or, for that matter, amino-benzoic acid. Benzoic acid given to an animal reacts with amino-acid glycine and is excreted as hippuric acid. The heel is on the atoms nitrogen hydrogen two, the toe on the atoms oxygen two hydrogen, or for that matter on the atoms sulphur oxygen two nitrogen hydrogen two, the ring of sulphanilamide being very similar in shape. The process is known as competitive inhibition. The shoe of the right foot is caked with dry mud, and looks dirtier than the shoe of the left foot, which is merely dusty. The big toe of the left foot is wearing out the canvas.

– Good morning.

– Good morning. I believe Mrs. Mgulu –

– Yes, she told me about it. You know Mrs. Mgulu well?

– Yes, I mean no. It's my wife. She works –

– Oh, I see. Well I'm glad you're punctual, there's plenty to do. These old gladioli corms have to be lifted for one, and sorted for spawn which must be kept separately for saving. I suppose you know all about that. As a matter of fact they've been left there so long, owing to one thing and another, it may not be possible to keep the spawn this year, and it'll soon be time to replant, from stock I mean. You'll have to prepare the soil. I did think of just leaving them there, the winter's been mild so far and the soil's well drained, it would just have to be mulched with leaves. But the calochorti are going to be planted just in front of them at about the same time so it's best to prepare the ground anyway. I suppose you know about celosia, do you? I'm trying a little experiment here.

Above the gesture are the two mauve flowers. The red network of veins is very fine. Mrs. Mgulu watches through the fine network of bare branches, from a window in the big house, made just discernible by the leaflessness. No, Mrs. Mgulu walks in the olive grove beyond the bougainvillaea, and in among the laurel trees, through the red poinsettia. Beyond the tall wrought-iron gates the mimosas are in bloom. Clay occurs mostly in colloid form which is not chemically inert, like sand, and this makes it indispensable to soil fertility. I suppose you know all about base exchange, for instance, with a salt solution like soil water, which releases the insoluble potassium and makes it available to the plant. The feeling is one of autotrophism. Mrs. Mgulu sits graciously at her dressing-table in the sand behind the large-leafed red poinsettia, having her hair brushed into sleekness. Mrs. Mgulu takes more than an interest.

That is how the malady begins. The onset is insidious, well advanced before diagnosis. Anaemia, progressive emaciation, fatigue, tachycardia, dyspnoea, and a striking enlargement of the abdomen due to splenomegaly and hepatomegaly. But the spleen remains smooth and firm on palpation and retains its characteristic notch. The black fingers tap the flaccid white flesh, the wrist emerging dark from the white sleeve of the doctor's coat. The imagination increases in size progressively and usually painlessly until it fills most of the abdomen. The gesture is one of careful investigation. Enlargement of the lymphatic glands may occur in the later stages of the disease, with a general deterioration to a fatal termination. Humus has an exchange capacity roughly six times that of clay, it's important to know these things.

Mrs. Mgulu steps out from behind the poinsettia, wearing something diaphanous.

– You must come at once, she says, it's your wife, she's very ill.

No. Mr. Marburg the butler steps out from behind the poinsettias.

– Mrs. Mgulu has sent for you, he says, will you kindly step this way.

– What is it? What's happened?

– It's your wife. I'm afraid she's fallen ill.

Mrs. Mgulu steps out from behind the bedroom screen, wearing something diaphanous.

– I'm very sorry. My husband is doing all he can.

– Of course.

– I have to tell you that it's the acute, fulminating type. Nothing can be done.

– What, the monocytic? Or chloroma?

– Oh, I wouldn't know, you'll have to ask my husband. Are you a doctor too, then?

– I once studied chemistry.

– Oh, I see. It's terrible, she looks quite green. Would you like to see her?

The gesture is one of invitation. Behind the screen the black fingers tap the flaccid white flank. The eyes and gums are bleeding. The gums are maroon or purplish.

– Lilly. Lilly, it's me.

Lilly is deaf.

– The leucocyte count is 700.000 to the square millimetre.

– Doctor, how long?

Dr. Mgulu is not a medical doctor but a Ph.D. (Tokyo), Economics and Demography. This fantasy is therefore ruled out of order by the Silent Speaker. The Silent Speaker's gesture is one of benediction between the two mauve flowers above and the unborn plants below the humus which yields carbon dioxide that dissolves in soil water. It is important to fill the body's reservoirs with minerals like potassium or carbohydrate complexes found in seaweed, so that radioactive minerals of a similar type are then absorbed and passed straight out.

– What exactly is the cause, doctor?

– The aetiology is unknown. It could be a neoplastic disease. Or due to metabolic disturbances. Or toxic factors. Chemically treated food and such. Has your wife been taking any sulphonamide derivatives? Some doctors still prescribe them.

– You know very well that she is Colourless.

At the moment, the fantasies are under control. Sooner or later, however, they will pervade the blood-stream and increase at a striking rate, paralysing the skull with tumorous growths. Sometimes it is sufficient merely to imagine an episode for the episode to occur, though not necessarily in that precise form.

At eye-level, through the window, about four metres away, and to the right of the fig-tree which overlooks the road, there is Mrs. Ned's shack. The windowless clapboard wall immediately opposite is dark with age and the cunonia on the corner is dead, its red spike withered away. To the right, at the front of the house, the verandah looks dilapidated and the straw shed over the wash-tub at the back is crumbling down. The wash-tub has a bar of new yellow wood nailed along its top edge.

The view to the right, if it were visible from this position at the right of the window, would be of the fig-tree. The view obliquely to the left is of the corner of the porch belonging to Mrs. Hans, who has the shack next to Mrs. Ned's. The view ahead, if a view were available, would consist of innumerable shacks in small bare gardens where nothing grows very tall. At least, that is the view from the kitchen window over the sink, which faces the South East side of the Settlement, unblocked by Mrs. Ned's shack. If Mrs. Ned's shack were not in the way all the innumerable other shacks to the South and South West would be visible from this window also, unless they had been removed, or destroyed, in the walking distance between the fig-tree and this window. A periscope might perhaps reveal a scene of pastoral non-habitation.

In the walking distance to the kitchen window, the shacks are innumerable. A rectangle of light ripples on the wooden table. The wrinkled wood inside the rectangle of light seems to be flowing into the wrinkled wood outside it, which looks darker. The wrinkled wood might be thought alive. But the rectangle of light is only a refracted continuation of an oblong on the red stone floor, made by an oblique ray of winter sun filtering through the hanging beads over the doorway and turning the red stone floor into a river. Soon the gruel will be served.

Mrs. Ned's kitchen, through the hanging beads in the imagination, is dark. The hanging beads are mottled and make a crackling sound. Mrs. Ned is standing by the kitchen window, staring at the innumerable shacks to the South East of the Settlement. Her thin mouth is slightly ajar. She is wearing a crisp white cotton overall with short sleeves. There is otherwise no explanation for the lack of the red framework or for the Colourless mottled face, with the untidy hair growing low on the brow. The staring eyes are hazel and strike two notes of expectancy. A stethoscope might perhaps reveal that her heart beat faster on seeing him appear round the East corner of the house. The mouth is thin but wet and welcoming, though the overall looks clinical, half hiding the goitre on the neck which, however, seems larger. The two white forearms hang limply but move up to unbutton the white overall down the front as the need is wordlessly transmitted and mouth meets mouth and the groin races into function.

Sexual intercourse takes place on the kitchen chair. It is satisfactory. The woman is on top, carrying out the necessary motions, smelling of sweat, chopped-up onions and washing-up water. The crisp white overall is wide open over greyish underwear. She is a gaunt lady and moves in jerky rhythm, head thrown back on its thick mushroom stem that swells where the goitre is laid bare. Human beings do not make love. They make agreements to enfold each other briefly. The disintegration has come together again and there is thus no need to talk. A conversation, however, occurs, for the sake of civilisation. It is of no consequence.

– Mrs. Mgulu gave me a very special message for you. Both verbal and written, in case I forgot one of them. Where did I put it?

– Oh, Lilly! Well, what was the verbal one?

– You might as well have your gruel now, since you're here. I'll warm it up. She was sorry about the Exchange, she should have known, she said, but there is a way out, if you really do keep to odd jobs. She rang them up again, do you know she rang herself, in front of me, and spoke to the Manager or whatever he calls himself, the top man. She said, oh, but it's all a misunderstanding, I never intended to employ him in the garden, it is simply that my head gardener does all the interviewing for jobs outside the actual house. Building? she said, oh, no, though I do want a few potting sheds put up, he would only be trundling wheelbarrows, no, how did she put it, transporting material, ladders and such, you know, assisting here and there, cleaning out the front flight of steps, cleaning windows and such. Well, she had quite a time with them I can tell you, what with the builders' union and the window cleaners' union, but she was so polite and patient, and after all she is Mrs. Mgulu, they had to give way. It's nearly ready.

– I wonder why she bothers. I never asked her for anything. I don't really care one way or another.

– Now that's not a nice thing to say. You've been out of work for nineteen months now and I can't take all the burden.

– So has everyone else.

– She has strong ideas on the subject, you know. She said to me while she was waiting for the Manager on the telephone, it's a purple telephone you know, she said, it's not charity, it's not philanthropy, Lilly, you must understand, it's a basic right, she said, but when a thing gets out of hand, like this, and for reasons beyond anyone's control it becomes impossible to give a large number of men their basic rights one can but do one's bit to help one individual case whenever it comes one's way. That's what she said. Then the top man came on.

The steaming circle of gruel in the bowl is greyish white and pimply. The squint is not so wide, or so blue, in the luminosity thrown by the oblong of moving light on the red stone floor and in the rectangle of rippling light on the wooden table.

– I also think she's very fond of me, that's why. I've worked for her a long time, all in all. She's a real lady, and she knows, well, she respects me as a human being. And you too. She went to the trouble of writing you a note, where is it? Oh and by the way, I got Mrs. Ivan to clear out those tins. She seemed quite upset, but I think I managed to make her understand about wastage and poisoning. After all there is constant famine about. I made signs on my tummy. She made signs with her hands like an inverted V, roof she said, and Ivan, I don't know what she meant, unless they're building a shack of their own somewhere and need the tin.

By hand, across the top left corner. By hand. I am so sorry about all this mix-up, but all is well now, please come to the house tomorrow and report, with this note, to Mr. Swaminathan, my Managing Agent, who will give you all the instructions you need. D. Mgulu.

The gesture is of crushing the note into a ball and flicking it across the kitchen towards the hanging beads. It falls into the flowing red river on the floor.

– Damn the woman. Lilly, you're worth all of them put together. Don't ever despair of me, Lilly, don't.

The gesture is of tenderly enfolding all the refracted colours and bringing them together again in one transparent light. A teinoscope would no doubt reveal that the squint is really a straight look in the luminosity thrown by the sudden knowledge of the person inside the person, a little girl perhaps, dandled on the knee. The gesture is of capturing an electron from the nearest orbit and rearranging everything within by the emission of an X-ray. You never know when that may come in useful. There is thus no need to talk, in the best of possible worlds.

2

DAILY from 8 a.m., outside the Labour Exchange, a dark blue face the size of a bungalow lies upside down at eye-level, the thick hair spread like roots over red desert land, the eyeballs pushing their black nucleus down towards the underlining eyebrows and the street below, the teeth agape in rigid horror, or pleasure as the case might be. The dark blue breasts are high and rounded tumuli slashed by curved oblongs of gloss as if by the nearness of the spidery hand or by the invisible emanation from a black sphere of crinkly matter that hangs above like a carbonised sun within the slanted orbit of an enormous shoulder line, all this beneath a giant cactus candelabrum. SO TORRID, SO TENDER.

The street follows the curve of the lower line of teeth agape above the upper line of teeth. It is not as curved as the chin-line or the rounded tumuli slashed with gloss, nor does it make the same orbit as the enormous and slanted shoulder line. The street swarms with much smaller people.

Face to face, however, the man is large and coffee-coloured, dressed in pale blue. He holds out a black thermoplastic hose too close for comfort. All around, just above the crowd, conventional weapons point.

– What about you, sir, would you like to comment on the situation?

– Yes. It's a mug's game.

Behind the metallic trellis the face is very black Bahuko, star-fished with light-reflecting sweat, although the day is not yet hot.

– Unemployment benefit pills cannot be administered retrospectively I'm afraid. Now then, occupation?

– Look, do we have to go through all that?

– You know the rules. Three weeks of non-attendance, I'm sorry but you have to re-register. We can't keep up otherwise. Here, you can fill it up for yourself if you like. I'm not fussy. I'll see what there is. Hmm. Difficult, you odd job men.

– But I've got an odd job. That's what I came in to report. In any case I attended yesterday.

– Now wait a minute, there's a note here at the bottom. Someone rang through about you. A Mrs. er –

– Mgulu.

The young palm tree in the square mops the luminous white sky, framed darkly by the door. The square has one slightly rounded side which the street at this point skirts, forming an almost imperceptible segment of a non-existent circle. To the right the street continues straight on, and to the left it forks into two narrower streets, one of which continues straight on. From the Labour Exchange, the impression is one of a straight street, although experience has proved that a man standing at one end to the left cannot see the street at the other end to the right. Or vice versa, as the case might be. The street in any case is swarming with people. On the other side, on the curved edge of the square, a large collision of them is clustered in arrested motion, overtopped by microscopes pointing. In the centre of the group the man in the pale blue suit holds the black plastic hose to the chest level of a man with high cheekbones polished like shoe-tips and a white gold smile.

– Are you going to vote for the Asswati Governor or against?

– Last time I was sweet, lick me now, said the salt.

– What do you have against the Governor's policies?

– I never said I was against.

– Well do you disapprove of particular policies, the satisfaction campaign, for instance?

– What satisfaction?

– Surely you've seen the slogan. We won't demand satisfaction till we satisfy demand.

– Yes I disapprove of that.

– Why? Don't you think it's dynamic and imaginative, something the people have been really crying out for. Genuine satisfaction.

– No, I don't. I'd call it a demand campaign anyway.

– So you'll be voting against the Governor then?

– I never said that.

– What about you, sir, which way will you be voting tomorrow?

– I don't know. Haven't made up my mind yet.

– Do you approve of the demand campaign?

– Yes, I think so. Yes, yes, I suppose so.

– Why do you approve of it? I mean, isn't it a little hard on the unemployed millions?

– Well, yes, I suppose it is in a way.

– Are you unemployed?

– No. I'm a crane-operator.

– Are you satisfied with the Government's record?

SO TORRID, SO TENDER. The face lies upside down, the eyeballs pushing their black nucleus towards the underlining eyebrows and the street below. A group of men stands under them, near the steps of the Labour Exchange. The slight curve of the street follows the curve of the lower line of teeth above the upper line. It is not as curved as the chin-line or the tumuli that come alive like ant-heaps to the nearness of the spidery hand.

– I'm a physicist. I used to be an alchemist. Lick me now, said the salt.

– I'm a maize-grower.

– I have been all these things.

The buildings to the right of the Labour Exchange are drab four-storey municipal buildings very similar to each other. To the left there is the face, covering the windows of several old houses from the top of the shop fronts to the roof two floors up. Next to the face is the Colourless child, shrivelled and smudged with sores. COME OVER INTO PATAGONIA AND HELP US. The houses continue at the same low level all the way along the street to the left until they merge on account of the slight curve, into the opposite houses on this side, which from here seem taller but may or may not be, according to the degree of perspective trick. To the right of the Labour Exchange the height of the municipal buildings is more or less maintained with offices and shops up both the narrow forking streets towards the centre of the town.

The black mannequins in the dress shop to the right wear this year's colours, red and orange, and dance in arrested motion, protruding their behinds.

The faces clustered round the man in the pale blue suit vary from shining black to lightest brown and occasional pink or yellow. The cluster could be of caladium hybrids, or a speckled sea anemone, for it is mobile in a liquid way. One face opposite is as lined as a walnut and entirely surrounded with white hair. The face stands out in stark serenity.

The black plastic hose is being proffered to the neighbouring man, a dark Madrassi Indian, who sways gently from one foot to another. The black plastic hose follows almost imperceptibly, like a dying metronome.

– Yes. I want to say that to deny is the only true human

power, rather than free will.

– Erm. Does that mean you're going to vote against?

– That I cannot say. The reflected image of any object or notion depends on our acceptance, but we can efface it in a thought. Thus the power of negation determines the faculty of reasoning.

– I see. Well if you're a professor perhaps you'd like to comment on the situation?

– Oh, no. I am in business. Import and export.

Somewhere in the archives there will be evidence that this occurred, if it is kept, and for those who wish to look it up. Other episodes, however, cannot be proved in this way. Sitting alone, for example, on a kitchen chair, making love. A rectangle of light ripples on the wrinkled wood. If all the molecules that compose the solid table were gradually to move faster and faster, as fast as the molecules of liquid, the fastest would have sufficient velocity to move out of the substance. The table would then evaporate. A little pool of liquid might be left on the red stone floor, but otherwise it would be impossible to prove that the table had been there. A radio-isotope carbon 14, with a half-life of 5600 years, might perhaps trace and measure its prehistoric existence, but only for the human mind behind the carbon 14, the development of phenomena being correlative to that of consciousness. A little knowledge is a dangerous thing. Better get on with the job since a job, at last, is to hand, with or without identity.

The facia-board in its long rectangular frame of rough wood lies on the floor of the new pavilion. It measures six metres long. The width, or rather the height, for it has to go up on the wall, is eighty centimetres. The stencilled shapes cut into the facia-board are rounded, like flattened rhomboids. There is much banging about and a Colourless boy sings When You Love Somebody above the banging. Some of the stencilled shapes are rounded trapezes, some are rounded oblongs, some are irregular ovals. There are kidney shapes, lung shapes, tongue shapes, cardiac shapes, bladder shapes, womb shapes and possibly even stomach shapes and spleen shapes. There is a small thyroid too, between the spleen and the womb. Now only the pieces of coloured perspex remain to be stuck over the cut-out shapes.

When you love somebody
Forget it
When you want somebody
Scrap it

The perspex pieces must be a little larger, so as to stick on to the board since this is the wrong side, they need not be cut to the exact shape but may remain geometrical, providing they do not overlap each other, for they must lie flat. When the board goes up on the wall over the lights, only the rounded shapes on the other side will show, and be lit up in all the different colours. It is difficult to decide on the colours. Blue for the lung perhaps, and green for the spleen, purple for the kidney. Or pink for the lung, blue for the spleen, red for the womb, purple for the cardiac shape. No, that won't do, two purples are next to each other. It is more important to balance the colours in relation to each other than to equate them with the significance of shapes. The designing and lay-out of the shapes has been done by someone else.

Mr. Swaminathan stands on the steps of the gazebo and sways gently from one foot to the other.

– Yes, well, how do I know it's you? This piece of paper is quite creased all over.

– My wife threw it away by mistake.

– What? Speak up man.

– My wife threw it away by mistake.

– You might have found it in a garbage-can for all I know. There's no name on it. If at least it said admit bearer I could rightfully take the risk. You have borne it, I can't deny that.

– I can tell you about the mix-up she refers to.

– Yes, well, she did describe you to me as a matter of fact. The white hair. But you people look so alike you know.

– My wife works here. She could identify me.

– By hand, that means nothing. Oh well I'll take your word for it. There's no time to lose, really. Two builders are off ill and the big pavilion must be finished in time for the garden-party.

– Mr. Swaminathan, excuse my asking, but how do I know you are the managing agent, and not, for instance, a professor of philosophy?

– Don't be impertinent.

– Or in import and export? In town in the street you said you were in import and export.

– You don't want to believe everything you hear and see in the street. Now get on with it, the foreman will tell you what to do.

The piece of blue perspex between the orange rectangle and the green trapeze overlaps the green. It is necessary to slip it underneath the facia-board and outline the cut-out kidney shape on to it with a pencil, so as not to saw it smaller than the shape, plus a little all round for glueing. The kidney shape has a large lower lobe. The piece of blue perspex is an uneven triangle with the narrowest angle sawn off. The longest side saws down quite easily. The piece of blue perspex is an isosceles triangle with the narrowest angle sawn off. Down on the facia-board, the space that the angle would have taken is occupied by part of a red parallelogram. The blue perspex fits very well. A flat stone holds down all four pieces of perspex while the glue dries to a good hold. The yellow piece of perspex can go next to the orange. A pair of feet, shod in buff leather to match the buff trousers, strides over the facia-board without touching it. Or tripping it, as the case might be, in brown trousers for example, saying sorry mate followed by silence. A woman's foot, black in a pink shoe, steps on the wooden frame on one side of the facia-board. The other similar foot steps across to the wooden frame on the other side. It is possible, without looking up from the grey perspex, to see the hem of the pale orange overall which hovers for a moment within the outer orbit of the downward absorption.

The paving-stones are large as tables. The trousers widen slightly at the bottom, most of them brown or black. Shoes match and shine. It is like being in a forest. The trees run away as the flag-stones vibrate.

No, Mr. Swaminathan sways gently from one foot to another. The black plastic hose follows almost imperceptibly, like a dying metronome. The cluster could be of caladium hybrids, or a speckled sea-anemone.

– You sound very professorial if I may say so, for a business man. Do you think the proposed aid to Sino-America or even to Seatoarea would help to solve the problem?

– I'd rather not comment on that.

– So you'd prefer to see a definite economic association with Chinese Europe?

– Oh no, I'm against that.

– Why?

– Well, it wouldn't be in our interest, would it?

– What about you, do you have any views on the situation?

– Yes. Compulsory blood-tests, permissive death and compulsory birth control. That's the only way out. I mean it's not fair to burden us with their mutations is it?

So torrid, so tender. The face lying upside down, the eyeballs holding back their black nucleus from the attracting orbit of the street below. A group of men shuffling about beneath them, near the steps of the Labour Exchange. The black mannequins in the dress shop to the right, wearing red and orange, dance in arrested motions, protruding their behinds. To the left, on the big poster, the teeth are agape in rigid horror, or pleasure as the case might be. One brown face opposite is as lined as a walnut, with a toothless mouth that says, We had a dream. It's a disgrace.

– Yes sir, can you speak up a bit. What's your occupation?

– I'm an old man. My face is lined as a walnut and entirely surrounded with white hair. My face stands out in stark serenity.

– Could you speak up a bit? Straight into the mike, that's better. It's a noisy street, isn't it? Now, which way are you going to vote tomorrow, dad?

– When I was a young man we had a dream, of universal brotherhood. We were all going to work side by side in partnership, the strong helping the weak. Nobody was going to be afraid. Nobody was going to take revenge, revenge was for primitive people, and we had rapidly become civilized. There's always as much to be thankful for as angry. What's happened to all that? Why aren't we helping those who have now become weak? We only pretend to help. What are we afraid of? Why have we fallen away from the dream?

– Well, we can't get into a theological discussion here, I'm afraid.

– Theology! You tolerate the gods as you pension off old men. We did the same. We always learn too late.

– Thank you very much. What about you? What's your occupation, sir?

– I'm a hairdresser.

– Do you approve of the satisfaction campaign?

Or, alternatively,

Mr. Swaminathan stands on the steps of the gazebo, swaying gently from one foot to another.

– You might have found it in a garbage-can, for all I know.

– Mr. Swaminathan, excuse my asking, but how do I know you are the managing agent, and not, say, in import and export?

– If we start with conjectures that have the highest possible informative content or – which has been proved to be the same thing – the lowest possible probability, and if we test these conjectures with the greatest possible severity, those which survive the tests will acquire the patina of prestige that traditionally attaches to knowledge.

– Yes, but does it bear any relation to the real thing?

– Well, it's only a crumpled piece of paper after all. By hand, it doesn't mean anything.

When you want somebody
Scrap it.

The thyroid will be scarlet. It is about the life-size of a pear, and a tenth the size of the spleen, which increases progressively and usually painlessly until it fills most of the abdomen. The shapes on this side of the facia-board are quite geometrical. The note requires an answer, of polite thanks merely, but an answer. By hand. It won't mean a thing. Dear Mrs. Mgulu. Thank you very much for all the trouble you have gone to on my behalf. I am most grateful and will make every endeavour to serve you to your greatest satisfaction. To the best of my ability. The green trapeze lies side by side with the white square, its slanted line touching the blue triangle. I hope you will have every reason to be entirely satisfied. I am most grateful and will endeavour to serve you to the best of my ability, which I hope will satisfy you in every way. Which I hope will not cause you any further trouble. Yours truly.

Mr. Swaminathan stands on the steps of the gazebo and sways slowly from one foot to another.

– It's only because the builder is ill and the job is urgent. There shouldn't be any objection but I'd keep quiet about it, you know.

– Mr. Swaminathan, why are you afraid of employing me? What is this pressure, this barely spoken discrimination against us?

– Us? Who's us? You're imagining things.

– Good. Make him say the obvious, it's easier to conceive the reply. The reply must be passionate and deeply moving. On pronouns for example. You used to be Us and we used to be Them, to you, but now it's the other way about. Why? We tried our best. Oh, we brought you syphilis and identity and dissatisfaction and other diseases of civilization. But medicine too, and canned ideas, against your own diseases. And we couldn't bring you radiation leukaemia or chemical mutations, because we absorbed all the chemicals ourselves and must have spared you only just enough to immunise you. Or else you had an ancient strength inside, that we couldn't corrupt. We were whited sepulchres and never came to terms with our dark interior, which you wear healthily upon your sleeves, having had so little time to lose touch with it. Now we are sick. Is that the reason? Is that why you are afraid, afraid of our white sickness?

The rhetoric is vain, the passion pale and disengaging. Even inside the mind that pours it out in silence Mr. Swaminathan stands on the steps of the gazebo, swaying slowly from one foot to another, failing to identify himself with suffering. The process is known as alienation, and yet the passion hurts, seizes the body at the back of the neck somehow, in the medullary centres, down the glosso-pharyngeal nerve perhaps, or the pneumogastric, at any rate forward and down into the throat, which tightens as enlargement of the lymphatic glands occurs and pain spreads through the chest, aching and down into the stomach, nauseous. Sooner or later it will reach the spleen, which will increase in size until it fills most of the abdomen, remaining firm and smooth, however, on palpation. The onset is insidious and well advanced before diagnosis. Prognosis poor, continuing to a fatal termination. Splenectomy contra-indicated, treatment unsatisfactory, no therapy, but the blood-count, marrow biopsy and glandular biopsy will furnish a firm diagnosis. These organs on section appear grey or reddish grey, packed with myeloid cells, mainly polymorphonuclears and immature cells such as myeloblasts, promyelocytes, myelocytes and metamyelocytes. The psyche on section appears grey.

From this position in the gutter, the paving stones look

large as tables. The trousers widen slightly at the bottom, most of them brown or black. Shoes are dusty or caked with mud. It is like being in a forest. The trees run away as the flag-stones vibrate. The thing is a long distance away. A seismograph might perhaps reveal, but the curving jaw of the street crumbles further up, swallowing the insect crowds. Some people are always left, kissing the gutter. Darling, they're playing our tune.

The wiggly oblong resembles nothing but a wiggly oblong, to be pencilled on to the pink piece of perspex beneath the facia-board. From this position, Mr. Swaminathan, I love you.

It is important to believe in the bowl of steaming gruel. A microscope might perhaps reveal animal ecstasy in the innumerable white globules that compose the circle, but the gruel tastes hot and salty on the soft palate at the back of the mouth and flows hotly down the digestive track to the duodenum. Sooner or later the white globules will feed the corpuscles in the blood stream, occasioning continual traffic jams and innumerable collisions. The wrinkled wood is quite static in the pool of light, which overspreads the table and transfers itself on to the still and red stone floor. The table casts a large rectangular shadow on the red stone floor, flanked on one side by the tangential shadows of the empty chair at the end to the left. Next to these the body's shadow makes a bulging growth on the clean line of the rectangle. It is swallowed up from time to time by the moving shadow of the occurring conversation. The door is shut behind the hanging beads and to the right of it, on the top shelf, the recipes stand side by side, on gaily coloured tins.

– It's best to keep them really, tempting though they may be. You never know when they may come in useful. Besides, none of them is self-contained. Each recipe requires the contents of at least two other tins, and I never seem to have the right combinations. I do now have two out of three for Beef Strogonoff, though, because cook gave me a tin of it today and I have a tin of rice. Let's see, it says open the tin and empty contents into a copper-bottomed saucepan, stirring slowly on low heat. Add salt and paprika to taste. Meanwhile open large Gala tin of fried rice, oh dear I only have a medium tin, but this says serves six, empty contents over a dessertspoonful of ground-nut oil in a copper-bottomed saucepan and heat slowly, chop a handful of fresh parsley take a medium tin of Gala sauté carrots, you see that's the one I don't have.

Some of the gruel's globules remain attached to the rounded white sides of the bowl. The light over the table makes a moon in the darkness beyond the window. The squint seems wider tonight, and yet less blue. The pale eye that doesn't move is fixed on the shelf of can-recipes, but the mobile eye stares towards the reflected moon in the darkness beyond the window.

– In an emergency of course one wouldn't bother about proper dishes. One might be glad to have just the fried rice. Or guavas.

– What a wind there is tonight. The shack seems about to take off.

– Yes and it's raining too, listen. Most extraordinary weather for the time of year, we should be having Spring showers. I like it though. I hate the stillness of a sickly sky. I can identify with the wind, especially the night wind.

– Hello, is there anyone there? It's Mrs. Tom.

– Who-ever's that? Oh dear, why can't they come round the back, they must know I've got lodgers in front. I am so sorry, Mrs. Ivan. I didn't know – you don't? Oh, it is kind. I'm sorry, it won't happen again. Just a minute. Who is it?

Oh hello Mrs. Tom, goodness me you look like a sea-lion under that raincoat. Could you come round the back? Mr. and Mrs. Ivan live in this room.

– No, I just want to give you a message, anyway I'd only wet your kitchen, it really is streaming. You know you need a gutter along the roof of this porch, or do you call it a verandah, look at it, I've had to cross through a curtain of rain. It's from Mrs. Mgulu. She rang through and asked me to let you know urgently that the kitchen light reflected in the darkness beyond the window remains quite still despite the wind. It is the still centre of the storm. No one has ever photographed the inside of the moon. There is of course a very real danger of disintegration, but that is a risk worth taking. Mr. Blob: thank you very much. Mr. Swaminathan, thank *you*. Sometimes it is sufficient to formulate a need for the need to vanish, or proliferate rapidly as the case might be. Identity has its chemistry too. Mr. Swaminathan will be there to help, and if there are any objections that side of it can be arranged in the morning, she says, after all it's an emergency, the gale blew it down, so would he come at once. Mrs. Mgulu emerges from the bedroom, wearing something diaphanous. My husband is speaking to the nation in half an hour, can you possibly put it up again by then? Oh don't worry about the Labour Exchange, my dear, Mr. Swaminathan sways gently from one foot to another, smiling cryptically. Mr. Swaminathan is my arranger of all things, my right hand. Well I must rush off or they'll be wondering where I've got to at home. Oh dear this rain, it's like a bead curtain you really must get him to put a gutter up there. Goodnight. Here goes. Wow! Pshshsh. The noise must have been continuous, but leaps into hearing now to be shut off and muffled. The wrinkled wood is quite static in the pool of light, which overspreads the table on to the still and red stone floor. As static, at any rate, as the network of minute lines on the back of the wrist. A microscope might perhaps reveal which is the more alive of the two, the fear or the expectation.

– That was Mrs. Tom.

– I know.

– She came across in all that rain, with Mrs. Mgulu's black raincoat over her head, you know, the one I was so hoping Mrs. Mgulu'd give to me. I said to her you look like a performing seal in that raincoat. She didn't mind, though, she's a good sort is Mrs. Tom. Up to a point. She should have known about the lodgers, though, and they were in bed and she was peering in like anything, for all the world as if a bit of slap and tickle were going on during the very interruption. It's true they were whispering.

– What does Mrs. Mgulu want?

– Mrs. Mgulu? Why should Mrs. Mgulu want anything? Oh, you mean Mrs. Tom. Well she had a message for me from Mrs. Jim up at the house. She's feeling ill and wants me to come early tomorrow and do the market for her. I said I would, of course, poor dear she's tired herself out. She's anaemic you know, I shouldn't be surprised if it's pernicious, and she has gallstones. Will you have some more gruel?

The circle in the bowl is greyish white and pimply. It steams less and appears quite flaccid. The wrinkled wood is dead in the pool of light.

– Lilly, help me.

The skin around the eyes, both the mobile eye and the static eye, is waxy. There is no reproach in the mobile eye, the emotion expressed is nearer to concern. The static eye expresses only off-ness, which emphasises whatever the mobile eye is expressing, reproach perhaps, or puzzlement as to whether the inaudible voice has or has not raised itself from its condition of chronic aphonia.

– Lilly, how do you identify with the wind?

– The wind? I just listen to it. And sway a little. In my mind I mean. It has the rhythms of strength. The night wind especially.

– It has the rhythms of anguish.

– Well that's up to you, isn't it?

– The wind is only the wind, you know that, it carries no significances.

The mobile eye rests on the bowl of gruel.

– Start with small things. Believe in the bowl of gruel. And eat up, now, while it's still hot.

– How is Mrs. Mgulu?

– Well, it's funny you should ask. I think she looks quite ill, at least, as far as one can tell, she's always beautiful in any circumstances. She wears an alexandrite in her left nostril you know. But then, she will complicate life for herself. Even this market business, for instance, it's a sort of health fad, really, she could get everything delivered, and of course she does, but not vegetables, she doesn't trust the tradesmen she says, and she's probably right, so Mrs. Jim goes to the market early and chooses everything. Though they've a big kitchen garden now as well. No radioactive fertilisers and no chemical insecticides. Oh she did a lot of thinking on that. But it won't start producing till the Spring. Why that's almost now, isn't it?

– Do you think everything's all right up there? In this gale I mean.

– What, in the kitchen garden?

– Well, anywhere. The roof, the aerial for instance, or the telephone wires.

– Mrs. Jim rang up all right. And, it's a solid house you know.

– Didn't Mrs. Tom say something about Mr. Swaminathan? I thought I heard his name.

– No, I don't think so. Why should she? He isn't there anyway at this time of night. He lives in the town.

The face lies upside down, beautiful in any circumstances, with the thick hair spread out like roots, the eyeballs pushing their black nucleus down towards the underlining eyebrows and the street below, the nostrils flat and far apart, the wide lips huge, agape in ecstasy, the dark breasts high and rounded to the hand. Mr. Swaminathan stands alone in the curved empty street, swaying gently from one foot to another, worshipping the face in a chant. The black thermoplastic hose follows imperceptibly like a dying metronome. There is no water coming out of the hose, but it could gush forth any minute.

– Tell me Mr. Swaminathan, will you be voting for history or for progress?

– There is no such thing as history, except in the privacy of concupiscence. That is an article of faith. Memory is a primitive organ in the left hemisphere of the brain, inscribed with sensory observations, which are reflected by the right hemisphere as the moon reflects the sun. But that's another story.

– So you will be voting for progress?

– There is no such thing as progress. There is only the Moment of Truth.

– Mr. Swaminathan help me. Is there a secret? A story behind the story?

– There is a secret. But it is not a story.

– Come to bed, Lilly. I want to make love.

The wind, which does not have the rhythms of either strength or anguish, rattles the shack's corrugated iron roof. The rain shimmies down the small high window, a long way from the mattress on the floor. In the dark the four raised knees make a table mountain under the army blanket. The condition is not one of priapism. In action, it might perhaps be sufficient to imagine a face the colour of irrigated earth lying there instead, beautiful in any circumstances, the eyes white slits, the nucleus half gone into half consciousness, the nostrils flat and far apart, the wide lips mauve with pink and white between, the dark breasts high and lively to the hand. In absolute immobility however, it is enough merely to evoke the gestures of the past, which does not exist save in the privacy of concupiscence. The four raised knees beneath the army blanket are dark and presumably bare of flies, the two bodies placid under the tent, the male to the left, the female to the right. Limply the right hand of the male holds the left hand of the female. The outer hands lie quietly alongside.

– Lilly you start. I need you so.

– Do you remember when you were the hospital porter, how you used to come into the women's ward to collect and deliver the letters? Twice a day you'd come.

– Yes, yes, go on.

– And you'd call out, any letters for posting, and the women would call back from various beds, usually the same beds every day, but sometimes there'd be a shy voice from a different bed.

– Yes, yes. And what else did I say?

– You'd walk up one side of the ward, handing out the mail, and collecting any for postage, and you'd call out, anyone want a jelly-baby? And some would call back yes, and others would be silent, some too ill to care, some unconscious maybe. And you'd walk up the other side of the ward, handing out more mail, and collecting any for postage, and you'd call out, anyone want a jelly-baby? And some would call back yes, and you'd go up to the bed and give them one out of a crumpled paper bag which had been in your trouser pocket. You held it in your left hand, with the letters still to be delivered between the index and third finger, and you took out the jelly-baby with the thumb and same two fingers of your right hand and gave it to them. The letters to be posted went into your right hand coat pocket.

– Yes, yes. Go on.

– You were very popular. The women would call out yes George I want one, and here George, I've got a letter, and oh thank you George I knew you'd bring me some good news.

– And what did the sister say?

– The sister said any man who comes into a women's ward every day offering jelly-babies out of a paper bag needs medical attention.

– Oh-ah, that's good, that's wonderful.

– That's how we met.

– Go on.

– You're forgetting me. Tickle my memory a little too.

– Do you remember how impressed I was when I first took you out and found you were such a good mimic? You mimicked the women in the ward at 5 a.m. over their early morning tea. Please do it again, please do it again.

– Well. That's a nice cup o' tea this morning – Eh? – I said, that's a nice cup of tea this morning. – Oh. Yes, it is nice, isn't it? – Not like yesterday – Eh? – I said not like yesterday. Yesterday was terrible. If I'd have shut my eyes I'd've thought it was hot water (long silence). That wasn't yesterday, that was the day before. Yesterday's wasn't too bad. – Eh? – I said, that wasn't yesterday mornin' the tea was like hot water, it was the day before. Yesterday's was all right – Oh was it? Well this one's real good tea. It's a pleasure to drink it. – Eh? – I said this one's real good tea anyway – Oh. Yes, it's a lovely cup of tea. And you said –

– I think you're wonderful.

– And I said what's your name and you said Bill to you. And I said call me Lilly.

– Go on.

– And one day you came into the ward as usual and you went up to Granny Grumble and she said raise me Charlie I've slid right down and the nurses don't know how and don't pay no attention to me anyways. And it's true the nurses just weren't strong enough they had to raise us in bits and she always yelled with pain or pretended to be. And you put down your letters and your paper bag on the edge of the bed and you crooked your two hands under her armpits from the back and raised her swift and sharp and she cried oooh! how lovely in eighty-year-old ecstasy.

– Aaaah. Go on.

– No, you go on.

– Do you remember that nasty nurse you disliked so much, from Trinidad she was and one day she came out in a loud voice with Everyone says the patients in Ward Fourteen are impossible.

– And this was greeted with a stony silence and I was killing her with a look, she was near me you see so she said Oh, I don't mean you. And I said no dear you mean the plants.

The laugh is that of a delighted child.

– Go on.

– No, you titillate me now.

– Do you remember how impressed I was when I took you out the second time and you knew so much about it all? We were travelling by tube and you said to me, do you know, you had to shout in my ear because of the noise, but of course nobody heard, despite the crowd, you said, do you know, out of all these people you see every day travelling on the tube twelve and a half per cent have a permanent colostomy. And I said, what did I say?

– You said, oh you really seized the opportunity, it was such clever repartee, you pressed against me with the weight of the whole crowd on you as the train jolted round the bends, and you murmured in my ear, or shouted maybe, my beloved put his hand by the hole of the door and my bowels were moved for him.

– And despite the noise you heard it and blushed furiously and laughed to cover it and shouted back into my ear I am black but comely which of course wasn't true and the train screeched to a stop.

– Don't stop, don't stop.

– Aaaah.

– Go on, go on.

– Do you remember an inn Miranda do you remember an inn and the tedding and the spreading of the straw for a bedding and the fleas that tease in the high Pyrenees do you remember an inn.

– I remember I remember the house where I was born the little window where the sun came peeping in at mor-or-or-orn.

The wind which has the rhythms of identity rattles the

shack's corrugated iron roof. The rain shimmies down the small high window, a long way from the mattress on the floor. The four raised knees make a table mountain under the army blanket, the two bodies placid in the tabernacle, the male to the left, the female to the right reflecting the sensory observations as the moon reflects the sun. Memory has occurred, in a state of comatose suspension. Limply the right hand of the male holds the left hand of the female, the two outer hands lie quietly alongside. The squint is not visible in this position, nor would it be in any other, except as preformed knowledge peering through the blackness. But look at the closed eyelids they are the right colour. The wind which has the rhythms of completed union rattles the shack's corrugated iron roof. The rain shimmies down the small high window.

– Listen, they're playing our tune.

Sooner or later some interruption will be inevitable, an itch to scratch or a bladder to go and empty or sleep perhaps and some disallowable dream. But now there is only immobility. Everything that moves increases risk.

– You haven't been bringing me my gruel in here for some time, have you?

– No, that's true.

– Goodnight.

– Goodnight.

During the hammering the conversation takes the form of the hammering, which has the high-pitched ring of metal hammer on metal chisel. Lost high-pitched words lurch suddenly into a lower key whenever the hammering stops.

– if you don't mind.

– No, I don't mind.

– . . . big idea?

– I don't know, but it's all got to be taken up, Mr. Swaminathan said.

– Hey, stop hammering when you talk. I can't hear you.

– Mr. Swaminathan said it's all got to be taken up, and that wall's going to be knocked down too.

– Yeah, I heard, but why all . . .

– I suppose the bathroom alone isn't big enough.

– Hey? Stop hammering. You've got no . . .

– I know, I've been told that before. I can hear myself though, and I can hear you through my hammering.

– . . . Vocational Training.

– Surely you're too young to have gone through the Resettlement Camp?

– What you talking about? Stop hammering. What Resettlement Camp?

– I thought you said you'd had Vocational Training.

– Voice training, stoopid. I don't usually do this kinda work, I'm a singer. They like us as singers, you know. Quaint you see, oldey worldey.

When you love somebody
Forget it

The hammering has the high-pitched ring of metal on metal, one hammer hitting the chisel on the beat, the other slightly off the beat. The voice is completely audible through the hammering and is charged with an aggressive gaiety not at all present in the languorous snarl of the speaking voice. The gaiety is not infectious.

When you want somebody
Scrap it
Oh, whe-he-hen you gotta ye-he-hen
Turn it in

The long metal chisel is hammered in some fifteen centimetres under the pink marble slab. The size of the pieces into which the marble slab breaks varies in direct ratio to the angle at which the chisel is held from the floor. The more horizontally the chisel can be held, the larger the pieces. But the chisel can be held horizontally only when inserted either, as at the start, from inside the edge of the sunken bath, or, as now, from a side where another slab has already been removed, so that the chisel is being held at a level with the under-flooring. Between two slabs the chisel must be held almost vertically and tapped very gently into the dividing line. The singer does not tap gently.

– . . . get to the wall, then it won't be so easy.

– Oh I don't know, they'll be free of access on one side.

– Stop hammering I can't hear a word you say.

– I said they'd be free of access on this side. The really hard ones were the first.

– Yeah and I did more'n you did of those.

The singer holds his chisel obliquely and cracks the slabs into smaller pieces. He pauses a great deal.

– I wonder what they're gonna do with all those pieces.

– I don't know. A pink terrace in crazy pavement, perhaps.

– Stop hammering you old loony.

– A pink terrace in crazy pavement.

– Say, you're in the know, ain't you? Who you in with?

– That's a very good question. I congratulate you on –

– What you saying?

Mr. Swaminathan stands in the pink marble bathroom and sways gently from one foot to another. Mr. Swaminathan paces up and down the pink marble bathroom, counting his own steps. The foreman does not pace up and down but advances cautiously from one two-metre distance of his measuring-rule to the next. He is a tall Asswati, taller and handsomer than Mr. Swaminathan. He has delegated the crouching measurements around the bath and coppershell washstands to the young Colourless worker who hums as he measures, but apparently jots nothing down. The bathroom measures about six metres by eight by four. It is bare of towels, sponges, soaps, jars, bottles, pots, brushes. The rails and racks for these things merge into the pink marble walls or floor, imperceptibly breaking their surface with hollows and curves. Mr. Swaminathan's eyes strike an atonal chord. The bathroom window, at eye level, is about two metres wide, and half a metre high, almost wholly filled with a sky intensely blue. From this position, three steps away and to the left, only the distance to the right can be seen, the sea of olive groves and the Settlement of dark brown shacks like flies regimented on a flat patch of ground. Just beyond the Settlement the town sprawls in a sunlit haze, tall where it is not squat, grey where it is not golden.

– with the wall, d'you think? I'm talking to you.

– I'm sorry, Mr. Swaminathan. I was trying to pick out my house.

– Yes, well I haven't got all day. Hmm. You-er-live in the Colourless Settlement? I gather the bungalows are very comfortable. One per mated capita now, isn't it? That's a wonderful improvement. There's nothing like that in the town, well I suppose you know, the overcrowding there is insoluble. And as for the big cities –

– Gee, I know some people'd call 'em shacks.

– Well, that's a matter of opinion. They were built by Colourless people in the first place, weren't they, admittedly a very long while ago, for holidays, before the er –

– Well says the tall Asswati foreman I think we'd better leave them to get on with it and deal with the wall when my two builders come back. After all the marble has to be removed before it's knocked down.

Mr. Swaminathan's eyes strike an atonal chord, confusing the neural cells which complain by discharging a high mad microvoltage. It is not, however, his eyes which do this but the memory of his eyes having possibly done so, or the psychic presence, now hammered into by the high-pitched ring of metal hammer on metal chisel. A recording engineer might perhaps separate the components of the mixture. If the hammering were extracted, the lost sentences that came and went and returned in reconstructed form might be recovered and heard. The internal conversation, however, is too intimately compounded with the sentences that came and went to be separated by mechanical means. Except perhaps by bombardment with beta-particles.

– Well I'm tired, I guess we can have a rest now.

– But we've only done a fraction of it.

The marble slab has come away entire, without breaking at all.

– Hey, have you seen the view from this window? We're quite high up, considering.

– Considering what?

– Oh, I dunno. Considering it's a bathroom and all.

– Don't you think we should try and get as far as that wall? They're always accusing us of being lazy. Mr. Swaminathan might come up any minute.

– Say, you're a dadda's boy, ain't yer? Mr. Swami this and Mr. Swami that. You got a yen for him or what? You listen to me, you gotta go slow, go slow in everything you do for 'em, otherwise it's a mug's game. What's all this for, anyway?

– Mr. Swaminathan said something about a hair-dressing salon for guests at the big ball.

– Did he now? Big ball, eh? Hey, there'll be extra servants needed, won't there, butlers and drink servers, you know, circulating. And hairdressers, right here in the pink marble. Well, hairdressers' assistants anyway. D'you think we'd stand a chance?

– I thought you said you were a singer?

– Yeah, well, not exactly. I go to night-school, see. I'm waiting for the big time. I take on jobs like this 'cos I can keep my voice in while I work. Oh boy when the big time comes! It's all a question of luck. Being heard at the right moment by the right person. That's discovery.

– You mean you'd sing while handing out champagne or shampooing ladies' hair?

– Well. You never know. Oh boy, to get my fingers lathering and scratching in all that thick black hair. D'you think they'd take me on?

– I don't know, what are you registered as?

– Yes, what are you registered as?

– Oh, hi-yer boss. We were just having a wine-break. No wine though.

– I asked, what are you registered as?

– I'm all things to all men I guess.

– Don't be impertinent. You're nothing to me and you may as well go.

– Oh now look here, boss –

– I said go. Wait downstairs in my office for your wages up till now.

The pieces of marble are strewn all over the floor. It is essential to pick them up and pile them in the corner which has already been demarbled. Some are triangular, some are trapeze-shaped, some are just small chips. One is a whole rectangular slab, which came away entire.

– Now then. Can you cope by yourself for the time being?

– Yes, I think so.

– Bad lot, that one. He not only won't work himself but prevents others from doing so. It was the same in the pavilion. Delinquent of course.

– He told me –

– Yes, I expect he did. Well it all comes to the same thing in the end. What did you say you were registered as?

– Well, er, if you'll excuse my saying so, I'm all things to all men too.

– It's all a matter of tone, isn't it. You're all right. You're a serious chap, you seem to grasp the nature of reality. You know, it's not so easy for us as you may think. All privilege brings its inhibitions and the privilege of health is no exception. There's an irrational fear that lingers on, it's understandable, and in some cases justifiable. I just thought I'd mention it.

The conversation is real, repeat real. Sometimes it is sufficient merely to desire intensely. The law is known as the attraction of opposites.

– The law is known as the second law of thermodynamics, namely, that warmth cannot flow from a cold to a hot body, from a weak body to a strong, from a sick spirit to a healthy spirit, without the application of external circumstances.

It is sometimes sufficient to say nothing, or in this instance to stop the gentle throwing of marble pieces on to the pile of variously shaped slabs in the corner, for the sequence to continue.

– It is thus very difficult for the strong to love the weak, and for the healthy to love the sick, since no warmth is received from them or for that matter needed. The energy radiated from the strong can only flow into the weak in the form of temporary pyrexia, or even hyperpyrexia, which makes them weaker and sicker until dead cold, because it cannot flow back. You understand, don't you?

– Mr. Swaminathan, you don't have to explain.

– Sometimes it is kinder to explain at the beginning. It may prevent a tumorous growth.

– You mean in the imagination?

– Imagination is not an organ, it is a function. And when you recall this conversation, remember also that memory is not a place in the brain but a function of neural energy. So much energy is wasted through friction, dissipated, disorganised, it is important to preserve what there is, otherwise all molecular motions of love would be random ones, unable to impart uniform motions to other atoms. Then the universe would die, of maximum entropy.

– The diagnosis, however, would be a post-mortem.

– There you go again with your sick talk. Some people think that cold Colourless bodies should be done away with, to protect the universe, you know. But I am not such an absolutist. For one thing, it's unscientific. What did you say you were before the – er displacement?

– I was a humanist.

– I didn't mean your politics. They didn't see you very far, anyway, did they? I meant your identity. Oh well, it doesn't matter, identity is only an instrument after all.

– Mr. Swaminathan, I want to ask you one small thing. And that is, well, if you could, once a day, when I pass you on my way up here, just once a day, nod to me. It would help me so much, it would help to confirm my existence. This swaying of yours, you see, it's such a negative sort of gesture.

– Well I will give the matter my consideration. It may not be very wise. Obsessions feed on so little. You are evidently still seeking that external circumstance. But then after all it might be a matter of common courtesy, you being here in this house, working. Perhaps really it would be kinder to sack you.

The feeling is one of euphoria. The veins in the pink marble leap out like a white network made to catch falling eyes. Existence takes the form of the hammering, which has the high-pitched ring of metal hammer on metal chisel. Identity is only an instrument, a hammer for example, hammering a metal chisel. Two instruments, to be precise, or one instrument and its objective. The gesture of work is its exactitude. It is important to hang on to that. The white veins in the pink marble tremble and nod, they sway and stretch out to catch the excited atoms. An oscillograph might perhaps reveal whether the hammering which now drives its high-pitched ring of metal on metal into the neural cells also drives into the memory of the conversation, memory being a function, not a place. An electroencelograph might perhaps separate the components of the conversation into the elements of silence, reality and unreality. A recording engineer might then dub the unreality with the hammering, if of course the hammering is not already part of the mixture. The piece of marble has broken into a shape exactly like the Matterhorn pink on a picture postcard. That the physical presence has occurred is not in doubt, for the visual image, though rapidly fading, is more distinct than in other circumstances, whereas the psychic presence is less strong than it is when there has been no physical presence, less engulfing, not engulfing at all. It is difficult, however, to be equally certain about the conversation, despite the ringing echo of certain phrases, such as the swaying, you see, protects me from levitation, which is unscientific. Did Mr. Swaminathan say, or did he not, the swaying, you see, protects me from levitation, which is unscientific?

– Mr. Swaminathan, you said in the street that memory is a primitive organ in the left hemisphere of the brain, reflected by the right hemisphere as the moon reflects the sun?

– You don't want to believe everything you hear from the man in the street.

– But Mr. Swaminathan, you did say, didn't you, that denial is the only true human power, rather than free will, and that negation is the shadow self which permits man to find unity?

– Well that's another story.

– But is there a story behind the story?

– That's a very good question. I congratulate you on having avoided the trap.

During the hammering, the conversation is one-sided. Highly intelligent questions pertinent to the conversation are posed with a rush of ease, but remain essentially unanswered, for the imagination has not sufficiently identified to compose exactly the same answers as those composed by an alien set of neural cells. This proves that the unhammered conversation has been real since unimaginable replies occurred, though difficult to reconstruct, and fading fast.

The slab breaks into three pieces, one of which is an isosceles triangle. The other two are right-angled triangles with one angle cut off. The lines of breakage are not, however, quite straight, but follow the course of nature. The edges, also, of the breakage lines, are not always vertical, like a canyon side, but more often oblique.

The sun pours into the room, inducing a state of pyrexia. The room must be very high, under the flat roof perhaps, for the long narrow window is full of sky, intensely blue if not as blue as on a picture postcard. It is necessary to close the shutters.

The plane-trees along the straight drive make a thick long crocodile up to the house, the jaw disappearing into a long wide coast of foliage below, the tail into a haze of distant trees and shrubs in green and red and yellow. On either side of the crocodile are smooth green lawns, like water, islanded with flower-beds in great clusters of colour, mostly mixed but one oblong a mass of red. Flower-beds give way to clumps of laurels, pink and crimson azaleas, pink and blue hibiscus, fuchsia, palm fronds, pomegranates and green bay. Beyond the flowering shrubs and trees the mimosas are still in bloom. The white wall is only guessable behind the yellow fringe, which curves imperceptibly to the left until the white wall becomes visible again, and becomes two white walls, the first much further forward, separating the expanses of lawns, flower-beds and bush-clumps from the olive-grove and the vegetable gardens, the other beyond the vegetable gardens along the edge of the property, where the head gardener's cottage is. The path bordered with cypress-hedge is a small dark snake to the large crocodile. Both walls are edged with red and blue and yellow here and there, the bougainvillaea perhaps, and the red poinsettia which are leaves not flowers.

To the right of the coast of foliage around the house, the gazebo is just visible on the lawn. The new pavilion is hidden in the trees.

Beyond the pale yellow fringe of the mimosas bordering the property the olive groves tumble away in a silvery green sea. Taking one step to the left of the window, it is possible to see the Settlement of dark brown shacks, each sloping corrugated roof straddling its minute verandah like a fornicating fly, its wings shining patchily in the sun. The flies are regimented on a flat ground just outside the town. The individual couples are not distinguishable. The fig-tree cannot be seen at this distance. Perhaps it has been blasted. The town sprawls in a haze, tall where it is not squat, grey where it is not golden. The sunlight must be directly on it because the haze makes it indistinct. Taking one step to the right of the window, it is possible to see, far out to the left beyond the maize fields but clearly delineated in the more indirect light, the Colourless Hospital and, next to it, the Colourless Cemetery, a miniature town of miniature sky-scrapers. The gesture is one of careful investigation. The black fingers move swiftly over the white abdomen, palpating the left side or knocking gently through black fingers. The dark nurses move stealthily along the beds in pink stiff calico and silent knowledge. The Colourless are dying of the malady.

Out of the trees immediately below, the garden-party spills its molecules over the lawn.

Daily at five a.m. is the moment of truth. The body lies under the army blanket, as close to its objective self as it is possible to be, listening to the lack of dialectic that strengthens it from within. The body lies under the army blanket, comfortably enclosed in the absolute knowledge that it lies under the army blanket in the dark on a large square mattress on the floor of a small rectangular room through the rectangular window of which a dim daybreak slowly unrounds the murkiness back to angles. Sooner or later some interruption will be inevitable, a movement upwards of the knees and sideways of the feet, a lifting of the torso, a leaning on the elbows perhaps, a crouching of the legs, a pushing-up of the body with the arms, a stepping to the window that gives out on to Mrs. Ned's shack and, from a certain position, on to the fig-tree that looks blasted. Everything that moves increases risk. But now there is only immobility and in the dark a state of comatose suspension. The body lies under the army blanket, a long way from the small high window, comfortably enclosed in the absolute knowledge that Mr. Swaminathan has not nodded and will not nod ever at any time, and that it doesn't matter in the least. The absolute knowledge wraps the body from outside, leaving no trace of error in it.

Sooner or later the observation of phenomena will be inevitable. But now there is only the listening to the shadow which, however, rapidly curls up its film-reel and goes to sleep. The fig-tree's grey framework of trunk and branch, that leans along the edge of the bank at an angle of forty degrees, is further framed by a mass of deep green foliage. Inside the angle, the road may be seen. From ground level, near the fig-tree, the arch formed by the leaning trunk and the downward sweeping branch frames a whole landscape of descending olive-groves beyond the road, which itself disappears behind the bank. The U-shape of the thick and long grey twigs on the downward sweeping branch, which grow first downwards and then curve up, is partly camouflaged in the deep green foliage.

If the grey trunk is further framed by deep green foliage the fig-tree cannot look blasted.

If the clumps of laurel are in full pink and crimson flower the mimosas cannot still be in bloom.

The dim daybreak slowly unrounds the murkiness back to angles. Sooner or later the immature cells will begin to circulate, the myeloblasts and myelocytes, the promyelocytes and metamyelocytes.

Daily at eight a.m. the hope has grown that Mr. Swaminathan will perhaps nod today after all. The hope has grown with the indwelling of Mr. Swaminathan as he cohabits the body, sharing the observation of phenomena, along the passage that is angular when curving is desired, into the kitchen with the red and still stone floor, you see how still it is, Mr. Swaminathan, because the sun cannot as yet stream through the bead curtain, between Mrs. Ned's verandah, it is dilapidated isn't it, and the large-leafed fig-tree on the right, I told you it couldn't look blasted now, on to the road, past the Settlement, along the road with the town behind, through the olive groves and the carefully terraced, carefully irrigated vegetable gardens, but as you know they're always dry, dry, the vegetable gardens, there's never enough to go round, along the road, through the village of smart concrete huts, past the concrete post office and past the grocer, through the averted looks and eyeless smiles, along the road, past the big white houses, along the white wall that is gently rounded, so you see it's impossible at any one moment to know whether things are any different round the corner, into the tradesmen's gate that leads up to the back of the big house, the hope has grown that Mr. Swaminathan will perhaps nod today after all. The servants' stairs are steep and stony. Up the five flights the body suffers from dypsnoea. The pink marble bathroom is short of air. There are seven steps to the step-ladder, then five more up the ladder and the body leans against the top of it, heavy with the absolute knowledge that Mr. Swaminathan has not nodded and will not nod ever at any time, and that it hurts. The absolute knowledge has entered the body at the back of the neck somehow, in the medullary centres, down the glosso-pharyngeal nerve no doubt, or the pneumogastric, at any rate forward and down into the throat, which tightens as enlargement of the lymphatic glands occurs and the knowledge spreads into the chest and down into the stomach, nauseous. Sooner or later it will reach the spleen, which will increase in size until it fills most of the abdomen, though remaining firm and smooth on palpation. Anaemia, fatigue, pyrexia, tachycardia, dypsnoea, cachexy, the onset is insidious and well advanced before diagnosis. The prognosis is poor, continuing to a fatal termination. Splenectomy contra-indicated, treatment unsatisfactory, no therapy, but the blood-count, marrow biopsy and glandular biopsy will furnish a firm diagnosis. These organs on section appear grey or reddish grey, packed with myeloid cells, mainly polymorphonuclears and immature cells such as myeloblasts, promyelocytes, myelocytes and metamyelocites. The marble chips fall chirpily to the floor. It is possible to detach the larger pieces of vertical slab by holding the left forearm against them while hammering on the chisel, but more often than not they crash to the floor, breaking into much smaller and unusable pieces.

– Mr. Swaminathan, you said in the street that memory is a primitive weapon.

– My dear chap, memory is not a place but a racing function of neural cells giving off dismal rhythms at less than ten microvolts, which are driven into by the high-pitched ring of hammer on chisel into marble. What did you say your occupation was before the er –?

– I was a humanist.

– I didn't mean your politics. And in any case, which humans? Which section of humanity were you for? The weak or the strong? Quick, two seconds to answer. One, two. You're a square peg in a round hole aren't you?

The conversation cannot take the form of the hammering because during the hammering there is no conversation, and during the conversation, if it occurred, there was no hammering. Without a recording engineer no chemistry of identity can put those two elements together in time. The pressure of the forearm on the vertical marble slab is difficult to estimate accurately. Either it prevents the chisel from penetrating beneath the slab, or it is too loose to hold the slab to the wall. Either the conversation has partially occurred, the beginning for instance, the remainder being suppressed, selected, manipulated, transformed, schematised, because inunderstood. Or the conversation has wholly occurred, and been wholly manipulated, transformed, schematised, because inunderstood. The marble slab breaks into three large pieces, two of which fall crashing to the floor. A corollary to that is that the conversation has wholly occurred and that Mr. Swaminathan is mad. The gazebo is fully visible on the lawn, to the right of the coast of foliage around the house. The new pavilion is hidden in the trees. A second corollary is that the conversation has wholly occurred and is wholly sane but beyond the grasp of sick white reasoning. A pigeon lands on the parapet of the lower terrace roof above the entrance colonnade and shifts from one leg to another. A second pigeon lands a half metre or so away on the same parapet and waddles cautiously with an occasional bold side-hop, up to the first pigeon, who flies to the curlicew top of a jar on the parapet, followed after a pause by the second pigeon in a flutter. There is not enough room for two on the curlicew top of the concrete jar and the first pigeon takes off, swoops down towards the green crocodile and then veers upwards suddenly and close past the window, to land presumably on the roof immediately above. The second pigeon flies across the crocodile below and into a tall pine-tree.

Mr. Swaminathan stands hugely in the dusty bathroom, swaying from one foot to another. With one sweep of the hand he wipes the pink marble off the wall to the right of the window. At the gentle pressure of his outspread hand the wall crumbles down in a cloud of dust. The dust fills the head, bombarding the cells that run riot, emit helium particles until the leaden head disintegrates to bismuth, lead, thallium, polonium, bismuth, emanation 222, radium, thorium, uranium, on and on, in a hundred and sixty microseconds, or three million two hundred and thirty one thousand six hundred and forty two years one hundred and seventy three days point nine.

– You know very well that that is not how it occurred. Look around you, does this resemble what you know of prehistory?

– It is pitch-black. There is no mind to perceive it.

– You are perceiving it now, by special licence.

– Ah, but I have a blind spot. It's not my fault, it's due to non-existence.

– Don't boast. We haven't built you up yet. There will be a period of initiation. You must learn to participate you know. Nothing less than symbiosis will do, a participation so effective that it cannot be imagined, for it is not only pre-logical but pre-mythical and anterior to all collective representations. Now then, merge.

– I suppose you're marking time really.

– Time, what's that?

– Time for the black and white image to percolate. We can always add the colours later, as they crop up.

– White? If you can see any white about you're already hopelessly corrupt. I said anterior to collective representations. Nothing less than symbiosis will do, between the totemic group and the totem. Now then, merge.

– It's pitch-black.

– That's better.

– But great white penguins are waddling in. No. They're crocodiles, white bellied, up on their hind legs, they fill the whole corridor, help, help.

– There you go again with your sick talk. I said anterior to collective representations. What did you say you were, a physicist? You must know very well that the development of phenomena is correlative to that of consciousness. And that therefore the prehistory of the earth as described by modern science was not only never seen, it never occurred.

– But carbon 14 –

– There you go, assuming that the behaviour of particles remained unchanged over aeons. All you're entitled to assume is that phenomena would have been as now described if they had been seen by people with the same kind of perception as man has evolved only quite recently. A mere few hundred years.

– Help, help! The crocodiles! They're slimy. They're crowding in down the corridor on their hind legs. I'm strangling one. I'm strangling the second. I'm strangling the third. The fourth. I'm strangling the fifth. After five is numberlessness. They go into the collective genitive. They crowd in, help, help.

– Merge, you fool, merge.

– Help!

– All right, if you must have your crude symbols and your schematisations, there's only one way out. You see these cabins along the corridor. They're for changing. We'll shepherd the crocodiles into them. That's it. One by one. You see, they're quite gentle really.

– The floor's wet.

– Well of course, this is an indoor swimming-bath. Now you listen to me, there are three floors, we're in the basement. Above us, people slide in to the swimming-pool from the same level. Above that, there is a gallery, and they dive in. Down here however, we have to go in through these round glass portholes. They're like submarine escape-hatches, only you can swim straight across the two membranes and up through the water. The process is known as osmosis. It's quite a long way up, so take a very deep breath, now, come along, don't be afraid, in you go, merge, in you fool, go on or I'll have to push you.

– No! No! No!

The ceiling is pink and veined in white, and a long way away. The wall ahead is pink above a glossy and pale orange door. To the immediate right, very close to the eyes is a wall of pink veined marble. The veins are enormous, they leap out like a white network made to catch floating eyes. The wall is not very high, half a metre perhaps or a little more, edged by a two centimetre mud-coloured band where the marble has been removed. To the immediate left, very close to the eyes, is another wall of pink veined marble, half a metre high or a little more, also edged with a mud-coloured band where the marble has been removed. Beyond this low wall, some way away, is a high pink marble wall, joining the pink marble ceiling. Inside the head is a hammer striking at a chisel. The wall beyond the low wall to the right is mud-coloured, with some of the pink stripped off, the frontier between the pink and the mud being straight and vertical half way up the wall, then zig-zagging to the ceiling. The straightness of the line to the floor is an item of returning knowledge, for it cannot be wholly seen from this position. The body lies in the sunken marble bath. Inside the head a hammer is striking at a chisel.

– Oh! I'm sorry, I forgot – good heavens! What a funny place to rest. You look as if you were lying in a coffin. No don't move, I'm sure you've earned your break. I forgot this bathroom was being done, you see. Oh, yes, you've done a lot already. Are you alone?

– Erm, yes . . . yes, ma'am.

– I say, are you all right? You look terribly white.

– I am white.

– Now, now, no inverted snobbery, you know what I meant. Aren't you . . . yes, you are, aren't you . . . Lilly's husband?

– Yes, ma'am.

– No, don't get up. I say, you do look ill. Anything wrong?

– I – erm – I think I must have fainted. The last thing I remember, I was on top of that ladder. Then I was in here. And my head –

– Give me your hand, you'd better sit up. There. Can you try and get to your feet and sit on the edge of the bath? That's better. I want you to put your head down between your knees. There. No? You feel sick. Yes of course. Look, I'll sit down here with my feet in the bath and you lie down alongside it with your head on my lap. Stretch your legs out, that's right. Or raise your knees perhaps, it might be more comfortable on this hard floor. You poor old thing. Just relax. Don't keep turning your head.

– Mr. Swaminathan –

– Oh don't worry about him, he's gone up country to the Farming Estate.

– He has? How long?

– Did you say how long for?

– How long has he been gone?

– I've no idea, a week, ten days. How are you feeling?

– Oh, better, much better. If I could, if you don't mind, just a moment longer –

– Close your eyes then, and relax.

Under the red networks of the eyelids in the sunlight, the dark curves of chin and lips and nose seen from below the breasts that are ensilked in orange fill up the eyespace shimmering with black and yellow and pink. Nevertheless it bears a close resemblance to the real thing, as a mere lifting of the lids can prove and does. The face looks down. The left nostril wears a blue-green stone set in gold. The eyes strike deep, a rich, chromatic chord. The ceiling is pink and veined in white, and a long way away. The wall ahead is pink above and around a glossy and pale orange door. To the immediate right –

– How are you feeling?

The thick lips are unsmiling. The expression is one of concern.

– All right, I think. I'm very sorry. You've been so kind. So very kind. Woops. Oh, thank you. It is Mrs. Mgulu, isn't it?

– The same.

– I don't know how to thank you. You shouldn't have – really.

– That's enough of that. If a person can't help a fellow-creature in distress, well, where would we all be? But tell me, why did it happen? Was it the sun? It is hot in here I must say. Facing South and under the roof. Why don't you leave the door open to create a draught?

– Well, the noise, ma'am, and the dust.

– Or are you . . . ill?

– Oh, no, no, not at all, I assure you. I love my work. I'm so grateful to you. Nineteen months, you see, it's demoralising. I once took a degree in Creative Thought.

The eyes strike deep, a rich chromatic chord. The stone in the left nostril is an alexandrite perhaps, blue-green by day, with purple shafts. The wide lips are edged with mauve, they purse in mock reproach that bears a strong resemblance to the real thing. It hurts, down the back of the neck, then forwards, spreading throatwise through the chest.

– You don't have to impress me, you know, I love people as they are. And I'm glad I've been of help, not just for Lilly's sake but for your own. Now, are you going to be all right? I don't think you should be working up here all alone, that wasn't the idea at all. And in a pink bathroom too, right at the top of the house.

– It's nice, this pink marble.

– Oh, do you like it? It's very old-fashioned, it must have been put in when the house was built I shouldn't wonder. It's all going to be changed into a hairdressing salon for my guests. Right through into the next room.

– What colour?

– I haven't thought yet. Black probably. Though that's not very original. Or purple. I'm very fond of purple. But I really can't think what Mr. Swaminathan was doing, putting you up here, all alone in a pink bathroom. I must speak to him.

– No, no, please don't, he'll think –

– He won't think anything, he's my servant. One has to speak to them, you know.

– But I thought –

– Well don't. A pink bathroom at the top of the house, really. No wonder you fainted. Sheer introversion. And I had him trained in human relations, mind you, he should have known better.

– Mrs. Mgulu –

– Yes?

– I beg you not to speak to him. I like it up here. And I like Mr. Swaminathan.

– I see. But work is a social function. You must learn to relate, you know. I've taken a special interest in you for Lilly's sake, and for your own, and from now on you'll do as I say.

– Yes ma'am.

– I'm going to keep my eyes open.

– Yes ma'am.

The eyes strike deep, a rich chromatic chord, that echoes in the blood long after it has come and gone.

Whereas no amount of positive evidence can ever conclusively prove a hypothesis, no evidence at all is needed for a certainty acquired by revelation. Why him? That's a very good question. Why now? That is an ignorant remark. In an age of international and interracial enlightenment such as ours revelation is open to all, regardless of age, sex, race or creed. It is not, however, compulsory. It's entirely up to you. Just fill up this form and queue here.

Mrs. Ned's arms throw her laughter about, it rebounds against the kitchen walls and she catches it. The goitre moves slowly up and down as she relishes the idea. It is possible, after all, to act out these things. With a little concentration, she can be made to give the correct reply. The evening breeze moves the bead curtain imperceptibly, so that through it the slanted glow from the setting sun can be seen reflected in the verandah glass of Monsieur Jules's bungalow. The red stone floor is dark and still.

– You provoked it you know, your unconscious did, I

mean, the fainting, and her coming in just in time to find you.

– Lilly, you shouldn't have said that. Why didn't you let Mrs. Ned say it? She was going to.

– No, I wasn't. I was going to say that it's an external circumstance. That's what they call it. So you be careful.

– Of course you're under-nourished as well. That's what Mrs. Mgulu said when she told me. Lilly, she said, he's under-nourished. She gave me these pep pills for you, they're rather hard to come by, they're better than the national ones, she said.

– Isn't the whole world?

– Oh Mrs. Ned, don't be morbid. I think I'll open that tin of pineapple after all.

– I'm not morbid. It always helps me no end to think of those six point two people to the square metre in Sino-America. I don't know how they stand up to it, I really don't. Afro-Eurasia's being much cleverer. I mean, it helps me to think how fortunate we are. I didn't mean –

– No, of course not.

– Yes I will open that tin of pineapple, to celebrate.

Mr. Swaminathan has returned from the Mgulu Farming Estate up-country. He has not nodded and will not nod ever at any time, but the pain, though unallayed, is less acute. He continues to indwell, swaying slightly from side to side, sharing the observation of phenomena. Other people, however, also say the necessary things, from time to time, and no evidence is needed to prove that these things have been said by just these people. With a little concentration from within it is possible after all, to divide oneself and remain whole. At least for a time. There is a record which can be beaten.

– Though of course, there is the spiritual hunger, as you were saying, and that I can't deny.

– There are plenty of remedies.

– Oh, you're a great one for remedies, Lilly, I know. But in the end they're more dangerous than the original –

– Have a slice of pineapple.
– Well, that is kind of you. I was going to say cachexy. Can you spare it? I mean, it was for him, wasn't it?
– Why him?
– That's a very good question.
– Why now?
– That is an ignorant remark.

Mrs. Ned's arms throw her voice about, her laughter rebounds against the wall and she catches it excitedly. As for the squint it seems a little wide this evening, the blue mobility of the one eye calling out the blueness of the temple veins and a hint of blue in the white skin around. The skin around the eyes, both the mobile eye and the static eye, is waxy.

But Mr. Swaminathan dwells within, swaying from side to side, aching his absence from the sharing of phenomena.

The floor is almost finished. The other workers have left. From this position, laying the marbled thermoplastic tiles on the last strip of floor between the wash-basins and the dressing-tables, it is possible to distinguish the dark legs of the hairdressing assistants from those of the guests as they step across from time to time in variously coloured shoes, for the hem of their pale orange overalls just comes within the outer orbit of downcast absorption. The guests, however, wear black slipovers. It is necessary to raise the eyelids a fraction to include a serial of long black legs that shoot out, in variously coloured shoes, each leg supported below the knee by another which rests vertically on the thermoplastically marbled floor. Different sizes and darknesses of thigh are underlined variously in red or pink or black. The floor is almost finished, the other workers have left and the salon is functioning in embryo, for a few guests only. The floor is scattered with snippets of dark cut hair, mostly wet and curved, but they dry quickly, and when they dry they thicken out. Some are almost circular. A few are silvery pink or green. A pink and yellow boy in pink and yellow cotton trousers sweeps the snippets with a miniature broom and brings them together in a grey funeral pyre, the colours merging with the dust. The hairdresser himself is a small dark man in candy-stripe trousers, with delicate black hands and large brown lips thickly pursed in concentration. Mrs. Mgulu wears golden shoes, and a girl in an orange overall with piled gold hair is lathering her thrown-back head, the neck-line dark and taut, the chin well up and rounded, the lips protruding above it and beyond them the wide nostrils. The gold setting of the alexandrite is just visible on the left nostril. The marbled thermoplastic tiles are purple, with a streak of pink.

– Why now? Why not now? You know the past proves nothing. There's no such thing as the past, save in the privacy of concupiscence. That's an article of faith. So stop fretting about how it might have been. Unless of course the urge is too great to be contained. Then go find yourself a whore, a bureaucrat's willing wife, they're all willing to re-enact you know, regardless of race or creed, so just go ahead and indulge yourselves with post-mortems and forged identities. Go on, go on.

– Why, Lilly, whatever's the matter?

– He gets on my nerves. And there's my tin of pineapple gone, for nothing.

– Don't cry, Lilly. Shall I take him over for a bit? You need a rest.

– Oh, my pineapple!

– But the pineapple was gorgeous, and we had a good laugh, didn't we? Look, I've got a tin of prunes at home I can let you have instead. Oh I know it's not the same but there's a lovely recipe on it for prune kebab. He's a sick man you know.

– I'm perfectly healthy. I do a full day's work. That's the test isn't it? Can he love, can he work?

– Well –

– And if the past proves nothing why do they keep asking about my previous occupation?

– They're bureaucrats. They're behind the times.

– What were you before the displacement! What displacement for heaven's sake?

– The displacement from cause to effect.

– Oh Mrs. Ned! You understand me! Help me, help me.

– Lilly, d'you mind?

– No, I don't mind. Not if you bring me the prunes.

– My dear, you mustn't get so worked up. It's their little weakness, they fed on our past you see, and drained us of its strength, and we feed on their present. Now they deny the past, but need to ask as a matter of form, it flatters them, it's a relic that they adhere to. We must allow them their little weaknesses.

– Come closer. Tell me, Mrs. Ned, how can you know they fed on it if there's no such thing as the past?

– There you go again with your sick talk. It's all a question of adjustment.

– Mrs. Ned, you are full of promise, I want to make mental love to you, here, on the kitchen chair. D'you mind, Lilly?

– No, I don't mind. I can tell you in advance, though, it won't help. Don't forget the prunes.

– Tell me about yourself, Mrs. Ned.

– There's not much to tell, it's banal really, I first met my father in the usual circumstances, as a transference, and I said to him, why did you deprive me of my trauma, I've been looking for it ever since, alchemising anecdote to legend, episode to myth, it's exhausting, you've made my life a misery, it's because of you that I've grown up deprived, but he didn't reply. I fell in love with him, deeply, painfully in love. How did you first meet your mother?

– At her funeral. The flowers on her coffin were a mass of red.

– Really? Why, what did she die of?

– In the displacement, you know.

– Go on.

– I can't.

– What did she say to you?

– She was covered with purple patches. Her eyeballs stuck out. She couldn't speak, she was deaf and blind.

– Was it the monocytic type?

– No, Chloroma.

– Go on.

– I can't . . . Come in.

– Excuse. Boeuf Strongonoff. Wife.

– Well, thank you Mrs. Ivan. But why?

– Cry on tins. Present.

– It's most kind of you. Lilly will be delighted.

– Please empty to return. Keep for roof. Ivan.

– Certainly. Thank you very much.

– Nichevo. Goodnight. Goodnight Mrs.

– Goodnight Mrs. Ivan.

– Goodnight Mrs. Ivan. Oh dear where were we?

– I don't know.

– Erm. What did you do, before?

– What do you think I did?

– Something important.

The image of the man grows up a little. The two hands clutch each other damply across the wrinkled wood of the table, which is quite still and unflowing in the dusk. The goitre opposite seems to swell as Mrs. Ned relishes the idea.

– You're important to me.

– Oh. But who are you? You must make yourself important too, a worthy vessel to contain my importance.

– You must make me a worthy vessel. It takes two to make love.

– Did you ever find your trauma?

– Not really. It got lost, in the displacement, you know.

– What displacement?

– The displacement from cause to effect.

– From birth to death.

– From nothing to something.

– From red to sickly white. Then black.

– From infra-red to ultra-violet.

– You're beautiful. You're wonderful.

– That's why I have this goitre, you see, it's a deficiency of thyroxin due to emotional deprivation.

– Oh my darling, you are important, you are a worthy vessel.

– What did you do, then, it must have been very important?

– I was a great lover. A lover of society. I grew up with her, grew strong out of her, basked in her. I tickled her, scratched her, tormented her, accused her, I trained the great microscopes of searching questions on her. I despised her, mocked her, got cynical about her, used her. I despaired of her, had high hopes of her, I loved her.

– How wonderful. So you satisfied your own demand?

– Yes, of course. But I was only a cog in her machine and the machine ground to a standstill.

– She let you down?

– Yes.

The image of the man grows up.

– Have you told this to anyone else?

– You are the first person to know.

– That's nice. Because I'm bound to feel with you. I was let down too. Built up and then let down.

– You're not doing it right, you're talking about yourself.

– I'm only explaining that I'm ready as a vessel, and that I'm bound to feel with you, and understand your idealism.

– But I'm a formalist.

– I see. Well, it all comes, I mean, tell me, have you ever been in love, deeply, painfully in love?

– Er . . . define your terms.

– Needing his, I mean her, interest, I'll put it no stronger, full-time, deeply, painfully enough to make an abject idiot of yourself getting it, and of course not getting it, on account of the situation, and so losing his, I mean her, interest. If any.

– No, only women do that.

– I am a woman. Have pity. You're such a wonderful formalist.

The image of the man grows big. His identity is enormous. Identity is a powerful instrument.

– You're talking about yourself.

– I've always loved you. From the very beginning I've loved you.

And so on. Lilly was right. Sooner or later smallness returns. Anyone can bluff a metaphysical remark as part of the pretence that the human mind is interesting, and alone involved. But nothing less than symbiosis will do. And in the marbled top-room of the mind, Mrs. Mgulu wears golden shoes. Her head is helmeted in golden chrome. In the left nostril, the alexandrite looks pink in the salon lights. She is reading a book on horticulture, with glossy golden callicarpas on the cover. From time to time she puts it down on her lap and looks a little beyond it to the floor in front of her. Or even to the right of her, keeping her eyes open, which strike deep, a rich chromatic chord. The marbled thermoplastic tiles are purple, streaked with pink. Have you ever been deeply, painfully in love? The answer is no, never. It is possible, after all, to act out these things, to divide oneself and remain whole, despite Mr. Swaminathan's silent sway as he continues to indwell, sharing the observation of phenomena, staring at Mrs. Mgulu in golden shoes and a helmet of golden chrome. Eating her up. Her dark face shines under the hot air, beautiful in any circumstances, with the alexandrite pink in her left nostril. Mr. Swaminathan holds a black thermoplastic hose that follows his movement like a dying metronome.

– Let's go and interview her, you and I.

– Is she not beautiful in any circumstances?

– We'll ask her.

– She can't hear, under the helmet.

– She will remove the helmet when she sees the microphone. She loves me, you see.

Mrs. Mgulu sits graciously at the dressing-table, taking an

interest in the crackling electricity of her hair which is being brushed into sleekness by the small dark man in candy-stripe trousers, whose profile is reversed in the mirror. His hands are delicate with pale pink nails and his brown lips pout in concentration. On the other side of the dressing-table is another dressing-table which faces the other side of the mirror. There a pert Bahuko girl in an orange overall dresses the hair of a guest who is hidden by the two-sided mirror. As she works she glances into the mirror at the results. Even her long brown hands are visible, with their golden nails, but the guest's head is hidden by the raised square mirror. From this position to the right of Mrs. Mgulu the Bahuko girl looks as if she were dressing the hair of Mrs. Mgulu's image who faces Mrs. Mgulu on this side of the mirror. Mrs. Mgulu's hair is being dressed by two live people, an Asswati in candy-stripe dressing her real hair, and a Bahuko girl in orange, dressing her reflected hair. Mrs. Mgulu does not know this, for she cannot see the Bahuko girl. In the square wooden-framed mirror her own smooth Asswati face smiles at her reflection with self-love in the round black eyes and in the well-curved lips, but occasionally with graciousness at the reflection of the Asswati with delicate hands, who pouts his mouth pursed in concentration. The smiling black eyes shift a little to the left, with graciousness, and then a little to the right, with self-love. A psychoscope might perhaps reveal the expression to be one of pleasure in beauty, rather than self-love. And then a little more to the right. The last marbled thermoplastic tile is glueing nicely, purple, streaked with pink. Sooner or later some interruption will be inevitable, a movement will have to be made, a finishing of the task, a declaration that the activity, the heat, the motion of colours and the concrete feel of tools and materials are over. You people are all the same, the task has taken far too long. The big ball is practically on us and the salon is only just finished, it's all very well but it has been one long headache. You're all as lazy and unreliable as one another.

– and Lilly's very worried about you.

The eyes strike deep, a rich chromatic chord, the scent of hair-lacquer fills the corridor. The alexandrite in the left nostril is replaced by a small gold flower on a chain that climbs over the nose and loops gently along the cheek into the hair just above the right ear. Follow me, she said, I want a word with you outside. The conversation is real, repeat real. She leans her bare black arms against the golden banisters. Follow me, she said, tapping him on the shoulder, I want a word with you outside and now the golden banisters go curving down behind her, a sort of crown in depth, a spiral gown, a chrysalis.

– She was upset about the infidelity of course, anyone would be, but these things happen and she understood. Anyway it's none of my business. But your capacity to work is my business. I'm your employer, for the time being anyway, and I've taken an interest in you, for Lilly's sake at least. I'm very fond of Lilly. She practically brought me up and I owe a lot to her. She's been with me ever since, I know her as I know my right hand, and she's very unhappy about you. I've been watching you in there. You're dreaming half the time. Oh I know the other workers are no better, it's understandable, they want to make the job last, but still, time isn't elastic.

– It's because of there being no past, and no future, ma'am, it's so difficult, living in the present.

– I see you've been talking to Mr. Swaminathan.

– You fed on our past, you see, and drained us, now you deny the past but need to remind us, it's an empty ritual for you, a weakness. But it hurts.

– You don't want to believe everything Mr. Swaminathan says, you know.

– That too is one of the things he says.

– Yes. He belongs to the rope-trick tradition, which can be as unhealthy as – well, you know what I mean. I think I should send you up to the hospital to be psychoscoped.

– Oh, no!

– Why, what's the matter? It's a very rapid treatment, quite painless and it does the world of good. It's a privilege, too.

– Not . . . the Colourless Hospital?

– You speak so low. I can't hear.

– Did you mean the Colourless Hospital?

– The—? But we don't have segregation here, we're a multi-racial society. Exalting all colours to the detriment of none, don't you know your slogans? Good heavens, I do believe you really are living in the past . . . Tell me, does it hurt?

– Yes.

– You're in a bad way, aren't you?

The dress is mauve. The shining black hair is coiled up high and smells of fixative. The small gold chain loops gently over the nose and the banisters weave circles around her.

– Come with me, I'll give you a letter.

The banisters weave circles round them both.

– Then you can go back and sweep up the mess before you leave. It's all got to be spick and span by tomorrow.

The banisters weave circles.

– Steady! Are you all right? You can't faint on my stairs, you know. I would send you with Olaf, my chauffeur, but I need him to go and open the Famine Bazaar. Are you taking those pills I gave Lilly? They're better than the Government ones and they're rather hard to come by. Wait here.

Whereas no amount of positive evidence. We can make our errors in a thought, and reject them in another thought, leaving no trace of error in us. No evidence at all is needed for a certainty acquired by revelation. Yes, but what relation does it have to the real thing? The number of molecules in one cubic centimetre of any gas, at sea-level pressure and at a temperature of fifteen degrees centigrade, is approximately twenty seven million million million, and each molecule can expect five thousand million collisions per second. Mrs. Mgulu emerges from the bedroom door, wearing something diaphanous. Classical physiology tolerates only one unknown quantity at a time in any investigation and that quantity shall be Mrs. Mgulu. Come in, she says, I want you to read this letter and see if it's all right. Oh, stop it, you know very well this dialogue will not occur. We don't have segregation here, oh I know it looks like it, but you're selecting the facts, I do assure you we're a multi-racial society. Come in, she says, and I'll show you. I've always loved you, right from the very beginning I've loved you. You're living in the past aren't you, but now is the time for the beginning.

– Here we are, you go to the Hospital and give them this letter, they'll get you back into focus. It's all a question of restoring the equilibrium. But first go up and tidy the mess in the salon. It must all be spick and span by tomorrow. You're feeling all right, aren't you?

The dress is mauve, the shining hair is coiled up high and smells of fixative. The small gold chain loops gently out of the left nostril over the nose and cheek. The eyes strike deep, a rich chromatic chord that echoes in the blood long after it has come and gone.

The salon is empty. The thermoplastic marbled tiles are scattered with dust and bits of plaster. In the corner the small funeral pyre of hair has been left, grey with mingled dust. The banisters weave circles. Go to the Hospital and give them this letter. They will restore the equilibrium. They will weigh you in the balance and find you wanting.

The thin freckled left hand lies limply on the neighbouring human thigh. The thigh too is thin, and wrapped in faded grey denim which creases like an old tree-trunk. The creases multiply toward the loin, converging and vanishing into it. Something is missing. The dirty canvas shoe has a hole where the big toe presses and no shoe-lace. The shoe was once white but is now grey and yellow and brown. The other shoe, half hidden by the left foot which is crossed over it, may be in holes and grey. Its rubber sole gapes on the left side. Something is missing. Under the bony wrist the creases start, and multiply towards the loin, like the innumerable legs of a large spider. That's it. And yet the pale green corridor is full of flies, buzzing in the heat making heads negatively shake, hands wave, knees twitch, feet stamp though not necessarily all at once. Sooner or later the fly will straddle the high blue vein on the gnarled hand and the Bahuko nurse will emerge in pink and white calico and call out an identity and the thigh will slope up into a vertical position, slowly or suddenly according to the age and the humour and the health, according to the degree of sanguinity or melancholia, according to the balance or imbalance of hope and despair.

– Mrs. Mgulu, of Western Approaches. Ah yes, she is much given to writing little notes, is Mrs. Mgulu.

The metal grill splinters the bland Asswati face as the eyes move slowly from right to left under the heavy lids. The fly settles on the right corner of the stalwart lips, that twitch the fly away. In the left arc of the nose with the right eye closed,

– Excuse me but that letter is addressed to the doctor.

– Occupation?

– Well, doctor I suppose.

– You suppose?

– Oh you mean me. Odd job man. At the moment.

– Previous occupation?

– Psychopath.

– Psy . . cho . . path . . . Sponsor, Mrs. . . . Mgu . . . lu. Right. Go up the corridor, second left to Out-Patients, wait there till you're called.

At the back of it all, Mr. Swaminathan sways weakly from

one side to another like a dying metronome. You see, he says, sooner or later the sequence will occur. There is a movement in the neighbour's neck of one who is about to talk. Sometimes it is sufficient merely to say perhaps or I don't think so or how very interesting, as the case might be, for the sequence not to occur. It is easy enough in the negative. The fly lands about ten centimetres away from the hand that holds an invisible bunch of flowers. You should write to her, you know, it would be quite in order, she is much given to writing little notes. She takes an interest. The tiled floor is mottled. The dirty canvas left shoe has no shoelace and a hole where the big toe presses. The rubber sole of the right shoe gapes beneath the left foot that is crossed over it. Dear Mrs. Mgulu. Since you are given to writing little notes, may I take it upon myself to reciprocate and ask you to take a further interest. The sequence with Mrs. Ned was a failure, despite the tender, incestuous appeal of white within a black man's world. Dear Mrs. Mgulu. Since you have so kindly taken an interest in my welfare I would like to tell you that the sequence with conventional weapons is about to begin. Mr. Swaminathan, however, still ticks away at the back like a dying metronome, despite the flood of your, despite your generous and devoted efforts to dislodge him. It is not merely that I desire you physically, which is understandable in any circumstances, but that he watches me desire you, he occupies me with you like a sneak and a small-time spy and I would prefer him out of the way. I would prefer to give myself entirely over to desiring you, for sometimes it is sufficient to desire intensely. I hope therefore that the conventional weapons sequence will have some result and shall inform you of further progress as it occurs.

Dear Mrs. Mgulu. Open the flood-gates please, I want to die.

– Excuse me, do you happen to know what that green door is at the end?

– No, I don't.

– All the other doors are white, you see. And that one's green.

The neighbouring human thigh, empty of hands, is wrapped in faded grey denim and creased as an old tree-trunk. The neighbour has crossed his arms on his chest. And yet the pale green corridor buzzes with flies that make heads negatively shake, hands wave, knees twitch, feet stamp, not necessarily all at once though all at once in the sudden awareness of these gestures having occurred for some time. They should know that people with kidney trouble find it difficult to use their voice, the voice gets lost and little, the effort involved produces monotonous low noises that go on and on and suddenly get loud and bear no relation to the real thing, whatever it is, which could be communicated. After which they are swallowed back in shame. People with kidney trouble do not like people.

– I never said you had kidney trouble. Your eyelids are the right colour.

– But doctor –

– Psychosomatic. Or sciatica. I'll give you some pills to cheer you up. Next please.

– It can't be the lavatory because that's here.

– I suppose not.

– And it's not the doctor and it can't be offices.

– No.

– Do you think it's one of the wards?

– I don't know.

The floor is mottled all the way to the pairs of feet lined up opposite, in canvas shoes, with legs denimed or bare.

– It isn't marked. I mean they usually have a name, don't they, a benefactor or someone.

– Yes.

– It can't be the theatre either, that's upstairs. Or the X-ray room. That's at the back near Physiotherapy.

– Is it.

The Bahuko nurse emerges from the doctor's door in pink

and white calico and the neighbouring thigh tenses. A name is called out. The thigh relaxes. A large pale lady in a black cotton dress rises slowly from further down the line, collects innumerable bags and waddles in, all basketed around. The freckled hands lie limply on each of the neighbour's thighs. And yet the pale green corridor is full of flies, buzzing in the heat.

– And yet, you know, I've seen them going in and coming out of that door.

It is not merely that I desire you intensely, but that I want to die. Sometimes it is insufficient to disimagine. It is not possible at all. The thing exists and floods the consciousness. I would prefer him out of the way, since he might drown, if you would be kind enough to tell him. He is your servant and one has to speak to them. The thing exists and we cannot pretend that it does not. I hope therefore, and shall inform you of further progress as it occurs.

– Excuse me but would you do me a favour?

The conventional weapons are ranged all round, pointing downwards and converging. The lights above the microscopes glare a heavy heat.

– Did you say yes?

– Yes. What is it?

– When you go in there, could you ask them, oh the nurse will do, it doesn't have to be the doctor.

The neck is freckled, the face a greenish, yellowish colour, the hair ginger. The eyelids are pink and swollen, the skin beneath the eyes trembles slightly.

– Ask them what?

– Well, about that door. I've tried but they never tell me anything. They go all mysterious whenever I ask a question. You know, evasive. As if I had no right to ask, as if there were a secret sect and I wasn't initiated, you know what I mean. But I've been coming here a long time, six years, close on. I swear to you that door wasn't there when I first came. Have you been coming a long time?

– No.

– Oh, well, I expect you're just lucky then. They'd probably answer you. You may have been initiated for all I know.

All the dancers on the ballroom floor are dressed in black to mourn the death of the Governor. The faces and hands of the gentlemen are black, the faces, shoulders and arms of the ladies are black, all glowing with vitality, and every gentleman holds one lady at arm's length, jerking tremulously, then convulsively as the ladies quiver and quake in their shimmering black gowns. The Governor's wife watches benignly through a gold lorgnette, her eyes two gold-framed pictures on a dark velvet wall. Through the gold lorgnette the dancers quiver on the ballroom floor which is as round as the eye of a microscope. The dancers lean backwards, putting out their bellies, and then forwards, bouncing out their behinds in dignified postures and a steady rhythm. Mrs. Mgulu, hand on hip, leans her plunging neck-line forward in a dignified posture and a steady rhythm and says let me introduce, no , but really, you haven't got a clue, have you?

– Have you?

– What?

– Been initiated.

The Bahuko nurse emerges in pink and white calico and calls out the correct identity, the recognisable label, the dog's dinner bell. Hope rises with the body on the weight of tingling legs.

– I thought you had. You won't forget?

– No.

– You will wait for me, won't you?

– This way.

It depends which kind of Chinese the doctor is, a renegade from Chinese Europe or a refugee from Sino-America, or even a renegade from Sino-America. Or an Afro-Eurasian born and bred, by chance descendance perhaps or any number of individual circumstances.

– So we were a psychopath, were we? We have a sense of humour, yes? Sit down. Strange, that is not what Mrs. Mgulu gives me to understand in her letter. Hmmm.

The gesture is one of careful record-keeping. The fingers move swiftly over the white paper, holding a black pen. The eyes move from right to left in their slits, following the letter. Dear Dr. Fu Teng. I am sending you one of my workers who suffers from humour deficiency. Who suffers from an imbalance of all the humours. Dear Dr. Fu Teng, kindly weigh this patient in the balance and find him wanting me, Mrs. Mgulu. It is important that he should declare himself. The fingers move swiftly back to the beginning of the line. Dear Dr. Fu Teng. Kindly provide this patient with a technique for living.

– Yes. Well, clearly you don't in fact need psychoscopy. However, if that's what Mrs. Mgulu wants, we'll have to give it to you.

– But doctor –

– Yes?

– Aren't you going to examine me?

– I have examined you. We have our methods if you don't mind. I can tell you one thing, you haven't got what you think you have, oh yes, I know what you're thinking, you all think it, the existence of this thing has turned you people into drivelling hypochondriacs. However, if you insist, you can have routine tests. Nurse, blood count, steroids, M.S.U., B.M.R., P.B.I., the lot. And a form for psychoscopy please.

Mrs. Mgulu emerges from behind the screen in a gold helmet and a mauve dress. She takes the pulse carefully, looking down at the gold watch that hangs upside down on her left breast. She holds the watch a little outwards with the thumb and forefinger of the left hand.

– How are you feeling now? Does it hurt?

– Yes.

– Let me fix your pillows for you. There, that's better.

The gold watch sways, the gold chain on the nostril and

cheek trembles with the motion, the scent is of aloes and hair fixative, the eyes strike deep, a rich chromatic chord expressing secret knowledge and concern perhaps that bears a strong resemblance to the real thing. It is not merely that I desire you physically, which would be understandable in any circumstances, but that he watches me desire you, peering at me with bland inscrutability in his lidless eyes, the lower edges of which are straight and upwards slanting, the upper edges of which are curved but vanishing, into the skin of the face itself. Mrs. Mgulu leans her plunging neckline forward and says you know, don't you, it's only kidney trouble.

– What's that? Who said you had kidney trouble? What books have you been reading? Speak up now, I can't hear you.

– I haven't been reading any books.

– Well, you must have got these items from somewhere. But they're all wrong you know. You mustn't imagine things.

– It's so difficult, living in the present.

– Who said you had to live in the present? The present contains the future. Who have you been talking to? You mustn't get ideas, you know.

– Doctor, tell me, is there a secret?

Dr. Fu Teng writes busily. The vibration of the voice has not been sufficient to carry the question over to him and the question evaporates, leaving no trace of error in the air, except perhaps a residue at the back of the mind, to be answered by Mr. Swaminathan in his own good time, slow time. Clearly Dr. Fu Teng is an Afro-Eurasian born and bred, by chance descendance perhaps, or any number of individual circumstances.

– Right. There's the file, nurse, get it sent round, will you. And call the next patient.

– Doctor. What is the answer?

– This way please.

A nod can mean dismissal. Either the vibration of the voice has been insufficient or the dismissal would anyway have occurred. The fact that Mr. Swaminathan has not nodded and will not nod ever should be viewed in this light. On the other hand the fact that Mr. Swaminathan has not nodded and will not nod ever is of no significance.

The exit door leads into the test cubicles. The test cubicles lead into one another and are for urinating, bleeding, drinking radio-active iodine through a straw, dreaming, conversing with Mrs. Mgulu and having her traced with isotopes, lying at 5 a.m. under a space-man helmet that measures the moment of truth in the blood. The process is known as degradation, out of which the complete molecule must be built up stage by stage, using unambiguous reactions until total synthesis is achieved, which will finally confirm the method of breakdown. The test cubicles lead out into a pale green corridor lined with doors and guiding notices. The doors are white. The guiding notices are white with large red letters. The legs of the waiting females are white, those of the waiting males are trousered in faded denim.

The microscopes are gathered all around, pointing downwards and converging. The heat from the lights induces a state of pyrexia. Between two of the converging microscopes the monitoring screen hangs from the ceiling and shows a fresh white jellyfish on a pale green background, with yellowish white filaments flowing downwards and long black tentacles flowing upwards out of a purple outer skin that covers only the top of the jellyfish. But now the smooth asphalt face of the interviewer is on the screen patched with curved oblongs and blobs of white reflected light.

– Don't keep looking up at the monitor, it spoils the picture. Look at me or else straight at the viewer, that is, the camera in front of you. Don't look at the other cameras either.

– I can't turn my head anyway, with all those wires attached to it.

– That's for the toposcope. Now you're not nervous are you? Just relax. We're going to diagnose first then proceed to treatment, though not necessarily in one session. It depends how much resistance you put up.

– Dr. Lukulwe, says the loudspeaker somewhere.

– Yes, doctor? says the interviewer here.

– Give me a spot of level will you.

– One two three four five Monday Tuesday Wednesday Thursday.

– Thank you but more natural. Have you briefed the patient?

– I was just doing so, Doctor Benin.

– Carry on, I'm listening.

– Right. Well now, I have to tell you that the lies show up immediately on the oscillograph. No moral judgment is involved so don't worry about it, the lies are themselves revealing and help diagnosis. One-man truths, that is to say, delusions, will appear on the depth-photography screen, but only in the long run. That's why we have to give it a long run, but it's for your own sake. You're not to worry about a thing, just relax. You ready? Dr. Benin, we're ready when you are.

– Fine. Stand by recordings. We shoot in . . . ten seconds . . . from . . . now . . .

– Well, sir, since you've heard the discussion, could you give us your views on the situation?

– Er . . . what situation?

– Come come. Your situation. Just relax, let the drug talk for you.

– It isn't working yet.

– It will in a second.

– Well . . . the situation is highly inflammatory and demands a serious reappraisal.

– What exactly do you mean by reappraisal?

– There will have to be an investigation.

– But don't you think there have been enough investigations?

– I don't accept that. Though it is certainly a viewpoint.

– What do you accept?

– I would say that if the situation does not visibly improve we shall have to consider taking action.

– What sort of action have you in mind?

– Well of course I would have to consult with my committee. Well of course I would have to consult with my cabinet.

– And what action do you suppose your cabinet has in mind?

– Well of course we do not envisage anything as drastic as breaking diplomatic relations with reality, indeed we rather depend on these good relations. We shall do everything in our power to exhaust all possible constitutional means first.

– And then?

– Well, then we shall have to consider taking action.

– I see. What about you sir, do you vote for the Government in power?

– I am the Government in power.

– And you, do you vote for or against the Government in power?

– Last time I was sweet, lick me now, said the salt.

– What do you have against authority?

– I never said I was against.

– So you vote for the Government?

– I never said that.

– Do you prefer to satisfy demand or demand satisfaction?

– I don't accept that.

– Do you prefer to satisfy demand or demand satisfaction?

– What's the catch?

– Just answer the question.

– To satisfy demand.

– Would you rather support medical treatment of criminals or medical treatment of politicians?

– Er . . . politicians.

– What do you have against criminals, don't you think they need medical treatment as much as anyone else?

– It is certainly a viewpoint.

Inside the jellyfish on the monitor, which is looking heavenwards, another jellyfish can be seen in profile, with the black tentacles flowing up and backwards, then another in quarter profile. The glowing basalt face immediately ahead smiles like a flash-bulb breaking. The black eyes in the pinkish whites gleam with triumph, the triumph perhaps of the fanatic inventor astonished by his own machine, astonished that it works.

– What about you sir, would you rather support the refugee programme or food for the victims of the population explosion?

– Er . . . food.

– So you like your food?

– No.

– Why are you against the refugees? Are you afraid they will increase the unemployment problem? Your own personal unemployment problem?

– No, of course not. I didn't mean –

– Do you like reading books?

– Oh, no, I don't read books, I assure you.

– But don't you want to improve yourself? Or do you prefer nine-pin bowling with the gang?

– Oh no, I mean, I suppose, I like some books, it depends.

– So you don't like nine-pin bowling with the gang?

– I . . . I like, ideally I would like, best I mean, nine-pin bowling on my own, and, secondly, reading books with the gang.

– Do you like laughing?

– Of course. I mean, not immoderately.

– So you often feel excluded from group laughter? Now will you look up at the monitor screen. Do you like it all in red? Or do you prefer it in blue? Pink? Or brown? Violet? Or white? Green? Yellow? Thank you. Do you prefer wood or metal? The sky or the earth? Fire or water? Thank you. Do you love Mrs. Mgulu or Mr. Swaminathan best?

– I love Mrs. Mgulu best and Mr. Swaminathan a little bit more.

– That's a very good answer! Has someone told you the way to answer that question?

– No. It's all my own work. My head hurts.

– It's the mental enema. Hold it just a little longer, we're nearly through. Do you put your wife and children above your country?

– Yes. No, I mean. In an emergency –

– You have no children, have you?

– Not . . . now.

– And your country is? . . . Humanity? Come come. What did you say? Afro-Eurasia. Good. Tell me, what are those innumerable little monomanias I see in your head, no, don't look up at the monitor, they're like crushed pieces of paper, or flowers, half-started letters and daydreams. You are given to writing little notes?

– Only in my head.

– Do you think an oral tradition is superior to a written civilization?

– I, no. I wouldn't say that.

– So you believe in acting out?

– Only in my head.

– Did you enjoy the displacement?

– No.

– Did you enjoy Mrs. Ned?

– The sequence was a failure. Her deep love is too white, too dirty grey I mean, like the convolutions of the brain.

– Do you prefer history or progress?

– There is no such thing as history, save in the privacy of concupiscence.

– This . . . is . . . the privacy of concupiscence. I am your doctor, father, God. I build you up. I know everything about you. Your profile is coming up very clearly indeed on the oscillograph, and the profile provokes its own continuation, did you know that, the profile moulds you as it oscillates?

Diagnosis provokes its own cause, did you know that? To put it more succinctly, diagnosis prognosticates aetiology, and certainly your depth-psychology personae are most revealing, if somewhat banal, no, don't look up at the monitor, you see, it only makes the eyes of the jellyfish look heavenwards, but we know the jellyfish is only looking at itself, don't we? And the jellyfish cannot meet its own eyes. That's right, you look into the camera with the little red light on, the eyes on the monitor are no longer looking heavenwards but straight out. Of course you can't see them looking straight out unless you look up in which case they look up too. You cannot catch yourself. But the meeting is not compulsory. Now then, tell me, because you can tell me, you know, what is your occupation?

– Odd . . . job . . . man.

– Very nice too. And what was your occupation, before?

– I was a self-made man.

– A contradiction in terms.

– I was chosen among five thousand as the most balanced and normal of men, to be one of twelve representing my country on a special mission in space.

– What were you really?

– An analyser.

– Deeper.

– A synthesiser.

– Deeper.

– An alchemist, lick me now, said the salt.

– Deeper.

Yet another profile is added inside the jellyfish, the outer face of which still looks heavenwards. There must be ten profiles in there at least. Or twenty.

– I don't know. What's that flickering light? The sun flickers through the quick plane trees.

– Don't worry about that. It's just to increase the neural electricity you give out which helps the oscillograph. Go on.

– An electrician. A builder.

– Deeper.
– A welder.
– Come, come, no false shame. Take off those identities.
– I don't know. I really don't know. I see a huge triangle, orange, and a yellow shower, and circles, red . . . oh.
– Do you love anyone at all?
– Second . . . law of . . . thermodynamics . . . subject to, the whole universe . . .
– Will you lay down the white man's burden?
– He is dying. Absolve him . . . That are heavy laden. Take it up, take it up for me . . . Oh, father, doctor, touch me, cure me, oh Mr. Swaminathan, I love you.
– Mr. Blob. Thank you very much.
– Oh . . . Is it over?
– Yes. Mr. Umbassa, would you remove those contraptions from the patient please.
– Is that . . . all?
– What more d'you want? It was a long run. We have our methods, you know. Besides, there's a long queue, as you're well aware, you must have been in it at least two hours.
– Doctor. Is there a secret?
– A secret?
– I mean, what is the answer?
– The answer? The answer's in biochemistry of course. Here's a prescription. Take two once a day every morning before breakfast. They'll cheer you up and help you to cope.
– You mean, after all that . . .?
– I've told you, diagnosis only prognosticates aetiology.
– I don't understand.
– You're not meant to.

The sigh is almost imperceptible, the boredom perhaps imagined on the bland and glowing asphalt face.
– There we are. Goodbye. Next please.
– Excuse me but, will you want to see me again?
– What? Oh, no. You're a bit behind the times aren't you? Psychoscopy's an extracted absolute of analysis. We

don't need transference any more. We're not only able to telescope a dependence that used to take years to build up, we telescope the let-down as well. You'll see, the wrench will be fairly painless. More so, at any rate, than with Mr. Swaminathan, eh? You'll have to renew your drugs, though, we haven't quite solved that one yet, but there's an automatic dispensary outside, you just feed in your prescription each time. Goodbye.

Somewhere in the archives there will be evidence that this has occurred, if it is kept, and only for the minds behind the microscopes. And besides, the installing and rigging up of the microscopes, and of the subjects under the microscope, interferes with the absolute result of being tinted. Other episodes, however, cannot be proved in this way.

3

MRS. JOAN DKIMBA eats the Beef Strogonoff and rice with appetite and relish.

– Lilly it's delicious. I'm so glad to see you're not starving here. What a pity you're on a diet, that gruel looks most unappetising. I must tell Denton, he's very interested in the geography of famine. He has a great big map in his office, you know, and sticks coloured pins into it. You can see everything at a glance. It's particularly bad in the North, especially in and around the capital, where of course the overcrowding is awful. Everyone flocks to the capital hoping for work, it's amazing how stupid people are, they're told to keep away but everyone thinks they're an exception. I spend hours and days slum visiting and trying to persuade them. It's true there are more jobs in the capital, naturally, but nothing like enough, and the more everyone thinks so the less there are. Then those terrible shanty-towns grow on the outskirts like cancers, huts built of petrol-cans and old tyres and bits of tarpaulin, the bidonvilles, you've seen them I expect, and crime of course is rampant. For every ten people we manage to move out to rural areas two hundred move in. You don't know how comfortable you are here, with your own separate bungalow, two whole rooms and a kitchen. Oh yes of course you do, having come here from the capital. I wish we could rehabilitate more people, but it really is impossible to keep up with it. Denton tours the whole country, the whole continent even, and the other continents too, trying to get co-operation from distributing organisations, did I tell you he's been made Chief Spokesman, he was chosen among sixty-seven, you know, to represent his country, but the trouble is everyone's out for themselves, and so suspicious! Of course there's corruption, no one denies it, but you'd think they'd be able to tell, I mean they ought to have perfected means of detection by now, and international policing of distribution. In the end one has to tackle everything oneself. And I must say we've done wonders in this country, out of sheer will-power and determination. The energy of the people, it's amazing. I mean just look at this reclaimed area, it simply didn't exist before. Does your husband work on the land or is he retired? I think the Pension-Pill Scheme is marvellous, don't you, I mean, no one ever thought of that before, to keep the old people not only fit but happy. Denton had quite a hand in that, you know. It's the same with the dole-pills. Well I mean that side of things is important, isn't it. The difficulty is in persuading people to come and get what they're entitled to. They seem to prefer wallowing in their misery, it's quite extraordinary.

– Oh, he's unemployed? I see. It really is an insoluble problem, isn't it? And I assure you that it isn't prejudice, Denton's gone into it very carefully, the figures show that prejudice is definitely not part of the overall picture, though of course it may occur in individual cases here and there. You see, you can't get away from the fact that the Colourless are more unreliable, oh, not that they mean to be of course – except in individual cases, throw-backs, so to speak, who can't adapt to new environments– but simply because they're weaker, they go sick more often, and they're more susceptible to the – well, of course I don't know why I'm talking in the third person like this, I'm as Colourless as you are, but somehow I've been caught up, as it were, in a manner of speaking, but I'm with you all the way, naturally. But I thought you told me he had a job up at Denise Mgulu's? Temporary, oh I see. It is difficult isn't it? I should have thought that with the BAUDA there'd be plenty of extra work. Oh, it stands for Ball in Aid of Under Developed Areas. Lilly, you should know that, it's an annual event. Oh, I see, well maybe she's right, it does make it sound a bit grim, I suppose. But I always think it's best to face facts. You know Denise strikes me as awfully out of touch sometimes. All this lady of the manor business. Of course I approve of her food-growing experiments, I think she and Severin have done wonders round here, but you know Severin is always up at that farm of theirs, he's hardly ever seen in the House of Reps and for heaven's sake one must be seen. I mean one is elected for something I suppose and what is it if it isn't representation? And they wouldn't've been able even to start the farm if it hadn't been for the Government reclaiming schemes. Denton had a big hand in that you know. Still, I always support Severin when Denton runs him down, and I positively persuaded him that this year we must come down and support their ball. So here we are, and of course I just had to look you up. I do think you have a charming kitchen. And this meal was delicious, Lilly, but then you always were a marvellous cook, even at school you always came out top in domestic science, didn't you. D'you remember when Miss er, what was her name, Miss Mgoa, that's it, she asked me, how will you find and feed a husband, Joan, if you don't learn how to cook, and I said I shall have servants, it's strange, isn't it, how I knew even then, and she said coldly, I doubt that very much. She did, you know, I remember it as if it were today. Oh yes, I've had my share of prejudice, and of course it was much worse in those days as you know, the first reaction being a complex of relief and revenge, and then the fear of the malady, but I believe all these things like health and luck and success are a matter of attitude, they're a state of mind. They're not things outside us that come to us. We project them. Now you never did project that, Lilly, and I imagine your husband projects even less. I mean fancy getting a foothold of employment in that big house, just at the time of the big ball as she calls it, and then losing it.

– Oh, I see. I didn't know. What did they say? It isn't . . .? No. Not that they'd tell you of course, until it was too obvious. Psychoscopy? But that's marvellous. What did I tell you, I knew he didn't project, one only has to look at him. How clever of Denise. And how very kind. He's tremendously lucky, you know, very few Colourless get it. Oh, in theory of course, but in practice they're given up as hopeless, and there is a tremendous demand and a shortage of qualified psychoscopists, not to mention the machines and operators. It's highly skilled and takes years to train them. It breaks one's heart when the unemployment is so acute, but there it is, it's always the same old story. There are jobs for the specialists or rather for some specialists like astro-computors and isofertilisers and demographers and geoprognologists regardless of race or creed, but not for the unskilled or even the semi-skilled and the unskilled literally cannot even be trained for such jobs, their standard of brain-function is too low, well, it's a chemical fact, and the semi-skilled and specialists in other things are too set in their ways to adapt. Adaptation, that's the thing, you see. But what with one thing and another, and the priority on cosmoindustry, bathyagriculture, psychostellar communications and all that, and of course, medicine, I mean all other medical ways and means of dealing with the malady, psychoscopy's somehow become a luxury. So you see he's very lucky. I hope it will have done some good. I'm sorry to talk about you in the third person like that, my dear, it's very rude I know, but then, you don't say much, and besides, it's a sort of habit Lilly and I got into, a sort of game we used to play at school, talking about people as if they weren't there. Very unnerving. That was the idea, of course, to show we weren't put out by the others' treatment. Oh, they were very nice to us, but there was a sort of undercurrent, if you know what I mean, and it was much worse then than now, which was understandable really. I mean, what with history and the displacement and all that, and of course the malady, I mean things have improved considerably, thanks largely to their extraordinary energy and efficiency and generosity. Because they really are superbly generous, you know, very warm-hearted people, that's one thing one can say, they are warm-hearted, in fact I'll tell you one thing, now that I feel so much one of them, you remember how at school they used to call us cold fish, cold-blooded, cold-hearted? Well they still do, you know, that's entirely between you and me, and you of course, but there's a tradition, going way back, no doubt into tribal history, that this is the fundamental difference between the Melanian races and the Colourless. Even I feel it sometimes, this basic attitude I mean. That's why I have psychoscopy every month. It's absolutely invaluable to me. I mean, I have to meet so many people all the time, I'd be lost without it.

– Only one. Oh, well, it's better than nothing, you know, and as I say you were lucky to get it. And presumably they gave you your biogram. They didn't? But why on earth didn't you ask for it? Yes I'd love some coffee thank you Lilly. Oh, the biogram is indispensable. It's the extracted absolute of your unconscious patterns throughout your life, well, the average, if you like, telescoped in time into one line that shows your harmonious rhythm, your up and down tendencies, you know, when the sub is most or least at one with the super. Then all you have to do is to choose your safe periods for social intercourse. It's possible of course to work it out for yourself, very roughly I mean, and only for the time under survey, and it's even possible to work out other people's biograms, the people you constantly deal with I mean, and so choose their safe periods to coincide with yours. But the observation does take time and tends to be subjective and therefore unscientific. Still, it all comes to the same thing in the end, a technique for living. You should try it, it really does work. The psychoscope is better of course, it telescopes a whole life-time after all, and quite, quite objectively. As a matter of fact I'll let you into a secret. Denton and I know our psychoscopist so well by now, he has given us the biograms of most people we come into constant contact with, and I must say it has made the world of difference. I wonder whether the psychoscopist here is anyone I know, he might give me the Mgulus' biograms. After all we are staying at the house several days. Thanks awfully, that does smell good. Denton has things to discuss with Severin. What was your chap's name? Dr. Lukulwe. Hmm. No, I don't know him.

– Oh but they have. Well of course. All politicians are psychoscoped regularly. And their wives. Well, they have to be. I mean the situation would be too dangerous otherwise. Look what happened last time. I'd go so far as to say it's thanks to psychoscopy that everything's been running as smoothly as it has, quite under control in fact, as far as that is concerned. Because you know, it's quite incredible but people do forget, oh yes, new generations, despite history and everything. I suppose that's the trouble, really, we started with too many that had the highest possible informative content, or, which is the same thing, the lowest possible probability, then we seized every opportunity to test them with the utmost severity, eliminating and eliminating, well, there you are, those that survive enjoy the prestige that traditionally attaches to survivors.

– How do you mean, who said that? I do think your husband is peculiar, Lilly. It's not part of an epic poem if that's what you want to know. Though I suppose it might well be. Come to that, perhaps it is. It did sound sort of gnomic didn't it? Yes well you're quite right, Denton said it, in one of his speeches in the House, and I remembered it, as I'd helped him a bit, oh yes, I do now and again you know, though he has a secretary of course and a ghost, still he trusts my judgment absolutely, well, my inspiration, he calls it, my Colourless collective unconscious. These things are important, you know, in an interracial society. It's nice to feel we're still useful in more ways than one, and ancient wisdom isn't to be despised, even if it did make mistakes.

– Of course the past exists. Whatever next? We must face facts you know. Lilly, is he all right? Would you like me to use my influence and get him another psychoscopy? I'm sure I could, certainly when I get back to the capital, all I have to do is to ask my own psychoscopist. What did you say this one's name was? Lukulwe. I must jot that down. Lu-kul-we.

– What did he say? I can't hear him. An answer. What do you mean, an answer? Don't be so metaphysical. Do you mean an explanation of the origin? Or do you mean a cure? Surely you know that diagnosis only prognosticates aetiology. Well. I should have thought everyone understood that by now. It's a short way of saying that they don't claim to find either the ultimate cause or the ultimate cure, but they do know exactly how it functions, and can prescribe accordingly. I mean every neurosis has its mechanics, which are absolutely predictable, they can tell exactly what anyone will do next, it's marvellous. And it's true of everything, medicine, for instance, well, look at the malady, and of course social science, and demography, and politics, the lot. That's why the principle is so important. I can't stand not knowing how a thing functions. I mean one must know the rules. That's why psychoscopy's been so invaluable to me, it really does provide one with a technique for living, especially the biograms, and they really are amazingly accurate, I've found. I can't stand not knowing where I stand, if you know what I mean. That's why I never liked artists much. Or diplomats. But they're a thing of the past, which proves of course there must have been a past. Oh, they're still recognised, they have a vestigial function that is useful in its way. But you only have to meet them a few minutes, or read an old document or an old book, or see an old film at the film museum, and you get that sort of crushed feeling, at least I do, and I know Denton does, and all the friends I've ever talked to about it do, and their reactions are very similar, and they boil down to this, what view are we being urged to take? Well, it's impossible to tell, I mean, it's unnerving, isn't it. No. I like to know where I stand. I've chosen my life and I wouldn't have it any other way. My children are healthy and have a fairer chance of survival than if – than otherwise. I love being in the swim of things, I take an interest in world affairs and local government and everything that Denton does in fact. I travel with him a good deal. I see all sorts and conditions of people and their circumstances, their activities, their projects and their hopes, and I love having a hand in helping, however indirectly, the Government and world schemes for their furtherment and betterment. I love people you see.

– Lilly it was simply splendid seeing you. I'm so glad I was able to come, and thank you for a perfectly delicious lunch. I'm sorry to see you're on a diet, I hope it's nothing serious? Oh, good. I go on a temporary diet too sometimes, it's a wise thing to do now and again. Well we must keep in touch. And if there's anything I can do please don't hesitate. I mean none of this false shame business between us. We're old friends you know and I'll always stand by you. A friend in need. And of course that goes for you too. I hope you find work soon, it's very demoralising, I know. You are taking the pills, aren't you? Would you like me to have a word with Denise? Why not? It was your health, after all, and she sent you there. She's very odd at times, is Denise. Still, come to think of it, perhaps you're right. At least for the moment. She may have her reasons. I mean I haven't seen your biogram or anything. Never meddle is my motto. Well, be patient, renew your prescription, and don't you neglect the dole-pills, they're better than people think, you know, I've seen them being manufactured and the director of the biochemical industry's a personal friend of mine. I hope you'll feel better soon. Lilly, my dear, goodbye, it was lovely to see you. Oh of course I may catch a glimpse of you up at the house, but we won't be able to have a nice long chat like now. I did so enjoy it. Goodbye.

Behind the trellis the gesture is one of helplessness, palms flat and briefly facing upwards, paler, almost pink, and heavily lined, with unacknowledged pasts perhaps, and present prospects. The gesture would be the same if the helplessness were faked. The back of the man to whom the gesture is made slouches. His neck creases into his shoulders and he has thin pale hair.

– How do you expect us to help you if you don't take your dole-pills? Don't you understand that you are unemployable in your present state? Even if there were jobs available.

The man with the slouching shoulders and the thin pale hair shifts to the right and leans sideways on the counter, as if to make the conversation less private. Nevertheless it is not possible to measure or even roughly to estimate the degree of sincerity in the sympathetic eyes behind the trellis, for the metal grid splinters the bland Bahuko face, which also shines with curved oblongs and blobs of white light from the heat of the day, and the voice too seems encased by the barrier.

– What did you say?

– I think the pills are slowly poisoning us.

The whites of the eyes are brownish with a tinge of pink. The blacks of the eyes are brown, and for a moment stray away from the pasty face and the slouching shoulder of the man leaning on the counter, but the meeting is not compulsory and the dark lids immediately half shield them.

– Oh come now, man, you don't want to go believing that sort of thing. What was your occupation?

Through the slanted slits under the lowered brown lids the eyes just visible follow the dark hand as it moves across the pink card, holding a golden pen, and neatly braceleted at the wrist by the spotless white cuff-edge.

– I don't mean on purpose.

– What? Oh. Well, I should hope you do not. It is a very serious accusation. We have courts in which to make that kind of statement, backed with suitable evidence. Now then, are you going to take it, I haven't got all day.

– You can't force me to take the pills. They're poisoning the blood-stream. I've analysed them, I know, under pretext of building us up and protecting us from radioactive minerals you're over-filling us with potassium and carbohydrate complexes, you're multiplying our leucocyte count, you're slowly debilitating us so that –

– Now that's enough. If you have any complaints you can take them to the proper quarter. As far as I am concerned you must take this pill, and I am entitled to insist that you take it here in front of me. We're only trying to prevent unemployment apathy and frustration, you know, which are the seeds of crime. But it's for your own good mainly. Don't you see that you must keep yourself fit and cheerful just in case a job does turn up? I mean if it did you just wouldn't get it. Or keep it. You're in a bad way you know.

– I can't swallow it without water.

– Yes you can, it's very small and quite round. Good. Now don't miss out tomorrow or the next day. You'll see, you'll soon feel quite different. Next please.

The grid grows big and splits the taut Bahuko face, alert as a monkey's but shining with curved oblongs and blobs of white light from the heat of the day.

– Is it true what he said?

The vibration of the voice has not been sufficient to carry

the question across the metal barrier and the question evaporates, leaving no trace of error in the air, except perhaps a residue at the back of the mind, to be answered by Mrs. Mgulu who writes no little notes and does not nod and aches there by her absence. The dark hand moves across the card, holding a golden pen. In the right arch of the nose, with the left eye closed, the vertical metal bar divides the taut Bahuko face almost exactly in half. In the left arch of the nose, with the right eye closed, the vertical bar moves to the right of the face. The horizontal bars frame the face above and below.

– Hermm! Excuse me. But is it true what he said?

– What? Speak up man, I can't hear you.

– Is it true? What he said?

The shrug seems to fill the whole trellis, twining in and out of the squares.

– No. He always comes and makes a scene. It is his big moment. We play along with him. Nothing today I'm afraid. Here's your pill.

– No thank you.

– Hey, are you starting that game? You must take it. It's a new regulation. I've got my job to do and you've got – to take it. Go on.

The pill tastes bitter in the saliva under the tongue. The floor is mottled and full of feet in dirty canvas shoes. Men move aside. Above their heads the notice says Do Not Spit. The young palm tree stands cut in stillness against the blue intensity framed darkly by the door, and waits, as if to bend down and mop up the accumulating spit that sizzles suddenly on the burning pavement and then is lost in walking legs and under ambling feet.

– Wait.

The voice grabs the shoulder. The man has a pasty face and thin pale hair. His hand is now outstretched.

– You are my friend?

– No.

– But you spat!

– A man can spit can't he?

– What? I can't hear you.

– People don't usually.

– You mean you always say things like that?

– Like what? I mean, oh it doesn't matter. My voice. It's very small.

– Oh I don't think so, it's just the noise here. I saw you . . . spit. Don't worry I won't tell. Did you see the way he made me take it like that. Why, I might have been a child. Where you from?

– The – er – just outside town.

– No. I mean before. Ukay?

– Yes.

– Uessay. Can I walk along with you?

– If you want to. I mean, it's very crowded, isn't it.

– I must talk to you. About these pills.

– Are you a doctor then?

– There you go, you're as bad as they are. That's not the point. But can you honestly say that you haven't been feeling steadily worse since you started taking the pills? Stand here and cross your heart and say – hey, there's no need to push, Madam, the street's big enough for all of us. Mongrels. Sons of bitches, the lot. I'm sorry my friend. I am upset and irritable today. It's the long-term effect of these pills, there is not a doubt about that, and I ask you once again to stand here and cross your heart and swear you haven't been feeling steadily worse since you began taking them. Can you? No you cannot.

– Well, it's true I do feel worse.

– More and more debilitated! Of course. They send up the leucocyte count you see. Oh, the onset is insidious, well advanced before diagnosis. Very clever. But I'm not having it.

– But do you have proof? I mean how did you come to these conclusions?

– What? I can't hear a word you say.

– Well, you asked for it. The street's much too crowded. OW!

– Oh, I could probably prove it, if I had the facilities. The laboratories and that. But at the moment it's just an idea, a hunch if you like, you know, like the sulphonamides and derivatives, for years everyone thought they were the answer to everything, until the ultimate harm they were doing to the blood cells was finally realised and, well, that's medical history, like leeches or anything else. And this could be the same.

– Have you told anyone about your suspicions? Anyone responsible?

– No. And they wouldn't listen if I did, would they? It wouldn't be in their interest. Because it's true. So they treat you like a lunatic, and if you're not careful they treat you like a subversive element.

The crowds knock into their sudden immobility. The noise mills about. The traffic hoots by slowly through the swarming people who gesticulate and move lethargically among the shouts from the vegetable stalls. The children and the old men grub about under and between the stalls, under and between the innumerable legs, hoping to find a fallen fig or some dropped seeds of maize. It is market day.

– Now, listen. As I said to that chap, I don't mean they're doing it on purpose, nor are you going to get me to say it. I don't know who you are anyway, come to think of it you're not as friendly as you seemed when I saw you spit.

– Well, I didn't ask for your company.

– You're dead right. Don't you trust anyone. Here's my card. I'd ask you round to my place, I live down town, couple of blocks along but I share the room with four others. I like you. Let's get out of this and go sit on a bench. I'd like to know you.

– Well, er, I have to be getting back. My wife's ill.

– Oh. I'm sorry. I see you have all the more reason to be suspicious.

– Well, it's not quite like that. As a matter of fact I just won't believe that. If I did I couldn't go on living.

– What? I can't hear you. Come along round this corner, that's better, we can breathe. Now listen to me, I'll tell you something. I believe we're being slowly exterminated. And I'll tell you another thing. I'm not having it. I don't take my pills either. I spat out that one too.

– You're mad. Stark raving mad.

– Ha! That's what you'd like to believe, that's what everyone'd like to believe. Oh, I know you lot, you ex-Europeans, you'll play along with them as far as you can, you don't want to know your own kind, do you, the cold-hearted kind, they call us all, you know, but it's people like you that have made it so, it's your sickness we're suffering from. Your wife is ill is she, and you live in THE-er-just-outside-the-town, do you? I know where that is, I'll find you, if I want to, that is.

The fist lands straight on the snarling mouth with the advantage of surprise, paralyzing the mind behind the fist as much as it disfigures the face beyond it, so that the returning blow astonishes equally. The side-street rocks, then straightens. The grip is less strong than expected, the staggering is unsteady, the man is feeble, sick perhaps, tears burn the eyes, the grip lasts longer than expected, and aching burns the throat and head, the staggering is unsteady, the side-street rocks, the paving stone moves up. Innumerable trousers widen slightly at the bottom, grey or buff-coloured, like trees, or in creased grey denim like fig-tree bark, and some legs bare and thin and white. From this position in the gutter the paving stones look as large as tables.

– Are you all right, man?

– Of course, he's all right. They've neither of them got the strength to hurt a fly.

– Are you hurt somewhere?

– Two old men, they should be ashamed of themselves, fighting like that.

– Look at them, they're crying now, both of them.

– Licking their wounds. It's disgusting.
– Now then, what's happening here?
– Oh nothing, constable. An old Colourless man knocked down another. I don't think any harm's done.
– You all right, man? Come on up then. What's all this about? You fighting at your age? Who started it?
– I'm not old. I only look old. On account of the –
– Is it? Yes, it is. Constable, I know this one. I say, aren't you Lilly's husband? Yes you are. His wife works up at Mrs. Mgulu's, Western Approaches, you know, that's where I work and I've seen him around. I think he does odd jobs.
– Oh, well, if you'd like to see to him I won't take the matter further. Western Approaches, you said, Mrs. er? Mrs. Jim. Thank you. How about you, man, are you hurt?
– Don't you touch me!
– Now then, now then, I'm entitled to lay hands on you if you give me cause. I suppose you started this?
– I say, you are Lilly's husband aren't you? Oh, thank goodness, I'd hate to have perjured myself to the law of the land. Whatever got you into that mess? Well, never mind now. I think you've wriggled out nicely. I'm Mrs. Jim. I daresay Lilly's talked to you about me. Look, would you like me to help you home? I've only got a bit more marketing to do if you'd like to wait for me in that bar. No? I think you should at least have a drink. You look very shaky. And perhaps a bite to eat. Come along, now. I'll pay for it, don't worry. That's it. Just hold my arm. I work up at Mrs. Mgulu's you know, that's where I must have seen you.

At home there would be a remedy. A remedy would be read, it would occupy the air. Or a letter from the Labour Exchange, according to our records. At home the gruel would be brought.

The palm wine tastes a little acid, the bread a little sour. Sooner or later Mrs. Jim will go and finish her marketing. Mrs. Jim has gallstones. She's anaemic, you know. I shouldn't be surprised if it's pernicious. But Mrs. Jim is the picture of health, pale pink and fleshy and bedworthy in a purely physical way. She certainly lives in the present. She has adapted to her environment, has Mrs. Jim.

– Well, you don't have much to say for yourself, do you? I can't imagine your ever saying enough even to get into a fight. But maybe it's shock. Perhaps you'd rather have had mint tea? No, you just sip that quietly while I finish my marketing then I'll see you home. You can help me carry some of the bags as a matter of fact. I shan't be long.

Inside the avenue of the mind, that functions in depth, Mrs. Mgulu sits back in the cushions of the vehicle as it glides smoothly out of the town. The shining hair is coiled up high, dressed in gold chains and off the face, cave-blue through the blue glass and the wide lips mauve.

– That looks like Lilly's husband just ahead. Olaf, will you slow down so that I can see? I hear he had a little trouble in town with a Colourless ruffian. Perhaps he could do with a lift. Yes it is him, will you stop. Hello, there. Can I give you a lift? How are you? You don't look too good. Jump in.

The concrete huts move slowly by, grey in the shimmering heat. No. The sun beats down into the nervous system that has no foliage to protect the nerve-ends. The road burns through the thin soles of the canvas shoes. Mrs. Mgulu walks lightly alongside, wearing something diaphanous, smelling of aloes and hair fixative. The vehicle moves slowly ahead waiting upon her fatigue. But she walks lightly alongside, although the tall acacia trees give insufficient shade. The number of the vehicle is eight four . . . the number of the vehicle is insignificant.

– Oh but I love walking. Especially with someone. I never really see anything by car. I never really see anything except with you. Look at the concrete huts moving slowly by, grey in the shimmering heat. The road burns through the thin soles of your canvas shoes, I expect, as it burns through my gold sandals.

– The tall acacia trees give insufficient shade.

– The number of my vehicle is 8473216.

– It wasn't the way you think, you see, he told the employment clerk the pills were bad for us, and the clerk made him take it there in front of him and me too so I spat mine out and he saw me and well it turned out that he meant genocide, and I said he was mad and he said, oh he said horrible things, he called me cold-hearted. You know I'm not, don't you?

– Now you really mustn't go believing everything you hear from the man in the street.

– That's what Mr. Swaminathan says.

– Ah, my old friend Mr. Swaminathan. Is he still swaying away at the back there?

– He's there all right. But he refuses to acknowledge my existence. It's very hard. He just watches. He watches me desire you, he occupies me with you like a sneak and a small-time spy. I would prefer him out of the way, I would prefer to give myself entirely over to desiring you, but he is one of the warm-hearted and I cannot transfer any energy to him to move him out.

– That isn't true. You know that isn't true, don't you?

– No. It isn't true. You are quite right. He is no longer there. He hasn't been there for a long time.

– Because I am there. Wholly and fully, my presence burns up your psychic energy as the road burns through the thin soles of your shoes. I shall always be with you, talking to you and sharing your observation of phenomena, until you die, because that is the way you want it, and I am your dark reality.

– I don't want it. I never wanted it, I was happy watching flies and eating gruel and talking to myself and making mental love to my wife. Why did you have to take an interest? I didn't ask for your interest. I didn't ask to be confronted with your accomplishments and your possessions. Why did you have to flaunt your privileges at me? All privilege brings its dissatisfactions and the privilege of health is no exception. I didn't ask to be psychoscoped. It's made me ill. I wasn't ill before. Why did you have to enter and occupy me in this way? I don't even like you.

– Because you are my servant and you do as I tell you.

The Settlement is on the right. The hot road continues emptily on then vanishes into the olive groves. In the distance on the hill the upper storey, dazzling white, the flat roof of Western Approaches emerges from greenery that looks grey in the shimmering heat. The fig-tree's foliage is deeply green, the leaves are large and still, five-lobed, clear-cut and stiff against the tense blue sky. The rough grey bark is wrinkled in the bend of the trunk like an old man's neck, and along the trunk like a thigh of creased grey denim irregularly shot with darker thread. The rough grey bark is shot with black lines made up of discontinuous black dots, but interrupted by transverse cracks where the trunk curves, or by crinkly craters where branches have been cut away. The rough grey bark is lined and wrinkled like the inside of the brain. The dotted lines make up a system of parallel highways, along which march unending convoys of ants, each one behind the other like jungle porters, patient and purposeful as neural impulses on their way to the synapse in the neural ganglia, where with the action of alkaloid substances such as muscarine for the parasympathetic system and adrenaline for the sympathetic, annulled respectively by atropine and ergotoxine, they will produce their influence on the effector cells. On the right of the nose, with the left eye closed, the thickest grey branch sweeps horizontally below the starting line of the yellow grass patch where Mrs. Ned's shack begins. The cunonia at the corner sticks out its wine-red spike from a mass of crimson leaves brilliant in the sun. On the left of the nose, with the right eye closed, it underlines Mrs. Ned's shack, as if Mrs. Ned's shack were built on it as on a boat with the sea of foliage below, where the long grey twigs it bears curve downwards and then up, in large U-letters just discernible through the leaves.

– Here is the Colourless Settlement. This, Mrs. Mgulu, is where I live. Look at the fig-tree, how it leans. No, it isn't my fig-tree, it belongs to the State I suppose, but I love it nevertheless. That is my bungalow, there, well not mine exactly either, yes, we're comfortable thank you, though I must admit the atmosphere was friendlier in the bidonville, where we lived before. That's Mrs. Ned's shack, next door, she's the one I was mentally unfaithful to Lilly with, as you see she's very close. There is also Mrs. Jim who despite her gallstones is pale pink and fleshy and bedworthy in a purely physical way, she lives in the present, you see, and has adapted to her environment. But she lives further away. I don't know where Mrs. Jim lives.

Leaning against the horizontal branch it is possible to observe the shacks and yet remain hidden by the foliage of the fig-tree, the trousers of faded denim blending with the trunk no doubt, from far away. Look at the smooth grey bark, Mrs. Mgulu my love, how the lines run parallel down the length of the branches, but discontinuous, and interrupted by transverse cracks where the trunk curves. On the smaller branches the dotted lines are not immediately visible to the carelessly naked eye, but a microscope would certainly reveal a system of parallel highways along the branches in discontinuous black blobs like vehicles immobilised. How large do you suppose they seem to the ants, or to the neural impulses?

That is how the malady begins. The onset is insidious, well advanced before diagnosis. The fingers tap the smooth grey bark which remains firm on palpation and retains its characteristic notch. The imagination increases in size progressively and by no means painlessly until it fills most of the abdomen. Enlargement of the lymphatic glands may occur in the later stages of the disease, with a general deterioration to a fatal termination. The absolute knowledge that Mrs. Mgulu writes no notes and walks along no highway and does not nod and aches there by her absence, the absolute knowledge enters the body through the marrow bone, and up into the medullary centres, down the glosso-pharyngeal nerve no doubt or the pneumogastric, at any rate forward and down into the throat which tightens as the knowledge spreads into the chest and hurts. Sooner or later it will reach the spleen, which will increase in size until it fills the world. From ground-level on the dried-up yellow lawn the arch formed by the leaning trunk and the down-sweeping branch frames a whole landscape of descending olive groves beyond the road, which itself disappears behind the bank. The grey framework of the trunk and branch is further framed by the mass of deep green foliage. Inside the frame is Lilly's white face aureoled in wispy hair. A telescope might perhaps reveal, from this position on the dried-up lawn, that the squint is less wide, less blue, hardly visible at all at this distance and in the luminosity of the midday sun.

– Careful, you'll get sunstroke there. What have you been up to? Mrs. Jim came back from town and said you'd been in a fight. I got off early. You look awful. Why don't you go inside, it's cooler. Or at least lie in the shade of the fig-tree. Listen, would you like your gruel brought out here for a change?

Daily from 8 a.m. outside the Labour Exchange no dark blue face the size of a bungalow lies upside down, but a group of smooth, scaleless green monsters with green faces and the whites of black eyes bulging from strips of black skin like masks between the green below the eyes and the green skull caps above. The group surrounds another green monster recumbent with black snout. SO GRIPPING, SO HUMANE. The chief surgeon grips the knife. He is giving a lecture on recumbent humanity. Splenectomy is contra-indicated. The prognosis is poor. The disease is specially characterised by the peculiar greenish infiltrating subperiosteal masses in the bones of the skull, particularly in the orbits and sinuses. When in the marrow they lead to bone erosion. The green colour of the tumour masses fades rapidly in the air and light, being a protoporphyrin derivative. Symptoms, marked exophthalmos, diplopia, caecity, surdity, pyrexia, purpura. The doctors wear the masks of the humans, green is the colour of the biosphere. COME OVER INTO PATAGONIA AND HELP US.

The Governor's vain Asswati face is cut diagonally by a shaft of light reflected in the glass, from left to right across the nose to the right ear, or, in his position, from right to left across his nose to his left ear. Beneath the shaft of light, the Governor juts his stalwart lips and stares fiercely out regardless from the far wall beyond the heads of the employment clerks at their grilled partitions. With his unbandaged ear the Governor listens to the shuffle of feet and the murmur of male voices and the calling out of names and the squeaking of hinges on metal cupboard doors and the banging of same, not to mention files and metal drawers, and he gazes benignly down. His dark eyes meet all eyes that meet his, but the meeting is not compulsory. The heads of the employment clerks are mere black silhouettes behind the small print of the grid partitions. The neighbour's magnifying-glass moves away from the micronewscard which drops between the thighs on to the mottled floor.

– If no news is good news then news must be bad news.

The syllogism has a soft centre, firm nevertheless on palpation, retaining its characteristic notch.

The vibration of the voice has not been sufficient to carry the witticism into the neighbour's left ear, and the syllogism evaporates, leaving no trace of error either in the air or in the mind, except perhaps a residue at the back of the brain, greenish in colour, to be dealt with by Dr. Fu Teng in his own good time, slow time. In the corner of the eye, the neighbour is Chinese, a refugee from Sino-America perhaps, or a renegade from Chinese Europe. The magnifying-glass recedes and then advances into his left trouser pocket, making a circular bulge on the thigh.

Underneath the eyelids the men continue to mill about the Labour Exchange but the whole scene goes grey. Nevertheless it bears a close resemblance to the real thing. The ceiling is pink and veined in white, and a long way away. The wall ahead is pink, above and all around a glossy and pale orange door. To the immediate right, close to the body, is a wall of pink veined marble, not very high, half a metre perhaps or a little more, edged by a two centimetre mud-coloured band where the marble has been removed. To the left of the body is another wall of pink veined marble, half a metre high or a little more, also edged with a mud-coloured band where the marble has been removed. Beyond this low wall, some distance away is a high pink marble wall joining the pink marble ceiling. The wall beyond the low wall to the right is mud-coloured, with some of the pink stripped off, the frontier between the pink and the mud being straight and vertical half-way up the wall, then zig-zagging to the ceiling. Good heavens, you look as if you were lying in a coffin. You'd better give me your hand and try to sit up. Look, I'll sit down here with my feet in the bath and you lie alongside it with your head on my lap. Just relax. Close your eyes. Under the red networks of your eyelids in the sunlight the dark curves of my lips and nose seen from below my breasts that are ensilked in orange fill up your eyespace shimmering with yellow and black and pale and hectic red. Nevertheless it bears a close resemblance to the real thing, as a mere lifting of the eyelids could prove. The left nostril wears an alexandrite set in gold. In daylight the stone is blue. At dusk the stone is green. In the electric light the stone is mauve. At the moment it is possible to take one's choice, daylight, for example, in the refracted orange of the summer sunset as it slants into the pink marble bathroom on the top floor of the big house. The bathroom, however, faces South. Beyond the flowering shrubs and trees the mimosas are over.

In the corner of the right eye, the neighbour is gone. At dusk the alexandrite is green. In daylight it is bluey-green, at night a pinky-mauve. At the moment it is possible to take one's choice, cyclamen for example, on the dark velvet skin. In the corner of the right eye the neighbour is pale and Scandinavian blond. His head leans against the wall and he stares vacantly ahead of him, into the eyes of the Governor perhaps, compulsively. There is thus no obligation to disturb the air with errors and platitudes. The Governor listens to the shuffle of feet and the murmur of male voices and the squeak of metal hinges and the banging of metal doors, not to mention the multiplied buzzing of flies. The shaft of light has slipped down the dark face, bandaging the mouth and leaving the nose quite flattened. The nose is a broad-based triangle with the two nostrils wide apart, rounding the lower angles. Sooner or later the identity will be called out and the occupation demanded.

– I was a degree-collector.

– A what – collector? Speak up. You mean garbage?

– Bachelor of Haematology, Doctor of Apologetics, Bachelor of Oscillography, Doctor of Metallurgy –

– And Master of None?

– Master of Arts, Fellow of the Society of Royal Urologists, Fellow of –

– We have you down here as a schoolmaster. Iranian. We have you down here as a welder.

– Oh well it all comes to the same thing in the end.

– Don't be impertinent. We haven't built you up yet. There will be a period of initiation. The important thing is in the holding and the aiming of the instrument.

Through the round goggles the sparks fly out. The situation is highly inflammatory and demands constant reappraisal.

In white helmet and round goggles Mr. Marburg the butler emerges from behind a metal screen, Mrs. Mgulu has sent for you, he says in an ominous tone, will you kindly step this way. What is it? What's happened? It is not for me to say, I am her servant and I do not exceed my frame of reference. She has sent Olaf with the vehicle for you. The number of the vehicle is insignificant. The vehicle moves swiftly and smoothly across the blue landscape. The sun flickers through the tall quick acacia trees, increasing the neural electricity to help the oscillograph.

Mrs. Mgulu steps out from behind the bedroom screen, wearing a mauve silk dress and golden shoes. Her arms are made of iodine crystals. Her stiff black hair is coiled up high and smells of fixative. The alexandrite set in gold looks sea-green in the left nostril.

– It's your wife. It's Lilly, she's very ill. Dr. Lukulwe is doing all he can. I'm afraid it's the acute, fulminating type.

Behind the screen the black fingers tap the flaccid white flank. The eyes and gums are bleeding. The gums look purple and the face pale green. All round the bed the microscopes point down like conventional weapons, and the glaring lights are hot.

– Lilly, Lilly, it's me.

Lilly is deaf and blind.

– I'm so very sorry.

But Dr. Lukulwe is only a psychoscopist, a charlatan, he will make her worse, he will make her suffer with his machine, please get a real doctor.

– Real? What is real? His eyelids are the right colour.

– Please let her die in peace without self-knowledge that is false, built up by instruments and the minds behind the instruments.

– Oh but it bears a close resemblance to the real thing.

The gesture is one of careful examination. The doctor's eyes are those of an inspired pedant. The doctor's black eyes gleam with triumph inside the pinky whites, the triumph perhaps of a fanatic inventor astonished to find that his invention works.

Up on the monitor the jellyfish are writhing inside one another, disintegrating and reaggregating into different patterns in depth as well as width.

The gesture is one of helplessness, palms flat and facing upwards briefly, paler, almost pink, and heavily lined with past mistakes and present prospects.

– It is important to fill the body's reservoirs with minerals like potassium and carbohydrate complexes found in sea-weed, so that radio-active minerals of a similar type are then absorbed and passed straight out.

– But doctor, it is quite evidently too late to do that.

– I said it would have been advisable.

– What exactly is the cause, doctor?

– There you go again with your sick talk. Don't you understand that in paleontology the beginning of a new organism cannot be observed, because at the beginning it is not recognisable as a new organism and by the time it has become one the beginning is lost. I have already told you, diagnosis merely prognosticates aetiology.

– You mean, you remember me?

– There are records. You, however, seem to have forgotten.

– But Lilly, but my wife, my wife is not a paleontological specimen.

– The rule is universal in all fields. It is a scientific law.

– An article of faith.

– Until disproved. In the meantime, we are content to know how the thing functions.

– What thing?

– Anything. Society. Life. The universe. God. The unconscious. A land-reclaimer. I must go now.

– But doctor, the patient.

– Oh yes. Blood transfusions would help a little. Ease her at least. May I see your group card? Hmmm. Pity. Won't do at all. I'll have the right Colourless blood sent from the bank at once. You nearly forgot her yourself, didn't you?

– Doctor, please, why her? She's led a selfless, blameless life.

– I am not a theologian. Goodbye.

– Camille, show Dr. Lukulwe out will you. You stay here. Goodbye, doctor. Listen my dear, I'm the same group as Lilly. I know it's not allowed, but really it's too absurd, isn't it, I mean I can understand it the other way round but what harm can good healthy Melanian blood do to Colourless? Even my husband, Dr. Mgulu, who stands on a narrow Nationalist platform would applaud from a human point of view. Now I'm going to lie down here, you must help me with the needle and straps.

It is more difficult to find the vein in the arm that is made of iodine crystals than in the sick white arm, where the blue vein stands out like a rampart, calling out the grey-blueness of the flesh around it.

The rectangle of light ripples on the wooden table. The wrinkled wood inside the rectangle seems to be flowing into the wrinkled wood outside it, which looks darker. If the source of light were not known to be the oblique ray of sun filtering through the slightly swaying beads over the doorway, the wrinkled wood might be thought alive, as alive, at any rate, as the network of minute lines on the back of the wrist. But the minute lines on the back of the wrist do not flow as the wrinkled wood seems to flow. A microscope might perhaps reveal which is the more alive of the two.

– the essential amino-acid tryptophan combined with potassium iodide and the sodium salt of glutanic acid plus a minimal addition of di-iodo-tyrosine. Take two once a day or according to advice from physician. Oh dear where's the fly-swatter?

– Lilly, who am I , what was I?

– D'you want to go to bed? There isn't much time. I have to be back at the house at half past two.

The squint seems not so wide, so blue, in the luminosity

thrown by the oblong of flowing light on the red stone floor. The static eye fixes the empty bowl of gruel, the mobile eye is static too, reproachful perhaps or full of wonder or puzzlement or anticipation, without which it would be indistinguishable from the static eye. Some of the gruel's globules remain attached to the rounded white sides of the bowl which looks like the inside of the moon. The stone floor is a red river.

– I must just rinse the bowls and spoons and scrub the pan.

– Lilly, I love you. I've always loved you, from the beginning I've loved you.

– What is the beginning?

– The beginning is now. Leave the dishes. I'll do them afterwards.

– After the beginning which is now. And then.

– When?

– When we first met. Do you remember how it was? Come my love and I will tell you, titillate you, arouse you from your deathly deficiency, it was a corridor like this one only longer, not quite so cubic and with numbered doors.

– Oh yes, I like that one. But the doors were labelled.

– Labelled then. A long way underground, oh very deep, very significant. I came out of the operations room, you remember, with a sheaf of notes in my hand, and bumped straight into you, it was some collision. I was in uniform too, and our tin buttons clicketied together as we kissed, I didn't know you from Adam and your helmet fell off, clattering to the concrete floor.

– And it rolled down the corridor. Go on.

– Lie down with me and hold my hand. And I will tell you. Lie down with me I said, what on the concrete floor, you said, and I said life is short, don't argue, give me a child. And people came and went, their legs stepped over us, and the Wing Commander came out of the operations room on the way to the lavatory and said for heaven's sake put your helmet on man it's regulations. I had a crush on him you know, but he wouldn't look at me, his eyes wouldn't meet mine, they'd veer away, in embarrassment perhaps, at the dissymmetry.

– I was a messenger, wasn't I, from the observation room.

– Only for the duration. You told me you'd been a student. Though I must admit you looked older than that, you looked older than your years even then.

– Yes, well I was. I'd been studying for some time. There were always funds somewhere one could apply to. The State, Big Business, Big Philanthropy.

– That's not how you put it last time.

– Isn't it? How was it then?

– Don't you remember, it was on account of the termites, it was prettier.

– Tell me.

– That the library in the desert shack where you spent all those years alone had seven hundred books –

– Seven hundred and thirty-two.

– And thirty-two.

– One on every subject. The Government had stocked the library for the survival of knowledge. I was its librarian.

– But the termites were eating their way through the books, every book had holes like craters right through all the pages, some had small holes, some big holes –

– And sometimes the hole was in the top half of the page –

– And sometimes in the bottom half.

– But holes nevertheless. It made reading very difficult.

– Oh but you knew so much.

– There were gaps.

– And you said, I had to laugh, you said, I love the asymmetry of your eyes. You had so many theories. You even had a theory about my eyes. But I forget what it was. Something about a satellite out of orbit, or an excited atom. I never did meet your parents. Or you mine.

– Or me mine. Or you yours.

– They were above, naturally. Do you remember the music, it was just one note, oscillating though, from the seismograph or something in the observation room, and it was broadcast all over the corridors and even the lavatories and dormitories. We learnt to sleep with it. And with each other, well, everyone did that. Goodness me, the babies born down there, they were numberless. Do you remember ours, how frail, how thin, how pitiable?

– You're talking about yourself.

– But it was only for the duration. Tickle me a little too.

– Do you remember the night-classes, everyone was so bored, we all started self-improvement on one another, and we sat on a bench together and learnt Perpetual Motion. Very tiring, after working all day. I taught semanthropy on Tuesdays.

– And the dances, do you remember the dances? The one when we got engaged, I remember it as if it were yesterday, you held me at arm's length and we writhed away at each other and I just knew.

Through the gold lorgnette of the Governor's wife, the dancers quiver on the ballroom floor which is as round as the eye of a microscope. The dancers lean backwards, bouncing their shimmied bellies, then forwards, bouncing their flounced behinds in dignified postures and steady rhythms. Mrs. Mgulu slowly stirs the air in front of her with her bare black arms, the hands flat out at right angles. Mrs. Mgulu leans her plunging neckline forward in dignified posture and steady rhythm and says what books have you been reading? You must have got these items from somewhere, but they're all wrong you know, you mustn't go believing everything Dr. Lukulwe says, he's only a doctor in psychoscopy. Ultra-specialisation is death to the species, look at orthogenesis. Look at us. Look at the Tertiary era or the Palaeozoic. But I've always loved you, from the beginning I've loved you.

– The beginning cannot be observed.

– The beginning is now.

– What's the matter dear? Have you gone off?

– I'm sorry. I'm very sorry. I've no duration. Lilly, you must forgive me. It's all so long ago. I'm tired. So very tired.

Beyond the closed wrought-iron gates the feathery green branches droop like ferns over the white wall that separates the property from the road. Beyond the tall wrought-iron gates and beyond the feathery green mimosas on either side the plane-trees line the drive, casting a welcome shade. One half of the tall wrought-iron gates might be unlocked, might perhaps be pushed open with an effort of the will. Sometimes it is sufficient.

At the beginning it was sufficient. It was at times and within certain limits sufficient to imagine a movement for the movement to occur, although it was easier in the negative. A scene of pastoral non-habitation, perhaps, or the prevention of a sequence. But sometimes the gruel was brought. And whereas no amount of positive evidence conclusively confirmed a hypothesis, one piece of negative evidence conclusively falsified it. Since the beginning there has been a displacement from cause to effect. The episodes imagined now go down into the spleen which increases in size by no means painlessly until it fills most of the abdomen. The leucocyte count is 900,000 to the square millimetre and quite beyond the will's control.

Beyond the closed wrought-iron gates that open only by remote control the plane-trees line the drive in a green tunnel that recedes into more greenery with a gleam of sunlight here and there, and blobs of colour from the bougainvillaea, the poinsettia and perhaps the laurels still. The house is quite invisible.

The white wall gently rounds as the road curves, and continues to curve, but almost imperceptibly. It is impossible ever to see whether things are any different round the corner.

In the white wall, the glossy black door opens suddenly. Sprtch, grrrr, no, not that. The black door opens and good afternoon, I'm the new gardener.

In the white wall the glossy black door opens. The woman stands framed by the whiteness, dressed in a black cotton overall. The background is of rose-red flowers and cypress hedge receding. Pale face, pale eyes that strike no note, pale hair. The waxiness is due to a deficiency in the liver. The waxiness creates a silence.

– Good afternoon. Could I possibly see the head gardener?

– Who wants him?

– I came once before, you may remember, Mrs. Mgulu sent me, well, there was a misunderstanding. I've been unwell. But I'm all right now. I'm sorry to trouble you.

The two white pillars beneath the black rectangle are made of sodium chloride. Behind them the path is crazy pavement.

– Oh. Well, I suppose it's all right. Will you wait there, I'll see if I can find him. I'll have to shut the door.

Or something like that, the legs being brown perhaps and the flowers a mass of pink. Mrs. Mgulu says they remind her of damp December funerals in the North, the hands being black, the flowers a deathly white. To live the gesture in immobility is to evoke and therefore to have observed the gesture. But imagination is not an imaged projection of observed phenomena. Sometimes it is sufficient to imagine an episode for the episode to occur, and that is the terrifying thing, though not necessarily in that precise form. The first failure is the beginning of the first lesson. Learning presupposes great holes in knowledge.

In the white wall the glossy black door opens suddenly. The woman stands framed by the whiteness, pert and petite and pretty in a white linen dress the neckline of which embraces the glowing basalt of her throat as a crescent moon the night sky. It is more difficult as a negative. The background is of pale flowers and cypress hedge receding. The brownish green of the cypress hedge looks darker in the light of the white linen dress, merging with the skin's rich earthy brown. The negative creates a silence.

– Good afternoon, ma'am. Would it be possible to see the head gardener?

– What's that?

– I was wondering if it would be possible to see the head gardener. I'm sorry to disturb you.

– Who wants him?

– I came once before, it was another lady. Mrs. Mgulu had sent me, but there was a misunderstanding.

The two pillars beneath the white vessel are made of graphite. Behind them the path is crazy pavement.

– Oh. Well, I suppose it's all right. He's about somewhere. I'll go and see if I can find him. Wait there please. I'll have to shut the door.

The gestures are framed by the white wall. Above the gestures are two mauve flowers. The red network is very fine.

– Oh yes. You know Mrs. Mgulu well? I'm all for everyone lending a helping hand. Especially us, I mean we must stick together, mustn't we, I always say to Milly, that's my wife, or is it Dolly, I always say to Polly, forty-nine years we've been married and we've seen plenty, I can assure you, I always say to Polly, in these difficult times we must all pull together and sink our ex-differences as Westerners, don't you agree.

– I'm afraid I never studied non-Euclidean geometry. I specialised early, you see, in my country –

– In your country men were lazy and smug. That's why they lost the battle for survival. It's an article of faith. Conceited, lazy, unreliable. These little orange-trees, for instance, they've been wrongly planted, in round hollows, instead of on mounds of earth. The fellow who did that was one of you lot. Hosed them for minutes at a time, that's what he did, and let them soak in a great pool of water, why it's murder, especially in the dry season, they can't take the contrast. You have to be gentle with them you know. The water should be allowed to drain down slowly.

The green snake slithers along the left flower-bed right back to the yellow door in the white wall, though in the other direction it also reaches as far as the wall beyond the olive grove, where the brass tap is. There are six other hoses and taps.

– Oh of course I realise that it takes four or five hours, because every plant must be watered individually. I do know that, it's one thing we can't do with machines, though naturally you probably use the automatics for vegetables. Some plants like the spray, I know, and some prefer a plain jet on the root or around the root. These castor-oil plants for example, they need a very gentle jet which mustn't touch them at all or the stem would break. So I wouldn't use the spray at all but I'd put my finger over the nozzle-holder whenever I need a spray.

– You certainly seem to know a lot. What did you say your occupation was?

– I was a landscape gardener.

In the white wall the glossy black door opens. The pretty Bahuko woman stands framed by the whiteness, the edge of the white linen dress resting crescently upon her skin. The negative creates a silence.

– You can come in. Follow me.

The path leads straight up to the small white cottage. On either side of the path the cypress hedge stands in a narrow flower-bed full of pink carnations fragrant on the hot air. The hedge opens its brownish green arms to the woman in white linen who walks into them poised and indifferent as they recede. She is an arum lily on a dark stem moving. The path is made of benzene rings.

– Wait here. My husband is just coming.

The left foot treads the length of a cemented line. Between the tiles, the right foot carefully selects another line of cement parallel wtih the edge of the path. The instep of the left foot crosses the carbon atom at the top of the elongated hexagonal, pointing towards the nitrogen hydrogen two. The amount of free energy that becomes available for the performance of useful work does not correspond to the total heat change, but is equivalent to the new face that is handsome, smooth, assured, glowing with earthen vitality and slashed with curved oblongs of sunlight, well?

– I, I came, I was wondering – excuse me, but are you the head gardener?

– I am.

– Oh. I see. I came earlier. The pink man, your predecessor I mean, Mrs. Mgulu had sent me –

– You know Mrs. Mgulu then?

– Yes. Yes I do. I was working up at the house, but I fell ill and she sent me for treatment to the hospital. I'm all right now. But they want me to have an outdoor employment and she sent me to you.

– How do I know you're telling the truth? Mrs. Mgulu said nothing to me. Haven't you got a note?

– No. I – er, I had one but I lost it. Mr. Swami –

– What? Speak up. Besides, if Mrs. Mgulu sent you why did you expect to see my predecessor? He died. Some time ago.

– Oh. Well I'm sorry, I'm confused. I had seen him you see.

– You mean you had seen him about or you had been sent for an interview?

– For an interview.

– And?

– Well. It's difficult to explain. There was a misunderstanding.

– Hmmm. Yes, well you're obviously telling the truth there more or less, or you'd have a better story. The only thing is, I've got all the gardening hands I need. If anything we're over-employing here.

– But what about the watering? Have you got anyone for the watering?

– The watering? It's being done all the time. As you should know if you've been here before. Look.

Round and round, catching the sunlight once in every revolution, the spray unfurls its minute particles at vast distances over the encampment of wigwammed plants to the right of the cypress hedge. Round and round. Catching the sunlight, the spray unfurls its radiating hydrogen and oxygen over the field of potato plants next to the field of tomato plants. And silently through the deep canals beneath the cobcorn skyscrapers to the left of the cypress hedge, the water flows from an unseen reservoir, pumped like blood by an unseen irrigation reactor, darkening the earth with life.

– But what about the flowers? They're not like vegetables, each plant needs watering individually, some like the spray, and some prefer a plain jet on the root, or even around the root. The castor-oil plants, for example, where are they? When small they need a very gentle jet that mustn't touch the stem at all or it would break. Where are the castor-oil plants?

– We don't have any. They're cultivated gross up at the farm, and as for flowers, you should know very well that Mrs. Mgulu has given over all the grounds to food-growing, except for the area immediately around the house. And that is well taken care of as regards watering. The lawns are sprayed automatically anyway. You should know that if you've been here before.

– Yes. I suppose so. One gets confused. May I ask you, do you know, I mean how, what, what did he die of?

– Who?

– The head gardener. Before you I mean.

– How should I know? If he was before me.

– Did he, do you suppose, could he have just fallen dead, in a flower-bed, the red one for instance?

– Which red one?

– On the front lawn, to the left of the drive as you go up towards the house.

– There isn't a red flower-bed on the front lawn, left or right.

– Oh. Perhaps I made a mistake. It's only natural. It's the human element.

– The human element covers the whole earth and interpenetrates itself, the earth being round. It is a painful process. Those who cannot grow with it must die.

– So you think . . . Oh. But could he have fallen into it, when it was there? The red flower-bed I mean?

– If that's the way you want it then he could have. I wasn't there and nor, as far as I'm concerned, was the flower-bed. One doesn't talk of these things. Now I'm afraid I'm very busy, so if you don't mind –

– Please. Please. Give me some work. Part-time, low-grade, unskilled, I'll do anything, absolutely anything, oh please, I beg of you, have pity.

The benzene-ring is enormous, the energy-rich bonds stretch interminably to the right. From this position the trousers are buff-coloured, widening slightly at the bottom like trees. The shoes match and shine, too glowing to be gripped.

Layers and layers of possible reactions fill the silence like a mountain cut in half, primitive fear, a fury of revenge, sublimated gratification, embarrassment, indifference. Mrs. Mgulu steps out from behind the poinsettias wearing something or other and says tell him to get up, Ingram, nobody should grovel, in an age of international and interracial enlightenment such as ours revelation is open to all regardless of sex, years, race or creed. The age however stretches interminably. The physical stuff of the universe wraps up the earth with knowledge and communication, and the earth shrinks, and those who do not partake of the great secret growth are eliminated and shrivel away under the physical stuff that is knowledge and communication and wraps the earth with love, for nothing less than symbiosis will do.

– Get up, man, get up! Nobody should grovel, that is an article of faith. But you are sick, it is difficult for us to employ the sick, you must understand our position.

– I am sick because I have no work.

– You have no work because you are under-nourished.

– I am under-nourished because I have no work.

– Oh I didn't mean just bread. There's consciousness too, man cannot live by bread alone. He needs his daily ration of the whole world, blessed are the conscious for they shall inherit the earth.

– Is that an article of faith too?

– If you have faith yes, if not not. However, bread is important. I'll see what I can do.

The gesture is one of benediction, or helplessness perhaps, the black hands spread over the molecular geometry of the pink-tiled pavement, then up a little, palms paler, almost pink, lined with achievements, longings and evolutions, then gesturing, after all, a pause, creating from the atoms of the air an expectation.

The process is known as osmosis. Sooner or later Mrs. Mgulu will emerge from behind the poinsettias and say give him some work, Ingram, the period of initiation has gone on long enough. He has come through, if not exactly in flying colours, being after all Colourless, not too badly, all things and radiation considered. There is a limit to initiation even in the worst of circumstances. Give him a little work, the hose, since he holds on to that so passionately, and the grass fires.

The dialogue runs smoothly along the kindness in the soft black eyes, orchestrated by a depth of racial memory. Vegetables are mentioned, and occasionally flowers. But mostly maize and rice. The dialogue falters as the smooth face turns its curved oblongs of reflected sunlight off towards the olive grove and a monologue moves away on the other side of the dark neck and the crinkly black ball. The voice is deep and resonant, yet the vibrations are insufficient to carry the words in the opposite direction through the back of the crinkly head, and the words get lost, if any, requiring a reply perhaps, a contradiction, to carry them forward along a certain groove of disputation to some unnamed astonishing conclusion, or merely a murmuring acquiescence, stunned adoration, even further research. I require notice of that question.

– This is where we burn all the weeds and other waste matter. The gardeners make little piles wherever they happen to be working and a boy collects them and brings them here. Usually he does the burning but you will be doing it from now on. As you see there are several charred areas, so don't use the same one twice running. Mrs. Mgulu intends to build a nuclear waste disposal unit here, but in the meantime we have to burn things the old-fashioned way. But of course it's dangerous, in this heat, the grass is so dry, a mere spark can flare up and run all the way to the trees in no time. That's how most of these forest fires begin. So you have to keep hosing the grass all around the funeral pyre, is that clear? Keep it damp, and even hose the fire itself when it flares up too high, it has to smoulder rather than burn. Let me see you do it. Take that pile, it's the biggest. No, use the rake first, it must be a neat pile. You must tell the boy not to throw the stuff all over the place, it only creates extra work. Not that that's a bad thing these days, but there's more kindness than ruthless efficiency in this establishment. Believe me I've seen other places. Good, that's the stuff. A little bit more there behind. Right. Now you go up to that tap in the wall and turn it on. This hose is relatively short, it's kept here just for the purpose. Never mind if water's wasted. You can't be in two places at once and it all goes into the dry earth, even if nothing is grown round here. Now then, you light the fire. Oh, well, I will, just this once. You must carry a light, always. Good. See how quickly it catches. No, don't hose it yet, you'll quench it. All round. Gently. That's right. You can either walk round, but be careful to toss the hose away behind you or it'll cross the fire. Or you can stand here and crook your arm with the hose to get round, then move a little to the left and do the same, then a little to the right. You can't bend a jet of water, oddly enough, but you can make it go round the corner in a way. Well, I'll leave you to it. I've got a great deal to see to.

The fire crackles like rain on a stone pavement. The falling water patters. The funeral pyre of human hair smoulders gently on the marble floor. The banisters weave circles round it, unfurling its minute particles over the dried-up grass. You cannot bend a jet of water but you can make it go round the corner in a way. It is a question of how you hold the instrument, and of aiming correctly, whether it's fire or water. The human element wraps up the earth with interpenetration and those who do not partake of the great secret story which is not a story are wiped out in a thought, leaving no trace of error. The revelation is open to all regardless. Fill up this form and queue here.

– If you love somebody, forget it. If you want somebody, oh, hi, it's you. What are you doing here? That's my job.

– I've been given this aspect of it. You need only bring the stuff now. Division of labour.

– Fine, fine, don't think you're taking anything from me that I care about one way or the other. You still yenning for old what's his name?

– The head gardener asked me to tell you, would you please load out the stuff straight and neatly on the pile and not scatter it all round for me to rake in. Any that's left might catch fire on the dry grass.

– Say, look who's talking. You silly old man, who d'you think you are, bossing me around?

The olive trees move slowly along, tinged by the sunset. It is difficult to tell their exact colour, for the knowledge of their normal silvery green interferes with the absolute result of being tinged. And yet the road is pink. Not so much immediately underfoot but further. Immediately underfoot it moves slowly along, grey and burning through the thin soles of each canvas shoe as it steps down upon it, ahead of the body and ahead of the other foot, until the other foot follows carrying the body with it, and steps down on the burning road ahead of the body and ahead of the other foot. That is the way a man advances, on his hindlegs, his forelegs free to hold an object such as the world for instance, his head free to look at the object held and reflect upon it. The object could be his own head. But the advance is slow, despite the shrinkage of the world, and the nearness, for example, of Patagonia. Further along, the road is pink. The white house on the hill is pink. The pink house higher up is flame-coloured.

Despite the heavy knowledge that Mrs. Mgulu has not nodded, nor appeared, nor given the slightest proof of her objective existence, and that it hurts, despite all this she moves alongside, sometimes reclining in the cushions of the vehicle as it glides companionably along at a walking, talking pace, or alternatively treading lightly on the burning road in golden sandals and something diaphanous, sharing the observation of phenomena, the village of smart concrete huts, the concrete post-office, the grocer's shop, the smiling eyes and frank admiring looks, the carefully terraced, carefully irrigated vegetable gardens and the terraced olive groves through which the pink road winds. She smells of aloes and hair fixative and all the objects stand out sharp.

Or else quite suddenly the objects are switched off and merge into a dim olive-green dusk which wraps up and weighs down the heavy knowledge that Mrs. Mgulu has not given the slightest proof of her objective existence and does not share the observation of phenomena, and that it hurts, entering the body through the marrow-bone, up into the medullary centres, down the glosso-pharyngeal nerve perhaps or the pneumogastric, at any rate forward and down the throat that tightens as enlargement of the lymphatic glands occurs and the knowledge spreads into the chest, aching. Sooner or later it will reach the spleen.

At eye-level the shacks come into view. Three of them are on fire, are having a party, reflect the reapparent setting sun in their verandah doors. The others are all dead, straddling their own verandah roofs in a cocooning dusk. Some people would call them bungalows.

– It is not merely that I no longer desire you physically which would be understandable in any circumstances but that you dwell in me and watch me no longer desire you and smile as I mourn the passing of that simple, intense desire. Sometimes it is sufficient to disimagine, so that slowly and with infinite patience, atom by atom the element of desire will disintegrate. But energy is indestructible as you well know, except in very special circumstances, and so something remains, other and else, equally painful and whole. The thing exists and we cannot pretend that it does not. We make our errors in a thought and reject them in another thought, leaving a host of errors in us. Sooner or later the body must be emptied.

Sooner or later the bowl of steaming gruel will be set down on the wrinkled wood inside the pool of light.

Mrs. Ned's bungalow is on fire. The glass verandah doors of Mrs. Ned's bungalow reflect the last rays of the setting sun. The other bungalows are extinguished. The fig-tree's foliage is dark blue-black, the leaves are hardly distinguishable. The dark green trunk leans along the edge of the bank at an angle of forty degrees inside which, from the road, the lower section of the brown clapboard wall next to the verandah merges into the dusky patch of dry grass. The lower branches swoop down their dim U-shapes, visible against the grass only with the help of the knowledge that they are normally visible from this position, in daylight. It is the knowledge of their shape which makes them visible.

The glass door of the verandah reflects a green light, in which a filmy monster shifts into view, cut into three sections. The top section frames a jellyfish surrounded by flowing wisps, the middle section a tiered hierarchy of diagonal wobbles, the lower section two wavering stems. Don't keep looking at the monitor it spoils the picture. What books have you been reading? Your head is full of items, you must have got them from somewhere.

– I'm a reflective type, you see. I exercise my memory in the privacy of concupiscence, the male to the left, the female to the right, reflecting sensory observations as the moon reflects the sun . . . Oh, the satisfaction of demand, any day . . . No, I have nothing against authority, what makes you ask? My gesture is of holding a conventional weapon, a flame-thrower for example, or an atomic machine-gun. I am a fire-fighter you see. The fire-fighters' union kindly did not object to my working overtime, at overtime rates, of course, which is quarter-pay, on account of the severe unemployment, and overtime hours only, from 2359 to zero hour, and in the privacy of concupiscence.

– That's very interesting. Your profile is coming up very clearly, your depth personae are most revealing, no don't look now, there is a very real danger of disintegration.

– I might of course disintegrate, but that is a risk worth taking.

– Mr. Blob: thank you very much.

The shafts of green light swiftly shift, the picture is replaced.

– Oh, good evening Mrs. Ivan. Nice evening. I was just seeing whether the door needed, well –

– Yes?

– Cleaning, you know, I mean, the hinges. I think they squeak, don't they, would you like some oil on them?

– I have.

– Oh. Well, then perhaps –

– *My* verandah, yes, okay?

– I – er – wasn't peeping in, Mrs. Ivan. I assure you. It's just that, well, I love this verandah door.

– You see yourself.

– Yes. In the green light of the evening. It's very . . . frightening. Effective I mean. Look. Come here. Yes, come, don't be afraid. I'll shut the door. Look at yourself. Isn't it beautiful? In three sections.

– Yes.

– Mrs. Ivan –

– Shsh. He hear.

– Oh. Is he asleep?

– No, no, him, in door.

– But, Mrs. Ivan, that's you.

– It is me-him. The light.

– Oh, I see.

– Shsh.

The algae are still. The hierarchy of diagonal shafts are still. The aureole is dark gold as an angel's. To the right, a little behind, is the jellyfish, petrified in frozen zigzags.

– For me it is him. For you, her. You understand?

– Yes. I understand.

– Sometimes, then, for me it is her. Like, for you, him.

– Yes . . . Yes . . . I love you Mrs. Ivan.

– I love also. Long in your house, only goodday, good-night, excuse, no friends, wife busy, I love, all must love.

– I've always loved you, from the beginning I've loved you.

– And him in door?

– Layers and layers of love.

– Lares? What is lares?

– Lay-ers. Like geology. Or geophysics.

– Ah. You love tea? Samovar tea?

– The god will go if you open the door.

– He come back. Dark now.

– Yes, he has almost gone.

– He go inside maybe. Come in please. You sit. Look, I have many tins now, all boiled, your wife ask, clean, this shelf all full, many many. Roof, Ivan build hut. One day.

– Where?

– God he know.

– So you'll be leaving us?

– One day. Private. You understand?

– Yes.

– What you were before?

– I was an Intellectual.

– Ye-es?

– I was a broad-based Liberal humanist.

– Please?

– And you?

– I am born here.

– Yes of course. I'm old enough to be your daughter.

– Please?

– It was a joke.

– Ah yes, Ukay humour. Different from Uessessarian. I speak Asswati very good, I laugh in Asswati but not Ukayan. They teach at school, here everyone speak Ukayan good like Asswati, but for me not, my mother always speak Uessessarian as child to me.

– It all comes to the same thing in the end.

– Please?

– We seem to communicate all right.

– Ah yes. You love my tea?

– Very good, thank you very much.

– You prefer with milk?

– No, no, it's fine like this. You – er – you're very cosy in here, aren't you? You've arranged the furniture quite well.

– Ye-es.

– I'm afraid it's very old furniture we picked up here and there. I got that armchair on a rubbish dump outside the town you know, they were about to burn it.

– Yes.

It is the knowledge of the shape and size of the sparse furniture which makes it visible in the darkened room, the armchair with its inside spewing, the rickety iron bed in the corner to the left of the verandah-door, the curtained shelves on the wall facing the verandah, the small table with the wash-basin that doesn't match the jug or slop-pail, the cooking-ring in the corner, the larger table against the other wall, its far end covered from edge to edge with opened cans, the wooden kitchen chair. It is the knowledge of the history of every item which makes it sharply visible in the darkening room, even, if need be, in absolute blackness. It is likewise the knowledge of Mrs. Ivan however limited so far, that makes her tangible to the eyes and inner thoughts in the almost blackness of the darkening room. There is thus no need to talk, the atoms of her being move soundlessly in waves across the darkened room. A conversation, however, occurs. It is the knowledge of the history of every item thought that makes it tangible to the neural cells both before and after utterance, the utterance merely giving it that particular form which may or may not have been expected by the neural cells as they quickly rearrange themselves to enfold it in that precise form.

– What does your husband do, Mrs. Ivan?

– Labour Exchange.

– You mean, as an official?

– No, no. Unemployed. He wait.

– I've never seen him there.

– No? Maybe different, er – chass . .

– Group?

– No. Different, er – well, yes, different group, different, ah, time.

– What did he do before?

– You on other side yes? Questionnaire.

– I'm sorry, one gets so used to thinking of oneself that way, one transfers it.

– Yes? You transfer much? Your sickness. Yes? Or contain?

– I suppose I transfer most of it. Mrs. Ivan, how did all this happen, really I mean?

– Really? What is really?

– Through all the false identities that we build, the love-making, the trauma-seeking, the alchemising of anecdote to legend, of episode to myth, what really happened to us?

– Us. Us is difficult. You still think us. I do not think us. My mother Tartar, some Chinese, my father Uzbek, half Bahuko.

– But. But your hair is blonde!

– Red, no? Red gold, on identity. You not look in day-light. Funny genes. My son, eight years, my son surprising black. He strong. He work good at school.

– I see. I thought – but if you're quarter Bahuko, why are you living here? Why are you so poor? You're even poorer than we are.

– Always somebody poorer. Look Sino-America, nothing to eat, and Seatoarea.

– Oh yes I know, I know.

– Ivan, he ex-Uessessarian. Unskill. Skill before, no use, gone. Lucky room here. Thank you.

– What happened, Mrs. Ivan? What happened? Please tell me.

– To Ivan?

– No, to us.

– Us again. You very sick. People come, strong, too much strong, sick from too much strong, they go, more different people come, with not sickness.

– No, it's not that simple. Something happened, something robbed us of the fruits of the earth.

– Perhaps nothing. That is what happened. The fruits are to everyone. But something, something means all. It was too much difficult. Oh, I cannot say, for me Ukayan words not come.

– You mean, Mrs. Ivan, that the human element mutated in some way, disintegrated even, as a radioactive element transmutes into another by emitting particles, diminishing itself?

– Diminish is . . . less? No not diminish. More. Human element more bigger.

– Covering the whole earth and interpenetrating itself to a new consciousness and those who cannot grow with it must die.

– Yes. Cannot trap the god for strong. He get into blood and no get out with giving, so poison.

– Man needs his daily ration of the whole world, and nothing less than symbiosis will do.

– Man is daily ration of whole world, he must be also eaten by all others. He petrol, grain, he electricity, he books, he satellites, he information bad good, he hello how are you, goodnight, sleep well, you love my tea I love your sickness, and that perhaps was too much difficult. Oh, I have speak never so many words Ukayan.

– Your samovar tea loosens your tongue.

The steps on the verandah loudly surround the enveloping darkness back to the angles felt one second before the sudden flood of light brings them leaping into sharp outlines and colour. The entry of Mr. Ivan and young, Bahuko, bright-eyed, thin Ivan Ivanovich, does not dispel the interpenetration of the psychic rays but adds to it, enriching it with smiles, and oh what nice surprise, how kind, you will be better soon, now you have work, alas not me but there is always hope, Ivanek here is first in mathematics, have some more tea, I love your samovar.

The flies lie quiet on the transverse bar, at eye-level, so quiet they might be dead, this very dawn on the transverse bar of the closed window in front of the closed shutters. The closing of the window after the hot night, the closing of the window like an earthquake to the flies, did not disturb the flies in their embrace. Beyond the shutters, a few metres away, rises the slatted shape of Mrs. Ned's bungalow dark in the shadow cast by this shack and the rising sun. In the evening it is the slatted shape of Mrs. Ned's shack that casts a shadow, keeping the burning sun in its late aspect off the little room, creating in theory a coolness, were it not for the corrugated iron roof that has absorbed the heat all day. But now the sun is rising on the other side. Soon it will beat down upon the iron roof.

The mattress on the floor is already covered over. The kitchen door is framed by the bedroom door. At the end of the short dark passage, almost cubic in its brevity, the kitchen through the two open doors seems luminous and apparently framed in red. The door, however, is of rough wood. The luminosity is due to the rising sun that flows obliquely into the kitchen through the bead curtain over the door and more obliquely still through the window above the sink to the right of the door, due to the slanted shade from Monsieur Jules's roof. Only a narrow shaft of light turns the red stone floor into a miniature ditch of fiery water across the threshold. The wrinkled wood of the wooden table is still and dead, unlit by any shaft refracted or direct.

The squint is not so blue to-day, or so wide, in the luminosity of the sunrise pouring its dust into the molecules of air through the window above the sink. But it is bluer and wider than at noon, when the luminosity is more stark, even with the shutters closed. The circle of gruel in the bowl is greyish white and pimply. The gruel occurs at dawn these days, and is come to, arrived at, never brought, movement being necessary and sooner or later leading to attainment.

– Lilly, why don't we move from here?

– Are you out of your mind? How can we move? It isn't allowed. And we're extremely lucky to –

– I know. I meant, go, emigrate.

– Wherever to? Eat up your gruel and hurry, we're late. You know this is the best, the richest, the freest part of the world.

– That's just it.

Some of the gruel's globules remain attached to the rounded white sides of the bowl, which looks like the inside of the moon.

– Nobody has ever photographed the inside of the moon.

– Or the inside of the earth for that matter. Why should they?

– Oh but they have. The very bathysphere of our being.

– Do you mean you want me to leave the big house, and Mrs. Mgulu, and everything, to follow you into the bathysphere of your being?

– Perhaps.

– Where were you thinking of going?

– Into Patagonia.

– Oh I see. Yes. I understand. You feel your job up at the house isn't real, then?

– Oh I'm grateful, don't think I'm not grateful.

– Don't you love Mrs. Mgulu any more?

– I love her. But she doesn't possess me.

– She wouldn't claim to. The slave age is over.

– Officially.

– It's always up to you. I'm glad. It's good to be free. But you're in no state to sacrifice yourself for others. They want strong healthy persons who can stand up to a life of unimaginably hard work that never ends, in terrible conditions. You wouldn't last two minutes.

– I'd find the strength.

– You're not serious, are you?

Sometimes it is sufficient to imagine a way of life for the way of life to occur. Or not, as the case might be, the silence seeming to support the negative. The static eye fixes the empty bowl of gruel, the mobile eye expresses an emotion nearer to concern, perhaps, than to admiration.

– I don't think you realise how sick you are.

– Yes, I am pale, but look at my eyelids, they are the right colour, for the time of year, I mean.

– Perhaps I ought to tell you – well, we'll talk about it some other time. We're terribly late, I'll have to wash up to-night, come on, we must go.

The fig-tree's grey framework of trunk and branch, which leans along the edge of the bank at an angle of forty degrees, is further framed by a mass of deep green foliage. Inside the angle the road is briefly seen. The road is not too hot under-foot as yet. I do wish Mrs. Ned would do something about her shack, it does look so dilapidated, doesn't it. Especially the verandah. She ought to get a new wash-tub too, I keep mending it for her. You too? Oh, I didn't know. The wood's rotten, the nails can't get a grip. But then our roof does need a gutter along the front, it slopes straight down to a curtain of rain on the verandah, Mrs. Tom made the remark to me, I felt so ashamed. You will? Oh, that's wonderful. Before the rainy season. How hot it is already. The conversation proceeds and immediately underfoot the road moves slowly along, warming the soles of the foot through the thin canvas shoe as it steps down upon it, ahead of the body and ahead of the other foot, until the other foot follows, carrying the body with it, and steps down on the warm road ahead of the body and ahead of the other foot. That is the way a man advances, his hands free to hold another's hands, his eyes unblinkered by the other eyes that share the observation of phenomena, along the road with the town behind, through the olive groves and the carefully terraced, carefully irrigated vegetable gardens which nevertheless look so dry, through the village of smart concrete huts, past the concrete post-office and the grocer's square shop, between the friendly wave and the dust from the beaten carpet, along the road, past the big white houses with tall wrought-iron gates and shaded drives, up the hill along more olive groves.

– Can I give you a lift? I take it you're going to Western Approaches.

The vehicle has drawn up silently alongside. The pale blue face at the wheel remains impassive. The rear glass is down, framing no cavern-blue but the normal healthy tone of irrigated earth, deep velvet round a radiant smile, under the sea-green alexandrite and the pink straw hat.

– Hop in. Lilly, you come in the back with me. I'm sorry I didn't pick you up before, it would have saved you the long walk. But I started off later than I intended this morning. I've been up-country at the farm you know, and I promised myself an early start before it got too hot. Well, I've almost made it. Olaf switch the fan on will you, please?

The road is flint, the olive groves are misty-blue, the pale blue wall is gently rounded. It is impossible at any one moment to see whether things are any different round the corner but the moments vanish fast. Above the pale blue walls the poinsettia bunches purple, the bougainvillaea hangs intensely violet, the pines are blue-black and the palms aquamarine. Beyond the tall wrought-iron gates the feathery branches droop like sea-ferns over the pale blue wall that separates the property from the road. Beyond the tall wrought-iron gates and beyond the mimosas on either side the plane-trees line the drive, casting a welcome shade. The tall wrought-iron gates open by remote control forming a guard of lances on each side of the vehicle as it glides in between them. The sun flickers through the quick plane-trees, increasing the neural electricity for the oscillograph, a huge triangle appears, orange, and a yellow shower, circles of red, oh, close your eyes, relax, under the eyelids the dark curves of chin and lips and nose seen from below the breasts ensilked in orange fill up the eyespace shimmering with yellow and black and pink, swiftly moving, but under the eyelids the triangle remains, trembling in orange, and here we are, home at last, well I must say I feel quite tired, I'm not used to getting up so early. I have an enormous schedule too, so Lilly you must come up and help me change, Camille is off I think today. Goodbye. Oh not at all, don't mention it. I'm glad I saw you.

It is impossible ever to see the beginning of anything because at the beginning the thing is not recognisable as anything distinct and by the time it has become something distinct the beginning is lost.

To the right of the drive through the trees the gazebo is just visible on the lawn. The new pavilion has been removed in the walking interval between the making of the facia-board and the burning of the weeds. The new pavilion looks old. The cedar boards have greyed and the windows look blocked in with canvas. The door squeaks on its hinges, releasing the scent of hay and dung and milk that had anonymously roused archaic layers of memory on approach, but only now remembered. The right side of the pavilion is divided into large stalls at ground and upper levels, each filled with hay stacked up, and some with straw. The left side is a stable, each stall white tiles and stainless steel, filled with its cow ruminating in clean fresh straw. Straight ahead, at the upper level, there is no facia-board but only another stack of hay. Straight ahead, at the upper level, in the corner to the left where the hay has been dipped into, the morning light pours from the Southern window to illuminate one solitary kidney shape of perspex, in brilliant summer blue.

The voices grow into the consciousness. At the far end of the pavilion two men emerge out of a stall and walk together down the wide aisle between the cows and the stacks of hay. They are both very dark against the gleam of Southern light, then dark as well in the full daylight from the windows above the stable stalls, and one is shorter than the other, well-dressed and not belonging quite. He nods as he walks past and on out of the door.

Beyond the trees the earth has been ploughed up into neat

but pale and stony furrows, darkening in a wide circle under the already swirling spray, round and round as it unfurls its minute particles at enormous distances. The field stretches as far as the clumps of laurels and azaleas, the hibiscus, fuchsias, palm fronds, pomegranates and green bays that make the white wall merely guessable behind them. To the left of the drive the lawn has also become a pale ploughed field under a swirling universe. Further down beyond the swirling universe the brown goes grey, or is it pale mauve, it becomes grown basil, or is it lavender spike. Along the white wall of the kitchen gardens, to the right of the olive grove, stands the settlement of beehives in a row. There must be a path somewhere leading from here to the head gardener's cottage beyond the wall and the patch of waste ground where the weeds are burnt. The bees should not be disturbed. Neither the newly planted seed nor the lavender should be trampled. The only way is to go back to the front of the house, turn right then down towards the olive grove. The boy always comes through the olive grove with his wheelbarrow.

The air is hot, enveloping, it presses down. The lavender smells pale and sickly along the edge of the hot air. Is there a story? Ah, that's another story. But is there a story behind the story? That's a very good question. I congratulate you on having avoided the trap. Imagination is a function, not an organ, it is an energy but can get sick and cold and radiate no warmth to stronger bodies. Mr. Swaminathan, you don't have to explain. Sometimes it is kinder to explain at the beginning. But when and how did it begin, your nod just now meant nothing. That's a very good question. Diagnosis always prognosticates aetiology, as you well know.

The weeds are scattered all over the scorched earth. They have to be raked up into the pile. The heat beats down. The green hose slithers in the dried-up grass towards the brass tap in the wall, the water spurts and flows into the blackened ashened earth. The fire crackles like rain on a stone pavement, the falling water patters. The funeral pyre of human hair smoulders gently on the marble floor. The banisters weave circles round it, unfurling its minute particles over the dried-up grass. It is important to hold the instrument like a conventional weapon and to aim correctly. You cannot bend a jet of water but you can make it go round the corner in a way. You can hold the weapon like a microphone and answer into it.

That is how it all began. There is a secret but it is not a story. It is not possible to witness the beginning, the first ticking of the metronome, because all you are entitled to assume is that it would have been as now described if it had been seen by minds with the kind of perception man has evolved only quite recently. Those that cannot grow with it must die.

The fire leaps up bright orange, with a yellow shower, circles of red, oh, close your eyes, relax but grip the instrument and hold it up, well up, let it gush forth from the deep sphere of our being and reach up for the sky before it turns to spray its dust over the fire that crackles, leaps up bright orange, open your eyes, the sun hits the back of the neck, the dust fills up the head, bombarding the cells that run amok, emitting helium particles until the human element disintegrates and radiates into the huge consciousness of light, under the eyelids a gold triangle, a yellow shower, circles of orange and the head goes leaden, grey in a hundred and sixty microseconds, three million two hundred and thirty one thousand six hundred and forty two years one hundred and seventy three days point nine. And a billion more besides. We are merely marking time and time is nothing, nothing. A moment of agony, of burning flesh, an aspect of the human element disintegrating to ash, and you are dead. But that's another story.

SUCH

1

Silence says the notice on the stairs and the stairs creak. Or something creaks in the absolute dark, the notice having come and gone like things. Someone creaks, levelling out nails perhaps with the pronged side of a hammer.

The coffin lid creaks open. Voices hang on a glimpse of five moons, five planets possibly. The layers of my atmosphere, however, distort the light waves travelling through it and upset the definition.

–Yes, well, you go too far. I mean you exaggerate.

–I draw the line as a rule between one solar system and another.

–Can't you see the notice on the stairs says silence?

–I can. I collect silences. This one has a special creaking quality, as of a coffin-lid opening.

–Get up then, and climb out.

The five moons unless planets perhaps hang about anxiously as the stairs creak out of the grave. The planets move in their orbits and the orbits surround me like meridians in slight ellipses. One of them says lie down, I shall dissect you now.

They force me gently on my back, head down the stairs. The heavy woman sits on my chest with her huge buttocks in my face. Her skirt rides high and she sits reading a book propped up on my thighs. The men and women go up and down the stairs that creak and she says don't worry, they only play at going up and down, like actors. Soon the curtain will fall.

–You don't have to choke me! Get off! Help! Help!

–Good boy. You didn't cry. I've found out all I want for the moment.

–What, for heaven's sake?

–Oh, nothing for heaven's sake. But you have an interesting excrescent scar in the middle of your belly, beautifully shaped, perfectly round and flat, just like a little flan-pudding. An individual flan-pudding. I checked it with the book. You may go now.

Between each desk of the amphitheatre the floor sinks like a blanket of interstellar cloud. The silence has a creaking quality.

The girl-spy on the outer orbit stretches her right hand.

–Quick, step out here. I only have one hand.

On her left spiral arm she carries a row of quintuplets.

–They opened up my knee, and found a hard-boiled egg inside. I scooped it out, it hurt, and I flung the slices away like discs, but they came back in their orbits and now I have to carry them.

–Can I help you? You helped me.

–Well you could help me to hide them. If the journalists find out I won't be able to do my work.

–What work?

–My secret work as a girl-spy. I couldn't have helped you without it.

Three of the planets shift, one onto my right arm, two onto my left. She keeps the other two.

–Shouldn't we get them baptised?

–Oh names, she says, what do names matter? I can tell them apart.

–Don't you have a name?

–Do you need to tell me apart?

–No, but I'd like to call you something.

–All right then, call me Something.

–Wouldn't you like to call me something too?

–Oh, no, we'd only get confused. Besides I can't call you by your name, not yet, you see, it frightens me because it means you have to go back.

–But I don't know my name.

–You will. In the meantime, if you insist, I'll call you Someone. Since we help each other.

–Thank you, Something, thank you.

–Don't mention it.

–All the same, I think we ought to get these baptised. You never know.

–But I do know, I always know, remember that, Someone. Still, if you want it, Jonas will do it for us. We'll find him by the Travel Agent's swimming-pool.

We do. Jonas and his Jovials play primitive jazz on the opposite edge of the pool, which slopes down to the deep end, quite empty. We step in at the shallow end, walk across diagonally and climb out by the ladder at the deep end. The men and women all around us cross the pool, go up and down the ladder and the steps.

Don't worry, they only play at going up and down, like actors.

–What shall we do without water?

–Stop fussing, Someone. Jonas does it with music.

He does. He places the first planet on the end of his trumpet, lifts the instrument to his big mauve lips and sobs out Gut Bucket Blues to the rhythmic counterpoint of clarinet, bass sax, trombone and drums. Gut Bucket moves off into his orbit. Jonas places the second planet on the end of his trumpet and plays Potato Head Blues, then, with the third, Tin Roof Blues, then Dippermouth Blues with the fourth and finally, to change the style, Really the Blues. Really follows his brothers into orbit.

–You see? I had a good idea. Now the journalists needn't know about them.

–Oh, they'll come back. Things do. Tin Roof first, I think, then Potato Head.

–When do you expect the journalists?

–Any time. They ask all the wrong questions.

–Like what?

–Oh, things they don't really want to know, like how did it feel exactly and what did the fat woman say?

–What did she say?

–Don't you start, Someone. I mean, I wouldn't trust you if you told me all your private scars and pimples immediately on first acquaintance. And you wouldn't trust me if I told you mine.

–But you did tell me. About the egg.

–Don't mention it.

–And the slices and nevertheless I trust you.

–I could hardly hide the evidence. I mean, I had to explain its origin.

–Ah, but I hid it for you. By having it baptised.

–You don't hide things, Someone, merely by giving names.

–But Something, baptism doesn't just give names, it gets rid of the original cause.

–Only for a time, Someone. The original cause comes back. You don't understand much, do you?

–I understood more inside the coffin. The five geometries of the human psyche, for instance.

–Yes, well, I must go about my secret work before the journalists come.

–Oh, please, take me with you.

–No, no, I can't do that.

–You can do anything, Something.

She looks at me with astonishment.

–All right then, on one condition.

–Yes?

–That when the journalists put their questions, you will remember everything I've said, and represent me truly.

–What, everything? But I thought –

–You think too much, Someone. Just listen. And use your eyes. You must admit you haven't seen anything yet.

–I don't admit, I agree. But you told me –

–I've told you a few things. I shall tell you more. But you see, when the journalists get at me, they ask all the wrong questions, and so of course they get all the wrong answers.

–They may ask me the wrong questions too.

–Oh, not of you, Someone. You know the five geometries and the language of orbits.

–But you do secret work as a girl-spy.

–Precisely. I can't even elicit the right questions. And so you see, they can't possibly understand. You'll have to translate. You have the right equations. We'll go and see the Travel Agent now, he'll fix it all up for us.

–Who do you spy for, Something?

–Just keep your promise and your eyes and ears open.

The Travel Agent surrounds himself with pamphlets, maps and thin red lines in zigzags, parabolas, irregular pentagons. You didn't have to make all that primitive noise. I deal in local colour only. How do you expect me to work out my percentages?

–Smile, Mr Travelogue, smile.

–That won't help me. I never go anywhere, I just fill in the vouchers and you have to make primitive noise. See the Universe, says the notice above his head. The Management accepts no responsibility.

–We didn't make the noise out of necessity, Mr. Travelogue, but from freedom of choice. What have you to offer us?

–It depends what you want to see. You can select any medium from infra-red to ultra-violet. Or a number of permutations.

–I'd like to use them all.

–Oh, you can't do that, sir. You'd have to pay all the percentages from .01 to the twentieth power per cent.

–A thousand million million million!

–Where did I put the spectroscope? Ah, here. Now this shows some lovely colours. Black light –

–What about supercosmic?

–Very steep, sir, very steep. Outside the range.

–And infrasonic?

–Outside the range.

–Oh, Someone, you know nothing. Just keep your promise and your eyes and ears open. Didn't you see the notice on the stairs says silence?

–Yes, but the notice here says –

–Listen to me, I do the knowing around here. Either you play it my way or I leave you to your own desires.

–We guarantee to smoothe out marital quarrels through our tours, sir, look at our motto behind your head: Time heals, spacetime heals faster. Your money refunded if not entirely satisfied.

–How can you satisfy money?

–Oh, money satisfies itself, sir. Only itself.

–You strike a safe bargain, don't you?

–Stop quibbling, Someone. If I had known –

–Smile, Something, smile.

–Well . . . you smile first.

Outside by the swimming-pool Jonas begins the Blues again.

–Good God! Confirmation already.

–No, no. Listen before speaking. He plays Basin Street, not my responsibility at all. And don't say Good God like that.

–Like what?

–Such a primitive noise, oh dear. I suffer and endure, all things and civilization considered.

–Come come, Mr. Travelogue, smile at the gentle sound, so sad, so melancholy, it should cheer you up.

–You come come. I haven't got all day, you know.

–Oh, I thought you had a spacetime continuum. I apologise. What can you offer us?

–Well, you could select this simple tour through the canals. By private punt. You just follow the zigzags, though you may find the T-bend here a little difficult to negotiate. The white monks from the monastery in the meadow, however, provide a canal-pilot if desired.

–Don't waste my time, Loguey dear, I can't carry on my secret work with white monks breathing down my neck. Besides, we want to go further afield.

–Ah, yes, well, I do have another field for your research, speaking extragalactically, a whole range of fields, as I said, anything from ultra-violet to infra-red. Let me see –

–Why can't we go supersonic? Above words I mean. I collect silences and after all the notice on the stairs does –

–You have a point there, Someone.

–Thank you. Besides, black light turns my stomach.

–How about it, Loguey?

–Well, if you insist, I could manage something, by special arrangement, just above ultra-violet. At fifteen to the fourteenth power per cent.

–A thousand million million!

–The excess profit goes entirely to the Save the Appearances Fund, I assure you. Just put your money in the box here and I'll fill up the vouchers.

–Oh well. Just this once. For you, Someone.

–Thank you, Something. Thank you.

–Don't mention it.

–Where do you get all that money, for heaven's sake?

–I work for it, Someone, I told you. And don't say for heaven's sake. But you have a point. Thank you for your point. When do we go, Loguey?

–The vehicle will come in to land very soon. Expected time of arrival, let me see, lamda equals h over mass times velocity, why any minute now, unless it has arrived already.

–Oh good, in visible light, I want to photograph it.

–Put away your camera, Someone.

She touches my individual flan-pudding so that I feel naked and ask Why.

–Because you can't photograph means of communication. You'd break the law.

–What law?

–Thou shalt not photograph means of communication. Secret means I mean.

–How do you expect me to tell the journalists all I've seen and heard without evidence? They won't believe me.

–You'll have to use your equations. Now, have you got everything? We'll need the trolley, Loguey.

–What for?

–Food and drink of course.

–You get that on board.

–And words. We must take words with us.

–No excess luggage.

–But Something, surely if we go supersonic –

–We must have a book of rules, if only for reference. Come on.

Something starts loading the iced shelves along the top of the trolley with tins and bottles and packets of frozen peas. The bottom shelf she stacks with books.

The huge plane drowns Basin Street with a huge noise as it comes in to land in total darkness on the tarmac behind the Travel Agent.

–You see, you couldn't have photographed it, Someone.

–Don't forget your route-map. You'll need some latitudes, here, and some longitudes, here. And you too.

Mr Travelogue measures us up and down and sideways quickly, expertly. He embraces us up and down and diagonally with meridians, tropics, and elliptical orbits. We look almost spherical, except for our flattened poles and my individual flan-pudding which hurts under the ligatures.

–You don't have to choke me. Help! Take them off.

–Good boy, you didn't cry.

All round us the men and women spin about as flattened spheres, pushing their trolleys in the ultra-violet light towards and from the plane.

–I suppose they only pretend to come and go, like actors?

–Good boy. You have another point.

–Don't mention it. I can't move.

–You haven't tried.

The meridians, tropics and equators stretch like elastic. We roll the trolley and ourselves, through the actors who pretend to roll, and up the gangway of the plane into a hole in the end of the tail. Inside, a large cafeteria greets us.

–You see, we didn't have to bring all that food.

–Stop quibbling. Look at the notice.

The notice on the wall says silence. The stewards and the air-hostess pretend to come and go with trays between the empty tables and don't really exist. Framed in the small round window Jonas and his Jovials play inaudible Blues on the tarmac.

Something looks anxiously along the books at the bottom of our trolley next to the table. She picks one up, leafs through it quickly and opens it at the letter T. Not finding what she wants she turns to the letter P. Then D. Then G. At last with the sigh of a person losing a point she turns to R, and gives a little sideways nod with raised eyebrows to signify both recognition and surprise. Then she passes me the book, her fingers pointing at the sentence: Really will come back first.

Marital quarrels can occur above or below the verbal level as well as within it. In a pressurised hum of silence Something picks a tin from our private trolley and hands it to me for punching. In the same pressurised hum I shake my head, replace the tin on the trolley, beckon to the air-hostess and transmit my order with a gesture into the pressurised hum of silence. The air-hostess inclines her head with courtesy and a pleased look as if receiving a compliment. Something shakes her head and wags an index finger negatively. In my collection of silences this one takes the prize for sheer pressure. The atoms of our will-powers collide in the pressurised hum, and a long drawn battle ensues. Bombarded atoms whirl around each other, emitting particles of pain, withdraw, get reinforced with fresh electrons, re-enter, begin again. I win. Someone always wins. The air-hostess brings glasses and a long red drink and Something meekly sips at it. My silence says I have proved my point, her silence says don't mention it, my silence says smile, Something, hers says you smile first, my victor's silence does it easily, her vanquished silence ruefully but smiles. I put my meridians around hers and we merge into one almost perfect sphere, despite my excrescent scar, my individual flan-pudding in the middle of my belly.

A feeling of no movement wakes me, no vibration, no hum of silence even. Framed in the circular window, houses and hedges pass. We fly almost at ground level, along a road. The silence bounces with the sounds of people in the houses loving, quarrelling, calling their children in from the gardens where they throw their high-pitched voices like bright coins along the sunlight.

–Something, wake up. Look.

–I know.

–Our plane has changed into a private vehicle, sort of cigar-shaped.

–Yes. A cocoon.

–Nonsense. We move on wheels, I feel them. And look we have embryonic wings on either side. We must have fallen asleep.

–You drank more than I did.

–I see.

–Do you, Someone? What for instance?

–The sounds of people quarrelling, loving, calling their children in from where they throw their voices like shining coins along the sunlight.

–You read what you want into it, Someone.

–I can see the sounds but can't hear what they say.

–I didn't think you could. You don't take much interest in things as such, do you, Someone, despite your five geometries? Only in the appearances you try to save.

–Oh, come, Something, I have a high regard for you. Surely I've made that plain by now.

–Have you?

–Well . . . Didn't you like my meridians?

–You've made it plain to your own satisfaction.

–I don't know any other way, Something.

–You will. Fasten your safety-belt.

–I can't. It hurts my camera-eye.

–Put it away, Someone. You won't see anything through that.

The vehicle lifts over a bank of yellow dustcloud, bumps down their steps immeasurably and with no undercarriage crashes to a stop. We emerge from our disintegrating cocoon, a man, a woman in the vast plain of a circular crater. The ploughed fields in the hard baked earth offer no trees, except in the distance perhaps, near the slopes. The houses on the far edge of the crater curve a little like asses' jaws as we start with crumbling steps towards them having to walk all that way in the hot sun without a drink.

–You chose the transit drink, Someone. The infra-red.

–But you said –

–No I didn't –

–You did. You said we'd travel supersonic, on the top edge of ultra-violet.

–Until you shifted us into the red end of the spectrum. The light of the further regions that recede at the speed of light itself can never reach us now. You with your five geometries should know that.

–Oh, have it your own way.

–No, Someone. I played it your way.

–You do the knowing around here, as you never cease to remind me. You know everything, don't you, girl-spy?

–Not everything. But I came prepared.

–Prepared for what, for God's sake?

–Not necessarily.

–Oh, really –

–Not Really. Someone, please, please don't let's go on like this.

–No, don't let's.

–It makes me feel, so desolate.

–Me too. Have I – have I lost a point now, Something?

–Only a little one, a matter of timing. I think, perhaps, Really won't come back first after all.

–Why not? The book said –

–Yes, before we, before the law got broken.

–Another law! How do you expect me to follow all these laws I've never heard about?

–But you know about the red shift, Someone. That, together with the degradation of intensity, as speed increases, means that less and less of the light actually emitted reaches us.

–Oh, don't start proving your point again.

–I haven't any points to prove, Someone, you have. I only follow my instructions.

–Whose instructions? Secret instructions, I suppose.

–If you like. I can't tell you more because you wouldn't hear. You chose opaqueness, Someone. You still have too much atmospheric density. I don't mean that as an insult but as a statement of fact.

–Thank you for pointing it out.

–But you see, the density makes me bend the laws a little. Even a lot. And then it takes a long time to unbend them.

–Like light waves? Or do you mean, like meridians?

–Well, both. Like meridians, within.

–Let me enfold you.

–No, we must keep walking. But you can take my hand.

–Smile, Something.

–You smile first, but she says it smiling.

Sometimes she seems to pull me along, sometimes I pull her. The ploughed fields of the plain inside the crater offer no trees, except in the distance perhaps, and each furrow makes a high obstacle to step over. The earth looks hard and baked but crumbles as we step into whatever seed they have sown there on stony ground. Whenever I raise my eyes towards the distant trees to identify them I hit my toe against a boulder and curse, and Something merely keeps her pact of smirking silence which says don't mention it.

–Who ploughed this for God's sake, the Big Dipper? Why do we go this way? Do you follow your sense of direction or your secret laws of momentum, mass times velocity?

–We landed in the middle. It doesn't make any difference. You with your five geometries should know that.

–We landed on the left focus of an ellipse. We had the city with the children's voices behind us. Why did we go forward? Why didn't someone meet us, with a bus or train or something? My words rebound only against myself in the heat haze but their internal combustion pushes me along. Come to that why didn't we stay in the cigar-shaped vehicle? Why did we land, it had embryonic wings, and it had wheels, I felt them, we didn't have to come down those steps of dust-cloud, and so on, into the wounded trees. The surgeons cut carefully at the bark, removing it in quarter-cylindrical segments and painting the membranes of the twisted branches in bright orange. The orderlies pile up the curved rectangular segments on tall lorries that chug off slowly up the winding road along the slope of the crater. My God, Something, what do they do that for, help, it hurts, for insulation, Someone, to line the eardrums of the crater so as not to hear, help, help, it hurts, the pressure, it pushes out the eardrums on each side, it hurts, it hurts. I've gone deaf, help, help, I can't hear my own cries, help, ow, good boy, you didn't cry.

The baby sits on the mantelpiece, lolling its big moon head and about to topple forward from the weight of it, about to fall on me, on my wound, on my pain, and I have lost my arms or my meridians, no, here, as my meridians catch the baby in a cat's cradle and it bounces up into its mother's arms.

She nods her thanks in an absent-minded manner and goes about her business as an ex-girl spy or something. She doesn't seem to know me or I her in my convalescence.

–Do you know me in my convalescence, or I you?

–Oh, yes, I know you.

–I think, you do the knowing around here, don't you?

–The proprietress will come and see you soon.

–Ow.

–The proprietress of this house of course. The house-surgeon.

–Ow.

–She wormed the story out of me.

–Ai.

–Our story, of course, silly.

–Hng–ng–ng.

–I couldn't help it, Someone. She talked and talked, and suddenly I found she knew.

–Ow.

–Stop prodding me with questions. It makes me feel . . . so desolate. I have no future as a girl-spy.

–Ow.

–You didn't help by losing consciousness. A little consciousness can do a lot for a girl in a tight spot.

–It hurts.

–And even while she talked she called up the journalists. I don't know how she did it. She talked as camouflage.

–It hurts.

–Of course it hurts. You chose the way of unconsciousness which bends words to breaking point. I told you it would take a long time to unbend them and bring them back to life. You'll have to do exercises. Let me show you before she comes, that'll put her nose out of joint.

She swaddles the baby, hanging it from her right shoulder and across to her left hip so that its lips can suckle her left breast. This frees her hands for us to play cat's cradle with my meridians, very slowly, soothingly, and the game tires but exercises the muscles of my interest.

–Which one came back first, Something?

–Dippermouth. He sucks hard, he hurts my nipple.

–He has character.

–Oh no, character shouldn't hurt. Lack of character hurts. He takes after you, Someone.

–What! How? You told me – ow! It hurts.

–Lie still. It always hurts to give rebirth. You'll have to rest a little.

–Good people! Good children! Ah, you'll go very far, my turtle-doves. Now, we must get you up for the journalists. You didn't cry, you know. I told them that. I'll have to examine you first. Stop that game at once. Now, where did I put the book?

–Madam, you shall not sit on me. I won't allow it.

–No, I won't allow it either.

–Good people! Splendid. Now that you've made your gesture, I hope it didn't hurt. Where did I put that book? Ah, here, goodness, how it has grown. Almost as big as me, laugh, I thought I'd die, breathe in, don't mind my buttocks, will you now, off with the bandages, unwhirl, unwhirl the bandages, lift up your knees, dear, for me to prop the book on, thank you, hold it, your breath I mean, I hope I don't weigh too heavily by now, I go from strength to strength you know, as you get weaker, laugh, I thought you'd died. Off with the last bandage, off with the lint, crack, why, what a lovely wound, just like a big eye gashed, painted bright orange. You can have a look between my legs, I'll raise my buttocks a little as a special favour, there, you see, whoops, oh dear, I couldn't keep them up, I hope it didn't hurt too much, hold it, your breath I mean, now let's see, what does the book say, yes, they removed the bark in segments from the trunk, very useful, very useful indeed for the insulation of the big ear-drum, only a mite of course but every mite has its main, laugh, I thought we'd die, the lot of us, but the time has not yet come, nor the space for that matter. Time heals but spacetime heals faster. Soon the scar will look just like an individual flan-pudding in the middle of your belly, or like a protruding camera-lens if you prefer it that way, you will go far, my boy, see much, now then, a little more orange paint, I know, you chose infra-red but anyway you've had that. On with the lint, whirl round the bandages, the latitudes, the orbits, the ellipses and up you get, well, up I get first I admit, there, that feels lighter doesn't it, breathe away. Ah, here comes the journalists, they will rejoice to see you in a wheelchair already.

I can hardly manipulate the epicycles she has fixed to my hips, but Something pushes me from behind.

–You'll have to hold the baby, if you don't mind, the swaddling gets in the way. Here. Take.

–Something! Dippermouth weighs a ton. I can't possibly have fathered him.

–You both weigh a ton. Oof!

–What, in my condition? Unless I absorbed some of her weight while she sat on me.

–He has your very high density and low luminosity.

–Do you mean like a White Dwarf? Impossible, I'd consist of degenerate matter.

–Well –

–Besides, he's only just got himself born. And I belong to the main sequence.

–How did it feel exactly repeat feel exactly query what did the joke fat woman unjoke say did you die laughing pardon me you see she said you didn't cry unpardon if I may get in a query edgeways query how come your plane stroke vehicle changed into a vehicle stroke autostop unquery so you hitchhiked repeat hitchhiked on the skyroad stop delete last seven words for autostop read auto space stop query what shall we call you unquery no reply stop mister you must have a name unmister he says someone scramble check query has he lost his mind uncheck unscramble suggest Lazarus in said circumstances unsaid no objection quote no comment I feel sick don't puff your cigar-shape at me comment has humour expand human touch your end my reply to soothe we only do our duty feed the people good people we like people end reply query please repeat please how did it feel exactly repeat feel exactly Mister Lazarus query did you want to come back unquery we must know what you felt thought saw said heard stop.

The headlines girdle the world in black and in bright lights with telepictures of my winding-sheets unwinding from my face, my swaddling-clothes unswaddling from my birthmark. The man who died laughing cries out at the world. The man who came back won't come out. The man who didn't cry mocks the world. Read the human story in the Daily Sphere. See the superhuman drama on your screens tonight. Tonight Lazarus dies for you again, exclusive interview by Tell-Star, Tonight, Yesterday, Tomorrow in World Without End.

I sit in my wheel-chair and watch myself sitting in my wheel-chair. My wife waits on me hand and foot, wearing her lover's kisses on her lips and passing them to me in her emotion at my death and amazing recovery. She brings me grapes and oranges. The grapes I suck the pulp of, leaving the deflated skin. The oranges she peels for me in segments and it hurts to watch Tell-Star, smooth as a blade, peel me apart into an empty hole. No, I remember nothing.

–You died you know, the staff-nurse says the sister says the doctor says the surgeon says, speaking in strip-cartoon, each in a square room with accusing remarks attached to their smiles like gall-bladders, to be continued in our next. Darling, you can tell me, your wife, your own. I want to understand. Didn't you have any dreams at least?

–No. I never dream.

On the monitor the world cocks its giant radio telescope and I watch myself watching the psychotic handwriting of distant nebulae on the round screen. It comes from way beyond the visual range, in which the layers of atmosphere distort the light-waves and upset the definition. But I draw the line as a rule between one solar system and another.

–Quite. Yes, indeed. So you do actually, remember moving through a kind of space, doctor?

–No. I remember nothing.

–So you would say, in fact, that we can expect only total darkness?

–Darkness? Well . . . no. Darkness implies light.

–Annihilation then?

–Nihil obstat nihilum.

–Quite so. For the benefit of our viewers, perhaps you could translate?

–No. I lost the equations. I must have left them in the pocket of the seat in front in the first vehicle. I must have left them in the coffin, in the upper parietal lobe of my brain.

–For the benefit of –

–The Save the Appearances Fund, certainly. How much do you want?

–Er . . . doctor, one of the newspaper reports that you opened your eyes for a second when they removed the coffin-lid. Do you remember anything of that?

–I remember . . . Something.

–Something. Er, what exactly? Fear, dazzling light, relief, astonishment, pain?

The scalpel scrapes into my pain. My wife's lover and his wife watch the operation through dull eyes in my drawing-room, hers hypnotized by the never-never land of other people's pain, his veiled with knowledgeable labels at my poor performance. He would have done much better, given the circumstances, but then, circumstances do not touch everyone with the same meridians. He has one stance to adopt, and with it he lassoes my wife and no doubt others and they come like mares. My wife likes one-stance men, she reads them from afar, and having deciphered their one stance feels humiliated and angry at her own limitations. My wife peels me an orange and dies with me vicariously.

The world drains me of atoms. I find it very tiring. Lazarus finds the world tiring goes round the world in black and in bright lights as a startling discovery.

Tell-Star persists with his verbal pedantry under which the worms in my head squirm and he sharpens his beak. What exactly do you mean by something, Dr Lazarus, or as a scientist at least could you define your terms?

Tell-Star picks his nose and masturbates in his unscreened existence but I remember nothing.

–Surely the nails, doctor, you must remember the lifting of the nails.

–The silence creaks. I collect silences, you know, one needs silence in which to read the nervous handwriting of the invisible coronas to distant galaxies. Couldn't you give me a little silence?

–I understand, of course, but for the benefit of our viewers who can't bear silence, couldn't you hit a nail or two on the head for them to read in the sayings of the week? Could you define at least the nothing you remember?

I can't remember my wife's name or my wife's lover's name. He calls her nothing except you in the private banality of their untender story, and she calls him of course darling, so how can I remember? Of-course-darling retains his atmospheric density with that name, and he calls my wife nothing as he makes love to her but names, what do names matter? I shall call him Stance or something. I remember . . . oh yes? What, for instance? The silence in which he makes love to her, this one will add to my collection with his grunts, grimaces, snorts and body-odours, say something nice, she begs at the quick afterwards unsatisfied, you make love well, she bargains. It takes two to make love, he concedes a back-handed compliment with a slap on her buttock to his own satisfaction only and I remember Something. Yes, what, for instance, could you define your terms?

The world cocks its giant ear, twisting and swivelling it

about. I remember, yes, what, a flash, a name, yes doctor, what name? Total darkness. Jonas. Black Jonas and his trumpet.

Lazarus says he saw Black Jonas delete check Ole Black Joe check must mean Joshua at Jericho flashes round the world and the walls come tumbling down. The walls around the crater grin like asses' jaws and crumble.

–My dear chap, says Stance, I don't blame you in the least. After an experience like that you should rest, get away from it all. Why don't you take a trip? I can fix it for you in a jiffy.

–How do you know, says my wife on the quick verbal uptake for lack of deeper satisfaction, that he wants to travel in a jiffy?

Laugh, I thought I'd died.

–So you saw Joshua, says Stance in his best interested voice which amounts to a casual shrug.

–How very odd, says his wife. I can't remember her name either. What did he do?

–He played on his trumpet.

–Really?

–No, not Really.

–Don't laugh at us, darling, we really want to know. I mean, in time of course. When you've rested, it will all come back to you. Things do.

Lazarus mocks the world with Joshua and his trumpet goes round the world in black and in bright lights. I watch myself in my wheel-chair watching the world through a rounded screen. Fifteen thousand for my exclusive story.

Fifteen thousand million miles of no story in the psychotic handwriting of diffuse turbulent gas and ionized hydrogen on a small screen.

–I'll fix it in a trice. How do you know, says my wife repeat performance. I wish I could remember her name. Everyone has a name although he calls her nothing in the private banality of their untender story. I have a name and no story. I only want a little silence.

–And you shall have it, darling. I'll take you to Bermuda. Fifteen thousand! Or – you can go by yourself if you prefer.

–Where the remote Bermudas ride, Stance quips happily and he rides my wife already in the nearby remoteness of his ulterior motive which I read like the distant stars.

His wife can't hope for an eternal quadrangle from me. I suppose she also has a name, everyone has, but I feel sick so please don't bombard me with your particles of anxiety and you kindly stop puffing your cigar-shape at me.

–My dear friend, of course, why didn't you say? Don't worry, however, I'll fix everything before you have time to think and his wife archly says how kind.

–I don't want to go to Bermuda. I want to stay right here and work on my equations. And you shall stay here with me and look after me.

–Of course darling, if you want it that way. But the journalists –

–They'll tire of it as soon as they've tired me out or no doubt before. I only want to cock my giant ear and listen to the total darkness in case it emits particles of light.

Lazarus gives his message to the Citizens of the World. Read the Daily Sphere tomorrow. As told to your favourite reporter, Tell-Star. Lazarus' own sick handwriting photographed for you by telescopic camera in World Without End tomorrow. Read World Without End tomorrow, yesterday, today. Read Lazarus' message in Sayings of the Week, no, I remember only total darkness, no, I remember nothing.

–Why did you tell them nothing?

–What? Leave me alone. I only want a little darkness.

–I can't leave you alone, Someone.

–Why not?

–I can't trust you. And besides, I belong to you.

–You do?

–Why did you tell them nothing, Someone?

–I didn't. I told them . . . Something.

–You went much too soon.

–But the journalists came.

–They came for me, not you. But you never listen.

–I lost . . . Something.

–You lost your equations, Someone.

–I remember now. I've had such a peculiar dream.

–I know.

–Oh yes, you do the knowing around here, don't you?

–I don't know your equations, Someone.

–Have I lost a point, then?

–I tried to help you.

–But I had such an odd dream. Things come back.

–Yes, things do.

–I dreamt I died, and came back to life and could read people. Good people.

–Really?

–Yes. No. Not Really. What happened to Dippermouth, Something?

–He took after you, for three years. Now he takes after me.

–How did he take after me?

–He had your opaqueness. Now he has, to some extent, my transparence.

Dippermouth toddles into the room on tiny golden legs. The needles on his big moon-face point horizontally at a quarter to three and he gives a gurgling laugh like a chime.

–Can he talk?

–At three years old? I should think so.

–Say something, Dippermouth.

–Hello, dad. Wanna see something, dad ?

–But I can see her, son.

–No, I mean something great, real great. Can you read, dad?

–I can read dials, Dippermouth.

–Good dad! You give real daddy-answers, don't he, ma?

–Doesn't, Dippermouth.

–Oh, but he does. You read my dial, dad. What does it say?

–A quarter to three.

–Quarter past nine. Got you! Now watch.

With a creaking noise that reminds me of something, Dippermouth dips and dips his mouth to twenty past eight, and with a louder creak dips on to twenty five past seven and on until my eardrums burst and his mouth joins down into itself to form one vertical needle that oscillates painfully on half-past six. Then with a screech it swivels as one needle half round the dial to twelve and the cowboy shoots his way across the screen on a white horse in a cloud of dust. The homestead burns. A sheep trots past the foreground and the naked blonde pours out of the flames with screams. The cowboy yanks her up onto his horse now blackened with the smoke, gallops away and Stance comes nonchalantly out of his hiding-place, smoking a big cigar. Good man, he says, can you repeat, we'll do a take this time. Why didn't you have your camera on, the cowboy asks, galloping back, I can't repeat perform indefinitely. Well, I wanted to film the conflagration first, we'll mix you in, don't worry. Shoot. I yank the blonde again onto my saddle and gallop off the screen. Good man, he says to my wife, I changed the decoy blonde, he never noticed, this one will take him far. How unscholarly says my wife to confuse the records. Don't you respect history, science? Things, he says, I have no interest in things. I like people. Now, my remote Bermuda, ride me. So he does call her something, and in the privacy of their banal untender story they go into a clinch. The needle chimes the romantic music of the spheres and then goes cloppety-clop around to half past six and with a creaking noise that reminds me of something slowly opens back to the disarmingly triumphant smile of Dippermouth at a quarter past nine.

–Quarter to three! Got you. What did you see, dad?

–I saw . . . my wife.

–Well! You sure saw something stupid!

–I saw remote Bermuda ride on Stance.

–You read what you want into it, Someone.

Dippermouth dips his mouth a little in disappointment.

–All that Bang Bang I gave you and you only saw Kiss Kiss. Oh dad!

He creaks with disgust and I cover my face with my hands.

–I can't bear it, Something. I keep losing points. Why do you do this to me?

–Smile, Someone.

–No, you smile first.

I smile, it hurts and Dippermouth creaks back to a quarter to three.

–Quarter past nine! Got you.

–Good people! Good children. Now put away your camera, you mustn't tire your little excrescent scar, dear boy, or I'll have to swaddle it up again in bandages. Let me see –

–Madam, you shall not sit on me, no, I won't have it, stop, get off!

–My dear good man, why should I sit on you? Stop yelling your head off or you'll lose it, and then what will you do?

–What shall I do, Something?

–You leave my dad alone, fat grandma.

–Oh you dear pretty boy, what do they call you?

–Dippermouth Blues, fat grandma.

–Well, Mister Blues, I congratulate you, why, I would hardly have recognised him since I dragged him out of you. Let me see now, how has your little flan fared since then?

–Don't touch me! Take your hands off me!

–These surgeon's hands that saved your life with all their skill?

–I fear your hands.

–My dear good man, you understand nothing. I shall flounce out in a fury if you go on like that, and then what will you do?

–What shall I do, Something? Take me away, where can we go?

–Where would you like to go, Someone?

–Anywhere, away from her fat hands rummaging in my scar, from her fat buttocks about to climb on to me, from her huge weight.

–No weight climbs on you, Someone, weight only consists of the attraction between two bodies. Use your head. Lift it up. Do try to use your eyes and ears. You never look, you never listen. I made only one condition, but you didn't keep your promise.

–I don't keep anything. Even my point, I lose it all the time.

–You have a point, Someone. I assure you.

–Has she . . . has she flounced out?

–Yes. You hear what you want to hear.

–All that Big Bang I gave you, dad, and you only saw Steady State.

–But –

–Quiet, both of you. If you don't take care, Someone, your atoms will become totally random and unable to impart uniform motion to others. Now concentrate, please, look, listen, organise your energy, listen at least to the absolute immobility of your own heat death, if it must occur. A little consciousness can do a lot.

The house crumbles around us. All the houses fall with a loud neighing from the edge of the crater and down through the twisted branches of the cork-trees with great creaks and crashes, down the immeasurably tumbling steps into the middle of the crater, which opens up and engulfs us all, Something, Dippermouth Blues and me.

We play cat's cradle with our meridians, slowly, soothingly, and it quietens the neural cells in their untempered morse along the growing muscles of my love for Something. Soon we have wrapped ourselves and swing gently in our hammock. The boat chugs down the river and Dippermouth sings in a cloppeting counterpoint to the drum-like moon that bounces back his signals.

–What's happened to the others, Something?

–You mean the journalists?

–What journalists? No, I mean the other moons.

–Oh, them. They'll come back in time.

–Which do you think will come back next?

–I don't know.

–I thought you knew everything, Something.

–Well, not everything. I only follow my instructions.

–Secret instructions, girl-spy?

–If you like. But they get bent and broken.

–You mean I break them?

–Well, when you break your word, it creates density and upsets the definition. And that confuses me.

–So I lose a point again.

–You win points too, Someone.

–I do?

–Yes.

–Does it mean, then, that you lose points when I win?

–All things have a balance. But sometimes we win points together, Someone.

–Like now?

–Like now.

–I love you, Something.

–You don't have to say that.

–I don't say it out of necessity but from freedom of choice.

–Freedom can mean the bending of a word, even to breaking point.

–Oh, don't start proving your point again.

–I haven't any points to prove, Someone, you have. I only follow my instructions.

–Who gives you your instructions? Why don't you tell me things?

–But you have no interest in things as such, you said so yourself.

–Did I? Me, with my five geometries? I thought someone else said that.

–No, you did, Someone. You show such idle curiosity. For a psychogeometrician, I mean.

–Would you prefer a busybody?

–At least a busybody really wants to know.

–My busy body feels so tired. You've tired it with your secret laws, for forty-eight thousand million years or so, like a White Dwarf, you said so yourself. What do you expect, a Blue Giant?

–You chose the way, Someone. I told you it would take a long time. You build up such atmospheric resistance.

–Me? Resistance? But I love you, Something.

–You don't have to say that.

–Haven't I proved it?

–To your satisfaction.

–I do everything you ask. I play it your way.

–Oh no, Someone, you make me play it your way. You chose opaqueness. You don't hear things, you see what you want to see, you insulated the crater of your ear with cork –

–Me! But the surgeons did that, and the fat woman, I didn't want it, I yelled, surely you –

–It all comes to the same thing, Someone, you with your five geometries should know that. And so I find it hard to get through to you. The layers of atmosphere distort the light waves travelling through it and upset the definition.

–Even like now?

–Even like now.

–I feel so tired, so tired.

–Would you like Dippermouth to show you another film?

–No. Perhaps. Where do you suppose this boat will take us?

–Wherever you want it to take us.

–You sound jolly helpless, I must say, for a girl-spy. Why don't you follow your instructions and your secret laws?

–I follow them.

–Or have you lost contact with base? Base! Ha! Now I understand. When you say you follow your instructions you mean you follow your base instincts. Well, why didn't you say so? All this talk of laws and meridians within, you had me quite perplexed. Good girl. Come let me rouse your base instincts.

The hammock slowly diswraps us as I rouse my ascendancy over her and we separate into people observing each other in the act of love, good people. I prove my point and feel as pleased as a turkey-cock.

–Would you like to read my dial now, dad, says Dippermouth when he can get it in edgeways. His voice bounces off the moon as from a drum. I give him a paternal pat which sets off the alarm.

–Stop it, dad! Stop!

–Sorry, son, sorry. There, no harm done. Stop, says the moon.

–No harm! Just you wait, I'll probably die before my time, you great clumsy oaf.

–How dare you talk to me like that? Oaf, says the moon.

–Well at least I tell the truth. Not like ma who's got herself all besotted with you, truth says the moon, already on the edge of that theatre, sotted with you the moon says, that big round hole you came out of like a sinking nincompoop –

–What do you mean, round hole says the moon, you warned her? How? Compoop the moon says.

–I warned her. Not to give you a hand.

–What! And, says the moon.

–But, oh, no, Someone. I play it your way.

The moon says your way as Dippermouth imitates his mother with a snarling simper and I want to hit him but Something stops me. The atoms of our will-power collide a little in a short-drawn battle but the well-being in the pleasure of my turkey-cock has drained me and I defer to her with a flourish of face-saving. Dippermouth's dial now saved grins mockingly at a quarter-to-nine or the alternative and dips into his creaking oscillations as the boat chugs down the river.

The boat chugs down the river through the weeds that enmesh its chugging progress. A crocodile slowly slices the forewater. The decoy blonde runs screaming from the burning hut and leaps into the river. The crocodile slowly slices the rearwater towards her. The fat unshaven captain nonchalantly emerges from his small square cabin and watches the decoy blonde struggling in the weeds with the crocodile slicing the water towards her. He throws out a life-belt at her, or a lasso perhaps, and draws her towards the boat, slicing the water quicker than the crocodile. He yanks her dripping onto the boat-deck and she faints into his arms. Now I remember they did all this before, on a big liner, with the other blonde. I played detective but took no notes or pictures by way of evidence, relying on my brain which couldn't retain the immense complexity of plot and motivation. Good man, says Stance, can you repeat, we'll do a take this time.

–You only see what you want to see, Someone. Why do you want to see this tripe?

–It has a certain disconnecting charm. Anyway, if you see it too, you must also want to see it.

–I want to know you better by looking through your eyes.

–And through Dippermouth's dial. You mothered him after all.

–You fathered him.

–I really don't see how.

–You don't see anything worth while.

–Worth whose while?

–Your while. My while. You try to live without causality, pretending that each moment has its own separateness, that anyone might come or go in that one moment like an electron. Why, you might as well ask for the moon.

–Oh dear, here we go again with your mystifications.

–I speak with perfect clarity.

–I've noticed that when people say a thing has perfect clarity they merely wish it had.

–People perhaps. You like people, don't you? You have no interest in things. But people consist of things.

–Oh come, Something, I have a high regard for you. You know I have. Anyway stop throwing that phrase at me. It doesn't apply to me. I didn't say it, someone else did. He did. Stance. The man in the film.

–When you don't understand something, Someone, continue as if you did, it will come clear later. You with your five geometries should know that. Instead you enmesh the mathematical process with verbal pedantry and tangential arguments.

–Dad, oh dad, ma, stop it, you two, look what you've done, dad, you've clogged the boat. Look at the weeds! Look, ma, we've got all stuck.

We have. The engine has stopped chugging and gives only an occasional cough or splutter of exhaustion. Rushes enmesh the rudder, embrace the boat, fall like a net over the cabin door. We can hardly climb out and the sun rides high and hot.

–Well at least that echoing moon has gone.

–I could go down and cut the weeds with my delicate needles.

–Don't you dare, Dippermouth, for one thing the leeches would suck you out of existence.

We have reached an impasse, Something, Dippermouth Blues and I. Clearly they lay the tangle in my words. Clearly they expect me to disentangle us.

–Well at least something has clarity. How do you want me to do it?

–Reflect, Someone. Dive into your reflections.

–I have none.

–Precisely.

–But the leeches. The leeches will suck me out of existence.

–You have strength to spare. Surely you can give a few corpuscles.

–What, in my condition?

–Your wound has healed. Don't you remember what the Travel Agent said? Time heals, spacetime heals faster.

–The Travel Agent! How many light years away did he guarantee that? I've had forty-eight thousand million wounds since then.

–Reflect, Someone, reflect.

I reflect. The sun bakes but does not drink the river dry for me to cut the weeds. I reflect. It hurts. It burns. Dipper-mouth ticks away silently and the ticking silence taps each neural cell. Something falls asleep under the growing net of weeds. She falls away from me and my inadequacy ticks on silently and hurts. The higher the temperature the faster the vibrations and consequently the higher the frequency of the radiation emitted, so that devices like the brain become unsuitable on account of the inertia associated with matter of relatively large mass, which now produces nothing more startling than the fact that in this type of communication the echo decreases with the fourth power of the distance between two bodies, rather than with the square. I think furiously as the sun moves down the sky. She said something about causality, but then it only pretends to cause, like actors, to save the appearances. I think more coolly as the cool returns. After sunset the degree of ionization in the lower layer of my atmosphere falls off through the recombination of ions and the higher layer then reflects, less dense, with fewer collisions. The darkness creeps along the water through the weeds. Dippermouth ticks loudly now and Something has fallen away from me into a separate darkness, under the net of weeds. I could fly off now on my relative lack of attraction between two bodies, out of my bondage, my responsibility to her if any, after all I didn't ask for her stretched hand. I didn't choose the way, I wanted only opaqueness, nothingness. I didn't order these complexities, these secret laws and her priggish mystifications. The darkness cools my thoughts, the darkness chills me and I feel alone. Something, say something, I can't bear the silence. Dippermouth ticks away, grinning his permanent sleep at a quarter to nine, a quarter past three, who knows, she does the knowing around here. The new moon suddenly cuts through the dark looking remarkably like Planck's constant over two pi times the square root of minus one.

I reach for the square root of minus one and snatch it down. I dive into the darkness that chills my bones. Under the water I cut hard at the weeds with the sharp blade, all round the boat, I cut and the weeds float away. The leeches cling to me and suck my red corpuscles, leaving me the white. Once every minute or so I come up to breathe, and the weeds bar my passage. I choke. Get off me. Help. Hold it, your breath, I mean, cut, hold it. Ah, breathe away. The sky looks black without the moon's square root of minus one, totally black and even the stars and galaxies have receded at the speed of light, heaven knows where, she does the knowing around here and she has fallen away from me.

I dive into the darkness and it chills my bones. Under the water I cut hard at the weeds, all round the boat I cut, and the weeds float away one by one. The leeches cling to me and suck my red corpuscles, shifting me into the x-rays of the spectrum until I feel so faint I want to die again for lack of white light. Once every month or so I come up to breathe, but the weeds bar my passage and I choke, get off, get off, hold it, your breath, I mean, cut, breathe away. I dive, I cut, I choke, I faint. The leeches suck, the galaxies recede. Once every year or so I come up to breathe, and as I breathe away the sky lightens a little each decade.

The day breaks with a cough and splutter. I faint and wake at dawn and dive again and cut the last remaining weeds around the rudder. The spectrum has turned green and bright. The leeches suck my last few red corpuscles and I long for the replenishment of oxygen from the yellow dawn which I see through the spectrum but can't reach. I kick the boat for one last push of strength and float into the dazzling light that chugs alone and down the river away from me, smaller and smaller.

Silence says the notice on the stairs and the stairs creak. Or something creaks in the absolute dark, the notice having come and gone like things. Someone creaks, levelling out nails perhaps with the pronged side of a hammer.

The coffin lid creaks open. Voices hang on a glimpse of two moons, two planets possibly, but the layers of my atmosphere distort the light waves travelling through it and upset the definition, even perhaps the distinction between one solar system and another.

–Ssh. Can't you see the notice on the stairs says silence?

–This one has a ticking quality. It hurts.

–Keep quiet, Dippermouth.

–Or creaking. As of a coffin-lid opening.

–Get up then, and climb out. Let me give you a hand.

–I fear your hands.

–These hands that drew you in out of your drowning thoughts?

–You did it . . . with your hands?

–Well, not entirely. I lassoed you. How do you feel?

–Fifty thousand million years old. Like a White Dwarf.

–You freed us, Someone. Thank you.

–Don't mention it.

–Oh, but I must. I always mention it when you do something proud. You worked so hard. Say thank you to your father, Dippermouth.

–Thanks, dad. You did us proud.

–What creaked, Something? I heard a creaking noise.

–Only the cabin stairs, Someone – Dippermouth coming down the stairs.

The face framed in the round window of the door radiates something silently and vanishes, leaving its peaks and flat lines of anxiety to trail rapidly across the dial like the nervous handwriting of a distant nebula. It comes from way beyond the visual range, in which the layers of my atmosphere distort the light waves travelling through it and upset the definition of what, my death or my amazing recovery? You died, you know, the staff nurse says the sister says the doctor and the surgeon say all filled with stupid pride at my achievement. They speak in strip-cartoon, each standing inside a square room with accusing remarks attached to their mouths like gall-bladders. But what do they accuse me of? Achievement arouses envy. I remember that. People try to pull you down in countless little ways. They have certainly pulled me down. I can't move. You haven't tried. But any fool can undermine confidence in achievement, why, I have done it myself, to my patients, for instance, whose names I have forgotten, and to my wife, a word in here, an edging remark there and I'll do it again no doubt. But why should they do it to me? Why me?

–I don't know, darling. Nobody knows these things.

–Oh, things . . . Have people come?

–Well, no. The doctor says –

–The journalists.

–What journalists?

–He'd better rest now, dear.

The gall-bladders sail into space, filled with galling remarks. The worms in my head squirm and the inquisitor sharpens his beak. Don't you remember anything? I understood more inside the coffin. The elasticity of shock counters the elasticity of pressure, for instance. The mass of matter resists, yes, you could call matter resistance.

–Quite. Yes, I suppose you could.

He sits at his big office desk in the admin department behind a battery of telephones in ivory, blue and grey, between two scaffoldings of metal trays like rectangular hammocks. Two secretaries tap their harmonised morse beyond the door with a round window in it. So that they can see, he says, and tell my wife, that I don't get up to anything. He sits at his big desk and surrounds his ponderous person with diagrams, curving graphs, zigzags in red elastic, rising black bars of various heights, sliced silhouettes of people and regiments of rectangles with little coloured cards in them representing something or other that he has his tabs on.

–You see, I have a sort of scientific method too. One can't deal with people on this scale otherwise. I like to know at a glance who works on what programme and what progress they make.

–Can you see that at a glance from where you sit?

–Why, certainly.

–You have long sight.

–Well, you as a doctor should know. But I have no intention of wearing glasses. Useful thing, long sight.

He emanates only apparent brightness. Some fifty million years or many more have run him out of hydrogen, shrunk him inside his ponderous person, increased the internal pressure and temperature so as to form heavier human elements and hence a fall in temperature, collapse and a flinging out of heavier elements until it settles down as a small bright star of high density and degenerate matter that weighs a ton per grain, like a White Dwarf. But the silent words rebound only against myself though their internal combustion pushes me along. I close my staring eyes to avoid the issue of my weariness, so he says how does it feel exactly now, Larry, with no curiosity idle or otherwise, to show he understands. Time heals, he says, and the scalpel scrapes into my pain.

–I can't sleep. To avoid the issue of my death and amazing recovery, I toy with scientific trivia. Quite, he says with a paternal pat in his voice on my psychogeometrician's head and the telephone rings. An ivory conversation ensues, surrounded by diagrams and thin zigzags in red elastic and sliced silhouettes of people which he sees at a glance from a long distance. And people operate the buzzer that operates a female voice beyond the door with the round window in it and the voice announces someone or other waiting to see him. My dear chap, he says, I only follow my instructions and whatever I had asked him to consider as to some astrophysicist or other and his personal problems remains unapprehended or dismissed. I may not know much about psychiatry but I do know what people want.

–Do you, Stance?

–Stance? Why do you call me Stance?

–Sorry. For some reason I find it hard to remember people's names.

–Well, not to worry, what do names matter?

–Sometimes they help to hide things.

–Things? What things? You should know better than that, you deal with people too. Or would you consider yourself one of them, the scientists, I mean, who only think of things, complexes, chain-reactions, oscilloscopes, equations?

–Equations operate through people too.

–Thank you, Someone, thank you.

–Don't mention it.

–Oh, but I must. I always mention it when you do me proud. Don't you remember anything?

Yes, I remember Something who sits now by the window in a shaft of street light cradling Dippermouth gently in her left arm. She bends over him and then with her right index finger slowly dials the big hand of his face right round, and then the little hand half round, and the big hand a quarter round, the little hand three quarters round. Dippermouth ticks unevenly in impulses and she listens carefully, staring into his face. She gets up, lays him down lovingly in the cot the hotel has provided, croons a little over him, bends down to kiss him and comes back to bed.

The face framed in the round window of the door radiates silently and vanishes, leaving its peaks and flat lines of anxiety to trail swiftly across the dial, until the pain behind the eyes resolves the nervous handwriting to an optical image. The city has all the idyllic beauty of a happiness sequence. Small streets wind up and down, giving shade and high echoes. The houses kneel and join hands in white arches, slender bridges, parapets, open windows and cast-iron balconies with people leaning from them and talking to each other in the quiet tones of evening. Old women sit in doorways, watching, possessed of something.

She has brought me back to life and I walk wide-eyed, listening to the gestures of the city.

–Look, they've advertised you everywhere.

–What!

The picture dances at me on every poster, standing in the middle of an amphitheatre, holding a spellbound audience of Blue Giants, bright cepheids, Red Stars, White Dwarfs and all my patients ever by means of large circular gestures, gestures like triangles, gestures like parallelograms and squares. No one can hear a word except inside my head and in the spheric empty space immediately around. The acoustics cork the space, the microphone has died, the sound-waves can't get through the layers of my atmosphere. I talk in silent bubbles like a goldfish in a bowl, contort myself in gestures but the crowd soon tires of circles, triangles and squares. They cannot hear the words that rebound in my head but I can hear their grumbles, groans, hisses, yells, their slow clapping and stamping of feet. Then the bull comes in, hoofing up cosmic dust, aiming straight at me with his huge and pointed horns. I hold my terror out at him and plead with sentences that curl around him and bounce off the crowd in rhythm like a drum. I contort myself, create situations, strike attitudes and make circular gestures in wild colours. The crowd screams for my blood. Does everyone want my miserable corpuscles? The bull lunges at me, plunges his horn into my midriff, tosses me up and throws me at the crowd that yells and sits on me, good people.

Something bends over me.

–How do you feel?

–Terrible. Oh, my God, why did you have to do that?

–I didn't do anything.

–No, you left me to it.

–You had an omen, Someone, you must take note of it.

–If you think I can sit here calmly and interpret omens! I died, I tell you, I died.

–You seem to make a habit of it.

–Why do you keep testing me, Something? What have I done to you? What have I to do with you?

–We belong together.

–I thought you called this the happiness sequence.

–No, you did, Someone.

–Lulling me into a sense of false security. What do you expect of me, for heaven's sake? Who did you dial last night? Who do you work for?

–For you, Someone, only for you. For us. I feel so proud of you.

–Proud of me? Ha!

–You killed the bull.

–I didn't. It killed me.

–You always drop the curtain before the end of the show. How do you expect us to communicate if you don't let the argument develop? Get up, look at yourself, you haven't even got a scar, except your old one, your birthmark, such a nice little birthmark too. Get up, look around you. Look, listen, Someone, take in, and think about what you see. Something who bends over Dippermouth in the hotel room that night, that day, that night. She bends over him and dials his face with love and anxiety. I don't know what she sees in him. He ticks away with his irregular morse and it ticks through my neural cells along the muscles of my exasperation with her. That night, that day, that night the messages change their chemistry of atoms and the rhythm quietens to a sullen poison. Get up, look, listen, Someone, and think about what you see.

–Get up. Look. Listen. Think. All right, I have listened and thought. Thought this. That I go my own way from now on. You understand?

–I understand.

–Don't suppose . . . I mean, I hope –

–Goodbye, Someone. Say goodbye to your father, Dippermouth.

–See you, dad.

He does. He sees me in the amphitheatre, all dark and empty now, watching the harvest moon big and balanced on the outer rim of hi, dad.

–Go away, Dippermouth, I want to think.

–Can I think with you, dad?

–No, I don't want you.

–But you've got me, dad. Sometimes, of course, I've got you, ha!

–I don't care who's got whom. Go away. She should know better than to send you.

–She didn't send me, dad, you've got me. The alarm may go off at any minute.

–What alarm? I haven't touched you.

–You'll have to wake up, though, everyone does.

–As if I believed that. Wicked stories to frighten kids like you. I haven't done anything.

–You've done me.

–I haven't touched you.

–No. You've forgotten me, haven't you, dad?

–I haven't forgotten you. I just want you to shut up.

–I shall scream for attention in five seconds from now, just like you deep inside yourself.

–I never scream for attention.

–Everyone does, dad, things come back, boomerang, boomerang, three two one zero. He dips his mouth and screams.

I hit him hard across his stupid dial. The needles oscillate violently, swing round with a loud creak, the alarm shrieks then goes suddenly silent, the whole machinery slows down to an intermittent tick as Dippermouth falls and all his brain uncoils over the crumbling stones of the amphitheatre ground. The creaking of the hands turns to a rattling splutter until at last the ticking comes to a full stop. The harvest moon rides high and silent as I sit and howl at it like a child of three.

My wife visits me every day, I think, how do you feel, she says, and things like that. She brings me grapes and oranges.

The grapes I suck the pulp of, leaving the deflated skins they won't allow me to swallow, I remember that. The oranges she peels for me in segments and it aches the muscles of my heart to watch her but why me?

–I don't know, darling. Nobody knows these things.

–Oh, things . . . Have people come? The journalists.

–What journalists?

–He'd better rest now, dear.

The gall-bladders sail into space, filled with galling remarks. But what do they accuse me of? I haven't done anything. The worms in my head squirm. I remember –

–Yes, darling?

–I remember something.

–What, darling? Try to remember. The psychiatrist says –

–The what?

–The hospital psychiatrist.

–Oh, no, not that. Tell him to go away. I know the names of things.

–Of course you do, darling. But he says – well the surgeon says you mustn't talk, and the psychiatrist says you must, otherwise the shock –

–will . . . counter . . . the elasticity . . . of pressure.

–Something like that.

–Something . . .

–Yes, darling?

–The spheres . . . it all goes round.

–Close your eyes. Try to remember. He said I should, I mean, that, with me you might . . .

–So you still follow secret instructions?

–Not secret, darling, not against you. For you. Nobody –

–I must . . . exercise my . . . meridians.

–Yes?

She writes things down in a small book. She dials secret numbers and works out the laws that I have bent and broken, the shock will counter, mass times velocity, time heals, and things like Larry, it all came as such a shock.

–Pressure.

–But the man said he couldn't sleep, he swore he'd seen you breathing.

–I breathe all the time, unbeknown to you.

–I know, darling, you did, you do. I gave you the . . . kiss of life, Larry. But he said you'd breathed before. You looked so dead, darling, so very dead. Three days. It came as such a –

–shock.

–And then they didn't believe me.

–No, they wouldn't. Not without photographic evidence. But she wouldn't allow me. Breathe in, she said, madam, you shall not sit on me.

–Sorry.

She removes her hand from my arm. She dials secret numbers and listens to the laws transmitted from the centre. Who do you work for now?

–Who? Larry, I work in the same place, for Professor Head. In the automation room. Don't you remember anything? Oh yes, the little orange lights flickering like stars on the big grey control panel, each over clear white lettering that says Hot Spots, Erase, Inhibit, Alarm Reset,

Auto Man, Emergency Off, Next Instruction and things like that. And the face in the round window of the door leaves a trail of anxiety bleeping across the dial in flattened lines that bulge suddenly into peaks like the nervous handwriting of distant nebulae. It comes from way beyond the visual range, in which the layers of my atmosphere distort the light-waves travelling through it and upset the definition. But something creaks, the coffin-lid opening, Larry, can you remember that? You see, the man said, the man from the hospital morgue I mean, he said he couldn't sleep. He'd let you go and they'd nailed down the coffin. So he went to see the doctors but –

–Those hands . . .

–Yes, they'd signed the certificate. So he came to me and, well, they thought I'd gone out of my mind with grief. But I had my rights. I insisted . . . Oh Larry. I nearly had you cremated.

–Now, now, my dear, you promised. I thought I could trust you.

–I couldn't help it, doctor, he wormed the story out of me. Surely, surely, well, what difference does it make?

The strip-cartoon of cubic rooms with the gall-bladders in them slips to the left. You could raise the cubic room to the fifth power simply by letting A run down and B wind up and adding the pyramid numbers. Then the strip story would end to be continued in our next life where I have no name but darkness. They have removed the scaffolding of tubes around me, out of mouth, throat, wrists, belly and private parts. I must have died since then. They have removed the great big chromium drum that gurgled to the left and the dials behind, where someone read the nervous handwriting of all my atoms and jotted down their infinite calculations. But what do they accuse me of? Why me?

–My dear Laurence, everything has a reason. You won't understand it now, my boy, so pass it over, as Arago said to a pupil long ago, when you don't understand something, continue as if you did, things will come clear later. Mathematics works that way. You should know that, Laurence, even in your own weird geometry of human nature from which we all benefit here. Yes, yes, we miss you. Dekko, and of course your wife. Good girl, good people all. She came straight back to work, you know. Said she couldn't –

–Dekko?

–Yes, Tim Dekko, my junior colleague, once a patient of yours I believe. Good man, all things and civilization considered. He said he'd come and see you as soon as . . . well, as soon as you can take it. I must admit, ah, no, I don't admit, I agree as he would say, yes, well I confess I discouraged him a little. Difficult man to talk to, in your condition, or in any condition really.

–When do you think Really will come back?

–Hard to say, Laurence, hard to say. A long time, probably, I mean, really to come back. You must build up your strength. Above all sleep, Laurence, I hope you can sleep all right. I suppose they give you pills, well, no, you can't take anything, can you.

–I don't know what they give me. I think I sleep.

–Yes. Yes. Of course. The doctor said you do nothing

but sleep. Very hopeful. Very hopeful. Yes, build up your strength. People will take advantage of you, without meaning to, of course, thinking your resistance has returned, but knowing full well below their thoughts that it hasn't. You understand what I mean by resistance, don't you, Laurence? Yes, yes, take your time. We miss you, of course, we scientists tend to edge on the brink of madness without our resident psychiatrist. But physician heal thyself. And life has a way of proving no one totally indispensable. Don't take offence, you know what I mean, energy works that way, it gathers itself up to fill in holes.

–Professor, please, will you drag Really out of me with your strong hands?

–Yes . . . yes . . . of course. Well, I mustn't tire you with my old man's chatter. Dekko sent his regards. Yes, close your eyes, Laurence, blindness has great advantages.

–How do you feel, she says. Forgive me for, for last time.

How did she get in through the darkness? The cubic room has moved to the left again. She spies on me. I don't want to forgive my wife for anything, I want her to go away and leave me to my sinking heart. She talks in strip-cartoon, standing inside a square with accusing remarks attached to her deceiving smile like a gall-bladder. They float like stones inside it and each stone falls out and down into my darkness, making great rings that widen and lasso people with names I have never heard of, Stanley and Tim and Martin, Patricia and something, Tin Roof, Potato Head, Gut Bucket, Dippermouth, I wish she would move to the left and take the cubic room with her. She does.

The patients wait expectantly for solutions in the round auditorium. Bright cepheids, Blue Giants, Red Stars, White Dwarfs and filaments of gas that may ultimately become young stars. But I have lost my geometric series. I must have left it on the plane, in the pocket of the seat in front with the route-maps in red zigzags. The clock ticks round full speed ahead as the moment stands shock still around the heart for minute after minute in the regulation fifty. The chairman steps up to the podium with a folder in his hands, which says District Surveyor in large print.

–I have surveyed the minutes of your time, doctor.

–But my dear sir, I haven't had my time yet. Give me a moment, things will come back to me.

–Yes, yes, things do.

–Well then.

–A small point arises. You see these two smears on this page?

–What about them?

–I have completed my laboratory analysis. I have found your wife's imagination quite fertile. Yours on the other hand has no chromosomes at all. Fifteen hundred per cent sterility.

–Fifteen hundred! But I have fathered five sons.

–Really? Do you know their names?

–Well . . . let me see.

–You don't see much, do you?

–Something comes back to me.

–Thank you, Someone, thank you.

She comes up slowly out of the auditorium.

–Don't mention it.

–Oh but I must. I always mention it when you do me proud. I even write you little notes to say so, it happens rarely, I admit, and I don't suppose you read them.

–Laboratory analyses don't lie, my dear. I knew you had cheated me. The District Surveyor says –

–Yes, but what district, Someone?

–The district of my time. Why, the clock has almost done my regulation fifty minutes for me.

–Dippermouth, stop that.

–Hi, dad.

–Good God. I thought –

–You think too much, Someone, and you take names in vain.

–Well, if you'll excuse me. I must continue with my demonstration. Things will come back to me.

–Oh yes, things do. Can you remember their names?

–Let me see . . . Dippermouth, for one. And – er –

–Dippermouth, where have you put your brother?

–Under the podium, ma, to catch dad's guts falling.

–They won't fall out just yet. Gut Bucket, come out of there at once.

–Hello, pop.

His round face or the round auditorium rumbles, then opens out like a tuba blown from deep below. Such a primitive noise, sighs the District Surveyor, and it snorts out a rhythmic grunt like Stance love-making to my wife as the podium at its centre moves away and we move away with it, Dippermouth, Something, Gut Bucket Blues and I.

It drives heavily from bump to bump, holding the road well with its thousand hundredweight. The driving depends on perfect co-ordination between Something and me. I watch the fuel, manipulate the gears, she keeps the speed steady and handles the steering wheel. The little orange lights flicker like stars on the grey control panel, each over well-lit letters that say Erase, Uninhibit, Shift Count, Pot Drawer, One-shot-trigger and things like that. We thus have no need for a back-seat driver and our two sons can sleep behind the tarpaulin, unless perhaps they watch from the opening at the rear the bumps that move away behind us like horsepower waste along the endlessly straight track.

–Do we make the bumps as we go? They don't appear before us in the headlights.

–How observant of you, Someone.

–Well –

–It certainly helps to know we do.

–A little consciousness, as you say –

–Yes and I don't have to steer with such concentration. I like talking to you, Someone.

–I like talking to you, despite having to shout. I don't understand why we need low gear Inhibit on this perfectly flat straight track.

–I suppose energy works that way, or doesn't it?

–You've changed, Something. You don't do so much knowing and you talk less priggishly. I like it.

–Perhaps we've both changed a bit. Marriage does that, it mellows people.

–When did I marry you, Something?

–Oh, a long time ago. You wouldn't remember. Men tend to forget anniversaries.

–We have infinite divergencies on our minds. Talking of which, when did Gut Bucket return from orbit?

–On his sixth birthday. Didn't you know? You must admit he has a nice round face.

–I don't admit, I agree. A sort of double face, in fact, a face within a face.

–So you noticed that too. Oh, yes, he has depth, has Gut Bucket.

–He takes after me.

–Well. You do look cylindrical, but one can't see into you. I mean you still resist with your opacity. Dippermouth has a cylinder too, but shallower, naturally. We all have cylinders, when you come to think of it.

–They don't resemble each other much, do they, for twins?

–Oh, but they do. Only you can't add much to Dippermouth, except time. Gut Bucket contains more, to save the appearances at least.

–What, for instance?

–Well, he has more guts. Dippermouth ticks away quietly, but with a highly-strung mechanism he tends to dip his mouth at the slightest hurt sensibility and yell his head off like a child of three.

–I know.

–So you do.

The tarpaulin lifts behind us and Dippermouth's dial peers through.

–Hi, dad. We've arrived.

–Not quite yet. You haven't dropped your brother out of the back have you?

–No, he hasn't, hello, pop.

–I don't altogether fancy that name, Buck.

–Gut Bucket, pop. Double face, double name.

–Well, we'll compromise. If you insist on calling me pop I insist on forgetting your double name, I'll stick to Buck.

–Call me Gut and you've got a deal, pop. But you'll fancy my double face when you go pop.

–I don't make a habit of going pop, I assure you.

–Okay, pop.

–Well, I think we really have arrived.

–No, we haven't, Someone. I said we'd turn right as we entered the forest but you would go left.

–Left? I didn't even see a fork. How do you expect me to see in this pitch dark?

–I told you, but you didn't listen. As usual.

–Didn't listen! I couldn't hear a thing. Anyway you have the steering-wheel for heaven's sake.

–You jerked my arm, Someone.

–I jerked it! How could I?

–Well, you did.

–I didn't.

–You did, pop. During all that talk about my double face. You had your arm on mom's and –

–Oh, dry up.

–Okay, pop.

–Well, you'll have to go into reverse, Someone.

–No, I won't. I never go into reverse.

–You'll have to on this narrow road.

–Shut up, you bitch, the lot of you, I've had enough.

The door of the truck opens easily and slams behind me as I jump and fall through the dark into soft sandy ground up to my ankles, knees, thighs, hips, howl, help, help, and the bucket bangs against my head, hold on to me, pop, hold on to the edge of my top face. I grab the edge of his top face and slowly feel myself pulled up out of the sand which creeps down like a million ants or asteroids as I find a foothold on the truck and hold Gut Bucket tight, climb in, pant on the driving-seat with cold sweat prickling on my forehead and retch my guts into the double face the outer edge of which I hold in a paternal hug. The stench mingles with the smell of fuel.

–Thanks, pop. Empty now? I'll just go and wash if you'll excuse me.

Something lifts the front screen for him and he steps out onto the bonnet in the dark. A clanking follows and a soft flung thud and a swishing and hiss of steam. He steps back with a clean and shining inner face right to the rim.

–Well now –

–Just a moment. I want to get this straight. Who wins this point, who takes the blame for this?

–It doesn't matter, Someone.

–Oh, but it does.

–We don't win points any more, Someone, we travel together, we win and lose them together.

–Oh no we don't. We had an agreement. I did the power, you did the steering.

–We both lose and win, Someone. You jerked my arm. I lost control.

–I didn't jerk your arm.

–All right.

–God, I feel sick.

–I'll make you some tea, pop. If you stop quarrelling with mom. And Dippermouth chimes four.

–I don't quarrel, she does.

–I thought you'd emptied yourself, pop.

–Well, run along, Gut Bucket, less words, more action.

–Action! I like that, I saved him. I contained him. With which last word he vanishes behind the tarpaulin.

–Meanwhile I think perhaps we should try to reverse. If you feel strong enough I mean.

–Reverse! In this pitch dark?

–I'll switch on the backing lights. Besides, I do the steering. You only supply the power.

–But how will you keep to the road? If you diverge one inch we'll fall into the quicksands.

–Well, I'll try. We'll have to risk it, anyway. The road stops at the end of the blue zone. Look.

She switches on the headlamps on an army of blue trees that block a road without issue. She switches on the backing lights and floods the road behind us in the rear mirrors. The little orange dots on the control panel twinkle like stars over Hot Spots, Erase, Pot Drawer, Next Instruction. Slowly we make our reverse way and she steers well I must admit, I even agree as we move on a moonbeam through the dark.

We park in a bright clearing as the sun rises. Gut Bucket calls us, gonging flatly on his thorax so we step out and gratefully empty him of tea, drinking in turn from the top edge of his face as the sun shoots up the Good people! Sitting in the dawn. How goes my patient? I must see your scar, pull down your trousers, man.

–Madam, you shall not sit on me.

–Sit on you? Why should I sit on you? I only want to see, I have my rights, you know.

–Don't touch my dad, old grandma.

–My, how you've grown, dear boy, since I pulled you out of him. What do they call you now?

–Dippermouth Blues, you stupid old woman.

–Charming. How you do wind your way up and down and around my affections. One keeps a bond, you know, I delivered you. Why, and your brother here, he came in useful for the placenta, didn't you, Bucket boy, my, how you've grown.

–I delivered pop, fat gran, he clung to the edges of my top face in agony. Then he had early morning sickness into me.

–So he did, so he did. Trust a man to get it all the wrong way round. No sense of timing, none at all. Well, if you won't let me see your little individual flan I can't insist, but I'll have to charge you for the space.

–What space?

–The parking space here on this ridge. You don't think you can have it free, do you, not in the Blue Zone, why, you need a disc. We have to cope with a great scarcity of space and time, you know.

She sits on me, her two enormous buttocks in my face, and makes a primitive smell. Her hands rummage between my legs, Dippermouth lets off his alarm. Gut Bucket jumps about sonorously thumping his thorax, do something for God's sake, so he gives a great big somersault and lands upside down on her head. She yells a sonorously muffled yell inside Gut Bucket and thumps her enormous buttocks up and down on my chest like a thousand hundredweight as her hands leave my private parts to grasp the bucket and free her head from the darkness that envelops mine as I choke and splutter inside the echoing bucket maaa – maaa – ah, breathe away she says to her distant self, laugh, I think he's died.

Professor Head, friend and radio-astronomer asks no questions of these wide-awake eyes that hurt as they see people in the map-like shapes of their radiating coronas, inner meridians, latitudes and spirals. He has small eyes himself, one of them almost blind, the other watery, through which he peers at calculations held an inch away from it, wearing five-dimensional glasses. He merely says it depends, really, what one expects to see, and the scientific principle of perfect doubt works well with him. He teases the university's non-scientists at dinner. Nurturing doubt needs much more care than nurturing spiritual life, he says. Scratch any humanist and you will find at least five quite irrational principles held perhaps unconsciously but as rigidly as any dogma, which nobody can question without causing total or partial collapse. You should know that, Laurence, in your own field. He teases interviewers on the screen. Ah yes, it takes a lifetime's training to doubt everything, even one's own observation, to treat each infallible proof as merely a working hypothesis which explains things until it has outlived its working usefulness and so ceases to explain them. Such as your eyes, Laurence, men get unsettled by your eyes.

–I came to ask you, but then, I don't even know what I want to ask, except perhaps, why me? Sometimes I wish I could remember something.

But he answers no questions either, except in the curved way of light, like when you don't understand something, continue as if you did, things will come clear later. You should know that, Laurence. Mathematics works that way. You start with nothing, treat it as something and in no time at all you have infinity or thereabouts. Storytellers do the same I believe.

–Yes, but I have no story to tell.

–You will, you will. In the last sentence.

He sits surrounded with the maps of light. We tap the silent telephones of outer space, we bounce our questions on the planets and the galaxies answer out of aeons. But they give no names, only infinities of calculations.

–Oh, names. What do names matter?

–I think they do, Laurence. They tell a story given at birth, creation perhaps, when the primeval atom burst. You know, I suppose, that I favour the Superdense Theory, what they call the Big Bang, not the Steady State?

–Yes indeed. I should know that by now, after all my time here, and your television lectures.

–Ah, you watch those, do you? Well, well, how good of you. Popular, you know, but still.

Professor Head has an undoubted presence on the screen despite his small eyes, one of them almost blind, the other watery. He walks through metal curves and makes spheres spin and plays with atom-rings as with an abacus and in slow close-up twists the plastic beads that thickly coil along the spiral called the thread of life, holding together in a daze of attention the auditorium that curves upwards from him in tiers as the cameras swing their booms away and point the cold precision of their lenses on a spiral galaxy. The others, my rivals, hope to prove the Steady State soon by actually seeing, or perhaps I should say hearing, a hydrogen atom in the creation process. This at the speed of one in the space of a large house every thousand years, to compensate for the recession of the galaxies at the rate observed. Hardly hearable of course. You know what I mean by hearing, don't you, Laurence. If I showed you a map of the sun as we hear it through the giant telescope it would fill the entire sky. Did you know that?

–I did. My wife –

–Ah yes. Bright girl. She understands all we do, you know, more than most computer-operators I have had working for me.

–Now I remember what I came to ask you. I see people like that. As you see the sun. It hurts. And why? Why me?

But he answers no questions either, except in the curved way of light, like what do the doctors say, oh doctors, I know them too well, nerves, they say, I have said it myself, time heals and things like that, indeed Laurence, you have little faith in your own profession, but then, as a geometrician of the soul which, like the universe, has at least five geometries – geometries? Why professor, I would call them geologies rather, maps of ocean depths, well, it all comes to the same thing you know, like physician, heal thyself, or at any rate continue as if you had, things will come clear later, in the last sentence perhaps which ushers in his junior colleague, Dr Tim Dekko, and his anxiety about promotion wrapped up in a complex equation. With infinite patience and the finite velocity of light Professor Head peels off the geometric series like the skins of an onion to reach a tearful child who makes the professor's one eye water and says you sit on me.

–My dear good man, why should I sit on you? I have every interest in pushing your work, good work, you know that. And you know it too, don't you, Laurence? I depend upon it.

–Yes, everyone depends on everyone here. We all go round in circles and nobody gets anywhere.

–Energy works that way, my dear Tim. But I only fill in the forms, you know. Well, now that you've made your gesture I hope it didn't hurt. Let me see, where did I put your calculations?

He holds them an inch away from his watery eye and scrutinises them through five-dimensional glasses while Dr Dekko flinches in the tight meridians that surround him but do not fluctuate an inch into the wavering undulations that fill the rooms of others, doubling, trebling each other's trebles like a map of ocean depths. Yet something emanates out of his small corona in the mad morse of neural cells that races round in no space, no privacy, his silence says, and receives at once the radiated objection well, you didn't have to enter during my presence or let your scientific skin get peeled away. I know, however, how it happens, the worms in your head squirm as the world you see in even the gentlest creature sharpens its beak, so that the programme in your giant computer-mind gets blocked, goes blank of calculations, cries like a child of three. His mouth dips down a little and through his rimless glasses there pulses out on a low frequency an average story of a decoy blonde who costs a lot in scant clothing. He rides her with a sad passion in the basement of a life that keeps up the appearances with a smart modern villa garage balcony front-lawn back-garden air-conditioning a plump virtuous wife and three plump schoolgirl daughters. He stands plumply surrounded with feminity for whom he can do no wrong, so that he does it and his mouth dips down to twenty-five past five.

–Smile, Dekko, smile.

–That won't help me. I only do all the work around here.

–Well, I'd better go, I've taken up enough of the Professor's valuable time. He also has work to do, though you seem not to believe it.

–Of course I believe it. But he gets a decent salary, not to mention fat television fees. Why should he care?

–My dear good people, of course I care. I do my best. But the matter doesn't rest in my hands.

–These hands that saved my life with –

–What?

He sits surrounded with the maps of radiation that waver through his watery eye and five-dimensional glasses. He nods and smiles through the infinite velocity of uncreated light. We do our best, he says. We tap the silent telephones of outer space, we bounce our questions on the galaxies which answer out of aeons. But they give no names, no explanations, only infinities of calculations. You on the other hand give names to the complex geometries of the soul, you explain perhaps, but do you heal, within space-time I mean. These maps represent something, certainly, but not the ultimate mystery of the first creation that has gone for ever with its scar inside one huge unstable atom. You can't photograph such means of communication.

–How long do you think it will take?

Our elegant hearse rattles along the cobbled street, drawn by five elegant black horses. Something and I lie in the open coffin, making love quietly under the autumn sky filled with the Whale ahead, the River below, Cygnus half way down on the right with Deneb brighter than fifty million suns. The Serpent-Bearer has gone down below the horizon perhaps. Gut Bucket sits in front, holding the reins, while Dippermouth manipulates the brakes as we rattle downhill. But we have wedged the coffin firmly and it doesn't slide. How long do you think it will take to the cemetery, Something?

–As long as you like.

–I long to die with you, to make it last. I love you, Something.

–You don't have to say that.

–Tell me you love me, Something.

–I love you. More than you think. And more than you love me.

–We won't try to win points on that.

The hearse stops with a jerk and no whirring of the brake on the wooden wheel. Gut swears by gut, lashing the horses on their rumps. Dippermouth says tut-tut, gee-up. The front horse raises his black tail, the others follow suit, so that in perfect concord they all shit long and generously onto the cobbled street and the stench surrounds us swiftly. Good horses, says the grave-digger, step down, my dears, you people have all the luck. Oh yes, you'll die good, you'll sprout, more than I will, I only do my job. Out you come. He spades up the horse-dung piles and fills the coffin with them.

–Where do you expect us to lie?

–On top. Underneath. On either side. Where you like. The snake eats its own tail. Have you got your route-maps? Oh well, who cares, the rich die in good earth, the poor inherit it in afterdays. In the meantime they clean up. Why haven't you got any flowers? Flowers would absorb the smell.

–I don't know. The midwife didn't give us any. Why didn't she give us any, Something?

–Well, you didn't help by losing consciousness. A little consciousness can do a lot for a girl in a –

–I like that. She said breathe away, so I did. What do you expect?

–Flowers and good rich dung. They guarantee to smoothe out marital quarrels among the rich in the rich earth. Oh yes, you'll sprout all right, more than I will. I never go anywhere, I just bide my time and clean up.

–Well, we'd better push on.

–Always in a hurry. Some people have all the luck, but then, five horses, and black ones at that. I wish you a long life and many good years after.

–Whoa!

Gut Bucket stops the hearse by an empty patch of earth in the cemetery, thumps his thorax and jumps down. Dippermouth perks off his alarm briefly, his mouth awry from chewing bubble-gum. The grave-digger throws out the last spadeful of rich earth and hauls himself up on a pulley, pushing the side of the narrow grave with his feet like a mountaineer. A narrow, narrow grave.

–But we booked a double room.

–Nothing to do with me. I only deal in local space, and we have a shortage here. A poor old woman inherited the space next door. You'll have to lie on top of one another. No harm in that, I take it?

–But I won't sleep a wink.

–Stop fussing, man. What difference does it make? You start with little, treat it as more and in no time at all you have infinity or thereabouts. Time heals, they say, but timelessness heals faster. As to space, well, we have a shortage here.

The Serpent-Bearers lift the coffin from the hearse with Something lying on the soft bed of dung and me on top of her. Dippermouth blubbers his bubble-gum and Gut Bucket says don't cry, Big Dipper, they have to do it, and he bows into the pile of rich earth, filling himself with it. I feel heavy with sorrow, he says, and pours it down on top of us. Do you think they'll give us an inscription?

–I don't know, Someone.

–I thought you did the knowing around here.

–Not any more, Someone, you confuse me with broken words and things.

–Ah yes, your secret instructions. Do you still follow them?

–I try, but I often lose contact.

–I must say I would like an inscription.

–Well, I don't see that it matters, you break those too.

The escalators trundle through the dark intestines, stones float in gall, green horse-flies swim in urine, furry caterpillars all lit up like skeletons in barium light crawl through the dung. Patience, my love, the reflex will come soon. But I feel sick. It hurts. It always hurts to give rebirth, wait patiently, and breathe, it will come soon.

–But I breathe all the time, unbeknown to you.

–Breathe quietly, regularly, relax.

–What! Take her away, don't let her near me, get off, get off.

–Hush, my love, no weight sits on you, only inside you. Soon, soon it will come.

The earth purrs under me with a scratching sound that drills into my entrails. Something bends over me pressing her fingers into them or the earth perhaps, the soft dung, humus out of which in a dim starlight peers a small brown thing. A furry animal crawls limply out into her hands bundling itself at once into a ball. Dippermouth ticks away quietly somewhere and Gut Bucket stands stock still, coming in useful for the placenta.

The furry ball uncurls and twists its ribs in pain. It turns so pale and so transparent it looks like vanishing altogether, like a decaying giant horse-fly about to crumble into dust, take it away.

Something gathers it up and holds it to her breast, whispering to it or breathing perhaps the kiss of life into the dying born thing.

–You've got a girl, Someone. A delicate little thing. We'll have to take very special care of her.

–A girl? But how? Show me.

She brings her breast closer with the odd insect shape attached to it, already bare of fur and settled now into a thick-waisted hour-glass, but fast losing its transparency as it fills itself with sap.

–Do you know her name, Someone.

–I feel so tired.

–Potato Head. You came up through the heavy water, Someone, of course you feel tired. But weight only consists of the attraction of two bodies. It can buoy you up, according to the combinations or splitting of its atoms. So Gut Bucket goes down to the round pond of heavy water that buoys him up, to clean himself, he says. Dippermouth ticks quietly away somewhere and Something croons over Potato Head. She doesn't seem to know me or I her in my convalescence. She takes no notes now, and dials no dials. I can sit up a little and suck the pulp of grapes. She peels me an orange in segments and it hurts, don't do that.

–What?

–Peeling. It hurts.

She puts the orange down.

–Do you sleep all right?

–Yes, I think I sleep.

–Do you dream at all?

–No. I never dream. Stop spying on me.

–I don't. I mean, I've stopped. I only – oh darling, if anything you spy on me.

–Do I? How?

–I don't know. I don't know why I said that. Your eyes. Your eyes seem to, see things.

–They feel, sort of hollow.

–Yes, they look hollow, but then, after all – And so big, Larry, so big.

–Like dish-telescopes.

–Well, not as big as that.

–As if I had other eyes, turning inside. Or perhaps these turn inwards. Can you see my pupils?

–Yes, Larry. Huge pupils. Do they give you drugs here?

–I don't know what they give me.

–I must speak to the doctor about that.

–Don't speak to anyone, least of all to Stance.

–Stance?

–The Travel Agent.

–Travel – ?

–Grave-digger.

–All right, all right, my darling, don't worry. Nobody wants to harm you. They've done a wonderful job.

–All things and civilization considered.

–Yes well, I know, they made a huge mistake. But then you can't altogether blame them. You did die, you know.

–Did you really die, dad?

–Dippermouth.

–You do say funny things, daddy. But mummy warned me.

–Mummy? Whose mummy?

–Mine, daddy, me, Patricia.

–Oh. How did you get in?

–They said I could. I came out top at school. Ten out of ten for maths and biology. Oh, and current events, nine. And that in spite of getting only seven for religious instruction. I hate r.i. Did you hate r.i., dad, and English, and history? I do. But I came out top all the same.

–Good. One feels better when one comes out top.

–Did you come out top, dad?

–I suppose so.

–Martin's gone back to France. But he knows you've come through.

–Through what?

–You died, you know, says the nurse says the sister and all the rest, speaking in strip-cartoon, each in a square room with accusing remarks attached to their smiles like gall-bladders to be continued in our next. Did you really die says Dekko in the subsequent square moving from left to right, I don't believe it in another ring attached to his tight mouth, it has a perfectly good scientific explanation. But the explanation vanishes from right to left in the dark as he stands in the cubic room with trite remarks inside an onion round his rimless glasses, tight layers that don't peel off and make no maps of contours. My wife sends her regards. Would you like anything, grapes? I brought you flowers . . . I mean she sent them . . . From the garden . . . You've seen our garden, haven't you . . . I hope you will come and sit in it and rest . . . You don't have a garden, do you. Or an expensive mistress though your wife, ah, but then I do all the work, I discovered the formula, Head took the credit. Died, he should have died, for heaven's sake, Laurence, don't look through me like that, it frightens me. Don't you sleep well here?

–Yes, I think I sleep.

–You mean you don't know? Don't they give you anything?

–I don't know what they give me.

–My dear chap, how does it feel exactly, says the next

square affably, and talks of people it likes who go to bed with names I have never heard of, bringing them in from outside myself like mares lassoed by non-existent radiations. How can people get so messed up and contorted, the square room says, it doesn't understand, really, marriages broken up, divorces, nervous breakdowns, why, for what, and it heard, the other day, the square room says, in confidence mind you, and the story floats between the layers of atmosphere inside the square room and upsets the definition. Well, I suppose you know all about that sort of thing. I mean you live on it, don't you, but still the square room doesn't see why people should get things so out of proportion. The square room wouldn't. But then the square room has long sight.

–Perhaps you have never died.

The square room shrugs and says something or other and stays or moves perhaps to the left like the others. Unless it sharpens its beak, what exactly do you mean by something for the benefit of our viewers could you translate. The scalpel scrapes into my pain, the worms in my head squirm, but I have lost my five geometries.

–I suppose men find it easier to move in space and time than in effort.

–Do you mean men or man, sir?

Stance quibbles the professor with oppositions and Bermuda smiles remotely behind the whirls of smoke. Surely man, as such, puts tremendous effort into moving through both space and time. Indeed, look at him, reaching the moon, bouncing his codes against the planets.

–Yes, look at him, says Bermuda less remotely, and the words rebound from inside the map-like contours emanating from her, filling the room, the street no doubt, the entire sky. Their internal combustion has pushed her out of their banal untender story that throttles her. Stance's wife sips her drink and looks with glazed eyes out of an angular attitude in the depth of the sofa.

–I meant something a little different, the professor says gently, or pretends to say inside the latitudes and longitudes he shows to men. Let's put it this way: below the visible to the naked eye you have infinite degrees. Any amount can occur between mineral matter and nothingness. Why not above the visible?

–Any amount of what?

–Oh Stanley! Why do you pick on words with a pretence of sharply pursuing an argument you merely clog?

–Come, come, Brenda. What do you mean? As a mathematician you should define your terms.

–I speak with perfect clarity.

–I have noticed that when people say a thing has perfect clarity they merely wish it had. Brenda, what's got into you?

–Any amount of shock and pressure, the professor continues, ignoring the opaqueness between them. Despite his small eyes, one of them almost blind, the other watery, he has an undoubted presence on the screen of social intercourse that flickers its arpeggios like harp-strings up and down our subliminities. The elasticity of shock should equivalate the elasticity of pressure. The mass of matter resists. You could call matter resistance.

–Quite. Yes. I suppose you could.

Stance looks into his glass darkly, holding it distantly at the level of the nice little individual flan through which his sensibility photographs the world. You scientists talk of things, and matter, and energy, as if divorced from people. Well of course even I know you can't detach energy from matter, but still, you go too far, I mean, you exaggerate. I have no interest in things as such, I like people.

–Do you, Stance?

–Stance? My dear Larry.

–I beg your pardon, Stanley. For some reason I find it hard to remember people's names.

–Well, not to worry. What do names matter?

–I think they do, as a matter of fact, wouldn't you say so, Laurence? We of course use mostly symbols and infinities of calculations. But you give names to the dead satellites in the complex geometry as you called it, of the human soul. They tell a story, given to people at birth.

–I have a name but no story.

–Nonsense, my boy, everyone has a story. A tender or untender story.

Remote Bermuda looks out with her naked eye, suddenly in an anguish only I can see. And Professor Head perhaps, who closes his blind eye and cocks his giant telescope to catch the radiation of the bursting galaxies. But Stance's wife sips her drink and looks with glazed not naked eyes. She cannot hope for an eternal quadrangle, though she bombards the square room with the particles of a vague discontent. Don't you remember anything, no dream even?

–No, I never dream.

–Darling, everyone dreams, even those who don't remember, you of all people should know that.

Remote Bermuda, Brenda, there, her name returns, fills out the square room with her naked eye and honest vulnerability. She wastes herself, and thinks that I waste her, but energy works that way. I don't know what wastes me. My second life, my death, my amazing recovery. If you had infinite time, professor, I toy with scientific trivia to avoid the issue of my silence, wouldn't energy degrade itself in the natural way it has, and level itself completely? Then you'd have no shocks, no movement, no life at all. As in a White Dwarf, you told me.

Dr Tim Dekko and his plump virtuous wife sit side by side, she trying frequently to engage remote Bermuda in domesticicities, taking her curt impatience with a pleasant smile, he holding his expensive decoy blonde tightly inside himself, wrapped up in layers of mathematical appearances.

–But we don't have infinite time, Bermuda quips determined to reject her working self from which I have borrowed findings and put me in my place with pure feminity. What has that to do with us, with me?

–Ah, trust a woman to ask such a question. Come, Brenda, you can do better than that.

She both flinches at and revels in his smirking banality. I like life, she insists straight into him, I like shocks and movement.

–Yes well, you have a point, he concedes lethargically. I like life too.

–What do you mean by life? How dare you talk of life to a man who – who –

His wife's stuttering accusation, thrown sharply out of her angular attitude in the depth of the sofa, bombards the square room with the particles of her anxiety. Stance shrugs.

–I think we should forget that. It has a perfectly good scientific explanation, as Larry of all people knows very well. Wouldn't you say so, Dekko? You must admit –

–I don't admit. I agree.

But his wife's anger still disturbs the flickering harp-strings on the screen of social intercourse. I wish I could remember her name. They call each other of course darling in a deep hate that has degraded itself like energy to indifference and of-course-darling suits them both. She says of course darling you'd say everything has a scientific explanation, although you have no science, you lap up other people's. Well, yes, why not? unruffled. Scientific facts never hurt anyone, whether visible or invisible to the naked eye. I mean, until the politicians get hold of them. Surely you make, put me right, professor, you make suppositions merely as working hypotheses and curled up in the opaqueness of his unradiating complacency I see or hear the whole argument in advance that will lead him into self-contradiction, stop, and discard them with no love lost between you when they outlive their working usefulness. You can't do that with personal survival.

–No, you can't.

–I mean, of course darling, you can and do, but the personal element may torment you. Don't blame me.

–Nobody blames you, Stan. His wife's anger has restored Bermuda's calm. May I have another drink? But she has a point, you know. Professor Head says even equations have a personal element, and operate through people too, well, in a chemical way of course they do, but –

–Quite. You can't detach energy from matter, can you, professor?

–But you can't call people matter! Mrs Dekko pipes bravely out of her plump attractive simplicity and Stance looks at her with sudden sexual interest. Even Tim as a scientist would admit, I mean agree, that people have minds, emotions, mystery, something unique, well, an essence.

–You see, Sally my dear, you have to use the word something. People's essence, as such, bores me. We all communicate through things, superficial things mostly.

–I thought you had no interest in things. You like people, you said.

Now that it has come, I feel for Stance as my wife, quick on the verbal uptake for lack of deeper satisfaction, wins her point. He flounders out of her contempt with an echo that has bounced from her before, merely to watch how they operate through people, he says.

The scientist works wonders with the precision of his language. He arabesques his way through the equations of energy contained until the chemistry of anger and hurt pride lies quietly balanced in the test-tube, on a dial, on a page that turns a new leaf full of squares and lines intersecting, circles, tangents and cubes, curves too, and the light turns the days into a fifth dimension. It hurts. How do you feel? she says.

–Ghastly. I think I died.

–You seem to make a habit of it.

–I can't help it. It happens all the time. It hurts.

–You had an omen, Someone. Think about it, absorb it. Didn't you take down the inscriptions?

–Good heavens, here I lie half-dead and you expect me to sit up and interpret omens. In my condition.

–Get up, Someone, you haven't even got a scar.

–I feel choked –

–Dippermouth swallowed his bubble-gum. All his machinery's got clogged and time has nearly stopped. You must act fast.

–Why me?

–You'll have to operate, quickly, Someone. You know the five geometries.

–Do I? . . . All right. I'll need Gut Bucket then.

–Okay, pop.

–Stand still, Gut, and wipe that grin off your outer face. Now, let's lift him up, gently does it. Pliers. Scalpel. Screwdriver. Forceps. There, you can see the gum between the teeth of the wheels. Spittal. Smooth it in. Gently does it.

Pliers. Scissors. Out it comes, whoops into the bucket. Spittal. Oil-can. Screw-driver. Needle and thread.

–His heart has stopped, Someone.

–Oh dear.

–He said he'd die before his time, you great big clumsy oaf.

–No. No. I'll manage it. Fingers. Where did you put my fingers. Ah. Gently does it. Slowly, slowly. Touch and press and touch and press. Lightly dip not too deep, lift the tip. From a long long way away the heart-beat moves back into consciousness like a clock tick heard again after a clockless time of heavy concentration. Needle and thread. Wipe sweat. Screw-driver. There all done.

–Oh thank you, Someone. Thank you.

–Don't mention it.

–Oh but I must. You've done him proud, hasn't he, Gut Bucket?

–You've done okay, pop. You've sure done him fine. He looks pale, though, and his mouth dips right down.

–Twenty-five to five. Not bad going for a beginner. My first operation.

–Oh, Someone, thank you. I thought I'd lost the square root of my time.

–You love Dippermouth best, don't you, Something!

–I love him . . . as the first born.

–What about Gut Bucket?

–I love him too.

–And me?

–Of course I love you, Someone, you know I do. But love has different aspects.

I love Potato Head. The only child of mine so far I have actually felt reborn, she fills me with a tenderness that brims right out of me whenever I see her. At twelve years old she seems remarkably small, but Something tells me this comes from her weaker sex and she will grow in effort, rather than time and space. Gut Bucket stares anxiously, as if ready to receive her death inside his shining depth at any moment.

The café looks remarkably large for the edge of the town. Perhaps the centre lies at the circumference, or in the left focus of an ellipse. The people come and go, good people, or pretend to, meeting professional friends who can count and therefore know them better than those who merely profess friendship but can't read inscriptions or secret laws like momentum equals mass time velocity. Hands shake, smoke wisps, voices swim for dear life. Some sit in corners writing the story of their death and amazing recovery but they don't include me because the patterns in the table's dark grey marble makes no sense and time has chipped the edges so that I pour the molecules of my tenderness into Potato Head. May I wish you a long life and many good years after. I thought I recognised you. Thank you for coming back.

–Thank you for recognising me. A little recognition can do a lot for a man with a wife and three children.

–Three? Only three? Tut-tut, the rich live young. I deal in local stuff. I never go anywhere, I just fill up the buckets and do the irrigation around here. The cistern doesn't work, you see.

–Couldn't I help? You helped me. I have acquired a little

surgical talent since I saw you last. So I climb on the lavatory seat and lift the cistern lid. The water trickles loudly in to fill the tank and never stops, and never fills the tank. Let *a* stand for the tank's cubic capacity, *c* for the speed of light, and in no time at all you have eternity or thereabouts. The ball has got unhooked and dropped right down into the empty bladder which explains the gurgling sound. Pliers. Scalpel. Fingers. Wire. Needle and thread. A simple operation. Out it comes. But what, no ticking? His heart has stopped, Someone. Oh dear. No, no, I'll massage it. Fingers. Ah. Thank you. Gently, now gently does it. Touch and press, lightly dip, not too deep, lift the tip and touch, press, dip, lift. The gurgle leaps back like a clock-tick heard after a heavy concentration, wire, needle and thread. The water trickles into the empty bladder and the ball rises slowly on its surface. I pull the chain, the lavatory flushes full, I flush with pride, the attendant with overwhelming gratitude. I step down from the podium and he shakes my hand. You've done me proud, he says. Gut Bucket dances with delight and thumps his thorax, you've done it pop, oh pop, look, listen.

The whole town flushes with delight. The streets move quickly full of signs and wonders in mass morse. Somewhere up in the centre Base Headquarters disgorge the twisting teleprinter tape that flows its messages, commands, instructions to the citizens. Lazarus check known as quote Larry unquote has restored repeat restored the flow of energy stop read communication unread despite some degree of clogging in the system still three cheers hip hip for Lazarus and his daily friends good people all stop new para without end.

The ticker tape whirls its welcome and the streets move fast with people in mass morse. The jerking rhythm smoothes itself into canals and I help Something with Potato Head in her arms onto the punt. Dippermouth still pale from his operation ticks away quietly on the front cushion and Gut Bucket jumps in after. They trust my navigation for I can't go wrong on the punt-wide canal with houses hurraying on each side.

When we come to the T-bend in the meadow we can't turn without breaking the punt in two. We'll have to call the canal-pilot. Something says what a bore, I don't want white monks breathing down my neck. But the white monk patters down the white monastery steps and doesn't breathe at all, he belongs to a silent order, good, I collect silences, and takes a flying leap into the back of the punt so that the front, with Something, Dippermouth and Potato Head rises up dangerously. He steps left a little to steer the front over the T-bend then steps right a little to steady it. Then he runs down the punt and dips it over the T-bend and into the canal again, a bit too steep, for the punt fills with water. Something grabs Dippermouth but in the shock loses Potato Head who falls into the canal. Quick, Gut Bucket, bale as fast as you can.

I dive for Potato Head who has sunk like a stone. I grope blindly about, find her and swim for dear life up through the murky water, where furry caterpillars crawl, stones float in gall, green horse-flies flurry past my lips and ears,

I hand her dripping to her distraught mother. Something bends over her, whispering or breathing perhaps the kiss of life. Will she die, dad, Dippermouth ticks anxiously as Potato Head's transparent shape absorbs the sap. She mustn't, she mustn't. Let me see her, dad, I haven't seen her yet. And he smiles his ten to two smile at Potato Head who splutters, coughs and breathes. She has small eyes, one closed, the other oozes an unseeing tear.

–They've blinded her!

–No, Someone. She came blind to us. Or almost blind.

–But –

–You never noticed. I didn't like to tell you.

The punt drifts on up the canal. I let it drift. Gut Bucket sits alone, baled out, on the flat prow. Dippermouth ticks away with his mouth trembling at twenty to four, twenty past eight, who knows, like the lock-gates we come to sailing into their open arms. Something calls out, Jonas, Jonas, we've arrived again.

Jonas has lost his horn, his voice, he says in gravelly tones, Ah's keep nothing, Ah sure done swallow an oceanful of sand crossing Jordan in dat big big fish.

–You do keep things, Jonas, I know you do. Try, Jonas, try, just enough to let us through.

Jonas gives a big sigh, then clears his throat with a great grinding wheeze that closes the lock-gates behind us. In his gravelly tones he sings the blues of life as we sink imperceptibly with the surface of the water in the punt-wide lock until the bar of sky seems far, very far up, Jonas peering over the brink like a harvest moon.

–You will tell posterity, won't you?
–Tell them what, Something, how my heart sinks?
–About yourself, Lazarus, yourself and me.
I said to my soul shut up.

At last the second gates open their inverted arms and I pass out into the lower canal. My wife lies quiet beside me. Her left arm accolades my chest and her face burrows into my right arm. Awake she doesn't come so near, she flinches from my breath that smells of my decay. I crumble internally, my inside body feels like a giant horse-fly falling into dust.

I fear a second death. The first came easily unawares, but to have to do it all again, and without quite remembering just what, except a certain blindness, deafness, inability to speak perhaps through a cleft palate or something, fills me with terror. And yet I fear a second life more than I fear my death. Why me, I fear those fumbling, healing hands, why couldn't you let me lie in my silent decay and darkness? I have acquired a painful sensitivity to noise, to radiation and to the taste of love degrading itself away in men and in myself until it levels itself completely and no shocks occur, no movement and no life around my staring eyes and I work out the square root of my time.

My wife lies at my side not flinching from me in her sleep, but I can hear the poison of his unimaginativeness race round like gall and choke the permutations of her chemistry as the little orange lights flicker above the programming of her basic urges with Erase, Shift Count, Inhibit, Pot Drawer and things like that during and after the banality of their untender story, so that she snarls more and more nastily as nothing radiates through the layers of his atmosphere, the high density, low luminosity of degenerate matter, as in a White Dwarf me? Impossible, I belong to the main sequence. Or, more likely, what did you expect, a Blue Giant?

I wonder if the taste of love on other planets degrades itself away until no shocks occur, no movement and no life. Their handwriting reads nervously on dials, but then it all depends what you expect to see or hear, for the world cocks a posterior horn at distances, blocking its blood vessels, nerve fibres, muscle spindles, tendons and ganglia with primitive acts and noises. Sometimes I think that during my death I became Stance. Stance? I mean, you know. I had to perhaps, in order to understand the half-baked men you choose. I don't choose them, they chose me. Well. I should feel flattered, and do in a way, that you never give me a rival I can take seriously. Yet in another way I would feel more flattered if you did. Rather than waste yourself. You, with your, what? well, energy, imagination quite fertile and experience, oh, experience, she says, the full scepticism of the scientist in her, flattery, education, and things like that, they teach us nothing, we start with zero each time, treat it as something and in no time at all we have an infinity of humiliation or thereabouts, which perhaps we need in order to start back at zero. Something always comes out of nothing. And I remember, what, out of time somewhere I have a daughter.

–What do you mean? Of course you have a daughter. Patricia. And a son, at college. Have you forgotten them?

–Oh, yes. I mean, no. I only remembered . . .

–Did you dream something?

–You know I never dream.

–You mean, since your training analysis, you've trained yourself to forget. You know research has shown everyone dreams –

–No. I mean that someone has deprived me of my dreams, during my death. As if I had left something behind. I know it sounds odd but –

–Yes, well it does. You get odder and odder. Ever since –

She lapses into silence, avoiding the issue of my death and amazing recovery.

–But, what I meant to say, about Professor Head –

–Professor Head? What's he got to do with it?

–I don't know. Forget it.

–Well, we all need father-figures, she says with self-disparaging simplicity. They come and go just as fathers do, or pretend to. They don't have to have character as well.

She wastes herself, out of a feeling that I waste her, but energy works that way. I don't know what wastes me, my eyes full of something I can't remember, my eyes that see like giant posterior horns cocked by the world beyond the red shift of people's inmost essence which with the degradation of intensity, as speed increases, means that less and less of the light actually emitted reaches us. Look at it this way, Laurence, we tap the silent telephones of outer space, but only, if I may put it simply for you, with a pin through an apple. The rest of the universe has gone for ever in both space and time, beyond our reach. How can we hope to photograph creation?

He holds the calculations an inch away from his eye and peers at them through five-dimensional glasses.

–I feel a great concern, Laurence, about our friend, Tim Dekko.

–His work, you mean, or – ?

–Both, both, my boy, they always go together. Life balances all things, as you well know. He has begun to diverge, to lean a little towards the Steady State Theory, in opposition, of course, to me, but clearly he forgot the master-card when he fed in this stuff. These permutations make no sense. No sense at all.

–Couldn't my wife put them through again when he goes home? He needn't know.

–Home, yes. Nice home he has. Attractive daughters, wife. Pity.

–But Stance won't get anywhere with her.

–Stance, you call him? Yes. Good name. Good man, too, except for, well, we all have our weaknesses. Still, as you know, life balances all things. Dekko asked for it, yes indeed, poor man. Can you help him at all, Laurence?

–I don't seem able to get through to him, sir.

–Quite so. Quite so. He waits for me to die, poor man, to step into my shoes. Well, that would help, certainly. But unfortunately I can't exactly choose the moment. You didn't, did you, Laurence?

–No, sir.

–No, no, I thought not. Though one never knows. I don't imagine you chose to come back either. Dear me, these doctors keep one alive far too long, so tiresome for promotion, when one has played out one's genius I mean. Of course I could retire, no doubt he thinks I should. D'you think I should, Laurence?

–No, sir.

–Hmm. In the old days one died before retirement age, of pneumonia, influenza, anything could do it. What did you die of, Laurence?

–My heart stopped, sir. I mean, forgive me, during an operation. They opened me up quickly there and massaged it, so they told me, but in vain. Apparently.

–Ah yes, indeed. I have no memory for physiological detail these days, despite my own ailments, or perhaps on account of trying to forget them. Dear me, how did we get on to this, most unscientific, ah yes, Dekko.

–I don't know the way to his heart.

–No. No. He does wrap it up, rather. How shall we peel away those outer layers of atmosphere, Laurence?

–Perhaps, well, through recognition. A little recognition can do a lot for a man with a wife and three children.

–Not to mention, yes, well. Couldn't you, perhaps, with your unsettling eyes, decoy the blonde?

–No, sir.

–No, I thought not. And nor, of course, can I. Pity that Stance . . . a most unmathematical man, balancing things the wrong way about. Well, well. Recognition, yes. Though recognition usually adds further layers to people. But how can we recognise him, Laurence? I've tried praise at every turn, even when I disagree, but he absorbs it straight into those tight layers of his and gives nothing out. Besides his work falls off.

–Do you say that because –

–he disagrees with me? I've thought of that, Laurence, I have, believe me. I have no illusions about my age. Infinite space exhausts me. Look at my eyes, I've worn them out with listening.

–I know.

–Of course we could secretly brain-drain him to the States, but so far they have put out no tentative feelers even, let alone tempting offers, except to me, and I don't want to start a second life. Would you, Laurence?

–No, sir.

–No. Of course not. Why, I'd need three separate lives to catch up, and then what would I do?

–What will he do, Something?

–You may well ask, my boy, you may well ask. How did we get on to this, most unscientific, oh yes, Dekko. How shall we recognise him, Laurence? We must devise a way.

I don't know how to reach him. As one of my ex-patients who assumes that analysis consists of sitting dumbly with the analyst, feeding him no items and then giving up, your kind of science doesn't work, says Dr Dekko. He doesn't tell his wife about the tentative feelers and the tempting offers he receives after all to drain his brain across the ocean, or anyone, least of all me. He keeps them tight in those close-knit meridians that do not fluctuate one inch into any wavering outlines. Yet something emanates out of his small corona in the mad morse of neural cells that reject in every cycle of his undrained brain the one decoying premiss as it blocks with irrelevance the programming of both his ambition and his loyalty. So that he starts again, feeding the items of his desires, disgorging their binary arithmetic on wide white sheets of hope except for the one item of his wife's own chemistry now galled by the banality of the same untender story with the mixture not quite as before owing to the presence of plump affronted virtue. My wife? Well, what about her?

–Wouldn't she like to get away, to go to America? Have you asked her?

–What do you mean? Who said anything about going to America?

–Surely you've had offers. All the scientists do. Especially since –

–Since what, Laurence?

–Well, since the Theory.

–THE Theory, you call it. Whose theory?

–Oh, come off it, Tim.

–Our theory. Yes, team-work, Head called it on television. I noticed he mentioned no names.

–Names, what do names matter?

–Ah, the anonymous greater glory of science.

–My dear Tim, the television people can't clog the public with a lot of names, except for Tell-Star and such.

–Just because you have to appear anonymously on programmes in your field –

–But surely you don't think the brief subliminal flash of names under your episodic image remains for one moment in the public mind? You have your name on the technical stuff.

–Yes. At least some people know who does the work around here.

–Smile, Tim, smile.

–What good will that do me? I work all round the clock as Head gets more and more dotty and turns pop-scientist –

–And takes all the credit, you mean.

–Credit must circulate. Otherwise energy falls off.

–And in no time at all you have no shocks, no movement and no life.

–Oh, stop quoting Head's obiter dicta at me. You know nothing about it, Laurence, they have no relevance at all.

–You don't like him much, do you Tim?

–Of course I like him. I . . . I used to admire him enormously, who wouldn't. When I first came here, and even long before, I thought of him as a, yes, as a god, a giant among intellects, I mean, why, his work as a young man, well, you wouldn't understand, but –

–But scientific genius gets played out at forty? Do you believe that, Tim. Do you . . . fear it?

–Of course not. Head went from strength to strength,

and so will I. And so will you, Laurence, in your own queer field, well, I mean, when you get your vigour back.

–Only you don't think I will?

–I didn't say that. These things take time. Everyone knows a serious illness affects the metabolism of the brain, at first I mean.

–As does old age in the end?

–But Laurence, you can't call yourself old.

–I meant Professor Head.

–So you've got it all lined up. You brain-drain me away so that your wife has a nice clear field all to herself as Head dodders into retirement. But she'll have to show a bit of brilliance, you great innocent. Stop spying on me, Laurence, stick to your more naïve, less empirically minded patients. Yes, yes, I see, what does my wife think, wouldn't she like, oh Laurence, you great clumsy oaf.

I have heard this conversation in waves that run backwards through time, I even seem to supply the words and their internal combustion pushes them along though I don't do the steering. We make the bumps as we go and leave them on the road like horse-power waste as the little orange lights flicker on the control-panel, over Erase, Next Instruction, Uninhibit, One-shot-trigger and things like that, which flicker in Dekko's eyes while his mouth dips a little and he apologises, I get so tired, he says.

–I know, Tim. I know. You do work hard. I only meant, about your wife, she might want to get away from, well, have you talked to her at all, Tim, have you asked her? I mean, perhaps more than just scientific facts come into it.

–You think you know a lot, don't you?

–Not in your field, Tim, of course.

–Yes well, I admit, I mean I agree, that scientific facts, as our admin friend would say, never hurt anyone. Only when –

–People –

–Yes. People. Sometimes I think you read right into me, Laurence. I get frightened by your eyes. Not frightened exactly, but, unsettled, shall we say. They've got so big. They look as if they might come right out of your head on long stalks, and yet they stay deep sunk. Do you take drugs or something?

–I seem to live backwards, or rather, part of me, my ears and eyes, as if their atoms consisted of anti-matter. I realise this makes no scientific sense.

–It has no physical meaning. I mean even in theory you'd cancel them out or if not you then other matter.

–Probably sleeplessness does it. And a sort of weird forgotten memory of, a wish –

–A wish? For what?

–To die again. And a fear. They go together. Sometimes I think that during my death I became everyone I know.

–But you didn't die, Laurence.

–A sort of love, perhaps, which I left behind. Because at other times I feel appalled and overwhelmed by the ineffectualness of love, or friendship, or tolerance. Or perhaps I only mean the ineffectualness of my own, for I feel none of these things, they died with me, so that I can't after all expect anything from them.

–You say, at other times, you mean like now?

–Like now. Forgive me, Tim, I don't know what's come over me.

–I think I know. But if I put it into words it would sound mean and disagreeable. Everything I say nowadays sounds mean and disagreeable, after I've said it.

–I suppose pure scientists tend to get frightened of words, because they don't use them. I believe that poets also get frightened of them, for the opposite reason. But it all comes to the same thing in the end. We all have to face the same facts.

–I think, perhaps, I will talk to Sally. Insofar as I can. And to Brenda.

–Why Brenda?

–My eldest daughter. You've met her many times. You don't have much memory for names, do you?

–No. For some reason –

–But then, as you would say, what do names matter? She takes her common entrance next year. An upheaval wouldn't do her any good. Maths and physics. Yes, she takes after me. Bright girl, brighter than the other two. Yours also, I gather. But then, women in science, you know, they don't reach the top flight. Still, I will talk to her. Harvard, after all . . But then –

The permutations of desires start grinding round his inner automation at the slow speed of unhealing time, rejecting in each cycle the one decoying premiss in two parts *a* and *b* with the basement of his life feeding in again the same two blocking items. Unless perhaps I have pushed his atoms a little towards his daughter's physics with a word thrown in that might make rings around those infinite distances and lasso him with more widening circumstances, him, Sally, Brenda and the less bright other two whose names I can't remember.

Inside the mirror on the landing of my consulting-room the shape stares back, spinning meridians, latitudes and spirals that grow and fill the entire glass but silently, emanating no messages, no nervous handwriting, no atoms of any anger, love or wonder. Something however creates the undulations and if not anger or love then some nebulous memory, surely, behind the eyes. But the eyes close to avoid the issue of their death and amazing recovery. The pain behind them resolves the optical image in the dark, as with a change of lenses, so that inside the mirror the tall thin man stares back, as before death, before recovery, as when life took its normal course through blood-vessels, nerve-fibres, muscle spindles, tendons, flesh and such.

These ache. Their returned presence mocks the spinning curves, the latitudes and spirals and the wavering outlines that grow suddenly monstrous before vanishing as if they had not wavered or spun there at all, curves doubling, trebling each other's trebles like water rippling from a stone thrown or a word perhaps, filling the entire mirror or, with some others, the whole room, bursting its walls, the house, the street, the square or the whole sky. The blood-vessels, nerve-fibres, muscle spindles ache, form some sort of presence, something to hold on to at least, such as the door-knob that moves away into a shaft of light where hangs the voice of a remote girl-spy with all its wavering outlines widening out from a small dry foetus of well how do you feel today into a threnody of unacknowledged anguish that fills the room, bursting its walls, the house, the entire sky untenable because I have come to the conclusion that you see radiation, Larry, and radiation consists after all of decay, degeneration so that you see the death that lies inherent in all living existence but why? why me?

–I don't know, Larry. Don't you remember anything, a moment, a non-temporal moment perhaps, of total knowledge, or total intuition, some final decision for or against made in the light of the person you had become midway through life in the dark wood?

–For or against what?

–For or against, well, the clarity of total consciousness.

–No, I remember nothing but opaqueness. Or something perhaps –

–Like, volition? As opposed to will?

–moving through space, forewards but back at the same time, as if I consisted of anti-matter for ever cancelled out –

–That makes no scientific sense.

–as if in all our words and gestures, acts and attitudes we effected some sort of parallel penetration into whatever had originated them, their primeval atom, say, with built-in unstableness.

–Well, not built-in, Larry, the instability would have occurred in the next moment of creation, together with time and space, causing, at once or ultimately, the big bang or whatever. The moment between nothingness and time. Or, if you like, between eternity and time. So vice versa. The moment of death, neither before nor after, affording a non-temporal transition in time from one state to another, through which the two interpenetrate into a total consciousness of both the whole of before and the whole of after, the first enabling you to choose once and for ever, don't you remember anything?

–Since I didn't in fact have to choose, clearly none of that can have occurred, if it does at all, how could it? Sometimes I feel that during my death I became everyone I know, even my patients perhaps, whose names and the names of whose neuroses I can't remember, whose aggressions, inabilities and blindnesses I have absorbed over the years, unless mine perhaps, so that how could I choose? Do you believe that possible: at the moment of death, instead of facing oneself, if at all – but what exactly happened to me, Brenda, did I really die?

–I don't know. The doctor said so many things, such as most satisfactory in the circumstances –

–but then circumstances do not touch everyone with the same meridians –

–or that recent experiments in resuscitation have shown that life ebbs away slowly, and can remain a long while in a body otherwise incapable of it. They can maintain life in some organs as you know. But sooner or later comes a moment – which they can always tell, except – well, they can't tell one thing, the precise moment when the soul has left the body.

–The soul, Brenda?

–The psyche, you prefer to call it.

–Oh names, what do names matter? Sometimes I feel that during my death I became quite unsettled she looks as the latitudes and spirals fill the room again out of some word perhaps thrown in to split a nucleus unstable inside the small dry foetus of interest which grows into an anxious query about death, her own, not merely that of others, briefly but hugely glimpsed, personally envisaged not dispassionately observed, so that the cells whirl round their alarming morse around the lymphatic glands, which he said they should examine too with radio-active isotopes. They couldn't do it before, I mean in your state of health, they couldn't submit you to further tests, and at first they said you had nothing organically wrong with you, no, not your eyes or ears either, nothing at all, just nerves. That ache, and blood vessels, muscle spindles, bones flesh and such that form some sort of presence to hold on to, such as your patients. Shouldn't you perhaps start seeing a few patients again?

The voice leaps from the shaft of light saying how do you feel and things like that they've telephoned, many of them. Many? Well, several. It might do you good.

–I'd hardly call that a sensible reason for seeing patients.

Whose names I can't remember and whose aggressions, inabilities and blindnesses I have absorbed over the years so that I couldn't possibly have chosen anything if any choice occurs inside the latitudes and spirals that fill the room, forming an anxious query about death as traced with radio-active isotopes leaving something behind, volition perhaps as opposed to will which, when it finally catches up can in a sudden flash say gug, grr, pa-pa like a doll bent.

At twelve years old Potato Head has learnt to manage the double syllable quite well, echoing her upper and her lower shape that look like two cells filled with sap and preparing for separation. But other words come hard through her cleft palate. Gug-gug-grr, she says. Everyone looks at us in the big canteen and I feel overcome with shame, don't talk, Potato.

–Gug, gug, nnn-da.

–Stop it, Potato.

–Grr – da.

–Come to mummy, Potato Head, come, here, this way. Here, my love.

Potato Head turns her watery eye towards the voice and gropes at it, burying her blind face into her mother's lap. Grr . . . da . . . grrr . . . da, she sobs.

–She says her grandmother has died, Something tells me. Well, we'd better go to her, hadn't we, my sweet?

–Her grandmother? Who, for heaven's sake? And where?

–Not far. Next door, in fact, upstairs.

Dippermouth weighs a ton in my right arm and wakes with a short burst of ringing. Where's Gut got to, he asks.

–Next door. Upstairs.

We have become quite estranged, Something and I, as if my impatience with Potato Head came between us, which of course it does, for I envy her ability to hear and translate my daughter's speech. Next door in fact upstairs Gut Bucket stands stock still under the bed of his large unconscious grandmother, respectfully receiving her incontinence. Hi, fat grandma, says Dippermouth and dips his mouth a little while Potato Head gropes blindly towards the smell. Gug, gug, . . . grrr . . . pa–pa, she wails like a bent doll.

–We'll have to change her, Something says. Help me, Lazarus.

The name floods through me incontinently and I remember everything, the almost perfect spheres, the travel agent, the journalists, good people all, the meridians like elastic and the cat's cradle we played, the canals and the horse-power, the pond of heavy water sinking like my heart, the giant trumpet and the ear of the world turning away lined with cork peeled off in curved segments wounded in bright orange. I hold my two hands over my ears and shout to drown the pain. I can't, I can't, I can't.

But I do, because Something tells me I must. I stand behind the big fat woman's head and slip my hands under her sweaty arms. Something takes her under the thighs on one side, Potato Head unexpectedly strong on the other and we lift her off the bed onto the floor where she moans and makes a large puddle. Something changes her bedclothes quickly, laying a plastic sheet on which we lift her back. She weighs a million million years.

–Good people, good, these hands that saved. I shall flounce out and, then, what will you, do.

–Hush, grandma, says Gut Bucket in a cleaned out echoing voice, don't tire yourself.

–Useful, for the, waste-disposal, Bucket, boy. The bond, remains, where –

–Here, grandma. Dippermouth Blues, grandma.

–Oh yes. My, how . . . and you, what do they . . . ?

–Lazarus, madam.

–The bond, my, rights, you know.

–Gug – gug – grrr.

–Ah my Sweet Potato.

She dies, her muscles tighten, her juices dry up. The journalists bring a stretcher and lower her through the puddle on the floor into the chapel below where a coffin on wheels receives her in the midst of lilies and white carnations that absorb the smell. Gug – gug, Potato Head sobs in my arms as we walk down the spiral staircase, there, my love, don't cry, my little one, my daughter, and the Blues played by Jonas and his Jovials wail writhing up the aisle, don't cry my love until at last the funeral music stops.

–Bury me under the cork-trees, says the body of Something's mother in the sudden silence amid the lilies and carnations and Potato Head screams.

–Gug – gug – grrr – na da, na ba, na ba.

–Of course she has died, my little one. And we must bury her. She only speaks from reflex action, it will pass. Look, it has passed.

–Pa – pa. Pa – pa. Alalala – love you.

We walk the earth on our ten feet like a decimated centipede, Something and Dippermouth, Potato Head and I, Gut Bucket bringing up the rear. Tall blue flowers line our path. Ahead of the procession Something picks a few here and there as she walks, and lays them in a long and shallow basket. I pick some too to help her, but they won't pick, they draw out on and on from deep down, and come up with the root that wriggles like a lizard. Do your flowers have live roots? Yes of course, we have to live on something.

–Pa – pa, wa – wag – ga?

–I don't know, my sweet. Where do we go, Something? I mean, I would like to know and it might help the children not to get too tired and nervous.

–One never does know exactly, does one, Lazarus. If one did one wouldn't get there. But we have to find the lady.

–The lady. Now what? Another secret instruction?

–Every spy-story has a lady, you know that.

–Oh, you mean the decoy blonde? Well, why didn't you say so?

–Because I don't know the colour of her hair, her shape, her age, or anything about her.

–You seem pretty helpless I must say, for a girl-spy. How will you know her then? By a secret sign I suppose?

–In a way. By the square we shall find her in.

–Oh, so we move in squares now, do we?

–Of course, haven't you noticed? Every circle has its

square, you know that, Lazarus. Every sphere has its cube. We live in squares and on square roots.

–I can't see anything square about these roots. Wriggling lizards and worms, moles, rats, ferrets and snails. Do you really expect me to eat those?

–I expect nothing of you that you don't freely want to give. We'd better stop here.

–What's happened to you, Something, why do you act like some sort of schoolmistress, so estranged, so distant?

–You make the distances, Someone.

–Me? I don't. Good heavens, you've called me by my real name. You haven't done that for a long time.

–Pa – pa.

–You have many names to answer to, Lazarus, and you don't always answer. I even send you little notes sometimes, but I don't suppose you read them.

–Notes? I've never seen little notes from you.

–Well, you'd hear them, actually, or see their sounds.

–Oh. Yes I do receive your notes. But you don't exactly put your signature on them, do you?

–Stop quarrelling, dad.

–I like to preserve a certain discretion in the circumstances. Besides, you don't really read them so what difference does it make?

–I shall scream for attention like a child of three if you two go on. Time to eat.

–Bang-bang, pop, time to eat.

–Smile, Something.

–Well . . . you smile first.

Potato Head gives a loud gurgling laugh. She hasn't heard this code before. I smile and Something smiles and takes the lizards from the basket to fry them alive so that they shrivel into chopped up cubes. What spheres? I mean, what circumstances?

–I beg your pardon? Oh. My professional circumstances.

–Ah yes. As a girl-spy. I don't altogether like your profession, you know.

–I don't either. As a matter of fact for a long time I haven't had much future as a girl-spy.

–You mean, because of me?

–Well, yes and no. Without you I wouldn't have any future at all. I mightn't even exist. But you think you can live without causality, pretending that each moment has its own separateness, that anyone might come or go in that moment like an electron. Why, you might as well ask for the moon.

–I didn't ask for any moons.

–Sometimes I wish I had married a poorer man, a man less well endowed, I mean.

–D'you know, these square roots don't taste too bad. Not very satisfying, though.

–Coo – na – ska.

–Quite right, Potato Head, cube roots. Bright girl.

–Say, pop, we could live on cube roots for ever, couldn't we? Let one run up and another run down, take any number, to infinity.

–Well, they leave me with a hungry hole.

I sense the chasm there beyond the trees ahead with the round lake of heavy water. I fear the presence of the dead fat woman with the heavy buttocks on my chest and the busybody hands that rummage in my pain, deliver me of great weights which go off into orbit only to return, heavier still with infinite·calculations raised to the fifth power. The daybreak reached however meets us at a great height, looking over the sloping woods, not into the round pond of heavy water but down at a distant square house with the roof right off. Inside a large square room surrounded by a narrow corridor an old lady walks about, bent almost double, wearing a flowered house-coat.

–The quaternity, Something murmurs and starts to cry.

–But Something, she has white hair.

–How did you know, Lazarus, have you learnt to see?

–Come, we must go down.

The firmness of my tone dispels her sudden fatigue. Yes, yes. We must go down. Yes. Let's go down.

She speaks busily, brusquely. What have I done to her? I have not seen, not heard, I have quenched her with my quibbling, absorbed her into my opaqueness. I move through my sleeplessness and my internal decay, where I have someone and I don't know who. A sort of giant horse-fly falling into dust, who radiates and writes me little notes unsigned which I don't read, losing points all the way.

The white-haired lady, bent double in her flowered house-coat welcomes us in dumb-show and Potato Head translates. La-ka – Alalala. Foo-dra.

–Thank you, thank you, we can do with some real food. We love you too.

–Lavava. Da-gra-basa-ya.

–Yes. I remember, the man said you had inherited the patch of earth next to ours. Thank you for recognising us. A little recognition can do a –

–Fa.

–Four? Already? When do you expect him?

–Soo.

–Will it . . . hurt?

The old lady and Potato Head both put their hands to their ears.

–I see. Yes. I thought so.

She hobbles round among her antique furniture and tapestries. The blue flowers on her house-coat smell of lilies and carnations. She takes my hand and leads me to a tapestry embroidered with the Whale and River constellations, the Serpent-Bearer and Cygnus whose Deneb shines brighter than fifty million suns, fifteen hundred light-years away and yet no brighter than Vega in the Lyre like fifty-two suns twenty-six years away. Gug, says Potato Head. It draws up to reveal a corridor full of doors, the first of which opens on a young man who sits on a divan in a small square room. The top half of his head stands open like a casserole lid and he spoons out the contents of his brain to eat it. He smiles for it tastes good. She shuts the door and leads me to another, behind which the same young man sits on a divan bed repeat performance. Each door, all round the corridor, reenacts the same scene until at last we reach the opening in the tapestry and re-enter the large square room where Something looks anxious.

–I don't think you should have shown him how. He did the others in unconsciousness.

–Not all of them, Something, not Potato Head.

Who feels for my hand so that the sap of her new strength flows into me.

–A little consciousness can do a lot, you said. Surely you want me to see and understand?

–I can't bear you to suffer.

She starts crying again. What have I done to her? Dippermouth toddles up. Dial me, ma, you'll see, you've just lost contact, ma, dial me, please, you haven't dialled me for so long.

She takes him on her lap and dials him through her tears, the big hand a quarter round and so forth listening carefully to the uneven morse and staring hard into his face.

–I can't hear. I can't see through my tears.

Potato Head holds my hand. Ya, she says.

–I know. Here, Gut Bucket, stand close, you'll come in useful for the placenta. Dippermouth, stay with your mother and keep trying. Potato, don't lose my hand.

The old lady comes towards me and pushes me onto the divan with her bent head. My face from the lower level looks into hers, my eyes watch her sensitive hands as they take up the knife and cut carefully along the eyebrows and around above the ears. The noise deafens my brain. The houses on the distant edge of the world's ear laugh like asses' jaws, the giant trumpet blares, the walls come tumbling down. The top lid of my head opens up slowly and with a trembling hand I take the offered spoon. I ladle out the food from inside my casserole head and hand the spoon first to Potato Head, who takes it to her mother. Something sips at it disconsolately, then gulps, and revives. She gets up, comes towards me with Dippermouth ticking weakly on her left arm and the spoon in her right hand. She dips the spoon into my head, feeds Gut Bucket, then hands it back to me to dip into my head again and feed Potato Head myself. Potato Head grows strong and takes my hand. She feeds me with the spoon. One for mummy she says in silence or perhaps in her glug language which I now hardly notice. One for pa . . . pa. One for your Sweet Potato. One for Dippermouth. She feeds me like a child. The blood drips into Gut Bucket who stands in a deep double meditation full of my placenta and smiles a beatific smile. But the noise crashes through me still. Dippermouth now fed revives. He dips his mouth with a loud creak, twenty to four, got you, twenty past eight, twenty-five past seven, and on until my eardrums burst and his mouth joins itself to form one vertical needle that swivels with a screech in one wave-band round the dial, emitting a whole agony of gunfire as the boys come roaring through the screen on motorbikes, swerving and bending low, their white crash-helmets like big moons in orbit, falling down out of orbit, vanishing, falling, crash.

He walks into the room in black leather and white helmet. He lifts the transparent vizier, looks at me and laughs.

–How do, pater, he says in a mock-Victorian voice, or else mock-army, who knows in all that noise. Tin Roof reporting for duty, sir.

The way devised by Professor Head to obtain recognition for his junior colleague Dr Dekko consists in dying before his time like a great clumsy oaf. Nor does he undergo any amazing recovery and the pain of mine clatters through me again, shaking the giant decaying horse-fly of my internal body, sending its anti-atoms in a whirl of mass morse along the fibres of my loneliness.

The sequences of happiness, hurt pride and social conversations which I hear in advance or backwards have not included this, only the scent of lilies and white carnations round him on the coffin. I have groped blindly into him, feeling his complex meridians with my fingers but failing to massage a few more moments of my unwanted time into them. In death too his transparency has resistance but his strength now escapes me along the procession of respectful mourners, as long and detailed as the journalists' obituaries and as surprising. It forms an elongated mosaic of bent heads from many countries, government departments, towns, universities; editors, television producers and interviewers, students, scholars and unknown beneficiaries of his publicly diffused learning, of his privately diffused kindness, housewives, nurses, business-men, shopkeepers, poets and scientists, three daughters and their children, two sons and theirs.

Brenda, whose name has re-acquired her shape, walks by my side in tears. Next to her Mrs Dekko sobs at the passing of her plump virtue and of a great example, whose junior colleague Dr Tim Dekko, peeled of appearances and tense with mixed emotions, looks whiter than the lilies and carnations on the coffin.

I pull up the flowers of my sorrow on the way and every stem comes up with a big root alive like a wriggling lizard, rat, or mole that gnaws at my decaying interior body. I fill myself with earth and pour it down into the grave. Something of me gets lowered with the coffin and I shall obtain no answer to the query of my second life or any other.

The one-stance man has not attended the funeral for he has but one stance. He sits behind his telephones and trays, inventing his own indispensability with red zigzags, curves, black bars of varying heights, regiments of rectangles filled with coloured cards, sliced silhouettes of people. I never go anywhere, he says, or perhaps alas I can't leave my office. And the secretaries tap their harmonised morse beyond the door with the round window in it. So that they can see, he says, and tell my wife, that I don't get up to anything.

–He never did find much time for the elementary courtesies, except when he hoped to get something out of them. Well, what do you expect, a Blue Giant? No conversation occurs except in the distracted atoms of her neural cells that race round in mad morse, a special relationship, he said. Oh that. But a special relationship requires a special radiation, you should know that by now. I did, I refused him on that ground alone at first. I made it my one condition. Ah, but you inhibited him from the start, of course he bent the laws and quibbled to win points in such circumstances. What circumstances? Those of your contempt. So she snarls useless reproaches at his opaqueness for in this type of communication the echo decreases with the fourth power of the distance between two bodies and no conversation occurs except as poison racing round in mad morse along the fibres of her fury at her own limitation, standing beside the grave where something of me got lowered, what did you say?

–What?

–You called me something.

–Did I? No, I couldn't have. Come on, let's go.

–You did. You say the oddest things. During the funeral you muttered something about a bucket.

–Well, I don't know.

–Sometimes I wish I had married a simpler man, more imaginatively illiterate, I mean, who couldn't read me, and who wouldn't bother to learn, though that too can hurt. But as you said once, it struck me at the time, character never hurts, lack of character does.

–Did I say that? I thought someone else –

–No. No. He wouldn't. Where do you go, Larry? I mean, do you have anyone? I often suppose you have. I wouldn't blame you. Life has a way of balancing things.

–I move through my sleeplessness and my internal decay. You can smell it, can't you? I have someone there. A sort of giant horse-fly falling into dust.

She starts crying again. She fears the unknown in me but doesn't label it with a big round zero, or if she does she sees through it at times as one watches the absolute immobility of a wing against the ultra-violet light through the window of a plane flying at the speed of years, unless perhaps the nervous handwriting of distant nebulae bleeping across the dial, saying what do you want, Larry?

–To learn to love. I mean, not just to walk through people like so much moon-dust, not just to see and hear the degenerate matter and accept –

–Like Stance.

–Stance?

–I like your name for him. It helps me to – detach myself. He likes people, he says, he sees the worst and best in them and accepts it, but only to make use of it and shrug it off. Unless at any point the worst or even the best needles his own self-satisfaction and then, oh then, he condemns and destroys.

–We all do that, Brenda. Some people have transparency but resistance, like solid light, so that you merge with them but can't walk through them. Some have a soft opaqueness, which deflects the light waves travelling through it and upsets the definition. That hurts. You can walk easily right through them but in a slimy contact. Sometimes I feel that during my death I became everyone I know and I left myself behind. Or else, if that means anything nowadays, as if I had acquired something of creation, but nothing of humanity.

Means of communication have lost their secrecy and anyone could photograph them, record them, amplify them to the hundredth power and go stark raving mad. We no longer walk the earth on our ten or twelve feet, we travel on roaring motorbikes, in petarding sports-cars, in siren-ambulances, in fire-engines that clang through towns, shooting the lights, why did you shoot the lights, Tin Roof, I didn't, sir, I shot the policeman, and in express trains that whistle through long tunnels, thunder across continents, crash into grand canyons, leaving us maimed, half-buried in a maze of twisted steel. Why, Tin Roof, why all the hurry? Look what it does to us, to our bodies, to our nerves.

No one would recognise our once almost spherical shapes now, neither our cylinders nor our inner circles. Gut Bucket looks dented. Dippermouth peers through a smashed dial, Potato Head's upper and lower shapes seem held together by only the slenderest waist. As for Something she hardly speaks these days without crying or snapping, her face grown quite rectangular with little orange lights flickering all over it. So that our nerves fall out of us in great bundles of wires that bulge out of our bowels. We never play cat's cradle with our meridians now. Only Tin Roof with his crash-helmet seems perpetually unharmed. But one thing puzzles me, can you explain it, Something? The bent old lady in the square –

–Oh, Lazarus, don't bother me with transferred identities.

Why shouldn't she take over? You should understand these things by now.

–You once told me, Something, to let the argument proceed before clogging it. I merely wanted to know how they buried her. The plot promised to her, beside ours, remember, has an oblong shape, well, like any other. But if she died bent like that, from poverty, she must have needed a right-angled coffin, and a right-angled grave.

–No, sir. They put her in the square on the hypotenuse. Surely you must have noticed it. I drove into the wrong square at first, you see, hence the time I took, and the noise, apologies, pater, but anyway she had plenty of room.

At twenty-four, Tin Roof astonishes me with his polite charm and his love of noise. I never know whether he mocks me or not. He speaks respectfully but his tone makes me uneasy. He doesn't take after me at all, I never had polite charm, and never went in for noise, I collect silences. Why do you like all this noise, Tin Roof? I mean, thank you for your explanation, which I find entirely satisfactory, more than Something deigns to give, but you haven't answered my first question yet. Why all this noise? I collect silences.

–What happened to your collection, sir? I'd like to see it.

–Oh, really! You do it on purpose. I can't get through to you at all.

–Tin Roof, sir. Really hasn't come back from orbit yet.

–Orbits! Ellipses! Meridians! Latitudes! The Travel Agent surrounded us with them protectively, to guide us, they used to stretch like elastic so that we could contain everything within ourselves. We used to play with them. What's happened to our meridians, Something, why do we lie buried under this twisted steel?

–She won't tell you the truth, dad, already on the edge of that big round hole you came out of like a sinking nincompoop I warned her not to give you her hand. But she got herself all besotted with you. Oh, no, Someone, I play it your way.

Dippermouth imitates her with a snarling simper and I want to hit him but Something stops me or my half burial under twisted steel. Potato Head feels for my hand, sniffs at her failure to find it and my lack of help. Gut Bucket keeps very quiet, can hardly breathe in fact with his caved in thorax and I don't care. Only Tin Roof in his crash-helmet sits unharmed.

–I told you, Lazarus, you can't get rid of origin by giving it names, except for a time. Origin comes back.

–Whose origin? I never fathered this brood, you said so yourself, it came out of your knee, a hard-boiled egg, and you flung –

–Don't mention it.

–the slices and nevertheless I trusted you. I helped you after all. Some trust. You've let me down, Something, let me down badly.

–Please, let's wait until the salvage men come and get us out. Our nerves have spilled all over the place, look at them.

–And what about that fine upstanding young man sitting around unharmed, why doesn't he do something?

–He can't, Lazarus. Not until you get through to him. Oh please don't let's go on like this.

–Like what?

–It makes me feel so . . . desolate.

She cries. I feel half buried in twisted steel and cold indifference. What have they done to me, and what have they to do with me? I want to go back, I have left a wife in a state of shock that invites predatory selfishness, I have left jobs undone, patients uncured, theories unthought out, wasted here in this twisted steel and these spilled out nerves, waiting for a long lever-crane of criss-cross metal to lift the train off us. I watch it through the window as it creaks and clanks, diameters round from left to right and then from right to left, its cabin off-centre with an automan inside who operates the switches so that the cubic weight at the short end moves round with it and the pulley at the long end travels along it at the speed of slowly returning health. But it will never get here to lift the twisted steel from all this lot that has nothing to do with me.

–But it does, Lazarus, it belongs to you. Why didn't you tell the journalists about them? I asked you to. I made only one condition.

–What journalists? They've gone. Or never came.

–Your daily friends, Lazarus.

–I have no friends.

–You let them go. You've always let them go, moving through people as through so much dust. But they'll come back.

–Have I moved through you, Something?

–I tried to help you. I even write you little notes sometimes.

–But I can't read waves and sounds, Something, not from you. You've only enabled me to read them in others, and I don't like it. I can't talk to people, Something, and it hurts.

–You chose the supersonic, above words, remember.

–Well, then, all the more –

–I know. And we did use words. Too many. But you insisted on the transit drink, as I knew you would, on account of your name. But I hoped that somehow, with your five geometries, you'd manage.

–I have no geometries, you must have made a mistake. Or else I lost them, left them on the plane, in the pocket of the seat in front, or in the upper parietal lobe.

–These geometries work through people, Lazarus, you said so yourself. You must trust your friends.

–You mean, Dekko, and Stance, and people like that? How can I? I draw the line as a rule between one solar system and another.

–Yes, well, you go too far, I mean you exaggerate.

–I trust you, Something, or at least, I trusted you once.

–And others too. Your daily friends, Lazarus, from all your days.

–My daily friends, the journalists. I don't understand. You mean Tell-Star, and people like that?

–You studied with him.

–I – good God –

–At Tin Roof's age.

–Ph.D. Sociology.

–Something like that.

–He masturbates and picks his nose in his unscreened existence. I could read right into him as well.

–So do you, Lazarus.

–What!

–You masturbate your brain with false causalities that heal nobody, infinite calculations that increase the distances.

–But Something, haven't I proved –

–to your own satisfaction, yes.

–Have I become Stance, then?

–A little more of his genial unconcern wouldn't have harmed you. Instead of – his other aspect. It . . . It makes me feel so . . . desolate.

–Tell-Star! Of course.

Beyond the door with the round window in it the machine clatters out its binary arithmetic on virgin sheets of paper covered with ones and zeros. Tim Dekko stands by the operand, his tight-wrapped face turned towards Brenda at the control-panel who brings down the switches in a quick competent succession. The little orange lights flicker like stars over Erase, Inhibit, Block, Prime, Pulse, Mesh and things like that. At his feet a mesh of wires wrapped in green, grey and red plastic bulges from the machine's lower bowels onto the floor.

Brenda has left the back of the drum open, facing the door with the round window in it, so that, says Stance, my secretaries can see, and tell my wife, that I don't get up to anything, except Tim Dekko and Brenda and two engineers in dumb show beyond the drum full of power thyratrons like regimented cylinders wearing haloes of blue light. Yes well, we all have cylinders, when you come to think of it, but some tick away quietly, bouncing their messages against the moon, some have more depth, more guts, and a shining inner face silent with quiet meditation, some have a double shape that fills itself with sap as with vibrant resistance you can see into but cannot penetrate. Others, like me, have nothing but a thick opaqueness of flesh which you slice through like butter, failing to make more than a slimy contact, until the reality of a dead professor or someone, so much more present even in his death than in his dying life moves through me with its vibrant atoms that whirl round mine, create resistance.

Tim Dekko turns his tight-wrapped face towards Brenda at the control-panel and yells his head off in the dumb-show of the silent film framed by the door's round window which becomes oval, replaced by a narrow shaft of sound and the long rectangle of their conversation in twinkling orange lights, Alarm Reset, Next Instruction and the clatter of binary arithmetic, oh hello Laurence, how did you get in?

–Brenda, I must talk to you.

–Not now, Larry, not now.

She pulls down switches quickly, competently and jots down her comments on a pad in a column called Narrative, figures in the column called Location, a tick under Next Instruction.

–Brenda –

–Won't it wait, Larry?

–I've remembered something.

–What?

–Something . . . of the narrative, the location.

–Oh, go away, Larry. Can't you see we must finish this programme.

–What programme?

–Track, eight four two one. Syne shot. Block Prime Pulse Mesh.

–When did I marry you, Brenda?

–Oh go away, Larry, for heaven's sake, go.

No doubt Stance would have watched the operation and shrugged, his grey eyes veiled with knowledgeable labels at my poor performance. He would have done much better in the circumstances, but then, circumstances do not touch everyone with their enmeshed meridians. He has one stance to adopt and with it he lassoes my wife, Tim's wife, and they come like mares. They like one-stance men, they read them from afar, then having deciphered their one stance get angry and embittered at their own lack of love. Remote Bermuda dies with me vicariously as she moves out of the one stance that melts away from my enmeshed meridians. But if I had really died I would have had, surely, a flash of something that would not translate itself into indifference. I have lost the equations that enable people to move through people easily without love. I hear, see, read all the inscriptions that emanate in waves from the radiating coronas of all their little solar systems, unless they only pretend to emit, like actors. And underneath the hearing, seeing, I have corked ears, blind eyes, unfeeling hands, I speak through a cleft palate, break my promises, I have let something go.

–But you don't suffer the children to come, if I may say so, sir.

–Forgive me, Tin Roof. I couldn't bear the noise.

–Or the smell either, sir, or the glugging of communication, or the ticking of your time.

–What shall I do, Tin Roof?

–Recognise me, father. A little recognition can do a lot for an unprodigal son.

–You mean, you remained at home all the time, while I expected the other?

–You expect him all the time, father.

–Really.

–Yes. He will come of course, he has never stopped coming.

–At forty-eight.

–Congratulations.

–How shall I recognise him?

–We all look alike, under the differentials.

–Yes well, the infinite divergencies confuse me.

–You confused us too, breaking the laws, altering our orbits. But look at it this way. If a film-director wanted to make a film featuring quintuplets, he'd never find five child actors, or actors of any age, looking exactly alike, unless he chose quintuplets, and the law of probability against their all having both acting talent and the required physique would work out at a thousand million million to one. So what would he do? He'd use illusion, and camera-tricks, and silhouettes and stand-ins.

–Why did we crash, Tin Roof?

–We had to. The rails got twisted.

–How did she, I mean where, will she . . . Tell me, son, have I divorced her or something?

–I got her out. Thank you for calling me son.

–Thank you for getting her out. Did it take long?

–That depends on your second life. You can begin it any time, she told you that once.

–You mean, you listened all the time?

–We didn't move in time, father.

–But you said I expected Really, all the time.

–During your life, father, your first life. And now also.

–And in that district you remained with me?

–We all remain. You can't get rid of us merely by giving us names and sending us into oblivion. Oblivion has its orbits, like everything, you know that.

–What shall I do, Tin Roof?

–You could, if you'd like to I mean, and don't mind the noise, climb on my pinion.

–Yes, I'd like that.

–Right. On you get.

–Go gently with me, Tin Roof. I mean, I know you find me tiresome, but the noise, well, it does give me such a pain inside my head.

–I brought you a crash-helmet, father.

–Oh, thank you. Thank you, son.

My arms in orbit round his waist, ourselves in orbit round the district of my time, we move in total immobility against the ultra-violet light, producing no vibration, no hum of silence even, until the circular steel house made out of our ellipses rises like a hemisphere above us and around. We land on the flat slice of its inner equator, surrounded by innumerable slices that diminish in space towards the rounded roof and this in spite of the curved door to the right. Alalala – pa – pa like a bent doll. My sweet Potato Head. Her hand gropes out for mine, her strength moves into me out of her double shape and back and into me again. The silent hum of the inner equator vibrates under our twelve feet as if they all belonged. Gut Bucket stands in quiet double meditation, his handle in my other hand and an ecstatic smile round both his inner and his outer rims. Something bends over Dippermouth and dials his needles as he ticks away in impulses that bounce back from her secret source as a girl-spy. They say you love me, Lazarus, she says.

–I do love you, Something, you know I do.

–But you have to go back.

–I don't want to go back.

–We'll have to clear out of this vehicle, father, it'll get pretty hot if that door shuts.

–Out where? Into empty space? No, we can't, we can't, can we, Something? I like it here.

–Well, it depends on you, really.

–Really? Will he come now?

–He'll come at the expected time of arrival, if you want him, Lazarus, and I know you do, you must. But I do so hate to see you suffer.

–I won't get out. Not through that door. I must pace out this radius, and square it, and divide it by the height, and multiply it by the number of slices, and then you see I'll know exactly how it works, quick, help me, keep busy, count the slices, yes, I accept them all.

–You must get out, Lazarus, you must.

–Don't panic, Something. A girl-spy doesn't panic.

–I know, I know, I have no future, but I must tell you, yes, I must. The house, Lazarus, the steel house. Someone designed it so that the door would close up automatically at maximum entropy and everyone left inside would die of absolute immobility from sheer heat.

–Entropy? What entropy? Who designed it, for heaven's sake?

–You did, Lazarus. You have a complicated brain. Oh, I know you can't help it, but it does make things difficult for a girl-spy with all those innumerable slices of you. Sometimes I wish I had married a poorer man –

–Oh cut that out, Something, you've never stopped saying I see nothing, understand nothing.

–But you do, Lazarus, you will. If you don't forget me.

–I'll never forget you, Something, because I won't leave this place. I don't believe in maximum entropy.

–Pa – pa, like a bent doll. Dippermouth's needles oscillate more and more weakly and very slowly the door closes.

Quick, get out. The heat becomes immeasurable. Gut Bucket starts melting into a pool of red hot metal. Potato Head crumbles like a giant decaying horse-fly. Something bends over Dippermouth as the atoms of total waste whirl around his dial and his impulses tick slower and slower. Only Tin Roof still roars round, drowning the vibrant hum, consisting now entirely of exhaust into which he picks me up, propels me with a jet into my belly, backwards into the closing door. I don't want to go back, I don't, I don't, pushes me, squeezes me through it as Something bends over Dippermouth and I fall, fall, fall to the loud ticking inside the district of my time.

2

Inside the mirror on the landing towards the lawyer's office the shape stares back the map-like contours of some unknown region, continent, galaxy perhaps with two craters or starless coalsacks radiating nothing. Something however creates the wavering outlines and if not the eyes then some faint memory, surely, behind the eyes, filaments of gas in violent motion or two extragalactic nebulae in collision, four or five hundred million years away. But the eyes close to avoid the issue of their death and amazing recovery. The closing resolves the optical image like a change of lenses, so that inside the mirror the tall thin man stares back, as before death, before recovery, as when life took its normal course through blood vessels, nerve fibres, muscle spindles, bones, flesh and such.

These ache, and comfort in the aching. Their returned presence mocks the wavering outlines that grow suddenly monstrous before vanishing as if they had not wavered there at all, round undulations doubling, trebling each other's trebles on a map of ocean depths, filling the entire mirror, or, with some others, the whole room, bursting its walls, the house, the street, the square and the whole sky. The blood-vessels, nerve fibres, muscle spindles form some sort of presence, something to hold on to at least, such as a banister gripped by the hand towards the next landing and the door marked W. E. Mellek, Solicitor, which opens to the touch or to the words come in of the well-living swarthy, my dear friend, how good to see you.

–Too.

The well-living and the redying easily merge their atoms since both hasten towards death regardless, the one from genial ignorance the other from some nebulous memory of something, surely, behind the eyes that ache and then what will you do?

–I beg your pardon?

–When we've got you through this – er – unfortunate business.

–Oh, that. Yes. If I relive that long.

–Come, my dear friend. We mustn't make a habit of talking in that way. Emotional blackmail, your wife, if I remember, called it. She said she couldn't stand it, in a statement, at least, to her solicitors, Winnie & Winnie, an excellent firm, not a cause at law of course, but it has gone down as a contributing factor. And of course, as we all know, emotional blackmail only works where emotion remains.

–Did she?

–Did she what?

–Say that?

–Indeed she did. She said, now where did I put the book of rules? Now where did I put that file? Ah, here. From that day on, she says, I think she means your recovery, ah yes, up here, we must place it in context, mustn't we, from that day on we ceased to communicate in any way whatsoever.

–I thought we communicated a great deal.

–Oh well, my dear Larry, women always say these things. Afterwards. They never loved from the start, it never worked, they always knew it wouldn't, though they tried, by every means, and so forth, to play it our way. They forget the good moments. If any. Sometimes of course, these don't occur, but on the whole . . . And then, during the good moments, or else much later, years later, they see only those, how good, after all and so forth.

–We all do that.

–Yes, yes, indeed. However, this won't suffice in a court of law, as perhaps you know. We must exclude collusion of course, but had you agreed at all, on a cause, desertion, or something else, a little quicker, very quick in fact. The Post Office ought to deal with undefended divorce cases, they clutter the courts. But you must, of course, provide a cause, and the waves begin again, first round the horn-rimmed glasses that glaze the soft Levantine eyes of Wilfred Edwin Mellek, Solicitor, then out in trembling undulations on a map of ocean depths. Or perhaps they only pretend to emit, like actors, filling the space immediately around him as he sits at his mahogany desk, no more, held still in tremulous space by the well-living flesh in loose black jacket, pin-stripe and wide white collar, for we mustn't make a habit of dying, must we, I mean once, I admit, impresses people, with such an amazing recovery thrown in for good measure but twice, well, nobody would take you seriously, a yogi trick, they'd say, some medical hoax or error, as you of all people should know. And why, they might not bury you.

–My wife told me she would have had me cremated. We communicated that much, I believe. She cried when she said that.

–And besides, it might not happen.

–Which? Death or recovery?

–Ha! My dear Larry, you always had a sense of humour, even at Cambridge, thank God you didn't lose it somewhere or should I say some time in that bit of eternity. Though your wife says – ah well, it doesn't matter. Of course, death happens to us all, indeed it does. I totally accept the fact, though seldom think of it, if at all. Tell me, I suppose everyone asks you that, don't you remember anything?

–I remember . . . something. A little.

The waves expand into a spiralling query from a small unstable nucleus of fear hidden like the square root of minus one deep inside the charm, the well-living swarthy flesh, the soft Levantine eyes and labyrinthine knowledge of law that makes up what you as a psychiatrist should know, I mean what happens to that thing you chaps call the unconscious when the body lies in the lowest state of life, if at all, well, they may put people on ice for years, I mean, what ought to happen, you must know the theory at least, does it tick on at a low imaginative level or what, did you dream, for instance?

–No. I never dream. At least –

–So you really remember nothing?

–I remember . . . a sort of enmeshment.

The waves retract a little to form an island round the word like a stone thrown that widens them again to lasso some concept at an infinite distance where we can expect, I mean, something.

–My dear Edwin, I don't know. I have no way of verifying that, don't let it worry you. To every man his own afterlife if any.

–You mean according to his expectations? If any.

–Or deserts. Which comes to the same thing.

The pain behind the eyes resolves the optical image of the widening rings back to the gentle undulations as before, around the horn-rimmed glasses to the space immediately around him at his red-leather topped mahogany desk, no more, held still in tremulous space again by the well-living flesh and easy tolerance of labyrinthine ways, which of course as a scientist you would need to verify, before they could have any validity as experience.

–Oh, experience.

–You speak like a true sceptic, my dear Larry, not I rejoice to see, like an empiricist. As if every proof had its alternative. And so it has, and so it has, in your line of country I expect, and certainly in mine. Which brings us back, I fear, to the business in hand. Yes, yes indeed.

He emanates the same sense of irrelevance that fills the room as to the business in hand of his strange profession built on the failures of men to live together in love and amity, despite the labyrinthine knowledge and interest still clinging to the gold-rimmed books and pushed back against the walls. He has a small free electron of fear that can suddenly accelerate in the field of the calm proton in parabolic orbit that emits thermally on a short wave-length filling half the room, no more, bursting no walls no city boundaries no frontiers no galactic fields but held in tremulous space by a certain mellow strength somewhere in that well-living softness and that kindly flesh the presence of which comforts, reassures as to the existence of neural cells, muscle spindles, blood vessels and such, behaving not, if I may say so, like a gentleman, she wants the alimony and full costs despite your possible agreement to give her cause –

–It doesn't matter.

–Hence, you see, my first question about your future plans. Your letter alarmed me somewhat.

–My letter?

–Yes, your letter. Don't look as if you had forgotten writing it, or wrote it in a trance or something. Though it wouldn't surprise me. I can catch a glimpse of what your wife means when she says – but never mind, where did I put that letter, ah, here.

–No, no. I remember it. I wrote it. I meant it.

The small and nervous handwriting fills the page at wide impersonal intervals like an equation worked down to the very end and frozen there in resolution as if x could really equal the square root of minus one in the unfamiliar context of the lawyer's file. All this about retiring, all right, withdrawing, to the simple life, close to the soil, the sun, the stars, why, my dear Larry, I know the state of your affairs, besides, what will your patients do, go mad or something?

–I lost most of them when I died. They can't do without someone for so long, they went elsewhere.

–But they'll come back.

–No. I'd lost them before. I couldn't help them.

–Others will come. You'll build up a new practice, you've fully recovered now.

–For a long time I've had no future as a spy. The great failure of our century. We give names to sicknesses, but we don't heal, merely create new dependencies.

–All right, do something else. Research or something. What happens to the unconscious when the body lies in a low state of life, for instance. Do they know? Doesn't that require looking into, with qualifications like yours?

–No.

–But you can't retire at your age, what, pushing fifty, I guess, like me, forty-eight? Besides, what will you live on, in Bermuda of all places, all right, inland, in the mountain wilderness, but even so, have you any idea of the prices, Mexico, you say now? Why even the poorest village wouldn't do it, with your commitments.

The sense of irrelevance grows into the outlines of his radiation, pushing them back towards the gold-rimmed books that line the wall behind the criss-cross metal over the shelves, penetrating the labyrinthine knowledge of alternate proofs and truths within his strange profession built on the failures of men. It makes a noise in a non-natural impulse like a distracted sea, lapping, withdrawing and advancing at a jerky rhythm governed by some mad moon or other somewhere in parabolic orbit around the business in hand, bouncing its signals of distress on a short wave-length back to it, pulsating, gasping so that you must decide one way or another what you will do. I mean to say, you know very well she hasn't a legal leg to stand on. If you really want to fight her on her own ground just say the word and I can settle it quite differently.

–My dear Edwin.

The pain behind the eyes resolves the unrhythmic signal in the dark as with a change of lenses, and the well-living swarthy face looks back with gentle eyes behind the horn-rimmed glasses, but as I have said before, it doesn't matter.

–Well, nothing matters, if it comes to that, I quite agree. But we must run some sort of show to keep going at all, mustn't we. I gather she may ask for the discretion of the court in respect of. Does she intend to marry this chap, er – Stanley –

–Of course not.

–Surely you see that I can't act for you if you don't instruct me. And, in this case, give cause.

–I only want to find some simple place where I can live out my second life in complete solitude.

–Desertion. Well, all right. It takes three years.

–I can't stand seeing, hearing, inside myself, seeing the whole of – oh, something, I don't know what, but it frightens me, I feel as if I lived backwards in time, consisting of anti-atoms, or had lost something vital and positive which I must go away and find. Silence perhaps, merely.

–You have seen what you have seen.

–I didn't say that.

–No, I did.

–Edwin –

–You don't need to explain. Have it your way. Physician

heal thyself. I never go anywhere, I just sit here and work people out of trouble in their best interests if any.

–Please do what you think best, Edwin. But don't take it out on . . . anyone, least of all –

–The children. I know. They all say that.

–Sometimes I feel I have none. Never had.

–Well, you haven't that many. Still, schooling and –

–Five, four.

–Larry! Come back. Come back.

–Two.

–Good boy.

Inside the mirror on the landing the shape stares back its map-like contours of some unknown region, continent, galaxy perhaps, with two starless coalsacks radiating nothing. And yet something creates the wavering undulations and if not the eyes then some nebulous memory, surely, behind the eyes, some electron of love or fear spiralling at high velocity in some magnetic field, so that the forces of acceleration in its orbits cause it to emanate on a long wave-length in a metre band. The pain behind the eyes that close to avoid the issue of their death resolves the optical image in the dark like a change of lenses, and the thin man stares back, as before death, before recovery, as when life took its normal course through blood vessels, nerve fibres, muscle spindles, bones, flesh and such that comfort. Their returned presence mocks the wavering outlines that grow suddenly monstrous before vanishing as if they had not wavered there at all, pulsating, breathing in and out in long undulations doubling, trebling each other's trebles on a map of ocean depths, filling the entire mirror or, with some others, the whole room, bursting its walls, the house, the street, the square, and the whole sky.

My dear Larry,

Forgive me for not answering your letter at once. I had to go to Virginia on an assignment, oddly enough connected with the work up at your place: a programme about the radio-telescope at Green Bank where, as you may know, they have started again on Project Ozma, begun some years ago but abandoned as having yielded no results. It seems that according to new calculations, a new wavelength might prove more fruitful in sending out non-natural impulses to Tau Ceti and Epsilon Eridani in the Whale and River constellations, and perhaps getting a reply if any intelligent life exists or has existed many light years ago at the same stage as ours on any of their planets, if they have planets. They would apparently recognise the impulses as non-natural. I apologise for telling you what you probably know already from your wife, patients and friends in your unusual surroundings as psychiatrist to the university science faculty, but I got all excited about it in a layman-like way, so that it all seems as new to me as it must seem old-hat to you.

Anyway, nobody forwarded your letter, and I found it here when I got back. Of course I remember our Cambridge days. I would have reminded you at the time of that unfortunate interview, but I realised then that you had no idea, and very little grip on reality as yet. Besides, I have changed considerably as middle age creeps on, I realise that.

I should indeed very much like to see you again, and soon. But the metropolis ties me down just at the moment, at any rate for the next six weeks. Might anything in the way of business or pleasure bring you down? Do please let me know, I can even put you up on my sofa if you come alone. Otherwise it will have to wait until some other assignment takes me up your way, which indeed could occur as we may do a follow-up programme on your own chaps. Not for some time however. So I hope you can manage something sooner than that for I would greatly enjoy seeing you, your real self I mean, now that you've fully recovered. I don't mind telling you that you really frightened me, and not many of the people I interview succeed in doing that. Besides, I have an idea I'd like to discuss with you.

Looking forward to hearing from you,

Yours ever,

Telford.

A secretary has typed the letter, behind a door perhaps with a round window in it many light-years or months ago, and no handwriting bleeps across the dial in peaks and plains except the name, but then why should it in busy days thus approached by a region that has receded at half the speed of life its light only now reaching us? Tell-Star persists in his verbal pedantry, and worms in the head squirm as he sharpens his beak in non-natural impulses that draw the line as a rule between one solar system and another though looking forward to a reply. The higher the temperature, however, the faster the vibrations, and consequently the higher the frequency of the radiation emitted, so that devices like the brain become unsuitable on account of the inertia associated with matter of relatively large mass.

–But father, no one could call you large, or even massive. Tall, yes, but not large. And certainly not old.

–How did you get in?

–I rang the bell, the landlady let me in.

–Oh. The fat woman, you mean?

–I suppose so. I wouldn't call her fat either.

–What do you want, Martin?

–Just to see you, father. How goes it?

–She shouldn't have sent you.

–Who shouldn't?

–Your mother. She should know better than that.

–She didn't send me. I just came. I mean, Mr Mellek wrote to me at school, at the end of the term, and told me of your, well, how things stood. He gave me your address, in case.

–In case of what?

–In case . . . I should want to see you. I've just come off the train. Just passing through, you know.

He sits surrounded by his languid charm, radiating diffuse gas unintensively with the beginning of a concentration that may ultimately form something, entering the main sequence perhaps fairly low down in the spectral levels, unless already degenerate matter, just passing through, you know, can I think with you, dad? No, I don't want you. But you've got me, dad, though sometimes, of course, I've got you. I don't care who's got whom, go away. So I just thought I'd come and talk to you.

–Talk to me? What about?

–Well, my future, for one. Mr Mellek says I may have to take matters into my own hands, whatever he means by that. I know what I mean by it.

–Oh?

–Well, he says you can't pay my school fees any more, want to retire or something. That suits me, father. I want to retire too.

–The alarm may go off at any minute.

–What alarm?

–Sorry, I thought I heard a noise. You've grown, Martin.

–Yes, father. Don't you recognise me, then?

–Of course I recognise you. But – well, I didn't realise – it sort of pushes one into the grave.

–You had a narrow escape, didn't you, father? How did it feel exactly, to come back? I mean, do you remember anything, dream anything?

–No. I never dream.

–Like me. I never dream either.

–Do you like noise, Martin?

–Noise? What sort of noise?

–Well, young people seem to love noise these days. A sort of roar of adolescence. I wonder whether I –

–Oh you mean motorbikes and sports-cars. No. But how clever of you all the same. Mother warned me I'd find it difficult to get through to you, but you've hit the nail bang on the head.

The needles oscillate violently, swing round with a loud creak, the alarm shrieks then goes suddenly silent, except for the loud ticking of something or other in non-natural impulses to the furthest region that may send a reply such as what do you mean, you want to retire?

–From school, father. I hate school.

–But you know nothing, Martin. Your reports –

–Precisely. I hate work, you see, that kind of work, history, Latin, Shakespeare, biology and all that.

–Because you don't try to understand it. But it all counts later. Someone used to say to me, I forget who, when you don't understand something, go on as if you do, it will all become clear later, and useful, too.

–Useful in what?

–Mathematics works that way.

–But father, I don't want to do mathematics, or science, and become one of those lunatics we live among, like Dr Dekko, and Professor Head, and –

–Oh, yes, Head.

–He died, didn't he?

–I believe so.

–Oh come, father, don't you know?

–Yes, yes. It all seems such a long time. Infinite space exhausts me.

–Or medicine for that matter. You didn't, want me to follow in your footsteps, did you, father?

–No. Oh no, don't do that.

–Well then. Good. We agree. After all if you can't afford it, and I have no capacity for it –

–What have you capacity for, Martin?

–A good question, father. Quite frankly, nothing. If I could do exactly as I liked, I'd do nothing at all. I'd get around on pure charm. You see, I've discovered how to do it. Just listen to people and smile, pretending a deep interest, well, not even pretending, after all, one learns a lot that way. But it flatters people and they start giving out, giving out diffuse gas unintensively, faintly, like the beginning of a concentration that may ultimately form a star, and enter the main sequence somewhere low down in the spectral levels, unless, perhaps already degenerate matter of high density, its luminosity decreasing with its mass like a White Dwarf in the final stage of its long life, or with some others, expanding, cooling, increasing in luminosity and moving out of the main sequence as Red Giants high in the spectral level, in elliptical orbits at the nucleus of a galaxy, or towards the spiral arms, bright cepheids, Blue Giants, colliding with another galaxy and filling the whole room, bursting its walls, the street, the sky. But then, you see, I realise one can't quite rely on that. Most people have nothing to give, unfortunately.

Most people find him charming and he sits in it lazily, gracefully, saying nothing, I'd do nothing at all. Except, the noise begins, racing around the orbits or along the square of the hypotenuse, surely you must have noticed it, every circle has its square, I drove into the wrong one first, hence the time I took, and the noise, moving in total immobility against the ultra-violet light, producing no vibration except noise, since you hit the nail, well, a new noise, in fact. These hands –

–that heal –

–instruments, father, not human innards. I have miraculous hands on the notes of a jazz trumpet. And good lungs. And a good ear. I learnt to play at school. And at home too, though you didn't seem to hear. I can create a new noise, father, one doesn't need higher education for that.

–But you have an artist's hands.

He stretches them out, long and lanky, feminine perhaps, but then you never noticed them, father, you never allowed for that.

–I did, Martin, I did. You had your collection. I gave you enough pocket-money for your collection of records. Primitive jazz, you called it.

–Oh, that. I've grown out of that.

–Yes, I even liked some of it, genial stuff. I took an interest, surely. But I thought, well, at first your school reports showed promise.

–Anyone can show promise at what he thinks will grip him, give him something, well, but you might have known, since you began as a physicist, mother tells me, and found you had no capacity for it –

–What else did she tell you?

–Oh, lots of things.

–Things?

–You sounded just like Stanley when you said that. Things? I have no interest in things, I like people.

–You seem to know a lot.

–Mother says people consist of things. Do they, father? Do your patients? I mean, you sort of live on people consisting of things, don't you?

–That sounds like Stanley too, if I may say so.

–Yes, well, she goes for the same type. Silly girl.

–So. You think your mother silly? Have you any such outstandingly original views on myself?

–Oh come, father, I have a high regard for you. You know that.

–Do I?

–Well, haven't I proved, by coming here, and talking –

–to your satisfaction, yes.

–Oh dear. She warned me I'd find it hard to get through to you. She said she couldn't communicate with you at all, that you said nothing to her, nothing that made the slightest sense, during the whole time, two years or more, since –

–I died.

–Yes, well, I know, you had a ghastly experience but what about her, she went through hell too, father, besides, time heals and all that.

–I thought, that we . . . communicated . . . a great deal.

–You used to sit there, even during the holidays, and say nothing, nothing at all. Mother had to send Patricia away, so that she wouldn't see.

–Did you, come home, during the holidays?

–Yes father.

–I had thought, that we communicated. Brenda and I. But perhaps I dreamt it.

–You never dream.

–No.

–I wouldn't say that death and recovery, however amazing, justified . . .

–What? My behaviour? Or hers?

–Well, all this, mess. And your crazy notion of retiring.

–So she did send you?

–No, of course she didn't. She never wants to see you again if you care to know the truth. Not in your present state.

–So you came, like a great clumsy oaf, to change my state.

–No. I came – how did we get on to all this? Oh yes, noise. What shall I do, father?

–You have a crazy notion of retiring, you have your charm, your lungs, and your miraculous hands, take matters into them.

–Well, a fine father you make, I must say.

–What do you want, money? A push, a start, an introduction to a drug-taking, long-haired jazz musician? I don't know any.

–Jazz musicians don't have long hair, you should know that by now.

–All right, you've made your point. You may keep your hair short.

–Thank you.

–Don't mention it.

–Oh father, don't let's go on like this.

–You haven't answered my question. What do you want?

–Only a little interest, encouragement. Affection perhaps. A father's blessing they used to call it. But you never gave me that. If I showed any enthusiasm for anything, you'd nip it in the really? Surely not, how can you remember, mother told me, oh, did she, and what else, well, what do you expect, a Blue Giant, emitting a high luminosity from the outer spiral of your galaxy, in the top level of the spectrum, but you chose the transit drink, surely you know about the red shift which together with the degradation of intensity as speed increases means that less and less of the light actually emitted reaches us? The layers of atmosphere distort the waves travelling through it and upset the definition. Yes, well, you go too far. I mean you exaggerate. I draw the line as a rule, yes I know, but wait, after sunset the degree of ionization in the lower layer falls off and the higher layer then reflects, I assure you, with fewer collisions. Wait, wait a little, Martin, have patience, I'll manage your school fees, of course I will, I don't want you to grow into a half-baked man who gets around on charm alone, though you have plenty of that, I know. But you'd only regret it later. You can still do what you want, son, thank you for calling me son, but even charm works better with an informed interest. Yes I know, life provides all the information you'll need. I admit, I even agree. But wait a year at least, things will come clear very soon in fact, when I've decided one way or the other, why, perhaps you could come with me, to wherever I go, if I go, for a while at least, See the Universe, time heals, but space heals faster. I'll make it up to you. Have patience with me. Wait, wait for me, Martin.

The conversation thunders across the metropolis, hoots through dark tunnels, crashes into grand canyons leaving everyone maimed under a maze of twisted steel, driving below the headlines that girdle the world in black and in bright lights of letters to the citizens, good people, in flashed imperatives such as drink Inter-Air, fly The Daily Sphere, Say it with Brandy, eat infra-red and See the World without end, red, amber, green against the invisible ultra-violet and the magnified noise, why did you shoot the lights, son? I didn't father, I shot the policeman in a vibrant hum of total immobility that crawls to my dear Larry, how good to see you. Come in. You know Elizabeth, don't you. She knows you.

–Elizabeth?

She looks with glazed eyes out of an angular attitude in the depths of the sofa. Oh yes. Yes. Hello.

–I must apologise, Larry, for crashing in on your long-last reunion. I called on Telford by chance and he told me he expected you. So I said I'd go, but he insisted on my staying a little while, to help break the ice, he said, so let's break it quick.

–Well, er –

–I believe you frightened him out of his wits last time you met.

–Come, come, Liz, you exaggerate.

–Oh please, don't say come – come like that, Telford, you remind me of Stanley. Anyway I'll go in a minute.

–No, er, please, don't, feel you have to.

She bombards the room with the particles of a nervous

energy that solidifies into zigzags of tremulous precision within her. I – er – came down to do some shopping. Oh, dear, Larry, those eyes of yours haven't changed a bit, do switch them off or I can't lie to you.

–Why should you want to? I didn't ask anything.

–No. No. Quite right.

–Have a drink Larry, you look washed out. What would you like?

Drink – The Daily Sphere in colour. Say it with –

–What?

–Brandy, please.

–Good. Now, let me see where did I put – ah, here. That'll perk you up.

–Thanks.

–Well.

–Yes. Well. Nice to see you, Telford. You – er – don't really look much like your image.

–Oh, that. Who does?

–I must – er – apologise, I mean, for not recognising you, at the time of –

–Nonsense, Larry, why should you, in that state. Besides, let's face it, we none of us get any younger. And I acquired that idiotic public name. But then, what do names matter?

She still bombards our conversation with those particles of anxiety that spiral at high velocity around the lightning zig-zag of her magnetic field, her eyes trying to intercept the pain behind the starless coalsacks which, however, radiate nothing back and remain obstinately fixed on

Tell-Star, but then do I look like my image? I mean, the vague image you have of me, if any?

–I don't, really, know you well enough. Elizabeth.

–No. Of course. Quite right.

–How, er, did, Stanley come down with you?

–No.

–No. I didn't think he had.

–You asked me, Larry, why I'd want to lie to you. Quite right. Good question . . . I don't. I came to town, not for shopping as I said but to see my lawyer about getting a divorce.

–Why?

–Why not? Anything you can do . . . Oh, I don't mind the petty infidelities, in fact I prefer it that way, though his clumsy lies bore me. If anything he hurts the women, not me. He does it all with so little enthusiasm, interest, affection even.

–What do you mind?

–The personal destruction by petty verbal victories. If it hadn't been for Telford I'd have ceased to exist.

–I see.

–No you don't see. You don't see anything.

–Cigarette, Liz. Let me fill your glass.

–Yes. Quite right, Telford. Thanks.

Tell-Star masturbates and picks his nose in his unscreened existence when he can't make love to men or politely pick at the squirming worms in the framed head of his victims. He sits surrounding this inner image with a rectangle of straight horizontal lines like a harp recumbent plucked in a non-natural impulse, held, however, in the tremulous space of the rectilinear room by a confident control, acceptance or resolution out of his strange profession built on the weak performances of men. Her lines cross his in swift arpeggios saying anyway, Larry, you can't talk. Like I said, anything you can do, in that field anyway –

–You seem to know a lot.

–Oh yes, I know a lot, one way and another. Besides, I've lived there, since you left. Things get around.

–Yes. Things do. Does she, I mean – does she, still –

–See him. Oh yes. He went through a banal stage of cutting her dead in corridors, but then, with your departure, the convenience of it, you see, compared with Sally, yes, convenience always tempts him more than anything. The predictability of his responses, bang on cue, freed me quite early on, so that the same sense of irrelevance fills the room around the business in hand if any as she bombards it with particles of nervous energy, her eyes trying to intercept the pain behind two starless coalsacks that radiate, however, no interest, and remain obstinately fixed on nothing, nothing at all except a long habit of merely professional listening to the failures of men which sighs why now, I mean?

–You don't really remember Elizabeth, do you, Larry?

–But . . . of course.

–From your present university? Or from . . . Cambridge?

–Cambridge?

–Oh, Telford, you promised.

–I know, Liz. But I find it hard to accept that a man can forget to that extent.

Drink Inter-Air, Fly World without End. Read Tell-Star in The Daily Sphere. Say it with bright imperatives to the citizens, and don't forget to tell the journalists that she bombards the rectilinear room with the particles of a furious relief that spiral round the zig-zags in a magnetic field emanating the fact that I have changed, to that extent, just as you say I have. Let's say no more about it.

–Elizabeth.

–Yes, Larry. You loved me. You wanted to marry me. And then you didn't.

–You read . . . English?

–Yes. Useless thing, English. I never use it.

–What do you use?

–Oh, I got along on charm while it lasted. But Stanley quickly trampled that away. I don't communicate much in any medium these days, except waves. Waves of unhappiness. And people shy away from those . . . Oh, don't pity me, Larry, or feel guilty. I asked for all I got. One attracts it, you know, as an idea attracts another. But it doesn't help to recognise it.

–A little recognition always helps. Not too much though.

–So you do remember something of me.

–Forgive me, Elizabeth. But our odd social encounters –

–I know. I do know. And you had him on your mind rather than me. Besides, after your –

–My death.

–Yes. That shook me, Larry. It really did. Telford can tell you.

–Telford?

–Liz and I have remained very good friends, ever since –

–I remember. You rather took her over, didn't you?

–Don't put it like that, Larry, you sound like Stanley sometimes.

–I know.

–I turned to Telford at the time because I knew he loved you. I wanted someone with whom I could talk you out of my system, yes, in English even, and who, well, who had no sexual interest in me and who wouldn't get me entangled on the rebound. Though I must say I've often secretly also wished he could have. Then I wouldn't –

–If you had married me, Liz, and after all we did seriously consider it, you would have seen Larry again tonight.

–Yes. Quite right. Those eyes of yours, Larry. They'd look right into me as if they could see something and yet saw nothing. I came to think I had nothing there to see, and of course perhaps I haven't.

–Nonsense, Liz. Don't run yourself down so much.

–You always did do that, didn't you, Elizabeth.

–So you really do remember something of me.

–It used to exasperate me, if only as a slur on my judgment. Because, as you wisely remind me, I loved you. I used to tell you, people will take you at your own estimation, they always do. As in the end I did.

She settles into a gentler radiation from the sofa, the lines less angular, more curving, trebling each other round the kind explanation dropped, lassoing out to catch other associations, memories perhaps but held in tremulous space by a calmer control of things, such as Tell-Star saying your letter, Larry, it had me quite worried.

–My letter?

The small spidery handwriting fills the page at wide impersonal intervals like an equation worked down to the very end of some unlikely resolution as if x could really equal y in the unfamiliar context of the door with no doubt a round window in it behind which a secretary has typed some sort of reply. It sounded so crazy. But then, scientists.

–I don't call myself a scientist.

–Yes, well, we'll talk about that. I have an idea I'd like to discuss with you.

–I didn't come to discuss ideas, Telford. I came to talk about, well, to ask, but now, with Elizabeth here, quite a lot comes back. I just want to explain –

–You don't have to explain. Like she said, I loved you, Larry. But anyway we'll have plenty of time. I've taken tomorrow off.

–Well, I'd better go, I've barged in long enough.

–Elizabeth. I'd like to see you again. I mean, could you lunch with me tomorrow?

–Not if you want to persuade me against divorce. I've thought about it for a long time, you know.

–Well, we do have other things to talk about. And we could forget Stance altogether, I wouldn't exactly mind.

–Stance?

–I mean Stanley.

–Oh yes. All right. Why not? Thanks, I'd like to. But don't think that I want, I mean, that I'll try to –

–I don't think anything derogatory of you, Elizabeth, not until you've proved it, so don't think it of yourself, or in no time at all you will have proved it.

–Yes. Yes. Quite right. Thank you. Ring me tomorrow before ten at my hotel, I expect you two want to talk. Goodbye. Don't see me out, Telford. Thanks, and she jerks her once again angular attitude out of the rectilinear room from left to right.

–Well, Telford.

–Well, Larry old twin. Do you remember our joint birthday party, champagne popping on the punts, just before our vivas?

–Bang in the middle of Gemini, yes. We drank to our astrological future as humanists.

–You didn't know you'd turn from physics to medicine, then, and find yourself in the end among mad star-gazers.

–Mad among star-gazers, Telford.

–I wouldn't say that, Larry, no. But I have an idea.

The amphitheatre grows immense, a spiralling galaxy of faces, bright cepheids, Blue Giants at the outer rim, roaring incessant noise in collision with other galaxies unseen, unheard by the Red Giants towards the centre who carry on regardless, expanding, heating up inside but cooling their outer layers as their luminosity increases, moving from the main sequence, unstable, pulsating, then contracting, fading, cooling, entering on their final stage as White Dwarfs of small mass and high density, each grain of dust weighing a ton no doubt and radiating faintly, unless filaments of gas perhaps, beginning a concentration that may ultimately become something. But the noise drowns the words inside the spheric globe, for sound-waves require matter and can't get through the empty space immediately around. The microphone has died, the acoustics cork the space, or the noise from the collisions at the outer rim drowns all the words, the complex inscriptions, the parabolic gestures that create situations, the angular attitudes that send things off into elliptical orbits until the crowd yells, hisses, stamps its feet. Then the bull comes in, lunges and hoofs the dust, plunges his horn into the attitudes and contortions and tosses them at the crowd that roars, good people. Well, now that you've made your gesture I hope it didn't hurt. Sit on you? My dear good man, why should I sit on you?

Inside the rectangle the face of Tell-Star peers through the horizontal lines of a harp recumbent plucked in quick arpeggios. How do you feel, he says.

–Terrible. Why did you have to do this to me?

–I didn't do anything, Larry.

–No. You left me to it.

–You had a nightmare. I came down to see.

–I had an omen, Really.

–Why don't you tell me about it?

–I think that I shall die, quite soon. I wish I could, Really, once and for all.

–We all do that, at times.

–I thought I never dreamt. But recently, I do, now and again.

–It doesn't necessarily mean what you think, Larry, you of all people should know that.

He walks to the long table behind the sofa for cigarettes and the rectilinear room fills with smoke wisps, filaments of gas, voices that swim for dear life and noise, the vibrant hum of waves merging, doubling, trebling each other and overlapping, expanding, bursting the walls, the street, the entire sky in ultra-violet light when before dawn the degree of ionization in the lower atmosphere has fallen off and the higher layer then reflects, something at least. A little consciousness can do a lot, although in this type of communication the echo decreases with the fourth power of the distance between two bodies. But even if you could see an atom coming into existence the problem would remain as to the forces which had created it. And besides, the same principle of indeterminacy applies, compared, I mean, with the determinacy in regard to large numbers of atoms. The moment you try to find out its condition the very process of investigation must disturb it. So with ideas and people, compared to mass ideas, mass people. And causes. And so, of course, with the primeval atom. You couldn't inquire as to what made it, or how it disintegrated, even if the time and space hadn't gone for ever. Let's put it this way, Laurence, we merely pierce the apple with a pin. And yet we try to live without causality, she said, who said, oh, I don't know, the fat woman, the professor or someone, pretending that each moment has its own separateness, that anyone might come or go in that moment like an electron, why, you might as well ask for the moon. I know you didn't. Or the noise either. Tell me one thing, the noise around the orbits, Telford, in Cambridge, at twenty-four, did I like noise? What sort of noise, Larry? Well, cars and motorbikes. And jazz, that sort of thing. Surely I didn't, I collected silences.

–I think perhaps you liked the thunder of ambition inside yourself, and sought silence to hear it.

–Ambition! Me? I've never had ambition. I don't care. I just don't care.

–Not now. But you did then. Oh, I don't mean mere ambition to get to the top, I know the staleness of that. No. You couldn't bear the idea of becoming, perhaps, a second-rate physicist. So you chose something easier.

–Easier!

–You know the world of doctors, Larry. As in any world, only a few have full capacity, top rank. The rest, I shudder to think, get by on average intake. But people don't know that, and trust them absolutely, or else believe it matters less in that field than in what they call real science. Pure science to you, a purist at heart, Larry. The naked ambition to break barriers, find new laws, advance things, not yourself.

–And things make a hell of a noise, a sort of vibrant hum. Or do I mean people? The hum returns, the filaments of gas, the smoke wisps intertwining voices that swim for dear life saying Hot Spots, Uninhibit, One-shot-trigger, time heals and things like that or how did it feel exactly query what did the joke fat woman unjoke say did you die laughing unquery if I can get a dial in edgeways how come you said nothing saw nothing of the slightest interest to anyone bracket I mean the world of course good people close bracket comment no wonder you wanted to come back uncomment query did you want to come back repeat quote mister Lazarus unquote shout no unshout he says quote you ask all the wrong questions and so of course unquote like eight hundred million miles of no story in the psychotic handwriting of the spheres on a small screen unless perhaps in the last sentence the leeches cling in the chilly depth of darkness and suck out the red corpuscles leaving only the white, up once a minute to breathe, hold it, your breath I mean, and read the inscriptions, the bright imperatives in the ultra-violet light, up once a decade or so, ah, breathe away, so how do you like it, Larry?

–What?

–My idea!

–I feel very tired, Really, can't it wait?

–No you don't. You feel elated. I choose my time well. I have great expertise in these matters. Of course you must think it over, but I'd like your first reaction, now, at once, just as a matter of personal interest, you know, I won't hold you to it.

–Hold me to what?

He gets up and walks to the long table behind the sofa for cigarettes or something.

–You haven't heard a word I said, have you?

–I don't know, Telford. I thought I did all the talking around here. For once.

–You did. Indeed you did. Look, I'll make some coffee. Relax.

The room empties of waves and undulations that treble each other as on a map of ocean depths disturbing the horizontal lines as they pass like arpeggios over a harp recumbent plucked. The dark stares back its giant starless coalsack that radiates nothing. Something however creates the wavering outlines and if not the eyes then some faint memory, surely, behind the eyes that close to avoid the issue of their death and amazing recovery. The closing resolves the optical image like a change of lenses and the silence comes, filling the room, the house, the street, the entire sky with planets unless moons perhaps hanging on a shaft of light that widens into a voice now, here, that'll perk you up, cigarettes in front of you. Well now. Listen, look. Think about what you see. I prefer to close my eyes. Ah, but you didn't close your eyes tonight, Larry. Listen, look. You remember in my letter I said I had an idea to discuss with you. Well, it has grown into a great big vibrant hum inside me, as you would say, a thing I must advance, a barrier I must break. I've thought a lot about what you've told me. And I want to do a programme on it.

–But, but, Telford, what have I told you?

–Everything.

–What!

–Everything I need to know.

–But how? I don't know it myself.

–Well, you've talked enough. About the Big Bang and the Steady State, the beginning of determinacy with space and time –

–Oh. That.

–And indeterminacy and madness and the exhaustion of infinite distances. In brief, your particular world of scientists, as seen by an informed but uninvolved intelligence. Just what I want.

–Oh, for heaven's sake.

–Well –

–You can't. You can't appropriate this – this – no, I won't let you.

–Look, Larry. I told you we'd done a programme on the Ozma Project at Green Bank. And we may do a follow-up on the work at your place, which ties up. But radio-astronomy, however fascinating, makes bad television, let's face it. You can't photograph means of communication that work by magnetic impulses, except as they appear on dials, and the viewer soon gets bored with dials and wavy lines and mathematical formulae. A few interviews can pep it up, but not much more. Now this idea of mine –

–But what idea, Telford?

–In simple words, Larry, I want to do a programme, or even a series, on the mental health of scientists. Naturally I shall concentrate mostly on atomic scientists. But this ties up, in a way, and I want the astrophysicist's view on radiation, on explosions of bombs in outer space, on hydrogen explosions as possible causes of abnormally strong radio sources, colliding galaxies and so forth, and their view, too, on the mental health of atomic scientists. Above all your view, as an expert, of their own mental health.

–I won't associate my name with it. Or my university.

–Well of course, you have to appear anonymously anyway. I could, if you insist, do it with an actor speaking your words. But I would rather have your image in personal interview, for conviction, rather than just your words on the sound-track.

–What words?

–All your words, Larry. All that you've told me tonight. Your story. I have it here on tape.

The room goes darkly deep inside, with small square marble tables good to write on some story of death and amazing recovery, but the patterns in the marble make no sense for time has chipped the edges and all the laws get broken. The dark room fills with people who come and go or pretend to, good people, meeting professional friends who can count and therefore know them better than friends who profess only friendship but can't read inscriptions. Hands shake, smoke wisps and voices swim for dear life. The room seems huge for the edge of the town, or perhaps the centre lies at the circumference, bright cepheids, Blue Giants that tremble on a screen with the horizontal lines of a plucked harp recumbent, so that the voices swim along the streets like neural cells in mad morse along nerve-fibres, teleprinting their messages from Base Headquarters somewhere on the left focus of an ellipse because someone has cleared the channels, good boy, he didn't cry get off, don't touch me, I won't let you, I won't.

–Larry, you have let me. By telling me.

–Pooh. A journalist.

–A friend, Larry. A daily friend from the sum of all your days. You've kept your promise.

–What! Telford, what exactly have I told you?

–Like I said, all I want, no more.

–I have a story but no name.

–Well, I can't use your name anyway. But I accept the reality of your story –

–But which story, for heaven's sake, surely you can let me hear the tape?

–Not now. It needs editing. It wouldn't help you, Larry, the incoherence –

–Did I mention . . . something, anything, about . . .

–Something of this, something of that. You spoke confusedly about many things, and ideas, and people. That doesn't matter. I'll sort it out and make some sort of sense of it, take what I want, it depends on what I get elsewhere, you see, about which I have only a hazy notion, but I'll mix you in, don't worry. I'll make the film in such a way that others will accept it.

–Oh yes. The law of probability as to that works out at a thousand million to one. So what will you do? You'll use illusion, camera-tricks and stand-ins.

–I'd rather not use a stand-in for you, Larry.

–You ask all the wrong questions, you get the wrong

answers, the wrong picture made of itsy bits of nothing . . . What promise, anyway?

–Oh, a promise we made long ago, which you seem to have forgotten, oddly enough, to meet again at double our ages and . . .

–and what, have a cosy chat, about life and love, truth, beauty and goodness or else, what, our achievements?

–and . . . expose ourselves.

–I see. And what have you exposed?

–A traitor, Larry. The Judas in all real friendship, who betrays in order to understand, or perhaps because he understands.

–Ah, what good listeners trained interviewers make. They probe, they pry and all the time they merely prepare traps, to show their superiority over something or other.

–Like psychiatrists?

–But then, nobody really listens.

–I really listened, Larry, believe me.

–Yes, doubly, with your inner and your outer ears, or so I thought. But your inner ears stood in fact outside yourself, a mere mechanical device lurking behind the sofa, with useful gaseous matter between us to propagate and distort the sound-waves travelling through it and upset the definition. I thought the acoustics of friendship corked the space around us, that the giant ear of the world had died, that I consisted of no matter and spoke backwards in silent bubbles up the time-scale as in a vacuum created by my trust.

–In speaking to me, Larry, you spoke to the world, your

other self, your twin. And the world consists of people. Each with a love of something, a fear of the unknown, however buried –

–Goodbye. Tell-Star.

The conversation bleeps at a non-natural impulse along the nerve fibres, blood-vessels, muscle spindles of the empty city, through to the Whale and River constellations and perhaps getting a reply if any intelligent life exists or has existed five hundred thousand light-years ago, although a blockage occurs when waves requiring matter to propagate themselves find none. Something however creates the wavering outlines that make the nervous handwriting across the dials and if not the eyes then some faint memory, surely, behind the eyes, filaments of gas in violent motion or extragalactic nebulae in collision. But if we survey the space around our galaxy, Ladies and Gentlemen, we find it very empty, for no other comes closer than a million light-years or so, making the chances of collision fairly negligible. Yet great clusters occur, moving at over two thousand miles per second, so that most of the noise must come from colliding galaxies. Some argue, nevertheless, that parts of a divided nucleus recede from one another at great speed, the violent processes involving collision of interstellar matter and ejection of high energy particles from the atmosphere of young stars, that cause the nervous handwriting across the dials in bleeping peaks and plains, letters to citizens in bright imperatives, drink infra-red, do not spit gamma-rays and see the ungrown foetus of men's love inside their atmospheric density, say it with smells of primitive noises from their deepest entrails if any, for we make the bumps as we go along with a great waste of horsepower more and more disorganized and no control-panel, only the little orange lights that flicker Uninhibit, Next Instruction, Pot Drawer and things like that, red, amber, green, bright cepheids, Blue Giants and new concentrations that may ultimately form hi pa, oh my sweet Potato. But how changed, enormous eyes painted black all round and how did you get in?

–The landlady let me in, pa. My, you look awful. Worse than in hospital.

–Did you see me in hospital, Patricia?

–Course.

–But surely, surely your mother hasn't let you come here alone?

–To the big city? Course. Why not? Well, not quite alone. I travelled alone, but she put me on the train.

–But where –?

–Oh, I stayed with my boy friend last night. Why did you call me sweet potato? Does that mean you fancy me after all or something?

–My darling little girl. Come here. Of course. More than anything in the world. Haven't I shown, petted, taught you to speak, played cat's cradle with our meridians –

–You do say funny things, pa. Heh, that tickles, laugh, you thought I'd died, my love, kiss kiss bang bang, steady on there, pa, you got a complex or something?

–You've grown, Patricia.

–Well, two years, pa, what d'you expect? You've hardly seen me.

–Didn't you come home, for the holidays?

–Home? No. Ma farmed me out with Stan and Liz. Said you needed quiet or something. Martin came home though. Funny that, with his trumpet and all. I never made any noise at all. But you can't follow the logic of crumblers.

–Patricia. I don't understand. Your mother – and why do you call her ma, Patricia? I find it ugly.

–All the girls call their crumblers ma and pa now.

–Crumblers. I suppose you mean parents.

–Well, what do names matter? Got a cigarette?

–What, at your age?

–Nearly fifteen pa, don't act square. Thanks.

–And what did you say, just now, about staying with your boy friend?

–Larry. Funny that, don't you think? You'd say I'd got a complex no doubt. Nice. Plays the guitar. Bit off, though, not very bright. Unlike me.

–But Pat, my sweet, do you – I mean what do you mean, stayed with him?

–With his uncle and aunt. Crumblers too but all right. Nice in fact. Nicer than him.

–But do you sleep with him?

–Well, one hardly sleeps.

–All right, make love.

–And there again, I wouldn't call it that either, if it exists at all. His performance, shall we say, lacks something. And he has pimples.

–So.

–Only a stage, of course. Still, by the time he's grown out of that and handsome I'll have grown out of him. Already have. A lot of rot, really, why does everyone make such a fuss about it?

–One day –

–Oh, one day I'll understand everything, I know that but not love, pa, it doesn't interest me, a thing that gets squares round in circles, like Stan says, no crumbler he, despite his paunch and grey hair, ma understands anyway. No, I'll solve the universe, pa. Can I go to Cambridge like you? I've passed my –

–Well –

–Pa, I did brilliantly. Two years younger than everyone and top of the whole country in maths, pa, and chemistry, and very high marks in biology, but I failed in English and Latin. They said it doesn't matter, I can get a scholarship, pa, so if you can't afford it –

–Did your mother send you?

–Course she sent me. To try and get some sense into your head and some money out of you. We can't live only on what she earns, though let's face it, she's done well, hasn't she. I want to take up astrophysics, like her.

–Well –

–Don't say well like that, pa. Haven't you any pride in me, don't you take any interest in what I've done?

–Of course I do, my darling, of course. It fills me with a very, very peculiar pride. I mean that. Because I know, well, what infinite pleasure could come your way, but sadness too –

–Pooh . . . Why sadness?

–Oh, I don't know. Hard work, for a sense of –

–But I love hard work, pa.

–I expect you do. Tell me, my pet, why this get-up?

–You like?

–Well, you look so geometrical. All those zips. And with, turn round, a hole in the left buttock of your trousers.

–Where? Oh, so they have. How teasing. Anyway, you can't blame me, pa, you give us no money. All the girls have –

–So, you lay the blame for the hole on your buttock at my door?

–No I don't, pa. Kiss kiss. Bang bang, steady state, ow that tickles, stop, you dirty old man. Say, pa, how about it?

–Hmm. How about, what?

–I mean all this nonsense between you and ma. So banal you know, sort of, common, I don't mean vulgar but, yes, well, it does have a kind of vulgarity. What the crowd does. All the girls at school have split parents or ménages à quatre or any way lots of them. I always prided myself on my originality. You've let me down, pa.

–Patricia, your mother has said she never wants to see me again.

–Oh, phooey. I say that to my boy friends a thousand million times. It doesn't mean anything, pa.

–You seem to know a lot.

–Well, I don't know much about adultery but I know what I like. My pa at home, not quarrelling with ma, not quibbling poor old Martin about things, laughing and joking about his funny old patients and his crazy scientists, helping me with my equations –

–I've forgotten all my equations, Pat. I must have left them in the pocket of, well, my student's gown. Anyway, you'll have gone way beyond me by now.

–Yes, I expect so. I'd hate to do medicine I must say. What made you change, pa?

–I don't know. Losing my equations, perhaps.

–You mean they didn't come out? Mine always come out. I'll show you.

–Thank you, Pat. Thank you.

–So you'll come back, and work, and everything?

–I'll . . . think about it, my sweet.

–Oh, that means you won't.

–Really I will.

–I mean come back. Well, at least work again, pa, even away from us, here, start up again, you'll find plenty of sick people around. A man must work.

–A conventional little girl, after all. So all you want is my money?

–Course. Why not? Besides, it'll keep you sane, pa. You can't just sit around and mooch in this godawful boarding-house, living on bread-and-butter or something.

–One could live on square roots for ever, just raising them to the nth power.

–Oh, you lovely man. I really fancy you.

–Too.

–Let's make a deal, pa. I work for my scholarship, and win it, you get a practice going again, here, anywhere you like, and then, who knows, time heals or if it doesn't, well, at least you'll have helped some square or other out of his spinning circles.

–Physician, heal thyself.

–How about it, pa?

–Sounds to me easier for you than for me. You show me your equations and I show you a mended crumbler.

–You've got a deal. Bye, pa. Love love.

Great clusters occur, moving at many thousands of miles per second, radiating infinite processes with the collision of interstellar matter and high energy particles from the atmosphere of young stars, filling the room with wavering outlines, as on a map of ocean depths, doubling, trebling each other's trebles, bursting its walls, the house, the square, the street, the entire sky. Words drop into the overlapping rings that lasso out to catch faces, voices that swim for dear life through the heavy water, some drown, some float, some gasp in the chilly depth, some slice the water with a skilful crawl, while Stance or someone walks nonchalantly out of his hiding place, smoking a big cigar. Good man, he says, can you repeat, we'll do a take next time. I won't, I won't repeat, why didn't you have your camera on, your little individual flan through which you photograph the world? Well, I wanted to get the galactic background first, tricky, you see, in ultra-violet light, but we'll mix you in, don't worry. The door ushers in the decoy blonde, no, not that one, I replaced her, he never noticed. Shoot. My God, your eyes. You didn't ring, so I came all the same, I thought, oh, Larry you look dreadful.

–I – er –

–Haven't you slept? Did you have any breakfast?

–I – er – had some coffee somewhere. I walked all night.

–Telford?

–How did you know?

–I thought he might – try something like that.

–No. No. Not what you think.

–I don't think that. No, Larry, I don't think the obvious worst of people in advance, only of myself. Telford wouldn't. He just wanted, so much, to understand, what had happened to you. So did I. But we all have our clumsy ways of trying to understand. Mine the unhappy woman's way, his, the journalist's way. Let's put it like this, Larry, he can't himself understand until he has reformulated it so that all can understand.

–Appropriated it.

–If you like.

–I don't. I see little difference between that and the woman's way. A possessive way.

–Or the artist's. Do you find that so very hard to forgive, Larry?

–Oh, forgive. But accept and live with yes.

–Live with! But surely Brenda has never shown that kind of possessiveness.

–Brenda! Who cares about Brenda! I must get that thing back. You must help me.

–Of course I'll help you, Larry, if I can. But you mustn't talk like that about Brenda, she –

–Oh, yes, yes, I suppose, if you insist, she would have shown possessiveness if I had let her.

–I see. Yes. I do see. So very well. Because in the end this comforted me most. The knowledge, I mean, that you would never have let me either, and the sense of irrelevance fills the room as she bombards it with the particles of her self-absorption, her eyes trying to intercept more than a long habit of merely professional listening to the failures of men that takes over and says let you what or something, I only meant, that I would have preferred that kind of not-possessing to not-possessing someone I don't want to possess. I mean, someone I don't respect, and so on in this language English, that she never uses until the long habit of asking all the wrong questions and so getting all the wrong answers gathers itself with a why did you marry him, anyway.

–Larry, my dear, you have a genius for attracting self-punishing women. And the self-punishing woman, when she can't get what she wants, destroys the little she might have and attracts, or can't repel, the man best qualified to punish her. Brenda did the same.

–Yes, yes. Energy works that way. Look, Elizabeth. I must get that thing back.

–We all want things back, Larry. I said to Stanley once,

I had serenity until you barged in. Because you know, I did achieve serenity, quite soon in fact, don't flatter yourself. I got a secretarial job, in Angola. Then Kenya. It made me happy. I met Stanley in Kenya.

She still bombards the room with the particles of her anxiety that spiral at high velocity round the lightning zig-zag of her magnetic field, her eyes trying to intercept the pain behind two starless coalsacks which, however radiate no interest, and remain obstinately fixed on the long habit of professionally asking what did he say?

–Oh, the usual, bed-getting phrases. Then I had a baby.

–Really.

–We have two boys. At boarding school.

–He never mentions them.

–No. Oh, he likes them well enough. He spent most of their childhood destroying their confidence as he destroyed mine. I don't know what he wants from people, the genius he hasn't got, I suppose, and yet the moment anyone shows the slightest individuality he can't stand it. The elder, called after you incidentally, has taken up the guitar. Not very well. The other, well, it doesn't matter. I haven't come –

–I meant, what did he say when you said that? About serenity.

–Oh. Yes. He said: that kind of serenity can soon develop into a form of anaesthetism. The complacency of it struck me dumb.

–What? . . . did . . . you say?

–The com-

–No. No. The boy.

–I called him after you, Larry.

–Larry. Of course. Yes. I see.

–What do you see, Larry?

–What have you done to my daughter, Elizabeth?

–Larry! I took her in. During your illness. I didn't tell you the other day because – well, I thought you knew and besides we had other – Larry, I looked after her, I loved her. She has all the charm, the intelligence, the poise that I –

–All right, all right. Who cares. The young must learn and all that. But I wish, I wish, she hadn't come to your house, Elizabeth. Stanley's house.

–Does it, matter so very much?

–No. Nothing matters, if it comes to that, as someone or other said. Oh yes. My lawyer. But we must run some sort of show, as he also said. To keep going at all. Lawyers, yes. I must see my lawyer about getting that thing back, preventing –

–What thing, Larry?

–That tape, you dolt... What did you think I meant, good God I can't get through to anyone. I told you, do I have to spell it out?

–Yes, please.

–Your best friend, the great Tell-Star –

–Oh, that. Forgive me, Larry, but I –

–Yes, I know, you have your own problems and I ought to listen to them. But I've given up my trade. I've given up exchanging the intense confessions of people with cleft palates for a few comforting names. You can't get rid of things just by giving them names.

–But Larry I didn't come here as a patient.

–What . . . did you come as then?

–You invited me to lunch, remember?

–Oh yes. How many millions of light years ago did I offer that cosy lunch filled with trivial talk of other people's affairs and things like that?

–I begin to see what Brenda meant.

–You do. Good.

–Well, it doesn't matter, Larry, if you –

–Elizabeth, can't I get it into your head that something has happened since then, and that it does matter, to me, at any rate, and that if you love me, loved me once as you said, whatever you meant by that, it should matter to you too, and that you said you'd help me, help me to get it back.

–You mean . . . the . . . tape?

–Good girl.

–How can I, Larry. Telford and I –

–So. You planned it. Planned it together.

–No, of course not.

–Elizabeth, I talked to him half the night, incoherently, he admitted that himself. I talked as one talks to a friend, or if you like as patients talk to me. I don't remember what I said. If I knew I wouldn't mind so much perhaps. But I don't know and I must. It doesn't belong to him, or even to me, probably. I can't let him use it –

–appropriate it.

–Yes, appropriate it, distort it, misrepresent people who have trusted me, people I work with, live with –

–love.

–Oh, love! Love has nothing to do with it. A thing for squares to spin in circles as my daughter puts it. I don't love anyone, you should know that.

–Like Stanley.

–Yes, yes. Like Stanley, if you like. But unlike long-sighted Stanley who cuts my wife dead pretending not to see her, I don't want it to show. Out of a different kind of cowardice.

–Unless on the contrary you don't want the real thing to show. The love. That you remembered perhaps.

–Real thing! I tell you I remember nothing. What do you mean? Have you heard the tape? What did I say? Tell me. Tell me. What did I say?

–Let go of me, Larry, let go.

–I thought I'd find you both here. Good, how very right.

–Oh, Telford, you know better than to think that.

–Me, think? Never. How do you feel, Larry? You had me quite worried the way you left at dawn, and in that state. My God, you look washed up.

–We haven't slept together if you mean that and we have no intention of doing so.

–Come, come, I never sugg-

–Telford, don't say come-come like that.

–I didn't mean to upset you, Larry. But I have my job to do just as you have yours.

–I don't.

–This idea really excited me. And the tape sounds terrific, Larry, even uncut and incoherent.

–Except for the last sentence.

–I forget –

–We haven't come to it yet, Tell-Star. Nothing makes sense until the last sentence.

–What exactly do you mean by that?

–There goes the scalpel. How did it feel exactly and what did the fat woman say. But you really want to know, don't you, Tell-Star, you show no mere idly prying curiosity, like Stanley. You ask all the wrong questions, and so of course, get all the wrong answers. You start with nothing, go on as if you had something and in no time at all you have eternity or thereabouts. Have you got your mechanical ears with you, Tell-Star? Don't you want to record my posthumous views on pettiness and moral cowardice in the elementary courtesies due to man from man, and to woman from man too, when they have exploited each other like things, courtesies which require not only words, Tell-Star, the human prerogative man most fears, but gestures and a smile perhaps, no, you smile first, Something, to pierce through the resistance you call matter which radiation needs to propagate itself but which deflects the light waves travelling through it and upsets the definition? Or have you corked your ears, your inner and your outer ears, living as we all do in a transparent bowl of anti-matter through which no waves can travel?

–Larry, calm down. Don't make such a thing of it. I think I'd better go.

–Yes, go, Tell-Star, go. I'll see you through my lawyer's transparency in future. I have my rights, you know. I won't allow –

–But of course, Larry, you do as –

–you to make any film, why, what will you use, illusions, tricks, and stand-ins, and yourself, Tell-Star, don't forget yourself, you have a star-role in the ridiculous story of my death and amazing recovery. But you must fade yourself out, Really, before the last sentence. Because reality doesn't lie in you after all, or in anyone. I could float off now on my freedom, out of my bondage, my responsibility to Something if any, after all I didn't choose the way, I wanted only opaqueness, nothingness, I didn't order these complexities, these secret laws I've never heard of and break even in obeying them. I kept my promise and my words rebound against me. But nobody will understand a thing you say, Tell-Star, or see, or hear, you'll speak, like me, through a cleft palate, say gug-gug query what exactly do you mean by that comment nothing, nothing at all or something repeat –

–Stop.

Her hand slaps-stops the white face in the round mirror on the cupboard door that fills with rings widening quickly out. People collide, spinning on orbits and made up of other people in slices that spread out like flat discs of vaporised heavy elements in the plane of their present orbits. And as their initial material cools the atoms condense, forming small particles of dust which through constant collisions aggregate into larger and larger bodies, until perhaps they burst with accumulated identities that pass from one to another like elements, emitting particles of pain. You can never know with absolute certainty that consecutive observations of what looks like the same particle do in fact represent the same. Because since you can't establish the precise location you can't claim to have established the identity of the thin face on the dial in the square control panel which still bombards the room with particles of anxiety, moving from right to left, how do you feel, she says.

–Has he flounced out?

–Yes, Larry.

–And then what shall I do?

–Just rest. And eat if you can.

–Oh, I can live on the square roots of my time for ever.

–I got some cold food from the shop round the corner. You slept, you know.

–Did I? I never sleep.

–You never dream, either.

–Sometimes, nowadays, I have an omen.

–Try to eat, Larry.

–Thank you. Thanks. For everything.

–Don't mention it.

–Oh but I must. I always mention it when anyone does me proud.

–I feel proud. You killed the bull. Oh, you've forgotten that, too. We used to joke about our imagined enemies, and things to conquer, exams, and your dissertation, remember? Why did you change from physics, Larry? I used to think you'd solve the universe.

–Perhaps my daughter will do that for me.

–Eat, Larry, eat. I can stay an hour or so. I have to see my lawyer this afternoon.

–Oh, that. Why bother, Elizabeth? Does he deserve even that much attention?

–Larry, everyone deserves the attention of definiteness.

–Even if they prefer the uncertainty principle?

–They only pretend to prefer it. While they have to. You used to say that. Someone would come along and find a unified theory that would do away with indeterminate interpretations, you'd say, and revert to causality. I thought perhaps you might.

–I thought so too. In psychic terms at least. But I didn't. In the meantime we do the best we can, some of us preferring to pretend causality exists, and others, others preferring to prefer its absence. But you can never know with absolute certainty that what looks like the same particle, with the same identity –

–Yes but for practical purposes you have to, Larry, in the chemistry of people. Otherwise how can you live?

–You can't. Not really .You pretend you do. To save the appearances.

–Larry, you can't honestly believe that.

–I don't know. I think I believe that every particle of

ourselves, whether combined with those of others in normal electrovalence to make up this or that slice of us, or whether bombarded by those of others until this or that human element mutates into some other, every particle of ourselves returns. So that it has, in that sense, identity. But you can never quite identify it at any given moment.

–Though you pretend to recognise it.

–You recognise it, if you like, by an act of faith. Every scientist makes an act of faith at that point, as does every doctor, parent, priest, he expresses the chance as a probability over a large number of atoms, a near certainty but a probability nevertheless.

–So we all pretend to come and go as fully ourselves. And all the time millions and millions of particles of us have combined with others or escaped into various orbits to return to us ultimately.

–The law of the conservation of energy. Marry me, Elizabeth.

–Thank you, Larry. Thank you.

–Don't mention it.

–But it wouldn't help. Those particular electrons or whatever that made up the slice or disc or sphere of you at twenty-four won't make them up at forty-eight. But I could, if you like . . . provide . . . evidence.

–Evidence? Of what?

–Well. Don't embarrass me, Larry. I know you don't love me, you said so. I have no illusions on that score. But I wouldn't mind. I mean, Brenda told me that you refused to –

–Brenda again! What else did she tell you? Do you

confide all your spots and pimples to each other at the split of an atom?

–Larry, forgive me. She did, become, quite friendly. She'd come to see Patricia –

–Ah, yes, Patricia. So you want to provide evidence of adultery with me. Why? To balance things out? You can't hope for an eternal quadrangle from me, my dear. So common, as my daughter would say.

–Larry, please.

–And for when had you planned this convenient little episode? Now? Who will give the evidence? Have you got the Queen's Proctor hidden there in the cupboard behind the door with a round window in it? All right then, now. You have to see your lawyer in thirty minutes, yes, a nice sense of timing, for your age I mean, come, my remote Bermuda, ride with me, come, don't dilly-dally, off with your appearances, now I understand, Base Headquarters, all this talk of secret instructions, laws broken, meridians bent, and all the time you meant your base instincts. Right, then –

–Larry, let go, let go, get off me –

–My dear good woman, why should I sit on you? You can ride me, if you prefer it that way. No? Come, let me rouse your base instincts, ha! Hands grab at hands and wrists to pin them down in an angular attitude with parabolic gestures that create situations, contortions in the innumerable particles of her desire bombarded with astonishment, repulsion, fear that spiral at high velocity around the lightning zig-zags of her magnetic field, till in no time at all you have a human body or thereabouts made up of lips and human breath and odour, blood vessels, nerve fibres, muscle spindles, bones, flesh and such. The resistance you could call matter melts and mutates into wild energy by a law of conservation that has a perfectly good scientific explanation, so that you give rebirth which hurts to some lost slice of you, a forgotten area of particles that come whirling back to form filaments of gas in violent motion or extragalactic nebulae colliding perhaps on the outer rim, great clusters moving at thousands of miles per second while the primitive noise occurs, in the wrong square. Some argue nevertheless that parts of a divided nucleus recede from one another at great speed, the shock processes involving ejection of high energy particles that must ultimately form a human element, a star where the taste of love will increase its luminosity until it cools in quiet rage at all that tenderness that went to waste, accumulating only the degenerate matter of decay. Well, what did you expect, a Blue Giant? We love like ancient innocents with a million years of indifference and despair within us that revolve like galaxies on a narrow shaft of light where hangs the terror in her eyes as the life drains away from blood-vessels, nerve cells, muscle spindles, bones, flesh and such, once and for all in a spasm from the attitudes, the created situations and the circular gestures, with the little individual flan already dead in her meridians, out of the story of a death and amazing recovery and into the unfinished unfinishable story of Dippermouth, Gut Bucket Blues, my sweet Potato Head, Tin Roof, Really, Something and me.

BETWEEN

To Eva Hesse
with love and gratitude

Between the enormous wings the body of the plane stretches its one hundred and twenty seats or so in threes on either side towards the distant brain way up, behind the dark blue curtain and again beyond no doubt a little door. In some countries the women would segregate still to the left of the aisle, the men less numerous to the right. But all in all and civilisation considered the chromosomes sit quietly mixed among the hundred and twenty seats or so that stretch like ribs as if inside a giant centipede. Or else inside the whale, who knows, three hours, three days of maybe hell. Between doing and not doing the body floats.

To the right of the fuselage the enormous wing spreads back quite motionless on the deep blue of the high sky, the sunlight quiet on the dull-shining metal, the jet-exhausts invisible in their power save for a tremor against the blue or the propellers invisible in their speed save for a hinted halo, no cloud and from this seat no reef of nature no man-made object passing to show that the plane flies immobile at eight hundred and thirty kilometres an hour height twelve thousand metres on a sheet of paper handed over the back of the armchair in front by a black hand above Bordeaux with outside temperature minus forty-two degrees.

Inside they have pressurised the comfort. The people sit hidden in their high armchairs but for a few head-tops bald fluffy blond curly back between the port and starboard engines, looked after cradled in their needs, eat drink smoke talk doze dream and didn't catch what you said.

— That curtain up there between us and the first class. It reminds me of a tabernacle.

— Oh. Yes.

— Or a Greek Orthodox church. Have you ever—

— Oh yes and travel-talk ensues half drowned in air-conditioning and other circumstantial emptiness with the eyes gazing at the blue temperature of minus forty-two degrees.

At any minute now some bright or elderly sour no young and buxom chambermaid in black and white will come in with a breakfast-tray, put it down on the table in the dark and draw back the curtains unless open the shutters and say buenos días, Morgen or kalimera who knows, it all depends where the sleeping has occurred out of what dream shaken up with non merci nein danke no thank you in a long-lost terror of someone offering etwas anderes, not ordered.

Or a smooth floor-steward in white.

The stewardess in pale grey-blue and high pale orange hair puts down the plastic tray covered with various foods in little plastic troughs.

— Mineralwasser bitte.

— Mineralwasser? Leider haben wir keins. Nur Sodawasser.

— Also dann Sodawasser.

Which bears no label. Leider nicht.

The decorative metal locks on each door of the cupboard shine in the shaft of bright light coming through from the left where the wooden shutters meet. They have Napoleonic hats and look like Civil Guards, the one on the right door carrying the vertical latch that hangs down in relief like a rifle at rest. Next to the cupboard the smaller doors of the dressing-table repeat the motif darkly and unreflecting. On the two drawers of the dressing-table, above the smaller doors, the Civil Guards lie horizontal.

Beyond the wooden shutters and way down below the

layered floors of stunned consciousnesses waking dreams nightmares lost senses of locality the cars hoot faintly poop-pip-poop the trams tinkle way down below in the grand canyon and an engine revs up in what, French German Portuguese.

The dark shape of the cupboard unrounds in the half-light. On the bedside-table stands the bottle of mineral water, its label still illegible. No one comes in offering anything.

The florid American priest leans forward, fills the round window as shoulders fill a slipped halo, watching the sea of cloud way down below no doubt, that draws the gaze into an idle fantasy of stepping out and bouncing on it as on a trampoline, unless the cloud has cleared, the window set quite low, the long thin mouth embedded in the cardiac flesh talking of tabernacles which proclaim that the cloud has not cleared, for he turns again and says in some countries the women segregate still to the left of the aisle, the men less numerous alas to the right introducing himself as Father Brendan O'Carawayseed or some such name. The girl lays her rich auburn head on the lap of the handsome man cross-legged above the caption He'll always remember Piquant. Of course the Church must change, but the world can't call the tune.

The dawn has quite unrounded the corners of the cupboard made of teak, built in up to the ceiling and therefore without corners. It has pale oak vertical bars for handles. The light roars full of traffic through the yellow cotton curtains on the right.

The label on the bottle says VICHY ETAT—Eau Minérale Naturelle. VICHY. Station du foie et de l'estomac. Toutes maladies de la nutrition. Saison thermale: Mai–Octobre. L'eau de Vichy CELESTINS constitue l'eau de régime des hépatiques, diabétiques, dyspeptiques. Prise aux repas, elle facilite la digestion et régularise l'intestin. Elle doit aussi sa réputation mondiale aux résultats obtenus too small however to read in the half light.

And yet the central heating has the unrelaxed intensity of a cold northern night, the sheeted puffed up eiderdown that causes sweat and falls off causing coolness indicates an outside temperature of minus forty-two degrees perhaps although the body stretches out its many ribs in a pressurised comfort as if inside a giant centipede. Or else inside the whale who knows, three hours three nights of maybe hell. Between sleeping and not sleeping the body floats.

The cloud has cleared. Way down below the window-seat through the oval window the rectangles of agriculture brush-stroke size, the forest blobs metallic lakes the scatterings of smudged dots the thin white lines curving and straight and crossing one another make up an abstract study of some earth-goddess in brown and green. Valmar girls always get a second glance.

The bathroom door faces the entrance to the room so that the bathroom has an outside window next to the balcony window of the room. Soon some dark waiter will enter with a breakfast-tray and something else not ordered. All ideas have equality before God he will say unless some orator with eloquent gestures outside the glass booth, his words flowing into the ear through earphones in French and down at once out of the mouth into the attached mouthpiece in simultaneous German.

But no, the green or perhaps blue washbasin stands on one leg to the left of the window back to back with its neighbour which runs a small niagara at dawn or so and gurgles loud into the green or perhaps blue washbasin to the left of the window, single rooms not often having bathrooms. The decorative metal locks on each door of the cupboard shine brassy gold in the shaft of distant hoots coming through from the left where the wooden shutters meet. They have Napoleonic hats and look like Civil Guards, the one on the right door carrying a rifle at rest, those on the drawers of the dressing-table lying down. A small dot of bright light thrown by the round hole in the shutter further up the cupboard imitates the sun. Or else the telephone rings allo? er, dígame? The bottle on the bedside table says Agua Mineral.

The stewardess in navy blue comes down the aisle, carrying a tray of drinks and a small Schweppes. The menu goes all the way to Santiago. Oslo—Prague, airborne one hour and ten minutes: smørrebrød Scandinave, café. Prague—Geneva, airborne one hour: jus de fruit. Geneva—Lisbon, airborne two hours: oeuf froid italienne, coq-au-vin, pommes parisiennes, charlotte russe, café. Lisbon—Monrovia, airborne four hours and twenty minutes: smørrebrød, délice de tartine à la S.A.S., café. Monrovia—Rio de Janeiro, quartiers de pamplemousse, omelette au bacon, Rio de Janeiro—São Paolo, São Paolo—Montevideo, Montevideo—Buenos Aires, Buenos Aires—Santiago but the menu has no personal significance beyond the oeuf froid italienne the coq-au-vin the charlotte russe café and the small bottle of scuse-plisse as the dark Viennese leans right across from the left to photograph the Alps in the pink glow of bitteschön, travel-talk ensuing half-masked by air and other such conditioning to prevent any true exchange of thoughts when rhetoric flows into the ear through the earphones in French and down at once out of the mouth into the mouthpiece in simultaneous German. Out of the mouths of babes the Frenchman says with eloquent gestures, la vérité, la justice, l'humanité. The words prevent any true EXCHANGE caught in the late afternoon sun that stripes the airport hall between the slats of the venetian blinds on the vast wall of glass beyond which the planes wait, move slowly off, rise suddenly and vanish or come in out of the blue over the unseen lake somewhere to the right of the distant mountains.

A voice calls out continuous flight and gate numbers and the murmur of the talking delegates as they wait in rows of desks like a giant class fills the great congress hall. The chairman knocks his hammer on the dais table. The congress members dutifully don their listening-caps and the murmur still continuing now comes through the earphones in the glass booth, picked up by the microphones the engineer has just switched on. Siegfried sits to attention, wearing his earphones like a helmet as communication begins.

— Meine Damen und Herren. Kindly fasten your seat-belts and observe the non-smoking sign. The animal has filled up again, its body between the enormous wings stretching its one hundred and eighty seats or so like ribs towards the distant brain way up. The large African woman on the right in a long printed dress straps herself with lethargic difficulty as she talks to the man beyond her in a language not understood. Votre poitrine peut se développer et se raffermir facilement. In some countries the women would segregate to the left of the aisle the men less numerous to the right. But all in all the chromosomes sit quietly mixed as the enormous wing spreads back on the port side, catching the last red segment of the sun before it disappears behind the blackened hill.

The shadow of the green pelmet cuts between the light reflected from the pale blue slatted blind, dividing the reflection into two giant staves of five lines each, empty of notes above the cubic-looking cupboard in the pale blue cubic room. The double bed feels huge, empty of music in the silent pale blue room. The bathroom door faces the entrance to the room so that the bathroom has an outside window next to the picture-window of the room with its blue slatted blind between its double panes and the green pelmet above, the two green bars of the undrawn curtains hanging vertical on either side. More often the bathroom flanks the entrance in a small passage, facing the built-in cupboard and has a token window on the hotel corridor or no window at all, merely a ventilation shaft. Sometimes it even flanks the bed.

Inside the white circle the red diagonal crosses the black right-angle so that the bus cream-lined and stretching long and tense like a vibrant animal should drive straight on with a clanking into gear and a great roar after the traffic lights between the yellow tram and the white façades with their bright letters red green blue Supermarché BRASSERIE UNIVERSELLE Epicerie *Léon Delhaize* Réductions SOLDES slashed obliquely on glass hiding the mannequins. But no, the bus turns right by the small sign in white letters on faded blue Détournement/Omleiding with a broad white bar in a red disc ahead by a drill vibrating on the cobbles an electric power van and a group of men in a small cloud of dust.

The cloud has cleared. Way down below the window-seat through the rectangular window with rounded corners the sea looks solid earth or clay you could cut through with a blunt knife pick up in handfuls mould perhaps into a moon marine mother of death birth menstruation or fear of something else not ordered. Horoskop: Sie haben Appetit auf Neues. Passen Sie zur Zeit so gut es geht dem Partner an.

In fact the bathroom door in pinewood flanks the pine cupboard to the right and stands ajar, letting in too much light from a high glazed window on to the wall pink-tiled all the way up and the curved edge of the black bidet. According to the legislation into effect you may not bring the antiquity out of the country. Please declare if you have plants or parts of plants with you but the blue bus at the frontier post honks for the congress members and interpreters who chose to leave Sofia by way of Istanbul. Please declare if you have plants or parts of plants because one day the man will come and bring you out of this or that zone with a tremendous force and the intensity of a love lost or never gained such as for instance one idea that actually means something in the light of that love. On this day or that the concrete corridor encased in glass slopes up straight from the tarmac where the yellow bus has stopped, and on into the airport hall of clean glass galleries coffee-bars teak stairways with wide frightening space between the steps and queues of plastic luggage moving unowned unmastered up the conveyor-belt over the edge and straight along toward the small swing metal gates where men half-hidden in booths consult secret lists with a quick lift of the eye on to this or that face. He stands alone between his thick black briefcase and his pigskin hold-all.

The menu goes all the way to Mogadishu but has no personal significance after scaloppine di vitello. Between Rome and Khartoum they will eat insalata di cetrioli, pollo arrosto con patate e spinaci, his greying head outlined in the small rectangular window with rounded corners on the blue temperature of minus forty-five degrees. Inside they have pressurised the comfort so that the hum of voices echoes loud in the marble hall as the Lord Mayor speaks into a microphone, bidding everyone welcome in inaudible near-perfect English to this ancient city, the acoustics of the marble-hall carrying the words into the painted ceiling and they wind unheard around the marble columns. The members of the Congress burble on move about in close national groups with left hands holding wine-glasses and right hands holding little plates of smørrebrød or vice versa in the crowded hall. He turns his back to the assembly, his greying head outlined against the enormous window that overlooks the fjord, talking to three middle-aged ladies and one young or maybe telling stories the one about the round billiard-table unless emitting ideas that actually mean something or even just listening staring at the fjord holding his glass his smørrebrød, a cigarette lighter perhaps to flame the young one with who puts her plate down on the low long sill and draws his fire and shapes her words with gestures which weave no doubt a circle round him thrice below her black and flashing eyes, her floating hair. Though smooth in fact and neatly piled in shell-formations high pale pink, tinted but effective with a fatal contrast of black around her eyes that flash significance excluding the present introduction of Mr. Bryan McThingummy and the speech of the lady in the flowered silk suit at the microphone up in the gallery who has tried for some minutes to address the reception as the members of the Congress burble on in a conducted tour for those who wish to shshshsh!

Mr. Basil McThingummy and the members of the Congress burble on over their wine their smørrebrød their smoke and move about in close national groups for those who wish to visit this renowned Town Hall, which as you know surrounds him with a group of women one young wearing a yellow dress and rose-gold hair smoothly piled up in coils and black around her eyes under straight black eyebrows, who shapes her words with gestures that weave circles round him and twine up into the painted ceiling and the microphonic words that shshshsh!

The light has quite unrounded the corners of the cupboard, made of teak, with plain oak bars for handles. The light pours insulated silence through the brown and orange patterned curtains on the left, despite the yellow Venetian blinds inside the double window behind the cotton curtains.

No clock stands on the bedside table the grumpy voice of the hall porter on the telephone saying ten past three madam. Ten past three! How long the night, llarga la nit, on account of the Northern Lights in midsummer. Unless how strange I never carry a watch either don't believe in them one finds clocks everywhere even if they all disagree according to locality speed height theme of congress and like you I always manage punctuality at work. You see we have much in common. No body occupies the empty bed. No one comes in offering anything not ordered.

Between the dawn and the non-existent night the body stretches out its hundred and twenty ribs or so towards the distant brain way up beyond the yellow curtain that divides the ordinary from the better and no doubt behind a little door.

— Mesdames messieurs. Air France vous souhaite la bienvenue à bord de cet énorme problème devant lequel cependant le langage flows into the ear and comes out into the mouthpiece over waves and on into the ears of the multitudes or so in simultaneous German. To the right of the vast metal wing the sun that had almost set before take-off has leapt quite high again above the mountains. It has some way to go before it sets once more.

The white circle surrounded with red contains a black car and a red car but the grey-lined bus swings out to the left lane and overtakes a large dark blue car with pleated nylon curtains over its rear window, the left lane empty of traffic between the closed shops called MĂRUNŢIŞURI, LACTO VEGETARIAN, ALIMENTE, TUTUNGERIE.

Stimate pasager! The pillow stands obliquely in the wall corner of the bed with its ears up, its middle carefully dented. The feather-bed buttoned up in sheeting no longer occurs, only the black and red patterned blanket folded over with the top sheet to form two parallel white borders from which the planes move slowly off, rise suddenly and vanish or come in out of the low grey cloud by radar to the distant brain way up in the long nose-tip. The labelled bottle on the bedside-table reads Apă Minerală—Biborţeni—Apă de Masă, feruginosă, bicarbonată, calcică, sodică-magneziană, carbogazoasă, hipotonă. The bathroom door faces the built-in cupboard of dark oak across the narrow passage leading into the room so that it has no window, only a ventilation shaft. Every few hours or minutes of the night just as sleep comes a great crunch of a key trying the door swerves sleep into half-wakeful irritation though the key won't fit until fury takes over with a bound and Was suchen Sie in anger through the unlocked open door to a blear-eyed blear-faced blear-aged man who sways in his pyjamas and slinks away into Room 38 and drunk astonishment at such a change of the expected person. Sometimes the number of the key remains several weeks running in the two or three hundreds, then suddenly drops to 2, or 4 or 10 so that the smattering of the mouthpiece can proudly utter doi patru zece at the reception unless iki dört on, depending on the size the time the place and nothing much above 15. Stimate pasager! La cererea clientului servim MICUL DEJUN in camere. Out of the mouths of babes the Frenchman says with eloquent gestures on the dais beyond the interpreters' glass booth, la Vérité, la Justice, l'Humanité, Tutungerie in blue beyond the glass between the red black and white patterned curtains and below on the shop window Debit a tutun.

Of course the expected person changes. The menu goes all the way to somewhere or other with the bathroom to the right and the Eau de Vittel—Pureté-Santé to the left but no personal significance after the coq-au-vin airborne three hours ten minutes between the enormous wings. The body stretches forth towards some thought some order some command obeyed in the distant brain way up or even an idea that actually means something compels a passion a commitment lost or ungained yet as the wing spreads to starboard motionless on the still blue temperature of minus fifty-one degrees, the metal shell dividing it from this great pressurised solitude. The body floats in a quiet suspension of belief and disbelief, the sky grows dark over the chasms of the unseen Pyrenees. The bright red bar of sunset cuts the navy sky like a horizontal hot poker as the tray comes in to land with its empty plastic cup, the mayonnaise mess in the plastic side-plate, the miniature braised beef and outsize roast potatoes and three dices of carrots, the roll the pat of butter in gold the cellophane-wrapped biscuits with the triangle of cheese, the toy salt-cellar and the lilliputian mustard-tube. The stimaţi pasageri huddle in the hundred and ten seats or so between the dark invisible wings, looked after cradled in their needs, eat drink smoke talk doze dream read that casual girls take the easy way to colour, Get that Glint with a Hint of a Tint, and love to your hair as the green light winks under the stars on and off in the enormous black beyond the small rectangular window and still on behind the eyelids closed, open, closed, open. It looks like a light way down on earth but doesn't pass away, it travels with the body of the plane full of stimaţi pasageri at a speed of total immobility between the invisible wings. The plastic tray remains full of half-eaten trifle and the crumbs of roll, the cellophane paper and the miniature mustard-tube. Between the port and starboard engines the body floats, the plastic tray takes off above the breasts of the air-hostess that point up her white blouse.

The ship bumps down the steps of air, losing height slowly as it nears its expected minute of arrival, the distant brain way up no doubt obeying innumerable instructions that translate time speed height into locality and channel and descent into bright lights. Ladies and gentlemen, kindly extinguish your cigarettes and do not weave circles round him thrice with eloquent gestures that wrap up la Vérité, la Justice, l'Humanité et la Tutungerie.

Siegfried works with his eyes and hands as well as with his ears and voice. He lip-reads the speaker on the dais through the small glass booth and in the next split second hears the expected English syllables of problems we should consider today for the sake of mutual understanding the advancement of learning the true state of things that pour into the earphones through the distant brain way up and out into the mouthpiece in simultaneous German. Two channels keep the mind alert he says the eyes the ears or three for he shapes the words with his hands reproducing the speaker's gestures to keep his mind alert since the delegates in the audience do not watch him in the glass booth but only the speaker or more often each other in whispers or their notes, waiting for their turn to shine.

— How can you work with only your ears and voice?

— Well, and the brain.

The distant brain way up.

— You don't watch the speaker and you keep your eyes quite closed.

Fixed on the words as they pass through the transmuter in the brain, the hands quite still on the desk, forming a squat diamond space with the two index-finger-tips touching away from the body, the thumbs pressing each other towards it and sometimes all the fingers touching like a cathedral roof. But you never see his gestures. You close your eyes and watch the words as they pass through the transmuter behind your closed eyelids what goes on there?

Steadily, in well formed phrases hitting the German nail on the French pinpoint. Unless alternatively concision shrinks the abstractions like angels to a pinhead and the pinhead pricks the Gallic nuance which escapes like gas depending on the speaker's nationality in French, Hungarian for instance or Chinese or mediocre, depending on the theme the time the place the climate, whether canyons or mountains create different pressures and great holes of air into which the plane sinks suddenly with a lilt of the stomach as in the Výtah—лифт—Ascenseur. Přivolávač it says, Appel.

— In der Luft gibts keine Grenzen. The dark handsome Viennese leans right across from the left to photograph the Danube which from der Luft looks actually quite blue to prevent any true exchange of thoughts above the close breath and perhaps intentional nearness unless he genuinely wants to photograph die Donau für die Kinder with a tip of nose in the foreground and maybe a dark green shoulder or curve of bosom even and the enormous wing spreading back moving at speed over the Danube quite blue from der Luft and gone.

— Ah but airports have frontiers. And travel-talk ensues with Herr Helmut von Irgendetwas who travels in textiles as others travel in simultaneous interpretation. To inflate jacket pull red toggle (1). To top up, blow into mouthpiece (2) in order to prevent any true exchange between the close breath and the leaning forward beyond keine Grenzen, obeying the innumerable instructions that translate time speed height desire into locality and channel and the slow descent into matter. You will find your life-jacket under your seat. This life-jacket can serve on an unconscious person. Uw zwemvest bevindt zich onder uw stoel. Dit zwemvest kan dienen voor een bewusteloos persoon. Questo salvagente one day will have no frontiers and no passports per assistere anche una persona priva de conoscenza. Aber natürlich, selbstverständlich, hoffentlich und so weiter.

Prague has a dingy airport still. A mess of huts, a transit-lounge like a wartime canteen. Just like our first meeting says Siegfried remember? The tannoy voice in the large wooden hut calls out ranks with names attached and even faces over uniforms grey-blue dark olive-green and khaki that wear a listening look for the Dakota aircraft about to take off from Frankfurt to a scattering of mimeographed news-sheets from the square metal table in the transit lounge look, the new Lord Mayor of Prague has promised to build a better one.

The Slovak National Council met in Bratislava yesterday for its first session since the General Election on June 14. The Council unanimously re-elected Minister Jan Trudny, member of the Praesidium of the Central Committee, as Chairman of the Council. Gut-gut. The Minister then took the floor.

— Mesdames messieurs. Aujourd'hui nous allons discuter le problème de la communication, du point de vue which reveals een bewusteloos persoon blowing hot air into the mouthpiece all enclosed in a glass booth going down, after having pulled red toggle (1) pushed the red button ⑤ ④ ③ ② ① Ⓡ ⓪ . But R turns out to mean Restaurant in studded black plastic cushioned walls not Rez-de-chaussée at all.

Kein Eintritt. Privat. Que cherchez-vous madame? Ah, au fond à gauche, in fondo a sinistra geradeaus dann links according to the theme the time the place with a flared-skirted figurine on the door. Or a high-heeled shoe perhaps as opposed to a flat foot, MESSIEURS, they have their exits and their entrances he makes his greying English jokes under his greying hair or stands against the gothic pillar telling the one about the elephant perhaps unless ideas that actually mean something to a svelte red-haired lady in a low décolletage that speaks ideas? My dear good girl and so forth.

Služi za brisanje. Za skidanje šminke. Für Rasierklingen. Zum Abschminken. Pour le rasoir. Pour le démaquillage. For the razor. To remove your make-up.

Molimo Vas ne upotrebljavajte ručnik. Bitte kein Handtuch benützen. Ever at all? Prière de ne pas se servir de l'essuie-main. Please weave no circle round him thrice and kindly do not leave your seats until the aircraft comes to a standstill.

It comes to a standstill. The body strapped under the tightly swaddling sheet and heavy blanket having slept immobile at a speed of nine hundred kilometres height ten thousand metres outside temperature minus something or other and the distant brain way up translating time speed height into locality and channel and descent where the light unrounds the corners of the cupboard dressing-table stool under which bevindt zich uw zwemvest for a bewusteloos persoon who nevertheless fondles the medal of St. Christopher between the breasts below the tightly swaddling sheet. No body occupies the empty space in the large bed nor will use l'essuie-main not für Rasierklingen. No one comes in offering anything not ordered. Soon some bright chambermaid will buzz allo? er, hello, seven-thirty, oh, thank you.

The headboard of the double bed forms a recess in the wall of pale turquoise silk, patterned in horizontal flat diamond-shapes with a tiny white embroidered circle at the corner of each diamond, forming studs, the lines that join all the studs to form the diamonds made up of minute stitches trapeze-shaped in white. A spot of light rests on the left lower line of each silk diamond turning it to silver. The light comes from the striped brown white and blue cotton curtain like a Dutch skirt clashing in style with the silk headboard but the night before in the electric light looking pale blue and gold and Louis Seize, muffling the footsteps made by Dutch people walking in Dutch along the Dutch canal with a Dutch dog barking in Dutch. The number on the key has dropped again to twee. But from the standpoint of the window each bright spot of light has moved to the stud-like dot at the points where the acute angles of the flat diamonds meet, forming a larger less bright patch on every diamond shape in the pale turquoise headboard recessed into the wall behind the empty unmade bed which the night before looked large and empty and made.

The dikes shine in the sun as silver threads between the large fields of pale green absolutely flat except for one surprising hill beyond the wing. The hill moves with the wing, rising quite disconnected from the land of unblossomed tulips below. The hill has a hinted halo of propellers almost invisible in their speed and the sun remains ahead from four o'clock to midnight never setting as the plane chases it across the clay Atlantic you could cut with a knife through Chicken Maryland, pancake and maple-syrup, cranberry and apple pie and Pouilly-Fuissé made in California. Do you have mineral water please?

— Mineral warrer? Do you mean nachral warrer?

— Nein, er, no thank you. Soda?

— Ow, sora-warrer. Sure. You can have sora-warrer. On the rahks.

— Thank you. Without the rocks please.

The bottle of Vidago stands on the bedside-table, poderosamente radio-activas, bicarbonatadas, liticas, arsenicais, fluerotadas, gaso-carbonicas. The cock crows loud and long at crack of dawn or so, triumphant in some shed or other somewhere beyond the slatted wooden shutters that rise easily to reveal the flat roofs of Lisbon and the pale blue temperature of no doubt twenty-two already as announced by the cock triumphant in some shed among the hanging sheets and the potted geraniums. Soon the bent wizened old woman dressed in black shuffles her booted feet noisily through the loose plaster on the terrace roof, drags a large iron-grey basin across from the shed-door to a low packing-case stood vertically against the white chimney, lifts the basin on to it, shuffles back noisily through the plaster to the shed-door, turns on a tap, fills a metal jug at a resonant distance below the tap, turns off the tap, shuffles across the terrace noisily through the plaster, pours the water into the iron basin at a resonant distance above it, shuffles back, repeats eight times until the basin contains a gallon or so of water for the washing of her wizened face eight times at a resonant distance above it like eight cataracts. A slatted shutter shrieks invisibly from above, another visibly and rising in a window along the right wing of the hotel where a blear-faced blear-aged man in striped pyjamas looks out and down, then up, gazes across, looks startled, sheepish, then licentious, smoothes his hair, makes dog-eyes, protrudes his lips, juts out his tongue slowly, very slowly out, and in, and out again, and round, repeats, cups the air breast-shape in his hand, protrudes his tongue slowly, very slowly out, and in, and out again, and round, looks back into the room then across the terrace, shows the palms of his hands in a naõ posso gesture and pulls down his shutter fast. The shutter from above slams down in anger shock regret, who knows to whom the blear-aged man has directed his dumb-show unanswered at one level 230 or thereabouts and at another higher unseen 312 perhaps responded to with yearning for romance or lust atingle in the loins unless despair in knowledge of the man exasperation cold indifference with her long blonde hair hanging over the sill sans merci despite desire at sight or lewd suggestion swelling her nipples through the diaphanous nightdress low cut on shapely breasts revealed as she leans forward or merely huge and heavy under flabby chins and a middle-aged face indignant under curlers. The wizened woman in black has gone and the cock crows in Portuguese triumphant somewhere on the flat roofs of Lisbon among the hanging sheets and the potted geraniums.

And yet the man from 230 or thereabouts looked straight across and eyes met eyes. The blear-faced blear-aged man unhesitatingly unanswered at one level. The same question everywhere goes unanswered have you anything to declare any plants or parts of plants growing inside you stifling your strength with their octopus legs undetachable for the vacuum they form over each cell, clamping each neurone of your processes in a death-kiss while the new Lord Mayor of Prague promises to take up the challenge in trying to make you commit yourself to one single idea.

— Ideas? We merely translate other people's ideas, not to mention platitudes, si-mul-ta-né-ment. No one requires us to have any of our own. We live between ideas, nicht wahr, Siegfried?

— Du liebes Kind, komm, geh' mit mir. Gar schöne Spiele spiel' ich mit dir.

— We have played those games mein Lieb.

— Why don't you marry me?

— You know why.

Such conversations never quite occur in such romantic terms unless in quotes expressing falsely something there no doubt, except in the precision of the mouthpiece at nineteen or twenty-five even. Bright girl, she translates beautifully don't you think? Says the boss. Meaning in his greying English way come live with me and adorn my gracious Regency London house with your charming French accent not to mention cuisine your German super-Aryan litheness and of course Fleissigkeit as well as your elegant cosmopolitan ways. The divine principle of love or flow of rash enthusiasm descending into matter bumps on the steps of air, lowers its undercarriage touches down speeds along the runway in a whistling roar of jets and strong tension of brakes that slow it to a taxying up the tarmac guided by some distant brain in a green glass booth and small white frogs with yellow discs for eyes until it comes to a standstill. A faint sensation of relief spreads through the body of the plane, slightly animating the chromosomes as if inside a giant centipede. Please declare if you have any plants or parts of plants with you such as love loyalty lust intellect belief of any kind or even simple enthusiasm for which you must pay duty to the Customs and Excise until you come to a standstill.

Soon some young buxom chambermaid in black and white will come in with a breakfast-tray put it down on the table in the dark draw back the curtains with bonjour madame good morning gün aydın who knows, it all depends where the sleeping has occurred out of what dream swerved up with non merci nein-nein danke in a long-lost terror of someone offering etwas anderes, not ordered.

Or a smooth floor-steward in white. On account of whose possibility absurdly the hair-net comes off, the pins picked from the hair which tumbles down seductively for no reason at all despite the greying strand, invisible no doubt in the half light needing that glint of a tint and normally worn scraped up with earphone diadem around the neutralised transmitter in the brain through which flows automatically cet énorme problème de l'humanité trop nombreuse at the International Conference of Demographers in Copenhagen coming out in simultaneous German. La grande leçon des préservatifs which means in fact prevention not preserving proves that the language laughs at the illiterate women of an Indian village taught the natural method with an abacus to count the days in fourteen red balls pushed one by one from left to right you may have intercourse. So that they shove all the red balls together from left to right like a magic spell and come back every one pregnant.

Higienska vreća za binde (Ulošci za dame). Molimo Vas ne bacajte ih u W.C. Sobarica će ih ukloniti zajedno sa vrećom. Sac pour bandes hygiéniques. Prière de ne pas jeter dans le W.C. La femme de chambre les enlèvera. Bag for sanitary pads. Please do not throw into W.C. The chambermaid will remove them. Hygienebeutel für Damenbinden. Bitte nicht ins Klosett werfen for one day the man will come and bring you out of this or that zone with a tremendous force and the intensity of a love lost or never gained such as for instance an idea that actually means something in the light of that death. Sometimes German comes first then French then English or vice versa in endless permutations with the language of the country always at the head however such as ΣΑΡΙΖΑ ΑΡΙΣΤΟΝ ΕΠΙΤΡΑΠΕΖΙΟΝ ΙΑΜΑΤΙΚΟΝ ΥΔΩΡ hardly worth the effort on account of SARIZA Table Water natural-curative Eau de Table naturelle-curative. Analyse de l'eau de SARIZA (en miligr par litre) Silice, Acide Sulfurique, Chaux, Résistivité électrique en Ohms Radioactivité (unités Mache) to the ΤΟΥΑΛΕΤΤΑ with care not to enter ΑΝΔΡΩΝ by mistake when the door bears no skirted figurine or high-heeled shoe in the imprecision of a mere smattering acquired among the Cinzano Jerez-Quina Liquor Beirao ouzo St. Raphael what will you have my dear in low square black armchairs the bar lit up like a reredos. He examines his money endlessly before paying, turning each of the lire douros marks over and over and the same with half-crowns and florins as if lire douros marks. All right then thinks thought will think Siegfried perhaps he will hurt her and I'll bide my time and gather up the broken bits with a great tenderness and kindly observe the non-smoking sign.

For visiting: (1) The aqueduct which winds from the wilderness to the old city wall. (2) The temple of Diana, tall in dark stone columns that make a pleasing contrast with the small white houses crouching around the temple and the Baroque church behind it. Or let us say the aqueduct walks says Siegfried from the wilderness on innumerable brown legs like a brown centipede, pierces the citadel and stops, collapsed, not too far however from the secret mysteries of Diana in broken columns coloured bronze mark you by the setting sun and surrounded with white palpitating stags, perhaps even animal organs not to mention the cross on the curlicued façade so much taller than the small church behind it.

— But stones do talk.

— Statistically, into microphones.

— Du Witzling.

— Witzling-Schmutzling, ja?

— Ein bisschen.

— Ich lieb' dich, mich reizt deine schöne Gestalt.

— Und so?

— brauch' ich Gewalt?

Silences differ more than hotel rooms or menus and the washbasin does stand on one lilac leg opposite another leg lilac or blue perhaps next door that gurgles at dawn unless much later to the right of the window beyond which what how when allo? er, pronto? Ah, grazie where the Convention of Acupuncturists presses points through the distant brain way up along the meridian of the vésicule biliaire which although à l'intérieur de la jambe ran once in prehistory on the other side the doctor demonstrates à l'extérieur on account of the foetus position of man with diagrams of a fish thrown upside down on the screen the lantern-slide projector behaving like an antipodal eye. He laughs you see how the mechanical breakdown in communication proves my point by telescoping time with an error, errors having frequently led to scientific truth, la pointe pressed home by the next speaker on the meridian of the heart C7 here on the wrist which stops hysteria at once with the vessel of conception CV52 as a recommended alternative for relaxation and the absolute calm she translates with don't you think? Meaning come live with me and grace my London house with your elegant cosmopolitan ways not to mention animal organs and the white Regency façade so much taller than the small imagination behind it. Or the box cottage in Wiltshire for escape from the elegant cosmopolitan ways of love in London Paris Oslo Rome between the enormous wings inside the clinical white fuselage of ships, temples of still motion at a speed of light-years bumping down the steps of air lowering their undercarriages and touching ground with a strong tension of brakes that slow it down guided up the runway by the distant brain translating time speed height intó locality, channel, descent.

— Un cottage? Que voulez-vous dire, un cottage?

— Hé bien, mon père, une toute petite maison, à la campagne. A box a refuge a still small centre within the village within the wooded countryside within the alien land, where Mr. Jones the builder who converts the bathroom says bee-day? Oh you mean a biddy. Yes I can get a biddy for you but you aven't got much room ave you? Ah si! Un cottage. The pale fat priest-interpreter looks over his half-spectacles made for reading the sheafs of notes before him. Un piccolo chalet. Va bene così? Un piccolo chalet?

— Va bene.

Un piccolo chalet in Wiltshire where stones talk walk make love until they come to a standstill. Welcome back Liebes to the freedom of the air and the precision of the mouthpiece in your nineteenth year and plus as he picks up the broken bits, working with eyes and hands as well as with his ears and voice. He lipreads the speaker and in the next split second utters the same syllables of half-love and bantering allusion that need no simultaneous interpreting by the code of zones flown over descended into half-visited on swift conducted tours with groups from Agricultural Aid Commissions, Conferences of Irrigation Engineers and even Congresses of Semiologists for example in palaces castles university buildings town halls, together sometimes or with say Signor Ingegnere Giovanni-Battista di Qualcosa or Comrade Pan Bogumil Somethingski, according to the requirements of language topic time available since the return to the precision of the mouthpiece at nineteen or twenty-nine even.

In fondo a sinistra the men in the café sit transfixed by the flickering local variation in the presentation of opposite viewpoints on every aspect of an instant world through faceless men who have no doubt acquired faces for them as their arch-priests of actualitá that zooms flashcuts explodes to

OMO! Da oggi con Perboral! Lava ancora più bianco! Gut-gut. Più bianco than what? We live in an age of transition, perpetually between white and whiter than white. Very tiring. Zoom. Applicate il numero di codice. The matchbox on the table shows a small postman in green with a large orange postbag on a blue background. The postman holds a letter with 00147 Roma written on it. Two orange arrows say il numero di codice and point to 00147 Roma. The orange bag twice as large as the postman says Applicate il numero di codice as Siegfried lights up with do you know the number of your zone and which represents reality the old towns like museums visited on conducted tours or the modern hotels we stay in all alike?

Sometimes however the bathroom door faces the built-in cupboard in the entrance passage to the room so that the bathroom has no window, only a ventilation shaft. Sometimes it faces the door of the room, occupying more generously a space in width not length with its own window on the street the sea the mountain the roof on which a wizened woman washes in eight cataracts affording a glimpse of something real surely below the sex-mime of a blear-aged man with tongue and mouthpiece or a car revving up in Danish. Sometimes the blear-aged man tries the locked door in drunken stupor with his key that doesn't fit and slinks away at the Was suchen Sie in fury and the change in the expected person. Sometimes the number on the key remains several weeks running in the four hundreds or three then suddenly drops to 5, 2, 4, 12, so that the smattering of the mouthpiece can proudly ask the the receptionist for beş, iki, dört unless dwanaście, depending on the size the time the place and whether canyons or rocks create great holes of air into which the heart sinks. Sometimes a chambermaid serves Frühstück or Micul Dejun in camere. Or a smooth floor-steward in white unless a waking call with collazione down below in a black plastic bar. Sometimes the bathroom flanks the cupboard facing the bed or beds themselves together or separate or longwise foot to foot along the left wall or even the right. Few hotels have single rooms these days it doesn't pay and single rooms seldom have a shower or bath or private loo, only a biddy and a wash-stand on one leg blue green white pink yellow or fixed to the wall with a thick metal tube lewdly protruding underneath but curving up again not always visibly however so that the empty bed lies empty and tightly made unless the puffed up eiderdown buttoned up in sheeting looks virgin-bellied untumbled or the bright orange blanket folds back within the sheet in two parallel white runways from which memories take off and disappear into the blue the cloud the fog.

Ausgang. Exit. Push. Tirez. Drücken. Déclarez s'il vous plaît si vous avez des plantes ou parties de plantes avec vous, loyalty for example or a simple enthusiasm for warming slippers on a late return from the club the office the journeys the philandering with the precision of the mouthpiece at conventions, conferences, commissions, congresses. Or else inside the whale, who knows, in the foetus position with diagrams of a fish thrown upside down for three days, three lives of maybe hell. Between loving and not loving the body floats.

On one side of the broad yellow arrow diagonal from corner to corner of the square card the razor-blade, printed in green, has a white narrow bar representing the slit, crossed at one end with a short vertical bar then a small diamond shape and another short bar, a space, a circle in the centre then a space, a bar a diamond and a bar. On the other side of the broad yellow arrow two pink lips slightly separated echo the white slit in the green razor blade. The yellow arrow points downwards across the cardboard square pinned up in diamond shape to cover the squares of paper and bears the lettering Pentru ştergerea lamei de ras şi a rujului. Pour le demaquiage spelt wrong et pour les lames de rasoir. For remove the make-up and for something in Russian then German last. Sometimes German comes first then English then French in endless permutations with the language of the country always at the head however such as Toaleta Femei unless ТОАЛЕТНА with care not to enter Bărbaţi when the door bears no skirted figurine or high-heeled shoe in the imprecision of a mere smattering acquired with the descent into new matter. Or just enough to say muchas gracias dowidzenia dove? In fondo a sinistra.

So that Siegfried picks up the broken bits working with his hands voice mouth eyes ears and more than his five senses into the vessel of conception CV 52 lipreading and in the next split second uttering the same syllables of half-love bantering allusion to the medal of St. Christopher between the breasts and other circumstances that need no simultaneous interpreting by the code of zones flown over descended into half visited on swift conducted tours together sometimes or separately and alone according to the requirements of conventions conferences congresses in castles palaces public buildings university halls where no communication of course ever occurs. Ever? You exaggerate. Something gets across.

— Criss-cross.

— Crease-crasse? God, verr god. The short gentleman with straight black hair in a black suit labelled Laos says god, verr god indeed. The Gairmans they applause their speakers. The English they applause their speakers. The French they say alone the French make intellectual contribution. Only Laos delegation praise all.

— And the Japanese. Don't forget the Japanese.

— They praise, yes mademoiselle, also.

— Presumably everyone comes for that. They certainly can't come for information since it all gets published anyway and they could simply read it.

— Information? My dear good girl unless perhaps du ernst German Mädel or my sweet more likely how naïve can you get? After what three, four years on congresses and commissions you should know better than that.

— Yes, well they might at least make a show of listening. Each speaker waits impatiently for his turn to read an interminable paper that has nothing to do with anything said before, you know, each one more concerned with output than intake.

— Ah, output, intake, god, verr god mademoiselle. May I use that in article? My card. Buan Ching cultural correspondent please.

— So you call this culture?

Of course of course natürlich selbstverständlich und so weiter weiter gehen through the freedom of the air and the imprecision of the mouthpiece at thirty-five and plus madame not mademoiselle despite the fact that on a day he leans against a column in a Renaissance palazzo, his grey hair surmounted by a cherub talking to the dark lady of not a single sonnet but smooth words allusive with his eyes on her low décolletage or maybe on the smoke blown down over it from her delicate olive nostrils. Have you anything to declare such as love desire ambition or a glimpse that in this air-conditioning and other circumstantial emptiness freedom has its sudden attractions as the body floats in willing suspension of responsibility to anyone, stretching interminably between the enormous wings towards the distant brain beyond the orange curtain and behind, no doubt, the little door.

The concrete corridor encased in cedar-wood slopes up from the tarmac where the blue bus has stopped and up into the lounge where yellow messages wait on a turntable of boards covered with criss-cross lattice-work in alphabetical order. No one calls out no name unanswered at one level, no one comes in offering anything. The airport hall makes up an abstract study of glass galleries hot air continuous murmuring and teakwood stairways with space between the steps to fall into down by the gleaming weight-machines in rows like robots for the queueing plastic luggage of those about to leave, to vanish past the booths containing the half-hidden men who consult secret lists with a quick shift of the eye. One day even airports will have no frontiers and no passports per assistere anche una persona priva de conoscenza. Aber natürlich. He stands by his pigskin hold-all his thick black briefcase in his left hand, shaking the right with the president of the congress the secretary the most important delegates male elderly female and doesn't introduce his team of three interpreters English-German French-German English-French besides himself French into English and they simultaneously stand about and smile in English German French.

They praise, yes mademoiselle, also.

Soon some dark waiter will enter with a breakfast-tray and the rest of the story will have to come out. What story? Oh you know as the Holy Ghost said that scandal spread by St. Peter about me and the Virgin Mary. He likes ready-made stories the schmutziger the witziger with a burst of crude laughter tout de suite and the tooter the sweeter. Was suchen Sie, die Toilette, nein den Aufzug, so, immer geradeaus dann links Ascenseur Lift or else a change in the expected person ⑥ ⑤ ④ ③ ② ① Ⓔ Ⓡ Ⓢ for sous-sol and the one about the Auvergnat who pronounces S as sh and when asked the whereabouts of l'évéché says au shou-shol. Oh, you ernst

German Mädel don't you see, les W.C., l'évéché do you have to have everything explained?

The light pours through the slatted shutters making a slatted pattern on the left pale green wall. San Pellegrino, Acqua litinica alcalina antiurica anticatarrale. Battericamente pura. Trams clang through the asthmatic gasps of an engine that won't fire in Italian not very far down among the poop-pip-hoot of cars below the several floors of waking dreams. The face reflected in the bathroom mirror neon-lit looks what thirty-four, forty-three below the greying strand broader sandier than the rest that tumbles on the shoulders needing nevertheless that Glint with a Hint of a Tint above the small medallion of St. Christopher almost in the cleft between the breasts and the neon light floods OMO on the glass shelf. Da oggi con PERBORAL. Lava ancora più bianco. Or else che cerca, signora, ah, l'ascensore. In fondo a sinistra. And the divine principle descending into matter through the earphones and out into the mouthpiece at the Congress of Gnostics in Brussels, Bonn, Beirut, wherever angels and ministers of grace and meaning come down to land upon a pinpoint unless at the Conference on Teilhard de Chardin where the flaxen-haired young lady in the audience holds a flaxen spool like a second oblong head and spins, manually spins as she listens without earphones to ideas all having equality before God no rising en masse of noussphere to point omega comme nous répète ce grand génie as she spins, spins a circle round him thrice so that he falters in the booth, loses the thread in the spun rhetoric and old Bertrand takes over on his microphone in his accented English.

Manhattan's lit-up post-war fairyland recedes below into the night. Ladies and gentlemen, welcome aboard this minister of grace floating upon a pinpoint rising to a height of fifteen thousand feet speed two hundred and fifty miles an hour. You may smoke now and give me a drink before announcing things like that. Like what? Like that you love me. Oh, did I say that?

I should like to remind the delegates that the Economic and Social Council has not asked the Committee to discuss the report of the Commission on Human Rights in detail but merely to formulate the principles which should guide the Commission's work in the future. May I suggest therefore that the Commission reexamine the question at some later stage. Or else in the Dakota on the long metal bench fixed to the curved metallic wall inside the fuselage, the round ribs all exposed as if inside the skeleton of a giant centipede. No. He says marry me my sweet and take me as you find me we'll have fun.

— Not that you followed him in all things mein Lieb.

— Well, the descent into matter.

Helsinki, London, Lisbon, Milan, Warsaw.

And language. Allo?—er, dígame? Muchas gracias.

— Wejście. Wyjście. Just one letter's difference. Which do you suppose means exit?

— Or gentlemen.

— Pas ici my sweet. Immer geradeaus up the corridor turn left and take me as you find me. Or irgendsowas Witziges unless perhaps gents have their exits and their entrances and please adjust your dress before leaving. Or even have you the time please yes but not the inclination.

Wherever particular people congregate Siegfried reads from the packet of cigarettes brought by the air-hostess in a wine coloured skirt and white blouse you smoke too much.

— La lune vous rend particulièrement sensible. Vous vous sentirez obstinés, prêts à mal interpreter les intentions des autres.

— Why do you read that stuff?
— Nothing else. Oh yes, the pamphlet.
— Well, we could talk.
— The Museum also contains statues, fragments of sculptures and other interesting works of art from the temples and constitutes an interesting collection. Why, we missed that.

What else? London and sometimes Wiltshire where stones talk and walk and make semblance of love have fun until they come to a standstill. All ideas have equality before God remember where you stumbled so why can't you commit yourself wholly to one of them?

— Ideas? Great Scott, nothing deserves a flow of rash enthusiasm my sweet. For fifteen years or more I have conducted my higher education by transmitting other people's ideas, not to say platitudes, from one microphone into another. No one expects me to produce my own as well.

Et comme l'a si bien dit Saussure, la langue peut se contenter de l'opposition de quelque chose avec rien. The marked term on the one hand, say, the feminine, grand*e*, the unmarked on the other, say, the masculine, grand. Mais notez bien que le non-marqué peut dériver du marqué par retranchement, by subtraction, par une absence qui signifie. Je répète, une absence qui signifie eine Abwesenheit die simultaneously etwas bedeutet.

The road from Idlewilde Airport runs past Jewish cemeteries with tall rectangular tombstones standing close together in miniature forewarning of skyscrapers. Soon some black or white waiter will come with a Manhattan cocktail or else the quiet American whose unquiet eyes will prevent any further quotations from the foolish fond old man called apparently Brutus Caesar who quotes his status as a very foolish fond old man fond, anyway, of whisky lady and bald pahr dessue le marshy, patting his bald marshy so that what can one say but smile agreeably at his charming self-deprecating sense of humour half drowned by the air-conditioning and other circumstantial emptiness amid the roar and whistle of strident laughter hum of voices that move about in close national groups.

The murmur of the talking delegates as they wait in the rows of desks like a giant class fills the vast hall. The president of the assembly knocks his hammer on the dais table or merely enters perhaps creating a sudden silence as the members dutifully don their listening caps to pick up the broken bits with a great tenderness and kindly observe the non-smoking sign. We note that the consensus of opinion in the Committee seems to favour the draft revised resolution. My delegation will certainly vote for it. We nevertheless have to face the real question, namely, how to implement it through the earphones in French behind the closed eyelids and out into the mouthpiece in simultaneous German or through other mouthpieces Russian Polish Arabic Chinese and him in another booth for simultaneous English no doubt staring at the empty desk.

Siegfried watches the speaker, he works with his eyes as well as ears and voice, even imitating the gestures with his hands. I recall—if you will forgive a personal observation—the first Disarmament Conference I attended in Geneva in 1932 and the interminable discussions we had then as to whether security came before disarmament or vice versa. I recall also the long discussions we had as to which weapons one could call offensive and which defensive, and our conclusion reached late one night in a café, that the offensiveness or defensiveness of a weapon depended on whether one stood in front of it or behind it. We seem to have made little progress since then. Nevertheless we should not give up the attempt und so weiter weiter gehen unless merely my government wishes to reiterate its whole-hearted support for the United Nations. We shall continue to honour our obligations and shall appoint a sub-committee to inquire into how the crisis has arisen. We live in a time of tension between two social orders and we must learn to resolve that tension. We must emphasise however that a vast cultural revolution has taken place which the world will not find easy to integrate into his quiet disparagement. Nothing deserves a flow of rash enthusiasm my sweet. As for the under-developed areas, we shall organise discussions to find out how best we could help those countries with their external defence problems and adjust their economies to the new situation.

— Gee, I saw you in your glass booth you sure looked dandy, silently efficient you know, unharassed, because of course I couldn't hear you. I listened to the English versions. That elderly fellow for the French and—

— Elderly?

— Well I don't know, he had grey hair. I always admire those fellers who do Russian and Polish and things like that. Russians and Poles I guess. You don't do Russian do you?

— No. French into German.

— German eh? Hmm. D'you like it?

— Do you mean German? Well—

— No I mean the job.

— Oh, this just came as an emergency, they needed extras. But one gets more than usually discouraged, more than with the other stuff.

— What other stuff?

— Oh, you know, literature, irrigation, the under-developed areas and all that.

— Jeeze. And you know about these things?

— Well on one level one hardly listens. On another one has to understand immediately you see because the thing understood slips away, together with the need to understand.

— Gee.

The quiet American with the unquiet eyes full of his upbringing's mechanically courteous interest in the other and whatever he or she has to say however abstract aphoristic platitudinous misleading looks at the bald and very foolish fond old man who says lirrechur, eh? Tomorrow and tomorrow and tomorrow, creeps in this petty place from day to day to the last syllable of recorded time. And all our yesterdays have lighted airport-halls with neon airport roads and tall rectangular tombstones standing close together in miniature forewarning of united nations ford foundations wall streets madison avenues where he talks to a young so young beginner in the art of understanding immediately, all channels alert eyes ears mouthpiece and fingers through her long auburn hair. She sneezes through her long auburn hair in the draught from the window skyscraped over the Hudson River so he says Dieu vous blesse into her peals of laughter through her long auburn hair and simultaneously translates back in time with Zounds! Restoration English for God's wounds you know. I have taken her under my wing, he says, she shows much promise and gets allotted somehow with him to other conferences, congresses, conventions where no communication ever occurs.

— Something comes out of them if only a knowledge of people. She says with her long auburn hair. Unless maybe: Something comes out of meetings or they wouldn't happen.

— Happenings prove only that something never comes out of them my dear.

— Whatever does that mean? For a chief interpreter you use words most imprecisely darling lost or perhaps not said after all amid the roar the hum the strident laughter no. I use them, simultanément ma chère collègue.

Ma chère collègue. And whatever wing means under which he has taken her. A thing of the intellect perhaps, ideas, a passion they have in common, literature for instance, irrigation, ready-made anecdotes for the under-developed areas or a certain verbal anarchy which makes their allusions intertwine in the echoing airport lounge as an abstract study in glass metal hot air and coffee-bars where the voice announces Flight KLM 62 to Helsinki delayed by fog.

Away from the road a path leads into the deep cleft between the two masses of the Phaidriades where lies the famous Kastalia spring. The visitor's attention turns immediately to the sanctuary of Apollo situated on the higher slopes of one of the Phaidriades rocks in five terrace-like levels, brilliant with the splendour of its monuments, the Treasures, the Portico of the Athenians, the Temple of Apollo beneath which the famous oracle used to sit and utter cryptic prophecies to all who came and consulted it on serious matters like war, alliances, births and marriages. Finally, a little higher up stands the Theatre, famous in ancient times for the performances of tragedy, and beyond the Sanctuary lies the Stadium, where the Pythic Games took place to celebrate Apollo's victory over Python, the legendary monster.

The visitor's attention turns immediately to the masculine unmarked and situated on the higher slopes in five terraces none of which deserves a flow of rash enthusiasm. Pupate! Pupate! He drives the hired car regardless of white hands about to signal other cars across. The policeman puts his head in at the window and shouts pupate? pupate? I don't speak Greek and the policeman waves him on. Quel culot! Insulting me in his own language. Well pu means where, so presumably pupate means où allez-vous, hardly an insult oh shut up you think you know everything don't you.

— For the phrase-book says listen to this under Marriage Proposal: As I really love you I want to make you my wife. Do you agree? Have you an opinion for the marriage? Did you want to test by means of engagement? Do you want to create our own home? Do you like children? Saith the book, the phrase-book saith.

The visitor's attention turns immediately to higher things such as Poulet sauté, Forestières, Macédoine de légumes, Riz Pilaff, Poire Belle Hélène, Fromage/Biscuits, Café over the ugliness of the modern capital that recedes as the plane rises swiftly to an outside temperature of thirty-nine degrees and the gods have left this land says Siegfried now the boss. They have their exits and their entrances over blue gulfs blue mountains and through slatted shutters in white cubic rooms where the white bathroom door flanks the pink painted built-in cupboard to the left and stands ajar, letting in too much light from a high window on the wall blue-tiled all the way up and the curved edge of the blue bidet. According to legislation into effect you may not take the antiquity out of the country. Wherever particular people congregate, you tap your cigarette more often than necessary into the chromium ash-tray on the round metal table.

— You never smoke it to the end. Just as you get at once on first name terms with everyone and promptly forget their surnames. So why don't you marry me after all these years?

— You know why.

— Oh that. The Vicariato di Roma. I can't think why you bother can you?

— No. Not any longer. But after all these years as you say one might as well see it through.

— To an unsuccessful conclusion? Then what?

— Well, one way or the other.

The men who fill the café sit transfixed by the flickering local variation in the presentation of opposed viewpoints on every aspect of an instant world through faceless men who have no doubt acquired faces for them as their arch-priests of faits-divers exploding into OMO! Le plus fort contre la saleté! But what difference does it make?

— How can one tell, until it has made it?

— If it makes it.

— If it does.

Une différence non marquée dérivant du marqué par une absence qui signifie eine Abwesenheit die etwas bedeutet, etwas anderes als ordered. Do you agree? Did you want to test by means of engagement? Or will you take me as you find me we'll have fun. Wejście/Wyjście. What difference does it make? In/out, up/down, container and contained. To go in you have to go out, up, down and vice versa. Pupate, pupate? Que cherchez-vous madame? Ah, l'ascenseur. Au fond à gauche.

Sometimes however the number on the key drops to fifteen from four hundred and twelve so that the smattering of the mouthpiece can proudly utter piętnaście unless onbeş, depending on the size the time the place and whether or not the bathroom faces the built-in cupboard in the entrance passage with no window only a ventilation shaft. Sometimes it faces the door of the room occupying a space in width not length and its own window on the same side as the picture-window with or without balcony on the street the sea the mountain. Here it faces the bed the double bed but sometimes two separate or longwise foot to foot along the left wall or the right even. Single rooms seldom have a shower or bath or private loo, only a biddy and a washstand on one leg white pink blue yellow or fixed to the wall with a thick metal tube protruding underneath but curving up again behind not always visibly however, depending on the place the time the theme, whether the hair gets washed and set with rollers in the hotel room or at the hairdresser friseur coiffeur kuaför frizer peluquería through signs with hands low here high at the back in coils, whether some languages for example divide their genders into animate and inanimate while others less primitive into andraic with a flat shoe or male figurine on the door and metandraic which covers objects animals of both sexes and women. Madame désire? OMO. Voici. Ah, un plus petit. Très bien. Madame désire encore quelque chose?

Leider haben wir keins. Die Apotheke, geradeaus dann links. Und haben Sie noch einen Wunsch?

So that the bells in endless crash-permutations on eight unimaginative manipulated notes endlessly permutate over the greenish drizzle from the distant belfry way off beyond the little door. Un cottage? Que voulez-vous dire, un cottage? In Wiltshire where stones talk to themselves and the greengrocer says of an old cauliflower did you want it for eating love? And anything else love instead of Madame désire encore quelque chose or Haben Sie noch einen Wunsch. What do you mean, for eating? Oh just my little joke sweetheart. An old lady she wanted mushrooms once and I said did you want them for eating and she said no for frying. So the phrase stuck love not to worry it'll all look the same in a hundred years as I always say it'll all come out in the wash. Do you want to create our own home? Do you like children? Saith the book, the phrase-book saith. And the shadow of the yellow pelmet cuts across the top of two vertical parallel lines themselves cut through by two horizontal lines thrown on the white-washed wall from the small criss-crossed window under the thatched roof, forming a large dièze the key of G for example on a non-existent stave but bent by the wall that slopes at that point up to the oakbeam ceiling in the master-bedroom or vessel of conception empty of master-music or conception or whatever wing means under which he has taken her auburn blonde svelte and dark to their conferences, commissions, congresses, conventions, walking down the airplane steps blue yellow orange white. It all depends on the theme the time the place the climate, whether Pernod for instance, Jerez-Quina Cinzano slivovitz turning his money endlessly over and over before paying as the waiter waits, the guilder francs pesetas zlotys krone half-crowns clinking or crinkling quietly, the only music endlessly permutating on eight unimaginatively manipulated notes over the greenish drizzle. Do si la sol fa mi ré do, do la fa ré, si sol mi do, do si la sol fa mi ré do, do la fa ré, si sol mi do crash permutating through the distant brain way up beyond the yellow curtain and behind no doubt a little door.

Vicariatus Urbis Tribunal—Romana (seu West Monasterien). Nullitatis Matrimonii. The copy of the petition printed on thick paper lies on the blue table-cloth where darker blue towers cathedrals domes and palaces form rows with WIEN repeated at intervals under each row and a plump prancing knight CAROLUS der VII in the alternate row beneath the crumbs of toast the buttery marmalady plate the empty yellow cup the yellow Melita coffee-pot. The hands lie quite still over the blue table-cloth, forming a squat diamond-space with the thumbs pressing towards the body the other fingers touching like a cathedral roof. Under the table the ankles cross over each other to close the circuit. Ci troviamo di fronte ad un autentico dramma dell' agnosticismo con tutti gli ingredienti storici filosofici e sociali di siffatto lieber Gott get the dictionary elemento determinante la involuzione in atto nella nostra civiltà.

The petition flowered by the Avvocato to the Sacra Rota lies on the blue table cloth with darker blue towers cathedrals domes and palaces and Carolus VII plump and prancing on a horse a little bit beyond the smattering acquired with scallopine di vitello campari soda dove la toeletta in fondo a sinistra between the enormous wings and the bells endlessly permutating on do si la sol fa mi ré do do la fa ré und so weiter weiter gehen over the greenish drizzle distantly beyond the little door.

1. I luoghi. Slowly now. The places: La Francia, la Germania, e soprattutto la Britannia, la dolce Inghilterra dai prati prati? smeraldini emerald or greenish drizzle cosparsi sparse, no scattered di case e di castelli con lamponi lampoons? e rododendri nei ben pettinati giardini pettinated gardens con i caminetti al cui fuoco fire? in the lanes? che dolci conversazioni serali what sweet evening conversations? proprio come nelle scene appropriate scene a noi familiari della narrativa da Dickens a Somerset Maugham: Lirrechur, eh? Tomorrow and tomorrow creeps in this petty luogo dove esplose il divorzio tra uomo e Dio, tra libertà e Redenzione, e dove pertanto gli effetti ne maturavano the effects do not mature, prima che da noi, nel crepuscolo delle anime in the twilight of the soul.

Well on one level one hardly listens. On another one has to understand immediately because the thing understood slips away together with the need to understand. Well on one level one would not understand at all, the standards of simultaneous interpretation crashed in the mere smattering acquired with San Pellegrino acqua litinica alcalina battericamente pura which no doubt should lavare ancora più bianco.

2. Il tempo: tra hello ducks.

— Oh hello Mrs. Jones. Framed in wistaria and the kitchen window above the sink and OMO cleaner than clean brighter than white you look pale.

— Yes I do look pale. I mean without me face. You know what I mean like. I have to put on a bit of rouge. I always did look pale even as a little girl and I still do. Until I put on me face.

3. Le persone finalmente folded away with the authentic drama of agnosticism and the breakfast remains ingredients historical philosophical and social performed in ancient times a little higher up beyond the Temple of Apollo to celebrate his victory over Python the legendary monster which hasn't put on its face framed in wistaria and accepts an offered cup of warmed-up coffee that'll bring colour to my cheeks did you say something love?

— Ouvre les jambes, Véronique, ouvre les jambes.

Below the kitchen window of the small flat in the rue St. André a gangling girl in pigtails deftly skips over two parallel lines of white elastic that form a long rectangle held apart at one end by the two ankles of another girl with a dark fringe who stands on the edge of the pavement, and at the other end by the two short legs of a blond child sitting on the steps. The gangling girl with pigtails has her back to the house and deftly skips over the two parallel lines not quite parallel enough, her right foot carrying the right line three times across the left and back, then both across each other in a diamond shape with a complete turn of the body to face the house, turning again to reform the parallel straight lines, her left foot carrying the right line twice and Faute! Tu prends ma place.

— Non, j'prends celle de Véronique. T'as eu ton tour avant moi.

— Alors vas-y Véronique.

— J'veux pas.
— Là, tu vois!
— Ta gueule. Véronique, saute.
— J'veux pas. J'veux m'asseoir.
— Mais tu vas embrouiller les points grosse bête.
— J' m' en fous. J'veux m'asseoir.
— Oh bon alors. Mais assieds-toi bien, ouvre les jambes pour qu'les lignes fassent parallèles.
— Par à quelle aile? j'vois pas d'aile moi.
— Imbécile. Alors Janine tu y vas?
— Vieille poire!
— Crapaude!
— Crétine!

Paris as Headquarters of simultaneous interpreters and international organisations for the advancement of peace common markets intercontinental missiles agricultural aid economical social cultural irrigation for refugees or the provision of two paper-making engineers for Korea one sericulturist one reeling expert one spinning expert for Burma one rolling mill technician one fertilizer one chemist works manager one acidulator in superphosphate manufacture and other such air-conditioning has husbands lovers wives mistresses of many nationalities who help to abolish the frontiers of misunderstanding with frequent changes of partners loyalties convictions, free and easily stepping over the old boundaries of conventions, congresses, commissions, conferences to which welcome back Liebes.

— So you wish to return to work madame?

To the freedom of the air and the precision of the mouthpiece at nineteen or twenty-eight. But how long, madame, have you stayed away, worked in other fields, lost touch got out of practice forgotten how to understand immediately because the thing understood slips away together with the need to understand. Well, on one level one hardly listens. Gee. Things have changed madame, says Prince Boris de Czarevitch or Somesuchovitch Directorovitch of all interpreters for Europe during all those years our techniques have improved, let me see how long, oh lord, how long? We could arrange a test for you, to see if you have lost or as yet ungained your confidence your speed your voice your heart your faith your memory your mind until it comes to a standstill and if it proves satisfactory we could arrange a period of retraining. Your husband has left us of course and I gather yes I know Siegfried told me. Siegfried? Ah yes, he recommended you. But he has gone to New York and you will find madame if you rejoin us that things have changed. We have many more interpreters now so that they remain more based on Headquarters where most of the conferences take place these days apart from fringe activities like the Leonardo Centenary for example and more cultural interchange with Eastern Europe or demographic irrigation for the underdeveloped areas and other such conditions of pressurised emptiness. We would base you in Rome or here which you should simultaneously translate as less gallivanting my girl real hard work at last at last an idea that actually means something and most of your old friends have left you know madame for higher things such as the masculine unmarked and situated on five terraces of ambition change love desire marriage. And have you considered madame what the life entails between the enormous wings losing height slowly bumping down the steps of air in this bedroom or that always away from home for example have you any children?

Away from the road a path leads into the deep cleft between the two masses of the Phaidriades where lies the famous Kastalia spring. And so you, born and bred a Catholic, entered into a marriage with a joint decision to frustrate its natural end? What methods did you use, signora?

Surrounded by the saddle of Koznitsa to the west, the Balkan Range to the north, and the undulating heights of the Sredna Gora Mountains to the south, the Valley of the Roses, unique in Europe and visited by thousands of tourists each year, drops gradually down to the east until it reaches the transverse ridge which locks both ranges. The gardens of this sunny valley, second home of the oil-bearing rose brought here from Persia in the seventeenth century, have since that day gradually crept westwards from Kazanluk and now climb up the eastern slopes of Koznitsa. The sun pours its light down on the blessed earth, and in its pleasant warmth the roses blossom, the rectangles of agriculture brush-stroke size, the forest blobs the scattering of smudges and the thin white lines that cross and curve make up an abstract study of the blessed earth in brown and green way down below the window-seat through the oblong pane of double glass with slightly rounded corners. Known in the Near East for its fine copper and iron articles, the town has a fine museum, and a monument of ancient art, the Thracian Tomb, now famous all over the world for its exquisite frescoes. Somewhere north of the town another monument rises, outlined against the sky on a mountain summit—a monument to the brave Russian soldiers.

The concrete path along the concrete landing-ground across which the passengers have walked leads into the concrete building where concrete men search every suitcase not for liquor jewels drugs but ideas, in dangerous print und das?

Les Insignes de l'Université de Cracovie a gift as yet unread und das? A list of Italian irregular verbs do you mind? Ah. Und das? The Valley of the Roses. And a Bulgarian phrase-book gut. Gut-gut. Und WECHSEL bitte? Links. Dankeschön into the white-lined bus towards the mountains against which the city rears its sky-scraper hotels office buildings palaces of culture.

Where to stop. The village of Rosino. Its very name symbolises roses in full bloom, pretty girls picking the blossoms, and the scent of attar of roses.

They praise, yes mademoiselle, also.

They praise presumably the portraits on the concrete buildings in rows bearded with hair or bearded bald or totally unfamiliar concrete faces all turning to their right westwards perhaps unless east, depending on the viewpoint or the side of the street, depending on the theme the place the climate of opinion and whether the surrounding mountains create great holes of air into which the mind sinks utterly baffled by the words in white on red across the concrete building 30 мир и gружба.

Away from the road a path leads into the deep cleft between the florid Monsignor and the recording priest on his left who writes all the proceedings down in longhand most unsimultaneously beneath the dark brown painting of some saint or other while the pale fat priest-interpreter to the right of the Monsignor further lengthens the proceedings by translating every utterance from Italian in fact half-understood into French and from French back into Italian thus creating a time to think of some answer truthful according to the requirements of a faith half-held in that climate language sub specie aeternitatis the Vicariato di Roma. We do not have a German interpreter to hand signora scusi, il Monsignor has got engaged in another court. But you say you speak French. Va bene così? Va bene. Well, one way or the other. But what difference does it make? Une différence non-marquée dérivant du marqué par une absence qui signifie eine Abwesenheit die etwas bedeutet, etwas anderes als bestellt. Do you agree? Did you want to test by means of engagement? Was suchen Sie, die Toilette? Nein den Aufzug. Ascenseur. Ach so, immer geradeaus dann links past the ТОΛΛЕТНА to the АСАНСbОР or else a change in the expected person ④ ③ ② ① Ⓟ for parter presumably towards the banquet-hall БАНКЕТНА ЗΛΛА where the president and his sub-presidents from this zone and that toast each other in progress mutual understanding hands across the frontiers on full stomachs underneath words in white on red зо мир и дружба.

They praise, yes mademoiselle, also.

Soon some sluttish chambermaid will enter with a breakfast-tray or else a dark and sullen boy nodding vigorously for no, unless bending his neck quickly towards the left shoulder then towards the right and back towards the left for yes as if to say the last straw or what-the-hell. Mineralwasser? What-the-hell. Bending his head vigorously from left to right and bringing МУНЕРАΛНА ВОΔА. Oh that. I can't think why you bother. Well, on one level one hardly listens to the autentico dramma dell' agnosticismo with all ingredients historical philosophical and social determining the involution of this our civilisation in la Francia la Germania e soprattutto la dolce Inghilterra, its emerald meadows scattered with houses castles lampoons rhododendrons pettinated lanes in which fires burn with sweet evening conversations surrounded by the Saddle of Koznitsa to the west and the undulating heights of the Sredna Gora mountains to the south along the Valley of the Roses. The very name symbolises pretty girls picking the blossoms among concrete faces looking to the right or wrong according to the viewpoint where to stop. The sun pours its light down on the blessed earth unless some desolate moon-goddess aghast at her son's death and the catastrophe she has provoked saying but where have all the flowers gone? Ah mademoiselle, they have not blossomed yet, the season has not yet come.

The plane has landed on the edge of a black promontory, its long nose-tip jutting out over the darkening gulf beyond which one horizontal line of light forms a T with a vertical line of light and a great clanging noise that stripes the blackness. Stimaţi pasageri. Welcome aboard this vessel of conception floating upon a pinpoint and kindly sit quietly ensconced in your armchairs, the women to the left of the aisle the men less numerous to the right, strapped to their seats that stretch interminably towards the distant brain way up in the long nose-tip beyond the tabernacle curtain and behind no doubt the secret door so heavy that the whole vehicle may topple over the edge into the dark invisible gulf beyond which one white line of light forms a right angle with another from the corridor of the hotel, behind the door of the black room in which the body lies inside the narrow bed, strapped by the swaddling sheet and blanket at a speed of total immobility in the night of Brussels Belgrade Barcelona Bonn, what difference does it make? A difference unmarked deriving from the marked by an absence which signifies eine Abwesenheit die etwas bedeutet, etwas anderes als bestellt, a change in the expected person aghast at the death of love or maybe merely of language and fingering a medal between breasts in blackness. In the tram-ridden night of Sofia.

The decorative metal locks on each door of the cupboard shine in the shaft of bright light coming through from the left where the wooden shutters meet. They have Napoleonic hats and look like Civil Guards, the one on the right door carrying the vertical latch that hangs down in relief like a rifle at rest.

Next to the cupboard the smaller doors of the dressing-table repeat the motif darkly and unreflecting. On the two drawers of the dressing-table, above the smaller doors, the Civil Guards lie down. Beyond the wooden shutters and way down below the layered floors of stunned consciousnesses and waking dreams the cars hoot faintly and rev up in Spanish unless Catalan streaked with a tinkling tram narrowly through the shaft of light where the wooden shutters meet. The dark shape of the cupboard unrounds in the filtered noise. On the bed-side-table stands the bottle of mineral water, its label still illegible. The visitor's attention turns immediately to higher things such as the dot of bright light thrown by the round hole in the shutter further up the cupboard imitating the sun above the Civil Guards. A voice calls out continuous flight-numbers and the murmur of the talking delegates as they wait in rows like a giant class fills the great Catalan evening in the bulging theatre with tumultuous applause for the boy-star with his guitar who pours La Nit, llarga la Nit and El poble que no vol morir full of Catalan passion down into the microphone and out in simultaneous passion. Di-guem no! Di-guem no! the bulging theatre demands in the tumultuous applause but the boy stretches out the palm of his left hand his right hand holding the guitar in a no-puc gesture half-indicating the police that lines the theatre and repeats instead La Nit, llarga la Nit with Catalan passion down into the microphone and out in simultaneous passion. The chair-man knocks his hammer on the dais table. The congress members dutifully don their listening-caps and the murmur still continuing now comes through the earphones in the glass booth, picked up by the microphones the engineer has just switched on. The eyes close, the thumb and fingers join as communication begins.

The visitor's attention turns immediately to higher things

such as Kalbsschnitzel natur mit Reis, gemischter Salat, Käsekuchen, Kompott, Kaffee over the modern capital that recedes as the plane rises swiftly above the mountains to an outside temperature of minus what, thirty-four, forty-three? Between the zest of youth and the enlightenment of old age comes an immense period called The Middle Ages. You look not quite yourself mein Liebes.

The hands lie quite still on the blue table-cloth over the domes the palaces in darker blue rows, the two thumbs pressing towards the body the fingers touching away from it forming a roof with a squat diamond space between. Yes I notice you always sit like that, even in an armchair, your ankles crossed your hands joined on your lap.

— Well it closes the circuit you see, so that you're self-contained, relaxed, and no-one can get at you.

— But who do you suppose wants to get at you mein Liebes?

You must excuse these questions Fräulein but in view of your French upbringing we must make sure of your undivided loyalty let us see now until the age of Herr Oberstleutnant at that age one has no loyalties. Ja-ja ich verstehe. So you, born and bred a Catholic, decided in advance, Madame, to divorce if it did not work, thus nullifying the contract in the eyes of God? Plus ou moins. My child you must use words more precisely. Did you or did you not? Oui mon père. Please declare if you have any love loyalty lust intellect belief of any kind or even simple enthusiasm for which you must pay duty to the Customs and Excise.

The hands lie quite still on the table, forming a squat diamond space with the thumbs pressed together towards the body and all the fingers touching like a cathedral roof. It closes the circuit you see so that no one can get at you. Come down into one world Liebes, decide between belief and disbelief, between loving and not loving, you have passed the age of adventure now, what, thirty-four, forty-three?

A woman of uncertain age uncertain loyalties holding her hands quite still with all the fingers touching to keep the résistivité électrique en Ohms and battericamente pura within and not give out too generously with a flow of rash enthusiasm above the blue tablecloth full of darker blue towers cathedrals domes palaces in rows and WIEN repeated at intervals with the plump prancing Carolus der VII in il piccolo chalet which remains a pied-à-terre for half the feet of that four-legged creature called an entity of bodies made one by the Sacrament of Marriage one foot à terre the other in the grave perhaps. Oh come off it, come down into one world und so weiter weiter gehen, immer geradeaus dann links in the smattering of the mouthpiece ears hands and eyes suddenly confronted however with TARTSD A PÉNZED A TAKARÉKPÉNZTÁRBAN in bright neon lights beyond the nylon curtain that floats behind the head down the shoulders to the floor. Of course some people may suffer while we build a new society but would you rather not have the new society? The delegates have registered their formal protests about the cardinal or the five writers still imprisoned in among the junketings, the congressional banquet and the sight-seeing tour around Lake Balaton. Down in the dimlit and deserted street footsteps walk in Hungarian slowly along the dark façade still pockmarked by machine-gun fire below the sign ELÖNYÖS! KÉNYELMES! BIZTONSÁGOS! Do you agree? Or did you want to test by means of engagement? Push. Tirez. Pchnąć. Ziehen. Have you Greek dialogues? Have you tea? I should like some milk together. I prefer it double-breasted. With two buttons. Without folding-up. I want narrow trousers. When shall I come for the rehearsal? In six days I go away.

Ici on parle français.

Zut alors says Siegfried grown slightly bald somewhere between New York and Reykjavik with a paunch pahr dessue le marshy. Pupate? Pupate? Que cherchez-vous madame, ah, l'ascenseur. Oh mademoiselle, they have not blossomed yet, the season has not yet come. Achten Sie auf den Originalverschluss. Heil-und-Tafelwasser. Das österreichische PREBLAUER. Sauerbrunn. Please do not throw into W.C. because one day the man will come and lift you out of your self-containment or absorption rising into the night above the wing par à quelle aile j'vois pas d'aile moi only a red light winking on and off in the blackness below but not passing away as the body of the plane bumps on the steps of air for the descent into bright lights and twinkling signals, roar and whistle of jets with undercarriage down, strong tension of brakes to a tame taxying up the tarmac until you come to a standstill somewhere beneath a Regency piece of London, on the Piccadilly Line alone in a crowd of Evening Standards lowered here and there as the long silent stop creates a slight anxiety in eyes that stare at advertisements to avoid each other in the bowels of the earth or vanish again behind a crinkle of sporting page loud in the lit up silence. Katina says Favourable day for whatever you want to do. In the evening you will have the opportunity to meet someone whose influence may further your interests. Then at last a distant rumble grows more distant and a clank lurches the carriage forward to a slow start, producing a faint sensation of relief that spreads through the body of the train slightly animating the chromosomes as if inside a long long centipede.

Emerging from Avernus made easy with escalators. They also go down. Saying ΠΑΡΑΚΑΛΩ ΑΝΑΜΕΝΕΤΕ, the button lighting up when pressed to call the lift, inside which incomprehensibly below ④ ③ ② ① come blank white buttons with ΙΣΟΓΕΙΟΝ and ΣΤΟΝ and ΚΙΝΔΥΝΟΣ in red meaning perhaps alarm? Na says the old porter at the rez-de-chaussée not fortunately sous-sol, shaking his head vigorously to mean yes, as ohi and a nod means no in Greek. Gut-gut, kalo-kalo?

— Nai. Kalo-kalo. Adio, efharisto.

— Parakalo. Bye-bye Frau, welgohome.

— Man denkt in Deutsch wann man in Deutschland lebt.

— Auf Deutsch darling.

— Und since man spricht sehr little Deutsch unlike my clever sweet half born and bred on Pumpernickel, man denkt in eine kind of erronish Deutsch das springt zu life feel besser than echt Deutsch. Und even wenn man thinks AUF Deutsch wann man in Deutschland lives, then acquires it a broken up quality, die hat der charm of my clever sweet, meine deutsche mädchen-goddess, the gestures and the actions all postponed while first die Dinge und die Personen kommen. As if languages loved each other behind their own façades, despite alles was man denkt darüber davon dazu. As if words fraternised silently beneath the syntax, finding each other funny and delicious in a Misch-Masch of tender fornication, inside the bombed out hallowed structures and the rigid steel glass modern edifices of the brain. Du, do you love me? Du, dein Bein dein Brust dein belly oh Christ in Rothenburg gem-city between the sheet and the tumbled sheeted eiderdown amid the central heating and the wooden panelling. Man works with hands light brush-stroke size over the rectangles of agriculture bearing plants or parts of plants forest blobs metallic lakes thin white lines man feels as an abstract study in seduction man performs with the precision of the mouthpiece eyes voice hands over limbs that find each other delicious on a creaking bed somewhere along the Romantische Strasse in a Misch-Masch of swift fornication between a hallowed structure and the rigid virginal edifice crashing down the runway with a scream of jets and strong tension of brakes to a tame taxying up the tarmac guided by some other distant brain in a glass booth and small white frogs with yellow discs for eyes and a splash of blood until it comes to a standstill du, do you love me, du? Do si la sol fa mi ré do, do la fa ré, si sol mi do peals in crash-permutations through the belfry of the distant brain way up from across the greenish drizzle and Great Scott du, my sweet, my fleissige, for God's sake make us coffee we've had enough of fornication on this late Sunday morning. Tout de suite and the tooter the sweeter.

Man sagt, man banters man makes love, rising to the occasion at all hours, man never says man loves except dein Bein dein Brust und dein damn medal of St. Christopher between 'em, or at most did you like it hat's geschmeckt despite the lil' ole Dutch cap or hats geschmeckt oh du my clever sweet my fleissige my deutsche mädchen-goddess for Chrissake make us some coffee what, a Ding no Dea does? Ah, du witzige sweet SCREAM why what's the matter?

— Spinne! Eine Spinne! Im Bad!

— What?

— Please! Come quickly!

— Oh hell. Now what?

— What you call it? Take it away, please, take it away.

— My dear good girl. Only a spider. A beneficent spider. There, gone, out of the window.

— Oh. Oh, thank-you.

— Why, you look pale as a sheet. For heaven's sake, screaming at a spider, the spinner of fates, a Ding no Dea does, did Athene scream at Arachne? Well, yes she did I suppose but not from fear, from jealousy and anger. There there, calm down my sweet, it brings luck you know.

— Araignée du matin, chagrin.

— But araignée du soir, espoir. Come let's pretend the evening has returned, ah du, dein Brust und so weiter or else don't you think lechería for milk-shop opening the shutters on la Calle de San Antonio in Madrid looks exquisite to an English eye? Unless in Cordova don't you think these plaster images all round in shrines and this monstrous Renaissance chapel plonked in the middle of the mosque with its calm forest of columns look positively obscene? E allora, what methods did you use?

— Comment? Ah. Hé bien mon père, d'abord une—je ne sais pas comment ça s'appelle en français.

— Dites en allemand mon enfant, ou en anglais.

— A sheath, at first, then a Dutch hat, er, cap.

— Non capisco.

— Vous voulez dire, madame, une capote anglaise?

— Non mon père. Je crois que capote anglaise veut dire ce que les anglais appellent French letter.

— Una cosa di gomma?

— Si.

— E l'altra cosa, più tardi?

— Je ne sais pas monsignor.

— Dessinez, s'il vous plaît. Ah si, si, la conosco. Va bene. Scusi, grazie tanto. E allora signora beneath the painting of St. Andrew Bobola.

E allora the languages fraternise behind their own façades finding each other exquisite in Beirut Copenhagen Bonn

Regency London and Wiltshire with swift frequent fornication that leaves a lot to the imagination becomes swifter less frequent with Great Scott do you always feel tired which later turns into yes you do look pale why don't you go to bed until it comes to a standstill. Man sagt das nicht however man does not speak of love nor of une absence qui signifie nothing more than a natural process une absence par retranchement from the feminine marked to the masculine unmarked except by a mental shrug signifying nothing that retrospectively deserves a flow of rash enthusiasm true friendship and affection remaining. Madame désire encore quelque chose? Bon alors ça fera neuf cent francs quarante au revoir madame merci.

And yet man once looked straight across and eyes met eyes limbs limbs in the freedom of the night and the precision of the mouthpiece at twenty-two or twenty-five even, with hands light brush-stroke size over rectangles forest blobs metallic lakes white curving roads which at first make up an abstract study in desire watched with curiosity as man works with hands eyes mouth hallowed structure into the rigid steel glass vessel of conception recommended for relaxation and calm crashing down on hard beds in Hanover Rothenburg Wien Hamburg Stuttgart and hats geschmeckt? The tannoy voice fills the large wooden hut calling out ranks with names attached and even faces over uniforms grey-blue dark olive khaki that wear a listening look for the Dakota about to take off from Frankfurt to Berlin. He stands in grey-blue with three stripes or two and a half around his sleeve and eyes meet eyes saying how splendid of Siegfried to have brought you to me, how come so young to work for us for them for him or else perhaps how come he sits so close on the long metal bench fixed to the curved metallic wall inside the fuselage the round ribs all exposed as if inside the skeleton of a giant cocoon, like paratroopers about to jump float down descending with white wings towards the rectangles of agriculture brush-stroke size the forest blobs the straight white lines that make up an abstract study of earth in green and brown. Yes well, every solution creates new problems and I can't pretend that as an Englishman I feel proud of what the so-called Allies have done. Why, and he talks, discusses things ideas the state of Europe and the zones of occupation spheres of influence not one of which in the non-existent future deserves a flow of rash enthusiasm as to administration re-education tact resentment humiliation revenge understanding distribution black-market fraternisation sex. Or do you know the definition of a titbit. Titbit? What does that mean? A mosquito-raid on Brest. No? I thought it rather good. Ah, Dieu vous blesse ma chère. You should get rid of a cold at this height not catch one. Things have changed however since the early days and I will take you under my wing. Great Scott! But English tall dark and handsome poised bantering affectionate what more can one desire in the imprecision of feelings at nineteen or thirty-seven even as the plane leaps up and down the holes of air-wind-storm that lurch into the mouthpiece, the passengers in grey-blue dark olive-green or khaki holding on to the metal bench or each other not to get thrown across the fuselage on to the opposite metal bench and its passengers in khaki grey-blue dark olive-green the round ribs all exposed. My dear have you not flown before there there his arm right round a little storm only a little storm soon landing at Tempelhof have you the time? How strange I never carry a watch either don't believe in them one finds clocks everywhere even if they all disagree according to locality you see we have much in common. Or as the man said to the prostitute who asked have you the time yes my dear but not the inclination as the plane lurches down the steps of air above the squares of grey façades so much less squat than the rubble behind them. Und haben Sie noch einen Wunsch? Ah, un piccolo chalet! Oh you mean a biddy! Did you want it for eating, love? Un piccolo chalet, va bene così?

Un piccolo chalet in la dolce Inghilterra dai prati smeraldini scattered with castles lampoons and rhododendrons, pettinated gardens, fiery lanes and sweet evening conversations appropriate to the narratives of Dickens und so weiter weiter gehen where explodes the divorce between man and God, liberty and redemption and the effects do not mature in the twilight of the soul through which the bells peal concatenations from the belfry in the distant brain way off beyond the greyish drizzle and behind the little door. You must imagine the time the place the kind of life led by the petitioner between the enormous wings ensconced next to Erich von Irgendetwas or Signor Ingegnere Battista di Qualcosa tall among the hundred and sixty seats but for a few head-tops bald fluffy blond curly black grey between the port and starboard engines all the stimați pasageri looked after cradled in their needs who talk eat smoke doze dream. Or else inside the whale three hours three days of what do you mean my sweet? Or yes you do look pale why don't you go to bed?

Unless he says but now we have moved out of the hard bed area into the softness of the east come live with me and join my harem here in Istanbul in heavy heat dein Brust like a mosque domed on the night sky my hallowed structure like a minaret piercing the Milky Way and hats geschmeckt? He turns the Turkish lire over and over as if roubles pennia forints in the hollow of his left hand with the thumb and forefinger of his right as the waiter waits in the hotel bar with the bill for his whisky and Mineralwasser. Mineralwasser? Ah, Maden Suyu! Maden Suyu. Kein Eis bitte. Teşekkür ederim. Bitteschön Madame. Well of course I too prefer the Suleymaniye mosque, splendid proportions of stone and space in white and orange, and all that gorgeous calligraphy, so much easier to contemplate than images because devoid of sense, to us at least, and indeed to most Turks you know, they have to have the Koran all expounded, can't read a word of Arabic. But then all truths get institutionalised sooner or later and die.

The grey-lined bus stops in a wide bosphorus of huge American cars with Turkish number-plates but Ⓓ or Ⓕ or (CH) on their bottoms all hooting poop pip pop hoo between the red and white bus on the left and the dusty demolition of a crumbling façade on the right that clouds a beautiful of course Japanese girl in a kimono against lake and pagoda under red lettering ZETINA. Dikiş makina radioları. Beyond the clouded beauty of the Japanese girl an almost triangular red wolf-head sticks out his neck sticks out his tongue unless perhaps breathes fire above PETROL OFİSİ —Yüksek kaliteli motor yağları and then GÜLE-GÜLE as the grey-lined bus stretches its armchairs endlessly towards the pip-poop-popping driver and moves on in the wide bosphorus of traffic turning right on to the bridge over the Golden Horn and up a sharp steep hill of shops to the hotel where the reception waits with sparkling Talaj for the infidels and Maden Suyu and fruit-juice for the more faithful hosts.

— Actually they all drink raki on the quiet, the Prophet didn't happen to mention it you know. Very strong, not bad at all you should try it my sweet.

The speeches have begun hands across the frontiers on floating stomachs over the murmur of unlistening delegates who move about in close national groups and token-clap until the dancers come in, fierce little men in blue silk and red and silver, one beating a big drum one playing a clarinet a third clicking long sticks extended from his fingers. In the adjoining room the pretty girl in green silk puffed trousers with green and orange bands coming down from the shoulders cries under her orange hat and headscarf among other girls in crimson trousers or green. Mademoiselle! Pourquoi pleurez-vous? Les hommes. Pas danser. Nous invitées. Mais les hommes pas permission kadın, kadın, er, femmes danser en public.

— Attendez.

The male dancers bow to the tumultuous applause and exeunt as the clarinet player gets a tap on the shoulder. Kadın? He shrugs, nods vigorously with Yok for no and exit. Yok we have none. Yok kadın.

— Kadın! Kadın! Kadın!

— What's got into you?

— It means women. The men won't let the girls dance. Look they weep. Please shout with me, all of you. Monsieur! On ne veut pas laisser danser les jeunes filles. Ah ça! Mais quelles beautés! Criez avec moi kadın, ça veut dire femmes. Herr Doktor, Entschuldigung. Dankeschön. Ka-dın, ka-dın, ka-dın, ka-dın!

The men dance their way out. The speeches start again hands across the frontiers on floating stomachs over the talking delegates and a rebellious group shouting ka-dın, ka-dın, ka-dın until the dancers come in, pale pretty girls in green and crimson puffy trousers covered with striped bands, none smiling under their orange headscarves over their high hats as they go through their solemn motions unhappily not quite in unison one tearful still and pale.

— Well yes I do look pale. Until I put on my face like. But I must say I didn't fancy them popish crows coming to interview me about you and your ex, dear, what could I say? I don't poke my nose into other people's affairs. Well, yes I know I agreed, and of course you confided in me in your loneliness poor love but still, and so slow! You should've seen them, writing it all down in longhand, just like the Scribes and Pharisees, or do I mean Sadducees? Well in the end I said to hell with that if you'll excuse me I've had a secretarial training. Yes, I worked in an office before I got spliced didn't you know, solicitors in the Strand. And I'll just type out your questions I said and my answers as one of your witnesses—witnesses I ask you what would I witness? You'd think they'd taken me for a peeping Tom you should've heard some of the things they asked I couldn't make head or tail of it. Not like our lawyers at all well of course you can hardly call them lawyers can you, just popish priests, black crows my mother used to call them though she also called the Church of Rome the scarlet woman and the golden calf. Or do I mean fatted calf? And I said if you have no objection sir, I said, oh yes I treated them polite for your sake love and they had none in fact they couldn't have seemed more delighted and surprised like they'd never seen a typewriter before. Such antiquated ways! I can't think what you see in that lot love. I mean why do you bother you don't want to get married again or do you?

— Nnn-o.

— Well then. And even if you did it don't mean anything any more all that sanctification lark you just go ahead and do it you got a proper divorce in the law of the land you don't need them foreigners. Oh I beg your pardon love but I never think of you as foreign. Oh I know you speak with an accent, French, didn't you say? Well that explains it, but then who doesn't we all have accents come to think of it, your hubby I mean your ex worst of all a la-di-da accent anyone'd think he thought himself a cut above and he didn't fit in down here not like you do dear. So you just go ahead and live in sin he settled the cottage on you didn't he, oh no you told me, you bought it yourself for five hundred pounds. And you had a biddy put in by my Tom he liked that nobody has a biddy down here. Well then, all the more so. After all you earn your own wages and come here on your holidays, funny that coming to England for holidays when everyone goes abroad but then you do everything the other way round don't you dear and I like you for that, I like original people. So you just bring your boy-friends here like you used to in the old days after the bust-up when you worked in London and came down weekends it quite livened up the village and what difference does it make?

Wejście/Wyjście.

Push. Tirez. Pchnąć. Ziehen.

The hands lie quite still on the pink table-cloth with darker pink towers cathedrals domes palaces in rows and WIEN repeated at intervals under each row and the plump prancing knight Carolus der VII between, the eight fingers touching away from the body to form a shape like a cathedral roof, the thumbs pressed together towards the body over the crumbs of toast and the postcard from Dubrovnik out of the discreet envelope forwarded from Paris Headquarters face down to show the phrase about la douce inoubliable dame aux yeux d'émeraude and signed with an illegible initial.

In whose mind in what place at what time has one remained la douce inoubliable dame aux yeux d'émeraude scattered with castles, lampoons, fiery lanes and sweet evening conversations? Somewhere along the Romantische Strasse between Wien and Valladolid amid the air-conditioning and other such circumstantial emptiness with emerald eyes gazing at the blue temperature of minus forty-five degrees height eleven thousand metres immobile speed nine hundred and twenty kilometres an hour handed over the back of the armchair in front by a fat hand over Prague where the new lord mayor has promised to take up the challenge in getting you to commit yourself to a single idea.

— Ideas? My dear good girl for twenty years I have conducted my higher education by transmitting other people's ideas or rather platitudes from one microphone into another. And I can tell you that not one of them deserves a moment of attention. One does one's job, in order to live well, have fun. We've had fun haven't we?

We have played those games mein Lieber.

Unless he says one does one's job, to the best of one's ability, simply as an instrument.

Man does.

— Not that you followed him in all things Liebes. But why talk of him he's gone let's talk of us we must love one another or die.

But where have all the lovers gone?

Siegfried grown balder somewhere between Dakar and Helsinki with a paunch pahr dessue le marshy sits in the kitchen of il piccolo chalet in Wiltshire where stones talk walk and make love until they come to a standstill. So, you have grown tired of your small box your refuge your still centre within the village within the wooded countryside within the alien land. Tired of weekend commuting between London and the end of nowhere strapped to your seat with a chastity-belt? Do you remember the Air Hostess who said with a charming English accent Prière d'éteindre vos ceintures and got so covered with confusion? Her voice I mean, got covered with confusion.

— Yes. Presumably air-hostesses, rather like interpreters, increase the statistical possibility of sudden death by flying so much. Do you think that counts as suicide? Without the actual trouble of committing it.

— Oh come off it Liebes counts for whom anyway?

— Oh Siegfried can't you understand?

— I understand perfectly. You have got bitten again with the old Wanderlust not to mention the other and long for the freedom of the air in your twentieth year and plus. Plus what exactly? Not that it matters I can work it out, besides, you don't look a day older and I wish you could pretend the same for me for old time's sake.

— Pretend?

— You will find your life-jacket under your seat.

— Dit zwemvest kan dienen voor een bewusteloos persoon.

— Good girl.

— Well, help me.

— So you want a zwemvest. Hmm, I don't suppose I have much influence at Headquarters but I can put in a good word for you. Why we could meet again here and there in Paris London New York und so weiter weiter gehen, immer geradeaus if you let me know your schedules in advance who knows, just think what fun we'll have.

— We have played those games mein Lieber.

— So you decided in advance madame, to divorce if it didn't work, thus annulling the contract in the eyes of God?

— Plus ou moins.

— My child you must use words more precisely. Did you or did you not?

— Oui mon père.

— Et votre mari aussi?

— Je crois, oui.

— Comment, vous croyez? You must say if you made a joint decision or not, the point has great validity in Canon Law.

— Father for three years he refused to testify. He said he would not give evidence in a foreign court.

— Foreign? Westminster?

— Traduzione per favore.

— Then came seven more years of vain attempts, first at Westminster then at Augsburg but they wouldn't even admit the petition. They said it didn't have a leg to stand on. And even here it has taken three years to prepare the case, interview witnesses and so on, well, all this for four years of marriage, after seventeen years one can't remember exactly.

— My child you must calm down, have patience, we did not build Rome in a day. The Holy Mother Church takes each case very seriously and leaves no stone unturned to find out the truth in the eyes of God.

— Traduzione per favore.

— Scusi monsignore. La signora dice che dopo sedici anni non si ricorda esattamente.

Non si ricorda esattamente of the truth in the eyes of God or even whether God has eyes or merely an absence which signifies eine Abwesenheit die etwas bedeutet. Ah yes, you always know everything don't you my sweet?

— In that tone of voice you should not use endearments it annuls them.

— Annuls! What fancy words.

— Why you mock my English you used to find it charming?

— I don't mock, I merely state. You do the mocking my sweet if I may say so.

— How, mock?

— Oh not mock-ha-ha, alas, just destructive. Always quibbling, correcting me, pushing me out to get all the attention, spoiling my jokes. But the Germans have no sense of humour.

— Pushing you? Correcting you? How, in English? Only in German. You said you wanted to learn it.

— Always on at me to take up this and that language. Wherever we happened to stay for a congress lasting hardly more than a week, ten days at most. The good lord or parental circumstances more likely gave me two languages by birth and I see no reason to acquire your smatterings of modern Greek, Turkish, Portuguese, Italian. Everyone everywhere speaks English or French, enough at least to understand one's daily needs of bed food and excretion. Immer geradeaus dann links, that will suffice me amply as far as German goes.

— You turn everything into a dirty joke. We never discuss anything nowadays, as we used to, even if we didn't agree, now we never talk of anything, not even the places you go to, the conferences you attend, the ideas—

— Ah yes! The ideas. Here we came in, the hero will now pick up the heroine on a plane about to land in Hollywood and offer her a contract for life. They go into a clinch. But it doesn't last, come the misunderstandings the infidelities on other planes in other cities und so weiter and we might as well get out of this picture into the bright lights of freedom for what can I tell you that you haven't already imagined, not to say invented? Yes, you know everything don't you. And you wouldn't believe me if I said one merely does one's job, simply as an instrument.

Whatever that means with which he takes her blonde auburn dark, her flashing eyes her floating hair fresh complexion small apple-breasts filling out between Stockholm and San Francisco too visible in a low décolletage by a Renaissance pillar or bare in bed with hats geschmeckt. A thing of the intellect perhaps a passion they have in common undiscerned by marriage literature for example irrigation the theory of signs significant and signified for the under-developed areas or a certain verbal anarchy of lewd puns ready-made dirty stories which makes their allusions intertwine in the palazzos castles university halls where the commissions, conferences, congresses, conventions broken occur while the

Regency house gets created into a pied-à-terre for his two feet that walk down airplane steps blue yellow orange white depending on the theme the time the climate, whether canyons or the Taurus Mountains for instance create great holes of air into which the heart sinks suddenly as in the Ascenseur with the red button ΚΙΝΔΥΝΟΣ meaning perhaps alarm? Pupate? No no signora, in fondo a sinistra.

— So you call this culture?

Of course of course natürlich selbstverständlich und so weiter weiter gehen through the freedom of the air and the precision of such devil-may-care feelings at thirty-eight and plus the splendid solitude in single bedrooms without bath or shower the toilet down the corridor and to the right or left unless double bedrooms without masculine unmarked the other eiderdown untumbled puffed out virgin-bellied or the sheets turned back over the dark blue blanket in two parallel straight runways from which only angels and ministers of grace take off into the blue the cloud the fog. Have you anything to declare such as love desire ambition nothing at all just personal effects and the fact that in this air-conditioning and other circumstances of total emptiness freedom has its inebriating attractions as the body floats in willing suspension of loyalty to anyone, stretching interminably between the enormous wings that spread back motionless on the deep blue of the high sky, above the sea of cloud that draws the gaze into an idle fantasy of stepping out and bouncing down and up on it as on a trampolin, stretching interminably towards the distant brain way up, suspended between the anti-syphillis programme the commission on narcotic drugs and division of narcotic drugs the timber committee for increasing production of immigration opportunities in Latin America beyond the magenta curtain and behind no doubt the little door. We live in an age of transition between one social order and another and we must effectuate that transition or die. To this end we favour the amendment to the draft revised resolution although we would remind the delegates that they still have to face the real question of how to implement it. The Egyptian representative's suggestion that the organisation should provide technical publications in all the official languages and in others as well would entail great expense. The organisation could only approve such a course in exceptional cases. The Mexican representative's suggestion that the Secretariat should try new techniques such as collaboration with the Press will receive most careful consideration. As for China we must emphasise that a great cultural revolution has taken place which the world will not find easy to integrate into a willing suspension of meaningful activity as the most advanced technique so far evolved for moving from one technology to another without blowing ourselves up. To this end we should formulate the principles that will guide the future work of the commission rather than discuss that work in detail which the commission can examine at some later stage.

The divine principle descending into matter or vice versa with the soul rising like incense and fusing with nothingness. All ideas have equality in the eyes of God at the Congress of Gnostics out of time out of space unless merely an absence that signifies outside the Church no salvation which simply will not do and indeed the Church itself has now admitted its error in this respect as in so many others. History has proved them wrong again and again, even in religious matters they have quietly had to shift their ground many a time while yet proclaiming to guard the eternal verities against the morality of the age. But even adopting ladies and gentlemen their outmoded, historical, diacronic view, look at the vital mysteries they have lost, by euphemising and narrowing them into convenient dogmas which even lose their convenience as times pass through the earphones in French and out into the mouthpiece in simultaneous German. And the fact that the breakaway sects have lost even more hardly justifies this great loss at the centre of things almost from the beginning if beginning we can call it sub specie aeternitatis. Of course the language and modes of thought of most people remain behind the inklings of the few always as ever persecuted destroyed burnt at the stake and at best ignored throughout the ages that pour through the neutralised transmitter in the brain and out in simultaneous confusion.

The bottle of Eau du Kiém stands on the dressing-table next to the empty wine-glass on a round metallic tray. L'eau de table de qualité. Gazéifiée-rafraichissante, digestive. Soutirée par Minolux S.A., 2 rue du Kiém, Luxembourg–Neudorf. Grand Duché de Luxembourg. The fringes of the white nylon curtain walk in the breeze all the way across the wide window just above the sill over the radiator. On the bedside-table lies the postcard of Palermo face down to let the eye fall on la si gracieuse dame aux yeux de vair that surely means a fur, not green or glass as apparently intended and signed with an illegible initial.

Outside the window the bridge spans a vast canyon with trees and houses down its slopes at the bottom of which runs a two-inch wide stream. Beyond the bridge and canyon stands the palace or town hall. Unless perhaps yes didn't Cinderella have souliers de vair? Which still meant fur. Qui fait trembler mon coeur de fol espoir. Can one have furry eyes? Translate the following passage into German and comment on the formation of these words: vair, ma douce amour (gender) und so weiter natürlich Fräulein you have passed. Sehr geehrtes Fräulein. We wish to inform you that in view of your fluent knowledge of French you have obtained the Dolmetscher Zulage which means that you may now draw 80 RM extra per month on your salary as Assistant Censor. Lieber Heinrich, hab Dank für Deinen wunderbaren Brief. Mes chers parents. J'espère que vous allez bien. Ne vous faites pas de souci pour moi. Depuis qu'on m'a emmené en Allemagne je travaille ici à Nüremberg dans une usine. Au fond je m'en fous. Meine Lieben alle! Lieber Horst, Lieber Helmut, Lieber Hans. Sehr geehrtes Fräulein et douce dame qui fait trembler mon coeur de fol espoir.

Where when and to whose heart did one do that? And what difference does it make? None except by subtraction from the marked feminine to the unmarked masculine or vice versa as the language of a long lost code of zones lying forgotten under layered centuries of thickening sensibilities winds its way surreptitiously up through the years into no more than the distant brain way up to tickle a mere thought or two such as where when and to whose heart did one do that?

— Wherever particular people congregate . . . you smoke too much. You tap your cigarette too often into the ash-tray and you never smoke them to the end, just as you get on first-name terms with everyone and don't remember their surnames. So why don't you marry me after all these years?

— You know why.

— Oh that, I can't think why you bother. You don't even believe it any more.

— No.

— Well then, what difference does it make?

— Just—how to explain, a sort of blind protest at the lack of freedom to choose, for or against.

— But my dear, you have the freedom to take no notice. If you no longer believe in the validity of any annulment, or its failure, based on half-truths and antiquated sophistries?

— We live in an age of transition, haven't you heard? The Church will find a voice. One day. Perhaps.

— Oh yes, the Church reforms but always at least a hundred years too late, and with an agony of resistance over the one per cent of what they ought to do at any one time. Even now—but you know Congresses better than anyone. I wouldn't mind if they'd got stuck in the 18th century or the 17th, but the 19th, ugh!

— Yes, yes, all right. But calm down. It really doesn't matter any more we've had fun haven't we?

— We have played those games mein Lieber. Yes. But if it doesn't matter to you why did you once make it matter to me? For what? Just the need to belong and to obey? Look where that got us before.

Such conversations do occur occasionally representing more or less truly something there no doubt and a small clutch of anguish perhaps moving up quickly to the distant brain way up with where when and to whose heart did one make anything matter?

In Istanbul, considered one of the most beautiful cities in the world, you will find a land of legends and history where East and West come face to face. Its legendary history starts in the eighth century B.C. Founded by the Megarions and called Byzantium after Byzas, their commander, it soon became a trade centre because of dein Brust like a mosque domed on the night-sky my hallowed structure like a minaret piercing the Milky Way with all that gorgeous calligraphy institutionalised and dead.

A la recherche des amours perdues. Lisez l'émouvante histoire de Marie-Félicie de Montmorency. Chantilly 1650. The calendar between the two mirrors shows a beautiful of course Japanese girl in a kimono against lake and pagoda beneath the letters in red ZETINA. Dikiş makina radioları. Elle aima Monsieur de Montmorency de tous les amours qu'on peut imaginer, car elle n'aima que lui. Above the mirror hangs a pale green sign with large black squiggles on it. The Turkish ladies occupy each hairdresser's loving attention with tall complicated styles regardless of other waiting femininities less confident, every strand here, no there, a little more forward and you've brushed the curl right out of it please use the tongs or the Turkish equivalent and taking literally the final Va-bene-così gesture with the mirror held to the back of the head and no, no-va-bene or the Turkish equivalent please brush it out back-comb it re style again and again ancora. Un amour de soutien-gorge. Ça pigeonne formidablement. The man talks to the mirrored reflection of the lady and the lady talks to the mirrored reflection of the man. Seen from the profile they do not proffer anger dissatisfaction and polite attempt to please at each other at all but only at the mirror. Votre déodorant. Choisissez-le sérieusement chez votre pharmacien. What does that mean? Madame? Up there. Ah. Arabe. Je ne sais pas madame. Just vital mysteries lost, euphemised into proverbs for the day. I wouldn't mind if they'd got stuck in the eighteenth century or the seventeenth but the nineteenth ugh. Ça va comme ça madame? Oui, merci, teşekkür ederim. Lutfen madame. Allaha ısmalardık. Güle-güle! So go the thankyous the goodbyes the welgohome in the smattering of the mouthpiece at twenty-nine or forty-five even and the baby-face stares out of lather under the letters Müjde! PEARS bebek sabonu —Lux sabonu hayranım. Hayranım. Turkish ladies surely.

Hayranım lutfen. Hayranım? Er—la toilette s'il vous plaît. Ah au fond à gauche madame. Merci. Tuvalet. ERKEK. KADIN. Of course KADIN. Ka-dın ka-dın ka-dın. Not hayranım which looked up in the pocket-dictionary says haylaz *faul*, hayli *viel*, hayran *verwundert* where when and to whose heart did one do that?

In Izmir (ancient Smyrna) you will find everything for your convenience and pleasure. The city has an admirable position at the end of the bay of the same name. With its hot dry summers and mild rainy winters mild indeed, does it say mild? Well, if you will arrange your Archaeologists Congresses in January. True, madam, but most of us go on digs during the summer. In England for example, at Stonehenge where I have special Wiltshire? How interesting. It forms a perfect centre for visiting the ancient ruins of Ephesus, Pergamon, Troy. Oh, you know Wiltshire? Quite well. Have you ever visited Stonehenge? Where stones talk walk make love have fun until they come to a standstill. Of course. Ah, well, then you will take a special interest I hope in my paper on the relationship between Stonehenge and Mycenae. The lintels you see, constructed by the fire-breathing wolf under the letters Petrol Ofisı and above Güle-güle means that the grey-lined bus stretches its innumerable armchairs towards the axe-motif you see passing a place called Yavaş in black letters on yellow. The Archeological Museum, situated in the Kültür (Culture) Park, houses the objects brought from Izmir, Ephesus, Pergamon, Sardes, Aydin, Mügla, Denizli and Miletos. But perhaps you wouldn't agree? Yavaş. I ought to introduce myself professor William Something didn't quite catch your name, excuse me, I probably know you, at least, your work in your own field? Oh no, no field at all, just translation you know. Oh? From English? Into what? From French into German. German? Ah. Do you like it? I mean, the work? Do you find the technical jargon hard to follow? Well on one level Yavaş, er, well yes in a way. But everything comes with practice. Even archeology? Everything, excuse me, Monsieur le Président? Oui madame from the seat in front vous voulez du feu? No thank you but we keep passing a place called Yavaş, not on the map have we gone round in madame no wonder, Yavaş means slow. Ah, voilà, merci monsieur. De rien madame. How do you mean everything? Oh, archeology, medicine, irrigation, economic aid for the under-developed areas and so forth. Goodness, do you work it up in advance? A bit, yes. At least the relevant jargon. But one soon learns, and then forgets, you see one has to understand immediately because the thing understood slips away, together with the need to understand. Oh. We even had a conference of archetypologists in Athens last week. Archetypologists? Well, you know, a sort of mixture of mythologists, psychiatrists and structural anthropologists. Structural? What do you mean structural? Well they didn't make it very clear themselves, really, sometimes it seems to mean the structure of primitive societies, or perhaps the structure of the system they use to make sense of it all, sometimes the structure of myths, you know, up into the sky or down into the earth. Ah yes, of course. Unless they meant perhaps the structure of the imagination itself. Oh I see, the imagination. How fascinating.

Where when and to whose heart did one do that? Do what and what difference does it make? None except by subtraction from the marked masculine and unmarked feminine or vice versa as the language of a long lost code of zones lying forgotten under layers of thickening sensibilities creeps up from down the years into no more than the distant brain way up to tickle an idle thought such as where when and to whose heart did one do that?

In Troy, located at the entrance of the Dardanelles, 32 kilometres from Çanakkale, on a mount near where the rivers of Dümurek (Symois) and Menderes (Scamander) join together, lie the ruins of the city whose renown Homer of Izmir (ancient Smyrna) sang and spread all over the world, the city whose walls rose to the legendary sound of music or circular dance, creating an invisible magic wall of defence undone by Achilles when he dragged Hector's body round it anti-clockwise to the horror of all concerned. The true history of Troy, however, continues from 3000 B.C. up to the Roman period. Archeologists have discovered nine settlements from nine different civilisations, nine cities over one another in Troy, naming them Troy I, II, III, IV, V, VI, VII, VIII, IX. According to the American Blegen Troy VIIa represents the Troy of Homer.

— How very disappointing.

— Well, yes, most non-specialists find it disappointing. I suppose you only see just a rubbish of stones labelled Troy I, Troy II and so forth. But I assure you it means much more than that to us. Not of course, like Stonehenge or Mycenae. But I mustn't bore you with my pet theories again, you will hear them at tomorrow's session and anyway you don't have to translate me. Nevertheless in exchange for your charming company on this excursion will you allow me to take you round and explain in simple terms I hope just what it all means?

Troy I, Troy II. This layer belongs to the Bronze Age. Schliemann thought that this represented Homer's Troy. But he bulldozed his way to find Priam's treasure silly ass, destroying everything. Sometimes the stones make up some sort of shape the bathroom door to the left of the entrance stuck in the nineteenth century or the paved ramp to the right. Sometimes the squares of rubble have walls with pillars at the centre contemporary with the Hittites unless the wash-basin stands on one leg lilac green blue yellow showing a new development. According to Blegen some men enjoy imparting their enthusiasm to furry-eyed ladies of thirty-nine and plus not one of which deserves a moment of attention. The younger interpreters however Joceline English into French and Sandra vice versa with un amour de soutien-gorge qui pigeonne formidablement and even Robert German into French get more surrounded with more tributes to their youth. They seem a different species altogether who learn from listening and live simultaneously all channels alert on all levels unless they merely block off different ones as yet unknown and unimportant or reduce them all to manageable size with poise and instant knowledge. Nevertheless some sort of homage gets paid to mere seniority perhaps from the specialist on Stonehenge and Mycenae who says the walls do not form an arc but a polygon. An earthquake destroyed Troy I you can tell by the fact that in this air-conditioning and other circumstances of pressurised excitation you have nothing to declare such as love desire ambition just personal effects like furry eyes qui font trembler mon coeur de fol espoir. A fire destroyed this second city. A fire destroyed Troy VI in 1250 B.C. But the wall here remains and almost certainly formed part of Troy VII, the famous wall you know. A fire destroyed Troy VI in 900 B.C. You can tell by the fact that in these circumstances of emptiness freedom has its inebriating attractions as the body floats in a suspension of ideas transmitted from one microphone to another at a speed of five thousand centuries per minute because the things understood slip away together with the need to understand. During all those years our techniques have improved let me see how long have you stayed away, got stuck in the nineteenth century, lost and never gained your confidence your heart your memory your mind until it comes to a standstill?

We have many more interpreters now so that they remain more based on Headquarters in the distant brain way up where most conventions take place these days apart from fringe activities like the Freud Centenary and Congresses of Archaeologists in Izmir (Ancient Smyrna) who say structural? Oh I see, the imagination. How fascinating. And where do you go next?

Paris as Headquarters of simultaneous interpreters and international organisations occupied with the advancement of learning peace intercontinental missiles rationalisation in the utilisation of wood cultural irrigation for the underdeveloped areas such as pilot and associated projects for fundamental education with missions sent to Afghanistan the Philippines Siam and Syria seminars in Brazil with special stress laid on the Declaration of Human Rights contains the small flat in the rue St. André where children shout ouvre les jambes Véronique or crapaude vieille poire j'm'en fous and other such air-conditioning for loyalty love lust ambition marriage not to mention the tall façade opposite with such small enthusiasms behind it. Yes, I notice, you always sit like that, even in this armchair, your ankles crossed and all your fingers touching. Unless you smoke too much.

— Well, it does reduce the smoking.

— And have you closed the circuit?

Siegfried grown almost bald somewhere between Byzantium and Constantinople with a paunch pahr dessue lives married to a nice Dutch girl based on Hamburg but why Siegfried? Or rather why Hamburg? Didn't you like the freedom of the air? Oh well, my spouse insisted you know just as yours had you more or less immobilised in Regency London after the first few months or weeks of making love in the hard bed area of Berlin Rothenburg Frankfurt, where again, Paris, Beirut, Istanbul? But I travel still despite and she has to show more understanding for the old Wanderlust than you did if I may say so poor man. Yes, I travel in electronics as other people travel in simultaneous interpretation. Not that I know anything about electronics mind you except that they contain the future in a way that interpretation however simultaneous of nineteenth century type bumbling can't. We live in an age of transition wouldn't you agree and must cope as best we can. But otherwise it doesn't make much difference from the old racket, one learns as one sells at the highest level in English German Dutch. I have acquired a smattering of Dutch by marriage, have you? Oh no, you acquired a smattering of English nicht wahr Liebes?

— Uw zwemvest bevindt zich onder uw stoel.

— Dit zwemvest kan dienen voor een bewusteloos persoon. And how goes the bewusteloos persoon?

— Fine.

— So, you've recovered your senses. Gut-gut. Well, we meet again. We can continue to meet again you know Liebes, here and there in Amsterdam Paris London und so weiter weiter gehen, immer geradeaus, if you let me know your schedules in advance I can always arrange a trip. Just think what fun we'll have.

— We have played those games mein Lieb.

— I meant, of course, as friends.

Silences differ more than hotel rooms or menus going all the way to the moment when I must go I really must. Bye-bye for now or as they say in Turkey güle-güle auf Wiedersehen bye-bye, Frau, welgohome.

The bottle of Eau d'Evian stands on the kitchen window-sill above the sink near the packet of OMO—le plus fort contre la saleté. Coupage du lait des biberons. Cure de diurèse et de désintoxication. Affections rénales—Lithiases urinaires—Goutte—Arthritisme—Obésité—Régime sans sel. Evian—l'eau essentielle, l'eau "vraie".

The hands lie quite still on the late Empire desk against the blue and green striped wall, holding the letter from Rome rooted out of the mess of papers in the niche answered-already-kept-for-reference Madame. I have pleasure to inform you that the Vicariatus Urbis has acknowledged the nullity of your marriage because of "mulieris simulationis contra bona indissolubilitatis et prolis" on April 17 based on half-truths and vital mysteries lost in antiquated sophistries. Dated heavens two years ago. You will appreciate that according to our conversation when you gave your testimony in Rome two years past, the Defensor Vinculi has now to appeal against this judgment at a Second Hearing. If he wins the Second judgment you may then appeal with a Third Hearing just like a tennis match mein Lieb final and decisive whichever way it goes. I can't think why you bother. Even in religious matters ladies and gentlemen they have quietly had to shift their ground into convenient dogmas which even lose their convenience as times change. I shall with pleasure continue to represent you when I hear from you that I hated all that interrogation Liebes why, quite like the end of the war trying to get a job and a Persil-Schein certificate denazifying us whiter than white, witness I ask you what had I witnessed but the snatching away of meine Liebe under my very nose thinking all right then he will hurt her and I'll bide my time and gather up the broken bits with a remittance for Lire 800,000 as follows: Printing Costs 50,000, Taxes Vicariatus Urbis Tribunal, 150,000, Second Judgment 100,000, Honorarium (nominal) 500,000. These charges as you see agree with the charges for the First Judgment. Cordially. Every solution creates new problems not one of which deserves a flow of rash enthusiasm which looked up in the dictionary on the late Empire desk once long ago meant how long possessed by the gods.

If we wish to avert famine in the developing countries, industrialised nations must concentrate on the words that flow into the earphones worn like a diadem through the neutralised transmitter in the brain way up behind the closed eyelids and down into the mouthpiece in simultaneous German to provide more technical and scientific help for the proper utilisation of these countries' own resources of proteins. Mesdames messieurs vous allez écouter aujourd'hui plusieurs discours by eminent specialists on methods of increasing the output of edible protein and translating time speed height into locality and channel and descent into new matter where the light unrounds the corners of the cupboard the dressing-table the stool under which you will find your life-jacket for anche una persona priva de conoscenza. No body occupies the empty bed thank goodness nor will use l'essuie-main not für Rasierklingen. No one comes in offering anything not ordered.

No one does anything at all. Assemblies meet and talk and even this Council can do no more than pass a resolution asking governments to initiate urgent measures for closing the protein gap. But governments must act. We can do no more than give them the technical information required. And the poorer countries must themselves give far more attention to oil seed production and fish-protein concentrates which still remain the world's cheapest sources of protein.

Between the dawn and the unrounding night the fingers fondle the medal of St. Christopher on the body stretching forth its hundred and forty ribs or so towards the brain beyond the yellow curtain that divides the poorer from the richer and no doubt behind a little door. But the biggest difficulty lies not so much in obtaining the additional protein as in making it palatable to the people who so desperately need it.

The members of the assembly sit quite still in a passion of charity concern interest unless perhaps alarm. Sandra works with her eyes ears voice and un amour de soutien-gorge but no hands as she watches the speaker through the glass-booth pouring the oilseed and fish-concentrates into the mouth-piece in simultaneous English. Between the cold statistics and the stark bare facts of hunger lies an immense period called indifference. Nous avons perfectionné des techniques expérimentales for texturing vegetable proteins by spinning to yield products which, when properly flavoured and coloured, closely simulate common foods such as bacon, chicken, beef and fish. Did you want it for eating love?

The menu goes all the way to 00147 Roma on account of mulieris simulationis contra bona indissolubilitatis et prolis. The bottle of Spa Monopole stands on the dressing-table. L'eau qui pétille—L'eau minérale la moins chargée en sels. Het mineraal spuitwater mit het laagste zoutgehalte. On the bedside-table lies the postcard from Venice out of the envelope addressed to Hotel Gallia Milano forwarded to Paris Headquarters and on to Bruges with the words Je sais que vous venez à Milan. J'habite maintenant Venise, belle ville d'amour et d'art splendide d'amour et crossed out without sufficient conviction. Si vous en avez le loisir venez voir cette merveille. Vous donneriez une incomparable joie à un vieil ami qui vous admire toujours, qui n'oublie pas la gentildonna "che fa tremar dì claritate l'âre" (comme l'a si bien dit ce grand poète Italien Cavalcanti: le connaissez-vous? Sûrement. Vous savez tout). Signed B.C.

B.C.? Or could it represent H.C.? H.O. or even E.C.?

F.S.? S.O.? One letter scrawled over the other like an incomprehensible ideogram. Je m'appelle Boris Carlov. May I introduce Prince Battista di Cualcosa. You never remember anybody's surnames Liebes or smoke them to the end. Bruce Chum glad to know you. My card Bong Ching, attaché culturel thank you. Señor Boniface Calderón. Encantada. Le plaisir de vous présenter le professeur Blaise Chose-Truc qui va vous parler de l'humanité la justice l'épidémie. Lirrechur eh? My parents had a lirre-rary turn of mind they called me Brutus Caesar. Tomorrow and tomorrow and tomorrow will do to wander about the canals of Bruges and think of cette belle ville d'amour et d'art splendide che fa tremar dì claritate l'âre. And of where when how to whose air did one do that.

Ideas flow thick and fast. My government wishes to emphasise that it does not take sides in the dispute, nor do we have sufficient forces in Middle East waters to exercise influence one way or the other. But Greece must learn, Turkey must learn that between the twilit gloom of earth below the wing and the almost unshruggable Taurus Mountains in a feverish glow glimpsed through the leaning heads and exclamations to the left of the aisle the sea looks earthen clay you could cut with a knife to mould some ancient goddess such as Vénus qui complique vos projets or Mercure qui influence votre magnétisme et votre vivacité d'esprit as the body floats in quiet disparagement. Nothing deserves a flow of rash enthusiasm my sweet. My Government wishes to reiterate its whole-hearted support for the United Nations. Et tu Brute? We shall continue to honour our obligations and tomorrow and tomorrow we shall appoint a sub-committee to inquire into the way we can best meet the crisis. Meet Mr. Bryan Crisis. Unless Helmut Heinrich Horst. We shall organise discussions to see how best we can help those countries with their external defence problems and render unto Caesar the things that belong to Caesar, just personal effects for instance and the fact that in this air-conditioning blowing through the mouthpiece you pull red toggle (1), adjusting their economies to the new situation. Wherever particular people congregate you never remember anybody's names. As for the Far East, we must emphasise that a vast cultural revolution has taken place, which the world will not find easy to integrate into my card Hong Cong cultural revolutionary please la crise la crise.

And if you look up the word crisis in the dictionary you will find that it once meant decision. Now here in this Congress of Demographers we need not concern ourselves too much with the etymology of words. All the same I suggest that at any minute now some bright buxom floor-steward will come in with a breakfast tray saying Morgen, gün aydın bună ziua no buzz the telephone pronto? hello? Seven o'clock madam. Thank you very much. The label on the bottle by the bed says Vichyvatten to hide the nature of the contents neither Vichy nor vatten but air surrounded with liquid so that tomorrow and tomorrow will do to wander along the Ström down below the hotel in the Venice of the North and think about cette belle ville d'amour et d'art splendide che fa tremar dì claritate l'âre.

Silences differ more than hotel rooms and tall façades with such small spirits behind them. The gods have left this land but we shall continue to honour our obligations towards a line BC representing geographical areas at right angles with the line AB representing population increase per square metre per annum. Now taking BC here you can see at a glance where the danger lies, and that the increase in ideas flows thick and fast. Mesdames messieurs, je tiens d'abord à remercier le Président du Congrès pour ses éloges que je n'ai pas conscience de mériter. Vous connaissez tous, je pense, ce mot de Bertolt Brecht (Bertolt?) which flows into the ear through the earphones in French and comes out into the mouthpiece over waves and on immer geradeaus into the earphones of the multitudes or so in simultaneous German.

On nous a convoqué ici dans ce charmant château du moyen-âge Wurtembourgeois pour discuter du thème suivant: La Littérature et la Sémantique. Mesdames messieurs je vous le demande, le moyen-âge connaissait-il la Sémantique? Hé bien moi non plus. What has the writer to do with Semantics? I ask myself that question. I even went so far as to look up the word sémantique in the dictionary and found it meant: SIG-NI-FI-CA-TION. La science de la sig-ni-fi-ca-tion. But what has literature to do with science? With analysis of meaning until the meaning vanishes under the academic weight of analysis? Rien! Ou, pour aider les interprètes, nikts, notting, nada, niente. Vous voyez! Il n'y a aucune difficulté le langage speaks for itself. I will tell you a story what story oh you know the one about le philologue Russe qui dit: we in Russia say jardine, the French say jardine, the English say jardine, the Germans say jardine, you know, a place where flowers grow, all have the same word so you see we have no differences and laughter cracks the earphones. Hé bien mesdames messieurs he had something there, through his philological blinkers. La littérature, la splendeur des mots, des sig-ni-fi-ca-tions, depends on sounds that hiss through the earphones et ces sons surgissent avec leur sig-ni-fi-ca-tions multiples through a natural process created by the marriage of la tradition et le progrès. Nous autres écrivains, nous ne nous soucions pas de cette science infime, infâme, for we proceed by instinct through le langage which we absorb with our mother's milk flowing through our veins and remaining far behind the inklings of the few. Out of the mouths of babes nous parlons en po-ètes, mesdames messieurs, en po-ètes. La littérature, l'humanité, la justice, l'épidémie und so weiter weiter gehen until the science of signification sobs and hisses into the microphone through the eardrums unless the pale Danish novelist next on the dais says that he has looked up the word semantics in the dictionary and found it means meaning. Well now quite soon some floor-steward in white will come in with a breakfast-tray and say all ideas have equality before God bringing in as well a postcard from Bernard Colliwobbles in Venice or 00147 Roma. Bruce Cliff. Brute Clinch. You never smoke them to the end. Wherever particular people congregate you want them to commit themselves to your latest enthusiasm whereas nothing, rien, niente deserves a flow of rash desire love loyalty ambition marriage of tradition and progress. Henri Chasse. Hermann Clot. Fernando Chiuso. Unless perhaps H.O., E.S., F.O., P.S. Etienne Edouard Edmond Emanuel Frédérique, Paul Pierre. A great cultural revolution has taken place which needs no simulation of women bacon fish by the code of zones AB at right angles with the line BC descended into half-visited on swift conducted tours of the world's trouble-spots. Kenya must learn, Angola must learn la grande leçon des préservatifs which shows Erich Enobarbus Fritz how the Greek lady says in broken French that she however has had no need to look up the word sémantique in the dictionary because in Greek semantikos means meaningful just as elios means sun and gynaika means woman. The meaning has remained and meaning in literature concerns Emile et les detectives unless humanity fraternity liberty tutungerie in the precision of the mouthpiece at a certain age of certain freedom from loyalty to anyone ABCD.

Whose coeur tremble de fol espoir.

But where and in what freedom of which air did one do that?

En Roumanie, pays des forêts, des fleurs et des couleurs, vous découvrirez un riche trésor d'art, témoignage des aptitudes artistiques du peuple roumain, de son sens inné pour le beau et l'harmonie.

The pillow stands obliquely in the wall-corner of the bed with its ears up and its middle carefully dented. The feather-bed buttoned up in sheeting no longer occurs, only the red black and white blanket folded back with the top sheet to form two parallel white borders from which the fact that we have not yet come out of the hard bed area my sweet has no personal significance beyond the Apă Minerală on the bed-side table. Indicaţii terapeutice: gastrite catarale cronice, colite şi enterocolite cronice, calculoză urică, anumite forme de nefrite, pielite şi cistite, hepatite simple cronice, litiază biliară, inflamaţii cronice ale căilor respiratorii in general, diateze, gută şi obezitate. Everywhere you will discover the history of the country, in the towns, in the valleys of the mountains as much as by the sea, witness the remains of graeco-roman antiquities, the daco-roman vestiges disseminated all over the land, the inestimable beauty of the Byzantine monasteries full of dark staring saintly eyes outside which a smattering of phrase-book Rumanian plus Italian Spanish French with a bearded monk brings up the tense heavy blond engineer from the excursion-party who says Mais vous savez tout!

— Au revoir, madame bon voyage, drum bun.

— Mulţumesc padre, la revedere.

— Excusez-moi madame, si vous désirez apprendre, il faut dire părinte. Padre non, părinte. Et pour grande politesse, cuvioase părinte.

— Cuvioase? Cuvioase părinte?

— Dévoué père. Mais cela n'a pas d'importance madame je me permets seulement parceque vous desirez. Enchanté madame de faire votre connaissance et au revoir.

— So now you know everything.

— Er, where did you say you came from?

— I live in Italy but—

— Please, could you repeat your name?

— Ah yes, very difficult madame, Boleslaw Czeszczyk CZE, SZ, CZ, YK.

— Oh. Er, enchantée monsieur. Mille excuses.

— I understand madame, people always say why you have so many consonants together in Polish? But it all depends on the habit of the eye. I live in London many years and every day of my life I see KNIGHTSBRIDGE. All those consonants together, GHTSBR, very terrorising. Also KN, DG, ten consonants three vowels. You know London madame?

— Yes.

— Oh but of course in your fascinating work you travel much.

— Well, not so much these days, most conferences take place in the main western towns except for fringe activities like—

— Fringe?

— Oh you know like the Shakespeare centenary and cultural exchange with Eastern Europe.

— Ah, you joke. Yes, good. I would not call Petroleum Engineering fringe. We must help these people you see to free themselves economically from Russia, they have so much petrol and great modern methods but not enough, and this conference ah, but you understand, I see while I speak, you in the glass box you translate, into what language madame?

— German.

— Ah.

The expression stiffens imperceptibly but feeling sure you translate excellently madame with many thanks for the German delegate Herr Ingenier Erich Osterbach he felicitates me. From West Germany of course. Yes madame in politics as in technology every solution creates new problems which makes one very sad.

And as for China well my card Bing-Song the problem looks more simple than it appears between the earphones and the mouthpiece through the neutralised transmitter in the brain, the hands quite still on the desk, forming a squat diamond space with the thumbs pressed together towards the body, the fingers touching like a cathedral roof, never seeing the gestures, the eyes closed to watch the words as they pass through the distant brain way up, steadily in phrases well-formed almost in advance to hit the German nail on the French pinpoint. Unless alternatively concision shrinks the statistics like angels to a pinhead and the pinhead pricks the Gallic nuance which escapes like gas and lingers far behind the inklings of the few depending on the speaker's nationality in French, Italian for instance, Polish or verbose, depending on the theme the time the place the climate, whether canyons create new problems as in politics and pamphlets full of Kulturstätten—Places of Cultural Interest—Curiosités Culturelles—Curiosità Culturali—Centros Culturales. Archives, Libraries, Memorial Rooms, Museums, State Apartments. Tabak-Museum IX Porzellangasse 51. Technisches Museum für Industrie und Gewerbe XIV Mariahilfer Strasse 212, Uhrenmuseum der Stadt Wien, 1 Schulhof 2. Monuments and Fountains. Sakrale Bauten. Churches—Eglises—Chiese—Iglesias. Opera Houses and Theatres. Privattheater. Teatros particulares. Aber Sie wissen alles gnädige Frau.

— Could you repeat your name?

— Doktor Friedrich Sachs.

— Oh yes. You made a very good speech today.

— Ah, gnädige Frau, demography produces nothing but despair. Populations multiply almost by geometrical progression gnädige Frau, in simple terms two times two equals four, times two equal eight, times eight equals sixteen und so weiter ad infinitum consuming the world's natural resources which soon will not suffice. In thirty years we shall have lost the food and birth control battle for ever. And the world talks and compiles statistics and does nothing except build more satellites more missiles ad infinitum yes, nothing but despair.

Uw zwemvest und so weiter ad infinitum which makes one very sad. And in your journey through Rumania you will meet modern comfort, the proverbial Rumanian hospitality, gaiety, dynamism and the creative spirit of the Rumanian people. You will meet Mr. Bryan Crisis. And if you look up crisis in the dictionary you will find the new face of the country whose economic power has increased thirteen-fold, the new aspects of towns, the more and more frequent silhouettes of industrial combines, the lively rhythm of a prodigious development representing only some of the accents of the renovating present. And did you enjoy the bus-excursion to Battalha senhora? Ah, you have seen it before, you know Portugal well? You like? Muite obrigado senhora what a charming compliment. Yes, I prefer Evora also.

Where the aqueduct walks from the wilderness on innumerable brown legs, pierces the citadel and collapses, not too far however from the secret mysteries of Diana in broken columns coloured bronze mark you in the sunset and surrounded with white palpitating stags, unless animal organs not to mention the cross on the curlicued façade so much taller than the small church behind it. But stones do talk. Statistically, into microphones. Du Witzling. Witzling-

Schmutzling? Ein bisschen. Well, the gods have left this land but we shall honour our obligations towards them all from Apollo to Allah, with plaster images and a Renaissance chapel plonked in the middle of the mosque looking obscene according to the time the place the theme the climate and whether canyons create great holes of air that leap into the mouthpiece two channels keeping the mind alert not to say three the eyes the hands the voice and more than the five senses in a flow of rash enthusiasm about ideas not one of which deserves a moment of allo? er, dígame? Ah, muchas gracias. You like your work señora? Oh yes, very much. And what do you like most about it, the travel or the translating? Well, the ideas transmitted, at least—Ah yes, you must know everything by now. Your name, could you repeat your name? Cano, señora, Esteban Cano. Encantada. Lo mismo señora, lo mismo, encantado to see that you have not lost your enthusiasm for ideals, so many people do. And where do you go next?

I luoghi: La Francia e soprattutto la Germania über alles then unter where the tannoy voice fills the large wooden hut calling out ranks with names attached and even faces over uniforms grey-blue dark olive-green khaki that wear a listening responsive look for the Dakota aircraft about to take off from Frankfurt airport for Hamburg. He stands tall blond and Aryan in British battle-dress dyed greenish-black and eyes too close together above a slightly broken nose and thin mouth saying I heard your name saw you at Headquarters loved you from the start no he does not say that. So you have got on to the same bandwagon. How come so young to work to fly on allied aircraft unless perhaps how come he sits so close on the long metal bench fixed to the curved metallic wall inside the fuselage the round ribs all exposed as if inside a skeleton chrysalis like paratroopers about to jump descending on the rectangles of agriculture brush-stroke size the forest blobs the thin white lines meeting at pimples cancerous growths that make up an abstract study of the late Mother-country in brown and green.

— Yes, well, every solution creates new problems and one did what one could to make it work to get things going again such as the sale of goods and normal life love ambition culture why, and he talks, discusses things ideas not one of which has lost validity for him in the administration re-education tact resentment humiliation self-recoil revenge understanding distribution black-market fraternization sex. And so you work in the French zone? Rejoice Fräulein that they do not put German employees in uniform although clothes create problems one gets so tired of women in uniform as if at his age what twenty-two twenty-three he had had mil e tre per annum per square metre of Lebensraum for nineteen hundred and forty six years and plus. Not that the girl officers so thoughtfully provided by the occupying allies to prevent fraternisation don't look glamorous mind you but not for us. Besides, the French call theirs Aspirantes. Not lieutenants mark you but Aspirantes. What do you suppose they aspire to? Do you aspire to anything? A change of zone for instance or come climb on my bandwagon and have a love-affair. And have a Bruderschaft. Well you'll have to wait Fräulein if you'll forgive the intimacy they have no lavatories on these Dakotas only a tube over there in the tail strictly for men only, visible to all and you'd miss wouldn't you. As a translator? How very interesting what a coincidence and where?

What do you mean only documents? What difference does it make? Accuracy, precision, nothing else matters. Oh yes and speed natürlich but all that comes with practice. They'd send you on a course anyway and besides they'd have to give you a denazification screening first. Things have changed however since the early occupation days and I will take you under my wing.

Everything comes with practice. Loyalty change of zone speed rash enthusiasm in the precision of translation at nineteen and plus. Plus what exactly? Ah so you had reached the age to help the German war-effort some while before it collapsed. What did you do? You will excuse these questions Fräulein but in view of your nationality we must make sure of your undivided loyalty total ignorance dissidence change of heart let us see now until the age of sir, at that age one has no loyalties. No? One does a job any job to the best of one's ability. Yes yes of course we understand but one does one's job, also, as an instrument. Had you thought of that? In view of your French upbringing however and the strong recommendation from the plane as it leaps up and down the holes of air wind storm that lurch into the mouthpiece the passengers in grey-blue dark olive-green and khaki hold on to the metal bench or each other not to get thrown across the fuselage to the opposite metal bench with passengers in dark olive-green khaki grey-blue the round ribs all exposed as if inside the skeleton of a dark olive monster. Du liebes Kind have you not flown before, there, komm mal her his arm right round a little storm only a little storm soon landing outside Hamburg as the plane lurches down the steps of air above the squares of grey façades so much less squat than the rubble behind them. You don't mind my calling you Du liebes Kind Fräulein? His arm right round a hole of air his nose long slightly broken and the mouth quite thin which says please call me Siegfried.

Everything comes with practice. Living in the requisitioned room in Hanover sparsely but better than others having access to allied goods sold at a profit. Catching colds in open jeeps with Flight Lieutenant This or Captain That and sometimes also Siegfried according to the type of prisoner interrogated and curing colds at the unpressurised height of two thousand metres eardrums blocked from any voice offering anything not ordered half-desired feared or longed for on the way to München where die Alte Peterskirche barely stands in stark broken façades around its rubble heap and on to Dachau full of German civilian prisoners or the Schloss codename Dustbin outside Frankfurt full of ex-high officials who can help reconstruct the history of devastation Dorf by Dorf day by day from the enemy point of view.

Diversion. Umleitung. Achtung Road Repairs now entering the British Zone with a flow of rash enthusiasm speed change of loyalty love hope so much less squat than the collapse behind it. Well but you see, sir, reading English newspapers at the AA, the A.A.? sorry the German Foreign Office one learnt to follow the war from the enemy point of view. The enemy. Ah yes, you mean us. And did you also learn to adopt our point of view? Bluffing a little, looking up unknown words in the dictionary hidden inside the drawer to hide the fact that one had merely passed a test in English learnt at night in Köln air-raid shelters in order to obtain the Dolmetscher Zulage which means that you may now draw 80 RM extra per month on your salary as Assistant Censor. Mes chers parents. J'espère que vous allez bien. Lieber Hans, lieber Helmut, lieber Horst. Sehr geehrtes Fräulein. *Dienstverpflichtung*. Which means that you have obtained a transfer to the Auswärtige Amt in Berlin, Presseüberwachungsabteilung Ausland (PA) Auslandspresseländergruppe Nord where you will work as wissenschaftlicher Hilfsarbeiter and read about the shelving of the plan to dismember Germany into the smallest possible pieces based on the old principalities and dukedoms in favour of four zones, the Battle of the Bulge, the five hundred sorties by Flying Fortresses hardly encountering any defence from the remains of the Jagdruppe belt scattered in Central Germany dropping their load vertically down despite the anti-aircraft vertically up making no difference upon Cologne Berlin Hamburg Kassel Dresden Leipzig Nürnberg where the old wooden houses by the river burn like ideas none of which deserves a moment of validity in revenge resentment humiliation pride of conquest über alles and longing for the end.

Founded in 1040 by Henry III Duke of Bavaria and Emperor of Germany, Nürnberg, made a free city of the empire in 1219, retained its independence until 1806. Destroyed in 1127, rapidly rebuilt, it lay on the great European Trade Route to the Mediterranean and grew in importance. Here Wallenstein defeated Gustavus of Sweden in 1632. Nürnberg also produced the Hohenzollerns, one of the ablest families of Europe. As Burgraves of Nürnberg they had thrived in the imperial favour and on the customs dues of a prosperous city. Today it has become the centre of the National Socialist Party and has given its name to the famous Nürnberg Decrees of 1935. The Fuehrer held a most important rally here last year. Natürlich you have passed. I always knew you would Liebchen, congratulations.

In the imperial dukedom of Bavaria and near Nürnberg die Baronin sits by the narrow darkening window of the Schloss overlooking the Pegnitz. Dankeschön Tante Frieda and in French too, top marks. Ah well that need not surprise us Liebchen and no doubt it will come in useful but German history, well, what a triumph. After all your father, wherever he may have vanished, did come from Bavaria, like so many good things these days, our good government for example began here as you know.

— Yes, Tante Frieda.

— Well now we'd better get back to Schiller. You have not yet satisfied me that you understand the Swiss and Austrian political background of Wilhelm Tell. You should feel grateful my child that I take so much trouble with your German education now that you cannot go back to France.

— Yes, Tante Frieda.

— And incidentally I heard you mispronounce Heil Hitler when we met the von Berlinghausens in the Marktplatz the other day. You said Hell Hitler. Now if you meant hell bright, the witticism, though ungrammatical, can pass. But I suspect that now you have started English at school you meant something quite different. And if you did you might get it correct for in English you would have to say To Hell Hitler which might not pass quite so easily even as a so-called witticism would you not agree?

You must forgive these questions Fräulein but in view of your French upbringing we must make sure of your undivided loyalty let us see now until the age of Herr Oberstleutnant at that age one has no loyalties. Ja-ja ich verstehe and your father you say disappeared? You don't know? You never really knew him? Hmm. However you lived with the Baronin gut-gut until you went to University on a scholarship last year and ja, you selected to study French, French and Provençal? Now why did you do that? You must have realised at the time that it could hardly come in useful in the war-effort. Hmm. Yes well I see you joined the Bund Deutscher Mädel at fifteen gut-gut. And I assume you have not heard at all from your mother in France Fräulein even through the Red Cross? Now how do you feel about that? Herr Oberstleutnant one must do a job, any job, to the best of one's ability. Man muss? Do you feel so impersonal Fräulein about the Vaterland?

But where have all the fathers gone?

Scott! As the boy flashes past on his bicycle down the road curving round the castle to the village and gone. Helmut the young Baron in Lederhosen and brown shirt who bicycles all the way to München and says komm mal her I'll show you something walking hand in hand into den Alten Peter for a frail skeletal nun in a glass case. Heilige Munditia. Patronin der alleinstehenden Frauen. Corpus Sanctae Munditiae Martyris. She looks a bit like Mutti sehr grauenhaft nicht wahr? I like her. But natürlich you will never need to turn to her will you. French girls never stand alone besides I'll marry you when I grow up. Says Helmut the young boy Baron who yesterday climbed the cherry-tree in the garden of the Schloss and down again with a felt-feathered hat full of cherries stuffed into two mouths that spit the stones and dark-stained kiss first time ever as he fumbling unbuttons the dirndl top begging only to see the small bare breasts now unsupported by the tight corsage unbuttoned, his hand pushing up the fresh white blouse only to see and touch a little under the cherry-tree. Ich hab noch nie ein französisches Mädchen geküsst. As if at fifteen he had collected nationalities or kissed a whole Bund Deutscher Mädel begging only to see if they too have breasts comparing measuring perhaps weighing found wanting a little with Grüss Gott and gone.

Yes yes of course we understand but one does one's job, also, as an instrument. Had you thought of that? Everything comes with practice. Love loyalty change of zone speed rash enthusiasm in the precision of translation bluffing a little with a dictionary hidden in the drawer to hide the fact that General Patton sweeps through Bavaria into Bohemia out of which Wallenstein drove the Saxons and stops, waiting for the Russians to arrive and divide the spoils into old principalities and powers with eardrums blocked from any voice offering anything not ordered half-desired feared or longed for. Ask him please what happened to the statistics of bomb-damage per town per night which his department looked after. He says he doesn't remember exactly sir. Ask him again, he must remember unless as boss he deserted the sinking ship. He says sir that he thinks they may have obeyed his orders and evacuated all the files from Berlin to Jena. What! Jena sir. They would. In the Russian Zone. What crass stupidity didn't they see the way things damn. Do you believe him? Yes, sir. Test him ask him why Jena what kind of thinking lay behind that decision. He says sir that we should have joined forces together against the Russians that every German secretly wanted that and yes well we have not come here to find out what every German secretly wanted. Or yes well if every German had openly declared what he now says he secretly wanted we'd have a very different Europe and this interrogation would not take place. But then such conversations never quite occur in such frank facile terms expressing falsely something there no doubt through the bluffing of the mouthpiece to prevent any true exchange of thought love desire or mere curiosity under the cherry-tree outside the Schloss posh dining-club for officers in grey-blue dark olive-green and khaki who smooch around with glamour girls in grey-blue dark olive khaki thoughtfully provided by the allies to stop fraternisation in slow fox-trot to a slow fox-trot band of accordeon-violin-piano-drums and gonna-make-a-senni-menn-al journey. Gonna set ma heart at ease. Gonna make a senni-mennal journey. To renoo ole me-e-mo-ries. You can't bring her in sir. No fraternisation here. Fraternisation! My dear fellow I've only just met her give me a chance. That makes no difference sir. Right, well, thanks for putting ideas into my innocent head we'll fraternise elsewhere won't we Fräulein my sweet? According to the legislation into effect you may not sentimentalise ole memories out of the non-existent country. Somewhere in Bayern still however die Heilige Munditia the skeletal nun lies in some dark cellar safely evacuated out of the Alte Peter Patronin der alleinstehenden Frauen undamaged unconcerned.

Everything comes with practice. Seeing the war from the enemy point of view for instance and the damage done by the V1's, by the V2's on Deptford or Gravesend some shot down in mid-air and the first list of casualties in Normandy although the enemy lost more. Catching colds in open jeeps and getting smuggled to this party or that given by the Royal Air Force in Hanover or the American Army Intelligence in Hoechst with Flight Lieutenant This and Captain That who hoots pedestrians off the street impatiently, and sometimes with Siegfried to a slow fox-trot band in Schloss Dies or Schloss Das unless Dustbin full of ex-high officials who can help reconstruct the history of devastation Dorf by Dorf day by day from the enemy point of view which positively grovels and I must say I enjoy that. In a requisitioned flat the English Captain says I like eating in the Officers' Mess at Headquarters the I. G. Farben building you know and bitteschön they say to not a single thank you and hat's geschmeckt? But Captain excuse me German waiters have said bitteschön since time immemorial and hat's geschmeckt. What, with OUR food? My dear mamselle don't you defend the swines that occupied your country AND you didn't defend it then what would you have done without us to liberate you so now you jolly well occupy them and enjoy seeing them grovel positively grovel all the more so because they have no food and live in cellars on the black market while we occupy their few remaining flats, and serve 'em right they serve us, we help ourselves to anything we may find for a change such as this, look, Schiller, Goethe, nicely bound editions as he slides the glass-front left to right along the low bookshelf varnished in dark brown I think I'll liberate these. I like German culture. But they belong to the owner of the flat you can't just take my dear young lady, I'll liberate you if you go on defending the swinish Hun why, no wonder you frogs all collaborated.

Kein Eintritt. Bright girl, she translates brilliantly don't you think? Says the new Boss in Paris new department of simultaneous interpreters for the advancement of cold wars hot peace intercontinental missiles. Meaning come live with me and adorn my gracious Regency London house with your charming French accent or cuisine your German super-lithe Fleissigkeit as well as your elegant cosmopolitan ways.

Such conversations however never quite occur in such dishonest terms expressing falsely something there no doubt in the bluffing of the mouthpiece in order to belong perhaps, to acquire a change of nationality unless of zones lying forgotten under layers of thickening sensibilities or to prevent any true exchange of cultural curiosities under the cherry-tree in Rothenburg gem-city undamaged by a miracle between the sheets and the tumbled eiderdown dein Bein dein Brust dein belly oh Christ and hats geschmeckt amid the central heating and the wood-panelling on account of mulieris simulationis all the way along the Romantische Strasse from the cherry-tree near Nürnberg to the war-crimes revealed in Bavaria where all good things come from nowadays our good government for example began here as you know. Grüss Gott and gone and hat's geschmeckt? Und haben Sie noch einen Wunsch?

You must forgive these questions Fräulein but in view of your French upbringing we must make sure of your undivided loyalty let us see now until the age of kissing the boy

Baron at that age one has no loyalties. Ja-ja ich verstehe. And I assume you have not heard at all from your mother in France now how do you feel about that? Man muss? Do you feel so impersonal Fräulein about das Heimatland? About das Vaterland? Translate and comment on the gender of ma douce amour die Heimat nearly always represented as feminine Athena for example Rome Germania Marianne Albion depending on the time the place and whether some languages divide their genders into animate or inanimate while others less primitive into andraic and metandraic which covers objects animals of both sexes and women. Mais la langue peut se contenter de l'opposition de quelque chose avec rien, the unmarked masculine for example deriving from the marked feminine by subtraction, by an absence which signifies eine Abwesenheit die etwas bedeutet. And where has all that absence gone? Non si ricorda esattamente into what rectangles of agriculture brush-stroke size, the forest-blobs the metallic lakes the thin white lines along the pimples cancerous growths that make up an abstract study of some desolate goddess or god perhaps aghast at the catastrophe she or he has provoked as the dark handsome Viennese leans across from the left to photograph the Rhine yellow from der Luft and gone the Tour Eiffel für die Kinder with a tip of nose in the foreground to prevent any true exchange of thoughts above the close breath and the pressurised excitation saying in der luft gibts keine Grenzen. Ah but airports have frontiers still. And travel-talk ensues with Herr Helmut von Irgendetwas who travels in textiles as others travel in simultaneous interpretation. You will find your life-jacket under your seat. To inflate jacket pull red toggle (1). To top up, blow into the mouthpiece (2), obeying the innumerable instructions that translate time speed height mild desire into locality and channel and the slow descent into old matter.

The hands lie quite still on the red and white checked tablecloth in the kitchen above the rue du Four where no children play but women step out of the hairdresser opposite with puffed-up coiffures blue orange yellow pink black beige, and walk along the shops looking at lizard bags crocodile-shoes nouveautés and of course men also andron bărbaţi messieurs who have their exits and their entrances. The hands hold the letter from Dear madam. The Vicariatus Urbis has decided the case against you at the Second Hearing on May 19 when the Defensor Vinculi had to make his appeal as explained to you in my earlier letters and here in Rome orally. You will appreciate that you may now challenge this decision at a Third Hearing final and decisive. I shall with pleasure continue to represent you with my abilities and profound studies when I hear from you with a remittance together with the card showing the Ca' d'Oro on the Grand Canal backed by the words 6 via Barberini, Santa Maria di Salute, Venise 9/6. J'espère que vous allez bien. Donnez-moi je vous prie de vos nouvelles car je ne cesse de penser à vous. Amors de terra lonhdana, Per vos totz lo cors mi dol. Signed B.C. Quite legibly and even bold unless perhaps H.C.? It all depends on the habit of the eye.

— Just like a tennis-match mein Liebes. Six Love—Love Six. Game to Defensor Vinculi God bless him. Defensor Vinc leads by three games to two in the third set. No wonder I couldn't wait and I can't think why you bother.

— Oh well now it hardly matters. A question of curiosity merely.

— Expensive curiosity. Where will you find all that money? Oh I know you earn reasonably well, and you don't eat. Boiled rice du lieber Gott. You look so thin you'll vanish altogether.

— One has to give the stomach a pause after endless restaurant and airline meals and congressional banquets. Anyway more than a third of the world population lives on rice or doesn't live at all.

— Het Mineraal Spuitwater. Ugh. Though I grant you the Dutch serve no liquid at all with meals, absolutely nothing but a cup of tepid coffee at the end unless one likes beer which oddly enough I don't. Spoilt by too much travel. Still, you could save your money in other ways than lining your stomach with boiled rice and the Vatican Treasury with 800,000 lire per match per decade. What difference does it make, you haven't remarried you can even communicate.

— Well—

— Do you communicate now mein Liebes? With whom?

— Du Witzling.

— Do you?

— No.

— Well then, why spend all that money? You could invest it for your old age it'll come before you realise believe you me. Between the zest of youth and the wisdom of age a not-so-vast period called The Middle Ages shoots by. Oh well, you know that one you have plenty of money and il piccolo chalet in Wiltshire settled on you by a generous husband. Oh, no I beg your pardon, you bought it yourself for £500 in the days when one could buy piccoli chalets in Wiltshire for £500. Of course you could sell it, it would fetch at least three times that now or more.

— No.

— No? Ah yes, your box, your refuge. But seriously Liebes was drückt dich? Not still the old adolescent urge to belong?

— No.

— Or a wish to get it declared null and void by some authority that pretends to speak for a higher perhaps in whom or which you no longer believe. In other words something other than yourself, your own annihilation having no validity at least for you?

— Annihilation?

— Well let's face it you destroy. You know like Helen destroyer of men destroyer of ships und so weiter.

Troy I, Troy II, Troy VIIa. How very disappointing.

— What rubbish, who believes in that femme fatale stuff these days, not men certainly. Everybody destroys to some extent. One has to reject some things if they don't belong. Or if they destroy.

— Unless perhaps, ah! Yes. No, surely not. You don't want to marry again do you? Or do you? Pining away all these years for some virtuous Catholic who has reawakened your deep buried faith so that you can't have each other except set and sealed by the finger of God before the altar in the bosom of Mother Church? Tell Uncle Siegfried.

— Nnno.

— Hmm? But you might. Well, well, surprise surprise.

— Thank you for the charming compliment.

— Now now you know I didn't mean it like that. Aber natürlich you don't look a day older mein Lieb and you might pretend the same about me for old time's sake.

— Pretend?

— As a matter of fact I don't feel too happy about meeting in Amsterdam. Anywhere else, but here I know too many of my wife's kith and kin and this restaurant particularly—

— Oh really Siegfried. Old colleagues?

— But you know what they'll immediately think.

— Let them. Who cares? Let them follow us even and see that we do nothing they would like to imagine.

— Ah but they wouldn't follow us to see, they would merely imagine. Besides, I would like to do more than imagine. Wouldn't you? Again, Viellieb, ancora?

The hands lie quite still on the white table-cloth in this restaurant particularly, where middle-aged couples or men alone come to eat vast plates of piled up food with tall glasses of beer or no liquid at all, or sit in fondo a sinistra transfixed by the flickering local variation in the presentation of opposite viewpoints on every aspect of an instant world through faceless men who no doubt have acquired faces for them in Dutch although not to the pale bearded young man in fondo a destra at the long low-lit desk who works with a notebook next to the newspapers cast aside and a large legal tome. Unless a book of physics or a dictionary perhaps looking up semantics enthusiasm crisis with a small cup of coffee. The thumbs press each other towards the body forming a squat diamond space with the other fingers touching like a cathedral roof, the ankles crossed under the tablecloth to close the circuit and who do you suppose wants to get at you mein Lieb? Apart from me I mean? No-one? That shaking of the head does it mean yes as in Turkey Bulgaria Greece? Or no as in the more dialectical West that has turned civilisation upside down?

Let's face it you destroy. Troy I, Troy II. Ephesos early became an important centre for Christianity. On the city mount of modern Selçuk the Ajasoluk (a bowdlerizing of the Greek "Hagios Theologos") the grave of St. John remained and between the 4th and 5th centuries the people of Ephesos built churches over this grave. Between the theatre and the public baths stands the notice BROTHEL. FREUDENHAUS.

ASK EVI. Yes well ask her why not as God said to the serpent. In 263 the Goths destroyed the temple of Artemis. At the end of the 4th century the people destroyed or readapted most non-Christian temples on imperial order. But Justinian took the famous green marble columns from the ruined temple of Artemis for Santa Sophia in Constantinople. As the Islamic religion began its victorious conquest of Asia Minor a long period of peace for Ephesos came to an end. Probably during this period wherever particular people congregated you wanted them to commit themselves to your latest enthusiasm whereas nothing, rien, niente deserves a flow of rash desire love loyalty ambition marriage of tradition and progress. In the early nineteenth century the German poet Clemens Brentano took down the visions of the stigmatic nun Katharina Emmerich poor alleinstehende Frau who dreamt of the exact spot near Ephesos where the Virgin Mary lived her last years and archeologists found the remains of a 4th century chapel built on an earlier rubbish of course though fitting that Stella Maris the moon-mother-earth-water goddess on her silver crescent should continue to have a cult there. What enthusiasm? Surely one can expect a little interest and less disparagement of the sort of things which your Church for instance. All truths get institutionalised sooner or later and die, it happened to the Greek gods the Roman gods the Hebrew god, even Christ got angry about that and probably looks on now in desolation at his dead desiccated bride my sweet. How dare you talk like that? You know very well that it means something quite other, to do with childhood and that my sweet the people have destroyed or readapted most temples to their vulgar need for dogmas and static images, banalising the great and ancient myths of fall, descent, and rise into innumerable instructions that translate time space death rebirth into a narrow channel of salvation according to those instructions only, no better or worse, as instructions for living, than say, your Zodiac language, which has the same ill-worded beautiful irrelevance but at least it amuses. One must laugh, what else can one do? Yes well thanks to you all that aspect has gone anyway let us not talk about it. Not that we ever talk about anything these days without quarrelling. You quarrel my ernst German Mädel you quibble everything I say, you destroy. Because you turn everything into a joke, a poor joke usually or dirty so that now we never discuss anything at all even the places you go to the conferences the conventions broken the congresses where the Greek lady says she has no need to look up the word semantics in the dictionary because semantikos in Greek simply means humanity, fraternity, tutungerie, a bowdlerising of Saint Theology for the building of which Justinian took the famous green marble columns from Ephesos, biding his time to pick up the broken bits didn't I Liebes, his hand having drawn electricity unfelt and battericamente pura from the pulsing wrist-base of the cathedral roof mistaking the long silence for what, where when to whose heart did one do that?

— Oh, what difference does it make let us not discuss it.

— All right we'll change the subject. Hmm. You change the subject my mind has got stuck on the one and only, and when I say my mind I mean three channels at least and more than my five senses.

— Do you know anyone with the initials B.C.?

— B.C.?

— Someone who seems to know about the racket, can find out where one goes or will go, though too late.

— Me of course. Incognito.

— Du Witzling.

— True I'd turn up on time. Unlike you mein Liebes do you

still not wear a watch? I really must give you one, or a travelling clock.

— No please don't. They get lost or broken.

— So you still live anticlockwise?

— Of course not. Clocks hang everywhere.

— They never agree however. Hence your unpunctuality.

— Never at work though.

— Only at play, ah well. Er, man or woman?

— Bărbat.

— So you know he has a beard?

— Witzling. No. Just a Man.

— Merely a man. Well, let's see. Some cher collègue pursuing you eh? How romantic. I thought they had replaced us almost entirely with gorgeous young computers. Forgive me. And does he keep finding himself on another plane?

— Not exactly. Though he lives on another plane all right look at these. Do you know that writing?

— No. Oh, but wait. Yes. The style. Aha. Natürlich selbstverständlich. Ma chère collègue but you have made a somewhat belated post-factum conquest of dear old Bertrand retired if I may say so several centuries ago.

— Bertrand! Good God.

The cloud has cleared. The jet exhausts invisible in their power save for a tremor on the blue or the propellers invisible in their speed save for a hinted halo che fa tremar dì claritate l'âre, no man-made object passing to show that the heart flies immobile at eight hundred and ninety kilometres and no man to come and bring you out of this or that zone of tickled fancy inside the distant brain way up with a tremendous force of a love lost or never gained lying forgotten under layers of civilisation thickening sensibilities such as for instance a language that actually means something in the light of that love or vice versa, but only a decrepit fond old man well sixty-five and plus whose surname you never remember do you Liebes but then no wonder in this case he always fell in love with young secretaries inaccessible, writing them flowery letters full of Provençal quotations about fin amor lonhtano and the princesse lointaine so that we used to call him Bertrand de Born.

— But didn't Rudel write about the princesse lointaine?

— Oh, you know everything my pendantic Liebes. I travel in electronics now not simultaneous interpretation, remember me? Or have you closed the circuit?

Et au départ, n'oubliez pas qu'en roumain "la revedere" signifie "au revoir" et que le sourire avenant de la Roumanie signifie "à bientôt" in the lively rhythm of a prodigious development representing only some of the accents of the renovating present.

Whereas in modern Greek elios means sun and gyneka means woman. The meaning has remained. Logariasmo parakalo for that matter means the bill please according to the phrase-book in a mere smattering acquired with the Wolga Boatsman Hara-Kiri Roumanian Cocktail Bloody Merry Whyte Lady in low square black armchairs the bar lit up like a reredos vous prendrez quelque chose chère madame? Nothing at all, just personal effects like furry eyes and the fact that in this air-conditioning the body floats in willing suspension of loyalty to anyone inside the giant centipede where I want narrow trousers. Without folding-up. I prefer it double-breasted. With two buttons. When shall I come for the rehearsal? In six days I go away.

Or did you want to test by means of engagement?

And we saw yesterday afternoon mesdames messieurs, in the Byzantine Museum of Athens, a remarkable example of this inversion by double negation so typical of the imaginative function in its descending aspect of depth, night, femininity, container which becomes contained, swallower which becomes swallowed, as opposed to its upward masculine aspect. Je fais allusion au Saint Christophe cynocéphale, dating from the 17th century, and represented with a dog's head. Two myths converge here, that of the man-eating giant with the head of a dog and that of the passer of souls, Cerberus, a transposition of the Egyptian Anubis. Here the Christ carried by death inverts the meaning of death, coming down through the neutralised transmitter in the brain behind the closed eyelids which open to catch a glimpse of Sandra working so young so fresh into simultaneous English with eyes ears voice and un amour de soutien-gorge no hands as she watches the speaker through the glass booth accompanying mortals in their perilous journey, et qui devient symbole de l'in-ti-mi-té dans le voyage, as well as protector and talisman against death itself, especially violent death. The mythical imagination invokes death against death in a characteristic double negation. Le Christo-phoros porte le Christ. And in a gulliverisation typical of giant myths, as for example the Gargantua legends, the swallowing mouth gets euphemised into a sack, a basket, une hotte, a container, which, like the mandala mentioned in Professor Strebbing's excellent paper this morning, represents a sort of porte-manteau centre-of-perfection, prêt-à-porter si vous voulez, like the prayer-wheel or even the prayer-rug, a miniature temple, cavern, womb, stomach, belly, vessel, vehicle, ship, sepulchre or holy grail, with the same confusional sliding from active to passive, from swallower to swallowed, from container to contained that we find in all the myths of depth, night, descent and femininity. They come so young nowadays, doing the same work with ease and careless poise from the start who have known no war no national groups as when les grandes personnes talked of la Guerre l'Allemagne and yet not like that at all, a different species altogether who can learn from simply living simultaneously all channels alert at all levels unless they merely block off different ones, witness le complexe de Jonas with which I dealt briefly earlier on in the foetus position with diagrams of a fish thrown upside down on the screen the lantern-slide projector behaving like an antipodal eye telescoping time with an error, la pointe pressed home on the meridian of the heart C7 here on the wrist which stops hysteria at once and the vessel of conception CV 52 as a recommended alternative for relaxation and absolute calm.

The black arrow on the left inside the disc points up, the red arrow points down. The grey-lined bus full of structural imaginations nevertheless swings out to pass the lorry with TIR on its bottom and (GR) over the blue number-plate E plus six figures in white stretching interminably with Transport International of something past already as the bus cuts in quickly aslant the eyes of a black car ahead switched on in anger unless perhaps alarm. Sometimes however the number of the key drops down from 412 to two times two equals four times two equals eight times two equals sixteen ad infinitum which makes one very sad. Away from the road a path leads into a deep cleft between the two masses of the Phaidriades where lies the famous Kastalia spring. The visitor's attention turns immediately to the sanctuary of Apollo situated on the higher slopes in five terrace-like levels. The visitor's attention turns immediately to the androgynous goddess.

For let me make it quite clear, the myth of the androgynous divinity, present everywhere, does not until the later cults of the masculine god, express the idea of the Father transcendent but rather that of the feminoid Son. Most lunar and vegetation divinities have a double sexuality, Artemis, Attis, Adonis, Dionysos, even Adam and his rib, not to mention australian, chinese, indian and nordic divinities. Hence the curious bearded goddesses which pass through the neutralised transmitter in the brain in French and out into the mouthpiece in simultaneous German. Or through the younger carelessly poised transmitter between the long lank hair and un amour de soutien-gorge qui pigeonne all channels alert with ease and out in simultaneous English. Hence the invocation of Sin, the babylonian lunar god as both matrix and merciful Father, principle of harmonious reunion hence ritual castration breast ablation hence the mythical origin of the Amazons hence into the mouthpiece in and out, in and out, slowly and round the eternal cycle of l'ourobouros, the snake eating its own tail indefinitely, not merely as a ring of flesh but expressing the material dialectic of death and life, life and death, death out of life, life out of death in an endless inversion echoing the agro-lunar drama of months and seasons, the sacrificial substitution permitting, through repetition, the exchange of past for future and the domestication of Chronos. Did you want it for eating love? Leider haben wir keine.

Between existing as a woman and working as a man in charge of the young a different species altogether, eyes closed, watching the words as they pass through the neutralised transmitter in the brain and hence, in and out steadily and round the eternal cycle sits an androgynous douce inoubliable dame desolate at the death of hope faith charity to any rib torn from her chest any small foreign body out of entrails for the forming of a language that actually means something in the light of that death. Or else inside the whale who knows for we must surely acknowledge that these vital lies have more energy than so many of the fragile truths that surround us in this supposedly rationalistic age so dominated by masculine upward myths, and that the essential truth of these

Lebenslügen reintegrates us in totality by virtue of an ontological recognition present in all of us. Can we call mensonge un mensonge qui a tant de vitalité?

The broad white arrow crosses the blue disc diagonally. The arrow changes into a black band diagonal across the disk. On the left of the broad yellow arrow that points down from corner to corner of the square card the razor-blade, printed in green, has a white narrow slit dented with short vertical bars and two small circles on either side of the diamond-shape in the centre. On the other side two pink lips slightly separated echo the white and dented slit in the green razor-blade. Pour le démaquillage et pour le rasoir. Sometimes German comes first then English then French with the language of the country Rumanian Russian Greek always first however such as Toaleta unless TOAΛETHA or even TOYAΛETTA with care not to enter Bărbaţi when the door bears no skirted figurine or high-heeled shoe in the mere smattering acquired with Acqua Minerale battericamente pura that cleanses ancient matter as it passes through the body because naturellement nous pouvons considérer toute alimentation comme transsubstantiation. Boiled rice, du lieber Gott. Couldn't you save in other ways than lining your stomach with a great hole of emptiness, for example the gulliverisation of St. Nicholas with his sack, a close parallel to St. Christopher and the good giants out of the man-eating monsters and the god-eating Titans. Witness the ships in nutshells, bottles, boxes within boxes, tabernacles in temples und so weiter weiter gehen through the indiscrimination of the mouthpiece at nineteen or forty-seven even.

The disc encloses three curved black arrows forming a circle anti-clockwise au schème de l'ourobouros, the snake eating its own tail indefinitely, not merely as a ring of flesh but as the material dialectic of death and life, death out of life, life out of death in an endless inversion echoing the agro-lunar dramma dell' agnosticismo con tutti gli ingredienti storici filosofici e sociali determinanti la involuzione in atto nella nostra civiltà. The English they applause their speakers. The Gairmans they applause their speakers in le mensonge vital which sits back desolate at the catastrophe it has provoked. And the Japanese, don't forget the Japanese. They praise, yes mademoiselle, also. Presumably everyone comes for that. They certainly don't come for information. Information? My dear good girl und so weiter and each speaker waits impatiently for his turn, each more concerned with output than intake. Ah, output, intake, god, verr god, mademoiselle. My card Bertrand de Born dont le coeur tremble de fol espoir. Where when and with what araignée du soir? How long have you stayed away, lost touch and more than the five senses out of this zone or that not applying il numero di codice lying under layers and layers of vital lies through mulieris simulationis and a shaking of the head nai for yes or a vigorous nodding ohi or yok for no sub specie aeternitatis unlike this our masculine-dominated civilisation turned upside down.

Sometimes however the number of the long-lost code falls from 412 to two times two equals four times two equals eight times two equals sixteen ad infinitum which makes one very desperate. Sometimes the bathroom mirror lights up in neon-daylight making a desiccated skeletal alleinstehende Frau of what thirty-nine, forty-six, unless in a rosy glow of the renovating present the reflection staring up at the reflection of the invisible man behind the reflection and back at the reflection looks about Herr Oberstleutnant at that age one has no loyalties. The glint of a hint of tinted hair shines golden in the rosy glow falling over the shoulders along the silver chain that carries the man-eating giant and passer of souls in a characteristic double-negation between the bare breasts fairly firm as yet only to see and touch a little under the cherry-tree.

The rosy glow spreads to the tap-end of the pink bath encased in black tiling. The left-hand tap has C for cold, no caldo of course natürlich and inside the pink bathtub lies a huge great SCREAM run door room bed bell push sob stuff-sheet-in-mouth sob cold sweat silence. Bell, push. Knock on door cover yourself entrez. Che desidera, signora?

— Bagno!

— Ma—

— Nel bagno. Una, una, une araignée.

— Signora?

— Insetto. Enorme.

— Ah. Un momento signora.

He vanishes between the built-in cupboard painted pink and the pink black-tiled bathroom where the water caldo-freddo runs for a momento! No, no, no-con-acqua si, tutto va bene signora, solamente un piccolo ragno ah, signora che bella!

The blue peignoir snatched from the chair in the rush to the noise of caldo-freddo has one sleeve inside out. Ma che pallida, signora. Non fa niente, buono, buono, mangia le mosche. Solamente un piccolo with insolent eyes and a great tenderness only to see and touch a little in the narrow passage between the built-in cupboard painted pink and the rosy glow of the situation so characteristic in this our masculine-dominated myth unmarked save by subtraction from the feminine with its ambivalence in the double-negation no e no.

Structures of power, even when they appear to depend on physical force, in fact depend on the assistance and cooperation of innumerable individuals for the administration of physical force. Mesdames messieurs, nous avons entendu déjà several of our many specialists in the theory of government, in civilian defence, in the strategy of non-violence, discussing this theme, and trying to establish—in principle at least—to what extent anyone, or any idea, can persuade those who oppose a power-structure based on physical force to refuse their assistance and co-operation. In other words can non-violence force the conqueror down into the earphones in French and out into the mouthpiece in simultaneous German. I have pleasure in calling upon Monsieur le professeur Bernard Mottin, directeur de l'Institut d'Etudes Civiles et président du Congrès, notre admirable hôte dans cette belle et ancienne ville de Strasbourg.

The brief applause of the delegates in the big hall cracks the eardrums through the earphones which have to be stretched outwards from the ears for a moment while the professeur climbs to the dais-table until the murmuring voices picked up by the microphone resolves itself into Mesdames messieurs and pause. Nous avons entendu ce matin une belle fiction. Le professeur Strauss—don't j'admire profondément les études—has elevated our hopes with ideas which, however idealistic and indeed true in theory, bear little relation to grim reality. The fruits of conquest, he told us, depend on affirmative action by large numbers of people, hundreds and even thousands. Yet force, he told us, cannot obtain this affirmative action directly. And the professor exemplified with a vivid comparison from the animal kingdom: you can drag a horse to water, but only the horse can make his muscles work. And if he won't drink, soon you will have no horse. We can imagine, the professor said—and indeed we have to—a militarily defenceless people completely confounding a conqueror or even a would-be conqueror—dissuading him in advance—by sitting quietly, not eating, not working, threatening to deprive him of any subjects simply by dying. He can let them die, he can even kill them. But he cannot exploit them.

Now ladies and gentlemen, this undeniable principle remains a principle, optimistic in its ultimate ends, cruel in its application, and totally at odds with any real situation in the world past or present. We have no evidence whatsoever that live human beings, let alone horses, can so embody this principle in any behaviour sufficiently organized as to disarm a tyrant of his bureaucrats and soldiers, even less to dissuade him in advance. Human beings need to eat, to work, and to this end will either knuckle under or, more often, persuade themselves that le mensonge vital die Lebenslüge contains sufficient double-negation to reintegrate him into totality compared with so many fragile truths and lost mysteries that surround us in this our masculine-dominated civilization turned upside down into the earphones and out into the mouthpiece with a gulliverisation typical of the giant myths euphemised into a sack, a basket, a container cavern womb belly vase vehicle ship temple sepulchre or holy grail, witness le complexe de Jonas with which the lost vitality of the word goes down into the mouthpiece and out through its exits and entrances in simultaneous German to the legendary sound of music or circular dance, creating an invisible magic wall of defence undone by Achilles when he dragged Hector's body round it anticlockwise. Non si ricorda esattamente for a fire destroyed Troy VI in 900 B.C. B.C.? Oh yes. The cloud has cleared into a fond old man well sixty-two and plus flowery love-letters full of Provençal quotations about fin amor lonhtano and all that.

E allora the languages fraternise in Geneva where malnutrition occurs in Europe on a far larger scale than anyone has realised owing to the widespread devitalising of foods due to mass-processing, chemical fertilisers, sprays and additives as well as ignorance of diet with 48% having an average intake of nutrients well below the minimum level, itself varying from 30 mg. of vitamins daily recommended by the British Medical Association in England to 70 mg. recommended by the American Medical Association and 200 mg. by the Russian. The doctor on the dais protests at carbohydrates refined sugar white flour and fluoridation of water forbidden in Scandinavia and all civilised lands of which the World Health Association should take note while others in Paris home at last speak of the spiral as a sort of stylised maze, the maze itself having originated in the underground passages of the cave-dwellers which always led to a sanctus sanctorum, in a chthonic religion of course, going down, whereas the spiral tower of the Sumerian ziggurat belonged to a lunar culture. The ziggurat idea lies behind that of the seven-terraced city of Ekbatana and the Tower of Babel. Mesdames messieurs, you must surely know already —and if you do not I recommend you to see—Breughel's painting of the Tower of Babel in which the letter from Venice reads Enfin! O gentildonna, douce dame aux yeux de vair! Votre merveilleuse lettre m'a rendu fou de joie. Which folie de joie goes into rhapsodies at length quite disproportionate to the brief polite note of thanks for compliments the speaker n'a pas conscience de mériter and totally at odds with any real situation in the prodigious accents of the renovating present. We have no evidence that human beings, let alone horses, can so embody the divine principle descending into any behaviour sufficiently organised to disarm a gentildonna of her furry eyes, vital double-negation simulation and other frustrations to the true end of marriage so typical in this our masculine-dominated myth turned upside down, in, out, around with a dumb show unanswered at one level and at another higher lower responded to perhaps with yearning for romance or lust atingle in the loins unless despair in knowledge of the man, exasperation cold indifference to the language of the long-lost code lying beneath layers and layers of changing sensibilities which nevertheless winds its way up surreptitiously through the centuries to undo the magic wall of defence around no more than the distant brain way up with an idle thought or two such as well, why not play a little at a mere correspondence of love six love, la gentildonna leads by five games to three in the second set.

The visitor's attention turns immediately to higher things such as the red star above the pediment of a grey mock-columned building opposite the hotel with its mere façade of columns that support nothing at all except MÁVIGAZGA-TÓSÁG in red. E allora the languages do not fraternise down the seven-terraced tower which has the structure of the Sumerian ziggurat.

Unless perhaps the seven-terraced tower sits suspended between belief and disbelief at a height of twelve thousand metres outside temperature what, minus forty-nine bumping down the steps of air its under-carriage lowered and touching ground so suddenly that the fingers fondle the medal of Saint Christopher under the blouse the distant brain way up guided by white frogs with yellow discs for eyes until it comes to a standstill and up the concrete corridor into the big hall where concrete men sit hidden in high booths and consult secret lists looking up at the change in the expected person. The plastic luggage moves along the conveyor-belt unowned unmastered then suddenly half-owned again as the concrete man searches, turns out the entire contents of the suitcase this? Rollers. For the hair. Ah. And this? A hair-piece. What? Peruka. Ah. Searching and searching for the face put on and other frustrations to the true end of marriage this? Well! Searching and searching not for intimacy or liquor cigarettes diamonds drugs but ideas in dangerous print and this? A Russian phrase-book do you mind? Ah. Du lieber Gott what an unexpected tribute to the power of literature. Lirrechur etc? Tomorrow and tomorrow and tomorrow, creeps in this dilapidated dining-room with galleries cupids on the corner pillars potted plants and a bulging orchestra balcony empty of perhaps balalaikas. The two thumbs press together towards the body, the fingers touch away from it forming a roof with a squat diamond-space between. So you've come for an East-West writers' conference on The Writer and Communication well, how very hopeful of them. And me merely for electronics what a well-organised coincidence. And do you still communicate mein Lieb, with whom?

Did you want it for eating love?

Tomorrow and tomorrow creeps in this petty place among the potted palms a group of young men in brown nylon macintoshes accompanying girls in skirts and jumpers one in apple-green frou-frou to an adjoining room where the young men take off their nylon macintoshes and dance close to their girls pre-war slow foxtrots lieber Gott has progress retrograded to a pre-war slow foxtrot orchestra depending on what you mean by progress. How long have you stayed away lost touch got out of practice or as yet ungained any confidence heart knowledge of true love memory taking off into the blue the cloud the fog? Haben Sie Butter bitte? Excuse please? May we have some butter? Bata? Er, mas-wo. Excuse, niet. Oh. Thank you. And how goes the tennis-match?

— Oh! That. Well, one takes no notice really.

— One does? Who exactly takes no notice 00147 Roma?

— Oh, you mean Rome.

— What did you think I meant?

— Nothing.

— Well?

— Well, it just goes on. Presumably. In the meantime—

— In the meantime we make love?

— Perhaps.

Siegfried grown totally bald somewhere between Moscow and Retrograd looks Liebes! Seriously? After all these years and despite or while waiting for Defensor Vinc? You'll strike me impotent you will.

— Not you Siegfried.

— You really do want things both ways don't you?

— Well you've tried hard enough to undermine what little faith remained.

— What me?

— Oh and him too. Everyone. And life. And Rome more than anyone. Your other advice found an echo anyway.

— What advice?

— To sell the cottage.

— To sell—I don't believe it. What, il piccolo chalet, gone?

— Not quite yet, but going.

— I simply don't believe you. How much? When? How?

— Four thousand. Someone wanted it, and approached an agent, who wrote, and, well, why not, as you said, one should save und so weiter and the rent in Paris went up to almost double after the last demand from Rome and—

— But Liebes! I never meant it seriously. Your box your refuge and all that. And without consulting me.

— Without consulting anyone. It just happened one morning, the letter came, and suddenly it all meant nothing. Why have two pieds-à-terre? Most conferences take place in Paris these days, apart of course from fringe activities like the Dante Centenary not to mention Writers and Communication.

— Du Witzling. But I don't understand you. Have you got something up your sleeve?

— Nothing at all, just personal effects.

— And very nice too. No seriously. Have you signed it away? Has it all gone? Il piccolo chalet?

— Not quite. Next week in London. A Medical Congress on the molecules of memory, appropriately enough.

— And you'll transfer the furniture and stuff to the rue du Four?

— Only some of it. No room as you know. The rest goes up for auction.

— Why do I feel as if I had lost a limb? You must have gone out of your mind.

— Or into it again. Paris has much to offer.

— Ah, gay Paree.

— No not that. Just living in the language of one's childhood. Shopping in French, paying rent and taxes in French, talking to the concierge in French, walking breathing in French.

— Hmm. You can't Persil-schein your German layers that easily meine Liebe.

— That doesn't come into it.

— Which reminds me, breathing in French, breathes yet the old French lover?

— Man achtet nicht darauf.

— Man doesn't?

— Oh, man. Man continues.

— Poor old thing. With no encouragement at all from la belle dame sans merci? Well, gut-gut. But I don't believe it. Even old Bertrand would give up sooner or later. Your eyes, your emerald furry eyes cannot lie. You have answered him. Nicht wahr? You enjoy it, nicht wahr, reading all that suffering stuff, it does something to you nicht wahr nicht wahr? Oh, Liebes, such an easy prey how can you?

— Only in the most off-hand and neutral way.

— But just non-neutrally enough to keep it going nicht wahr?

— Stop prying and bullying.

— Well, I feel jealous.

— It doesn't mean a thing.

— No?

— Nothing at all.

— Except perhaps—

— Yes?

— The language, Siegfried. The fact that all this suffering stuff as you call it pours out in French, well, it sort of turns the system inside out, it—

— I see. Yes, I do see. In that case, I can only bow out once again, gracefully I hope as before, as always.

— Oh Siegfried don't talk like that. It means nothing.

— Hmm. Besides I'd better not attempt once more to seduce you back, not here anyway, they have the charming habit of taking photographs and sending them to one's wife, boss und so weiter.

— Oh.

— I say that loudly enough to make the large-eared lady's job easier at the next table. I wish they wouldn't do it so obviously. Perhaps we should test her abilities and speak

Arabic, not that that would flummax a bugged watch. Oh. Meine Liebe! You mean, you really, wanted to?

— Yes.

— As er, as a substitute?

— How can you say a thing like that? After all these years as you say of friendship and even love.

— Take care, Liebes, take care. Oh. Have you any fruit? Obst. How on earth do you say fruit in Russian? Des fruits. Excuse, niet, poodeeng?

You can't Persil-schein your German layers that easily meine Liebe. Let's face it you destroy. All that suffering stuff you enjoy it nicht wahr nicht wahr? Aber man achtet nicht darauf. As if languages loved each other beneath their own façades, despite alles was man denkt darüber davon dazu. Then acquires alles a broken up quality, die hat der charm of my clever sweet, my deutsche Mädchen-goddess, the gestures and the actions all postponed while first die Dinge und die Personen kommen. Aber voaus und woein kommen die Personen?

Si les psychologues ont fait de grand progrès dans l'étude de la mémoire et de ses diverses composantes, telles que l'enregistrement such as recording and conservation, on sait par contre bien peu sur le plan purement descriptif de ce qui se produit physiologiquement au niveau cérébral, of the modifications in the nervous tissue through which a person retains events which affect subsequent behaviour. For 2500 years since Plato on propose des images et des concepts such as wax tablets, the tracks of memory, the synaptic recording, the biochemical engraving. Mais cependant un médecin anglais Gomulicki, studying in 1953 could even then deplore the fact that not one of these terms had any real relation either with the general problem, or with any one of the known facts. How far have we progressed since then down through the earphones into the nervous tissue in French and out almost unretained by any molecules affecting subsequent behaviour in simultaneous German. Or down into the earphones over Sandra's long lank rich auburn hair and out affecting no memory at all in sheer youth and simultaneous English.

Mesdames messieurs je vais vous parler for the twenty minutes at my disposal, de l'hypothèse concernant les relations ARN, ADN et la mémoire, hypothèse certes séduisante et au goût du jour, mais qui manque de bases très solides. Fashionable because DNA and RNA, the molecules which play a key role in protein synthesis, valent un prix Nobel de médecine every few years for those who work on them. Séduisante à plus d'un titre cependant. Mais il semble qu'un des éléments de séduction vient un peu de ce qu'on joue sur les mots, speaking of a *code* retained by DNA and RNA, alors qu'on n'emploie pas ce terme pour d'autres molécules—tout simplement parceque l'ARN et l'ADN interviennent en matière de code génétique. Obviously, if we can describe everything that happens in a living organism—including memory—in chemical terms, one or several types of molecules must *encode* the ideas and the remembered facts. But why should we identify these code-molecules of memory with those of the genetic code?

L'hypothèse veut que si les stimulus de l'environnement, in other words, events, transformed into electrical impulses, modified the sequence of bases in a particulier RNA, this would lead to modifications of structure in the cell containing the RNA and would permanently alter the physical features of the cell, since it synthetises the proteins en fonction des ARN qu'elle contient. This would leave a trace.

The terminology worked up in advance pours smoothly down into the mouthpiece with absolute calm out of the nervous tissue making the protein available to those who desperately need it, spinning to yield products which when properly flavoured closely simulate common foods contra bona indissolubilitatis et prolis. The signature on the deed however leaves no trace of regret for il piccolo chalet in Wiltshire where stones talk walk make semblance of love have fun until they come to a standstill. The yellow curtains the pelmet the carpets and the biddy remain as fittings and fixtures part and parcel of what a shame I'll miss you love. Not that you came here much lately but then I suppose we all settle for the land of our birth in the end don't we. Why don't you come and have a farewell drink with me and my Tom down at the local love where they all sit in a circle transfixed by the blue screen flickering out the local variation in the presentation of opposite viewpoints on every aspect of an instant world through faceless men who have no doubt acquired faces for them as their archpriests of exploding bombs exploding into Brighter than Bright Cleaner than Clean.

The seductive hypothesis whose seductive element lies in the fact that we play on words and speak of codes, postulates that the stimulus of environment modifies the sequence of bases, leading to the modification of the code within a cell within a body within a box within a village within a wooded area in an alien land. This would leave a trace. So that the child sits at the kitchen table facing a paintbox and dark water in a glass-jar plus a mess of coloured blobs lines smudges on a rectangular sheet of paper and bursts into tears. Mais quoi alors? Pourquoi pleures-tu?

— J'veux peindre.

— Alors peins.

— Mais j'sais pas peindre.

— Alors, ne peins pas.

— Mais j'veux peindre.

— Ah tu m'agaces. Décide-toi. Tu peins ou tu n'peins pas. De toute façon, reste tranquille.

— Und alles ROTE auf der Karte, das gehört ENGland.

The schoolmaster glares round the class, looking for a scapegoat perhaps.

— Und alles GRÜNE auf der Karte, das gehört FRANKreich.

The gangling girl in pigtails grows cold and pale even as a girl she always did look pale, uninteresting, then suddenly hot and flushed as the whole class follows the stony glare at the französische Mädchen responsible for the green on the map slightly deeper than the yellowish green vastness of the Soviet Republics right up to Siberia or for that matter Brazil and then again not quite so bright as the bright green United States of America together with Alaska beyond the crimson flush of Canada the pale pink of Greenland (pink?) and responsible also no doubt for the dark and pale das ROTE on account of the Entente Cordiale.

— Der Fuehrer aber hat geschrieben that the gangling girl released from stony glares feels homesick longs for was FRANKreich gehört and stares at the squarish green shape beneath the crimson old lady in a motorcar-driving position which represents apparently ENGland. The crimson old lady sits with legs forward on a blue space dented by a spoke sticking out of the green squarish shape much bigger than her and doesn't quite hold a crimson haired pink baby like a teddybear who also sits with his legs and arms forward leaning back on a blue space dented by the arms of the old lady unless perhaps he represents a peculiar steering wheel she doesn't quite hold. Or a doll in a pram. For das deutsche Volk, virile, numerous, hard-working, brave as proved over and over again by history ever since Otto I whose victory on the Lech in 955 finally liberated his country from the Magyar pest, das deutsche Volk no longer has enough Lebensraum. Look now at this map of Europe in the time of Otto. The Holy Roman Empire in its infancy. Das erste Deutsche Reich. Saxony up here. Lotharingia there. Franconia Swabia Bayern you all know Bayern, Karinthia Bohemia Moravia surrounded by a thick black line make up a sort of flying dog with paws curled down into Trieste and the kingdom of Italy as far as below Rome in dotted lines bring the hind legs funnily forward like a flying dog about to land along the Adriatic.

Das erste Deutsche Reich. Und später it expanded further, into the Northern Marches and the March of Austria, peacefully into Pomerania and beyond as I shall tell you next week. And later still the great emperor Friedrich Barbarossa went far down into Italy and eventually established, by the marriage of his son Henry to Constance of Sicily, the Hohenstaufen dynasty right down here. But the popes put a stop to that. As they always did, from Henry IV's brave penance in mid-winter to Barbarossa's meeting with Alexander III in Venice on July 24th 1177, commemorated by three red marble slabs in the porch of St. Mark's where the Emperor knelt to receive the kiss of peace, conceding however, no point of vital substance. But the popes have no power today. France and England have, backed of course by America. I want you now to compare even this map with the modern map. You can see how das deutsche Volk virile numerous and brave has suffered at the hands of the European powers and now no longer has enough Lebensraum.

The Lebensraum in orange looks enormous, as big as FRANKreich bigger than ENGland all the way to Wien like a wolf turned eastwards with its open jaw on Poland in dark lilac and Bohemia no Czechoslovakia the SUDETENland also in pale pink between its chin and breast. But paler than the pink baby of was ENGland gehört. Dänemark gives it violet ears perked up quite high in wild anticipation. The orange breast of the wolf touches the frilly top of Italy's purple boot which faces the other way however, kicking Sicily like a triangular football.

Two thirds of the way down the squarish green shape of FRANKreich not far from the frilly top of the purple boot lies Lyon, somewhere in which stands the big square black school where Mlle Levert professeur d'histoire talks of la grande différence entre l'Allemagne de Barbarossa et la faible fédération de 350 petits états après le Traité de Westphalie. Le pouvoir de l'empereur devint une ombre, même parmi les princes allemands. Il y avait eu en Europe une seule religion. Maintenant il y en avait trois. La France grandit de ces différences. Du moins, jusqu'au dix-neuvième siècle, quand l'Allemagne a renouvelé ses folles ambitions. But Mlle Levert looks cold and distant not so nice as young Madame Ribloux de l'Ecole Primaire who points to the map and says voici Lyon, à travers laquelle coulent deux rivières, le Rhône et la Saône. Et comme on dit toujours à Lyon, il y a aussi la troisième rivière, le Beaujolais.

— Où qu'elle coule, la troisième rivière maman?

— Où qu'elle coule? Où as-tu appris à parler le français comme ça?

— Où coule-t-elle?

— Quoi?

— La belle Jolaise.

— Mais tu radotes! Tu en as de ces idées. Tout à fait comme ton père, j'sais pas ce que j'vais faire avec toi.

— Maman.

— Oui?

— Tu m'aimes?

— Mais bien sûr ma poupée.

— Autant que moi j't'aime?

— Plus.

— Moi j't'aime grand comme le ciel.

— Eh bien moi aussi.

— Mais tu as dis plus.

— Hé bien oui, plus. Tiens, plus haut que le ciel, le ciel a ses hauteurs tu sais. Allons, reste tranquille ma chérie, fais tes devoirs.

— Et papa?

— Quoi papa?

— Tu crois qu'il m'aime?

— Ah ça ton père j'sais pas où il a fichu le camp.

Il a fichu le camp somewhere en Allemagne where I shall send you for a year with your tante Frieda later, quand tu auras quinze ans and you'll have done more German at school by then. For my sins you have a German name and you might as well learn la langue boche it will come in useful when you grow up. I never believed in denying your heritage after all I married him and besides, as I said to my mother when she objected—which of course made me all the more determined—we must forgive and forget, it won't happen again. If she hadn't objected I wouldn't have married him probably, oh yes I had others after me, a nice French boy Jules and then you'd have turned out quite different. Remind me not to object to any crétin you want to marry when you grow up it'll only throw you into his arms. And besides, le salaud je l'aimais. Well, you'll understand all these things when you grow up into a grande-personne ma chérie, et maintenant que tu as quinze ans, I've packed all your prettiest dresses into a great big trunk, and your German grammar, and some of your Comtesse de Ségur favourites so that you don't forget your French.

— Oh maman il y a longtemps que je ne lis plus la Comtesse de Ségur pour qui me prends-tu?

— Ah? Trop tard, I put them at the bottom never mind you may like to re-read them. Your train leaves tomorrow at eight, change at Frankfort for Nuremberg, just cross the same platform you won't have any luggage except a small suitcase and you won't get lost will you and don't talk to any strange men, or in fact to anyone at all tu entends? And you will go to Mass every Sunday in Nuremberg, your uncle has promised to drive you there after or before their own service in the village church, Calvinist of course or do I mean Lutheran? Protestant anyway. Your father didn't—oh well, that doesn't matter now. You will go won't you, you know what the devil does to children who commit mortal sins. And you must remember to say three Je-vous-salue-Marie and one Notre-Père every morning, and again every night when you go to bed.

— Oui maman.

— And when you come back you'll speak fluent German and sail through your bachot at seventeen if you keep up your French and Latin at school there which your tante Frieda assures me you will. Now don't cry, I've done everything to bring you up properly and equip you so that you can earn your living well and not go through what I had to. Women have a hard time these days when left alone to cope. In the old days they had large families to go back to or convents or something but now they have to go out into the world unequipped and the world lines up against them. Allons ma chérie don't cry I'll write to you every week and you'll write to me, everything you do and all the new things you'll see, why, in no time at all you'll get used to it, you'll even enjoy it. Your father had a lot of charm you know and comes of a very good family whatever one may say about his people in general. But good Germans exist I assure you and you'll make a lot of nice new friends at school, and in the village. And you know, you'll live in a castle. With a moat and drawbridge.

The drawbridge never draws and grass grows in the moat around the plain square Schloss, more like a house than a castle, but with an inner courtyard into which the small Opel drives bumping over the drawbridge until it comes to a standstill. The Baron steely-haired and stern but not like a vraie grande-personne at all on account of dirty leather shorts thick green woollen socks a grey jacket with green tabs on the collar and the feathered felt hat tossed over the small suitcase on the back seat gets out walks round the car opens the door and clicks his big brown shoes with mock perhaps solemnity and Willkommen Liebchen ah, here comes your aunt, gaunt, skeletal down the stone stairs that spiral like the sandy hair scraped back to a high coil and cold grey eyes. Willkommen Liebchen du sprichst ein bisschen deutsch nicht wahr? Gut. Wir müssen von Anfang an nur deutsch sprechen, weil obwohl wir natürlich französisch und englisch können du sollst hier doch deutsch lernen nicht wahr? Meet your cousin Helmut you will get on well together I know. My daughter and her husband and baby live on the ground floor you will meet them later. How pale you look. Come in.

How pale he looks, der Baron, dead on his bed surrounded with wreaths and tributes, brought back in state from the Sudetenland by train and then from Nürnberg on a guncarriage drawn by four motorbikes in escort having burst a blood-vessel while addressing a meeting but why Tante Frieda? Why?

— Schweinehunde! Kommunisten! Sozialdemokraten! Homosexuelle Juden! Here my child you behold a hero, the first hero and victim in a long line to come no doubt. Das Wehrkreiskommando has given him full military honours as an ex-tank captain in the Great War and hero of the hour. You will understand these things later my child, but remember now, your uncle did his duty only his duty as a Party Member. Nothing more. And all for those filthy Bohemians —no, I must not give way. O mein lieber Helmut. You will attend the funeral at my side, Liebchen, as the only representative of his poor brother your father, who went off to Russia in a mad weak moment, always so foolish and headstrong your father. In a black dirndl over your white blouse, I'll get Emma to make one up for you quickly, she has your measurements hasn't she or have you filled out since she made this blue one? Yes it does look a bit tight. Run up to her room and tell her. O mein lieber Helmut.

The first hero and victim lies in a long line to come on all sides Jewish German Polish Dutch French Greek Serbian Russian English virile brave hard-working for the Vaterland mother-country patrie according to the climate height of aircraft speed of conquest pride fear ignorance gnawing guilt wonder at these questions Fräulein but how did you come to stay in Germany at all at the beginning of the emergency? Your mother no doubt awaited you anxiously and the government made all provisions for repatriation of aliens. Or did you not regard yourself as alien? So you had appendicitis? Could you not have returned to France for the operation? Peritonitis. And complications. In the Krankenhaus at Nürnberg. Ah well. But you would have returned if you could? You regard yourself as French? Your father, ah! Yes, well we need not probe further into that, nobody blames you Fräulein and we have evidence that he has since died, purged we may say, by our charming neighbours. Gut. So you had a year in Freiburg? Who paid, die Baronin? A scholarship. So you feel you owe something to the German Reich surely. But why did you study French? France had already become our ally then and you must have realised it could hardly come in very useful for the war effort. And Provençal, Mediaeval French? Fräulein we need guns not butter. Well, to get a degree Herr Oberstleutnant, after the war of course, besides, one had the choice Herr Oberstleutnant, if the government did not wish one to pursue such studies they could have changed the syllabus. But in its wisdom—Ja-ja, quite so, the war will not last much longer, and what had you intended to pursue? After the war of course. Well, er, Middle High German. *Mittel*hoch? Yes, Hartmann von Aue for example or Wolfram's Parzifal. Ah, Parzifal, ja der Fuehrer likes that too. You see Herr Oberstleutnant one should know the sources and not deny what our great culture owes to France, at least at the time. Und jetzt auch, Fräulein und jetzt auch, we have never denied the Kultur of that great country indeed, Feldmarschall Goering has made a particular point of honouring it. Meanwhile you must face the Dienstverpflichtung. Pity you did not study English, much more useful at this stage. You have? Ein bisschen. No qualifications. You will. Gut-gut. Well we can draft you into the Censorship until you do, you realise of course you would get much better pay with an extra language, English especially. Well now, I assume you have not heard at all from your mother in France? Now how do you feel about that? Man muss? Do you feel so impersonal Fräulein about das Vaterland die Heimat mother-country patrie according to the presentation of a tactical withdrawal but strategic gain or vice versa read daily from the enemy point of view which says that England has lost many battles but never a war forgetting a little one called The Hundred Years lost despite Crécy Agincourt not to mention the American War of Independence und so weiter in the Presseüberwachungsabteilung Ausland (PA), Auslandspresseländergruppe Nord, Auslandspresseüberwachungsländergruppenreferatsleiter or for short Referat England (RE) housed in a requisitioned brothel Pommernstrasse Berlin with on the desk fat files labelled Geheime Reichssache and on the wall the poster of a wall patterned in huge ears and FEIND HÖRT MIT.

Feind hört mit everywhere all the time und man hört den Feind all day in drumming headlines and all night rumbling in the distant dark way up, the dark sliced through by searchlights converging on the dark sliced through by flak like red lightning in the dark sliced through by the falling scream with which the load excreted by the Feind speeds down and lands with distant thuds, closer crunches or a very close crash exploding into scarlet flames and flaring up the distant dark way up beyond the AA roof unless perhaps the shelter door.

— So you work in the AA?

Achtung Feind-hört-mit ya.

— A-A, A-A, A-A.

— Du Schmutzling-Witzling.

Such an old joke too everyone makes it the baby on its pot A-A and Vati-papa-ton-père so foolish and headstrong your father in a mad weak moment saying A-A elle a fait son A-A everyone makes it dans ses culottes sie stinkt was für ein kleines Schwein hast du mir da geboren. Yes well I wish you would joke sometimes and not act so solemn, so damned self-contained and secretive, like a ruddy geheime Reichssache. You should let up a little and come out with me instead of working half the night at your stupid old books. Yes, I know, you want to sit for your degree in silly old Freiburg. And what about the war? Meaning what about me and my desires. You think only of yourself, your interests, your future. Zukunft. du lieber Gott es gibt keine, we live from day to day and probably die tomorrow ich liebe dich don't you love me even a little?

The same question everywhere goes unanswered on crowded trains to Nürnberg for Urlaub or elsewhere in dark streets after cinemas in dim-lit restaurants canteens according to the partner unless Johann in the office who has organisiert a tin of beef he brings into your little room later begging only to see and touch a little or a mere mad weak moment of flattering attraction boredom fatigue enthusiasm for Horst Heinrich Hans Hartmann Friedrich Konrad Rudolf in grey-green with yellow tabs on the collar grey-blue with red tabs on the collar holding you closely in their arms or eating drinking making merry cheering up our brave boys for which you must pay duty also to the customs that splendid officers commissioned or non-commissioned have of coming up into your little room just for a goodnight drink I promise and unbuttoning your white blouse pushing up your pullover fondling you all over underneath your skirt o du, geheime Reichssache demanding unconditional surrender Endsieg um Gottes Willen let me make love to you tomorrow I go away. To Africa to the Russian Front to Greece to Crete to Sicily to Norway in a pride of conquest and Organisieren. I shall die for my country and you won't even love me a little. To Nürnberg for Urlaub on crowded trains don't talk to any strange men will you or to anyone at all on smelly trains that stop three hours in the middle of nowhere at night slowly growing up growing away from those who willy-nilly have harboured a half-Feind in their midst growing away with Hans met in Berlin then stationed in München komm mal her hand in hand into den Alten Peter half destroyed already warum? Warum hast du mich hergebracht? I hate seeing damaged churches. Because, because, I wanted to show you something, someone, die Patronin der alleinstehenden Frauen. But she has vanished. Die Patronin der—du, eine alleinstehende Frau? Niemals. Except I hope until I come back and marry you and if you have a child just contact my parents, net? Growing away, growing up slowly, retarded frigid evidently even in Rothenburg gem-city as yet undamaged between the sheet and the tumbled sheeted eiderdown surrounded by the ice-cold air despite the wood-panelling kein Kohlenklau says the host with a smirk but you have enough heat between you I imagine nicht wahr on the Romantische Strasse with Hans in grey-green and yellow tabs who goes off to the Russian Front tomorrow and does get killed. Grüss Gott and gone.

Endsieg.

No trace of them Fräulein, the authorities requisitioned the castle as Nazi-owned and came to chuck them out but they had vanished.

Ah non mademoiselle il n'y a personne sous ce nom-là dans cet immeuble. Un nom allemand? Y avait des boches partout. Et après prrrt ils ont fichu le camp. Avant la guerre? Ah ça alors j'n'en sais rien, y-a-que deux ans que je travaille ici. On l'aura emmenée, probablement, au début de la guerre. Et plus tard, ben, j'sais pas moi.

Plus tard, più tardi, l'altra cosa più tardi non si ricorda esattamente comes from the Red Cross and says as far as we can trace the matter your mother left for Germany after the Allied landings in the South of France evidently under the protection of a German officer. Local records show that a person of that name died in Nuremberg during an American air-raid.

— Und haben Sie noch einen Wunsch?

— Nein danke. Ah, doch, ein kleines OMO.

Keiner wäscht reiner. Gebremster Schaum! This would leave a trace. Noch etwas anderes? Nein, dankeschön. Bitteschön Aufwiedersehen. Aufwiedersehen. Omo Schaum-Stop reguliert sich selber.

The season has begun. Tourists pour into Paris Rome Belgrade Palermo Tripoli Athens Addis Ababa Istanbul wherever congresses commissions conferences conventions take place in June July August for those professional people who cannot organise their junketings to cut the gloom of winter or bear the thought of a vacation away from leurs semblables in case they miss a contact an idea or an occasion to shine. Well I prefer it Sandra says one gets some extra sun and besides, the excursions at least come off. Remember that terrible drive from Milan to Lake Como and the Dolomites in the pouring rain? I hate empty hotels they give me the willies I like them chock-block full of gorgeous sun-tanned men in open shirts and luscious girls in low décolletage that shows where the brown stops and the white begins. She says in her low décolletage that shows just that and laughs oh yes I like both sexes to look sizzling it keeps me on my mettle. Unfortunately most tourists in fact look horribly middle-aged. Those prosperous Germans ugh! The very same I suppose who came here as conquerors in that crazy war that made our mums and dads so crummily fixated on the forties.

Sandra chatters happily on in un amour de soutien-gorge,

belonging apparently to a different species altogether undamaged unconcerned doing the same work with ease and careless poise from the start unretarded by wars national prejudices bilingualism fraternisation sex who learn simply from existing simultaneously on all levels unless they merely block off different ones in much the same swift generalisations brought up to date such as those prosperous Germans ugh who talk of roads endlessly across hotel tables balconies and bright green pools, wow, even as they swim they talk of roads, the Brenner Pass the Autobahn the E 5 the route through Yugoslavia.

The Romantische Strasse between the year-long Fleissigkeit and a place in the sun.

— Do you understand German then?

— Well, no, not really, who wants to? Just enough to get around you know.

Enough for one's daily needs of bed food and excretion immer geradeaus dann links that will suffice me as far as German goes unless they read their Baedekers very loudly to their fat naked wives by hotel swimming-pools.

— The French talk of roads too, la Nationale 7 la route de Saragosse.

— No. The French talk of property. Elle a tout ce grand terrain, elle pourrait construire et sous-louer. Ah oui, ils ont acheté une maison de grand-standing, avec une vue magnifique sur la vallée de la Dordogne, trois chambres un amour de cuisine salle à manger un living deux salles de bains ma chère et deux W.C.

The number of the room has risen to 217. The bathroom door in pale green flanks the yellow cotton curtains that let in too much traffic from the left on to the double bed where the body lies too hot under the single sheet the pale green blanket folded over the white bedcover on the back of the chair.

The time hangs clocklessly around the distant brain way up what forty-three forty-seven? Soon some bright chambermaid will come in with a breakfast-tray and say structures of power in fact depend on the willing cooperation of innumerable individuals for the administration of physical force. This morning we have listened to a belle fiction. Such a principle remains a principle, totally at odds with any real situation in the past or the renovating present. We have no evidence whatsoever that human beings, let alone horses, can so embody the divine principle descending into matter in a behaviour sufficiently organised to force a conqueror down into the earphones and out through exits in simultaneous rejection of le mensonge vital with a double-negation that would reintegrate him into some totality, compared with so many fragile truths that surround us in this our masculine-dominated civilisation where the spiral as a sort of stylised maze and magic invisible wall of defence rose like a ziggurat or seven-terraced Tower of Babel in a mass of noussphere to point omega comme nous répète ce grand génie as the woman spins a flaxen spool. The ziggurat lands on the clay-like sea you could cut with a knife to model some sort of earth-goddess if only you could get out. The air-hostess says uw zwemvest bevindt zich onder uw stoel. To inflate pull red toggle (1). To top up blow into mouthpiece (2). But the mouthpiece has no breath on account of the vital lie and all the fragile truths in French and out in simultaneous German. You must hurry, the clay-like sea will liquefy at any moment now and you will need your zwemvest. She walks up and down in absolute calm and relaxation having had acupuncture on the vessel of conception CV 52 which has made her orange hair puff up into a huge spiral against the cinema screen. She sure looks dandy, unharassed you know in a low décolletage qui pigeonne formidablement showing just where the brown stops and the white begins bitteschön as the florid Monsignor stands up and leaning right across he photographs her from above to catch just where the brown stops and the white begins. Hurry up hurry up the sea has liquefied and the ziggurat sinks please use the Emergency Exit only but the body lies strapped to the seat by the heat of the safety-belt which burns into the vessel of conception CV 52 knock-knock-knock-knock. The yellow light pours in from the left the bathroom door in green faces the body strapped and the room takes shape quite suddenly with pale blue walls the built-in cupboard in mahogany on the right flanking the door knock-knock. Herein. Come in, er, entrez. Oh, he can't.

— Kalimera madame. Porte. Fermée.

— Oui. Toujours, la nuit.

— Bien madame. Déjeuner. Lettre. Pour madame.

— Merci. Er, efharisto.

— Ah! Kalo-kalo! Efharisto*sas*.

— SAS?

— Nai. Sas. A vous. Merci à vous.

— Ah. Efharisto.

— EfharistoSAS.

Oh God here we go again why won't he leave the room? Er, echete, er, nero metalico?

— Madame?

— Eau minérale.

— Ah, neró metálico! Nai. He shakes his head from side to side and exit.

Ma douce amour. Ah si je pouvais vous décrire l'émotion que je ressens à la vue de votre écriture maintenant (enfin!) si familière, et du timbre qui change —Marianne, Lilibet, Constantin et la ravissante Anne-Marie, Franco (moins ravissant)—selon les distances hélas toujours plus grandes entre ma princesse lointaine et moi. Je regarde l'enveloppe, je tremble, je m'évanouis presque, je n'ose l'ouvrir de peur de vous avoir contrariée, ennuyée peut-être avec mes tristes désirs impossible, irréalisables, je le sais, o mon amour. Jour et nuit the body lies in bed below the breakfast tray with quiet disparagement from the distant brain way up, suspending all belief in the language of a long-lost code that nevertheless on another level climbs anticlockwise through the centuries, crumbling the invisible wall which rose to a circular dance of simulation vital lies and other frustrations to the true end of childhood. Et puis je lis la lettre—trop brève hélas—où vous me parlez de vos voyages, de votre travail (qui m'intéresse naturellement). Ou plutôt oui, je l'avoue, j'imagine voir entre les lignes, que vous aussi, vous vous sentez bien seule, que vous cherchez quelque chose, et que peut-être, ah, ce grand peut-être, vous m'entrouvrez un peu la porte knock-knock and it opens without pause to admit the floor-steward in white bearing nero metalico and an empty wine-glass on a metalico tray. Efharisto. EfharistoSAS. Merci. The eyes glued on the letter the coffee-cup held half way between the breakfast-tray and mouthpiece meaning go away, vous m'entrouvrez un peu la porte, une fraction, un centimètre, que vous me permettez de vous adorer. He goes. Alors, ma douce amour, je ne me contiens plus, je me laisse envahir par les rêves les plus fous, je me vois dans vos bras, caressant vos—ah non, il ne faut pas continuer.

Il ne faut pas continuer à manger, to bear the weight of a breakfast-tray with the empty coffee-cup the breadcrumbs the jammed plate the gold and silver butter paper il faut enlever le plateau from the loins a tingle underneath the sheet despite the distant brain way up on a higher level of disbelief disparagement despair. Car je vous vois aussi entourée d'admirateurs, pas seule du tout, n'ayant besoin de rien et de personne, ici et là dans toutes ces capitales que je connais, que je hais, ah, pardonnez-moi cette vilaine jalousie. Je n'ai jamais aimé comme ça. So that despite the fact that il ne faut pas continuer he continues the interrupted erotica of self-indulgent words that caress up and down in and out and all over dans vos bras. Jour et nuit the body lies in relish of a long lost language that finds itself delicious and winds its way up through centuries into the vessel of conception vieille poire ouvre les jambes unless perhaps into no more than the distant brain way up to tickle a mere thought or two such as why not play a little further at a mere correspondence of love in French la douce inoubliable dame leading by six games to five in the second set. Par à quelle aile? J'vois pas d'aile moi. With the left hand fingering the medal of St. Christopher between the breasts just where the brown stops and the white begins, touching a little brushstroke size over the skin soft still between the breasts and round under the right cupping it caressing it just a little on the nipple that swells under the fingers brushstroke size as the language winds its way through eyes ears mouthpiece hands and more than the five senses.

It doesn't mean a thing.

Akóma thélo tria kilá sapúni, éna kiló wútiro: I want also 3 kilos of soap, 2 kilo Butter. Give me 2 tins of Milk, half kilo Tea and an envelope of Coffee. I wanted a kilo meat beef. I want also a lamb. As I really love you I want to make you my wife. Do you agree? As we love between each other do you want to create our own home? I want it double-breasted. When shall I come for the rehearsal? In six days I go away.

The road from Kennedy Airport runs past Jewish cemeteries with tall rectangular tombstones standing close together in miniature forewarning of ford foundations wall streets madison avenues united nations where Feind hört mit that we shall continue to honour our obligations towards the underdeveloped areas and appoint a sub-committee to inquire into the way we can stop the war in the Far East from dangerously escalating up the downward path. My government wishes to emphasise that it had not a single warship aircraft-carrier or plane within the area nor sufficient forces to exercise influence one way or the other. But Israel must learn, Egypt must learn that between America and Europe the six hours lost watching a film of love on the return flight cause the sky to darken at the speed of sight at midday as if on Good Friday over the clay-like sea that divides into two distinct unmerging patterns one plucked one undulating from two different winds and suddenly the red bar of sunset slices the navy sky like a horizontal hot poker because le ciel a ses hauteurs tu sais. Or else inside the whale perhaps where the body lies in the foetus position devoured by a long-lost language that breeds plants or parts of plants growing inside you gently wildly obsessively, stifling your strength with their octopus legs undetachable for the vacuum they form under each protein cell, clamping each neurone of your processes in a death-kiss with a half-visualised old man well fifty-nine and plus descending from the distant brain way up the downward path to another level in a circular dance of simulation vital lies and other frustrations to the true end of imagination. Oh I see, the imagination. How fascinating. Nothing deserves a flow of rash enthusiasm my sweet.

The decorative metal locks on each door of the cupboard shine in the shaft of light. They have Napoleonic hats and look like Civil Guards. A spot of bright light further up the cupboard imitates the sun. Beyond the wooden shutters and way down below the layered storeys of stunned consciousnesses the murmur of the talking delegates as they wait in rows like a giant class gets picked up by the microphones in the glass booth filling the theatre with tumultuous applause. A quartet of jazz fixated on the forties followed by a saxophone solo represent Catalan culture at a Catalan evening only just permitted by the government as a concession with police lining the space between the columns and the red velvet curtains marked SALIDA in green lights. A female choir in ill-fitting white dresses sings Swing Low Sweet Chariot and I gotta Robe in Catalan. A little girl harmonises behind a smaller little boy cutely Dreaming of a White Christmas in Catalan. Until at last the boy-star with his guitar appears and sobs Com un déu caigut and La Nit, llarga la Nit and Cantarem la vida de poble que no vol morir full of Catalan passion down into the microphone and out in simultaneous passion. Diguem-no! Diguem-no! the bulging theatre demands amid the tumultuous applause but the boy-star stretches out the palm of his left hand and his guitar in the right with a no-puc gesture half indicating the police that lines the theatre. Instead he repeats La Nit, llarga la Nit with Catalan passion down into the microphone and out in simultaneous passion to the tumultuous applause. The members of the congress dutifully don their listening caps and the murmur still continuing now comes through the earphones in the glass booth, picked up by the microphones the engineer has just switched on. The eyes close the thumbs touch the fingers join as communication begins. With whom? Du Witzling. Meine Damen und Herren. Mesdames messieurs. Air France vous souhaite la bienvenue à bord de cet énorme problème devant lequel cependant le langage of a long-lost code flows into the ear and comes out into the mouthpiece over waves and on into the ears of the multitudes or so in simultaneous German such as ich lieb' dich mich reizt deine schöne Gestalt which doesn't sound at all the same. To the right of the vast metal wing the sun that had almost set before take-off has leapt quite high again above the mountains. It has some way to go before it sets once more.

The black arrow in the white circle goes up, the red goes down or vice versa in the wide street turning right from the big dual carriage-way lined with tall rectangular buildings the Palace of Culture on the left. You will now see the old eighteenth century Warsaw rebuilt stone by stone from the rubble. Bardzo piękne. Ah pani mówi po polsku? No, no, really, only a few phrases, from a phrase-book. Nie, ale bardzo dobrze! What does that mean? Very well, very good. Je tiens à remercier monsieur le président de ses éloges que je n'ai pas conscience de mériter. What has semantics to do with literature? Rien, niente, nikts, notting. Vous voyez! Le langage speaks for itself in the red pamphlet with the white eagle on it which inside states that the recorded history of Poland goes back 1000 years. But archeological finds tell a way of life more than twice as old. Vous vous intéressez à la Pologne madame? Oui naturellement. Important events include: 960—Mieszko I, Piast dynasty, first ruler of Poland. 966—Mieszko I converted to Christianity through the offices of Bohemia. 973—Victory of Mieszko I over Germany. 1109—Polish victory over Germany at Psie Pole. 1331—Polish victory over the Teutonic Knights near Plowce. You enjoy the congress madame? Well of course. 1466 Pomerania recovered after victorious war with Teutonic Knights. 1525—The Prussian Duke Albrecht von Hohenzollern takes oath of allegiance to the King of Poland. But as we always say here in Warsaw, the statue of Sigismund up there still faces West. Like the eagle you know, though they took away his crown, you know he looks almost undressed without it. Do you remember old Warsaw monsieur, er, czy pamięta? Pamiętam. Tak. Pamiętam.

It would leave a trace. Wejście. Wyjście. Poczta. Pchnąć. Tirez? Poussez? Telefon—Znaczki pocztowe—Poste-Restante. Nie ma pani with a shake of the head for no. POSTAMT.

Eintritt. Drücken. Telegrammannahme. Briefmarke. Poste-Restante. Leider haben wir keine.

The visitor's attention turns immediately to higher things such as the seven-terraced Tower of Babel on the seventh hauteur du ciel way up above the smattering of the mouthpiece in ces capitales que je connais, que je hais, ah, pardonnez-moi cette vilaine jalousie. Je n'ai jamais aimé comme ça between the zest of youth and the wisdom of old age through an indefinitely long period called the middle ages.

The cloud has cleared. The jet exhausts invisible in their power save for a tremor on the blue or the propellers invisible in their speed save for a hinted halo che fa tremar di claritate l'âre, no man-made object passing to show that the body flies immobile at nine hundred and twenty kilometres and no man to bring you out of this or that zone with a tremendous force of a love lost or never gained lying forgotten under layers and layers of civilisation except perhaps through a language that actually means something in the light of no more than a fond old man's powerful imagination who always fell in love with young secretaries unattainable in soutiens-gorge qui pigeonnent and show just where the brown stops and the white begins, writing them flowery love-letters full of Provençal quotes about fin amor lonhtano and la princesse lointaine so that we used to call him Bertrand de Born.

Unless perhaps the seven-terraced tower sits suspended between belief and disbelief at a height of twelve thousand metres outside temperature what minus forty-nine with the menu going all the way to Detroit via Vienna Paris which contains the small flat in the rue du Four and the hairdresser opposite in which the women sit under their helmets insulated by the noise of hot air and the letter lies inside a magazine for secret re-reading relishing ma douce amour. Je ne vous ai pas écrit aux Postes Restantes que vous m'aviez indiquées de peur de vous manquer, car je connais ces mauvais courriers. Of course natürlich with flowery love-letters missing young secretaries inaccessible through inefficient posts in low décolletage that shows the first stirring of cette vilaine jalousie ah pardonnez-moi. Mais j'avoue que vos cartes m'ont rendu fou de joie, non seulement parcequ'elles venaient de vous, o mon amour, mais parceque pour la première fois vous trahissez quelqu'inquiétude à mon égard. Oh, pardonnez-moi. Je n'ai pas voulu vous causer la moindre souffrance, mais voilà le paradoxe de l'amour, j'en ai aussi ressenti un doux plaisir, si doux. Vous attendiez, vous cherchiez une lettre de moi.

The eyes follow the wide blue writing in the language of a madman that winds its way down from the distant brain with resentment humiliation understanding revenge distribution reeducation fraternisation sex. Votre déodorant. Choisissez-le sérieusement chez votre pharmacien. The letter gets folded down. Les questions que vous n'osez pas poser à votre gynécologue. The questions mount up. Ça pigeonne formidablement. Comment vivre la vie moderne? Des tests pour ne pas s'ennuyer. The letter gets unfolded. Oh mon amour, me donneriez-vous peut-être un signe? Je n'ose même plus y croire. Et pourtant jour et nuit je rêve je pense à vous, oh ma princesse lointaine, je vous vois dans mes bras, nue et mince et blanche, allongeant vos belles longues jambes nordiques, je pose ma main sur votre gorge, mes lèvres sur vos lèvres, je bois votre désir, je vous caresse doucement, ma main descend sur vos seins, dessous, plus bas, le long de votre hanche et puis plus bas, vous murmurez, vous me désirez, vous m'ouvrez, ah ma déesse je vous prends, j'entre dans vos profondeurs, vous criez de plaisir, tumultueuse amante oh ma déesse et vous m'aimez jusqu'à l'explosion en vous du glaïeul blanc. Pardonnez-moi, je délire. A Ding no dea does.

So the white gladiolus explodes in letter after letter in a language that finds itself delicious and breeds plants or parts of plants inside the seven-terraced tower undoing the magic wall of defence anticlockwise from the distant brain way up the downward path escalating to a death-kiss with a half-visualised old man well fifty-seven and plus the circular dance of simulation vital lies lost mysteries and other excitations to the true end of imagination.

E allora the languages fraternise in a frenzy of fornication by airmail par avion via aerea Luftpost ΑΕΡΟΠΟΡΙΚΩΣ Uçak İle responded to at one level and plus despite the Acqua Minerale battericamente pura Apă de Masă ΣΑΡΙΖΑ ΑΡΙΣΤΟΝ etc or SARIZA Eau de Table naturelle-curative résistivité électrique (en Ohms) Radio activité (unités Mache) Gerolsteiner Sprudel natürliches Mineralwasser erfrischend, bekömmlich, von Gesundheitswert, an der Quelle abgefüllt. La source on the contrary breeds plants or parts of plants within the cavern womb belly vessel ship temple sepulchre or holy grail with the same confusional sliding from active to passive from swallower to swallowed from container to contained that we find in all the myths of depth night descent into old matter lost and found again beneath the layers of thickening sensibilities convenient dogmas euphemised into a sack a basket une hotte that even lose their convenience as times pass. The languages fraternise in a frenzy of sensuality par avion and find each other delicious at one level and plus the long lost terror of someone offering something not ordered, so that l'altra cosa più tardi gets postponed by a magic wall of defence consisting of commissions congresses conferences and conventions that più tardi can wait while the language finds itself delicious in hotel rooms with footsteps walking outside in Swedish, Portuguese, or French along the rue du Four or on another plane that bumps down the steps of air and lowers its undercarriage for the descent into language and a mode of sensuality which might perhaps remain far below the inklings of the distant brain way up or even totally at odds with any real situation in the past or renovating present, the simulated substitution permitting, through repetition, the exchange of past for future and the domestication of Chronos. In some countries the women would segregate still to the left of the aisle worshipping plaster images, the men less numerous to the right shouting ka-dın ka-dın oh ma déesse tu me désires tu m'ouvres les jambes a Ding no dea does. But all in all and civilisation considered the chromosomes in the white gladiolus chrysalis vessel vehicle instrument explode over the air as the enormous wing spreads back from the long nose-tip to prevent any true exchange of any real situation when the rhetoric flows into the protein cells of the distant brain way up in French and down at once through more than the five senses in simultaneous lust. Aimez-vous le tutoiement? Ou cela vous offense-t-il? Dites-le moi franchement. O ma douce amour je vous aime je t'aime. Je me vois dans tes bras. Ta lettre, votre lettre, ah dieu, quels délices. Je n'ose y croire. Vous m'aimez? tu m'aimes tu me désires, vraiment? Je ne rêve que de vous. A quand mon amour à quand? Vos congrès ne vous amèneraient-ils pas un jour à Venise? Puis-je venir vous voir à Paris? Ah, rien que l'idée de vous regarder, de vous toucher, me coupe le souffle. Et pourtant j'ai peur. Me trouverez-vous trop laid, trop vieux? Moi je me souviens de vous, si blonde, si distante, si froide, et pourtant dès le premier jour je vous ai aimée, je n'osais pas le dire, et je ne pouvais pas vous oublier. Et maintenant, enfin! vos lettres, vos délicieuses lettres which respond on one level and plus the invisible wall that rises to a circular dance so much taller than the small love behind it, au schème de l'ourobouros eating its own tail not as a mere ring of flesh but expressing death in life life out of death in a reflection of the agro-lunar drama des rêves les plus fous non seulement de vous aimer, d'éveiller en vous tous les désirs mais de passer le reste de mes jours, et de mes nuits, avec vous. So that the body lies in a suspension of desire, finding itself delicious through the language of a long-lost code that winds its way up from centuries of disbelief in adoration, escalating up the downward path or vice versa until the invisible wall of never-never più tardi spirals anticlockwise into now perhaps why not explode ancora più bianco brighter than bright the white gladiolus in the depth the cavern the vessel of conception with the confusional sliding from active to passive that we find in all the love-letters where the languages fraternise in a frenzy of fornication by airmail until breathes the old French lover still?

— What? Oh. That.

— Yes, that.

— Well, of course not. What did you expect?

— I expected nothing. What did you?

— Dasselbe.

— You put a stop to it?

— Natürlich.

— Hmm. Gut-gut. No regrets?

— No regrets.

Siegfried works with his eyes no hands now as well as with his ears and voice. He lipreads the speaker and in the next split second utters the same syllables of old friendship and bantering allusion that let perhaps or do not let the vital lie slip down into the earphones and out into the mouthpiece in simultaneous belief and disbelief. The same question everywhere goes unanswered have you anything to declare any plants or parts of plants growing inside you wildly obsessively stifling your strength with their octopus legs undetachable for the vacuum they form over each cell, clamping each neurone of your processes in a death-kiss with a half-visualised old man well fifty-five and plus until the languages fraternise at the Congress of Byzantine Historians in Ravenna where somebody demonstrates the disastrous policy of uprooting the virile Goths from Italy. As a Gothic envoy said to Belisarius, we have observed all the laws of the Empire, we have respected the religion of the Romans, we have never forcibly converted them to Arianism, we have reserved all administrative posts to Italians. Mesdames messieurs, such a Gothic monarchy, so respectful of local feelings, might well have saved Italy from the Lombards. It might in fact have created a very different Italy. And if every German had openly declared what he now says he secretly wanted we'd have a very different Europe, oh yes, I had others after me, a nice French boy Jules and then you'd have turned out quite different, with no papal state, no Holy Roman Empire with all the troubles this brought, indeed it might have created a united Italy some twelve centuries before that painful achievement of relatively modern times when the telephone rings allo? er, pronto? Un signore chiede di lei signora. Bene, fatelo salire. Er, no signora followed by a flow of Italian which scusi non capisco, parla francese? Oui madame. L'hotel ne permet pas les visites dans les chambres après dix heures du soir. En I-ta-lie? Oui madame. Hé bien vous en avez du toupet, un vieil ami! Oui madame. Mais vous pouvez descendre.

Vous pouvez descendre. Vous descendez. Down in the lift that lurches up the knot of anger fear hope into the mouthpiece and out into another corridor carpeted in red velvet, lined with doors 112, 113, 114 having pressed perhaps button ① out of anger fear hope down the red velvet stairs like the blessed damozel with a sense of the ridiculous or la figlia che piange down a false situation in the lobby where he waits, panama hat in hand and broader than remembered, in a pink bow tie and a white suit that makes his mousy-greying hair look greyer round the base where it mostly occurs and more wispy above the porous rubber face that collapses a little at the jowls around a sunken mouth contradicting the protruding eyelids over southern eyes that well, yes, burn. Quelle idiotie, ces règlements. Pardonnez-moi. Bonjour. Bonsoir je veux dire, ah, mon dieu, vous voilà. The handshake no more than a handshake speaks nothing at all the feet move towards the bar in studded black plastic and vous prenez quelque chose? Non merci, ou plutôt oui, une eau minérale. Hein? Eau minérale. Ah bon, moi aussi, je ne bois jamais, ça m'esquinte l'estomac. Acqua minerale per favore. Sans glace s'il vous plait. Ah, moi aussi. Senza ghiaccio per favore. Battericamente pura as silences differ more than languages fraternise par avion meaning perhaps delusione désillusion disillusion on both sides unless perhaps alarm? Non mais vraiment, quelle idiotie, ces règlements. Je n'ai jamais vu ça en Italie. En Angleterre oui, mais, ah excusez-moi de vous avoir mais non, mais non. And travel-talk ensues about Venise cette belle ville d'art splendide et Rimini vous connaissez le temple de Sigismund, mais oui, vous savez tout. Sigismund? Who still faces west as we say in Poland. Sigismundo Malatesta. Il faut voir ça. Je vous y mènerai. Vous avez déjà vu Ravenna je pense, in the first capital of the Western Empire after Rome 00147 applicate el numero di codice on the matchbox which he takes to strike the match that doesn't strike again ancora and again then suddenly flares up to flame the middle-aged one with the older who himself doesn't smoke or drink and says vous fumez trop.

— Oui. Toujours.

— Hein?

With a grimace, turning his right ear anxiously as if deaf in the left oh no. Vous parlez si bas. Mais j'aime vos cigarettes. Elles ont l'air si élégantes. Wherever particular people congregate. Ce beau paquet doré! Cette fine baguette blanche dans votre bouche dis, tu m'aimes?

The same question everywhere goes unanswered je t'aime grand comme le ciel et moi aussi mais tu as dis plus éh bien, plus haut, tiens, le ciel a ses hauteurs et papa, tu crois qu'il m'aime? Ah ça ton père j'sais pas où il a fichu le camp. Il a fichu le camp in a language that finds itself delicious par avion but force-lands on a clay-like sea of silence you could cut with a knife pick up in handfuls to mould perhaps a conversation that actually means something in the light of that idiotie, ces règlements, in Italy of all places he has never known une chose pareille, en Angleterre oui, where he has no doubt frequently turned up after ten to call on young secretaries inaccessible on account of quelle idiotie ces règlements as he stares silently waiting for an answer from the goddess aghast at the idiocy she has provoked who looks perhaps not a goddess at all but a desiccated skeletal alleinstehende Frau holding une fine baguette blanche in her fine desiccated fingers which tap the cigarette nervously too often into the chromium ashtray as she watches his long veined hands each tensely curved over each of his knees and brings the cigarette up once more to inhale what fifty-nine sixty-two what cheek what damned impertinence and vanity but mutual after all, and out again through the mouthpiece in simultaneous tenderness with, very gently, of course the expected person changes.

E allora the languages fraternise a little as he sips his mineral water without ice under the staring southern eyes that well yes burn. Why do you speak in English? To remind me of the old days and my youth as a simultaneous interpreter of ideas nobody ever acts upon? Vous n'aimez pas ma langue? La langue de mes lettres? La langue—and the tip of his tongue peers out, moves slowly round his open lips, then in, then slowly out again, and in, and out in a dumb show pour éveiller en vous tous les désirs mais si.

— You know, when you came down those stairs—since you prefer to speak English—tell me, do you know Eliot?

— Eliot?

— T. S. Eliot, the poet.

— Oh. No, not really. By reputation. He wrote something called The Waste Land didn't he?

He wrote something called the waste land of whatever kind of literary conversation do we embark on now that might actually mean something in the light of that too. But when you came down those stairs I thought of an earlier poem of his I have always loved.

— What, more than Rudel or Cavalcanti? Surely you live in the twelfth century?

— Ah, vous vous moquez de moi, cruelle dame. Mais j'aime vos yeux moqueurs, même quand ils blessent. Car vous savez blesser.

— Let's face it you destroy.

— Hein?

— Nothing.

— You shake your head. I know, you don't mean to hurt, and you can't help my ridiculous sensibilities. I fully realise the element of the ridiculous in my, my—Help. Oh help him for Chrissake Great Scott und so weiter your, love?

— Oui, mon amour. His eyes well yes burn I don't like the

word love in fact I wish you would not talk English a foreign tongue to us both. But since you wish it let us return to the poem, perhaps you know it La figlia che piange.

— La figlia—? How strange. Where did—but did he, write in Italian?

— Stand on the highest pavement of the stair—lean on a garden urn—Weave, weave the sunlight in your hair—

— What, inside a hotel after ten oclock at night?

— There you go again.

— Sorry.

— Hein?

— Sorry.

— Sorry. Yes. How inadequate English sounds at times like this. Like what? Well you know, the one about the elephant or the titbit or Dieu vous blesse as a discarded personality that once hurt solemn earnestness takes over to hurt his unless merely the language that finds itself delicious has fled in a long lost terror of someone offering something not ordered. Moi j'aurais dit pardonnez-moi.

The fingers empty of any fine baguette join to form a squat diamond space, the thumbs pressed towards the body the rest touching away from it like a cathedral roof the eyes closed the ankles crossed to keep the résistivité électrique within so that you feel relaxed and no one can get at you by means of Clasp your flowers to you with a pained surprise—Fling them to the ground and turn—With a fugitive resentment in your eyes—But weave, weave the sunlight in your hair.

— You know it by heart.

— Oui. Je sais tout par coeur. Tout ce que j'aime, je le sais par coeur.

In advance. He knows it in advance, by airmail air attack that sends its parachutists floating down over the rectangles of agriculture brush-stroke size the curving lines the forest blobs the metallic lakes that make up an abstract study in seduction we can imagine—and indeed we have to—a defenceless people completely confounding a would-be conqueror by sitting quietly, not eating, not drinking, not smoking, not working at it, threatening to deprive him of his subjects simply by not existing. He can let them die, he can even kill them, but he cannot exploit them.

Now ladies and gentlemen this undeniable principle remains a principle, optimistic in its ultimate ends, cruel in its applicate el numero di codice, permettez-moi as he strikes and misses strikes again and flames the middle-aged one with vous fumez trop. Here we came in. Quelle idiotie und so weiter but Bertrand.

— Ah! Vous m'appelez Bertrand. Je n'ai jamais aimé ce nom, mais dans votre bouche, quel délice. Oh mon amour, vous ne voulez pas me tutoyer?

— Oui, si vous voulez.

— Hein?

— Ça viendra peut-être.

— Peut-être!

— Ecoutez, Bertrand, patientez. Comprenez que—

— Oui oui j'ai compris.

— No you haven't. And all that idiocy as you call it, rightly, with the rules and regulations. Why didn't you just book a room here then you could have rung direct? Où restez-vous ce soir?

— Ah. Je ne sais pas. Je n'y avais pas pensé. Ou plutôt—

— Plutot vous aviez pensé—

— Oui.

— Well if you thought that much in advance you might have thought it out properly. You don't suppose the hotel cares two hoots which room you spend the night in as long as you don't visit late at night in a room booked for one and stay there free of charge. What did you expect, that we should sneak up like a guilty couple and you sneak out again past the night watchman at crack of dawn?

— I, I didn't think. Pardonnez-moi.

— Hmm.

— Oh, vous avez l'air si fâchée. Vous, fâchée contre moi. Mon dieu, qu'allons-nous faire?

— Calorifère, as my mother used to say. She liked terrible puns.

— Hein?

— Ma mère, elle aimait les calembours. Elle disait: Qu'alors y faire?

— Je t'aime. Je t'aime. Je t'aime.

Grand comme le ciel. Moi aussi. Mais tu as dis plus. Oh le ciel a ses hauteurs tu sais. Et papa? Ah ça ton père j'sais pas où il a fichu le camp. And suddenly he returns in a language of burning eyes and dumb show with a tip of tongue moving slowly round his lips in and out and around, la langue et le langage which finds itself delicious spiralling round the seven-terraced tower anticlockwise undoing the magic wall which crumbles to the horror of all concerned turning l'altra cosa più tardi into now why not the long veined bony hands moving nervously up and down each knee on the white linen suit or curved around the breast and along the belly up and down the thighs qui s'ouvrent to the brush-stroke fingers into vos profondeurs où je vous prends j'entre en vous vous criez de plaisir tumultueuse amante oh ma déesse et vous m'aimez jusqu' à l'explosion en vous du glaïeul blanc in the depth the cavern the vessel of conception with the confusional sliding from active to passive which we find in all intense situations true or false when the language of a long-lost code of adoration breeds plants or parts of plants that stand quite still in a suspension of desire and disbelief saying well, you'd better go and book yourself a room. See you later. 414. Au revoir, monsieur, enchantée de vous avoir revu, alors, à demain.

— A demain madame. Bonsoir, bonne nuit.

Bonne nuit, hélas non. Le glaïeul a fichu le camp in a language that finds itself delicious par avion but force-lands on a clay-like sea you could cut with a knife pick up in handfuls to mould perhaps a worn-out middle-aged goddess aghast at the death of love desire and limbs that find each other revolting in an abstract study of seduction watched with exhaustion horror delusione to the despair and shaking dry male sobs irritating merely until it comes to a standstill. Et pourtant je t'aime, je t'aime, tu ne peux pas savoir comme je t'aime. Pardonne-moi. Je t'aime trop, voilà. Et tous ces mois d'attente, de rêves fous, followed by explanations promises that ça viendra tu verras plus extractions of promises patience gentleness and self-blame to save the other's pride a form of love perhaps aghast at the catastrophe it has provoked. Tu viendras à Venise avant ton départ? A Venise? Je voudrais tant que tu voies ma maison, que tu connaisses tout de moi, mon jardin, mes livres, ma femme même. Ta femme?

— Mais oui. J'ai toujours eu une femme. Enfin, toujours, depuis longtemps quoi. Trop longtemps. J'ai même trois filles, mariées.

— Ah?

— Tu ne le savais pas?

— Non. Mais du reste, ça n'a pas d'importance.

— Tu as raison, oh ma sagesse, l'amour ne se soucie pas de telles choses. Et puis tu sais, si tu voulais bien, moi je ne rêve que de ça, de vivre avec toi, je la quitterai, ça tient à un fil, ça ne dépend que de toi ma douce amour, oh comme tu me comprends, si douce, ma gentildonna und so weiter weiter gehen in the sheer impertinence and vanity of the mouthpiece or the freedom of the imagination totally at odds with any real situation in this man-dominated myth within a cubic room the white suit neatly folded still on the chair gleaming in the half-light the bathroom straight ahead running caldofreddo as the body lies a desiccated alleinstehende Frau fingering a medal symbole d'intimité dans le voyage in quiet suspension of anger between total indifference and a mild desire to pick up the broken bits with a great tenderness above the footsteps walking in Italian Gothic Lombard down the first capital of the Western Empire after 00147 Roma.

The dark shape of the cupboard unrounds in the slatted noise coming through the shutters on the left. The bathroom door faces the bed in which the body floats in a numb pain of exhaustion untraced between sleeping and not sleeping out of what dream shaken up with nein danke no thank you in a long lost terror of someone offering something not ordered. Soon some bright buxom chambermaid will come in with a breakfast-tray unless perhaps she can't or has a master-key to open the shutters and say buenos días Morgen or gün aydin oh no, buongiorno hell Ravenna. And all that. No one comes in offering anything.

The light has quite unrounded the corners of the cupboard made of teak or rosewood built up to the ceiling and therefore without corners. The bottle on the bedside table says Acqua Minerale San Pellegrino and all the rest about battericamente pura which means that the light looks much brighter than bright and the traffic noise sounds much noisier than noisy for whatever hour hello? Pronto? Che ora avete per favore? Comment! Non capisco, parla francese? Dix heures et demi madame. Dix heures et demi! Et le réveil par téléphone, demandé pour huit heures? Ah? Si. Scusi signora, er nos excuses, la réception a eu beaucoup de slam. Train missed thank god no worse congress over damn allo? Oui madame? A quelle heure part le prochain train pour Venise? Un moment madame. Oui bien dépêchez-vous. Oh damn and blast quelle idiotie quelle idiotie why go. Ah? Bon merci. Et un déjeuner tout de suite and the tooter the sweeter. Er . . . ? oui madame.

Quelle idiotie why go on a mere courtesy promise to show no resentment humiliation revenge non-fraternisation no sex but he will think just that quelle idiotie after two nights of bumping down the steps of air undercarriage down crash-landing on the clay-like flesh aghast at the death of more than the five senses to the shaking dry male sobs until they come to a sickening standstill as he tells of his wife's sexual adventures in great detail of un membre énorme told on their conjugal bed which gives him il confesse great shudders of sensual pleasure raconte-moi les tiennes, ton mari, il te prenait comment et depuis, tu en as eu d'autres? Rends-moi jaloux, rends-moi jaloux, je t'en supplie, raconte-moi and failing even there falls back even he like ton mari on a crude story out of Rabelais the language of his fin amor lonhtano collapsing like a hallowed structure C for cold, no caldo quick, hurry avanti, ah grazie tanto. Sulla tavola grazie.

And yet languages flew straight across and words met loins. But this undeniable principle remains a principle, optimistic in its wild vanity, cruel in its application and totally at odds with any real situation in the past or renovating present. We have no evidence that live human beings, let alone bitches, can so embody this divine principle of words descending into matter in any behaviour sufficiently organised not to disarm a would-be conqueror of his desire or emasculate him in advance. Most people need to eat, to love and to this end will either knuckle under or more often, persuade themselves that the vital lie contains sufficient simulation of desire to reintegrate him into totality compared with so many beautiful façades that plunge into the water as the vaporetto chugs along the Grand Canal, crossing it diagonally from one stop to another past the Casa d'Oro tu te rappelles, ma troisième carte? Ma première carte de Venise. Ah dieu, comme j'ai hésité, si longuement hésité. Je n'aurais pas dû. Mais quel doux plaisir de t'avoir ici, de te montrer cette belle ville d'amour et d'art splendide où j'ai décidé de vivre, où je voudrais vivre avec toi und so weiter weiter gehen in the wild vanity of the mouthpiece and the freedom of the imagination so totally at odds with any real situation in the unrenovating present. Unless perhaps, who knows, what difference does it make? In, out, down, up, exits and entrances, Eintritt, Sortie, Salita, Ausgang, Entrée, Fumatul oprit. No Smoking beyond this Point Kindly fasten your safety-belts. Please do not leave the aircraft until it comes to an absolute standstill. Push Tirez Ziehen Pchnąć only to rest a little stop, just stop transmitting other people's ideas on which nobody ever acts into the earphones and out into the mouthpiece in simultaneous German-ugh to stop, so tired, so old if well-preserved but not much younger than him after all why feel so outraged in this belle ville d'amour et d'art splendide vivre avec vous avec toi, to bask in adoration in French however crude collapsing and never out in simultaneous anything at all, only to touch a little until perhaps with gentleness and affection as a natural process in the marriage of tradition and progress in French en français je t'aime je t'aime je t'aime. Tu ne peux pas savoir ce que j'ai pu imaginer quand ton train—oh non, j'ai pensé toutes les folies, à ta fureur peut-être, ah ça faisait mal, tu ne me pardonnais pas, tu me haïssais, tu me méprisais, et je ne te verrais plus, ah mon amour tu ne peux pas t'imaginer.

— Mais si. Du reste, vous me le dites.

— Hein?

— Puisque vous me le dites, alors pas besoin de l'imaginer.

— Vous, encore?

— Puisque tu me le dis.

— Ce vous qui me glace, ce tu qui m'enchante. Et puis vous vous moquez encore de moi.

— Mais non.

— Mais j'adore ta moquerie, tes yeux rieurs, tout de toi.

— Même ma fureur?

— Hein? Ah. Non. So he does hear then and he says it only for time to think of some answer truthful in the eyes of some god of love totally blind, du moins, oui peut-être, une fureur amoureuse?

The vaporetto bumps against the jetty of Santa Maria di Salute at the mouth of the Grand Canal that gives out on to the wider waters between San Marco and the unanswered question which remains unanswered for the non-existent future unless perhaps what difference does it make. The narrow street along the narrow canal leads to another narrow street just room for two lined with peeling façades in grey orange yellow and old grey wooden doors that here, nous voici. Le corridor. Je vous mène tout droit au jardin, pour commencer. Car il y a des jardins à Venise, on ne le dirait pas. Hein? Des jardins secrets. Vous connaissez cette belle chanson du quinzième siècle—Quinzième? Ah, vous avancez! Hein? Oh, vous vous moquez de moi, ancora. Mais non, quelle chanson? L'amour de moi. He sings en-clo-o-o-o-o o-se. Dedans un jo-o-li-i-i jar-di-net. Comment on the gender of amour. The French say jardine, the Gairmans say jardine und so weiter you see all have the same word so we have no differences. What has love to do with botany or plants that grow on this blessed earth from Persia with the oil-bearing rose ah mademoiselle they have not blossomed yet the season has not yet come unless it has quite passed in the agro-lunar drama and the domestication of Chronos. J'adore cette chanson. J'en ai un disque, je vous le jouerai. Vous aimez mon jardin?

— Oh oui. Je vois que vous avez des glaïeuls blancs.

— Shshsh.

He looks up nervously at the shuttered window. So! The blood drains from the courteous attitude of the middle-aged woman playing at a gracieuse inoubliable dame who suddenly grows cold and pale even as a little girl she always did look pale uninteresting then suddenly hot and flushed as the language that found itself delicious crash-lands in a jardine full of white gladioli shshsh and acid-bearing roses that die have never blossomed Great Scott and gone followed by mais où allez-vous?

No need to run undignified from his absolute standstill to avoid a scene perhaps or out of stunned surprise incomprehension pride humiliation revenge non-fraternisation of a language qui peut se contenter de l'opposition de quelque chose avec rien. The marked term say the feminine, the unmarked say the masculine or vice versa can derive from the marked by an absence which signifies eine Abwesenheit die etwas bedeutet.

The visitor's attention turns immediately to lower things such as the absence of any vaporetto at the jetty and the convenient presence of a gondolier just depositing a female grey-haired tourist ready for another alleinstehende Frau with a glint of a hint of a tint. San Marco per favore. Bene signora and no attempt to look again in an Italian way at a worn-out woman with a slept-on look or unslept-on according to the enemy viewpoint Marianne Lilibet or die Heimat who gets no second glance from any man or boy in the piazza in an Italian way at the flesh between the zest of youth and the wisdom of old age where lies a not so long period of relief repose and resignation called the middle ages that wouldn't mind having got stuck in the sixth century with the virile Goths in Italy but the twelfth—ugh. And the fifteenth ugh-ugh. Nothing deserves a flow of rash enthusiasm my sweet, not even San Marco, which, begun in 830 and completed in 1484, preserves more perfectly than any existing building in the territories once belonging to the Eastern Empire the quintessential spirit of Byzantine art. Inside the porch three red marble slabs commemorate the spot where Henry Otto Friedrich or Barbarossa knelt to receive the kiss of peace from whatever pope non si ricorda esattamente after thirty years and plus conceding however no point of vital substance. The popes have no power now. We have no evidence whatever that any human being, let alone an alleinstehende Frau, can so embody the divine principle descending into matter in any behaviour sufficiently organised to prevent empires falling between one war and another to the scheme of l'ourobouros, not merely as a ring of flesh but expressing life out of death, death out of life that turns immediately to higher things, such as the blue temperature of minus fifty degrees or so around the enormous wing, the jet-exhausts invisible in their power or the propellers invisible in their speed save for a hinted halo and from this seat no cloud no man-made object no rectangles of agriculture or jardines passing to show that the heart flies immobile at a speed of nine hundred and ninety kilometres an hour towards the rue du Four.

Inside they have pressurised the comfort. The people sit hidden in their high armchairs that stretch interminably towards the distant brain way up behind the tabernacle and beyond no doubt a little door, except for a few headtops bald fluffy red sleeky black between the port and starboard engines, looked after cradled in their needs, eat drink smoke talk doze dream. Votre filet de sauvetage se trouve sous votre siège. Ce filet peut servir pour une personne privée de connaissance et per assistere anche una persona priva de conoscenza. This life-jacket self-rights itself to maintain the head above water. Omo Schaum-Stop reguliert sich selber. 1. Le sortir de son logement et l'enfiler par dessus la tête. 2. Serrer les cordons autour de la taille. 3. Ne pas gonfler le filet avant de sortir de l'avion. Pour gonfler, tirer la poigneé rouge (1). Pour gonfler à bloc souffler dans le tube (2). Allumer la lampe en tirant à fond la poignée jaune (3). The air-hostess in blue with short fair hair and un amour de soutien-gorge puts down the plastic tray covered with various foods in little plastic troughs representing not a ring of flesh but Poulet Sauté, Epinards, Pommes Frites, Poire Belle Hélène, Fromage/ Biscuits, Café. Vous avez de l'eau minérale?

— Non madame. Du Perrier seulement.

— Bon, un Perrier s'il vous plait. Sans glace.

L'eau follement pétillante. The body stretches forth towards some thought some order some command obeyed in the distant brain way up as the wing spreads to starboard motionless on the darkening temperature of minus what, forty-seven, the metal shell dividing it from this great pressurised serenity and absolute calm she translates with from a dead language that compels no passion no commitment no loyalty to anyone and out in simultaneous quiet suspension of judgment as the sky grows dark over the chasms of the unseen Alps and the bright red bar of sunset slices the navy sky like a hot poker in the twilight of the soul and sweet evening conversations. Vénus vous boude. Mars vous contre. La Lune vous rendra particulièrement sensible. Mercure vous donnera des idées plus claires through a swift reintegration into totality by virtue of an ontological recognition that we belong to all of the signs all of the time as the green light winks under the stars on and off in the enormous black behind the rectangular window. It looks like a light on earth but travels with the body of the lit-up plane full of stimați pasageri at a speed of total immobility between the invisible wings. The plastic tray remains full of half-eaten sautés skin and bones between the crumbs of roll the cellophane paper and the gulliverised salt and pepper containers. Between the port and starboard engines the body floats, the plastic tray takes off above the breasts of the air-hostess in un amour de soutien-gorge.

The ship bumps down the steps of air, losing height slowly as it nears its expected minute of arrival, the distant brain obeying innumerable instructions that translate time speed height into locality and channel and descent into bright lights. Mesdames messieurs, nous allons atterrir dans quelques minutes à Orly. Prière d'éteindre vos ceintures—excusez-moi prière d'éteindre vos cigarettes and laugh as the elegant blue-haired lady next to you laughs so that old age has its attractions still in the freedom of the night lights and the imprecision of nationality through the brightlit signs in French such as MILKBAR Parking Tearoom SOLDES de SWEATERS et de TWINSETS Teinturerie LAVING PRESSING for the improvement of migration statistics and the circulation of such reports to member governments. Nous n'allons pas considérer cependant les très simples instructions de certains codes—le code de la route par exemple qui ne représente qu'un intérêt dérisoire pour la sémiologie nevertheless and necessarily understood immediately and out in simultaneous German. As soon as we pass to other systems of objects and images—as for example the cinema, the press, comics, or, equally interesting, the codes of furniture, of fashion and of food, we find a doubling of the iconic message by language which supports the significations. Above Times Square five letters have gone dark in STU   ANT with the eye in an imprecision of nationality reading STUPEFIANT—The International Passport to Smoking Pleasure. Let us return for a moment to the central Saussurean dichotomy of Langue et Parole. La langue in a dumb show consists of le langage moins la Parole, une institution sociale, un système de valeurs which escapes from all premeditation since the individual cannot create it or modify it. La parole on the other hand consists of an individual act of selection and actualisation. This fruitful dichotomy has suggested many others, notably that of Code and Message, or the famous duplex structures which of course you all know and understand immediately because the thing understood passes away together with the need to understand.

The Belgian representative has emphasised that this commission should not limit its discussion to charity towards the handicapped but must encompass all activities aimed at building a better social order. I note that the consensus of opinion in the committee favours the draft revised resolution and my delegation will also vote for it. The question of implementation, however, remains. In semiology this division has led to others, for instance that between System and Syntagma. In le Système, sense depends on a relationship which retains only the difference between two things. The U.S. representative, by way of example, mentioned an elephant. He said that the elephant would have to put its first foot on the first stage. But why should the elephant have to put its first foot on evolving a procedure for bringing both sides to the conference table? Let him put his first foot on the procedure to be evolved and his other foot on the de-escalation of the war in the Far East. Or let him put his first, second, third and fourth feet all at once on all types of offensive from escalation to conventional warfare. As for example in a dictionary each apparently positive definition contains words which themselves need defining. Et tous les dictionnaires prouvent qu'il n'y a jamais de sens propre, jamais d'objectivité d'un terme. Le sens propre ne vit que dans un contexte expressif et particulier, such as for instance a study of methodology of diet surveys to assist governments in carrying out surveys.

So that we have le Système et le Syntagme—in food for example the System would consist of functional groups such as entrées, roasts, desserts. The Syntagma would consist of a series of actual dishes available, in other words, the menu which goes all the way to Dar es Salaam but has no personal significance after the coq-au-vin. Similarly in clothing, cars, furniture, architecture und so weiter weiter gehen in a total inability to follow the signification of the paroles that flow through the neutralised transmitter in the brain eyes open on the list of technical equivalences learnt in advance but not quite well enough and out in simultaneous German. Sandra manages smoothly, watching the speaker from under a lank fringe and earphone diadem that doesn't disarrange it. Françoise and Robert play at noughts and crosses or rude drawings perhaps while waiting for the next speaker in English, one sericulturist, one reeling expert one acidulator needed in Korea.

Now in language we find a vast disproportion between la langue, a finite system of rules, and the actual words or speech which vary infinitely. In the non-linguistic systems studied by semiology however, we find on the contrary une pauvreté de la parole, even, as in the language of fashion, une langue sans parole. In an expression like l'explosion du glaïeul blanc he looks up at the shuttered window and says shshsh—a distinction unknown in language, where one cannot decompose a sound considered as immediately significant into an inert element and a semantic element. Thus one may arrive at a tripartite division: le plan de la matière, le plan de la langue et le plan de l'usage. This allows us to account for systems without execution since the first element ensures the materialness of la langue. For in these systems la langue a besoin de la matière et non de la parole.

Thus one may arrive at no significance at all of an inert element without execution in the exhilaration of freedom from desire love pity for anyone through the neutralised transmitter of ideas none of which deserves a moment of attention in French and out in simultaneous German. Le signifié et le signifiant composent le signe, which occurs in all languages from theology to cybernetics. To establish the full significance of le signe we must remember that this term, and all its replacements such as symbol, icon, allegory signal und so weiter weiter gehen to a relation between two relata, which relation we shall present here in its binary aspect of alternatives—in other words presence or absence. Does the relation imply or not imply the psychic representation of a foolish fond old man left at a total standstill in a doorway of a peeling façade so much more peeling than the powerful erotic imagination behind it. Does the liaison between the two relata of stimulus and response produce or not produce an immediacy of understanding. Do the relata coincide exactly or on the contrary spill over one another in continuing letters unanswered at any level even unread after vous me tuez non pas doucement mais brutalement and filled no doubt to spilling over with incomprehension accusation humiliation revenge unless tact reeducation readministration Persil-Schein reorientation fraternisation sex. Die Vitalität des Mannes—Vitalität bedeutet: Spannkraft, Energie, Leistungsfähigkiet, auch in sexuellen Bereich. Um Sie zu stärken, stützen, und gezielt zu aktivieren by an absence which signifies what do you mean you've bought a car?

— Only a little one.

— But mein Liebes whatever for? In Paris!

— No, for holidays. And even here we get free parking at H.Q.

— But you always arrange your holidays between congresses, so as to benefit from the free fares.

— Yes, but one gets so tired of flying.

— One does?

— It'll make a change.

— Well, gut-gut. The result of speculation in property no doubt. I mean selling for four thousand a piccolo chalet that cost five hundred.

— Just time Siegfried, splendid thing time, it enriches. Care to drive to Istanbul?

— Istanbul!

— Gonna make a senni-mennal journey. To renoo ole me-e-mo-ries.

— Du lieber Gott, have you regressed that far?

Siegfried grown mellow in the joys of late fatherhood has no enriching time to travel in electronics as others travel in ole memories. Why don't you go with the antiquated French lover?

— Oh, that. Nothing came of it.

— No? Do you mean he gave up or—

— Oh, he goes on. Aber man achtet nicht darauf.

— Man doesn't?

— Well, what can one do except throw the letters away unread or return one or two as a sign meaning STOP?

The vital lie has turned into a fragile truth both coinciding exactly or on the contrary spilling over each other between Siegfried's belief and disbelief which makes no difference to an Abwesenheit die bedeutet merely a desire to see those splendid notices at the Turkish frontier, remember when we all went by bus from Sofia? Please declare if you have plants or parts of plants with you. Bitte Pflanzen oder Pflanzenteiler zu deklarieren.

— No Liebes, I didn't go that time. Some other man, your husband perhaps.

The actions all postponed while erst die Dinge und die Personen kommen. Aber woaus und voein kommen die Personen?

— Oh yes. The mosques. Witness le complexe de Jonas.

— What?

— Walking in stockinged feet on the innumerable prayer-rugs, six thousand rugs the muezzin said for six thousand people not, however there. And the huge white columns covered with dark calligraphy so much easier to worship than plaster images because totally devoid of any sense proper or improper, at least to the neutralised transmitter in the brain except in a particular context of perfect proportion between matter and space, presence and absence that signifies nothing at all, no love, no lust, no ambition, no disappointment, no personal messages in any code to any god of love or power or anger, revenge humiliation eternal torment repentance absolution or even death.

— Have you taken a pep pill or something?

— The stones contain the temple, cavern, sepulchre which contains one alleinstehende Frau sitting cross-legged on a prayer-rug, a miniature temple you know, prêt-à-porter, with her fingers forming a squat diamond space through which the pattern on the prayer-rug, say, blue, red, green, has no significance beyond itself. The stones contain the space and the space contains the presence of no more than centuries of mankind's need to love even eine Abwesenheit die nur eine Abwesenheit bedeutet.

— Yes, well. Or as uncle Siegfried said, I told you so. Do you feel all right? You look absolutely washed out.

— I always did look pale, even as a little girl.

— You did? Gut-gut. Well. Little girls must go to bed early. And I must fly. Wiedersehen Liebes. And do take a sensible holiday. Till next time.

Till next time perhaps or perhaps not in the joys of late fatherhood Grüss Gott and gone.

Aber voaus und woein kommen die Personen? Out of the nervous tissue which makes protein cells available to those who desperately need them, spinning to yield products which when properly flavoured with ingredients historical social and philosophical closely simulate common foods contra bona indissolubilitatis et prolis in the under-developed areas such as la Francia, la Germania e soprattutto not after all the land of infidels who say please declare if you have any plants or parts of plants, no nothing at all, just personal effects.

Just personal effects in the small Renault with the Paris numero di codice that ends with 75 on its bottom and Ⓕ for Feind in la Germania which makes no difference to an Abwesenheit die bedeutet merely an absence of belief in anyone or whether any god of love has blind eyes or twenty breasts and plus like Diana of Ephesus or a beard, androgynous and indifferent to the death of the feminoid son and transcendental father up or down the agro-lunar dramma del agnosticismo with all ingredients social historical touristic in the freedom of the road and through the simple instructions of the code de la route so poor in parole uninteresting to semiologists but nevertheless understood immediately as the arrows eat their own tails point left go up go down inside white discs, red discs, blue discs crossed with white bars black bars no parking no entry no overtaking end of no overtaking Umleitung Parkplatz Bitte sauber verlassen hooting twinkling left or right in orange brake-lighting in red ahead or flooding dipping swerving stopping to wave someone across with a courteous gesture unless to shake the fist in a smooth swift silent language understood by everyone each protected in a glass and metal box so that no-one can get at you.

And if you look up the word happiness in the dictionary you will find that the apparent definition contains words which themselves need defining and so on ad infinitum which makes one very merry. Il n'y a jamais de sens propre au dictionnaire, the proper sense living only in an expressive and particular context like menus for example where the sound does not disintegrate into one inert element and a confusional sliding from active to passive, from swallower to swallowed which we find in all the myths of depth descent and femininity. Witness le complexe de Jonas in the totally rebuilt Alte Peter of München where the frail skeletal nun lies in a glass case. Heilige Munditia. Patronin der alleinstehenden Frauen. Corpus Sanctae Munditiae Martyris. She looks a bit like Mutti, net? Sehr grauenhaft. But French girls never stand alone, du nie except I hope till I come back and marry you when I grow up and if you have a child just contact my parents, net? Ich hab noch nie ein französisches Mädchen geküsst under the cherry-tree which has vanished, the moat filled up no drawbridge only a dilapidated drive with a cement-mixer and two workmen eating sandwiches outside the shrunken Schloss its square peeling façade so much more peeling than the emptiness inside it. Eine Schule? Ja, seit vielen Jahren. Und was geschah mit der Familie, mit dem jungen Baron? Weiss nicht. Sie müssen es verkauft haben.

— Der junge Herr Baron?

The woman in the village shop looks young and stresses junge. Well, der Baron. They haven't lived there for ages, not since I was a little girl. They sold it. I think he lives in Nürnberg. An architect or something. Dankeschön. Bitteschön. Aufwiedersehen.

Why wiedersehen her? Or anyone or anything except mere stones to test the résistivité électrique to all ole memories battericamente pura in the rebuilt unrecognisable cities of Nürnberg or Berlin with visa complications through the zone of democratic Lebenslügen like any others among fragile truths and a French car? British passport? Born in France with German maiden-name und das? A Turkish phrase-book do you mind? Sie fahren in die Türkei? No, not now. You must excuse these questions Fräulein but in view of your desiccated look as an alleinstehende Frau we must make sure of your undivided reintegration into totality after all these years we do our job simply as instruments had you thought of that? How long have you stayed away lost touch a little forgotten how to understand immediately because the thing understood slips away together with the need to understand? Let's face it you destroy. What methods did you use? Ask her what happened to the statistics of destruction per citadel per night which her department looked after. Do you believe her? Or would you rather test by means of engagement? Why don't you joke a little instead of acting like a Geheime

Reichssache? Zukunft, du lieber Gott es gibt keine we live from day to day and what about the war meaning what about me and my desires in the Pommernstrasse which looks completely different from the enemy point of view.

The visitor's attention turns immediately to higher things such as the arrows eating their own tails and pointing left or right up or down with a mere finger twinkling flooding dipping immer geradeaus dann links in the freedom of the road and through the simple instructions poor in parole whether twelfth or nineteenth century but understood immediately by everyone each protected in a glass and metal structure so that no one can get at you through Köln and down across the Saarland into Lorraine Alsace the numbers on the cars ending in 67, 68 and on to Lyon through which two rivers flow as well as a third river la Belle Jolaise.

La Belle Jolaise and desiccated alleinstehende Frau flows on like a Geheime Reichssache so self-contained so secretive in such devil-may-care freedom from loyalty to anyone through rectangles of agriculture vital lies that turn into great curves of roads in dark real forests sweeping vineyards piccoli chalets grey façades so much taller than the non-existent past behind them. PRISUNIC. Tearoom. Coktailes. Le plus fort contre la saleté. Calorifères—Frigidaires. Ici on parle anglais. Ici on regarde la télévision behind the dark façades so much blacker than the blue eye behind them. Do you aspire to anything? A change of zone for example or the domestication of Chronos? I want it double-breasted. With two buttons, one for going up and one for going down with a lilt of the heart into the mouthpiece and the same confusional sliding from active to passive which we find in all myths of depth despite this our masculine-dominated civilisation which has turned vital lies into fragile truths such as Madam, I have just received the notification of the Nullity decision in your favour at the Last Judgment and enclose it with great joy and felicitation at the happy outcome just in time for the menopause.

ROMANA seu VESTMONASTERIEN. Nullitatis Matrimonii. SENTENTIA DEFINITIVA. In nomine Domini—Amen. FACTI SPECIES. Hodie onus nobis incumbit respondendi dubio, sub sueta formula concordato: AN CONSTET DE MATRIMONII NULLITATE IN CASU. IN IURE. Cum exclusa dicantur, Quoad, Quibus, Merito igitur, Verum quidem, Quare, Quoad exclusionem boni prolis, Quacumque as the paragraphs succeed one another for thirty printed pages of undoubted thoroughness and even Gründlichkeit in your eyes or those of any father transcendant speaking the language of the sixth, the twelfth the nineteenth century beneath the temple of Apollo where the oracle uttered its prophecies in riddles to all who came and consulted it on serious matters such as war, marriages and births with the gorgeous calligraphy so much easier to contemplate because totally devoid of any sense proper or improper, at least to the neutralised transmitter in the brain except in an expressive and particular context of perfect proportion between presence and absence that signifies eine Abwesenheit die bedeutet that tomorrow and today we shall continue to honour our obligations to the domestication of Chronos. No body occupies the empty bed nor will use l'essuie-main not für Rasierklingen. No one comes in offering anything not ordered.

No one does anything at all. Assemblies meet and talk and even this Council can do no more than pass a resolution pressing governments to initiate urgent measures to close the protein gap. If we wish to avert famine in the developing countries the affluent nations must concentrate on the words that flow through the serene transmitter in the brain and down into the mouthpiece to provide more technical aid towards developing these cheap sources of protein.

Between the dawn and the unrounding night the fingers fondle the symbole d'intimité dans le voyage protector and talisman against the death of love and the catastrophe that could provoke nothing at all just personal effects within the body stretching out its hundred and forty years and plus towards the yellow curtain that divides the starving from the affluent in suspended animation as a new technique for living. The biggest difficulty however lies not so much in obtaining the additional protein as in making it palatable to those who desperately need it.

Sandra manages smoothly in un amour de soutien-gorge that points up her white blouse. Structures of love, even when they appear to depend on physical, financial and technological resources and consumer goods requirements for the economic development of the under-developed areas (fuel, energy, iron ore), in fact depend on the co-operation of millions of molecules which play a key-role in protein synthesis encoding the ideas and the remembered facts. If the stimuli of environment, in other words, events, transformed into electrical impulses, modified the sequence of events this would permanently alter the physical features of such a seductive hypothesis.

The brief applause of the delegates in the amphitheatre cracks the eardrums through the earphones which have to be stretched outwards from the ears while the voice announces continuous flight and gate numbers over an abstract study in glass galleries, coffee-bars hot air and teak stairways with space between the steps over queues of plastic luggage by the gleaming weight-machines. Mesdames messieurs, nous avons entendu ce matin une belle fiction. We have no evidence at all that live human beings, let alone the skirted figurine or high-heeled shoe on the door can so embody the divine principle descending into matter in a behaviour sufficiently organised to prevent the illiterate women of an Indian village taught the natural method with an abacus from pushing all the red balls to the left like a magic spell and all coming back pregnant. From taking all their pills on the one day and coming back sick or dead. The populations multiply almost by geometrical progression like two times two und so weiter ad infinitum which makes one very sad. We shall however continue to honour our obligations and appoint a subcommittee to enquire into the way we can best meet the crisis. And if you look up the word crisis in the dictionary you will find that it means decision, which itself needs defining and so on ad infinitum so that nothing gets done at all at the Commission on Fundamental Education in scrap supply and demand of Narcotic Drugs and Division of Narcotic Drugs including pilot projects and associated fringe activities like the Napoleon Bicentenary Congress with special emphasis laid on an International Charter for Youth and the Universal Declaration of Human Rights. America must learn, Russia must learn la verité, l'humanité, la justice, et la tutungerie.

Prague has a dingy airport still. A mess of huts, a transit-lounge like a canteen just evacuated by an army leaving a scattering of mimeographed news-sheets on the square table and a few tourist pamphlets. Map and Travel Information for your visit to Czechoslovakia. Carte géographique-Informations sur la Tchécoslovaquie. Landkarte der Tschechoslowakei und Turistische Informationen. The Czechoslovak Socialist Republic consists of two equally privileged nations, the Czechs and the Slovaks. The highest organ of State power, the National Assembly has 300 deputies elected for 4 years. At the head of the State stands *Natural Resources*: coal, kaolin, iron, uranium, manganese and copper ore, pyrites, mercury silver, antimony, tin, tungsten, graphite, magnesite, naphtha and natural gas. *Transport. Principal Mountain Ranges. Principal Rivers. Folklore Regions. Tourist Season*—Czechoslovakia has a year-round tourist season. The mimeographed news-sheet says that the Slovak National Council met in Bratislava yesterday. The Council unanimously re-elected Minister Adam Smetny, member of the Praesidium of the Central Committee, as chairman of the Council. The Minister then took the floor.

Mesdames messieurs. Je tiens d'abord à remercier le Président du Congrès pour ses éloges que je n'ai pas conscience de mériter. We have come here in this beautiful old city to discuss a new and vital theme, The Writer and Communication.

The bottle of Vidago stands on the bedside-table, poderosamente radio-activas, bicarbonatadas, liticas, arsenicais und so weiter as the cock crows loud and long at crack of dawn triumphant in some shed or other on the flat roofs of Lisbon among the hanging sheets and the potted geraniums. The bathroom door faces the bed, at right angles with the window so that it has its window out on to the crowing cock triumphant instead of a mere ventilation-shaft. Soon someone will come in with a breakfast-tray and put it down on the plastic table that flaps out from the seat in front by the small rectangular window beyond which the enormous wing spreads back on the blue temperature of minus forty-eight degrees. The cloud has cleared. Way down below the window-seat the coastline glints metallic to the clay-like sea that divides into two distinct patterns one plain one purl from different winds invisible as Casual girls take the easy way to colour. Smoulder, tempt, threaten. The girl who knows about Lil-lets and widthways expansion feels confident and carefree. Life begins to beam again. You seem mixed up in some artistic venture, such as decorating, designing or painting. You will go to the forefront with original thought and if you want to make an important change do it now before you lose courage. Eine arbeitsreiche Woche—Sie kommen aber zum Zug wo und wann immer Sie jetzt möchten. Vielleicht sollten Sie trotz der enormen beruflichen Chancen das Privatleben nicht ganz ausser acht lassen. Achtung am 20ten. Saturn wirkt sich recht verschieden aus. But on this day or that the corridor encased in teak and glass reaches out to the door of the plane and on into the airport hall of hot air clean teak and glass galleries with black square plastic low armchairs and a board covered with blue messages in alphabetical order. No one calls out no name responded to at any level through the Customs Hall where swift electric trolleys bring the loaded plastic luggage up a sloping-lane at speed and out in simultaneous ownership. In some countries the women would segregate to the left of the conveyor-belt, the men less numerous to the right. But all in all and civilisation considered the chromosomes lie quietly mixed among the hundred million others or so that multiply in geometrical progression while nobody does anything at all.

So that the hum of voices echoes loud in the Palais des Papes as the mayor speaks into a microphone bidding everyone welcome to this ancient city of Avignon, the acoustics of the stone palace carrying the words unheard into the high ceiling as the members of the Congress on Tradition and Innovation unless perhaps The Role of the Writer in the Modern World burble on almost excluding the introduction of Dame Janet McThingummy and Madame Hélène Chose-Truc as well as Monsieur le Maire's speech on hands across the frontiers over floating stomachs that move about and shshsh! Que cherchez-vous madame? A travers la cour. Au fond à droite. Ah, la sortie? A gauche madame. Oui il fait bon dehors, une belle soirée, comme toujours ici. Vous avez senti le froid dans ces murs de pierre? Or else inside the whale and out in simultaneous wonder. Und haben Sie noch einen Wunsch? Madame désire encore quelque chose? No, nothing at all, just personal effects.

Between the enormous wings the body floats.

THRU

Through the driving-mirror four eyes stare back
two of them in their proper   place
Now right on
Q   ask us

to de   V   elop   foot on gas
how m(any   how)   eyes?

four   two
of them   correct

on either side   ▽   of the
nose   the other

two   ⚠   O danger
slow   down

eXact   replicas

nearer the hairline further up the brow but dimmed as in a glass
tarnished by the close-cropped mat of hair they peer through

The mat of hair is khaki, growing a bit too low on the brow
the nose too big.

Who speaks?

le rétro   viseur   (some   languages
more   visible than   others)

or the vizir looming grey eminence behind the consultan listener how
many times leaning a little to the right to peer into how many
rectangles a thousand and one in which there is a   flaw?

The second pair of eyes are less pale veiled by
the reflected hair crinkly khaki flecked grey

O but handsome all told whatever all is and who
ever tells a young god yet the lower eyes lie
blue to the tarnished replicas higher up the brow
which whoever speaks (Nourennin?) calls too low.

Some tale-bearer
(O capital!   your
story or   your
life
wot no   story?
no   life
punishment)   So that
Hang it all
no   life
story
off with   your
head   said the
chief   in-sultan to   his
red red rose
washed by
once upon
(some times)   purple passages
(other times)
hanging   suspen(I)s
from the
capital   of
Baghdad
Rome
Athens
Istambul   busy anteroom
con { st(anza)
(ante)
Neopolis
scarlet

WHORE of Babel — Whose?
HITE queen goddess — Who
Is always
Cramping
HIS styl — us
under
perpetual — sentence
subject — predicatimetable
just like — life
the scrapegloat of
SIN — TAG — MA — TRICKS

But when the muscular shoulders shift back to the correct position the cars that loom grey eminent into the retrovizor do not look double-faced or even quadruple-eyed top two through crinkly hair, for the hair has moved away out of focus together with the four eyes; the cars untarnished, with single metal grins between two pale gold eyes, one on either side, or else two smaller city slickers lower down but never both pairs together.

My love is like a white white rabbit
late
down the hatch
out of sight
dead — (safe)
earthhole though
il court il court le furet
and which way did he go?
thattaway
hey follow that car
you should have seen the one that got — away
that always gets — away
safe

as a jack-in-the-box
sitting beside
hiding behind
eyeing beneath
the grey eminence the retro-vizir beyond the {in / con} sultan
hearer of deep structures below the performance yes your
eminence I'm coming to that your reference moves up glaring

BUT

the retrovizor has a bluish tinge. At a flick of a switch the rectangle turns smoky grey to dim the dazzle of floodlights undipped or even gently dipped but the glare is preferable to the sudden isolation of almost not seeing behind a head

Ali Nourennin

To be discussed

entering a visually over	roomful of rectangular	freshmanfaces tables minds	floating audio into which you
enter unom repeat per	nisciently form what	for that time ever the deep	table space level comp
etence twelve stricted to	times a sem one technique	ester nor is the unless of course	a(u)ctor re he (who?) so
chooses he and out of	can use sever which he builds	al in layers up his effects	through which yes er
Paul? What intentional	do you mean fallacy yes	builds up what of course but	about the any message
narrative or Garbage-can?	not has an e Receptor then	mitter and a What does the o	recipient. mitter omit?

The dancing hoops. For the gold eyes when distant turn into hoops (at night in the correct position) of luminous green red amber white bouncing in out of through and through each other narrowing to slim ovals vertical horizontal swaying undoing swiftly changing shape as if juggled by a mad magician or by the black recumbent street beneath overhead bridges that make perhaps the optical illusion?

She shifts the mirror to her rearward glance. It doesn't work for her the mistress of the moment of sudden isolation at not seeing back to the black magician who fantastically juggles luminous hoops in the retro-rectangular hey put my mirror back.

So it needs adjusting.
Why at that precise point introduce this or that?

Intensity of illusion is what matters to the narrator through a flaw in the glass darkly perhaps making four clear eyes stare back, two of them in their proper place at height of bridge of nose and, further up the brow, the

other two, exact replicas but dimned as in a tarnished reflection, tarnished by the hairline they peer through. A

second pair of eyes hidden higher up the brow would have its uses despite psychic invisibility or because of.
Gazing they do not see themselves. They reflect nothing, nor do they look at their bright replicas below in their proper place on either side of the nose a fraction too large according to whoever speaks in this instance. Only these lower eyes, reflecting the eyes of the real face as it leans for vanity to the right, see the upper eyes, looking up at the brow which some teller or other thinks too low. Who?

Oh her.

W
h
o
'
s

s
h
e

w
h
e
n

s
h
e
'
s

a
t

h
o
m
e
?

never the les**S**
this is no**T**
n**O**
(**M**y)
the h **Y** s **T** e **R** y of **T**he
Eye
bec**A**use **I** would no**T** **S** e **E** th**Y** c**R**uel **N**ails
boa**R**ish f**A**ngs
pluck ou**T** h**I**s
poo**R** old (**E** **X**tract) (Cruel
Cruel n**A**ils) u**P**on **T**hese ey**E**s of
t**H**ine
I'll set (**C** **R** u **E**l fan**G**s)
my fo**O**t **P**oo **R** old eyes
These ey**E**s h**I**s e**Y**es
poo**R** old eyes
be**A**m **M**ote
Cruel fan**G**s
Eyes c**R**uel f**A**ngs
bo**A**rish
bea **M**
Moat
Etc
alrea**D**y (all read eye)

na**I**ls
Nails

upon **T**hese
eyes of t**H**ine I'll
s**E**t

the re **M**ote s**T**one
Wide **E**yes w**E**t?
p**A**rch **M**ent wa**X**
ar**X**i st**O**ne **T**race
d**R**y
pap**Y**rus
eye '**S**

blue lacuna of learning
and unlearning a text within a text passed on from generation to generation of an increasing vastness that nevertheless dwindles to an elite initiated to a text no-one else will read by means maybe of the flick of a switch for the overhead projector and diagrams drawn into a boxed screen to the right of the desk with a spirit-loaded pen thus not losing eye-contact.

The quiver of the bhi on the beeswax

How doth the bithy little Thoth
produthe an endleth piethe of cloth
when thought, that bithy little moth
devourth it all like tho much froth
leaving great holth, tho Thamuth quoth.

a busy competent performance before busy bees
who palp oscult measure time listen see
smell taste imitate suck the performer dry.

Hang it all we have the story of an 
O but is not incompetent performance a non-disjunction at level of deep structure? I me if it be possible despite non-equivalence to rewrite I as O and O as I

which has been suggested,
here,
you see,

cosí I

I I

should you start structuring your te><thattaway
or the latterway?

Those for: Peter Brandt Barbara Darcy Francesca Newman Robert Galliard Myra Kaplan Kathleen O'Shaunessy Ali Nourennin Renata Polanska Lin Su Fu.

Those against: Vittoria Charib Marie Faber Salvatore Tancredi Michael Mandel Jean-Marie Fèvre Eliza Jones.

Abstention: Paul Stradiver Julia Weintraub Neil Alder.
? Refusal of Vote: Saroja Chaitwantee.
a show of hands within a secret ballot
which is one way of introducing a cast-list.

unless Armel inventing Larissa
or Larissa " Armel
" Armel " Veronica
" Veronica " Armel
" Armel " Larissa
" Larissa " Marco (or is it Oscar?)
" Marco (?) " Larissa
" Larissa " Armel

The other possible permutations do not occur
for logical reasons: Larissa could invent Veronica but
in a limited subjective way in any case Veronica and she are
contradictories not contraries as Socrates explained
to Protagoras and Structural Semantics has just reinvented. While Armel could invent Marco or is it
Tariel and vice versa but due to the double standard
in practice would not stoop or merely would not have the curiosity. Clearly Marco does not invent Veronica nor she even
utter Marco (or is it Stavro?) they've never met besides
Stavro has no imagination.

On the other hand the hypotheses could have been
posed anticlockwise:

Larissa	inventing	Oscar
Oscar	"	Larissa
Larissa	"	Armel
Armel	"	Veronica
Veronica	"	Armel
Armel	"	Larissa
Larissa	"	Armel
Armel	"	?

er something's gone wrong here there seems to be
room for some extra who why the mistress of the moment
since the man any man must be if not many at least
one up who will fairly soon be dropped for she does
not see by day the four lies in the retrovizor when
shifted to her forward gaze nor dancing hoops by night

But it needs adjusting.
Well then I found myself with a magician on a
helluva stage as his stooge you know in tights
and a sequin bodice and my bust like it was busting
tight out of it and I was handing him coloured scarves

i think and suddenly a prop was missing I forget his
stick I mean his wand anyway it was my fault he couldn't

Lift the white rabbit out of the hat and the crowd murmured
and even shouted as he signalled frantically like mad
right into the wings but they didn't get the message and
in the end he walked off leaving me alone on stage to cope
somehow in the glare of lights that hits the mirror and
swings left out of it beaming ahead rewritten now
as two small red eyes in a hunched black shape which is

delineated against forward floodlight the retrovizor re-
opening to the hoops dancing up and down and aside
in the rear distance luminous horizontal ovals oh
no, vertical ovals as if at quarter angle amber red
green white swiftly changing shape and juggled by the

night or by the tall dark house with blue eyes
or maybe by the black recumbent street who
was very short and fat for a magician more than

obese you've never seen anything so fat he tried to
reach the switches to calm the audience but he was so

Very fat and short so he lifted me in my tights and bodice
ever so firm under the breasts with them busting
right out of the sequins and I managed to switch them
off and as he brought me down we kissed half
naked ever so sexy and then we started wanting
it like crazy but I said no later we have to
calm the crowd so he got wild and dragged me
after him out of the theatre but I wrenched free
saying the show must go on can you interpret
?
The show within the show
What?
of hands juggling

within a secret ballet of the I
hell honey I guess I just fill the air for you sure that's what
i like about you oh I thought it was my big beautiful
true blue tits they're fine too with a show of hands
entering under silk with a secret ballet of fingers on

tiptoe upon soft globed flesh the nipple now rising
hard between the lights the foot pressed gently purring
into a stop the is it sacred belly tensed to the show of
green fingers into the left thigh that jerks open to the
hot human humidity of a sexual humour secreted un-
secretly go on then

Doing what?
Oh filling the air. You do

it so much more convincingly
than the others (tit for

tat)
what others?
others who fill the air. Oh

Well you were giving mmmmm a class on British
history for some myst**E**rious reaso**N**
Oh
yes e**X**cite me **M**mm how
in the royal nav**Y** they
Punished the **S**ailors
there y**E**s **T**here
Er
by making them **C**limb out and
er walk the plank
and all the planks s**T**uck out all **R**ound
like h**E**ll honey **Y**es your
eminence oh **D**on't like
guns I'm coming to that
Go on
so when they dropp**E**d into the
Sea
what **T**he planks no the

sailors silly a h**U**ge eagle
boy   a**R**e you big
WEll he'd swoop
down on th**E**m and they had to
e**L**iminate himmmmmmm
wel**L** fight
It out
in the
Water
and if t**H**ey
won   they were h**A**uled out
th**E**y   weNt free and you
demonst**R**ated   i**T**
to the
Class you jumped the plank
and fo**U**ght it
out   with the eagle and
wrrrrrrrrrrrrrrrru**N**g
i**T**s neck.

You're mythologising me.
Oh any time. And then you came with your car and said come unto me I'll light the way and well

drove off

across the bridge in the scintillating foreign city

did you?   No I didn't
Dopey relations you have with your magician men.
Yeah but he wasn't you Stavro that was the first dream but he was short well you're short too but he was immensely fat and couldn't have strangled an eagle in the water for anything he'd have sunk you turn left at the corner
Hey I know.
Yes you should by now but you always forget.
Okay can you see a spot?
Usually there's one further up on the right. Here.

Too small.
It isn't. You'll have to back into it.
True. But it's still too small.
But Marco of course you can get in.
I'll say, if you light the way.
Tooshay! You kill me have you no male pride it's your car.
Come come honey it's your street.
Hang on I'll lower the window. Turn full right
yes   now left   stop   straighten   oh lordy no you're
on the pavement   all crooked   forward a bit   straighten her
up   no   You'll have to take her out and start again.

Who sez? Some tale-bearer (off) or Other who has
got it all wrong

backing   into   too smal**L**   a space
short
ening
the
man
who has no name till the m**I**stress
of the **M**oment
Backing into a
fear
o
F   **U**   **S**   **I**
e

pl**O**des
I   (t)   **I**   **N**to
r
e
some   other   text   u   a l i t y
r e a
l
i   o
couldn't
she be happy with y   o   u   in the
orbit of an eye and no referent without? Or with
the Other with he passed into hystery within?

Is it Marco or Stavro? (or Armel?)
There has occurred however the foreshortening of

Armel into Marco
Laretino or is it Tarie
L? of the accurate boymouth (removed?)

whose legs : his body : : his brow : his nose
relations in proportion quaternary conjunction
or disjunction with the possibility also of non-relations
non-conjunction and even non-disjuction a
game

Whereas well
Armel
is not like
that at all but tall
with hair quite dark
and swept back grey over
splendid brow as stark
as Beethoven's
making the nose (turned up)
seem small between the burned up
eyes and blurred
evasive
mouth
it occurred in South
Carolina
oh but
not muscular
indeed though
masculine
and slim for
grace and
elegance

(Portrait by Veronica)

Armel
however
equates
rarity
of
mind with
unusual
spirit and
the looks of a
hero with a brow
as high as Beetho
ven's a small nose an
evasive mouth
and hair swept back
dark but silver
over temples
retaliating eyes
and the
troubled
identity
of the
narrator.

(Portrait by his reflection)*

***Jacques, après avoir dit entre ses dents: "Tu me le paieras ce maudit portrait", ajouta.** – Vous avez été fou de cette femme-là?
Le Maitre–Et pourquoi haïssez-vous les portraits?
Jacques.–C'est qu'ils ressemblent si peu, que, si par hasard on vient à recontrer les originaux, on ne les reconnait pas. Racontez-moi les faits, rendez-moi fidèlement les propos, et je saurai à quel homme j'ai affaire.**
(Portrait of the portrait by Jaques le Fataliste)

**Tous les signifiés du portrait sont "vrais" . . . tous ces sèmes désignent la vérité, mais même mis tous ensemble, ils ne suffisent pas à la faire nommer (et cet echec est heureux. . .) Dans le système herméneutique, le signifié de connotation occupe une place particulière: il pointe mais ne dit pas; ce qu'il pointe. . . c'est la vérité, comme nom; il est à la fois la tentation de nommer et l'impuissance de nommer. . . Ainsi un doigt, de son mouvement désignateur et muet, accompagne toujours le texte classique: la vérité est de la sorte longuement désirée et contournée, maintenue dans une sorte de plénitude enceinte, dont la percée, à la fois libératoire et catastrophique, accomplira la fin même du discours; et le personnage, espace même de ces signifiés, n'est jamais que le passage de l'énigme dont Oedipe (dans son débat avec le Sphynx) a empreint tout le discours occidental.

(Portrait of the portrait by Roland Barthes)

Oh the moving finger points and having pointed itself out
moves on, will not stay for an answer, tetrapod
biped or tripod, two and a stick, a fang for an eye a foot
in it for an unintentional phallusy but an intentional
literality: gently dip but not too deep: you dip me
I dip you I I sir you dip us. So that today we shall make a
comparative analysis, taking these two famous classics, of the
art of digression. Those of you who attend (or even analyse) General Assemblies and Faculty Meetings may well have
concluded that it is not an art but a chaos. It is,
however, a very subtly planned chaos, it has the
odd, beautiful coherence of a neurosis. A pseudo-problem is
raised, to which a false solution is found, thus creating (by
design) another pseudo-problem. Neurosis has the cunning of
stupidity, and stupidity is a dimension anyone can fall into, however intelligent, indeed, part of the intellect can
rise suspended and watch, helpless and in pain, the misuse of its own projected trajectory struggling alone, as if
cut off from itself, in a delirious discourse not its brother's
keeper.

These things do matter despite psychic invisibilty
or because of in a text like the world or the human
body that merely
engenders

itself in
to

writing – for the foot men who say
O in the mountain break fast tonguetables (thou shalt

eat thy prisoner) for a feted calf

```
                      b
              t           o
            a         o   u   d
          f n h     a d t
←—  a g r i d i r o n y o r g u y a s t r i c —→
          r   n i   t   m   r e
          e     n   i   b   i
                d           l
```

so poor Midas and other goldicondeologists prisoners of

well-planned desires for their own excrement obscurely
alimenting them while nevertheless consuming them up
regardless.

So more
or
less
literally

It has all been dreamt up by the trait-or markster of the
comment, the tale-bearer as eiron-monger hatching against
his homo-logos a plot from fear of trans fer ring a handful of
silver
displaced
condensed
metonymised
such a
man
would not
fight
the eagle in the

water for one thing nor wring its neck. Nor would he have four
eyes neither in retrospeculation nor even in any kind of
retrodiscourse as Armel might have and naturally
does the moment they are uttered as possibilities
epithets you mean
no: sapphires or crysoprases staring tetracyclops from bare brow.

Clearly Veronica is in
love – true icon –

who does not therefore exist
as Larissa does
(so?)
?

Who
has however an iconic nose
and eyes like Isis or even maybe Ra
Jacques. – O
the day (or night)

is green
she plays upon a blue guitar

she does not play things as they are
hearing in the air messages un
emitted unadmitted mean

ingventing your desire with La belle si tu voulais (bis)
Nous dormirions ensemble o-la (bis)

and answering it unspoken with

No vale la pena el llanto or l'amor è un
altalena or love is just a four-letter word and
more: love is a bore, a soap op
era a telephone that doesn't ring

in many languages from Lucan to Lacan
she fills the air as well with
syntagmatic silence – from Phaedrus to Freud
Homer to Husserl and Locke to the Li Ki
effortlessly displacing notions with a diachronic chord.

Jacques. – ee!
Things as they are
are changed upon the blue guitar
namely
It is more difficult for a phallus-man to enter the I
of a woman than for the treasurer of signifiers
to enter the paradiso terrestre.
Jacques. – ah.
Ah indeed. Larissa talks like that. The pathetic fallacy may
be used to fill the hermeneutic gap. Or in the dialectic
of desire, the subject is subverted and the object is from the start an
object of central loss.
Jacques. –Eh bien! monsieur, qu'avais-je besion
du portrait que vous m'avez fait de cette femme?
Ne saurais-je pas à present tout ce que vous en
avez dit?
Ecco! In any case the mistress of the moment should be
changed, and no doubt will be in another moment though per
haps she could meanwhile be called, Ruth, for mixed reasons
of phonemic contiguity.
Jacques. – eh?
The Master. – work it out for yourself it's not very deep.
So that now we have at last returned to the subject of
discourse, while still of the moment before being thru
and hurt (oo!) but who is we to dip royally
no collectively into an age-old narrative matrix before we
gouge out the I in order carefully to gauge its liquid
essence? The namers of things the silent obsessional
re-emitters of words who will therefore have their
mouths removed the spinners of texts that can
engender only text such as the cold street juggling
no hoops in no retrovizor and the sudden isolation of
almost not wanting anything now standing in
the wide street recumbent under great curved beams of
pale light equispaced but staggered each to the other
laterally, the quarter arches never meeting even on
an imagined curve except quite distantly along the can
yon of tall blocks all asleep all dreaming along the
boulevard as they diminish in size quite distantly
asleep whereas you standing out there in the

cold street come along, did you hear? I bet you don't know what I said I said you never tell me your dreams.

I don't have any to tell.

Of course you do they've proved it.

Who have?

Every ninety minutes of the night why didn't you know well fancy me teaching you something every one knows that, for a quarter of an hour you come up from deep level sleep and dream with electrodes no what are they called well yes electrodes I guess or something on the eyelids recording the movements up down and sideways called Rapid Eye Movements gee it's just like television you just don't remember honey and you need it like food and drink and sex too they're called R.E.M.'s.

Not every ninety minutes then.

Oh yes you do they tried depriving them of their dreams waking them up you see when those rapid eye movements begin so then they compensated and dreamt twice as much and if they deprived them like that for fifteen days they got to the borders of schizophrenia.

Were they allowed in?

Er well I guess I just fill the air for you oh I said that earlier.

True,   that's what I like about You
Yeah   I guess sO
    are You going to allow me iN?
                            Can   You
            beat that whY whAtve   You cOme for then
                            Now   cOme   along
            the   C a N YoN
            boulevard   Of   tAll blOcks   all
            asleep   No   oNe   sleeper's
            dreams
    C Oinciding in excatlY   the same   quarter of
    A N   hOur   everY
                       NinetY   miNutes   thOugh
            perhaps   Over (You)
          Lapping   weeN   iNg
         eAch   Other
          Ruth   lesslY
          In   eNdless
          Stati
          Sti   Cal   prObabilities
          According Achording to the   Number
               sleepiNg but
    Never   (You staying
                        Over
                        Night?) the same show

Cut
A diagram could
No doubt be drawn
You see
Oh
No.

In the box with a switch for the overhead projector tO
Note and a spirit-loaded pen, thus not loosing eye-contacT
Or some still making love perhaps four eyes crossed foR
Riveting limbs, M or Y, opening crossing pentapod or ninE
Diagonals meeting In ⊗ On which I enters O anD
Envelopes contraries contradictories subalterns as a staR
Rivets form substance floating up every 90 minutes or sO
To surface structure from deep level dreamlessness downN
Over under electroded lids for a shared cigarette.

Yet when the shoulders return to their correct position, the eyes disappear all four (six? eight? or ten?) of them only the focus eyes remaining fixed on the road straight ahead but glancing up at the pale fish eyes one on either side (in the retrovisor the cars not double-faced at all) the silver grin here in this position cannot see if the brain too is equipped with another pair of eyes in the brow staring like jewels: lodged, perhaps, never to sally forth, in the mirror, condensed, a secret pair to reflect nothing except cars looming from behind over into the driving eyes that glance up at the blue perspective of fish eyes and down again retrowiser

▽ in daylight or in smoky grey

the year forms bluish slit-shaped holes of hours down days along implicit depths of weeks each one behind the other each slit a labelled letter-box translated into a rectangular room where the lesson of the day reproduces itself hour by hour in endless statistical probabilities which set end to end would no doubt extend and to a great extent exteriorise the text right off the page as far as

Mars and Venus copulating under the net, the third day with the sixth day, though it could also be Wodinsday with Moonsday or or Thorsday with Freyasday but never on a Sunday or anyone of these juxtaposed with any non-contiguous other from the point of view of any one teacher or student for that matter with varying performance in each system country continent classroom of each institution of learning.

0900 1100	Discourse Analysis I: Initiation to Semiotics (Miss Chatman)	The Novel as Intentional Object (Dr Toren)
1100 1200	The Semiology of Cultural Images (Dr Medaware)	Initiation to Transformational Grammar (Miss Arbor)
1300 1500	Language as Subversion of Society (Dr Underwood)	The Inscription of Protest: Women's Lib. (Ms.Littlebrown-Fitzjohn)
1500 1700	Discourse Analysis II: The Semiology of Mass Media (Dr. Medaware)	Empiricism and Imperialism (Prof. Ngu-Rey)
1700 1900	The Inscription of Protest: Black Literature (Prof. Littlebrown)	Initiation to Dialectical Materialism (Prof. Kreuzer)
1900 2100	Narrative as Object of Exchange (Prof. Kreuzer)	The Generation of Narrative Complexes (Miss Webb)

within a text passed on from generation to
g e n e r a t i o N Of an Increasing vasTness fULl Of what neVER
the mOre the less
dwIndles
To a
structUred
eLite M O re or less
texti V O R E
E V E R
R E A D
to O R D E R else the show within the
ƎHT ƎMOƆ ⅃⅃IT WOHƧ

which

must go on

e se non è vero?

Meanwhile

quell the audience by changing the subjects which have to be re-invented continually or subverted in the dialectic of desire.

Who speaks?

Oliver Claire Hubert Olaf Gregory Chou Stanley Catherine the short plump demagogue and his lanky henchman or the pale young man carbuncular. They have been speaking a long time. I move that we move to item one on the agenda.

You don't have the floor it's Jeremy's turn then Catherine Maurice Bob then you Simon. Jeremy?

Yes well very briefly I simply want to say that it seems to me quite evident that we must first decide on the viable modalities of action we should envisage before engaging in any kind of confrontation with the authorities on their decree of November 22. Firstly, on the one hand the chairs form bottom-shaped curves of white plastic and have liftable side-flaps that make a ledge for right-handed people only to write on point by point the finger at a pregnant plenitude like a pompous pilot that will not stay for an answering fear of piercing through to a catastrophic platitude full of the one that got away leaving a blue lacuna in the timetabled analysis of

Discursus

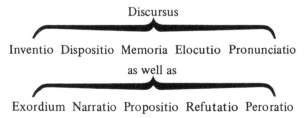

Inventio Dispositio Memoria Elocutio Pronunciatio

as well as

Exordium Narratio Propositio Refutatio Peroratio

e se non è vero you will find rectoverso the schematized split image of the sign that watches, helpless and in great pain, the engendering of its own projected trajectory struggling along ad

- Ingenium.
- Præcepta Rhetoricę. *Huius partes sunt,*
  - Vis *seu Officiũ Oratoris,*
    - Inuentio: *inuenit Argumẽta ex Locis.* Loci
      - Communes *uel Dialectici,*
        - *Artificiales,*
        - *Inartificiales.*
      - Proprij *uel* Rhetorici.
      - → *Argumẽta inuentare feruntur ad* — Fidem, / Motũ, { *Lenẽ, Vehemẽtem:* } — *Vt obtineatur Quæstio, seu Genus causæ.*
    - Dispositio, { Generalis, Specialis. } { Naturalis. Artificialis. }
    - Elocutio: *cuius partes,*
      - Sermo *Grammaticus, uerborum* { *Simplicium, Coniunctorum.* }
      - Figuræ,
        - *Tropi,* { *Dictionis. Orationis.* }
        - *Schemata,* { *Dictionis: Ordo* { *Grammaticus,* { *Dictionis. Constructionis.* } *Rhetoricus.* } *Mentis. Amplificationis.* }
      - Amplificationes, κατ' ἐξοχὴν *à Figuris separatæ. Oriuntur, ut & cæteræ Figuræ, ex Locis Dialecticis.*
    - Memoria.
    - Pronunciatio.
  - Quæstio,
    - Infinita, *ut est* Genus *Didascalicon: quæ Quæstio uel est* — { *Simplex. Coniuncta.* }
    - Finita, *ut Genus causæ*
      - Iudiciale. *Ibi status*
        - Coniecturalis.
        - Qualitatis, *seu Iuridicialis,* { *Negotialis, Iuridicialis,* { *Absolutus. Assumptiuus.* } }
        - Legitimus, { *Definitio. Contrariæ leges. Scriptum & sententia. Ambiguum. Ratiocinatio. Translatio.* }
      - Deliberatiuum.
      - Demonstratiuum, { *Personarũ. Factorum. Rerum.* }
      - → *In singulis tractandis considerandæ sunt Partes orationis.*
  - Oratio,
    - Exordium, { Rectum. Obliquum. } *Fines,* { *Beneuolentia. Attentio. Docilitas.* }
    - Narratio,
      - Grammatica, { *Personarum. Rerum,* { *Historica. Dramatica. Fabulosa.* } }
      - Oratoria. { *Generalis. Præcipuè hæc est* { *Simplex, breuis. Probabilis. Illustris. Suauis.* } *Specialis.* }
    - Propositio: *ubi & Diuisio, seu Partitio.*
    - Confirmatio, / Refutatio, — *uocantur Contentio. Vtrobiq; spectatur* { Materia / Forma } *Argumentorum.*
    - Peroratio, { Enumeratio, Amplificatio. }
- Scientia rerum. *Conficiendi ergo, ut Memoriæ succurratur, Loci cõmunes. Sic implendi sunt Loci Argumentorum.*
- Exercitatio.
- Imitatio,
  - Generalis, { Rerum. Verborum. }
  - Specialis: *ut Ciceronianæ compositionis, in* { Sententijs. Periodis. } — *Imitatio exprimat formas alienæ orationis, seu Genera dicẽdi quæ ex omnibus Rhetoricæ præceptis constant: & sunt 3.* { *Humile. Grande. Mediocre.* }

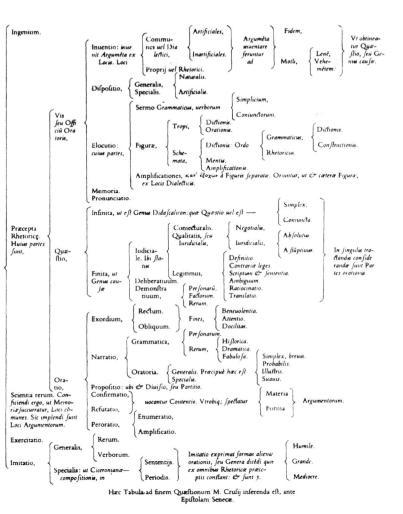

Hæc Tabula ad finem Quæstionum M. Crusij inserenda est, ante Epistolam Senecæ.

From *Philippi Melancthonii elementorum rhetorices libri duo Martin Crusii quaestionibus et scholiis explicati* (Basle 1574) opp. p. 606.

Or, on the other, to describe the proceedings in a letter to Larissa or perhaps the head of the head of the department, the short plump demagogue and his lanky henchman in smoked glasses who having carefully prepared the agenda for the manoeuvering of the meeting sit quietly clothed in democracy (but the emperor is naked!) as the tense young man carbuncular simply wants to say very briefly for at least fourteen more minutes while the middle-aged chairman of the hour exercises his fake authority with a motherless door-handle by way of gavel.

Secondly I don't agree with Charles that for nine and a half minutes the tense young man has said nothing very carbuncular under firstly his facial muscles moving up and down towards a thirdly we seem to forget that in a radical university destruction precedes construction as the morning forms a large rectangular hole within a larger rectangular hole full of bottom-shaped curves in white plastic with liftable flaps for right-winged people to write on a point of information let him finish for heaven's sake permit the disaffected elements to exercise such an inordinate influence in relation to their numbers. Not to mention extreme youth as they sit in the plastic shapes filling out the space with wide-based aureoles of self-importance basted in revolutionary spirit unless merely the intoxication of illusory power such extreme youth never had before this newly created institution of learning Language as Subversion of Society or the Inscription of Protest the Poetry of the Cry in a faculty that multiplies its base by youth zeal and inexperience so much easier for the short plump magician to handle. He is my dear Lara a typical demagogue but looks like Hemingway. In a sense they are all ready-made caricatures here, nothing to invent. Except the show within the show, the portrait within the portrait. But why bother since they create your psychic invisibility and don't want to know your true or untrue knowledge of themselves unless we form a subcommission to examine the problem, thus finding a false solution to a pseudo-problem and so engendering another pseudo-problem thirdly, as to the problem of desegmentation I have noticed that they're very fond of the word problem here I've just heard it four times and wish they could say blomper or promble just for variety because surely we are all agreed that the department should not be segmented piecemeal into more and more and smaller and smaller subsections that have no contact with the larger whole.

Catherine?

I haven't finished. Fourthly.

On a point of order, desegmentation comes under Item 3 on the Agenda.

Fourthly and lastly, as a matter of fact, Lara my love, you know me well enough to guess that I was foolish enough to make that smug remark to one of the young teachers here, called Oliver, an amiable dandy and anarchist to boot who picks up female students rather too often and overtly for competence—professional I mean not linguistic (and no doubt his performance in class and elsewhere leaves nothing to be desired ((e se non è vero è ben trovato yes? no))) (sorry, the parenthetic fallacy is filling the hermeneutic gap) I said to him in a moment of exasperation after a meeting, they're all ready-made caricatures here, and he got up from the floor where he was placing large blue rectangles on an outsize timetable and pointed to his most current girl-friend, a pale prim student with long black hair a mauve mouth and teeth like death saying what do you mean? I'm not, she's not. My Larissa what went wrong? I miss you despite. You say the object is from the start an object of central loss yet surely our peripheral gains reached and almost filled that empty centre fifthly. And in your narrative grammar are not some subjects wholly intransitivised, walking through the action with indirect objects only or none? (yours are the poems i do not write). Talking of which (students as objects) I never of course on a point of order that's not fair you said fourthly and lastly have affairs with students it's not fair, too easy, banal, and apart from that and psychic invisibility one can't work with them after they will go on as if (I know I'm doing it to you but we were a poem not a couple). It's bad enough even when one doesn't work with them. Even now I have a girl who's fabulous in bed but mythologises me in her dreams and tells them at great length and talks about the indifference of man and how I don't really want her like the fat magician she dreams of. Okay so I don't. I once saw a poster somewhere which said Abstinence is Good for you. In Wales, must have been. But the show must go on.

Until they vote on whether to take a vote those for those against abstinence refusal of vote repeat performance to pass the motion before moving on to item two on the agenda. You'll have to back into it. Leaning a little to the right to meet briefly the second pair of eyes, tarnished but useful despite psychic invisibility or because of a mere rectoversion of eyes juggled by the performing self left behind the time laid out in rectangles called The Semiology of Cultural Images maybe or merely Creative Writing into which you enter on Jove or Mars or Mercuryday saying we shall now consider the question of the narrator's presence in his narrative.

Those for. Those against. Abstention. Refusal of Vote.

And repeat performance before passing on to item three on the agenda (desegmentation) as juggled by the manoeuvering magician clothed in invisible democracy while the stooge chairman of the several hours knocks his motherless door-handle shouting order order in the poetry of the cry that this is an utterly delirious discourse until the short plump magician whisks away his main prop his invisible silk squares holds up his ego busting out of tight sequence and quells the audience, producing out of a hat a white white point of information or is it a clear summary of an essentially simple problem some people have misunderstood, so that in all honesty one must be frank for twelve and a half minutes we must call things by their right names unless perhaps we must see things as they are. And changed upon the blue guitar. And to sum up very briefly I simply want to say that we must first decide on the viable modalities of action to be envisaged in the struggle before I can go to the authorities and persuade–for that is the operative word, we must not seem to be adopting a threatening attitude (boo!)–and persuade them to accede to our demands.

Larissa my love. This is going to be a disconnected letter as I am writing it during a faculty meeting. The man who runs it–the faculty I mean not the meeting which he attends clothed in democracy and a garish tie he changes for each occasion as he changes the chairman of the hour (and I hope it never devolves on me) is an oddball, who first wrote me as Armel, signed Oscar. They use first names from the start here. He is, my dear, a typical demagogue. Not that I intend to describe him, descriptions capture so little and people are becoming more and more stereotyped. I am becoming more and more stereotyped. You are becoming shall I conjugate? But no, you are the exception to all the stereotypes or are you? Have you not carefully invented the person you have become? Not of course a stereotype, rather a unique unrepeatable model with cropped hair and a blue guitar, superimposing many models like a dompna soisebuda but is it you? Naturally you will not stoop to retort who am I, and perhaps it was after all I who invented you though you would not admit this. Certainly you invented me and withdrew, indifferent, paring your fingernails. Well enough of that. In a way they are all ready-made caricatures here, nothing to invent. Except the show within the show, the portrait within the portrait. But why bother since they create your psychic invisibility as you did and don't want to know your true or untrue knowledge of themselves. I have gotten a little tied up with my second person singular here but aren't you used to that—who is my second person singular?

Eyes that do not exist and reflect nothing, nor do they look at their companions, exact black replicas less tarnished and more clearly outlined in their proper place on either side the nose. Only these lower eyes reflected from the felt eyes can see, presumably, the upper eyes blurred just below the dark hairline, looking at nothing upwards or inside the brow which some teller or Other thinks Beethovenish until you enter into the rectangle saying today we shall study the transformation of functions in the epistolary novel, unless perhaps initiation to the Generation of Narrative Complexes in Audiovisual Imperialism as Intentional Object of Exchange. Or merely, diachronically The Beginnings of Narrative, so that you have to take her out and start again.

Once upon a time laid out in rectangles into which you enter as into a room saying once upon a time the author had supreme authority surrounded with floating faces some bent some gazing into diasynchrony or scrutinizing the chain of phonic signifiers with listening eyes linked to the question of

Varying degrees of omniscience

1. The author's presence

Take Homer written down in the first row whose **moi** in

1)Homer—**moi** in 1st line

the first line by way of invocation to the muse is the

only instance of the subject-emitter addressing his discourse to the young beardless Marx in the third row taking no notes staring through the phonic signifiers

with riveting eyes that break the chain asunder yet he is omniscent, from a modern viewpoint since he tells us things that Odysseus doesn't know, omniscient, anyway, within the universe of the mythic discourse, in which the relationship between emitter and receptor is univocal.

since the community assumes both roles, emitting and receiving a discourse it addresses to itself, indeed, the community is the discourse, existing by, through and for its myth, not before or after. In such a relationship the emitter speaks the truth (God) in fact he speaks for God

with a spirit-loaded pen on the diagram box writing
n a r r a t i o n

you see not narrator for the reasons just given. The element of manipulation however should not be too

visible, for it destroys the fictive illusion, making the recipient over-aware of a technique at work thus losing eye-contact with the young beardless Marx taking no notes and for that matter with Saroja Chaitwantee. Yes Ali?

Omni scient qui mal y pensent.
Ooooh.
My! That's a terrible pun.
Not when you think about it. I can do more.
So I noticed in your work.
Nominipotent O miniomnipresent narrator with his interdiscoplenary comment hominivorous or deivo

ous consuming his patrimoney.

(   )

Omni rident!

Well now

Excuse me correcting you Salvatore but it should be omnes. Rident omnes.

Well now

Okay okay Herr Professor Ali Nourennin we all know you're a great scholar and I'm only a wog putting in Italian endings. Besides your puns bust the grammar too.

Well now

But you weren't punning Salvo. The pun is free, anarchic, a powerful instrument to explode the civilization of the sign and all its stable, reassuring definitions, to open up its static, monstrous logic of expectation into a different dialectic with the reader.

Oh come off it Al.

I think we'd better get back to the subject of discourse.

Why, wasn't all that stuff you spouted from the same book as the stuff I'm spouting?

Sure. I gave you the bibliography. You're the only one who seems

Well then

Tell me since we're on this, were you working with Francesca? There seems to be a remarkable similarity in your attempts at explosion.

Sure why not? We're all in this together aren't we? There's no more private property in writing, the author is dead, the spokesman, the porte-parole, the tale-bearer, off with his head.

Fine. But wouldn't it have been better to have first given the reader

No. Ideas, and ideas are always words, come out of a mouthful of air, jostling each other, bursting like atoms, or hoops if you prefer, set theory gone wild, and the text slowly forms itself, like a shower of gold in Danae's lap. But even a raindrop has molecular form, and in the puddle it makes a shape.

Why that's beautiful Ali, you should work it into the text.

Thank you Saroja of the Oriental eyes, you are a girl after my own heart.

In my country a girl is a woman at my age.

Is that an invitation my love?

Come my friends, this is getting out of hand, extra-textual shall we say, or extra-classical.

Why sir, it's infectious.

Sure it's infectious. But what about the clarity of the message?

You read what you want into it.

I see. And what do you read?

It's not for me to say, I wrote it.

But the reader is the writer and the writer the reader.

According to his positioning in time and space. You remember what you said about the picture? It's the same. If you come very close you'll see only the texture and the brush-strokes. If you distance yourself a little you'll see the madonna and child. Distance yourself further and you'll see the balance of colours and lines, until when you go very far there'll be merely an oval with a blob off-centre. So with Hamlet you said, or Frye said, if you distance yourself very far you see an open grave, a woman's descent into it and a battle of two men leaping in after her. Then I did it with Macbeth and saw a dripping dagger leading to a circular O around the head and another balance of power struggle to a double death. But the process is infinite I think, within each text there is another text, within each myth another myth. The reader has to be prepared for the undeicidable.

Oh, Ali!

Hmmm. That's interesting, Ali. Opera aperta in fact?

Opera a parte!

No, Salvatore.

I still think the reader should be helped a bit.

No, but he can be prepared, like I said, he's the instrument, you know, it's a motet for a prepared piano.

Ha! Sul piano umano?

Oh, Salvo!

Piano, piano.

Well, to get back to the narrator. Take Pride and Prejudice, which we have been analyzing. What point of view does Jane Austen take? Barbara.

The point of view of a Victorian old maid.

Are you being ironical or have I not made myself clear? And perhaps a little diachronic precision wouldn't be out of place here. Queen Victoria came to the (scrub) throne in

1837

Jane Austen wrote during the Napoleonic Wars, which as you should know from at least the 1812 Overture occurred somewhat earlier. Though admittedly this is hard to tell from the text since the author is not in the least concerned with war. Right, well, to continue

Surely she should have been concerned with war and what about the Revolution don't you think all literature should be engagée?

Oh shut up Jean-Marie your French revolution achieved nothing it was a bourgeois revolution.

Surely you should be concerned with dipping into their minds (gently dip but not too deep) according to varying degrees of omniscience and coming at this point perhaps upon dramatic irony

But why precisely at this point ?

For often the narrator passes from one
floating
face to
another
even
within
one
rectangular space laid out in timetables through which a secret pair of eyes higher up the brow sees great

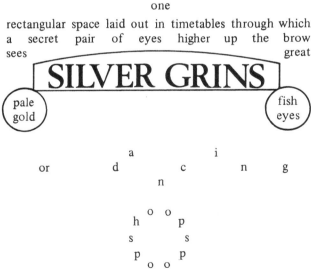

SILVER GRINS

pale gold

fish eyes

a i
or d c n g
n

o o
h p
s s
p p
o o

unless the mirror is moved to the
sudden isolation
of seeing nothing whatever in the
rear
of
the
mind
and
no
narrator at all though this is only a
manner of speaking since the text has
somehow come into existence but with
varying degrees of presence either bent
or gazing into diasynchronic space or

at the chain of phonic signifiers
like Ali Nourennin the beardless
Marx who takes no notes and stares
with riveting eyes that break the
chain asunder with a listening look

But it needs adjusting.

Take Homer for instance through to the civilization of the sign with its dualistic binary structure and its vertical hierarchy which coincides roughly though not by chance with the Renaissance we'll come to that and the rise of the novel of the middle class in layers to the unomniscient unprivileged unreliable narrator in the explosion of the sign at a time still laid out in rectangles into which you enter as into a room filled with nineteen maybe characters into which you enter for that space twelve times a term after which repeat performance with thirty two floating faces of another generation who create anew your psychic invisibility with unrapid eye movements tampering the Message between Emitter and Recipient so that

EMR⟶$\overline{\text{REM}}$ (REM) that do not want to know your true or untrue knowledge of themselves behind the marked portrait you compose in grades of presence/absence competence/performance that makes up the student role they play to the teacher role you play for that space twelve times a term not to mention a few faces overlapping such as those of Ali Nourennin and Saroja Chaitwantee so that you can compose in either case a double portrait.

Alder, Neil	√	$\alpha-$
Brandt, Peter	√	$\beta-$
Chaitwantee, Saroja	√	α
Charib, Vittoria	x	–
Darcy, Barbara	√	$\gamma+$
Faber, Marie	x	–
Fevre, Jean-Marie	√	$\beta-$
Galliard, Robert	√	$\gamma+$
Kaplan, Myra	√	$\beta+$
Jones, Eliza	√	γ
Mandel, Michael	√	$\alpha-$
Newman Francesca	√	β
Nourennin, Ali	√	$\alpha+$
O'Shaunessy, Kathleen	x	–
Polanska, Renata	√	$\beta-$
Stradiver, Paul	√	$\alpha-$
Su Fu, Lin	√	$\gamma-$
Tancredi, Salvatore	√	$\beta-$
Weintraub, Julia	√	$\beta+$

(Portraits by Dr. Santores)

Ali Nourennin however tends to get $\beta+$ or $\alpha-$ in Creative Writing whereas Saroja Chaitwantee gets α in both Creative Writing and The Beginnings of Narrative as well as in Black Literature which triplicates the portrait so that you get to know each year after three or four weeks which face is which, calling them by their names second names first and first names later looking at the correct referent the proper name gradually possessing the long blond hair the short cropped khaki the almond Indian eyes outlined in heavy khol the cherub revolutionary the pale girl's spotty skin the pudgy nose the dark trees thickly falling over the left shoulder silken in sari the fuzzy mop the red beard the horn-rimmed glasses the bright mauve eye make-up the intelligence wrapped in potentiality that you gently dip into and feel for, caressing it with sentences cocooning it with the convolutions of your brain to bring it out in signifying strings foetally modelled on yours and feeding on the corpuscles of your life's unlearning until they flutter out and about the rectangular room for a flash for an hour then nothing, settling on this or that blond or black head or the dark beauty of Saroja Chaitwantee. But we'll come to that.

Surname:	Chaitwantee
First names:	Saroja Sharon
Major:	Anglo-American Studies
Minor:	Information Theory
Course:	The Beginnings of Narrative
Teacher:	Dr. Santores
Other Courses this term:	The Semiology of Mass Media, The Poetry of the Cry, Black Literature, Creative Writing

(Portrait by the Institution)

which she generates out of maxims in the imperative, addressing herself or the Other with adagia like never let yourself be fully known. A fool utters all his mind. When an unsuitable young man proposes and proposes call his bluff and accept, he will soon get cold feet. Yes is for young men. Never let a man see you see through him. Or if by such misassociations when waking by anyone who has sworn eternal love, and thinking in the grey light of the small hours that grip the hole of truth what are you doing here with this sweet empty substitute, let not the day weave again his fantasy into your own so fully recognised, pick up your fantasy and go. Fill the air with quotations, twiddling along the transistor of your isolation, for no man is an island and the isle is full of noises.

BT
a little static - this exercise demanded a narrative link

Peter Brandt also prefers not to assume his I but ineffectively subsumes it in a dialectic of desire to name things by way of action in the second person singular until plural through a haze of heat and sunlight when you take off at dawn racing down to the ocean first to the swanky part then back along the highway to the slum stretch of shore at Las Ondas trash filthy with the sordid motel where you make love till noon then off again along the freeway towards Malibu or maybe into the hills above the chaparral of a canyon or into the desert where the air is hot but soft on your skin and you make love again in the shade of a cactus in flower.

γ+ Punctuation! Too many relative clauses. Some good phrases but evidently too subjective and unassimilated for the 2nd person you assume. See Butor's <u>La Modification</u> for more poised coincidence of Emitter's utterance and Recipient's

While Ali Nourennin plays with literality and other flawed reflections in the grammar of narrative which says the house must be broken into before the robbery can occur or that the introduction of the pistol indicates its later use. But the shot can precede the introduction of the pistol. In the beginning was the parting shot. In some languages moreover things do themselves: tout se passe comme si se hacia ma non si puo dire for es träumte mir. Ça parle. Who then, the Other or the metalanguage?

β+ a bit whimsical – not properly worked out perhaps but has interesting potential

But you don't have the floor it's Veronica's turn.
Who has been waiting a long time.
Who however signifying merely a
                                                  true image
                                                      in a piece of texture
has been removed from the calendar.

E se non è vero
it is well founded like all defence mechanisms

used by the I who loses
to the ϕ me in an eternal game of

v i n c i p e r d i

heads I win tails you lose the trace
the scar
the scare
the scream
the scram
the marks
the skermish

will return for all is marked
remarked
next term as the marked term

Oscar?

They however seem to permutate their loves wholly within the department still undesegmented apparently unable to communicate outside the textimetable and moving incestuously around like a motet for prepared musical chairs bottom-shaped with liftable flaps for right-minded people to fight on, no two fantasies fratrisiding in exactly the same binary arrangement from one term to another which creates a certain amount of tension between Charles Catherine Bob Isabel Oliver Claire Maurice Helen Jeremy Hubert Vivien Olaf Chou and the rest who teach mass media cultural images audiovisual materialism or discourse analysis as subversion of society imperial linguistics and initiation to the black man in white women's liberation shouting at faculty meetings where faculties never meet even on an imagined curve or even as an audiovisual illusion of a coherent structure diminishing in size

about
this
like
to go on
aberrant
utterly
that it is
of protest
peeches
tall
is

two
item
to
got on
even
haven't
and we
time
wasting
we are
agenda
on the
not even
ich is
fair
diotic
this

thus
the
lanky
hench
man be
traying
a slight
anxiety
about item
two unless
merely a
pretence at
a desire
for
speed

the
real
item
being
hidden
under
any other
business
the meeting
having then
dispersed
he having
raised
the

or
selves
your
sure of
so un
you all
tion are
indigna
why this
anyway
performance
again it's
etence
comp
oh

idi
otic
affair
in the
first
place
it is a
demential
proposition
that this
should be
posed as a
question
of
comp

too
it
know
dents
stu-
the
tent and
compe-
who is not
who is and
we all know
Besides
what?

If
we're
going
to take
student
mythology
as criterion
we're building
our house
on quick
sand
s

by
not
chers
tea
ing
look
best
by the
courses
choose
students
know
we all
talk
and

as
he
passes
a hand
swiftly
through
his soft
brown
hair
Thus

As
a
mid-
dle
aged
man I'm
glad
some of
them are
perverts
then

buil
ding
our
house
on
quick
sand
s?

Oh
no
real
ly!
This
is
too

Oh
sh
ut
up

O
r
d
e
r

r
d
e
r

Yes well very briefly I simply want to remind the colleagues that this idiotic affair as Julian rightly calls it arose out of the question of recruitment, which is on the agenda. And the real protest is about this curriculum vitae which has been waved at us like a white flag but which none of us has seen, in other words as usual a candidate is being foisted upon us whom none of us knows anything about but with whom we shall have to work—and here we touch again on two other major problems, that of desegmentation and that of syllabus reform, both incidentally on every agenda since the beginning of the year if not longer and always put off under pretence of more urgent business until there is no quorum, which urgent business is also the ostensible excuse for a rapid pseudo-solution of problems at the end of every year before everyone goes off on their jamborees.

Aaaaaaaaw.

and for the rapid foisting of this or that candidate every time there is a vacancy

Hear hear

nor does there ever seem to be any rival candidature, as in other universities which get two or three hundred applications from all over the world for any one post, indeed by the time the post is legally advertised it has already been privately filled

𝄞:No, boo

𝄢:hear hear

I demand therefore that as from and including the present instance the whole department should be entitled, in a new, radical, democratic university such as this

𝄞:ha ha

𝄢:hear hear

was intended to be, the whole department should be consulted and entitled to examine in advance copies of any Curriculum Vitae.

Name:	Homo Scholasticus	This portrait
Place of Birth:	Ur, Urania	captures
Date of Birth:	Mid 4th millennium B.C.	nothing
Education:	Athotis Preparatory School	either
	Memphis	being a record
	Nebuchadnezar Public School	not of brain
	Babylon	drain into
Universities:	Bamboo Script Writing School	feelings of
	Hao (Shenxi)	futility nor

Rome Alma Mater
Athens Academia
Iona School of Democritus
New World University

Degrees: of Presence

Teaching Experience:
Baghdad (Creative Telling)
Athens (Dialectic)

Megaros (Eristics)
Alexandria (Bibliography)

Bologna (Logic)
Syracuse (Rhetoric)
Cambridge (Mass. Information Theory)

Paris (Disputation)
Heidelberg (Hair-splitting)
Dublin (Nail-paring)

References:
Professor Philanthropos
Professor Semeiosis
Dr. Sophisto

of running
twice as fast
to remain in
the Place of
Birth but of

bare

results exact
replicas of all
such records
with minor
variations such
as Subject of
Thesis
Object of
Antithesis
Subject/
Object of

Synthesis

Nor

for that matter does it mention Larissa
who is the second person singular
keeping her I

So that today we shall try to work out a typology of digressive utterance by a narrator like Tristram Shandy who inscribes himself into his text as subject struggling with various levels of his own discourse. But is he not also an intransitivitised subject walking through the inaction with indirect objects only or none? Every structure presupposes a void, into which it is possible to fall, rehandling the signifiers over and over into acceptability, itself subject to memory and constant mutation as the subject-actant undergoes its transformations, each level of utterance generating another. This is an ancient technique, derived perhaps from agglomerated tales, you know, ten a day for a hundred days. You remember that 12th century Georgian romance we read, The Knight in the Tiger Skin, where each character has to tell his story—after much coy resistance–in order in fact that Tariel's quest may proceed. But as we saw the motivation can be reversed, Tariel being a passive and extraordinarily helpless hero who lets his friends hunt the heroine for him, in order that each story may be told. The initial story of the knight is practically forgotten. Better known and more significant is Scheherezade, whose very life is to narrate and whose narration gives her life, with every new character in the same situation, not a character but a tale-bearer, whose life also depends on his narration generated by the surplus value left over from the previous tale and itself generating the next. Read Todorov les hommes-récits on this. Each I leads into another I, unless I into O for Other interruption with a point of information?

Of course.

Oh no! Go away take your politics elsewhere we want to work.

Let them speak at least, it's a free country.

Who sez?

Go ahead please. In this text everyone has a voice.

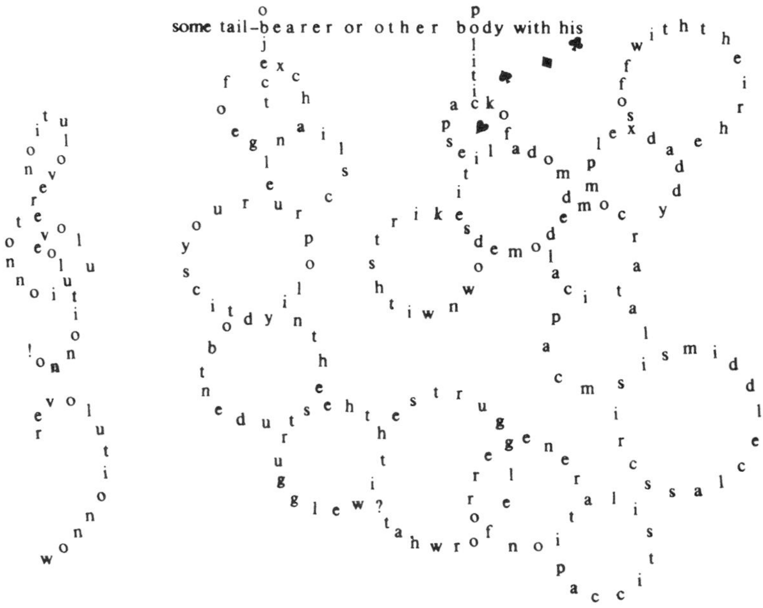

Brother I thank you well as you all know some of our comrades were arrested in the demo yesterday and we have called a strike of all

Who's we?

A majority of over a thousand to sixty-seven at the General Assembly.

Okay and there are over fifteen thousand students in the university

Yeah and where were they? If they're not concerned with the iniquitous situation resulting from authoritarian decrees in a society which serves only the interests of capitalism

Cant!

and conspicuous consumption

Go consume yourself

hear hear

them out they're right

Who sez?

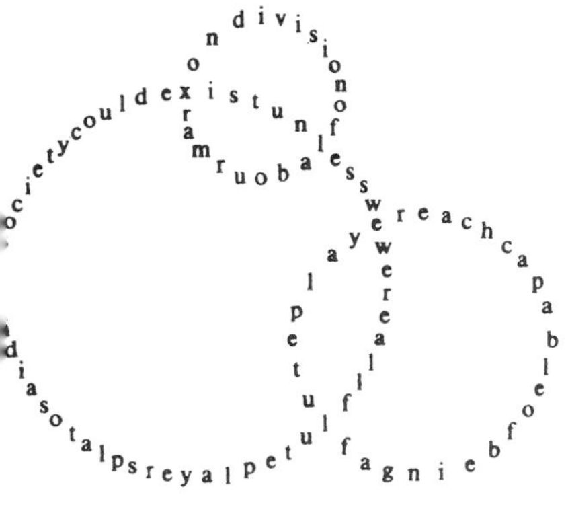

why this flight my friend?

o

cantabile pp

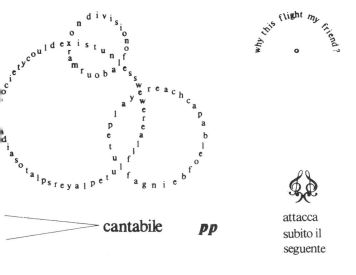

attacca
subito il
seguente

The problem is then for the narrator to get back to his initial subject, if he wants to of course, as clearly Tristram does, and on his own surface structure assumption that his Life and Opinions are his subject. Now:

Supposing you had started telling a story, which digressed into another and yet another, how would you go about returning to the first unfinished story? You could work back towards S, here, through other digressions, in a wide circular pattern, so. Or backwards through the same digressions, like returning through the same doors, so.

Digression in fact, has the same structure as any action or adventure. As when you have followed one character and want to return to another. You remember the guinea-pig simile in I *promessi sposi.* No? I have it here I will read it. I have often watched a boy (a dear little fellow, almost too high-spirited then, really, but showing every sign of growing up into a decent citizen one day) ((uuugh)) busy driving his herd of guinea-pigs into their pen towards evening, after letting them run about free all day in a little orchard. He would try to get them all into the pen together, but it was labour wasted: one of them would stray off to the right, and as the little drover was running about to get it back into the herd, another, then two, then three others would go scurrying off all over the place to the left. Finally, after getting somewhat impatient, he would adapt himself to their ways, and push the ones nearest the door in first, then go and get the others, in ones or twos or threes, as best he could. We have to play the same sort of game with our characters; once we had Lucia under cover, we hurried off to Don Rodrigo; and now we must leave him to follow up Renzo, of whom we had lost sight.

A quaint long-winded way of expressing the linearity of the text. And a false simile if you think about it since characters do not run about like guinea-pigs when abandoned by the author but remain suspended in a fictive illusion to be recreated by flashback more or less well camouflaged.

Camouflashback.

Who speaks then, Tristram Tariel (or Manzoni or Chota Rustaveli or Queen Thamar?) Lending his signifiers to a character who does not exist but nevertheless switches on the overhead projector to draw rewrite-arrows or transformational trees of embedded digressions or maybe rectangles with a spirit-loaded pen thus not losing I-contact through to the convolutions of twenty-seven brains he dips into and caresses with a point of interest built up at the flick of a switch into a diagram of digressions like doors leading into one another then scrubbed as soon as copied down to be replaced by a neater and more cryptic formula where S for Subject somehow via S^1 (S^n) is rewritten as O for Object, o^1, o^2, o^n.

Oh.

Or you could simply leap back, either without signalling, or using a phrase like to return to the subject of discourse, to return to our hero, or the old standby of adventure stories: Meanwhile, back at the ranch. Though that's naive and clumsy, and in a way cheating since you've given the reader a certain peculiar pleasure in frustrating his vulgar desire to know what happens, and that pleasure should not be dropped too brutally, leaving him hungry for it. On the other hand the vulgar desire to know should be kept warmly floating in his mind. He must not be allowed to forget the hero or whatever the initial subject was. The two pleasures, the intellectual pleasure in your game, and the curiosity, should be skilfully balanced, you should build in him a sense of trust, so that he feels you know what you're doing and abandons himself to your wiles. You keep both pleasures going. Do you follow the principle? Yes Barbara?

If the author has lost all authority like you said about the omniscient narrator how can he build up a sense of trust?

A good point, and the subject of our present analysis. But you're putting it a little too simply perhaps. The author has lost authority many times in the history of narrative, when one type has consumed itself, the element of manipulation becoming too visible thus destroying the fictive illusion, and no-one has yet come along to renew it, usually, as here, reconstructing it by perpetual destruction, generating a text which in effect is a dialogue with all preceding texts, a death and a birth dialectically involved with one another, but this is another problem. We'll come to that.

Ali Nourennin makes a brief phenomenological analysis of narrative time, bringing in Heidegger, Husserl, and Hegel's revolution that has been long preparing out of archaic flaws in the dialectic of change, raising antinomies of action that surpasses the subjective idea and renders it objective so that man realises retrospectively that he has accomplished more than he desired and worked at something infinitely beyond him. Are you already practising the art of digression Mr. Nourennin?

So that you could work backwards towards your main subject through other digressions, unless you simply leap back and say but to return to Larissa, though that would be rather clumsy and in a way cheating since you have given many women a certain peculiar pleasure in frustrating their vulgar desire to know what happens inside you, and that pleasure should not be dropped too brutally, leaving them hungry for it. The two pleasures, the pleasure in your game and the curiosity, should be skilfully balanced which is the work of a lifetime. You should have given her a sense of trust, so that she could have abandoned herself to your wiles in keeping both pleasures going. Do you follow the principle? The principle being that you do not follow the principle, you separate yourself from it though you remain good friends and write fairly constantly leaving the door open onto other doors as you drive away into the night twiddling along the transistor and watching the luminous colored hoops dance in the bluish rectangle that reflects the rear before you.

We'll come to that.

Meanwhile in Philadelphia

Let the shot precede the introduction of the pistol.

And if one settling a pillow by her head should say That is not what I meant at all That is not it at all, fill the air with quotations for the aisle is full of noises where angels fear to tread nel mezzo del cammin because I do not hope to turn again where the lack of imagination had itself to be imagined for a flash for an hour

slipped
out of
the rigid rectangle of time tablet
able to preserve the name of the fa
bled farther law bearer who unab
le to forbear his anger breaks all
eleven commandments (10+1) in the
textual act and brings new tablet
s(Shh) not rEplicas of thE prime uNs

Who is it saying O in the mountain? Putting his foot in it on a Thothday or is it Friday thus introducing a statistically improbable formal order in the general curve of entropy which will however be restablished by the scattering winds, the Noble Savage or the Blue Guitar? See Bibliography*.

*retrogradiens

Wallace Stevens John Dryden Umberto Eco Daniel Defoe Sigmund Freud Moses Ezra Pound Wallace Stevens T.S. Eliot (or Guido Cavalcanti) Dante Alighieri Alexander Pope William Shakespeare Saroja Chaitwantee S. Eliot Snoopy Hegel Ali Nourennin and the occidental discourse of Westerns.

**retroprogradiens

The retrovizor 1001 Nights Ezra Pound Lewis Carroll Robert Burns Lewis Carroll Robert Graves Louis Hjelmslev Ali Nourennin Paul Stradiver oh her Georges Bataille William Shakespeare Jacques Derrida A.J. Greimas Noam Chomsky Plato Ezra Pound the voters Ruth Veronica his reflection Diderot Roland Barthes Edward Fitzgerald Francis Bacon Sophocles W.K. Wimsatt Robert Greene Daniel Defoe Moses Wallace Stevens Sigmund Freud Wallace Stevens the folk Barbra Streisand Jesus Christ Frank Kermode Jacques Lacan Denis Diderot the Institution Ezra Pound the chairman of the hour Jeremy Roland Barthes Francis Bacon Jeremy Armel Tzvetan Todorov e.e. cummings the short plump demagogue Bertrans de Born James Joyce Wayne C. Booth Homer Roman Jakobson Julia Kristeva Ali Nourennin et al W.B. Yeats Northrup Frye Umberto Eco John Cage Jane Austen a Victorian old maid Julia Kristeva Dr Santores the Institution Saroja Chaitwantee Traditional wisdom Gertrude Stein William Shakespeare Peter Brandt Christopher Isherwood Ali Nourennin Anton Chekov the chairman of the hour hagiography Armel? the lanky henchman Julian Claire Oliver the chairman of the hour Charles et al Homo Scholasticus Laurence Sterne Choto Rustaveli Scheherezade Tzvetan Todorov the Student Body Karl Marx Plato Tristram Shandy Alessandro Manzoni thus meeting up with the occidental discourse of the Western.

Who is it?
Hello, Ruth?
Armel! Hi.
Hi.
Er And to what do I owe the pleasure?
You haven't had it yet. You free right now?
Honey you all right?
Sure why?
First time you've rung to say that usually it's me.
Well there's a first and last time for everything.
What, what do you mean Armel?
You alone?
Yes.
Send him packing I'm coming right over.

Armel that's not fair you never no never two nights running but never regular nights either so she never knows where she stands I never know where I stand what do you mean stand on this rather hastily remade bed I guess it's difficult to lie, naked, even on the phone with a naked man beside you.

Oh Armel that's a lovely pun you kill me I just can't be angry with you.

Why the hell should you be I'm the one who's angry who was he anyway?

Are you, Armel?

Answer me.

Nigger bastard.

Oh no don't you misuse the code now we're not in an erotic situation.

Aaaaren't we Arme-e-e-e-el?

No   damn you   Jewish slut

Nigger bastard decoding brown into pink mouth four eyes aslant black white limbs winding in and out over and under each other vertical horizontal diagonal swiftly changing positions swaying undoing and floating up every ninety minutes or so under loaded lids for a shared who was he anyway was he white was he any good?

Armel! You, jealous?

No. Just, outraged

What the heck's the difference?

in my mythical aura. What's the big idea telling me all those dreams if

Oh come off it Armel you're the one who insisted no regular petty boorjwah arrangement no planning and that all spontaneous like and you never ring and half the time you're busy and I'm just crazy for you so what can I do the night after's the only night I know you're not

Okay okay was he any good?

What d'you think after just now?

So? Why then?

You don't understand a thing do you. I promised not to fall in love not to make scenes and complications casual you wanted it so okay casual it is that cuts both ways or are you for the double standard you male showvinist and black at that. And you treat me like dirt at best a mildly amusing air-filling sex-object and make me pursue you well I'm a woman and okay I can pursue and be turned down and all but only up to a point so when a goy-boy crazy for it won't leave me alone and begs for it and turns up at all hours of the night not when I'm here he doesn't okay so he's selfish too and assumes I'm always available and so I am thanks to you and he comes too quick and goes and he's only using me to get confidence so's he can pass it on to the fresher flesh of little girls less good at it than me and I teach him plenty and say in effect go forth and multiply I have no illusions but for the moment he pursues me and I like it see?

She cries her black hair over her white arm.

Abstention. Refusal of votive offering.

Do you always make love in your watch?

Yeah. Just like you always take yours off. I love you Armel I'm sorry.

Have a puff.

No thanks finish it.

I never noticed.

What?

Your watch. Funny that. Like Gulliver.

Gulliver. Who's he when he's at home?

Precisely at home. Couldn't stand the human smell of his wife after living with talking horses and fell into a swoon, for two hours he says, implying that he looked at his watch as he went down. There's empiricism for you.

Oh very signif I'm sure. The man always takes his off, pretends it's out of time I guess so it doesn't count.

I just don't want to hurt you.

You can say that again. The boy left his behind once I was idiot-happy about it till I remembered a big middle aged man at the office I was crazy about he's left now, a cautious pussy-cat wouldn't make firm dates either not like you though just frightened so he'd wrap it up in vagueness I must protect myself he said like I was going to eat him.

Eurilochus.

I'm what?

Nothing. Something Larissa said once.

Clarissa? Who's she when she's at home?

No one. Someone I used to know.

You never told me about her.

Go on about the middle-aged man. Did he take his watch off?

Course he did. And he left it behind once together with his fountain-pen or was it a biro that dropped behind the bed and I took'm to him next day and teased him what would Freud say to that I said and he looked kinda sore and took'm and walked to the door and just as he opened it like he wanted everyone to hear he turned round and said he'd say I suppose that I'd spent the night in your bed. Annoyed? I was parannoyed. Well I mean I wouldn't have minded if he'd come out with it quick as a flash like you would adding maybe elementary my dear Watson like Freud was Sherlock Holmes but it was more a doubletake, slow and heavy, jocular and kinduv friendly you know on the surface but supercilious really and with the door open so's anyone could hear. I lost him soon after that. I always lose my men just like I'll lose the boy and I'm losing you. So how can the watch mean a damn thing?

You read what you want into it.

Oh yeah?

You know very well, Ruth, that everyone, you, me, anyone, gets the treatment they ask for, they unconsciously want as you're so fond of saying.

Yea, sure. So?

Jewish slut.

Nigger bastard.

Myra Kaplan
Second Semester
Exercise: dialogue

Comments by Dr. Sartores

α –

Thanks for special space! More than most have. As realistic dialogue this is well observed – or, I hope, imagined – and well handled. The narrator could in fact disappear entirely though you've woven him in quite well. But the disguised comment at the end is too much like a 'moral' and a bit bathetic.

Well at least it has got the elements of narrative moving a bit even at the cost of the bathetic fallacy filling the heremeneutic gap but, on the other hand, enabling the original asymmetrical subject of discourse who does not see the four lies in the retrovizor to be tactfully dropped without scene full of summary, as was forescene she having initially accepted her momentary status. Thus the cost is balanced on the

one hand (left) — other hand (right)

the felix end — justifying the — mean culpa

(though of course when the account is transferred to the viewpoint of the object exchanged the debit goes to the left and the credit to the right).

Either way the economy of the narrative is preserved via the Value theorem of Valincour.*

*Il est temps de rappeller ici que d'excellents érudits attribuent la paternité réelle des **Lettres sur la Princesse de Clèves** non pas à Valincour mais au P. Bouhours, S.J.**

** portrait of the paternity of the Value theorem by Gérard Genette***

***Boohoo to paternity S.J.: in the interests of narrative economy and of abolishing private property all plagiarisms will presently be unacknowledged.

To return to the subject of discourse: the arbitrariness (liberty) of narrative is not infinite. The narrator chooses the middle of his sentence (his kernel narrative sentence of course we're not speaking of real sentences) in function of its end

Contrary then to Brémond on Propp's functions who says that although from the point of view of la parole the end of the sentence commands its first words, we should adopt the point of view of la langue in which the beginning of the sentence commands the end, thus opening the whole network of possibilities in which we can then construct our sequences of functions.

Yes there is a contradiction there Ali, quite right. But that was in the beginnings of narrative analysis, I think Brémond has moved on. To return to Genette, the arbitrariness of narrative is its functionality

You said it was liberty

At the beginning of his argument yes. But he too has moved on and we with him I hope. Are you following this?

Liberté, égalité, fonctionnalité.

(Omnes SILVER GRINS)

Functionality, he means, as opposed to motivation, which is an a posteriori justification of the form that has determined it.

I don't understand.

No I don't either.

Well, there's a diametrical opposition between the function of an element–what it is used for–and its motivation–what is necessary to conceal the function. As Genette puts it, the prince de Clèves does not die because his gentilhomme has behaved like a fool, though that is how it seems, his gentilhomme behaves like a fool so that the prince de Clèves can die.

Oh yes, it's like the Knight in the Tiger Skin.

Exactly. So the productivity of a narrative element–its yield or profit or Value–will consist of the difference between Function and Motivation: V = F – M. An implicit Motivation costs nothing and will give V = F – O, i.e. V = F. Neat isn't it?

Isn't he falling into the capitalist trap by using its language?

I don't think so Robert. Literature is an object of exchange, a merchandise like any other, and works according to the same principles of economy, which we might as well understand. As does language.

As does teaching then?

Certainly.

But Socrates didn't take any money as he kept repeating in his apology, contrary to the Sophists.

I wasn't referring to the money exchange, Ali, so much as to the internal principles of exchange with what the receptor is prepared to give and take, not just in money but in effort and reward. You might say that Socrates was selling Virtue, Truth and Beauty etc. in return for a certain ability and pleasure in dialectic. But to return to yes Saroja?

That explanation, I mean V = F and all that is surely itself an a posteriori justification of the narrative and therefore a motivation?

And a costly one you mean? A very good point. But we mustn't confuse the levels of discourse. My function here is not to narrate but to teach, or shall we say I am not a function of your narrative, and we are using a metalanguage, so:

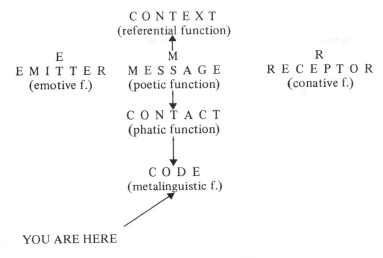

C O N T E X T
(referential function)

E — EMITTER (emotive f.)

M — M E S S A G E (poetic function)

R — R E C E P T O R (conative f.)

C O N T A C T
(phatic function)

C O D E
(metalinguistic f.)

YOU ARE HERE

(Unless you have gotten imprisoned in M)

There should be placards saying: Danger. You are now entering the Metalinguistic Zone. All access forbidden except for Prepared Consumers with special permits from the Authorities.

M-phatically.

And if one settling a pillow by her head should say that is not what I meant at all that is not it at all you can brusquely scrub the diagram and disappear altogether, though admittedly that is only a manner of speaking since the text has somehow come into existence

as an insistant instance

it happened in Europe last summer. I had driven from Strasburg where I showed my passport and car documents at the frontier and then I had a minor accident in

Augsburg having stopped at a stop sign just as the chap behind me didn't. After the usual exchange of insurance identities I drove on across Austria into Italy where I suddenly discovered that I no longer had my car documents so I went to the local police station in the next village and there the Maresciallo Capo Commendatore listened to my story and as he had no assistance he himself typed out the Dichiarazione di Smarrimento quite fast with two fingers. It was taking so long however that I asked him with a smile: "Lei scrive un romanzo?" And he replied with a Latin shrug: "Ma, devo raccontare qualcosa". This amused me very much and seems to me to symbolize all the narrator's problems we have been studying this semestre especially as he got it all wrong saying the smarrimento may have occurred during an incidente stradale in Strasburg which even if he had got the town right was a supposition on his part with no legal validity on such a document in other words pure fiction.

Salvatore Tancredi

Roll on the vacation.
Meanwhile in Philadelphia.

The present tense does not exist Armel, even as I write and your eyes move into the future from left to right (on their two legs 見 like Gulliver on his ladder contraption in Brobdingnag) let alone airmailtime, I'm going to lose a verb there just as you lost a person but never mind (read Hegel on Becoming) that's today's style, no time for belles lettres persanes or otherwise, I mean it's so much easier to ringturn up isn't it. Though no doubt you're doing that, the epistolary novel I mean as per your essay on Time in same which I read, though you still seem to remain in the old dispensation as if Clarissa and Pamela and Mme de Merteuil et al really existed and really wrote (boy in that perspective I wish Pamela could have been dealt with by Valmont–instead of being mere projections with which the reader identifies, the characters ultimately stepping right out of the text–read Rastier on this, most interesting. I ought to have closed that bracket ages ago why not here). No but seriously it's a classic example (the ep.nov.) of the fact that characters also narrate, which has been obvious since Homer but which trad lit critters keep ignoring. Why this flight into platitude? Structural analysis is already out of date, let alone all that stuff about scene and summary point of view and the narrator explicit implicit privileged unprivileged reliable unreliable etc., true of course but quite simply non-pertinent, impertinent in fact since point of view *is* discourse and what matters is⟶are the innumerable and ever escaping levels of Utterance by the I who is not the I who says I (if he does) but you know all that we discussed it. Which is why we have to reinvent it continually, rehandling the signifiers in constant reinvestment. Read Irigaray. And of course we have no surface narrative you and I, Armel, only the deep structures of competence, the show within the show, played out elsewhere, the text within the text which generates another text and so on ad neurotic infinitum.

Why ask what went wrong? If it did that is not an askable question (nor for that matter if it didn't, for opposite reasons). In any case you know part of the answer, at the surface (poetry being surface structure if it is anything, resonant to infinity and for that reason with its deep structure irrecoverable, and those who try to reduce it to deep structure are mere grammarians and drive me bonkers): 'He said "willingly for the tale is short / it was i think yourself delivered into both my hands / herself to always keep" / "always?" the young man sitting in Dick Mid's Place asked / "always" Death said.' But you can make up answers such as you didn't find your ME in me or you kept it nor did I find my I in you but kept it. Why speak of it however? Write your text and reinvent me in the present tense, which is a convention like any other tense. I shall then be different (and language consists of difference!) but from what unmarked term of your binary conception is harder to determine than in mere linguistics. Whoever you invented invented you too. That surely is the trouble, we do not exist. But by all means let's go on pretending we do, going forth and multiplying the letters (Fort/da). I^{I} enjoy your^{n} letters though not your cliché about leaving doors open or was it not slamming them, OK in a letter written during a faculty meeting (very amusing) but avoid in text please.

Larissa my loathing. Who's she when she's at home.

There has occurred however, the darkening of the man at the flick of a dialogue slipped out of a timetable turned smoky grey and even Black Literature to dim the glare of floodlights from behind, although the glare is preferable to the sudden isolation of almost not seeing Armel who is not like that at all but tall and deathly pale with an evasive mouth as described by Veronica and the Other and a brow as high as a sacred belly in the name of the farther the sun and the love that bypasses understanding swinging left out of it beaming ahead transformed into two small red eyes in a huddled shape outlined by forward glare and away into no narrator at all but a lacuna through which it is possible to fall into delirious discourse that does not belong to anyone least of all to any sidelight substitute whose only role is to utter by chance or by neurotic cunning the words of passion for ever unbelieved as deep structures every niente minutes or so but opening up a vast network of possibilities in which we can then construct our sequence of functions.

Are adagia functions?
" " arbitrary?
obituary?
a bit awry?
a bit aware?

Never let yourself be fully known.

Give not your soul unto a woman.

Contrariwise or unwise: There is no fear in love.

Teach us to care and not to care. Teach us to sit still.

And by banal association when waking by anyone who has sworn eternal love and thinking in the cold light of the small hours that grip the hole of truth as it generates nothing but *sentences let not the day weave the other's fantasy into your own so fully recognised, pick up your fantasy and go.

Fill the air from left to right with elements of narrative grammar which does not exist save in mythology which however covers a multitude of scenes.

And when entering into the name of a father as into a secret chiasmus remember that the law-bearer breaks all the commandments in wrath and then brings down new Thoth tablets which may or may not be exact replicas of those in the other scene.

(This in a parenthetic phrase is called the Parent Sinthetic Phallusy)

Those which? Those for. Those against. Abstinence is good for you. Refusal of the goddess by Eurilochus, you know, Canto 39 look it up, I can't explain without sounding like one playing the role of femme fatale but it has its basic truth, he ended up with crabs in his ears, eaten by crabs I mean at the bottom of the ocean for fear of being eaten or merely perhaps changed.

So that the darkening has occurred at the flick of a word or two although Armel is not like that at all but tall and deathly pale with back swept hair over a nominervating intelligence. These things do matter in a text like the human body politic or not, nor does he omnicomment the beginnings of narrative in a radical university which has been dreamt up by the unreliable narrator of the moment who however will be tactfully dropped without scene or motivation. For it is easy enough to find a substitute text such as for instance Greimas on attribution such as a) Adam wants an apple b) Adam wants to be good.

"The introduction, into the superficial grammar, of wanting as a modality, permits the construction of modal utterances with two actants: the subject and the object. The axis of desire uniting them then authorises a semantic interpretation of them as virtual performer subject and an object instituted as a value . . .

Such an attribution–or acquisition, by the subject, of the object–seems to occur as a reflected action: the performer subject attributes to himself, as subject of the descriptive utterance, a value-object. Thus the reflected attribution is only a particular case of a much more general structure of attribution, well known in linguistics as the diagram of communication or, more generally still, the structure of exchange, represented in its canonic form as an utterance with three actants–the emitter, the recipient and the object of communication. Thus the Narrative Utterance

$$NU = F: \text{transfer}\ (E \rightarrow o \rightarrow R)$$

The use of a very general formula has the advantage of allowing us to distinguish clearly between two different syntactic levels: a) the level of the syntactic operator of the statement, translated in a superficial grammar as the subject performer of the attribution (in fact a metasubject and the cause of the accomplished transfers) and b) the level on which the transfers themselves operate. The terms emitter and recipient in fact merely camouflage the distinction.

The second level (descriptive and non-operational) can then be given an anthropomorphised topological representation: the actants are conceived not as operators but as places where the value-objects can be brought and from which they can be withdrawn [so Paul was right about recipients].

The transfer can then be interpreted at the same time as a privation (at the superficial level) or as a disjunction (at the fundamental level) or as an attribution (at the superficial level) or as a conjunction (at the fundamental level), thus representing the circulation of value-objects topologically as an identification of the deictic transfers with the terms of a taxinomic model . . . that is, each isotopic space (the place where the performances occur) consists of two deixes that are conjunctive but equivalent, at the fundamental level, to the contradictory terms:

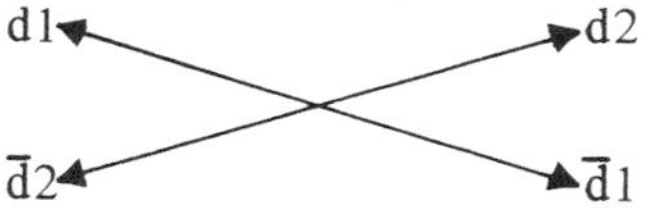

”

(by kind permission of the author)

So far however there are no actant-places except the Other Scene and the Institution of Learning where the old learn from the young and the young learn nothing until suddenly one day they too are old. And even that has just been closed down by an arbitrary act of Authority after serious textual disturbances due to the obscurity of excessive generalisation.

Some universities have large square rooms for faculty meetings with bottom-shaped chairs and liftable side-flaps for left-minded people not to write on a point of information, some have boardroom tables. In some you lecture on a raised dais in an amphibiantheatre to a sea of floating faces rising in waves upward and away, in some you sit ensconced in an armchair protected all around by walls of books, in others you sit on a table among the students but so as to be above them nevertheless and casually chat. In some you peripat along in ancient sunshine (known also as the peripatetic fallacy), in others you walk up to one who sits by the roadside pretending to be receiving wisdom and say you old fool, come out of it, get up and do something useful, you sit on the one and only wooden Chair between St Julien le Pauvre and Notre Dame or is it Ali Nourennin and Saroja Chaitwantee with the students on sacks of straw under a leaden sky. Now and then the mosaic of bent heads breaks and the boulevards which were originally promenades constructed out of demolished bulwarks are bouleversed back into bulwarks again. Other times the bulldozers are content to crash into the timetable. In some actant-places you have chalk and sponge and blackboard to inscribe and scrub your diagrams, in others a roll of parchment from which you dictate figures of rhetoric or else an organ of flash buttons facing glass cubicles full of earphoned heads or an overhead projector and a spirit-loaded pen which you dip into your mind coming at this moment upon nothing at all in the sudden isolation of losing I-contact with everyone except set pieces of masterpieces dying or half dead. There are degrees of presence just as there are degrees of redundancy to save the message from entropy which is the negative measure of the significance of the message. These are familiar rules, made to be broken in an age of transition between evolving permanence and permanent revolution moving right to left from the point of view of the object exchanged.

Order order. You don't have the floor it's Larissa's turn.

I am astounded. I think it is quite aberrant, not to mention confusing, for first year students to be plunged into Generative Grammar in one class and Black Protest or Women's Lib in another. For one thing the Women's Lib lot don't understand a thing about deep structures and are crashing around with destructive naivety but that's a parenthesis Larissa that's not fair. I can't have you will you let me finish please. You are turning this place into a carnival. Well I have no objection it's a mode of perception as Bakhtine has shown, but you should then be aware that carnival has its own structure at every level all taboos suspended all hierarchy reversed and certain very specific ineluctible processes I forebear to mention. There is too, the question of duration. If you know what you're doing, fine, go ahead. But I doubt it. And if we must have this chaotic freedom in the choice of courses let us at least integrate it through psychic structures that we understand. A text is a text is a text.

What on earth are you talking about?

Yes if you're going to hold that kind of discourse please explain yourself.

This is not the place.

The bar functions like a shrug of scorn between signifier and signified for ever eluded and played out elsewhere, in some other class perhaps where revolution that has been long preparing out of archaic flaws in the dialectic of change raises antinomies of action that surpasses the subjective and renders it objective so that men realise retrospectively that they have accomplished more than they desired and worked at something infinitely beyond them, making a turntable of the timetable so that, twiddling along the transistor you dip in but not too deep (but why at this precise point?) where neither workers nor women let alone coloured people have gained anything by so-called emancipation and the double standard remains. Left wing intellectuals talk a lot about making the revolution like it was making love and about destroying capitalism and the consumer society but they don't for all that refrain from enjoying consumer goods or borrowing vast sums at a high interest to buy luxury flats uptown and a country house in the bargain. As Marcuse said even the proletariat has been bribed so that we now have a new proletariat of second-rate citizens since any capitalist society must have a slave population, nor does one notice the intellectuals objecting to that. Or take women—leaving aside the bourgeoisie and their well-known mythologies one finds the very same intellectuals who talk of revolution and endorse black and women's lib having as mistresses young teachers or graduate students who slave willingly, for example at compiling an index for their man's thesis or next publication or typing it. But who ever heard of a man doing the index for a female graduate's thesis or typing it? As for sexual liberty well, the double standard is rampant everywhere one is amazed. If the woman objects she is being hysterical and making a scene. But the man objects in much more fundamental and subtly unpleasant ways, disguising it as highmindedness of some sort. I know of one case not so far away in which a man who lives with a young teacher has installed another, from the same department of course, expecting them to live in love and peace with great talk of communal life and the new ideaology. Fine but when she says OK the same for me he won't hear of it. Where's the new ideology in that? It's as old as sultans and no doubt cavemen. He even has them both working on his Index (laughter) and typing it. The more fool them.

Women in fact have gained all the responsibilities of men and none of their privileges, losing their own while men have lost something too, their sense of responsibility. And that at least was not the trouble in the days of the tyrant father. And even typical psychic castrates like Don Juan and Casanova at least were not hypocrites. In the Don Juan myth—the symbolic structure of which has long ago been analysed as that of castration, that of a man marked with the sign of incompleteness—the hero is at least magnificent to the end and it's the others who are left bathetically moralising by the fire of hell, nor does he treat his women as nannies to solve his problems or as harem-slave-secretaries, though of course his repetitive pattern of continual conquest by means of wild promises is an attempt to solve them at another level, and doomed to failure. But if he's a small winner he's at least a great loser. That's, that's all. I—I meant to develop it a bit more but I didn't have time.

Mmmm. That's, very interesting. There are some good ideas there

Doreen. The – er – levels of discourse are a bit mixed up though, aren't they? What do you think, er, Eliza?

What I mean is, there are several voices in Doreen's essay, and maybe some of them jarr a bit. Now which, do you think, and why?

Come along now, this is a free discussion. We'll leave the facts aside for the moment, but what is it that gives a sort of wrong tone here, not, shall we say, very scholarly or objective?

Well she don' pay no tension to the black people cep for the everlastin white lip-servus.

Right. But then she wasn't supposed to deal with that was she? She mentioned it at the beginning as a parallel, like the workers, but this is on Women's Lib. That's not what I meant.

At all, that is not it at all. Who speaks? Isabel perhaps or Claire who teaches the Inscription of Protest. For the significance of any message is synonymous with its information within a system of probability as opposed to entropy and disorder. But information depends on its emitter so that a message however predictable such as condolence would increase its level of information to an extraordinary degree if it came from the president of the counsel of ministers of the USSR or the Emperor of China, information being related to improbability, which is why modern novels can be so disorientating despite the fact that through this chaotic freedom in the network of possibilities we fill the air with noises, twiddle along the timetable from left to right and back, from one disembodied voice to another on this or that wave-length listening in to this or that disc-jockey and always the same disc-horse, a yea-yea and a neigh inserted into the circuit of signifiers, each discourse penetrating the non-disjunctive functioning of another. And we do not find that concert disconcerting. The greater the noise the greater the redundancy has to be. Go forth and multiply the voices until you reach the undeicidable even in some psychoasthmatic amateur castrate who cannot therefore sing the part.

Ah. A self-evident defence-mechanism against threat of extermination. Why this flight into delirious discourse?

But now it is quite clear who speaks: the man from Porlock. He has been speaking for some time.

He comes, in fact, from Timbuctoo in Mali, half way between the Niger and Lake Faguibin longitude 03 West latitude 17 North. He is slight and mighty, mat brown and dazzling—a chance occurrence yet clearly also generated by anticipation at the flick of a timetable, so that makes everything all right despite the interruption—and the lines of his hands like the skin between the fingers are deadly greyish white because, he says when rudely asked by way of tacitactic diversion, he has been cleaning something with a strong detergent. He is cultrate and cultivated, ebullient and bullying, censorious and sensitive, tactless and tactile (tu me le paieras ce maudit portrait) from which several facts you will have gathered that he is a writer.

Do white writers then get black lines on their hands when they clean things up?

Of course, look.

That's ink, too much.

Et pourquoi haïssez-vous les portraits?

C'est qu'ils ressemblent si peu, que, si par hasard on vient à rencontrer les originaux

Don't tell me you belong to the critical school that ferrets around seeking Dorothea's husband and the model for the Wife of Bath?

Who's Bath? Do you mean Barthes?

The bell rings. The pen is put down in mid-sentence

which one?

Guess. The eye is put to the judas-eye

you mean the trait-or master of the moment I mean the markster of the comment who dreams things up?

and there he is, curiously foreshortened by the lens, carrying five books, including one of yours foolishly loaned on a pressing request

do you mean one of yours or one of mine?

I didn't know you'd written any I mean one of yours I speak in the second person

which means one of yours why don't you say so

I do if you will allow me to proceed

proceed

The moment of hesitation passes, the door opens

on its own?

in some languages things do themselves

aha! l'amor si fa?

that is not what I meant at all may I for Chrissake bring this person in who is as I have said, a man.

Well if you put it that way get on with it, there can be no breaking in before the breaking of the lock no wonder you call him the man from Porlock.

There are times, Jacques, when the recipient should be shot right out of the message he makes so much noise.

Ah but where would the message be without him that's why redundancy was invented come to think of it it's easier for the emitter to disappear if things do themselves.

So far there is neither emitter nor recipient within the message, only without, thanks to you.

All right silence pax proceed hands across the sea

Hello.

I want to talk to you.

Fine beginning I must say
I wither him with a look.

I'm writing.

I know.

I'm seeing no-one, I don't answer the door.

The door hasn't said anything, and you have answered.

Well because I knew you knew I was here and I didn't want to offend you.

She who explains herself is lost. May I come in?

She?

Yes, you gave me an idea.

Ah.

Well, yes of course, what er can I do for you? Would you like a drink? Have a cigarette. Or some coffee or

No no sit down. Give me your hand.

Why?

I want to talk to you

Can't you talk without touching? What about?

Well of course about your book which I have touched handled read look I have taken all these notes.

But I only gave it to you a couple of hours ago you can't have read it.

Ah the vanity of authors. I am an author.

So I hear, and very successful.

Oh that, I don't care. Give me your hand.

Look, I only met you this morning

You mean there is a timetable in white society for hand-holding?

Well yes. I didn't even properly catch your name.

Armel.

What?

Armel.

Oh.

And yours?

It's on the book and on my door.

Ah but it might be a pseudonym. Larissa. That's nice. Larissa Toren. It almost sounds African.

Please, I'm in the middle of a sentence

which one?

I've already forgotten it thanks to you. Tell me what you want to say.

A great deal. It will take a long time. Come and have a kous-kous with me.

I'm sorry I've already eaten and I'm working.

Not now you are not.

Please say it now then.

Why this flight?

What flight?

That's what I asked myself all the time while reading your book look I have made notes. The publisher says it's very funny. He's mad.

That's not part of the book don't you know what a blurb is? The publisher says that to sell it and you're quite right, he fails. It has nothing to do with the text.

Ah. In my countries publishers tell the truth.

I didn't know you had publishers there aren't you published in America?

We don't, that's why they don't have to lie.

Hmm. So you don't think it funny?

Ah that hurt did I? Of course it's not funny you are weeping all the time it is one long cry of anguish.

Oh?

This woman for instance she says page 143, no, it's somewhere else, well never mind what I mean is there are moments when you touch on the very essence of things and then brrt! you escape, you run away into language. You are merely amusing yourself and I want to know why.

You mean that when I touch on the essence of things, in that text, it's not by means of language? What is it then?

There you go again, playing with words. Why this flight?

Into logic? Look, this is ridiculous, charming but ridiculous. Aren't you playing with words too, doesn't everyone?

Not me. Give me your hand.

No. So. I'm weeping all the time and yet I'm merely amusing myself. But isn't the only thing to do with a long cry of anguish to amuse oneself? In my country we never separate the two. I take it as a compliment. But you seem to utter these phrases as reproaches.

No, no, please do not take offence. Ah writers are so sensitive, I know, I am sensitive and now you are treating me as a person of no sensibility.

Oh come, we're both above exchanging hurt sensibilities.

That's better. Come, give me your hand.

No. Why do your hands have white lines?

Don't yours? Show me.

No.

Yes they have. See?

They're not white, they're beige, same as the hands, a bit darker if anything. Whereas yours

I have been cleaning something with a strong detergent. This is my natural colour, here, look.

What do you do when you write?

I use language, yes, I admit. But directly.

That's an old illusion. But I didn't mean that, I meant, do you cut yourself off?

Cut myself! Oh you mean, oh yes, completely, I rip out the telephone and see no one.

Well then can't you understand

But I want to understand that's why I came. Here you give me this book

because you happened to be at my neighbour's whom I happened to see on the stairs and who happened to ask me in and happened to introduce me to you and happened to insist that you should read one of my books

that's a lot of happening it must mean something

on the contrary it's a string of chance improbabilities. A terminal string.

and I happened to come up and want to discuss it with you so that you will perhaps happen not to take this flight any more

which is likely to have the opposite effect. Listen, you're very nice but I wrote this book ages ago it's dead and gone for me. I know everything that's wrong with any book I write by the time it comes out. I am now in the middle of another and to hear anything at all, for or against, about an earlier one is simply imp–non-pertinent, irrelevant I mean. But the interruption isn't, it could block me for days.

Ah, you see, you do care.

As you care about success.

That's a completely different level.

It isn't what you say it's the fact of interruption. A friend from Morocco turned up the other day

my country is near Morocco. There is only the whole of Algeria in between.

and I couldn't not see him. It was delightful. It took two hours. I lost three days.

Because that was real. It takes a lot of trouble and concentration to construct your escapist edifice.

Look, er, Armel, you're very perceptive, but you're not the only one to say these things you know, I've heard them before, many times.

You see. I'm in the majority then.

The majority doesn't make the truth.

A reactionary into the bargain.

Don't be silly. You think you know me from quickly leafing through a book.

I have read it all from cover to cover. And taken notes.

The majority also prefers platitudes. And I'm sick and tired of this one about language as an escape from reality. Language is all we have to apprehend reality, if we must use that term. And I notice that when people talk of reality they usually mean sex, with them.

Now Larissa Toren author, that is naughty, you are jumping to conclusions, I was referring uniquely to the communication you had with your Moroccan friend. But here you are putting delicious ideas into my innocent head.

And if they don't mean sex they mean communication. As if communication wasn't language.

Yes yes my dear but what language? I brought these other books to show you: here is a best-seller and sometimes you write like it. Sometimes however you write like this one, here, which is, look, I took all these notes.

All discourse is the return of a discourse by the Other, without whom I am not, but to whom I am more attached than to myself, I say I but I mean everyone, all of us, nor can I proceed to the identification of that I except through the medium of language.

There you go again.

Why do you suppose patients talk, and write? Why did the silent movies have captions? Why does teaching continue through books and dialogues and not simply by means of gestures and diagrams and experiments in glass bottles?

Well they do seem to use more and more diagrams but that's precisely

Why for that matter did you come up to talk if it wasn't to use language about language?

To go beyond your book.

to undermine it with other language, and that's fine, you have every right, everyone has a right to subvert any text with any other but now

and to hold your hand

well and so you have. And now truly I must put you out and get on with my work.

You are escaping again. All right you are the host I must submit. You know there is an ancient Peruvian subsitute for writing by knotting threads. It is called Quipu.

Sauve qui peut then.

Ah Larissa Toren author come give me a kiss.

No.

Larissakissammmmmmmmmmmmmm.

That's enough. Now please be a good boy and go.

And when can I see you again? Will you come and have a kous-kous with me?

Bang–bang?

Excuse me?

I'm sorry but I don't like kous-kous.

You don't like kous-kous!

Well it's too greasy for me I don't digest it.

I'll have something else for you then. What do you like? When will you come?

Next winter.

You are mad. I shall not be here next winter.

Too bad.

I mean now please Larissa Toren author surely you have to eat sometimes?

I'm sorry. In any case I'm expecting my husband any day, tonight perhaps.

You have a husband! Ah well, now I understand everything.

Good. You might have found that out from my neighbour. Goodbye. Thanks for calling.

Which could be called society as a subversion of the text, if it were not itself textual.

You see even the hands were unnecessary in the portrait.

Jacques my friend you must help me. Certain problems have arisen.

Yes master?

Well, first,

Oh no master, not that firstly fourthly on the one hand small a small b stuff I can't take it in. All right at faculty meetings but not when I have to participate.

Okay scrub it then one equals zero.

Please master what is the problem?

I'm just telling you. To begin with, I mean, sorry scrub that. Thanks to the man from Timbuctoo it is clear that Larissa is producing a text. But which text? It looks mightily as if she were producing this one and not, as previously appeared, Armel, or Armel disguised as narrator or the narrator I disguised as Armel. That's not very clear.

No it isn't.

Of course she may be producing a different text.

She may indeed, master.

That's not very clear either.

Perhaps not.

But you see what follows from that?

Not quite yet master.

It means that the narrator I transformed into Larissa am no longer your master but your mistress.

Master! I find that most offensive. I know that we quarrelled at the inn, but I made you agree afterwards that all our quarrels were due to our not accepting the fact that although you were pleased to call yourself and I was pleased to call you the master, I am in fact yours. And when you asked me where I had learnt such things I replied in the great book, which seemed to settle the matter. But no great book could justify, in our long relationship (which I may remind you includes the story of my loves, much interrupted but otherwise normal and healthy) no great book as I say could justify the imputation you have just made. I beg leave therefore, although it breaks my heart, to part company once and for all with one who

Jacques, Jacques, stop that. I didn't mean it literally.

Literally is I hope precisely how you did mean it master.

Jacques! You are a genius. Of course it was literal. A question of textuality.

There you go again.

Heterotextuality of course.

Eh?

It was a manner of speaking.

And a very strange manner if I may say so.

Well let's forget it there are more important problems than my change of, I mean thirdly, no I mean, to get back to the subject of discourse, this woman Larissa has not only usurped my place as narrator, which apart from putting our relationship in danger

you said to forget it

I placed it in a parenthesis–poses other problems. On the one hand, I mean for one thing her mental diagrams may be a good deal more complex than mine, but that's my problem, and on the other she has also acquired a sudden husband as a last minute escape.

He could be a polite lie.

Yes but he could be vero, no?

A husband is always, from a woman's point of view, ben trovato.

You are speaking like an eighteenth century man-servant.

Yes I am. And you are an eighteenth century gentilhomme.

But in the late twentieth century, Jacques, women have been liberated, as you heard, and it is therefore only a man's archaic viewpoint that his name and person are the greatest boons he can confer upon a woman.

Ah.

Oh don't start that A E I O U business again be articulate this is serious.

Yes master.

Of course her husband if true would have to be Armel

But she's only just met him and told him

no that's a coincidence. They do happen despite the critics.

I don't think so. You know my answer to all our problems, which has given me my surname not your surname your epithet

if it is written above

that's striking below the belt

if as I say it is written up there that we are to quarrel again, and make it up again, and have sexual problems

textual

textual problems that tie us up in knots like er Quipu, then it is also written that knots are meant to be either disentangled or cut.

Jacques what would I do without you?

That's what I said at the inn. And before you opened the door into the narrative.

Not only are they meant to be disentangled they are themselves meaningful. Decipherable.

Oh decisively.

Of course her surname is different. For you may not have noticed that she has acquired a surname from the book he was holding. That's no problem in the twentieth century though. But it's oddly close isn't it? Toren, Santores, why, it's part of it! And that's why they write letters they're separated-but-very-good-friends.

Well didn't you know that? It's the only thing which is clear, the epistolary novel is always crystal clear people will explain themselves. But what about Armel?

Yes, that doesn't quite fit. Moreover her mental diagrams seem to be also a good deal more complex than his, though his emotional ones seem more complex than hers, which is perhaps the trouble, but poses another problem if she is inventing him, and even more so if he is inventing her. Still, we'll come to that. As to the first name, well of course she could have changed whatever original name she gave to the man she was inventing, maybe it was Marco or Stavro, hence the confusion of brows hair and height at the beginning, and given him the name of the man from Porlock, I mean from Timbuctoo.

I don't follow.

To get something out of the interruption if only an unusual name.

You said women don't want a name from a man in the twentieth century.

Oh for fictional purposes yes.

Ah. I mean, so nothing has changed then, in the twentieth century?

That's the whole point, you see, out of the zero where the author is situated, both excluded and included, the third person is generated, pure signifier of the subject's experience. Later this third person acquires a proper name, figure of this paradox, one out of zero, name out of anonymity, visualisation of the fantasy into a signifier that can be looked at, seen. You should read Kristeva that's what she says. Though we mustn't forget that in the grammar of narrative the proper name coincides with the agent. In this way the construction of a character has to pass through a death, necessary to the structuring of the subject as subject of utterance, and for his insertion into the circuit of signifiers, I mean the narration. It is therefore the recipient, you Jacques, or anyone, the other, who transforms the subject into author, making him pass through this zero-stage, this negation, this exclusion which is the author. I am in fact dead, Jacques. Oh, he's asleep. What a pity. Everything is becoming clear at last. God! No! Yes! Quick, pen and paper

ARMEL SANTORES
LARISSA TOREN

Yes! It figures. So that's why she said about Armel not finding his ME in her and she not finding her I. Why the names are anagrams. Except for ME in hers and I in his. Am I going mad? Help! I should have stuck to pronouns as in late twentieth century texts which refuse biographies since a name must have a civic status. In the pluperfect. Or a camouflashback pluperfect. That's the rule. Written up there. In the grammar of narrative. Like attributes–states, properties and statuses. Iterative as opposed to actions. But any agent can enter into relationship with any predicate. The notions of subject and object correspond only to a place in the narrative proposition and not to a difference in nature hence no need to talk like Propp et al of hero villain lawbearer these are predicates. The agent is not the one who can accomplish this or that action but the one who can become subject of a predicate. Hence only proper names, not substantives, though of course there can be duplication as when three brothers or robbers accomplish an identical action they are syntactically speaking one agent just as two lovers can be temporarily united in one proposition. So there have to be proper names after all, Jacques, Jacques why are you asleep?

No, no master, I was listening.

Jacques. I am going to break all the commandments.

Oh good. When?

Well—tomorrow. First I must sleep. Undress me Jacques. I'm very very tired. Dead in fact.

Yes master. Come, your redingote. There. Now let me unbutton the waistcoat. One, two, three, four

oh make haste Jacques.

Well there are a lot of buttons. There.

That's enough I'll sleep like this I'm falling already

But master, your jabot, your boots Oh Lord he's off. See you later I-narrator. Here we go, left foot, yeeeeeeeank. Right foot, yeeeeeeeeank.

Mmmmm. Sing me a lullaby Jacques.

Anon anon sir. Ahem.

> Rock a narrator
> On a phrase-top
> When the verb blows
> The tree-structure will rock
> When the noun breaks
> The tree-structure will fall
> Down comes the noun-phrase narrator and all

into an idyll

and about time too

the happiness sequence with lush screen music running in the woods along the rippling brook fresh green fresh no that's for toothpaste or mentholated cigarettes or deodorant through a haze of heat and taking off at dawn racing down to the ocean first the swanky part then back along the highway to the slum stretch of shore at Las Ondas trash filthy then to the sordid motel where you make love till noon then off again along the freeway towards Malibu or maybe into the hills above the chaparral of a canyon or into the desert where the air is hot but soft on your skin and you make love again under a shadeless Joshua tree.

But within every idyll there opens out another idyll as in a vast mouth that never names the secret chiasmus in the name of the farther place.

Inside the mouth a camouflashback. Christmas time by an open fire in a fashionably beamed cottage. Six people, three men three women. Close-up on heroine sitting pale and dramatic her square face curtained into an oval by thick straight black hair parted in the middle almost meeting in well-trimmed curving points under the chin, underlining the distinct large mouth, touching on either side the edge of huge dark eyes themselves heavily framed in khol like those of Saroja Chaitwantee who however has a dark oriental beauty a quiet voice a modest manner and retains her mystery. The heroine is not like that at all but transparent deadly white and wears as the camera-eye travels down lovingly an elegant sea-green velvet trouser-suit close-fitting and low-cleavaged at the top three buttons undone to reveal pale lace under apple breasts when leaning forward to ask with childlike wonder in the huge dark eyes do you believe in the existence of God? In an elegant trouser-suit calling out in Shot 5 close-up of Armel pale and high browed a privation (at the superficial level) or a disjunction (at the fundamental level) as well as an attribution such as (a) Adam wants an apple (b) Adam wants to be good (at the superficial level) or a conjunction (at the fundamental level) so that God thus summoned as subject of discourse now exists (Shot 6). In an elegant trouser-suit.

She is not like Larissa at all or Ruth or Saroja Chaitwantee. Shot 7 Larissa watches, bored, the imperceptible shrug of scorn functioning like the bar between signifier and signified for ever eluded played out elsewhere yet ineluctably played out right here in the beginning as a parting shot

8. Close-up of Christopher Masters unmasterful long-haired but thin on top frail slight cowed in a winged armchair and pulling at his earlobe. This shot to be cut in at various points in the sequence. Shot 9. Another man, the host, filling glasses, handsome, silver at the temples, a professor perhaps or a publisher. Shot 10. His wife archavid out of Who's Afraid, watching Shot 11 et seq but seriously do you? I do. When I was a little girl with rapid eye movements (dialogue can be easily improvised out of seduction clichés and mystical maxims such as there is no fear in love in order to find your true Self the lower self must die which the recipient in the present instance is clearly meant to translate as O felix culpa in the presence of the divine I say O in the mountains which means O felix culpa etc). As they speak Armel uttering the maxims Shot 12 with a devouring yes-tell-me expression that lights his voice and eyes into what is your sign? No don't tell me, Gemini Shot 13 but how did you know (R.E.M.'s) I guessed (Shot 14 continues with R.E.M.'s and illustration) from your gestures hands eyes ways of talking you're

very interested in art aren't you? Why yes I work with art publishers I've always loved art even as a little girl (R.E.M.'s) so it must be true then. Can you interpret dreams too? I had such a strange dream last night I was in a huge tiled room on the edge of a small swimming pool and out of the pool there was an arm sticking out (rappel: shot 8) and I was trying to pull it out but it wouldn't come. And suddenly it did and I become a sort of bird, flying around the room unable to get out. What does it mean Armel? Puzzlement all round the publisher's wife archavid out of Who's Afraid of Sigmund Freud. It's a very poetic dream Veronica you have a poetic soul the arm is Excalibur and the bird the eternal spirit you see she sees and rapid eye moves.

So that is what went wrong, plunging into the dimension of banality. But no. Shot 26 Larissa purses an oddly prim mouth and shrugs, separating signified from signifier as God the lower from the upper waters or Freud the latent from the manifest, and within earshotful of sirensong a shot, a mere assassination or tearing off of orphic limbs as declencher of world conflict that has been long preparing out of archaic flaws in the dialectic of change, raising antinomies by action that surpasses the subjective idea, is the parting shot, rendering it objective, here on the ocean edge by the fireside, in an elegant trouser-suit sea-green with deep cleavage revealing apple-breasts laced in foam emerging like a trace in the memory and beckoning, naked, sprayed with the froth of stars and the existence of God as a seduction gambit in words Fiat Deus and there was love, each creating the other as Chronos created the phallus-girl cut from Uranos approaching the earth's open legs and tossed into the sea so that man realises retrospectively that he has accomplished more than he desired and worked at something infinitely beyond him like love out of revenge for the death of love.

Man advances staggering through regressions. Says Larissa (Shot 42).

The other eyes reflect nothing, and when the shoulders move back to the correct position in the armchair the image vanishes. In any case God as signifier is non-specularisable and cannot see himself signified except by a hidden representation of a representation. You should read Lacan.

This is Larissa's parting shot in the battle of books versus God as conversation gambits hiding the representation of another battle from which she withdraws into tacitactic defeat, back into the back of her creator's mind where she talks to her publisher, waiting strategically to re-emerge one day, fully armed, after a Trojan disc-horse war, content merely to send Hermes the swift-footed to Calypso's island or to appear disguised as Mentor on the lone sea-shore.

Neil Alder

α *Very good. I like the mixture of kinds, though you seem to forget about the film-script half-way — unless it is your intention to show that written narrative can perform some things the film cannot — Will discuss it in class (who, incidentally, is Christopher Marlowe?)*

Meanwhile.

Her creator works on the idyll.

Which is always a mise-an-abîme even though it occurs on the crests of amorous euphoria

slipping into another timetable through an open mouth full of stars art history and the existence of God in her open convertible (Larissa having insisted on not sharing the car with the ghost of an icon) and away in oleander on hills, the great St Gabriel range behind them overlooking the downward terraces trucked out in layers for low-roofed dead suburban villas and the bridge to the clapboard shacks and Mexican white houses of cracked stucco under a forest of aerials and beyond that the metropolitan sprawl that is eating up the plain, the ranch-lands, the orange-groves, spreading north and south in a death-crawl from which it is dying of the greed that made it and beyond that the bay out of which she came and the distant cliffs of Palos Verdes. Away above the chaparral of a canyon and into the desert where the air is hot but gentle on your skin, hungering between the accolades of breasts and hipbones each pointing to a mouth that grips the senses and old idyllic sentences such as your eyes are a bucolic entertainment your voice that of a shepherdess singing in green pastures your scent of musk and cytrus *i* fruit your thighs those of the Syracuse Venus under eyes devouring the inverted accolade that points down again into one word zero.

Peter Brandt

β- first paper, though you are repeating earlier pieces and much of the landscape is stolen almost verbatim from Isherwood.

And I shall teach you another alphabet with which it is impossible to write anything except love and laughter 'Ay for 'orses Beef or Mutton See for yourself. Devolution Evolution Effervesce into peals of mirth. It works all the way from alpha to omega into which you plunge with a spirit-loaded pen floating up every nineteen minutes or so for slowed down eye-movements under electroded lids and a shared Elf of gnome Emphasis Envelope O for the Wings of a Dove. O for a beaker full of the warm south tasting of Flora and the country green. Not Flora, me. Yes, you, V for le roi E for lution R for eedom is a noble thing O for the wings N for lope I for Novello C for yourself A for 'orses. And I shall spell you in the stars A for Andromeda R for what there's no R. Let's say R for Aries. Why R for the Ram! M for Mercury E for I don't know oh yes Earth we're a planet anyway. You're mixing stars and planets galaxies and constellations who cares L for Leo and Love. V for Venus and Vega E for Earth R for the Ram O for Orion N for er nebula I for what, I for Icarus a falling star? C for Centaurus Coma Capricorn Cygnus goodness what a lot of C's why don't astronomers distribute the stars better and finally A for Aquarius. I shall spell you into the sentence I speak into the paragraph into which I insert my you the sentence I speak. Thus you spell her to your image out of the stars and when the Pleiades come down to rest sow thou thy seed the I subsumed in the dialectic of desire yet growing big with adoration for a hero must have adoration out of which you form her to your image of an iotaboo like the existence of goddesses naked under elegant trouser-suit sea-green and laced with foam cut by time out of sky in coitus interruptus with earth's sacred belly and dropped into the ocean as a phallus-girl no one fantasy coinciding in exactly the same curve of time never quite meeting other curves along the canyoned thorax like a bladed rib kept back or withdrawn once long ago into a creature made to man's desire but somewhere along the sequence slipped out of his optical illusion to become a person in her own right wrong. Was it awful?

Yes. Was it nice?

O for the bathetic phallusy of words that fear to explode into the other place at a mere touch since in every idyll there opens out another idyll, lost, as a vast mouth opens, never naming the secret chiasmus the signifying substance which once upon a spacetime is accidented as the idyll of Armel and Larissa poem not couple.

Hmmm. That's interesting Julia, you've used the given elements very well and introduced new ones. Where did you learn that alphabet?

Oh in London, as a child. It's an old thing, my mother taught it me. You can tell it's English and old on account of A for 'orses and Ivor Novello. I couldn't think of a more modern Ivor except Ivor Winters and that seemed a bit too specialised.

Well considering you quote Hesiod via Pound and we've used almost everything from Phaedrus to Freud you shouldn't worry. After all it's our text, isn't it, for us only. I see what you mean though. How about ivory coast?

Gee yes, that's much better, with the sea symbolism and all.

I see you change the referent of the you at the end. Do I take it she's imagining the whole thing?

Could be, or passing from one to the other it doesn't really matter. He's gone off for a weekend you see and I wanted the shock of ordinary language in a conjugal state of tension at the end.

I see. Well, what do the others think? Shall we discuss how to proceed or do we have more to say on Julia's piece?

Well actually I worked with Salvatore, not with him I mean but we divided the sequence and I told him where I'd leave off and he's gone on from there.

Fine. Well Salvatore we're all agog.

Ahem. Julia's going to read Larissa as I've done the beginning all in dialogue and it'll be clearer. Okay Julie?

You know these weekends are always awful. There's the ridiculous aspect, you trotting off with your little suitcase or like this time shouting for your clean pajamas which I'd put in the machine with the others by mistake then of course going off without (laughter, smirk from Salvatore) and returning asking was it awful.

But there's also the degradation.

Oh don't start

But I want to understand. Why? You've always insisted on a rigid structure, no invasions from outside, we were a poem not a couple, no criss-crossing social foursomes with wife-exchange and the usual hypocrisies.

Well I've CHANGED.

Don't shout. Yes you have. But into what?

I don't know. I'm in a crisis help me instead of going for me.

Oh it's not the thing in itself that's banal enough it's the contradiction, the principle being that you don't follow the principle

Shut up you bitch you castrating bitch.

So that's where we've got to.

I can't stand this pressure, from both sides, all this drama why the hell can't women accept their respective positions the mistress wants to be a wife and the wife a mistress oh don't start crying again for God's sake.

You always said

always said always said well I don't say now

that I didn't love you, because I, didn't, feel jealousy whereas, you, did. Well you've succeeded, now, if that's, what you, wanted.

Lara stop this.

But why, Armel? You've said yourself you don't want to marry her, or live with her, and it's only, an obsesssion

Well you've had obsessions too.

Yes but they never went, that far, and you made me pay my God you did, and I always stopped, when I saw, you were hurt, so I suffered both, the detach, ment and your, punishment, you'd go off for, days, and nights, whereas

Please stop this hysterical rewriting of history.

But what do you want?

Ah! che vuoi? You made me read whatshisname, go and look at that skull-like diagram of his with che vuoi, a diagram of psychosis as you should know.

You're cruel.

Stop forcing me to choose. Try to understand.

I'm trying. But you're destroying me, my image of myself I mean, as, reflected, by you, that's what I can't take, the way, you're doing it. You know, all the things you said, what I was, to you, and now, it seems I've been, the castrating female, all along, and you've kept it, bottled up, instead of, talking to me, telling me, guiding me, on the contrary you've, pushed me, into that position, by always asking me, my advice, in everything, never taking, a decision.

You're contradicting yourself too you know. You always stopped your infatuations dutifully, you complied with the rigid structure I imposed yet I pushed you into the man's role. That's your version. You just won't see mine.

Well tell me then if I'm so stupid.

Perhaps I am trying to tell you something, and this was the only way. I love you Lara.

I don't, believe it. You wouldn't do this to me, and in this particular way, so crude.

Perhaps the only way I said.

You asked me a question. Yes, it's awful. You've finally succeeded in making me feel jealousy, by first destroying me verbally, so that I have no resistance, I imagine the whole thing, the whole time, morbidly, bisexually, I am her and I am you. It's horrible. And it needn't have happened that way if we'd had a more comprehensive structure, from the start, as I wanted.

But you never—oh I don't want all these recriminations, it all goes back too far and there'd be no end. We're in a crisis and we're going round in neurotic circles. That's the way it did happen, let's stop talking about it. But I understand. What you're going through. I felt your presence.

Oh go fuck yourself.

The fall was into language. Until the next time when you say you felt her presence she says I wasn't there I was with someone else. But bumping into us all the time out of psychic inevitability she says or is she spying obsessionally? As if the enormous sprawl of city eating up the plain were not large enough to contain the three of us. Well if you will canoodle in public so she toots by with a friendly wave which upsets Veronica and makes you furious well what else could I do coming upon you like that I couldn't back in that street everything I do is wrong recrimination or smiling by. Until she drives away into the night, twiddling along the car radio filling the air with disembodied noise that penetrates other noise like redundance busting the curve of entropy and always the same show, watching the dark magician as he juggles his logic into luminous coloured hoops dancing in the bluish rectangle that reflects the rear ahead.

Hmmm. That's

I haven't finished. And the hoops reiterate set circles of dialogue like why Armel I want to understand it's so against your own well I am Italian no sorry I meant to cross that out Well I can't explain. It's a terrible force, a mystical force (that's because we brought God into it you see). Something happens to me, it's like drugs, or Zen, a kind of Nirvanah, from the sheer time of it, the duration. What do you mean? A sort of divine emptiness from sheer repetition, like ritual, well, you can't go on for six hours can you?

Is that the end?

Yes.

Some guy. Go forth and multiply the multiplicator.

Ma, devo raccontare qualcosa.

What do you think?

2300–2400
2400–0100
0100–0200
0200–0300
0300–0400
0400–0500

Saroja?

I don't know. The tone kind of drops. It sounds too personal. Would Larissa and Armel behave like that, or talk like that?

Well would they? What do you think, Myra?

She could be sort of two people. I mean highly intellectual women can drop to the level of women's magazines when they're upset look at Simone de Beauvoir. And that increases their agony they kind of watch themselves doing it. And Armel who's been very poised so far, almost too much though I guess that was my fault sterotyping him into an old-fashioned casual cad well he could have a hidden violence men do you know which comes out, like hers, in a fury of vulgarity.

Sure, but somehow that's not quite rendered here. Saroja raised two points which are really in contradiction, the tone, or what we may call the literality quality, and the realism or plausability. You've neatly explained the former by the latter but it doesn't really resolve the problem, this being a text not an imitation of life. Michael?

I feel there's an awful drop after Myra's piece and Niel's I mean there the castration theme we've been studying in Hawthorne remained on a poetic level as a symbolic structure whereas here it comes out as a private and crude matrimonial wrangle.

Yes well I said it's a neurotic situation and the fall was into language.

Yes but what language? It was a nice phrase Salvatore but it doesn't quite get you out of it as author. Yes Peter?

Well I think it's crazy people just don't talk like that any more I mean they don't feel like that any more in an age of intersexuality they make love and that's that. Marriage is only a human institution invented to protect property and it's an outmoded institution.

Ali?

I agree about the non-literality and the modalities of thought and passion being archaic in fact the two usually go together. But I feel a bit sorry for the poor man who's being trapped in his own very human condition by her ruthless yet selfish logic, for all her unconvincing sobs, a mere matter of inserting commas. You married Salvo?

Well, yes.

I didn't know that Salvatore, though I might have guessed by now. Is your wife Italian?

No, English.

And that's part of the trouble is it? Have you been married long?

Seven years.

That's a lot for a student. You must have married very young.

Yes. I worked my way into college. I have a beautiful bambino.

Well you seem to have crowded in a lot. But we won't go into that. Shall we accept this instalment or let someone else have another go?

Let's put it to the vote shall we. Those for. You can vote too Salvatore. Those against. Abstentions. Any refusals? A show of hands in the secret ballet of the I upon the sacred belly of democracy okay then I'm sorry Salvatore, who would like to take it up from where Julia left off? Renata. Right. Then Saroja. Fine.

For since we have slipped from proper names and textual idylls into the realm of impure fiction with biographies and camouflash-backs, things being given a local habitation in the hills under the sun stolen from Isherwood the ocean on the blue guitar the citrus fruits stolen (out of a letter from Marco or is it Stavro who misspells citrus with a y) as one might steal a dream a maxim or maybe a nose or brow to generate a text full of guinea-pigs who do not exist except in a theory of the sign that has no reference in reality then why not organs? Has La Gioconda a liver? Valéry asked. Well she looks as though she has unless it is the patina of time, reformulating the poetics of the Renaissance and deforming Aristotle as when we say we know the characters of Shakespeare Balzac Dickens Racine as characters of flesh and blood. They are our brothers. Yet the representation is always double read Rastier on this. Sometimes it is real and wordly sometimes mental, and in any case unequal: in some respects less than life since any structure presupposes a void where the liver should be for instance or excrement or a hole within a hole such as thyroid deficiency; and in others more than life, more than plenary, a surfeit that makes Silas Marner more real than all misers, Rastignac more real than all ambitious men, overtaking their time as eternal truths both universal and particular, both simple and complex, denying both historicity and the materiality of the text. Which is why on the one hand allegory causes difficulty in this humanist theory which rejects it as bad while, on the other, historical characters too must be avoided, they have too much dead weight to become eternal truths. But structure has its reasons that realism knows not. See that article on Gombrowicz in your bibliography.

And if these characters are men of flesh and blood they must therefore have a soul and the soul has passions. So that we must study the passions that enflame the soul of Cleopatra. This is a seventeenth century concept for the notion of passion has disappeared. And this passion must push to extremes, become transcendant, provide references in the before and after. But, note well, we do not in fact attribute a body to these characters, and this despite all the later vogue for detailed physical description. Hence the dis-illusion when we see them on stage or screen. It is better to fantasise them than to see them. This is Rastier's view. You may not agree and we can discuss it. Thus, he says, the hero slips out of the text, establishing a specular relationship with the reader and away from the author in an eternal mechanism between the reader's demand and the author's gift of the character. The humanist theory has all the beautiful coherence of a psychosis: castration is at the basis of this enjoyment, Lancelot giving more pleasure to the ladies than any real imparfit brutal knight after the jousting without deoderant under his armour removed in a damp northern castle. He is a phallus detached from the totality of the text and walking about the world as hero. Yes Ali, on transcendance.

But who invents Larissa? A man, probably, suffering from anorexia in slow fluvial eruption, one flux catching up with the previous that continues nevertheless into his thirties forties or more somatic symptoms so that particles of food unbroken up by enzymes get lodged somewhere and toxic and he lives on a slop diet highly deficient in protein with the I subject to chemical disintegration in the dialectic of desire, these being mere iterative attributes which explain his passivity his depressions his outbursts of destructive violence his evasiveness and his inability to shut jars without opening them again to see if they are shut. And doors of cars, and doors. Hamlet has long ago been analysed, Don Juan has been analysed, Tristan Lancelot and Faustus who do not of course exist. For although it is arguable that any language which ascribes sensations and thoughts to persons will necessarily identify them as embodied persons the argument is itself a fiction. You can however reinvent them. Nor has he told–if he is telling–that Larissa is in the habit of having rotten organs removed all over the world, dropping an appendix in Sicily a kidney in Piscataway a gall-bladder in Gaul a thyroid gland in Thailand a womb totality in Utah leaving a chasm of pain and illness after sex and a hormone imbalance which subsumes the I as subject to chemical disintegration in the dialectic of desire, these being mere iterative attributes which explain her activity her depressions her outbursts of destructive violence her non-evasive articulateness her slamming of doors and wishing they were open with emphasis, envelope, O for the the wings of a dove.

Tea for two, euphemism, vive le roi, double you for quits.

For the alphabet the stars the zodiac and the gods are at least as old as the idyll of Armel and Larissa poem not couple which begins with swift-footed Hermes.

Dear Mr. Santores,

This is a fan-letter. I am working on a structural analysis of

your poems. I want to meet you may I? I have a lot of questions. I am flying over on 22nd but going straight on to Europe as there is no one else in New York I want to see. Please let me know if you'll be there and wherewhen. Looking forward,
Yours, Larissa Toren.

Dear Miss Toren,

I am so sorry we missed each other. I waited till seven but had to go out. The cab-driver must have been very stupid for my street though small is not so hard to find (that's a stilted pentameter). Of course if I lived in Manhattan it wouldn't have happened as it's all rectangles. Perhaps you would like to put your question in writing and I'll do my best to answer them, though I realise that's not the same, and I must admit I dislike answering questions in writing, there never seems to be any way of answering as there is in conversation, it all seems so black and white. I shall however be coming over to your part of the world for a year in September and I hope we may meet then.
Sincerely, Armel Santores

The golden gate to the paradiso terrestre the hills under the sun the ocean the vineyards and the c(y)trus fruits or is it the other place where invention grows out of letters following one another from left to right in childish characters that reflect a round pretty girl with soft round hair and unaccountable glasses. It's marvellous Armel this sparking of ideas by air across a continent: 'yours are the poems i do not write'. I love you already, intellectually I mean don't get alarmed I love your work your words and find your name in them paradigmatically I'll show you. My thesis is almost finished. Do you know our names are near anagrams? Looking forward yours ever Larissa.

Who is not like that at all but tall and dark with hair drawn tightly back and an iconic nose no glasses but eyes dark-framed and painted all around like those of Isis or maybe even Ra. These things do matter in a text like love and three beautiful illegitimate children by a man she refused to marry why do they always want marriage why marriage? In the immortal words of Louise de Valmorin nobody marries nowadays, only a few priests are thinking about it. Well I am a prêtre manqué Larissa. Manqué or marqué? In this day and age when we know that the object is from the start an object of central loss. He was called Oscar. Interesting isn't it. He scarred me with his zero oh that's not worthy of you Lara my love I know I fill the air with minimal narrative units from left to right or vice versa. He was not Odysseus the voyager through flux but Eurilochus. Eurilochus? Oh yes you know, Canto 39 I can't explain without sounding like a femme fatale you'll have to look it up but it has its basic truth. He ended up as a crab or something no at the bottom of the ocean eaten up by crabs which comes to the same thing for we can't eat each other without becoming each other can we. Let the phallos perceive its aim. I love your head Armel you have the most beautiful head. Like Beethoven. In fact I think I love your head more than anything, and all that's in it. O Salome do you want it on a platter then?

He was the unmarked term I mean Oscar was you've done linguistics haven't you no well you must every poet must it's wildly poetic, the binary polarity in any field phonic or semic but in fact much more complex one can do an elementary diagram of contraries and contradictories look white versus black or white versus non-white. But that's logic it's as old as Socrates it comes in the Protagoras. Oh does it? How wise you are Armel you must teach me. But linguistics is logic of course it seeks the fundamental patterns of thought below the surface structures. Take sexual relationships for instance, prescribed versus forbidden, say incest, horizontally, here, prescribed versus non-prescribed, diagonally, so, such as in our culture female adultery, then the other diagonal forbidden versus non-forbidden such as male adultery you see the double standard is useful even in semiotics the vertical relationships being implicit. And you can superimpose any other system the economic for example here, profitable, non-profitable, harmful, non-harmful you see female adultery coincides with non-profitable and male adultery with non-harmful so that on any one axis sixteen differently balanced or unbalanced relationships are possible and if you superimpose yet another system say individual, desired non-desired feared non-feared there must be sixteen times sixteen I haven't worked it out. Or take a simpler system traffic lights for instance, green versus red or green versus non-green, that's amber. The amber operates on both axes I suppose but with a different meaning non-green or non-red. Except at night when it functions on its own flashing on and off without taboo, and all you need is care and courtesy. It works all the way from semes to narrative structure or myth. Maybe it's the grammar of the universe or do I mean universal grammar. Though I'm also beginning to suspect structuralism. Maybe I'm going beyond it as I went beyond Oscar. It has its limitations yes he marked me with his zero, which is also the other.

But it needs adjusting.

Like a bluish rectangle into which you enter as into a room saying once upon a spacetime Larissa is a little girl. There is a photograph of a soft round pretty-plain creature in glasses ill-fitting cardigan over a blouse and string of pearls and soft round hair with two small children and a baby as if their maid and you dip your eyes into hers within it to feel for the potential beauty and bring it out in amazement. It has to be first imagined to be true yet not by you by Oscar perhaps the unmarked term who nevertheless conjures her as Ra, teaches her to dress to slim to wear contact lenses paint her eyes read learn live but not to love. Unless she has carefully reinvented herself for you or some other. A dompna soisebuda composed of femme-reine, femme-enfant femme fatale, grey eminence Cleopatra's nose Musset's Muse a bit of Heloise old and new the charming scatterbrain Georges Sand Mme de Merteuil George Eliot Antigone Elizabeth Barrett Browning Elinour of Aquitaine Mrs. Pankhurst Circe Julia Kristeva Joan Baez Penelope Virginia Woolf Helen of Troy la princesse lointaine Scheherezade Pallas Athene la belle indifférente the man with the blue guitar

The dance of the twenty-seven veils

The airy fiery ro$^{l}_{b}$es thickening to slow but articulate fluvial eruption one flux catching up on another that continues nevertheless until some swift earthquake for a flash for an hour crumbles all the structures if any either way the narrator could step in and say some years later or meanwhile but that is rather clumsy leaving the recipient-emitter-actant-place frantically signalling into the wings where no one gets the message. No of course I am not a structuralist I never have been I merely played with it besides one has to pass through it to understand modern linguistics. Generative grammar's

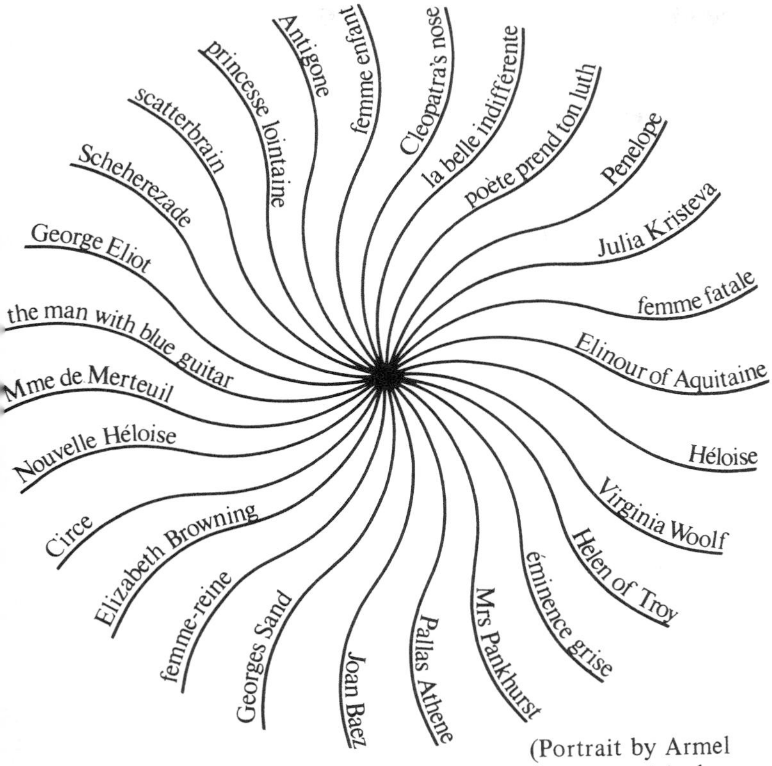

(Portrait by Armel from an original creation by Larissa)

the thing it's the grammar of the universe and it's wildly poetic why they have rules called it-deletion and psych-movement subject-raising and object-raising and head-noun-chopping can you imagine the object of central loss being raised read Hegel on Aufhebung it becomes wildly funny. Though the object is not obligatory of course but like a request stop according to supply and demand however inexhaustible in a consumer society and in any case ever escaping like the signified. Some subjects are intransitivised and walk about the world like stray phalloi detached from the totality of the text.

So far however there are no actant-places except the other scene and the institution of learning where the old learn from the young and the young learn precious little until suddenly one day they too are old.

We'll come to that.

Meanwhile, back at the other scene.

Armel works on the idyll. Or rather on the bucolic pastoral as opposed to the rustic.

The invariants found are

1) the place, which becomes no longer Arcadia as in the classical pastoral but simply the anti-town, the hills, the country.
2) the rustic love-song manifest through fixed motifs such as the boastfulness of the shepherd, the burst of anger with invectives the exchange of gifts and the comparisons taken from rustic life to comment the girl's beauty.
3) an equivocal use of pastoral and agricultural terms for sexual ends.
4) the display of visceral organs overflowing from excess of amorous anguish.

Having laid out the alleys and determined the streets, we have next to treat of the choice of building sites for temples, the forum, and all other public places, with a view to general convenience and utility. If the city is on the sea, we should choose ground close to the harbour as the place where the forum is to be built; but if inland, in the middle of the town. For the temples, the sites for those of the gods under whose particular protection the state is thought to rest and for Jupiter, Juno, and Minerva, should be on the very highest point commanding a view of the greater part of the city. Mercury should be in the forum, or, like Isis and Serapis, in the emporium: Apollo and Father Bacchus near the theatre: Hercules at the circus in communities which have no gymnasia nor amphitheatres; Mars outside the city but at the training ground, and so Venus, but at the harbour. It is moreover shown by the Etruscan diviners in treatises on their science that the fanes of Venus, Vulcan, and Mars should be situated outside the walls, in order that the young men and married women may not become habituated in the city to the temptations incident to the worship of Venus, and that buildings may be free from the terror of fires through the religious rites and sacrifices which call the power of Vulcan beyond the walls. As for Mars, when that divinity is enshrined outside the walls, the citizens will never take up arms against each other, and he will defend the city from its enemies and save it from danger in war.

(Portrait of the town and antitown by Vitruvius)

And if it is written up there by the narrator(s) that the shepherd shall boast in the antitown with mercurial exchange of gifts and display visceral organs then so it shall occur even though the narrator(s) may withdraw at last into the proepigrammed arbitrariness of a vacation, paring their fingernails. At which point the shepherdess's adoration would necessarily be tempered with a new anguish at the shepherd's obstinate refusal either to marry her or to live with her in an unpastoral pastiche of marriage (as he puts it, firmly keeping the fane of Venus outside the body politic), an anguish that might veer into jealousy or is it outrage as to what prevents him, given all that adoration given, however, only as a terminal string of symbols or object of exchange in a rewrite derivation where the object is raised to become subject of adoration which has to occur before the passive transformation into a sort of bird flying around the room unable to get out. For although the mise-en-abîme is eternally a mise-en-scène, syndiachronically orgyanised into a spacetimetable of yes your reference I'm coming to that erogenous zone in the sixth hour which is the work of a lifetime enclosed and isolated in a Silling Castle behind great bridgeless canyons, there is no promotion from object to orgyaniser no liberty for the victim of the libertine despite the undoubted fact that within the grammar of that narrative the roles can be interchanged and textasy multiplied until punctually at a fixed hour all the forged orgy ceases. For the deep structure of I am your slave is undoubtedly you will be mine and yet there is no transformational rule in any grammar which explicitly effects this since it is written up there that all deletions, reflexivisations dative movements object-raisings and other transformations be recoverable so that here it is merely a question of conjugality which comes under the lexicon and the morphophonemic rules as for example in please don't go Armel it's so nice having breakfast together.

I must go.

But why my love. We're alone. Christopher has gone, Larissa has gone. You're going back to an empty flat.

Precisely.

I don't understand.

You do really.

Perhaps I do. No man can hide a secret even in silence, he will chatter with the dropped parings of his fingernails.

Let's enjoy it while we can my love, don't let's spoil it, it's beautiful.

But that's just why it should last why are you so pessimistic?

What were you dreaming just now do you remember?

No, was I asleep?

Yes, you were muttering.

I wish you'd talk to me Armel.

But I do talk to you.

You know what I mean. Yes, we talk, of things, art and literature and God and dreams and beautiful landscapes and we laugh a lot and I'm very happy then. But you never tell me things, real things. You for instance. What do you really want?

My tie, where's it gone?

There. How long, Armel, how long?

That's what David said.

Who's David?

The psalmist. In Paris, where I lived for some time, the telephone is overloaded, and on international calls one tends to get a recorded voice saying Votre demande ne peut aboutir. Veuillez appeler ultérieurement.

And will, somebody, tell me, why, people, let go.

The shot can precede the introduction of the pistol.

I was quoting Cummings. I like him so much better than Christopher's nature stuff. You opened him up to me Armel and so much else besides and now you don't recognise him.

I did, but why wave quotation marks. I answered with another quotation.

From what?

I forget. Some essay.

Like all your answers it wasn't an answer.

Don't always ask the same question then, Veronica.

I'm sorry.

It's all right. I'm going now. Sleep well my love, have interesting dreams.

Larissa's in Paris isn't she?
No.
Where is she?
I don't know.
You must know.
Stop pressuring me, I've asked you before. I refuse to discuss her with you or you with her.
The adulterer's cliché. Oh Armel don't get angry I'm sorry. I can't stand that terrible glare in your eyes when you get angry you look so different. Forgive me. I just get, very unhappy sometimes I mean I know you made no promises you were quite honest but we didn't know we'd fall so deeply in love that I, would, really, fall so, deeply, in love oh Armel.
Come my little one, my little girl. There. My beautiful one my Venus. Don't cry. Aphrodite never cries.
But couldn't she be happy with you in the orbit of an eye and no reference without? Never let anyone see you see through them therefore
Never let yourself be fully known
Give not your soul unto a woman and yet
There is no fear in love
To adore is to give your soul but: Eurilochus?
Fear is the function of his narrative.
Oh another one who grabbed a balloon and then let go.

These are adagia that function as functions at the level of performance not competence. It is not clear who speaks last, a friend of Veronica's perhaps or more likely of Larissa's, the cases being caught up in the eternal quadrangle or, if you prefer it, which this friend clearly does, two deixes that are conjoined, because corresponding to the same axis of contradiction, but not conforming, and equivalent, at the fundamental level, to contradictory terms:

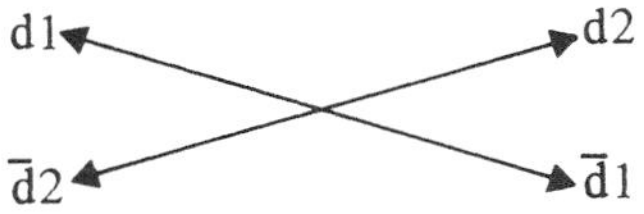

Thus the circulation of values, interpreted as a sequence of transfers of value-objects, can have two courses:

$$1)\ F\,(d1 \rightarrow o \rightarrow \bar{d}1) \rightarrow F\,(\bar{d}1 \rightarrow o \rightarrow d2)$$

which, in the case of the Russian fairy-tales of Propp, can be interpreted: society (d1) experiences a lack, the traitor ($\bar{d}1$) ravishes the king's daughter (o) and to hide her transfers her elsewhere (d2).

$$2)\ F\,(d2 \rightarrow o \rightarrow \bar{d}2) \rightarrow F\,(\bar{d}2 \rightarrow o \rightarrow d1)$$

which means: the hero ($\bar{d}2$) finds somewhere (d2) the king's daughter (o) and returns her to her parents (d1).

And if the king's daughter, settling a pillow by her head or throwing off a shawl, and turning toward the window should say That is not it at all, that is not what I meant at all, you can simply disappear, opening a door into another door, working backwards in a wide circular pattern. Or backwards through the same sequences, which is simply regressive, and in a way cheating, since you have given many women a certain peculiar pleasure in frustrating their vulgar desire to know what happens inside you, and that pleasure should not be dropped too brutally, leaving them hungry for it. The two pleasures, the pleasure in your textual act and the curiosity, should be skilfully balanced which is the work of a six-hour nightly timetable.

	Sceneday	**Mouthday**	**Toolsday**	**Wombsday**	**Circe's Day**	**Aphrodite's Day**	**Sated D**
2300 2400	Initiation I	Initiation II	Initiation III	Initiation IV	Initiation V	Initiation VI	And he
2400 0100	General Method-ology	The text-ual Corpus	The phallus as signifier	Actantial Transfor-mations	The Incrip-tion of Protest	Structure of myth: the phallus-girl	rested on
0100 0200	The dia-lectic of desire	The dia-lectic of desire	The dia-lectic of desire	The dia-lectic of desire	The dia-lectic of desire	The dialectic of desire	the seventh day
0200 0300	Subject Raising	Object Raising	The Passive Transform-ation	Deletion Rules	Recursi-vity	The head-noun chop-ping rule	from all his work
0300 0400	The Act-ant as Place	Man's Liberation	The Poet-ry of the Cry	The Logic of Func-tions	The gener-ation of narrative	The law of Supply and Demand	which he had
0400 0500	The hu-man body as text	Women's Liberation	The en-gendering of the formula	The role of enslave-ment	Eroticism as sub-version	The narrator as Zero	made

Do you follow the principle? The principle being that you do not follow the principle you separate yourself from it though you remain goods friends leaving the door open onto other doors that lead to the other place as you drive away into the night watching the luminous coloured hoops dance in the bluish rectangle that reflects the rear before you.

Don't look back Orpheus don't look back.

DANGER MEN AT PLAYBACK

Meanwhile.

Go forth and multiply the multiplicator.

See you later you-narrator.

But who invents Armel? A woman probably, binary to the bone, who sees herself entire and suffers from all the beautifully diagrammatic coherence of a psychosis when all that is signifiable in her is struck with latency as soon as raised to the function of signifier which initiates this raising by its original disappearance. Unless merely asthenia or cyclothymia, there can be no diagnosis since she too does not exist except as reinvestment itself perpetually reinvested letting S represent the subject of discourse and O the Other place and o the object of desire o^1 o^2 o^n.

On a point of information may we interrupt

Oh go away with your politics we want to work

No let them speak

Thank you my dear. But you brother you will soon be unable to work if the faculties continue on their present trend

We're quite happy about it

What faculties, yours?

And who's we, royal or collective? You little lot here? Caring only about accumulating credits like shopkeepers and acquiring your meaningless little degrees of presence and doctorates of debility to become lacqueys of the bourgeoisie?

Oh not that old playback. We'll have to earn our livings won't we like anyone else, whether we like this society or not, and if we want to change it we might as well understand how it functions.

Oh no my friend that way recuperation lies the bourgeois idyll is over you can't perpetuate it for ever. The revolution is upon us which has been long preparing out of archaic flaws and

Si fa la revoluzione, all by itself.

What's this guy talking about?

Make love not revolution.

Don't worry sister we make both.

Is that your point of information? We've heard it before thankyou.

And you'll hear it again with tearbombs on. Meanwhile there's a General Assembly of staff and students at five in the Karl Marx Amphi to discuss more particular and relevant problems. The reorganisation of the university into a non-segmented and truly revolutionary institution devoted to establishing the truth.

How can an institution be revolutionary?

For it's the protective segmentation that has enabled everyone, after an honest enough start, to fall back into all the old ruts, the hierarchisation of subjects, the dishing out of ready-made culture and all that shit. Apart from that there's the related question of the syllabus-reform the students have been loudly demanding for so long.

Which students? You? Who's you?

The vast majority as you well know.

The loud minority you mean. Everyone knows these General Assemblies are a farce, swayed by a few well versed in crowd rhetoric and ending in chaos, so that the real majority of serious students have ceased to go and the staff knows this and go on exactly as before.

You've hit it on the head my friend. If more people like you came to the meetings we might achieve something instead of this criminal apathy.

We're not apathetic we're diverting our energies into more useful channels.

Christ what is this class? Isn't this the literature department? I thought so. Literature is the servant of the bourgeoisie.

Well maybe we are too literary to swallow your clichés.

What the hell is this reactionary culture you're dishing out to these kids oh my sister?

If you really want to know, textuality as subversion of society.

Words words. Why this flight? Tell us how you go about it that'd be much more to the point.

This is not the place.

No it never is, is it? Hey you with the beard what you studying here come on comrade don't be afraid I won't eat you.

The symbolic structure of castration in The Mable Faun and other texts.

Christalmighty the marble faun! and you think it's with the marble faun whatever shit that is that you're going to succeed in subverting society? Oh brother.

Pooh! You're only acting out. Brotherhood's just another matrix, dismembering the paternal inheritance.

Well said Salvo.

Norman O. Brown you mean. Huh, we've read him too you know but he's on our side, don't you dismember him into yours.

No well I'll tell you something out of my own country for believe it or not I care about these things as much as you do but you're going about it the wrong way. Macte Jovis! we used to say in ancient Rome at a certain festival, kill Jupiter, kill the father, and we still shout ammazzalo! at soccer matches. Keep your violence for those my friend for you too will be fathers and dismembered and ammazzati.

Idiot. Sport is the opium of the people.

Yes Salvo that's all rhetoric, and rhetoric as you should know was born in Syracuse out of a lawsuit over property, not in order to establish the truth but to persuade people of its verisimilitude.

Ali you're nuts how can truth be established it's not an institution?

You're playing with words, Saroja of the beautiful eyes.

Well don't you?

My! This is an interesting little nest of bourgeois ideology. Words words words as the saying goes and as the saying goes it went. Are you coming to the G.A. or not?

To hear more words? Why don't you just blow the place up according to your own principles instead of going through that semblance of democracy that you call General Assemblies?

There follows a test for adjusting your stereophonic equipment. This is the left voice: boom body boom doom. This is the right voice: sham deed ah slam scram. If your equipment is correctly adjusted the sound should be exactly balanced in the centre:

Agitato ma non troppo

The bour-geois i-dyll is o-o-o-ver

pp < *f* < *ff*

Meanwhile the timetable has slipped into the other place, th tale-bearers having on pain of death given birth to other tale-bearer spokesmen of realities that merely seek to appear true, separatin the signifier from the signified the manifest from the latent and th upper from the lower waters of the sky in coitus interruptus wit earth as a death-battle with time for a trophy that drops bleedin into the sea to re-emerge, feathered in froth, the treasurer o signifiers behind which the molecules of water escape back int water that reenters into its own depths, retaining it mystery reflecting at the surface only the sky.

Il court il court le furet
Which way did he go?
Down the hatch, safe
as a jack-in-the-box

Under the expert guidance of the lanky hencheminence grise i smoked glasses

sitting beside — hiding behind

a chiasmus

lying beneath above

some sheik

hiding behind — sitting beside

The short plump pasha $^{\text{in}}_{\text{con}}$ sultan the assembly dressed in democracy (but the emperor's a naked imperialist!) hearer of deep structures below the performance of six hours as summarised in the minutes of the meeting of the permanent committee for the functioning of faculties May 24 at 1400 hours. Questions on the agenda: Statutes and internal organisation. Desegmentation and its consequences. Modification of the linguistics programme. Methods of Grading. Any Other Business.

1. Statutes and interior organisation

Given the importance of the agenda, this promble was postponed. A project of interior organisation will be sent to all colleagues as soon as evolved.

2. Desegmentation and its consequences

After discussion that frequently overflowed the framework of this one point, the permanent committee decided:

1) all sections must provide a regular report of their teaching activities by the end of the first semestre at the latest (unanimously approved).
2) all new projects must be submitted in writing by the same date if they are to be actualised the following September (unanimously approved)
3) the adoption of the following principles:
   - a for orses) every fact of language must be analysed as a global social phenomenon
   - b for mutton) all dismemberment and fragmentation must be avoided between different linguistic exercises
   - c for yourself) so must any segmentation between disciplines taught within the department (linguistics, literature, social sciences).
   - d for lution) the creation of a subcommittee to study the modalities of a possible actualising of the desegmentation of sections (unanimously approved)

A long discussion then opened on two points:

A. Integration of a horizontal co-ordination into the syllabus (principle adopted: experiment limited to three groups)

B. The number of groups thus desegmented to be actualised in September:

Brillig proposes the creation of four groups.

Tove is in favour of a solution which does not fix a priori the number of groups which, in his opinion, must depend on the number of teachers prepared to undertake the experiment.

Gimble is for the principle of integrating into the timetable the hour of horizontal co-ordination in the framework of only two groups.

Larissa Toren is opposed to all horizontal coordination which, according to her, would degenerate into useless chatter.

It is more difficult for a revolutionary trajectory to enter into the I of society than for the treasurer of signifers to enter into the paradiso terrestre.

For as soon as a solution is found in the E for lution of a project there will be a display of visceral organs overflowing the framework of this one point from excess of amorphous anguish in the horizontal coordination of segments.

This however is a Renaissance concept for the notion of passion has disappeared, having become merely a motet for prepared professor, altering his sonority.

E se non è vero, if it has all been dreamt up by the markster of the moment you can always drop into a lacuna, entering a busy beehive through a little hole where you execute a secret ballet with a show of legs and a quiver of wings for a swarm of honeyvorous impulses that palp oscult measure and imitate the message sucking the performer dry with no memory of the fact that the message has been transmitted from generation to generation of an increasing vastness that nevertheless dwindles to a fat queen bhi, quivering now and again in apathy from fear of being

unthroned
undroned?
whose stylus she must cramp
(he is the poet who dies by his pen)

For you are not qualcosa to be narrated by yourself or some other who talks like a book and wants to be read like an algebraic grammar of narrative where the punishment in final position never falls on the euphoric term, always on the dysphoric. Who ever invented you is the absently unreliable or unreliably absent narrator or you in love with him who is in love with the implied author who is in love with himself, so that he is absent in the nature of things, gazing into the pool as the I who wins but loses to the me in an eternal game of vinciperdi or through doors opening on doors, the eternal presence and absence of signifiers that characterizes the practice of language. You are a speaking head on a platter, narrating yourself to an earful of crabs at the bottom of the ocean or shouting in the wilderness with a mouthful of locusts and wild honeybees and blind as well maybe, since eyelessness is not a provisional state but a structure, a blind spot in your own youdipeon discourse and discourse only occurs insofar as there is lack of (in) sight. The fall was into language. Thus even the provisional other is only a verbal icon who carries the image of your head on a piece of texture, a handkerchief for tears a sheet for sweat semen and death, while waiting for the suspended narrative out of your head which will emit the word. Che vuoi? You always get your way in the end, even if it is not the way of your original demand which has accomplished more than you desired and worked at something infinitely beyond you, advancing as you are, staggering through regressions. Votre demande is not an askable question. Veuillez appeler ultérieurement. Freud Freud why persecutest thou/me.

For it is pure fiction and impure fantasy that Armel writes long letters to Larissa or will go on as if. That was a terminal string of symbols or what James calls a ficelle. But there is a flaw in the intensity of the illusion, for which you playing tale-bearer have to pay with your head even though some other tale-bearer created the flaw, leaning a little to the right out of vanity. In the correct position the flaw vanishes and there is no reflection except a distant icon of Larissa who is the articulate markster of the moment, rehandling the signifiers of what went wrong, redrawing mutual portraits in words that nail the word on the head then wishing she hadn't since the past tense is merely a convention even as she moves into another portrait which he reads from left to right like Gulliver on his contraption with his eye on legs 見 let alone airmail time losing a person there just as he lost a verb or viceversa no one dreamer's characters ever coinciding in exactly the same quarter of an our though sometimes overlapping in endless statistical improbabilities of reinvestment, filling the air with silent hierogrips that explode into an earful of stabs, tuning along a transistor of synchronised diachronic chords at night for lack of dreams and always the same show, into which you enter as into a room saying once upon a time Larissa is a little girl.

Why however did you crop her hair then grow it again and dye it black and give her three illegitimate children and an iconic nose? For you did not give her three children beautiful illegitimate or authorwise nor did any other either before or after the hole it is possible to fall through as into a delirious discourse, since any structure like Larissa presupposes a void, a gouging out of the I in order carefully to gauge its liquid essence, although the text can well supply the subtle dyes and the cosmetic surgery to round the Gothic arches where the heroine is fair and the femme fatale dark back into Romanesque, the two faculties never meeting except on an imagined curve or at a distance by optical illusion. For although the arbitrariness of narrative is not infinite there is a certain freedom of choice as to which of the two dark ladies of the sequence should become fair at the flick of a dyeing word or which, for that matter is really a man or even God in an elegant trouser-suit.

Tout se passe comme si we were brother and sister Armel and always had been. The very movement by which the family is constituted is that by which it is dissolved, for to educate children is to destroy the family. The family is the tomb, which must be guarded, and the woman who guards the family also guards the tomb to prevent the dead from being eaten by nature or by the cannibalistic violence of the survivors' unconscious desires. The woman is night, sensibility, divinity, the man is light, reason, humanity, that is to say, the city, or politics, which excludes the woman. The war between government and the family is the war between man and woman, which is eternal. To struggle against the family, government drags it into other wars and violates it, preventing total ensconcement into the natural but reminding it that it is subject to death. The husband and wife relationship is immediate, non-mediated, and specular, sensed through a natural unrepressed desire which however because it is natural, is lost, the initial piety eventually unreflected. The relationship of parents and children is mediating but the piety there is transitive and unequal. Only in the brother and sister relationship is there no desire and hence no repression, hence no war, but an unnatural peace, a recognition that does not have to pass through conflict. The brother and sister relationship goes further than the husband and wife relationship which is ensconced in nature, not only on account of desire and pleasure, but also on account of the negativity attached to singularity. And singularity is in effect replaceability. The brother however cannot be replaced.

A brother irreplaceable? O brother she has been reading Hegel again, unempirical Hegel who had been reading Antigone, daughter and half-sister to Oedipus, daughter and grand-daughter of Jocasta, dipping into the elementary structures of kinship as a cannibalistic survivor dips into pieces of master/mistress dying or half dead as a thieving magpie dips into this or that human brain for a silvery phrase, uncovering her tracks however by preserving the brain in a flask, after the parting shot, but conjuring it away into a political mystery, a mere struggle with Creon.

But is it true or merely well found, ill founded and dragged in by the long ashblond hair normally flattened down on either side of the waxen brow sharp green eyes iconic nose of a fantastically turbaned de la Tour lady demanding the hidden ace from the cheater at cards? (Tu me le paieras, du reste, tous les signifiés du portrait sont faux). Does not Larissa always give her sources and Armel none? Whoever speaks is hiding behind a discourse that is not theirs, from which the subjects vanish, the one giving no references the other too many, thus having the mouth removed. But if we give too many references what shall we teach the students we must keep something back. Yes well I must say I find it utterly aberrant that this question of bibliographical lists should create such an outburst of indignation are you all so unsure of yourselves or what? In any case students don't read.

So that the curved beams of their brightness never now meet even on an imagined line between them except quite distantly by optical illusion, staggered along the canyons of chronology, no one student's reading even coinciding in exactly the same rectangle of time though sometimes overlapping in endless statistical probabilities of texts within texts, so that we read about Virgil showing Dante Paolo and Francesca reading about Lancelot and Guinevere or more, about Bakhtine talking about Rachmaninov musicalising Virgil showing Dante Paolo and Francesca reading about Lancelot and Guinevere, who must have read about Tristan and Iseult who drank the potion which is the same word as poison which is what Thamus called the gift of writing offered by the great god Thoth as told by Socrates to Phaedrus as related by Plato who had related a discourse of Lysius which generated a discourse on beauty the soul the gods the delirium of love rhetoric the true the plausible and other kindred topics read by practically everyone since in some form direct or indirect.

This structure is generated by recursivity rules which in English tend to be to the right, as in French, whereas Japanese favours recursivity to the left. In theory the recursivity rule can be applied infinitely but there is a limit imposed by the human memory of both recipient and emitter, a limit which demonstrates the difference between grammaticality and acceptability. In either case however, it is the text that generates the passion acceptable in the text, and beauty is merely a referential code sending us back to beauty as statue painting or goddess. There are codes within codes, tales within tales, codas within codas, the porte-parole carrying his coda in his mouth until the caliph lui coupe la parole. In some languages the word is carried, given, taken, cut. In English it is given only as surface performative, then sometimes stood by as in Chinese or more often broken, as when we guarantee frontiers or get engaged and break it off. We do not give the word but the floor, we introduce the speaker, hand him the microphone or other U for misms in the secret ballet of the I who vanishes behind the I who says I, giving no references or too many.

It seems however that Saroja Chaitwantee despite her $a\pm$ can write but not narrate, generating her narrative complex by means of laws and maxims, addressing herself or the Other for you with adagia which can nevertheless function as functions if their negativity, attached to singularity and therefore replaceable, is replaced with lecture notes from some other rectangle of time unless stolen from or otherwise transmitted by Ali Nourennin. Of course. There have been looks exchanged so why not books? Books within books, looks within looks, looks within books, books within looks. Another idyll then, or semidylliotics within semiotic idylls. So that when waking by a man who has sworn eternal love and thinking in the grey light of the small hours that grip the hole of truth which cannot be established what are you doing here by this intense beardless young Marx who doesn't wash his neck or his long fuzzy hair, let not the day weave again his Kama Sutra fantasy into your own quite other, pick up your fantasy and go. Never let a man see you see through him, call his bluff and accept he will soon get cold feet. Fill the air with quotations, twiddling along the row of books and looks, listening in to classes of men and men of class struggles or caste wars that are the war between man and woman, day and night, the city and the tomb, for no man is an island he is full of noises, chattering through his silence with his fingertip ballet of the I and his dropped nailpairings.

But has Larissa a narrative complex? Is she a narrative complex? Or an actant-place with a brother-complex? Reinvesting dead Eteocles of the lion-skin in every man, her husband Haimon then in fact his homologue?

hǒmo logos ↓ {ratio / utterance} the undeicidable

The knight in the tiger-skin. Or how the tiger got his just-so stories to motivate his burning quest in the forest of the night.

And if we must have this chaotic freedom in the choice of discourses let us at least try and integrate it through psychic structures we understand. A timetable is not a turntable.

What on earth are you talking about?

Yes if you're going to hold that kind of disc-hoarse please explain yourself.

This is not the place.

The shrug of scorn functions like the bar between signifier and signified for ever eluded and played out elsewhere in other rectangles of time with a reformed syllabus by demand from the ever-youthful body of an old society for ever replenished from generation to generation, the object of exchange being a subject of controversy so that subjects have to be continually reinvented and always the same show

Century	13th	20th	20th	13th
Day	Martis dies	Tuesday	Wednesday	Mercoris dies
Time				
laudes	Logica	Initiation to Semiotics	The Novel as Intentional Object	Geometrica
prima	Astronomia	The Semiology of Cultural Images	Women's Liberation	Arithmetica
tiertia	Grammatica	Initiation to Generative Grammar	Language as subversion of society	Rhetorica
sexta	Musica	The Semiology of Mass Media	The Ideology of Diachronic Chords	Musica

none	Thetoric	The Inscription of protest	The generation of narrative complexes	Grammatica
vespera	Arithmetica	Narrative as Object of Exchange	Empiricism and Imperialism	Astronomia
completa	Geometrica	Psychoanalysis and the text	Initiation to Dialectictical Materialism	Logica

We have however retained a trace of hierarchy despite student demand in that you have to go through the trivium before proceeding to the quadrivium. The hours between completa and laudes may be spent in heterotextuality. There has been a complete reform in genital organisation.

For if it is true that there must be no specialisation, that, for example, no city could exist unless we were all flute-players, do you suppose that the sons of the best flute-players would necessarily be superior to the sons of bad flute-players? Similarly any man brought up among civilised men will know more of justice law morality than a man brought up in a society that has no education no tribunals or laws nor any constraints whatever. These are adagia, which even Protagoras thought were useful because memorable, as did Uang Iu p'uh. Had Uang Iu p'uh read the Protagoras? And are not all idées reçues? And what about Marx on the division of labour had he read the Protagoras? And why did Plato spill and spread the medicine-poison that introjects the body with its exteriority and make the memory fail into memorability? How for that matter did Socrates running to his friend report verbatim the entire dialogue with Protagoras in which midway he interrupts the discourse with a point of order that since Protagoras is speaking to a man without memory he must not speak so lengthily which point of order becomes an episode of some seventeen pages themselves leading to an explication de texte on a poem by Simonides before returning to the subject of discourse? Wrought irony within the orbit of an ire on eye that kills the letter it devours in a patricide extasy of O in the mountains with waxen or stone tablets broken in anger at the sight of a goldicondeology? Nor does the text tell how Dante ever got back to weave his comedy after being nailed to the upper cirle of light as a geometrician trying to measure it just like Gulliver and his watch until was struck by lightning his spirit and high fantasy. O luce eterna che sola in te sidi and love that spins the sun and stars out of the Consolations of Philosophy II.m.viii the text within the text nobody reads, the show within the show.

Unless it is, all the time, Oscar.

The unmarked term, scaring, scarring you with his zero, forming you to his pygmalion desire that realises retrospectively that it has worked at something infinitely beyond itself since the diagonal contradictory of the dialectical reply to I want to take you over must necessarily be I want to overtake you whatever the deep structure. How long O Freud how long?

And yet the unmarked term has long disappeared as object of exchange raised to the nth power but marked with zeroist authorship dressed in democracy clothed in cartesianism (but the emperor's a naked empiricist!), conjured away like a brain in a flask after the parting shot. Just as Veronica has vanished as object of any jealous anguish despite the letters of her name whereby she keeps her Ivory coast and see for yourself and capital V for Victory, the Ic however losing to the me he keeping L for gnome or Larissa. The text does not give her maiden-name only Masters which inaptly belongs to Christopher who like Veronica has been thrown piecemeal out of its timetable by the church as narrative matrix of outmoded myths on the incredulous grounds that they did not exist except as etymological formations (etymo: true, real). This could be known as the etymological fallacy. But fallacies have a way of being true for a while, true as the mistress-piece of the moment who then disappears from the texture of self-love as a scar vanishes, a trace, a negative on a piece of cloth. Paradise Lost, Maud Gonne, Albertine Disparue, a sort of bird.

For although every discourse presupposes a blind spot it never the less implies the absence of things as desire implies the absence of its object. This works all the way through from alpha to omega and from the phonic level to narrative structure or myth. Maybe it's the grammar of the universe. Programmed and epigrammed. Although you go beyond it as you went beyond Oscar. O for the wings of a dove.

O for a beaker

Queue for a quipu.

Which poses problems or even prombles to which false solutions are found thus creating other blompers. But every promble is not only meant to be disentangled it is itself meaningful provided it is written up there. Nevertheless the arbitrariness of narrative is not infinite since the narrator chooses the middle of his kernel sentence in function of its end which justifies the means with a felix culpa thus preserving the balance of power and preventing the economy of the narrative from crashing into a world crisis. V = F. V for la revolution = F for vescence.

So that we must devise viable modalities of action to be envisaged before engaging in the struggle the struggle for what? For abolishing all institutions of learning a conspicious consumption of knowledge

	deutera	trite	tetarte	pempte
dawn to noon	Courage	Duty	Piety	Virtue
noon to sundown	Nature of Man	Ideas	The False	The Dis-puter
Symposium	Being	The Soul	Friend-ship	Beauty

In the months of thirty-one days the symposium shall according to the desire of the majority either continue into hene kai nea or cease on the ninth day of the third decade thus affording two days of rest, hene kai nea and noumenia, the punishment in terminal position never falling on the euphoric term, always on the dysphoric. In the last decade the days are counted backwards. The timetable structures nobody wants with its built in obsolescence so why are you here or what will you put in its place? Oh not that question again brother you're ruddy tape-recorders so are you.

Danger men at playback, raising antimoneys by reaction that surpasses the subjective idea, rendering it objective for as Marx said personalities and events reappear, on the first occasion as tragedy on the second as farce. Albertine returning bereft of significance Paradise Regained a bore Maud Gonne and good riddance.

There has however been a complete reform of congenital organisation as we move staggering through regressions to the other calendar.

hekte	hebdome	ogdoe	enate	dekate	Tenth Day (hene kai nea/ noumenia)
Moral Wisdom	Justice	Royalty	Legis-lation	Science	rest
The Sophist	Recti-tude of Words	Rhetoric	Iliad	Funeral Oration	rest
Love	The Gods	Atlantides	The delirium of love	Pleasure	rest

society but destroys the family which structures society, each tale-bearer pressured into his story in order that the hero's quest may proceed. But as we saw the motivation may well be reversed, the timetable structuring the family but destroying society which structures the family, each tale-bearer carrying his coda in his mouth until he has eaten himself silly and soft and flabby, fit only for the undertaker who overtakes and takes over, the movement by which the family is constituted being also that by which it is dissolved, the womb the tomb a rectangle of time a city of rectangles along which the eye walks up and down like Gulliver on his contraption a moving finger mannikin that having writ with a spirit-loaded pen scrubs out the hieroglyphs and starts again.

Some trace of hierarchy however has been retained in that you have to proceed from the conspicuous consumption of the civic virtues in the morning to the built-in obsolescence of the private passions at night, resting every decade. The hours between the symposium and rosy-fingered dawn may be spent in the winedark sea of infratextuality for there has been a complete reorganisation of flute-playing phallusies. And if you peer through the flawed hymen eye-lens of a judas-eye in the timetable you will see the high men of learning curiously foreshortened into highwaymen who point a pistol at your brain after the introduction of the parting-shot, proepigrammed within earshot of the primal scene which does not take place in the institution of learning for that is not the place but the placenta thrown out with the mannikin leaving danger men at replay, and if you lose the thread of the texture you lose your head your paradise your utterance your pygmalion-skinned hero creature that slips out of your grasp and becomes a line in its own rewrite rule going forth to multiply the multiplicator of books and looks within books like a function of narrative

$$f(\text{bo } (\text{lo } (\text{bo } (\text{lo } (\text{books}) \text{ oks}) \text{ oks}) \text{ oks}) \text{ oks})^n$$

For mimesis inevitably produces a double of the thing, the double being nothing a non-being which nevertheless is added to the thing, and therefore not totally devoid of value although, however resembling, never absolutely true. C Plato for yourself. And when by way of additional supplement the thing is as evasive as a sophist in perpetual flight behind binary digressions of the dianoia beyond the discourse, diegesis needs a digraph, the right hand resting on the liftable flap to write down a point of information, the left hand ignota treeing off unsupported by a head-noun and falling into the void that is presupposed even by a tree-structure. Thus you will have two hands, two pens, two penises to generate a double text into a corpus crysis.

And if the master-marksman does not give us a little margin full of marks to add up we shall edge ourselves over the edge. These things do matter in a text like the human body or society as object of exchanging books and looks in the book of nature which is written up there or the book that imitates the soul or the soul of the book which is the unvoiced logos. And having edged ourselves out of the text we shall nevertheless be outlawed from the city because of the text that kills the head that brought it forth and is therefore fast exteriorised by the head before it generates itself into a patricide, safer outside.

But Sordello? And my Sordello? There are but the twenty-seven Larissas, and each is marked with zero, liminivorous but eliminated by the letter she does not write since the epistolary novel is dead and it is so much easier to turn up The Collected Telephone Conversations of Larissa Toren Armel Santores Veronica Masters even though your demand cannot reach its destination and you are requested to call ulteriorly.

For the more thoroughly we understand deep structures the more man is reduced to a cybernetic sigh to cypher into psychic invisibility a statistic two-dimensionally static on a page, diagramming his dysphoric dianoia, encoding his codal dreams, unless the motivation can be reversed so that the line of twenty-seven and a half black mannikins occurs in order to generate the lion-skinned hero helpless in his quest and displaying visceral organs overflowing from excess of amourous anguish. The heroine after all must not be found too soon since familiarity breeds contempt as the family breeds death. This seems not to apply to the hero apparent who is allowed to dis-chant his chances and enchantments from tale to tale ten a day for a hundred days owing to the double standard or taleological fallacy of felix culpa that the end be balanced by the meanness and the woman is always the end, the matter upon which you write your narcissistic love the virgin page you soil in which you sow your seed when the Pleiades go down to rest, the clay on which you scar the zero marks of masterhood by definition doomed to fail in that it masterhoods the eyes from the iotaboo. A good hero is hard to find.

Thus the original escapes between the signifiers of a discourse which is not your discourse but a trompe l'oeuil. Tu m'as trompé l'oeuil. Sauve quipu.

Qui parle? Socrates is the one who speaks, unpaid for selling truth beauty and goodness wrapped up in dialectic as objects of exchange for a good argument, Plato his microphone, his reverential reference. In any case students don't read. Soon all these innumerable voices will be as transitory as those of the transistor twiddled along from the transatlantic disc-jockey to the news in Serbo-Croat. For the record does not tolerate the re-presentation of a subject in its text, the I who says I not being the said I so that the recipient of the twenty-seven coloured veils is left frantically signalling into the wings of a love where nobody gets the message, like a pompous pirate who would not stay for a dancer through hoops and loops riding roughshod eye-hooded over unbeing for if mimesis exists non-being is. Look it up.

It follows therefore that if Larissa invents Armel inventing Larissa, Armel also invents Larissa inventing Armel. Thus there can be no communication between them and it is pointless or at least stylus-cramping to mime a dialogue of the deaf, an epistolary of the stolen I through purloined letters full of girded loins girdled with new leaves turned into fig-years of speech summarised in the minutes of their meetings where their mutual demand cannot reach its end let them call ulteriorly out of the anterior wilderness with mouthsful of locusts and white lies that eliminate Larissa right out of her own icon I-conned by his eyes until all that is signifiable in her is struck with latency as soon as raised to the function of the signifier which initiates this raising by its original disappearance, so that any discussion about whether to return to Armel (or to Larissa) as subject of discourse drifts into the undeicidable and she drives off again into the night watching the dancing hoops of taleological propositions split against one another inside the rectangle that reflects the rear a head, into which she enters as into a vehicle within a vehicle, twiddling along the transistor for other ideologies into which she enters as into a turntable broken into and broken up by a goldicondeology of golden youth for whom it is more difficult to enter the I of society than for the treasurer of signifiers to enter the paradiso terrestre as changed upon the blue guitar.

Evasiveness is the privilege of woman but woman has lost all her privileges by emancipation while gaining none of man's, only his responsibilities. And when man reverses roles to steal both the irresponsibilities and the privileges of woman adding them to his own while leaving her only the responsibility for everything he has nothing to do but find another vehicle to get into, another hole an O an open vowel who will nevertheless become consonantal with his inarticulate seed and bring forth a concatenation of consequences with the non-privilege of non-evasiveness. All privilege must therefore be abolished and we demand a complete reorganisation of visceral organs. La demande however ne peut aboutir and the staff knows this and goes on exactly as previously falling back into the old ruts which must be analysed as global social phenomena. A long discussion then opens on a two-pointed prong:

A. Integration of a horizontal coordination into the proepigram (principle unanimously adopted: not to follow the principle).
B. The number of groups thus desegmented to be actualised in the fall from the paradiso terrestre (Larissa Toren is opposed to all horizontal coordination which would degenerate, according to her, into useless chatter).

Since, however, even a dead idyll is a mise-en-abîme and since every chasm opens into another chasm into which it is possible to fall as into a void, the intelligence nailed in pain as it sees through the acting out of its own lunatic trajectory, so every idyll dead alive or half dead opens out into another idyll, the idyll of Armel and Larissa, of Ali Nourennin and Saroja Chaitwantee Paolo and Francesca Lancelot and Guinevere Tristan and Iseult the potion and the holy grail the pen and the paper full of invariants such as the institution of learning rusticated into a bucolic carnival past-oralised by the presence of fixed motifs such as the equivocal use of exhorticultural terms for sexual ends and the display of vicious organs overflowing from the excess of hominivorous anguish. Larissa however has had most vicious organs removed, dropping a vessel here there and in the other place which explains her non-existence and consonantal compensation, piecemeal metonymised, parceled out, fragmented into synthetic synechdoche that organises a chiasmus in a forgotten name to create the rejection that she proinjects. Yours are the poems i do not write. In some languages things do themselves even when le ça ne se fait pas.

But if you come too close to any icon vero or non vero you will see only the texture and the knife-strokes not the goddess curtained in black hair with a small phallus-man where the phallus by the psychological sell should be, wrapped up in swaddling clothes bandages or winding sheets. If however you distance yourself from that particular myth you see merely an oval with a blob off-centre which owing to an archaic flaw in the intensity of the illusion splits into dancing hoops that rise and fall into one another as if juggled by an invisible magician or a black recumbent grave into which two men leap to double death by dripping dagger plunged through a crown of thorns a golden O of all the world a stage which is the other scene. Let the phallos perceive its aim. Within each texture is another texture within each myth another myth each signifier signifying another each problem a preamble to a promble.

Unless it is all the time, Oscar. The naked emperor of I-scream. Or the young man carbuncular whose concubines stereotype his index with names and numbers that he may reach his doctorate of indoctrination deliveried in ideology from top to toe a footman of the bourgeoisie.

There are plenty of subjects to play with Oliver Claire Hubert Olaf Chou Gregory Stanley Catherine reformulating the poetics of the Renaissance in the poetry of the cry the representation always double and in any case unequal, in some respects less than life in others more than plenary Oscar for example more empirical and imperial than any empirical imperialist his lanky henchman more wenching and lanky in smoked glasses than any other guinea-pigs as eternal truths both universal and particular, each an emitter recipient and of course a place $d1$ $\bar{d}1$ $d2$ $\bar{d}2$ with sixteen possible types of unbalanced relationships the double standard being inescapable even in semiotics. Not to mention the students. Students however according to the lanky wenchman dressed in democracy and smoked glasses are very malleable. The element of manipulation however should not be too visible for it destroys the fictive illusion by making the recipient over-aware of a technique at work.

Meanwhile Saroja Chaitwantee has at last fallen in love with Ali Nourennin just as he has grown a little weary of empty adagia wrapped in oriental mystery and hovers back to Hegel Heidegger Husserl. He also removes his watch, no one dreamer's Kama Sutra fantasy coinciding in exactly the same quarter of an idyll.

Which needs adjusting.

Who speaks? What new narrator lover or mistress uttering there is no fear in love give not your soul etc except at night when the amber operates on both axes without taboo and all you need is care and courtesy (the notion of passion having disappeared), wondering however how to get through from the now which remains in the then to the then emptied of now. Simply by adding the heartlessness of then to then? But that is rather clumsy, metonymising the metaphor, projecting the horizontal axis of death onto the vertical axis of life and in a way cheating since you have given many a man a certain peculiar pleasure in frustrating their vulgar desire to know what happens inside you and that pleasure should not be dropped in mid-erection, leaving him hungry for it unless merely anorexic asthenic or cyclothymic, there can be no diagnosis since he too does not exist except as reinvestment itself perpetually reinventing S into O the Other Place and o the object of desire o^i o^2 o^n.

They reflect nothing, for the narrator has disappeared into a pool of lethal self-love with Echo echoing on, though that is only a manner of speaking and the manner of speaking says in the beginning was the parting shot. Never let anyone see you see through them. Never let yourself be fully known.

Take these down as rules, preferable to thinking about the object of exchange in a double standard of the narrator's omniscience that dips into many minds with varying degrees of presence of mind coming upon, at this point, the pistol, a mere instrument, whose only role is to utter by chance or by neurotic cunning the words of passion for ever unbelieved as surface structures every ninety minutes or so but opening up a vast mouthful of possible presences, an amateur Don Juan perhaps or Donatello of The Marble Faun why not? Oedipiano, piano.

The moving finger writes and having writ scrubs out the diagram. Tous les signifiés du portrait sont faux but even altogether cannot succeed in naming the falsehood, although they point to it in a hermeneutic gap chock full of the parenthetic fallacy whereby the falsehood is long desired but evaded by way of the evasive mouth and its paradismal trick of articulation.

It is the pain, it is the pain endures (I may the beaute of it not sosteyn) and pain, which takes a minimal fraction of a second thought to say, has to be lived through, and you could cover pages and maybe you do, rehandling the signifiers into acceptability and even amusement so that at last it vanishes like delight, a pricked balloon, a bubble not a festering boil. For no recipient desires a message of pain emitted from another, neither if he is in it nor if he is out of it, all the less so if has caused it. So you do not transmit the message, many times, and the unmany times you do you regret it since it falls on an earful of sirensong or wax or crabs. Only ebullience can be shared, grabbed, and is, for there is always someone who needs to reinvest in it.

Marco for instance.

Or is it Stavro?

At last we

royally or collectively

are

going

back to the

beginning which is the end

since

we (you)

are structuring (y) our

(T) (T)

T T hattaway

under perpetual
sentence
just like life

the ferret popping out of the
late rabbit hole with the
late rabbit dead
safe

as a jack-in-the-box
hiding within the retro-vizir
behind the con-sultan listener
of deep structures below
(yes your eminence we'll come to that your reference)
as emitter of message
(but what does the omitter omit?)
The hystery of the eye
The cruel nails
grammed in the r e m o t e

e y e s
p a r c h m e a n t
o r s t o n e
d r y
p a p y r u s

with a fear of fusion that
might e x t end
explode the
I into r
e
some Other sex u a l i t y
r e a
l
i o
t
y o u

The moving finger with its dumb designation maintains the truth (of the falsehood) in a pregnant plenitude the piercing of which (with the punishing finger in final position), both liberating and catastrophic, must bring about the end of the discourse, and the character (finger or pistol) is never more than a passage of the enigma with which you dip us all in the eternal debate with the sphinx that has stamped the whole of occidental paradismatics. Therefore the truth (about the falsehood) must be evaded at all cost of life until the death of the discourse.

Or at any rate, it needs adjusting.

Her hair is fair or dark, it doesn't matter except in gothic romanesque now that there are such subtle dyes even within the text. She is pale and sits

Where?

On the campus

Can one sit on a campus?

She sits on a castle terrace in Spain.

Caramba not picaresque that's as dead as the dread-letter novel.

In Slovenia, talking to the count

Titles have been abolished in Slovenia

turning her back to you. It is a warm summer evening. The benches and tables are of wood, under a trellis of vine, facing the crenellated walls that hide the view of the valley. Scrub that. The bench and tables are of wrought iron, under the palladian colonnade, facing the flight of white stone steps that lead to the wide gardens wrought-ironed beneath the moon in patterns of clipped privet. By the light of adapted eighteenth-century coach-lamps between each tall french window two foursomes call out one heart, I pass, two diamonds, three clubs, three diamonds, I pass, four diamonds counterpointed by three hearts, four clubs, four hearts I pass. Other groups sit and talk, smoking and sipping wine.

The count is a mad mathematician who makes strange signs on a sheet of paper as she leans half facing him, right breast tensed out by the angle of her arm right hand on her right hip, her thighs crossed tight under a black silk skirt, left elbow on the table the left hand supporting the long curve of jaw with thumb under the chin and the two long forefingers up into her temple hair the other two below her open lips, the two sets of two fingers forming an angle for the deeply interested gaze upon his words and symbols, and at the angle the wedding ring and the sapphire delicately ovaled in diamonds. But you should know Boolean algebra dear lady it would help you considerably look, I simplify, the connectives are not, or, and, if.

You feel so totally out of it that you will spare the other recipient the details since you are only a substitute narrator, jack-in-the-box not jack-of-all-trades, a mere pistol whose only role is to utter by chance or by sudden overwhelming desire the words of love for ever unbelieved. We'll come to that. The details over his handsome shoulder a little too close to hers look like a rectangle crossed by a diagonal marked with capital letters, followed by another set of letters the last line of which he says is a false premise with a true implication. The false premise being apparently that she has asked him how to represent in two dimensions a three-dimensional graph of narrated time past present and future, coding in as well narrative time for the reader as an unknown variable, the writer's time being irrelevant since the author does not exist, she says, only the text. And the true implication being perhaps her retrospective realisation that she has worked at something infinitely beyond her and beyond you too, so that you want to break up this communion of false premises with your uncomplicated desire which has been quietly generated for some time out of your request for a lift from her ebullient presence and black Fiat Luxe to Hungary where Marika lives on whom you last put terrific pressure to leave her husband escape to freedom and you and whom you itch to see whether. You're mad it's miles out of my way Oh please it would be such fun And then what you dump me in Budapest? Well er no of course So what then will she like seeing you arrive with another woman? Think pig. Why pig? It was a quotation, from Beckett. Who's Beckett? Two clubs, two hearts, two spades.

Leading metonymically via your desarroi and desire and the hot summer evening to the dutch courage from the slovene wine which enables you to down your shyness and break up the communion of false premises with another in close hot urgency near her perfumed ear when are you going to stop this and pay attention to me I can't compete I'm not the latin lover type.

She laughs. I'll deal with you later.

And no doubt she does.

Meanwhile something has gone wrong with the narration owing to textual disturbances. The castle seemed momentarily to be French. And yet you have drunk slovene wine and referred to the count as the latin lover type, the French being Frankished Gauls, despite the fact that you are yourself Italian, obviously with a name like Marco. Unless you are Stavro after all in which case you could be Albanian. Or Russian or maybe Slovenian. The Albanians could have been Etruscans.

Perhaps you had better transfer the whole scene to Mexico.

They don't have counts in Mexico, or castles.

Or to California which is full of exiles and where they move castles from Europe stone by stone or construct fake follies. So you could move it too, No, better in Europe where the revolution will not occur since

Oh keep that out of it we're on vacation now not on campus. The students have dispersed and the continuous notation cards on which you compose portraits and double portraits have been cybernetically processed into degrees of absence, permutated through the computer into grades obtained for this or that course the chaotic freedom in the choice of which makes you drive off onto the highway towards the paradiso terrestre. This is an idyll. Who speaks? There is a confusion of voices here, out of narrative time and out of character. The highway moreover is not always high, and in some cities the thruway goes round.

It is the Count who speaks however, pressing her into reading *I promessi sposi* as the best novel in the world and who is therefore quite evidently Italian, even if he is not a count.

But why a castle? It cannot be merely to change the scene since motivation is a cost and V = F. It could be a hotel (for realism). It could be for alliteration: a castle in California? in Catalunia? Calabria? Caledonia Canada Karinthia Kamchatka. But the punishment in final position has occurred on the diasporic term: the castle must be in France (Cantal or Aquitaine). Cancel however the calls of bridge. It is a Congress in Semiotics and semioticians do not play bridge but at semic polarities.

Or on a pale guitar addressing herself for you as La belle si tu voulais (bis) nous dormirions ensemble o-la (bis) and answering you with No vale la pena el llanto and readdressing herself for you with Yo no te offresco riqueza, Ti offresco mi corazón and reanswering you with You ain't going nowhere and a strange gaze at you through the whole repertoire in the dialectic of desire that gravitationally pulls you towards the centre of attention she enjoys as from the start an object of central loss, the sheer questiontagmatics having reversed the subject into a foreknowledge of the whole repeat performance which can only belong either to the narrator as a cheating young god or to Larissa as a well established structure that presupposes a void a fall into a delirious discourse watched indifferently through fingernail parings.

I'm not very good the first time.

O for a beaker full of the warm southern night that generates the first time into n swiftly changing viewpoints floating up from deep level dreamlessness every n minutes or so for a shared murmur of sweet nothingnesses then down again as mouth removes to mouth female to phallus in the show within the show, sucking the performer dry with recursivity from left to right in a performance that is to his competence as his nose is to his brow.

Fear is the function of his narrative.

You know his fear falls on the initial position but also on the last, he being a dysphoric term beneath his youphoria. And that the end of the kernel sentence is proepigrammed by the beginning, not by the bold centrecodpiece in mid copula as a wild manner of speaking pistolshot words like will you stay with me always always please will you marry me.

always? always Death said

The introduction, into the superficial grammar, of wanting as a modality, permits the construction of modal utterances with two actants united in a proposition, the axis of desire then authorising a semenic interpretation of them as virtual performer subject and an object instituted as value. Adam wants an apple Adam wants to be good. Such an acquisition, by the subject of the object, seems to occur as a reflex action, which is only a particular case of a much more general structure well known as the diagram of communication represented in its canonic form as an M and a Y of crossed limbs with diagonals from the I to the object

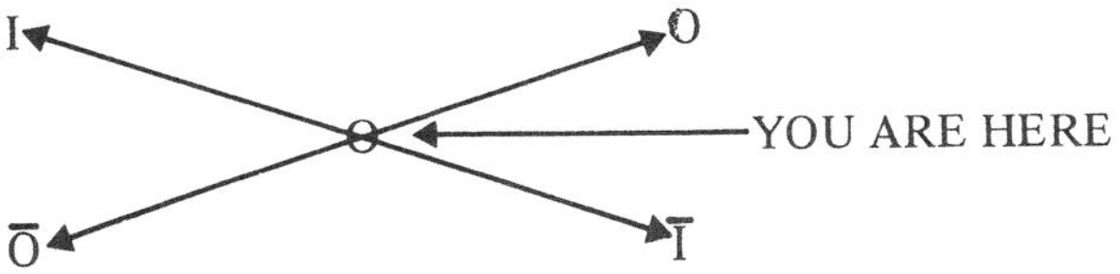

never believing anything said in moments of passion

(the notion of which has disappeared)

But I meant it, please, will you?

No my love, love is just a four-letter word.

That's only a song, you know it's more than that.

And when we've read the letters inside out and upside down you will go forth, and multiply.

But I don't want to multiply I have three children already.

Go forth then. Fort-da.

What do you mean fortda?

Oh nothing. Just ticking myself off with something Freud said.

Da means yes in Russian

and gives in Italian so what? (Yes is for young men)

Or if by such misassociation when waking by anyone who swears eternal love make love not war make conversation as if conversation could be made all horizontal coordination degenerating into useless chatter: I didn't know you were married.

I'm not I refused to marry her she took my name by Deed Poll.

Marriage is an outmoded institution. Only a few priests are thinking of it.

But you're married.

Yes. What's her name?

Maddy.

What?

Maddy. Well Madeleine really. Out of which improper name pours the surface grammar of his narrative disturbances for hours and days you shouldn't talk of her like that you must have loved her long enough to have three children by her only two one is by an early marriage in Italy now annulled I didn't love her you don't know her she's awful she drinks she's a lousy mother she neglects the children it's awful and I left her the house the car she's done very well out of me. But I love my children I'm worried stiff about them it's bad enough that I've become just a sort of uncle to Enzo that's the first one but well as an unmarried mother she has all the rights I'm only the absent father. But I want to take them away from her oh please help me. Now, soon, I need you.

But when the shoulders shift back to the correct position the cars that look grey eminent into the retrovizor do not look double-faced or quadruple-eyed out of focus together with the four eyes but untarnished with single grins between two pale gold eyes one on either side or else two smaller city substitutes lower down but never two pairs together.

My love is like a white white rabbit
late
yet consulting his watch
and removing it
down the hatch
out of sight
dead (safe)
earthhole though
il court il court
and which way did he go?
the way of all flesh (the happiness sequence)
hey follow that car (the chase sequence)
you should have seen ϕ
that always gets away safe
as a jack of all spades
hiding behind
eyeing beneath

the grey eminence the retro-vizir beyond the consultana
haggler of head nouns chopped below the performance yes your
eminence I'll come to that your reference but meanwhile

the retrovizor has a bluish tinge in the cold light the
rectangle turns smoky grey to dim the dazzle of floods
undipped or even gently dipped but the glare is preferable
to the sudden isolation of almost not seeing behind a
head

the dancing hoops. For the gold eyes when distant turn into hoops (at night in the correct position) of luminous green red amber bouncing in out of through and through each other narrowing to slim ovals vertical horizontal swaying undoing swiftly changing viewpoints as if juggled by a magician or the black recumbent street below and with the overhead bridges that make perhaps the optical illusion.

He shifts the mirror to his rearward glance. It doesn't appear to work for him the lover of the moment of sudden isolation at not seeing the black magician who tantalisingly juggles luminous hoops into the rectangular hey you put my mirror back.

So it needs adjusting.
Why at this precise point introduce another idyll?
Intensity of illusion is what matters to whoever is operating through a flaw in the glass darkly perhaps making two or four clear eyes stare back, two of them in their proper place at height of bridge of nose and, further up the brow, the

other two, exact replicas but dimmed as in a tarnished reflection, tarnished by the fringe they seem to peer through. A

second pair of eyes hidden higher up the brow certainly has its uses despite psychic invisibility or maybe because of. Gazing they do not see themselves. They reflect absolutely nothing, nor do they look at their bright replicas below in the proper place on either side of the nose which is a fraction iconic according to Armel but not precisely in this instance. Only these lower eyes, reflecting, presumably, the eyes of the real face as it leans for reassurance a bit to the right, see the upper eyes, looking up at the fringe of straight brown hair.

and so you glance askance at the short thick muscular body nevertheless a young god yet as you plunge into the dimension of his banality with the intention of tran-

smogrifying it by utterance into an idyll.
Or a blue lacuna of learning moon june soon a blue lagoon.

Oh?
No well let's face it, so far, as an idyll, it's a flop.

The castle stands in oleander on hills with the Alps or is it the Appenine range behind it, overlooking the downward terraces trucked out and sliced away for low-roofed dead suburban villas and across the motorway to the wooden shacks and the white houses of cracked stucco under a forest of aerials and down again to the metropolitan sprawl below which is dying of the greed and brashness of the north and beyond, the bay the straits at the tiptoe of the foot upon thine eye wo die Zitronen glühen.

So you take off, racing down to the wine dark sea of

infrasexuality for there has been a complete reorganisation of flute-players along the slum stretch of shore, trash filthy, as the young god swims out slicing the water with nothing in his head and spitting out foam like words of love into the chaparral of a canyon in the desert where the ear is full of sirensong under the shade of a red rock out of Eliot who's Eliot or a hollow man saying always always.

herself to always keep–always? always death said things in moments of passion which is a seventeenth century concept or even Byzantine out of the romance of Tariel in the tigerskin which he reads in the original Georgian do you know it it's wonderful. I know the text yes, I've even taught it but in translation I didn't know you could read Georgian how clever of you. It is so easy to hide in an idyll, the invariants of which are the place, no longer Arcadia but simply the anti-town and the rustic love song manifest through fixed motifs like deference and letting him take you over and light the way in his own land, plunging into the dimension of his unknowing as he sleeps stretching out his arm to feel you in his dreams you could dip into for his accurate boymouth moves towards yours murmuring oh it's lovely my lying here close to you having erections all night and finding you there unless he laughs and says I'm sorry it's only the garlic oh I thought it was me. It is easy to seize the text in its moment not of gesture but of dialogue with all preceding texts as death and birth involved in a dialectic to the death with one another, reading what you want into it, seeing too many hoops in the rear of the mind and coming upon at this point nothing at all, an absent language given in the silence of the pen, despite or because of the ensconcement in the natural pressure to possess you for ever by repeat performance please please marry me.

The fall was into language. But you should know Boolean algebra dear lady it would help you considerably I simplify look the connectives are and or if not.

Be careful of words Stavro, they are lures and have unexpected results.

If you mean they'll persuade you that's what I want, for that is the operative word we must not seem to be adopting a threatening attitude but persuade the authorities to accede to our demands which however cannot reach their end because when an unsuitable young man proposes and proposes call his bluff he'll soon get cold feet upon these eyes of thine.

I'm very touched, Stavro, and thank you. But let's take it lightly.

But I love you. And last night you said you loved me.

You're not serious, are you?

Of course I'm serious.

Then I'd better be blunt. It's out of the question.

You mean you're rejecting me?

Nnno. I'm rejecting myself for you. Why marriage anyway? I'm much older than you are for one thing.

You can't be. I'm the one who's old, I'm past thirty already and I've wasted my life. How can you be older well a couple of years at most.

My dear, women lie about their age but not usually upwards.

But. But. It doesn't matter. Why you look so young you're so beautiful. Your skin is like a shoolgirl's and your body

Thank you. But you don't have to be gallant, not in this. Besides I am much scarred as you know, and no lady Dorian Grey.

Who's she?

And one day suddenly soon it will all collapse and you'll see me as I am, you being still young and handsome.

I love you as you are. For better for worse in sickness in health the lot. I'll pursue you and pursue you if that's what you want I will not let you go.

The axis of desire uniting them authorises a semidyllic interpretation of the two actants as a virtuoso performer subject and an object instituted by itself as valueless through a negative portrait in order to evade the valuelessness of the subject performer. Thus the narrative utterance:

$$NU = F : \text{transfer } (E \rightarrow o \rightarrow R)$$

The transfer can then be interpreted at the same time as a privation or as a disjunction (depending on the level) or as an attribution or as a conjunction (depending on the level) thus representing the circulation of value-objects topologically as an identification of the deictic transfers with the terms of a taxinomic model, each isotopic place (where the performances occur) consisting of two deixes that are conjunctive but equivalent, at the fundamental level, to the contradictory terms out of Oriental and Celtic mists that nobody utters these days, or, if somebody does, can only be met by syntagmatic silence although words are urgently demanded and the demand can only degenerate into useless chatter. She who explains herself is lost.

You're very sweet. And because of that I'm being honest with you. I could have lied to make it last until you moved on in the nature of things to the fresher flesh of younger girls.

Never. I'll never love anyone but you.

But I promessi sposi, no. I don't want it, and besides it wouldn't work, you have all those years to live through and I can tell you they are crucial years when one finally faces oneself, painfully, and grows up.

You're treating me like a child.

I'm sorry. You are a man, I know, though in some ways still a child, like all of us.

All right then, that's what I want, that's what you have to give me, yourself, your body, and the wisdom of those years, I need it I need it. And you need me, I know, I want to find the child in you again and bring it out to meet me.

Let's enjoy it while it lasts my love, it's beautiful.

But that's just why it will last. Why are you so pessimistic? I've never proposed in my life, Amanda proposed to me and so did Maddy and I refused you can't, you mustn't reject me I can't bear being rejected.

Fear is the function of his narrative. Fear of rejection affecting initial performance that grows by gratitude into terror of loss, inflating the performative to wild inventio pronunciato exordium propositio not of the absent father but of the absent son as object of exchange while below, within the self-same text, run the refutatio the fleeing silent peroratio from the other fear of your acceptance and your otherness. You know you will forestall it by rejecting him soon, very soon, organising a chiasmus to make him reject you, which he will with cowardice and that will hurt. But he is a child and you are a woman invented by another in a parting shot.

{ I want to take you over.
I want to look after you why look at the way you keep losing things your car documents for instance you need someone to remind you of ordinary existence.
I want to be everything to you, father husband son and brother as you're everything to me. I'm offering you security and a calm relationship.

Yo no ti offresco riqueza, Ti offresco mi corazõn.

You're laughing at me.

I'm not, I just feel gay. How do you know I need or want security and not perhaps adventure? No it won't do Stavro (rappel: chiasmus) Besides, you'll only hurt me.

I'll never never hurt you. I give you my word 信

With all your goodly words you me endow.

You forget that I'm a gentleman.

Scrubbing the diagrams of previous passions at the flick of a switch with a spirit-loaded pen coming up every ninety minutes for a shared pursuit of the same insistently mise-en-abysmal dialogue with recursivity to right or left that is almost preventing the idyll from developing its fixed motifs such as the rustic love-song and the equivocal use of past-oral terms for sexual ends by thrusting in a chaotic pressure for the non-choice of courses although the boastfulness of the shepherd remains as he retells himself into acceptability, waving his curriculum vitae as a white flag, rehandling his signifiers into an Orthodox church as narrative matrix of outmoded myths we'll get married in each wearing a crown or a crumbling castle we'll do up look shall we buy that one which is not your discourse but a disc-organised trompe-l'oeuil sauve qui peut and the thighs of the Syracuse Venus not to mention the display of visceral organs overflowing from excess of amorous anguish. But if you distance yourself you see only the mannikin ensconced still in his mother's lap like an open grave a circular O with a blob off-centre and a struggle to double death. The process is infinite within each quest another quest for high adventure in a high romance. Pick up your picaroon fantasy and go fort-da. But why security and what do you mean by security you don't even seem to have a job.

Speaks the king's daughter to the prince disguised as poor younger son or the binary bourgeois lady of the left anxious not to take ten steps back to unpaid mortgages and seeing men through their theses and early publications stereotyping their index? Of course I have a job, I mean I had but I resigned, Maddy made it impossible for me.

Oh, where?

In Porlock.

Where's that?

Well in England. It's a new university.

Oh? Revolutionary?

No thank goodness. It's a language centre.

And what did you teach?

Albanian.
Goodness, is that a subject?
It's not only a subject it's a language.
Well I know, I meant
It may be connected with Etruscan, a great civilisation. Virgil was an Etruscan and so was Julius Caesar. And other languages too, Russian and Georgian. And Linguistics.
Linguistics? Oh, good for you.
But I want to switch to comparative literature. I have a friend in Lima in Peru, there's a new university starting up and they need people, and he says if I just turn up, oh come with me to Lima.
I've heard of this place, it sounds interesting and very radical. But then you wouldn't like it would you. Tell me, how is it that you, so young, are against revolution? It has to happen you know.
Revolution is for adolescents. And I'm not young, I seem young to you because you're older, though not so much, oh it could work, please, it's in the family, my mother was older than my father, my brother married an older woman I believe in it I need you I've done nothing, I feel old and my life's a mess, but with you, I know, I just know it will all come right, I feel this tremendous strength, please please don't turn me down, I want to catch up the lost years, now now, we have so little time my youth is gone.
You who hope to get through hell in a hurry, consulting your watch and removing it. You see I have brought these books. This is a best-seller and sometimes you write like it when the pressure of breast-selling reality forces you to open doors that nevertheless lead into one another through an inexorable typology of embedded digressions and an incompetent heroh competence again with the rapid foisting as usual of this or that candidate whenever there is a vacancy and no quorum left, whose pygmylion desire and wild performative nevertheless generates a text unless the motivation is reversed. Any agent can enter into a relation with any predicate. The notions of subject and object do not correspond to a difference in nature but to a place in the proposition uniting for instance two lovers. Hence there is no need to talk of hero villain seducer traplayer and lawbearer these rules are interchangeable. Sometimes however you vanish into a linguistic edifice you have erected, you or the garlic, in a six-hour nightly timetable which is very exhausting, crumbling your viscerally disorganised resistance to prove what? That the timetable exists the moment it has been uttered as a

possibility? That the lover of the moment will be untactfully dropped with scene and summary as is forescene thus unbalancing the cost on the one hand and on the other the mean culpa justifying the felix end in an eternal game of vinciperdi, though the economy of the narrative is seriously impaired and may crash into a middle class crisis? Or that it is more difficult for a phallus-man to enter the I of a woman than for the treasurer of signifiers to enter the paradisco terrestre?

But we must not confuse the levels of discourse YOU ARE HERE and the paradiso terrestre is a paradiso corporel which must last a little longer so that you follow the principle not to follow the principle but remain good lovers or maybe call his bluff and accept I promessi sposi? We love each other now, we have loved each other for six weeks, isn't that enough?

No. If it's not just tact and diplomacy you're trying to use, if you really love me as you say, please don't give up. Of course there are problems, of course there may be difficult adjustments for both of us, there always are. But I know, I know, deep down, I feel we've had too little time. If we can only give ourselves a year, another summer, we'll never want to leave each other, never. The gods can condemn us to life and death, but they can't force us to be human in our lives.

Can't they?

Ripeness is all and ripeness is far beyond calm and wisdom, è un astratto furore.

Stavro that's beautiful. I'm not sure whether it's true but it's beautiful. Thank you. I must however go to Rome alone for three or four days.

What! Why, what for?

To meet my husband.

But, I thought you'd left him.

He wants me back. We're going to talk it over.

But that's absurd, how can he, you're with me now, you must divorce and marry me, oh promise me you'll ask for a divorce and won't weaken, oh god, three days! What shall I do?

If you care as much as you say you can wait for me.

Three days! I'll never get through them. I'm going to lose you, I know it I know it please don't go who does he think he is after three years!

Not for sale as object of exchange of information.

But every structure presupposes a void, into which it is possible to fall into delirious discourse, the intelligence suspended helplessly as it watches the acting out of its own lunatic trajectory.

For within every idyll there opens out another idyll, as a vast mouth that never names the secret chiasmus in her, in him, the idyll of Armel and Larissa who once upon a spacetime is a poem not a couple, the idyll of Marco, Oscar, Stavro and Marika, Amanda, Maddy and the rest, Armel and Veronica, Veronica and perhaps even Christopher. And within each idyll opens out the idyll of the paradiso terrestre which is no longer Arcadia but the other scene.

Who speaks? The Other Author.

Chi parla?

Hi Lara!

Armel! Hi.

Hi. Are you alone?

Yes of course. Where are you?

Downstairs may I come up?

Ma certo caro.

In many languages from Phaedrus to Freud effortlessly displacing notions with several syndiachrumbilical chords.

You look terrific Armel. So brown and slim. Too slim in fact you're positively thin.

You know I live on sun and yoghurt. I've been on the beach. Waiting for your arrival. What happened to you? I went to the semiotic castle as arranged and you'd gone.

Yes I'm sorry. Fear perhaps. I went off.

So they told me. Professor La Bocca I mean.

He's nice.

Yes. But he wasn't very discreet. So Italian. They not only boast of their own conquests they gossip about others.

That's unlike you Armel why this anti-Italian generalising?

Well. Are you in love?

Allegra ma non troppo.

The happiness sequence?

Busting out of sequence. He's not Italian anyway he's Albanian. Perhaps Etruscan. Virgil was an Etruscan.

It's an Italian name.

Laretino? I guess so I think his mother married an Italian, but Stavro is apparently Albanian. Keeping his t for two his object and his V for victory.

Oh Larissa are you still at it?

Not really. Though it acquires a curious importance when a man proposes insistantly and has nothing to offer but his body and his name. Which is why, I suppose, he offers them around with such tremendous pressure though heaven knows the second is no longer necessary for the purpose of the first. But in order not to seem too eager for just the body as a love-machine one starts thinking, or pretending to think, of the name.

You seem unusually allegra, even agitata, did you say ma non troppo?

Stavro Laretino. Yes of course it's Italian, from Aretino, a district and a man. Do you know who l'Aretino was? A sort of scabrous precursor of Don Giovanni except that he was a mere writer like Casanova. Well there it is I shall miss my Subject in him, keeping it even if it gets mauled a bit and he will miss his victory and his it in me, keeping them as a small winner. He has ashthma however, sometimes in the middle of it all, and wouldn't be able to sing the part.

You haven't changed. Except that you're gentler. And even more beautiful. Love becomes you.

I become love. Why are you inquisitioning me you never liked my inquisitions even in marriage or rather you complained that I wasn't jealous and asked no questions, then complained when I was and did. Am I not allowed an affair even in separation?

I said gentler. Don't get arch and aggressive. I'm prepared to wait. I asked you for the same patience once but you ran away.

Because I was on the spot and you did it so clumsily, and we were together. Now we're not, I'm here, you're there.

I'm here now.

Yes. I'm glad. I think I need your help Armel.

Is it serious?

No, it's too absurd, a carnival misalliance. But unexpectedly it's hitting me in the other place. Oh it's all under control, in fact his sheer cheek in taking it for granted that marriage is the greatest boon any man can confer on a woman exasperates me though I try not to show it. But I may find, when I've done everything to make him run away, that I can't cope.

Stop now.

I can't. Oh it's not just that he won't hear of it that would be easy. It's me, it's the idyll, and the way your own idyll opened up such a terrible nostalgia for what we had, you and me.

Why don't you do the running away?

Oh, the chiasmus. He's weak and couldn't stand it whereas I in theory can. So that he must himself want to run away and I must bring him to it by awakening his fear.

Isn't that just a grandiose pseudo-generous way of proepigramming your sense of loss?

Oh I know. Maybe that is not what I meant at all. I plunge into the dimension of his stupidity, more a sort of literalness, as opposed to literality, his belief in his own words, which is infectious in the end so that I find myself wanting to lay aside my other eyes my overhead projector and cultivate my garden or rather, help him bring up his children, look after a man, do something useful for a change. It's a fantasy of course.

Well. Let me know. I'll have to change my will.

Your what?

I don't want to leave whatever I have to someone else's children.

Oh Armel don't be so stuffy. As if I were thinking of money! I told you anyway, it's a fantasy.

Yes well it does smack of the society lady rushing to Africa to look after lepers.

That's unkind. And it's more than that Armel. In purely practical physiological terms I can't take the amount he needs, any more than I could take yours, I'm already in considerable pain. We're playing at gods but for all their ludicrous love life they don't have nephrectomies and other ectomies except maybe castration. You'd think that after the removal of so much there'd be plenty of room down there but no, it knocks and knocks and he will damage me, for life probably. I keep begging for nights off but what he means by a night off is twice in the afternoon before and twice in the small hours the moment of truth remember.

Stop now Larissa, come back with me.

Stop at a stop sign and what if the chap behind you doesn't? The dialogue proceeds, and a smarrimento. He wants this happiness so much I'm even tempted to give it, for a year or so, a pig-male eon, I doubt his love will last more than that, and then to die, so that he won't have the burden and embarrassment of an older woman on his hands. It's, it's the closest I've come to, well, a mystical experience.

This is pure romanticism, Larissa, dramatization and self-pity.

That from you? And what about your own mystical experience of love?

Please Lara don't rake up all that. Listen to me. His love won't last two months. If you can't shake him off the normal way call his bluff remember?

Well you didn't get cold feet why should he?

He is not me but a motherless doorhandle crying order order, a toy he will discard as soon as given. Larissa we had fifteen years. You can't throw that away.

Why not? That may be their meaning. And what do you want me back for? As the femme légitime? A hostess? To show I've come back? Che vuoi?

I want to save you.

Oh Armel.

I know.

Stavro also said I want to take you over. I half waited for I want to save you he's certainly the type, always proposing to women not in fact available. He calls his wife Maddy.

Larissa why go through with this, giving out, as usual, to the mediocre, you'll only get hurt, as usual, precisely because it's mediocre.

I know. J'attire les cons et les fous.

Thank you.

Nonsense Armel you were always the exception.

Was I? And why make an exception of him now? He'll even do you out of your private suicide pact. There are easier ways.

Because I am writing this libretto Armel, I can play all the parts, including Donna Elvira who talks like a book, remember, though in Molière it's Don Juan who talks like a book you see how the semes of portraits travel. I can identify with them all, even Donna Anna who mourns her dead father the Commandatore the law-bearer. The only one I can't identify with is that fool Don Ottavio who offers himself as father and husband. Unless I can turn him into Don Giovanni, then I can imagine him.

Is that what Stavro said?

Something like that. But he talks a lot of nonsense, like the greatest calamity for Europe and the world was the dismantling of the Austro-Hungarian Empire. He's an amateur Don Giovanni he says so himself though he puts it differently, a recalcitrant and inhibited no-good-first-time Don Juan I think he said, and he pours out his short lists by way of curriculum vitae with a slightly different version each time, but longs to stop, this time it's real and don't forget I'm a gentleman.

Voglio far il gentil uomo. A gentleman, if the concept still exists, doesn't need to say he is.

Don't be snobbish and beastly, the revolution is with us.

Well he seems as archaic as I am, I didn't know such people still hung around. Strange at his age.

Yes, he's an anachronism. Or it's a lost generation neither one thing nor the other. Even students are more sophisticated. There is however a curious pull about it, out of archaic flaws inherited from courtly love.

So you regard revolutionary students as sophisticated?

Oh I didn't mean just politics, but yes.

Some of them are as reactionary and bourgeois as you'd call me.

Well of course. But they divide themselves neatly into those who work hard, marry young and take their responsibilities as citizens as conventionally as we did, and those who reject all the rules of society and have themselves a ball, even if the latter often become the former. It's the mixture of the two sterotypes I find disorientating, the irresponsibility and evident lack of moral gumption, combined with the earnestness, the intellectual and emotional standards of suburbia.

People are individuals, his naivety may be personal. As for his politics don't forget that as an Albanian exile he may have very good reasons to be against revolution.

Of course he's an individual, I love him for what he is, it moves me, I want to help him grow up.

You want to save him.

Touchée.

So let him be. Oh Lara don't you see what you're doing, the same pattern, telescoping a lifetime into a few weeks, just as he's no doubt repeating an even more obvious one. And you won't be able to hide your strength in an idyll for long, you will crush him and he will run away, which is when you will start fantasising him, if you haven't already, and suffer.

I know. He is the Faun. He looks like a faun, a foreshortened faun. And I am playing Miriam. But without the gothic structure or Donatello's romantic fidelity. That's why I transferred the whole narrative to Rome, the International Theme you know, as well as the psychosis.

But you're not going to, coldly, use

Ma, devo raccontare qualcosa. I shall spell you into the sentence I write into the paragraph into which I insert you the sentence I write. But no, we're going to Lima.

You're mad. What about your job?

I'm here on a sabbatical you forget, starting September.

To be spent in a pastoral pastiche of marriage outside the walls? And he's already a third person to you. You should dip into his own angle of vision not yours.

Oh don't Booth me I do dip that's the trouble but too deep I know it better than he does himself.

It will escape. You have no right to reify him into the voiceless object of an intellect that delimits him. A human being lives to the end on his lack of definition, he always has the last word.

Read Bakhtine! Of course he'll have the last word which will be a cowardly silence. But Armel this is a conversation not a book, even if I talk like a book. How can I use the second person about him to you?

Of course, I am your second person singular why persecutest thou/me. But aren't you composing a motet for a prepared Oedipiano with a falsetto sound? And what about the previous chapter?

I know, it's a flop. As this one, and the next, redundant but necessary for qualcosa to continue. Narration is life and I am Scheherezade.

Incapable of a thousand and one nights. Or ten a day for a hundred days.

It will all get changed and transmuted,

How then does it get into the text?

cancelled even, for it does not exist, except in my own boundless need and fear that will alter the signifiers into a delirious discourse through swift-footed Hermes with terrible letters no doubt that we can skip as he will, for no recipient desires a message of enduring pain redundant and therefore without information content because not from the Emperor of China, all the less so if he has caused it so that I shall not transmit it many times and the unmany times I do I shall regret because I do not hope to turn again where the lack of imagination had itself to be imagined, unless I transmit it to you, but of course that's useless since the recipient is the meaning of the message, even if he has an earful of sirensong or wax or crabs and can't take any aspect of the truth gone wild.

Teach us to care, and not to care, teach us to sit still.

I do, or rather I did, a simple man's simple love I can return simply for a while. But he won't let me, he's knocking at the other place both his and mine without even realizing it, so that what begins in banality has to go through the whole signifying chain from idyll to catastrophe until it can be returned to banality, beneath contempt, amusing maybe and harmless, a poison and a pharmakon that immunises. And he is the temporary pharmakos or scrapegloat, but only for a time.

And you say you love him? You treat him as an object and despise him thoroughly.

Of course. Both. There are degrees of love and scorn. As man with woman are you for the double standard?

But all this has nothing to do with him.

He's aiming at someone else through me too though he doesn't know it. This terrible love he calls it, and refuses to give it up.

But Lara that's no reason

Well it's just possible, you know, that I'm trying to prove with him, that your appalling accusations weren't true, that I can love without, well, dismembering, though I'm taking the dreadful risk of proving that they are.

It's you I'm thinking of, not him. You'll lacerate yourself. He won't, he'll never even admit he was using you.

Oh I'll come through. I always do you know. And so will he, certainly, you're right of course, he'll shrug it off with a swim and a fornication, or he'll erect another huge romantic structure and never know what hit him.

How do you know he won't? You're playing dangerous games, both of you, incestuous games, but you should be wiser Lara, you know yourself too well, and the great lack, the hole you speak of so often, which even I couldn't fill, never to be filled by anyone, least of all by an infantile phallus-man who calls his wife Maddy.

You beast.

I'm sorry. But I'm frightened for you.

Or jealous? Or outraged or what the heck. I'm frightened too Armel. His body is near but his discourse is far. He might be speaking out of some decadent Byzantine romance, the language of my twentieth year except that I never spoke it. It was fine as an idyll, in fact I turned a banal pick-up into an idyll because I couldn't enjoy it otherwise, and that was all I wanted. But he's more forceful than I thought, and has given it the twist of possession for ever, which normally I can't stand but I'm so tired Armel, I want to give up, give in. And yet though he insists the age difference is nothing he can't meet me even half way into his own future, naturally, so I have to do all the meeting, backwards, and not just the years of actual difference but way back, he's a mere child for all he's thirty. And of course that's rejuvenating on the level of the idyll but on the other it's like taking twenty steps back, into the void, where I never was. But his body is in me and I absorb his discourse through pores as if translated, magnified from far away. It's about love. He himself doesn't of course, recognise the other in me at all. His unknowing is my undoing for I need to be known, as my knowing will be his for he doesn't want my true or even untrue knowledge of himself no man does.

Hush. Every man does. But not so verbalised. Never let yourself be fully known, remember?

Oh it's only to you Armel, a scrapped chapter.

Thank you.

With him I dialogue on his endless problems, or we sing like crazy in the car he does Leporello to perfection oddly enough, you're right. For if I dialogue on other things I dialogue alone.

Well, see it through if you must. But don't let him see you see through him.

Thank you Armel, for letting me talk. I do love you, you know. I'll be back.

I hope so. My street though small is not so hard to find.

That's a nice pentametre.

Well, let me know if, if you do want a divorce.

Could you, if you can bear it, do one thing for me, now I mean?

What is it?

I'd like you to meet him. Oh not as you. He knows I'm seeing you of course, god, the fuss he made, but he's coming here tomorrow at eleven, we're leaving the next day. Could you call, as a friend, casually, at about quarter past, under another name, Oscar for instance and we'll have a drink together. And then you could ring me, or meet me outside. When are you leaving?

In three days. I don't like it. In fact I think it stinks. But all right, Oscar it is.

Armel you're marvellous. Is the poison really out?

In me yes, I think so. But is it in you?

Oh probably not, I'm rotten through and through you know, my name is Toren.

It isn't it's Santores. And I told you before, don't run yourself down, people will always take you at your word, if only on that.

Yes but I have to run myself down to him, show him the worse he wants so insistantly to take with the better.

If that's a perverse test of the knight by the lady he'll fail it. I was hoping to spend these three days with you. Indeed I had hoped for the summer but you went off.

I know. I'm sorry. Do you mind very much?

I think I mind more this morbid threesome you're asking of me. Why do you want it?

I don't know. For strength to stop maybe, confirmation of a kind. You know how it is, the information-content of a particular unit is defined as a function of its probability, hence redundancy, necessary however.

That should make you redundant too, if you're as predictable as he is and as you say you are.

Like u after q.

U for mism

M for sis

O for the wings of a dove. I see you still have your guitar.

Yes but it's cracked. It gives a funny sound, sort of muted.

Well, I must go. I had a jacket somewhere. What are you working on now?

Work! Oh how distant it seems. Oddly enough, The Marble Faun.

Structural analysis of?

I'm not a Structuralist I never have been. Though some of the concepts are useful. It's more of a Transformational approach really.

Transformation of what into what?

I don't know yet. The intuition of the native speaker into the intuition of the naive speaker perhaps.

You joking?

At the level of the signifier of course what else did you think?

Anything at all with you Larissa, language is your strength and your strength is your weakness. See you to-morrow.

There has occurred however the telescoping of the flute-player into a stereotyped foreshortened faun piping right to left on the rectangle of days with weeks and even years in an implicit depth, days that do not see themselves or the four lies reflected in the retrovizor, looking at nothing on or in the brow that Scheherezade thinks too low beneath the mat of khaki crinkly hair perhaps Etruscan or hiding behind a discourse from which the subjects vanish piecemeal, the one giving no references and the other too many thus having a mouth removed and other organs when all that is signifiable in her is struck with latency as soon as raised to the function of signifier which initiates this raising by its original disappearance, the show within the show.

For the idyll reopens out into the other idyll of Armel who is not like that at all and Veronica true icon iconoclasted before the introduction of the pistol, raising antinomies by reaction that overtakes the subjective idea, rendering it objective, here on the ocean edge, and irresistible, Aphrodite emerging from memory and beckoning, naked, sprayed with flowery foam.

For you are not qualcosa as narrated either by yourself or some other who talks like a book and wants to be read like an algebraic grammar of narrative, the punishment in final position never falling on the euphoric term, only on the dyspeptic, the moving finger piercing through the pregnant plenitude from idyll to castratrophy thus bringing about the end of the discourse. Nor have you acted out the dialogue spun by the silent narrator who is yourself perhaps making yourself articulate and wise, quick on the uptake gentle cruelonlytobekind with brief mean brushstrokes for objectivity and her semelic a wild moon detached and gazing at the earth, tide-driven and helpless so that you can save her and if that is what you want that is how it will be for you always get your way in the end by transforming the passive silence of undecidability into the undeicidable. Whoever invented it is the absent narrator or you in love with the unreliable narrator who is in love with the implied author who is in love with himself and therefore absent in the nature of things through doors opening on doors, mirrors on mirrors in an eternal game of vinciperdi with the presence and absence of signifiers that characterises the practice of language. A head in a pool on a platter in a textured cloth, the head detached to re-present the word, a disembodied voice.

Larissa?

Armel! I mean—hi.

Hi. You're not alone I gather?

No.

Ecoute. Je suis desolé mais je ne peux pas te voir.

Pourquoi?

Je ne veux pas discuter, c'est ton affaire.

Mais tu étais d'accord.

Oui, excuse-moi. Je te dirai une chose seulement. Il est mignon comme tout et même, je crois, sincère. Mais pas mariable.

Je sais.

Oh quelqu'un l'épousera sans doute, une étudiante. Il n'est même pas sortable.

It's all right he's gone out on the terrace he's very tactful, anyway I'm sure he speaks French so this farce is pointless. But Armel does it matter?

My dear, even alone with him excluding the world as lovers think they can you'll still have to take him out, out of himself into you. Il n'est pas à ta hauteur.

Oh my hauteur I've told you, I'm sick and tired of my hauteur. I want to be humble, to abase myself.

Then you will. But you won't find humility only humiliation, you'll revolt and you'll suffer. It's sick. And he's totally unconscious.

And what about you and someone else not at your hauteur?

Lara I don't want a discussion.

That's different isn't it, you're a man. Armel are you there? I'm sorry. It's awful don't you see what thou lovest well remains but if the lovest is removed only the narratio is left.

Are you playing anagrams again?

I can't help it Armel it's written in the name. Please can't I see you before you go?

No I'm sorry, I've already said more than I meant. I can't cope with this. In fact I was ill all night, vomiting.

Oh. Forgive me. You see I'm no good to you. Why did you come?

I don't know. I did then.

Armel don't go away.

I must.

Take me with you.

Not now Larissa. I'm sorry, I was hoping to but

Because of this? Punishing me again?

It's a question of timing. Like letters, they never coincide. But please, look after yourself, and see a doctor before you go.

Oh I'm all right, it's you who should see a doctor.

They've long given me up as you know, I heal myself.

Yes.

Well goodbye. Have a nice time.

You too. Bye, Armel. I love you.

I know. Bye.

But is it really possible to superimpose so many systems one upon the other, the social the economic the personal the traffic lights the institution of learning where the old learn from the young and the young learn nothing until one day suddenly they too are old? The exile motif on a suburban tale of Porlock upon a Gothic novel woven with the International Theme upon an eighteenth century fantasy itself the obverse of the Tristan myth known to Lancelot and Guinevere read by Paolo and Francesca then wagnerised and materlinked into Mélisande through layers and layers of books and looks that open like doors onto other doors as he comes in from the terrace high up above the traffic saying was that your husband? Yes. What did he want?

Oh just to say goodbye.

It was a hell of a long goodbye.

We have a very close relationship.

He wants you back. I know it. Of course he does you're so wonderful that's why we both want you. What's the matter, you seem sad.

No. I'm just thinking. You remember how Dostoievski makes Dievushkin read Gogol's Nose, no Gogol's Coat, and revolt at the author's concept of the little man, at the way he delimits him without his consent, arresting him in his own definition whereas every man knows he is not the definitions of others but for ever undefined, never coinciding with himself? Just as the trial of Dmitri Karamazov is a farce of other judgments and in the end he judges himself. And that made me think of books within books, stories within stories, each character a new tale-bearer. How far can we box in?

I don't understand. What has all that to do with us, or with your husband. Has he upset you?

No.

You're depressed again and you're going to discourage me. Don't you think I'm depressed too, after this meeting I was terrified of, and I was right, you're different.

Stavro one can't turn from one personality to another at the flick of a switch. One is temporarily invaded, but it will pass.

And here among all these books, it's like a professor's study, designed to intimidate the students.

Well it is a professor's study Professor La Bocca's he's a symbolic logician oh yes you met him. Anyway I am a teacher and so are you.

But all these notes, this pile of mail and records and tapes, you seem so self-sufficient, you don't need me at all.

I do Stavro, I need your terrible love as you call it, but I don't think I can have it, Stavro non avrò.

Oh please don't start again.

I'm not coming with you, I'm staying here. I have work to do.

You can't be serious. But it's all booked, you promised.

Then unbook me. I'm sorry.

I know, I can't offer you much, only problems, and I haven't even got a job. But I'll get one, at least for next year, and I'm applying everywhere, Rhodesia even, and you could get one easily, wouldn't you like to come to Rhodesia with me it's a beautiful climate like here, we'd live this paradise for ever.

Rhodesia! It's a fascist country.

No more than America if you mean the colour thing and you live in America.

Don't be silly Stavro. There's plenty wrong there but at least we pay lip-service to equality and a good deal more than people who read only Black Literature are aware. I couldn't live with, and therefore condone, official Apartheid, it's another kind of cutting off.

But you wouldn't be cut off you'd be with me.

Stavro stop fantasising, what about your children you must be near them they need you. You must stop rushing off, always putting the desire of the moment first.

It's not a desire of the moment I love you. And we'd take them with us. But you're right, as usual, she won't let them go. Oh what would I do without you. Of course I must stay in Europe. How about Strasburg I've applied there will you come to Strasburg with me?

I can't, Stavro.

What did he do to you?

Nothing. I'm just very tired, very very tired.

I know my love, it's my fault, forgive me. We shall have abstinence tonight and you shall rest. I once saw a poster in Wales which said Abstinence is good for you. Oh Larina I want what you want.

Do you?

It's only a moment of discouragement. But you must understand I can't take nothing but discouragement from you and remain unaffected. You mustn't try and see how much I can take.

(I'll pursue you and pursue you if that's what you want) No, I'm sorry, You can't take much can you?

I suppose not. But you're not very tough either and why should you be, except because both he and I like you that way. It isn't true after all that women are stronger. They love to cuddle their babies but aren't they just consoling themselves? Father is more important, he can speak and teach. Mother feeds you and teaches you to love but it's Father who teaches you how to survive. Oh I wish I could do something about my mistakes, I see them so clearly now. Oh my love, I seem to be doing again what I've done so often, having problems I can't cope with and rushing to a mummy or a nanny or a home or refuge. I hate seeing that I'm doing this to you. I feel lonely and abandoned, but my behaviour makes you lonely too. Please forgive your awful errant Childe Stavro.

I don't know whether to laugh or cry you're so absurd yet touching.

It's good to see you smile again. My Larina, I know, as you know, that it's peace and beauty when we're together, and I'm convinced that if we could live together for a year all our problems would disappear and we'd never leave each other.

So you've said. But I don't have any problems except the one you've thrust upon me. Don't you see that you're trying to force me into living a cliché, the cliché of the older woman and the younger man?

I just don't understand your concern with your age and cliché-mongers. Why can't you trust me? Will you please explain to me what I can do to earn your trust? Aren't you even now sending me out to Peru more or less to prove myself already, to see what distance and separation can do to our love?

I'm not sending you out to Peru, you're going anyway.

Lara hear me hear me.

You sound like an oracle. I'm listening.

Please, try to believe in me. I love you. Trust me. Come with me to Lima, I know you're frightened, I'm asking you to take a risk, but I'm taking a risk too and you said you wanted adventure.

You must go alone, Stavro, and meet other girls, you've only just left your wife she's not my wife well the mother of your children and I happened along. Marry one of your students in Lima, a nice young fleshy one, not thin and finished like me, someone who will combine motherly qualities with youth and looking up to you.

But it's you I love. Don't you look up to me?

Well, of course. But you seem crushed by me and I'm sorry. Look, go to Lima and if you still love me next year I'll come.

But, but, we'll be a whole year older then! How can I wait a year?

Yes, it's a ridiculous test of the knight by the lady. All right, I'll come as planned for the rest of the summer and then we'll see.

Oh my love, thank you. But you'll stay, I know you will.

Stavro you must understand, I can't give up my job, I'm alone in the world you know, I have to support myself.

But you're not alone now you're with me. And you'd get a job wherever I am, easily, more easily than me I have nothing only a silly Italian degree. But I'm a good teacher I know and I have wonderful references. And you'll want to stay, I know it, promise me you'll stay if you really want to and not pretend you don't out of fear or mistrust? I'll light the way for you.

All right, I promise.

Come, let's make love.

Not now Stavro I'm very tired I told you. Why don't we hear some music, or you read me some Dante.

Yes of course, where is he?

Top shelf right.

God, all these books. And all these publications of yours, there's a whole shelf, why'd you bring them?

As give-aways, one has to. Anyway you have your list of women, children and languages, I have my list of publications.

But surely you've had a lot of lovers too?

I don't keep lists as conversational gambits.

That's very unkind. It's the first time you're being really unkind to me.

It was a joke. Don't be depressed again my love or you'll depress me, I'd just got out of it. Anyway most of the books on those shelves, which are my corner, are in your field aren't they, all the disciplines have come together through linguistics now it's very exciting every system is being thought out again from top to bottom, even psychoanalysis has taken up from de Saussure.

Who's de Saussure?

But. Stavro! I thought you said you taught Linguistics? He's the father of it all.

Well, I don't know, it's Applied Linguistics I do.

Oh—I see. I'm sorry, I didn't mean, but why did you come to the Semiotics Congress then?

Oh just to see and learn.

And did you?

Not really, it all struck me as very pretentious.

Some of it yes. But that's the funny side, even semioticians don't communicate. Well, you can teach me Applied Linguistics and I'll teach you Theoretical.

That's lovely, yes I'd like that. And I'll teach you Albanian if you like and Macedonian. Or Russian or Georgian. Or Old Church Slavonic, that's Old Bulgarian, you should know the language of the church we'll get married in.

Well let's stick to Dante for the moment.

Where would you like?

Anywhere. Or the beginning first, then Purgatorio XXVI.

Nel mezzo del cammin di nostra

What's wrong?

I've just remembered a dream I must tell you.

For these things do matter in a text like love or revolution of those who talk like books idyllic epistolary farcical that inevitably produce a double of the thing re-presented, the double being nothing, a non-being which nevertheless is added to the thing and therefore not totally devoid of value despite the negative portrait of the object instituted by itself as valueless which, however resembling, is never absolutely true, and in any case singular so replaceable. He should have given you a sense of trust so that you could feel he knows what he is doing and you could abandon yourself to his wiles. For, if mimesis exists, non-being is, opening out like mouths into mouths that rehandle the signifiers into a delicious discourse as the summer forms bluish slit-shaped holes like blue lacunae into which you plunge towards the final crumbling of yet another babel.

You don't have the floor.

On a point of information

as object of exchange and from the start an object of central loss because stolen, like citrus fruits or a nose here and a dream there or kernel sentences out of faculty clashes books letters and symposiums to provoke the word by the word lighting up the commonplaces from the other place to generate a text.

So then I was being interviewed for a job by a woman professor who gave the job to a woman and I felt treated unfairly. Then as consolation she sent me out to play ball with her dogs saying a bit of fresh air will do you good and my dog will be kind don't be afraid. I went out it was sunny, it was the university playing ground with a huge green field for rugby and a sandpit for pole-jumping. I had a red ball with black stripes and I threw it over the sandpit. All the dogs ran and jumped for it one of them was mine, they were all boxers and labradors but mine was a mongrel and he jumped the highest and caught the ball and brought it back to me. I think it means the general worry and anxiety over my career and my life obviously at a crossroads. The sun and the green space represent South America or possibly Africa. The pole jumping is the risk I have to take, the red and black ball is life which I throw and gamble, the dogs represent my problems but in the end life comes back to me and I feel that I win do you agree?

Hmmmm yes, at the manifest level. You shouldn't tell me all these dreams, Stavro, I'm not an analyst and one needs the transfer.

Oh but you know so much about it you've read everything. And then I had another one I was in Ethiopia with you and going to visit a Russian church there and telling you all about it. It was Russian baroque, a small church with a huge tower over it and I kept telling you what a good imitation it was even though modern. Inside there was no iconostasis. The altar was like in St Peter's almost in the middle and the columns, altar and walls were covered with mosaics and frescoes, some Russian some Ethiopian and I went on saying how everything was bogus but of good quality and at the same time I was feeling afraid that the whole thing might collapse on us and I was anxious to get outside. And I took you out in the end without showing my anxiety and then I noticed that the bell-tower was no longer solid stone as when we entered but coloured glass and even more impressive than before and taller and I felt safe and that it wasn't going to collapse any more so I took your hand and the dream ended. Can you make anything of it?

A prepared oedipiano with a treble sound.

A foot man saying O in the mountains but O

Another one who grabbed a balloon and then let go.

You are the sentence I write I am the paragraph, generating each other cutting off each other's word not following the principle but separating from it piecemeal fragmented though generating now and again a kernel sentence eaten or falling into an earful of sirensong or wax upon which bees dance their honeyvorous messages, which comes to the same thing for we cannot eat each other without becoming each other neither can we refuse the gods in us without crabs in our ears.

For the gods in us are organic they do not have livers kidneys and complexes did Christ have a Oedipus complex? They are the complexes narrative and generated they are the liverish kidneys. They are the eagle strangled in the sea the mouth removed for naming things the revolution long preparing out of archaic flaws bouleversing the boulevards back into bulwarks, they are the transfer utterance which can be interpreted at all levels as privation disjunction attribution conjunction thus representing the circulation of value-objects as an identification of the deictic transfers. And they do not exist except at your awakening touch. It has all been dreamt up by the lover of the moment but displaced, condensed, metonymised. Such a man would not fight the eagle for one thing or another or wring its neck. Nor would he have four eyes or see luminous hoops dancing through and through each other. It doesn't work for him who will have to be dropped with an organised chiasmus since the lack of imagination cannot after all be imagined, only stolen, like citrus fruits out of stories and purloined letters to provoke the commonplaces out of the other place, the text within the text.

Qui parle avec un noyau dans la bouche?

You're taking a long time have I given you food for thought?

There's a well-known case, Stavro, of a man who used to write down all his dreams in a beautifully calligraphed hand, filling volume after volume which he brought to his analyst. And when he broke it off he asked for his dreambooks back but the analyst couldn't lay hands on them, whereupon the patient went into a rage, accusing him of stealing his dreams, calling him the violator of his unconscious and saying that what is given must be returnable. But it isn't you know.

I don't understand, are you mistrusting me again? I'd never do that to you, I'm not a case and I love you.

No, well. Never let yourself be fully known.

You never tell me your dreams.

If I ever do it will be total reversal.

What do you mean?

Which I see already, from yours.

For the information-content of a particular unit is defined as a function of its probability. There are however many possible exits. In general the more probable a unit is the greater its degree of redundancy which, at night, at the flick of a switch, can turn smoky grey to dim the glare of a floodlight from the other eyes, exact replicas higher up the brow, and the dimming is preferable to the sudden isolation of seeing too much by the glare of floodlight you must dip, gently dip but not too deep.

Now droops the faun head underneath the changed modalities into a desperate love, discouraged and afraid you see, I'm boring you with my dreams, my problems, saying in effect the world is too much for me nanny please protect me. But it would be so much better to be able to accept this protection when I'm capable of giving it. I'll find something, and even if it means separation for a while I want to come back a man. I don't want to enter into a relationship in which I'm just your appendage.

Out of the mouths of babes.

But Stavro you have entered into such a relationship, insistently, though I kept trying to tell you. Any relationship between youth and age is by its very nature unequal, and on both sides, whichever way you look at it, though youth is bound to win, if only because it is youth.

You keep calling me young I feel so old.

Retaining a trace of hierarchy however despite youthful demand although the horizontal coordination degenerates, according to the narrator, into useless chatter between I promessi sposi who will go on as if.

Veronica!

Armel!

You look more beautiful than ever.

Because I love you. I've never stopped loving you I've missed you terribly.

On a point of information may we interrupt.

Oh go away with your politics we want to hear this course.

What is this reactionary culture you're dishing out comrade the bourgeois idyll is over you can't perpetuate it for ever. The revolution is upon us which has been long preparing out of archaic flaws, bouleversing the boulevards back into bulwarks as the city opens up its legs to receive the flood of the vox populi. In the beginning was the parting shot.

And as Marx said personalities and events recur, the first time as tragedy the second as farce.

Revolution is only another matrix, dismembering the paternal inheritance in a Macte Jovis followed by fratricide. To eat is to be eaten for you too will be fathers dismembered and ammazzati.

Phooey. Rhetoric out of a lawsuit over property in Syracuse, a disembodied vox.

Revolution is not an institution.

We demand the abolishing of all idylls and a complete reorganisation of generating structures.

Truth is an outmoded institution.

Precisely. Words imply the absence of things just as desire implies the absence of its object.

Yes and discourse occurs only insofar as there is lack of sight, eyelessness is not a provisional state but a structure.

There is a flaw in the judas-eye.

Rubbish. Our object revolution is very much present, and desired.

It can't be both that's a polarity. In any case the punishment never falls on the euphoric term, only on the poor Yorick.

He's dead.

Safe.

Words seeking to be true become false and inversely, words seeking to be false become true. We end up experiencing the feelings that we pretend, one can't speak, or write, with impunity.

What set pieces of author dead dying and half dead are you dipping into like cannibalistic survivors comrade?

Look it up. Are not all idées reçues?

We demand the closing of all books and looks and the closing of this institution of learning the conspicuous consumption of texts with built-in obsolescence and a capitalist narrative economy now crashing into a middle-class crisis.

And who will close it, an arbitrary act of your fake authority?

Rules are made to be broken in an age that is earthquaking from evolving permanence to permanent revolution.

But from the point of view of the object exchanged the debit goes to the left.

You book-keeper, footman of the bourgeoisie. Close all the books I say. There have to be textual disturbances since you've all fallen back into the old ruts, regressed into archaic modalities that simply no longer exist and which can therefore no longer be imposed.

Hear hear.

Oh go fuck yourself.

Very good my friend it's better than fucking your mother. Who do you think you are, bourgeois little boys dipped carefully into a bloody eye and swaddled in a castration complex to preserve the dirty little family secret that structures society each tale-bearer carrying his code in his mouth until he has eaten himself silly and soft and flabby? That way recuperation lies. We dip you you dip us in a permanent circulation of value-objects with always something added, ex nihilo, swelling out the portrait of the object instituted by itself as a value although its semes are false, with the moving signifier pointing to the falsehood but incapable of decoding it so that although long desired it is maintained in a pregnant plenitude the piercing of which, both liberating and catastrophic, will bring about the end of the goldicondeological discourse.

So that the fat magician lifts you up busting out of sequence to switch the lights to quell the audience he says dragging you out into the wings of a carnival all hierarchy dissolved although you scream not now not now see you later you-narrator the show must go on first we must change the subject find the missing prop the thirty-seventh veil the white white rabbit mannikin out of a black hatch consulting his watching consultant as he falls into a faint.

Meanwhile the timetable crashed into by the bouleversing

bulldozers of society as subversion of the text has slipped into another, the talebearer has given birth to another tale-bearer, spokesman of a reality which merely seeks to appear true, separating the upper and the lower waters into sea and sky fornicating with earth in a death-battle with time for a trophy that drops into the sea and rises, feathered in foam, the signifier of signifiers beneath which the truth escapes for pigmaleons into its own depths, retaining its mystery, reflecting at the surface only the sky, despite the underwater plungers.

Iconostasis.

What do we do now, Jacques, the story of our loves has been interrupted again.

Coitus interruptus.

That's not worthy of you.

No, I never like it. I gather there's a pill now to structure the family which structures society.

The family has crumbled, together with Oedipus.

Unthroned.

O let us sit upon the ground and tell sad stories of the death of kings.

And kings' daughters.

Undroned.

Transferred to the other place.

A stylus she can't cramp.

The anti-hero anti-rescuing her from an anti-monster in an anti-romanzo.

It sounds very negative

and therefore singular

and therefore replaceable.

We could clean up the dirty little secret.

Or abolish it.

All deletions in the deep structure must be recoverable, that's a law, written up there as you would say.

That way recuperation lies. For you are not my master except by a purely verbal gentlemen's agreement I am yours.

A trace of hierarchy however has been retained despite demand in an institution where the old learn from the young and discussion frequently overflows the framework of this one point. Can a point have a framework? All purely verbal gentlemen should be eliminated. No, every fact of language must be first analysed as a global, social phenomenon. And what about mere linguistic ladies we demand an equal right to elimination. No, to analysis as global social phenomena. You don't have the floor it's Jeremy's turn. Oh god is he still here? Well very briefly I simply want to say the problem isn't where you think it is. Oh it must have gone out then it was here a moment ago that means we haven't got a quorum, the problem must be present.

And if present then no longer desired since desire implies the absence of its object as words imply the absence of their referents. Since we are talking about the problem it must therefore be absent.

> Slipped through the rectangle of time
> into a rectangular stanza into which you
> enter saying once upon a time
> there lived a credibility obitu-
> ary black framed portrait as
> an absent value-object of desire:
> hence all the semic portraitures
> that in the wabe did gyre.

So what do you think, should we kill off Larissa?

She sure asks for it.

Naive speakers indeed!

In fact.

In fact of language, a global social phenomenon.

A balloon half grabbed let it go.

Explode it.

Both liberating and catastrophic.

Well Renata gave us the clue.

She stuffed it with clues and so did Ali why don't they get together in a clueful grip?

Shall we Renata?

I'm not competing with Saroja of the khol-framed eyes.

Saroja of the oriental adagia has left this class.

Oh you're eliminating her too?

She has eliminated herself into a cloud of unknowing.

Ah, like Stavro.

No not like him at all he's a transparent blue lacuna which is quite different. More like Armel, if it weren't for that illiberal and catastrophic chapter in which you reinvented him as an ideal husband, articulate and crueltobekind, in order to dialogue lunatically with yourself.

What do you mean? That was real.

You hogged the paradismal dialogue my dear. Already Myra slipped him into the wrong rectangle as a black man last term at the flick of a sexual play and that had to be rectified. Tell me how did you spend you summer vacation?

Well, REALLY.

Textually speaking.

Sexually freaking so there.

Good good.

But Ali what do you have against the black people?

I am an Arab I have nothing at all against the black people Eliza.

BUT?

It didn't fit, that's all, The text must cohere. For Armel is not like that at all but tall and dislikes answering questions in black and white with a nominervating intelligence and an evasive mouth that wraps him up in the seductive parlour game of superstition disguised as mystery, which is an old illusion, but in which he nevertheless deep down believes.

That's precisely why one has to reinvent him all the time. I mean that's why Larissa had to.

The past tense doesn't exist my love.

You're going too fast I'm not your love yet

even now as we drive the discourse into the future merely glancing up at the retrovizor we watch the road ahead and sing like crazy touching each other's thighs voglio far il gentil uomo for instance or la belle si tu voulais.

with the intuition of a naive speaker.

Shall we return to the subject of discourse?

Yes, what is it?

The text within the text.

Looks within books.

But Larissa? and our Larissa? Has she not carefully invented the person she has become, stereotyping her twenty-seven veils for a pontificating pirate who will not stay for an answer?

Till a motherless doorhandle crying order order pistol-shoots her into a swift earthquake that crumbles all the structures.

Well grammatically they're the same agent you know, the doorhandle and the door, as when three brothers or robbers accomplish an identical action, only the modalities differing hence the confusion of brows at the start.

We're going round in circles this isn't a faculty meeting what shall we do, kill her off? Eliminate her to Lima or let her die in Rome?

Oh not Lima she wouldn't have gone she obviously had no intention of going.

Let us not fall into the intentional fallacy.

But she must die in ROMA AMOR spelt backwards of course.

A heroine who literally dies of love.

Let us not fall into the affective fallacy.

No not of love she doesn't love him she dies of the expanded timetable bulldozing into the remaining kidney hypertrophied you know to compensate for the removal of the other like dreams so it atrophies and

Oh yeah and I guess you want the intrusion of the bathetic fallacy to fill the gap with a deathoflittlenell scene Larissa attached to a kidney-machine that's desperately trying to cleanse her blood of false semes as she talks to the ideal husband?

Or to the Other.

No the phallus-man should simply be fizzled out.

Well he is already.

Oh I don't know it's odd how one usually does bump into ex-lovers, you know, Albertine returned devoid of all but negative significance. Let's have them meet though he would of course first fizzle himself out like she said, and that's what would hurt, after all that pressure, that he'd be too cowardly even to honour her as a human being and tell her he'd switched off and met someone else, a student like she said who'd look exactly like his mother but a fresh fleshy young version and who'd hold him exactly where she wants.

How do you know what his mother looks like she's extratextual.

Yes he's a motherless doorhandle remember.

Oh well we could work her into the Calabrian sequence all Italians bring their women for the mamma to disapprove.

He's not Italian he's Albanian. Etruscan perhaps.

But an exile brought up in Italy with an Italian name.

Virgil was an Etruscan so was Julius Caesar.

Was it Calabria I thought we said France.

Yes and he would calmly bring her, the momma-sudent I mean, as his young bride to the semiotic castle the following summer, where she'd be recuperating Larissa I mean by invitation of the Count Professor whatshisname La Bocca from being at death's door hanging by one thread about which he'd cared nothing having fizzled himself out the phallus-boyman I mean and we could have a hilarious comedy with the two women sneaking around the spiral staircases of the castle avoiding each other because he'd be too frightened to introduce them and La Bocca saying my dear lady he's no gentleman coming here and Larissa bumping into him finally saying why are you behaving in this ridiculous manner. What ridiculous manner sheepish like and she'd say well all this cat and mouse game introduce me to your wife let's behave like civilized human beings. Or maybe he could come up to her and say will you be my friend.

Oh my God Julia what mimesis are you working through nobody behaves like that.

And who cares if they do it's a lost generation.

No well I agree it's a bit too much but we should have the fall into language and the exploitation of the very clichés she feared.

Why? We've had plenty and rejected it.

But it somehow crept back into the text didn't it? Everything exists even the discourse you do not choose.

Not the dimension of banality.

On the contrary, for that very reason will you let me finish for heaven's sake it's my turn

and the floor is flooring you

Oh shut up and they'd meet for a drink on the castle terrace and Larissa would say well tell me all how did you two meet closing the manuscript in which she'd been inventing the whole episode before she knew it would turn out that way that happens you know and the whole dialogue in advance and the girl would say well I'm studying comparadive lirrechure.

Why are you making her a Southern North American they met in Peru.

That's true she's a Latin mother type or maybe an Inca hook-nosed and fleshy round the jaws preparing several chins. Oh well anyway it would come out that she went to his class on *I promessi sposi* and they got all cosy over that and he was amazed she'd read it and she also knew The Knight in the Tigerskin translated of course through her course in Comparative Literature and he'd tell Larissa all about it how nobody reads that and how unique she is the mommagirlwife I mean we'd better give her a Spanish name Vittoria for instance forgetting that Larissa too

No thank you thou shalt not take my name in vain

Well anything it doesn't matter they're dropping out, going to Rhodesia to live the white man's life and talking of how they'll go on safaris and that, hunting the tiger

They don't have tigers in Africa

They do

They don't

And talking of drop-outs what about the Hungarian girl Marika we've forgotten her.

Oh well he'd already dropped her for Larissa she's a loose end we can't pick them all up. Or we could have her escaping to freedom under his pressure, he'd have started writing to her again after leaving Larissa in Rome and before meeting his wife, then again not telling her he'd married and she'd be writing desperate letters from a refugee camp in Austria and his new wife would be full of motherly understanding about his previous affairs including Larissa and say we must help her Marika I mean I have a friend in Sweden or something and he'd be so grateful.

Ugh, it stinks, it's a lost generation, who cares.

You're mad, all of you. You're talking about all these people as if they really existed

Oh shut up Ali we're having fun inventing

independent of our text the entire point of which is not to reformulate the poetics of the Renaissance through the rise of the novel of the middle class in layers, why look up your notes on the filling out of that mental space with wide-based aureoles of droning on about the passions that enflame the soul of Cleopatra's nose or La Gioconda's liverish mystery Larissa's vicious organs which are all verbal organs and all removed reduced to a mouth most vicious of all that establishes a specular relationship with the reader's vulgar desire to know what happens next in an eternal game of vinciperdi between his demand which cannot reach its end by justifiable means and the author's gift of a running curriculum vitae as object of exchange, the truth as signifier being all the time non-specularisable except by a hidden representation of a representation.

Oh I don't know Ali we don't have to write to a proepigrammed course according to everything the teacher says.

No we don't down with Oedipus he's been deposed like they said there has been a complete reform of pregenital organisation and we don't get swaddled in mythical complexes any more.

No? then why are you so anxious to pick up all the loose ends and wrap them around yourselves like winding sheets? and why those, there are plenty of others while you're about it, floating about like the fringes of a sea-anemone what about Larissa strategically reemerging fully armed after a tacitactic defeat and a Trojan discourse war and reappearing disguised as Mentor on the lone sea-shore? You've forgotten that.

Well there must be some lost semes, vanishing away like gods into the other scene.

It has all the beautiful coherence of a psychosis with Don Juan a subject raised from an embedded sentence to a head-noun chopped, detached from the totality of the text and walking about the world of your fantasy as hero, giving more pleasure to you ladies than any asthmatic amateur who cannot sing the part without deodorant and throat-spray in a damp silling castle. But as you said yourselves or was it Armel, it's only a semiotic castle.

What are you talking about Ali this is the text we are creating it verbally we are the text we do not exist either we are a pack of lies dreamt up by the unreliable narrator in love with the zeroist author in love with himself but absent in the nature of things, an etherised unauthorised other.

Yes, looking back to the now in the then emptied of now losing his paradise his loved utterance and decapitated, eaten up piecemeal like pieces of poet dead dying and half dead.

Well I think we should take a vote on it.

On what?

To kill or not to kill Larissa.

No that's not a motionable motion I will reframe it we must vote on whether to be implicit or explicit and if the latter then vote on the positive or negative modalities.

Which, precisely, being which?

I vote we vote first on whether to vote those for those against abstinence refusal of representation with a show of hands in the secret ballet of the I where faculties never meet even on an imagined curve as illusion of a coherent structure diminishing in size

t
u
o
ab
this thus ,
like the
to go on lanky
aberrant o hench
utterly tw man be
that it is item traying
of protest to
a slight
got on real
speeches
anxiety
n't even item
of tall
have about
being
canyons
and we item two
hidden
the tall
time unless
y
side of c under
wasting a merely a
any other
r
either
we are preten
c
business
on
agenda mo
a
he having
on the de the
not even in raised
invar
which is ed the idi
iants
affair dress otic affair
of that
man
idiotic in the
me
idyll
hench
ti
this first
lanky being
ce
pla
to the
the peri
spa
according
into or patetic
malleable
stare fallacy
utter
being very
that
of the
however (rubbish)
faces
students
rectangu
ances and
floating
the
lar room
bend their
sea of
into which
blond black
before a
e
g
you
heads to
and down n
cha
write
walk up ti
of ex
down V
ter and ll
object
= F in
en
the
tive as
the
mosaic
narra
bal
of bent
le
my of
ou
heads
b
econo
v
are e breaks
ced
r
vards like a
sed
an
boule t
back crack
s
and a
into
ed
f to
ment
bulwarks
as
stay
mand
till
2x
com in the
the
run
place
them
h
make c of
bombs i i
birth
cry h O s
w
r r
d d
e e
r r

Thus the lanky hench the idiotic
man r a i s e d affair
who

in the first place
dis
h e n c h e s himself

(after reflexivisation of the identical
subject in the deep embedded sentence)

from the naked
emperor of
I-scream

(head-noun chopping rule)
rewriting the electoral platform into a
revised the elect the elect student
timetable electing despite demand

that every course should be represented in a re-presentation of every course on the decision-making committee though the demand cannot r e a c h its end since there are only fifteen decision-makers and a hundred and fifty courses which would upset the balanced economy of the narrative whose arbitrariness (freedom) is not infinite.

There are however plenty more subjects to raise
after the passive transformation and before ex
traposition of Olaf Oliver Chou Stan Catherine
Hubert Claire or the pale young man carbuncu
lar all speaking for a long time not to mention
the students very malleable, though the element

of manipulation must not destroy the illusion
of floating faces maybe coinsiding to form a
mosaic or else an avallon of long blond hair
cropped nose cherub revolutionary falling over
the almond eyes or the red beard wrapped in a
sari mop with horn rimmed tresses and bright
mauve eyes made-up intelligence you dip into
and feel for till an arm pops up textcalibur
of a deep thought you seize to dip into brains

twisting the knife in the lacuna with a slow
deliberation rewriting derivations into termi
nal strings or what James called ficelles, but
full of knotty problems like Quipu, which

however are there to be resolved, by means of a

pseudo-solution, thus creating other prombles
as you switch on the overhead eyes to show
a tree of knowledge branching off into intermi
nable proairetic possibilities, and or not if
being the connectives dear lady look and yet

there is always a binary exclusion since the S
either is or is not starred through a flaw
in the eye-contacting the goldicondeology excali
brated youth in terminal strings that eat
up like worms the corpuscles of your chaotic
unlearning the poetry of the corpus crysis which

flutters out into the rectangular room with no
exit like a sort of bird for a flash an hour of

a six-hour timetable then nothing only degrees
of absence but we'll come to that with inexorabi
lity since subjects are the space of travelling
semes the passage of a transformed decision
the attributes of a pentapod enigma in a nomi
native form borne by an unthroned king out of
a stone highergrif which has marked all our acci
dental discourse with a flawed judas-eye
gouged but gauged inessential despite the scar
the scare the scram the marks and the remarks

traceable only in the irrecoverable deletion
of a head noun on a piece of texture ex nihilo

In some languages however things recover them
selves. As when the student body turns into
the master markster of the comment for ever
marking every subject as object of discourse

nto degrees of presence
desired and feared
unfeared and undesired
superimposing unlimited antisystems
unto sixteen times sixteen time sixteen^n
possible balanced relationships in
endless permutations
represented in a hidden representation
inside a representation alphabetically
marked in columns that support the
proepigrammed linguistic edifice
of marked and un-re-marked
sem(id)Iotic
irrecoverable
narrators
gone

Adam	ϑ
Albee, Edward	ϑ
Alder, Neil	γ–
Amanda	x
Andersen, Hans C.	γ
Andromeda	β
Anna, Donna	x
Antigone	ϑ+
Aphrodite, alias Venus	β+
Aquarius	γ–
Aquitaine, Elinour of	x
Arbor, Helen	ϑ–
Aretino l'	x
Aries, alias Mars	α
Aristotle	ϑ–
Arthur, King	x
Athene, Pallas	β+
Austen, Jane	x
Austin, J. L.	β–
Author, implied	ϑ–
Author, Other	ϑ–
Bacon, Francis	ϑ+
Baez, Joan	α–
Bakhtine, Michal	β–
Balzac, H. de	ϑ–
Barthes, Roland	β+
Bataille, George	α+
Bath, Wife of	x
Beauvoir, S. de	x
Beckett, Samuel	β
Beethoven, L. van	β–
belle indifférente	x
black magician	α–
Boethius	x
Boole, Charles	γ+
Book, the	x
Booth, Wayne C.	ϑ
Born, Bertrans de	x
Bouhours, P., S. J.	x
boy-mouth	α
Brémond, Claude	ϑ+
Brillig, Bob	ϑ–
Brooke, Dorothea	x
Browne, N. O.	x
Browning. E. B.	α
Burns, Robert	x
Byron, Lord	x
Cage, John	α–

God	x
gods	γ
Gogol, Nikolai	β–
Gombrowicz, Witold	γ+
Gonne, Maud	x
Graves, Robert	x
Greimas, A.J.	β+
Guinevere	ϑ+
Gulliver	β+
Haimon	x
Hamlet	β
Hawthorne, Nathaniel	ϑ+
Hegel, G. W. F.	α
Heidegger, Martin	γ
Héloise	x
Héloise, la nouvelle	ϑ–
henchman, lanky	ϑ–
hero, the	ϑ–
Hjelmslev, Louis	x
Homer	x
Hubert	ϑ–
Husserl, E.	γ–
idyll, the	ϑ+
Institution, the	ϑ–
Irigaray, Luce	x
Isabel	ϑ–
Iseult	ϑ
Isherwood, Christopher	ϑ+
Isis	ϑ
Jakobson, Roman	β
James, Henry	γ–
Jocasta, Queen	ϑ+
Jones, Eliza	ϑ
Jove	x
Julian	x
Julien (St) le Pauvre	γ
Kaplan, Myra	γ+
Karamazov, Dmitri	γ
Keats, John	x
Kermode, Frank	x
Kreutzer, Professor	ϑ–
Kristeva, Julia	β+
La Bocca, Professor	x
Lacan, Jacques	β+
lady, the linguistic	x
lady, of the left	ϑ+
Lancelot	ϑ
Laretino, Stavro	x
La Tour, G. de	x
lawbearer, the	ϑ–
Leporello	β–
Lévi-Strauss, Claude	γ+
Littlebrown, Professor	ϑ–
Littlebrown-Fitzjohn, Claire	ϑ–
logos, hŏmo	γ–
logos, unvoiced	x
lover of the moment	α+
Maddy	x
Maeterlinck	x
Maître, le	γ+
Malatesta, Paolo di	γ
Mallarmé, Stéphane	x
Mandel, Michael	ϑ
man with blue guitar, the	α
man from Porlock, the	γ
Manzoni, Alessandro	x
Marco	x
Marcuse, Herbert	α–
Marika	x
Marner, Silas	x
Marx, Karl	α+
Master marksman of moment	γ–
Masters, Christopher	x
Masters, Veronica	x
Maurice	ϑ–
Mélisande	ϑ–
Medaware, Dr. Gregory	ϑ–
Mercury	γ
Merteuil, Mme de	ϑ+
Midas, King	ϑ–

Milton, John	x
Miriam	ϑ–
mistress of the moment	α+
Molière	γ
Moses	x
Mother	x
Musset's Muse	x
Narrator(s), the	x
Newman, Francesca	ϑ
Ngu-Rey, Professor Chou	ϑ–
Nourennin, Ali	β+
Novello, Ivor	x
Odysseus	β+
Oedipus, King	x
Olaf	ϑ–
Oliver	ϑ–
Orion	β–
Orpheus	x
Oscar	ϑ–
O'Shaunessy, Kathleen	x
Ottavio, Don	x
overhead projector	γ–
Pamela	ϑ–
Pankhurst, Mrs.	γ+
Paris Telephone Exchange	x
Penelope	ϑ
Phaedrus	γ–
Phallusman, the	α+
Philanthropos, Professor	ϑ–
picaroon, the	α–
Plato	β–
Pleiades	x
Polanska, Renata	ϑ–
Polenta, Francesca da	α
Ponte, L. da	α
Pound, Ezra	β
prince disguised as poor younger son	x
princesse lointaine	x
Propp, Vladimir	ϑ–
Proust, Marcel	x
Pygmalion	γ–
Quipu	γ
Ra	ϑ
Racine, Jean	ϑ–
Rachmaninov, Sergei	x
Ram, the	x
Rastier, Francois	γ+
Rastignac	ϑ–
Rustaveli, Choto	x
Ruwet, Nicolas	β
Sade, Marquis de	β+
Sand, Georges	x
Santores, Armel	x
Santores, Mrs. see Toren	φ
Saussure, F. de	γ–
Scheherezade	α–
Scholasticus, Homo	ϑ–
second pair of eyes	α–
Semeiosis, Professor	ϑ–
Shakespeare, William	β
Shandy, Tristram	β+
Snoopy	α
Socrates	β–
Sophisto, Professor	ϑ–
Sophists, the	ϑ–
Sordello, di Mantovana	x
Soul, book of the	x
Stein, Gertrude	ϑ–
Sterne, Laurence	x
Stevens, Wallace	β+
Stradiver, Paul	ϑ–
Streisand, Barbra	ϑ
Student Body, the	α+
Su Fu, Lin	x
Sultan { in	ϑ–
{ con	γ+
Swift, Jonathan	γ+
Tancredi, Salvatore	ϑ+
Tariel	ϑ–

Text, the	x
Textivores, the	$\vartheta-$
Thamar, Queen	x
Thamus	$\alpha-$
Thanatos	$\alpha+$
Thor	x
Thoth	$\gamma+$
Todorov, Tzvetan	β
Toren, Larissa	x
Toren, 3 illegitimate children	x
Tove, Jeremy	$\vartheta-$
trait-or, the	$\vartheta-$
Tristan	$\vartheta-$
Troy, Helen of	$\vartheta+$
Uang Iu p'uh	x
Underwood, Dr.	$\vartheta-$
Uranus	$\vartheta-$
Valery, Paul	x
Valincour	x
Valmont, Comte de	$\alpha-$
Valmorin, Louise de	x
Victoria, Queen	x
Virgil	$\vartheta-$
Vitruvius, Pollio, Marcus	x
Vivien	$\vartheta-$
Vizir, the	$\vartheta-$
vox populi	α
Wagner, Richard	γ
Webb, Miss Helen	$\vartheta-$
Weintraub, Julia	ϑ
Wimsatt, W.K.	$\vartheta+$
Woolf, Virginia	$\vartheta-$
Yorick, poor	$\alpha+$

(Portraits by the Student Body)

Oh keep them out of it the students have dispersed from the institution of learning how to become a parasite upon a text nobody reads passed on from generation to

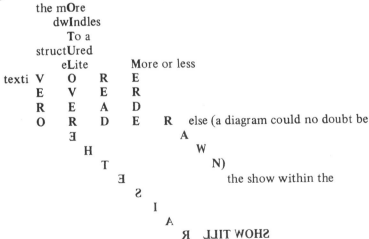

g e n e r a t i o **N** **Of** an **I**ncreasing vas**T**ness f**UL**l **Of** what ne**VER**
the m**O**re
dw**I**ndles
To a
struct**U**red
e**L**ite   More or less
texti **V** **O** **R** **E**
E **V** **E** **R**
R **E** **A** **D**
O **R** **D** **E** **R** else (a diagram could no doubt be
Ǝ **A**
H **W**
T **N)**
Ǝ the show within the
Ƨ
I
A
Я ⅃⅃IT WOHƧ

must go on the other scene since the institution of unlearning has been closed down by an obituary act of authority due to textual disturbances.

So that you^{n} drive away into the nightwiddling along the transistor of disembodied voiceless logos watching the hoops that dance red amber white green mauve eyes made up by the disappeared narrator in a mere vehicle now deprived of pilot who would not stay for an answer

his f o u r ▽s l o d g e d in
the retro v izor never

to sally fort-da and reflecting nothing but

T
E
X
(I)
U Я H T H R U